THE LUPIN COLLECTION

*Over 25 Arsène Lupin Adventures from: The Extraordinary
Adventures of Arsène Lupin, Gentleman-Burglar, Arsène Lupin
Versus Herlock Sholmes, The Confessions of Arsène Lupin*

MAURICE LEBLANC

Translated by
GEORGE MOREHEAD

Translated by
ALEXANDER TEIXEIRA DE MATTOS

CONTENTS

THE EXTRAORDINARY ADVENTURES OF ARSÈNE LUPIN, GENTLEMAN-BURGLAR

I. THE ARREST OF ARSÈNE LUPIN

It was a strange ending to a voyage that had commenced in a most auspicious manner. The transatlantic steamship 'La Provence' was a swift and comfortable vessel, under the command of a most affable man. The passengers constituted a select and delightful society. The charm of new acquaintances and improvised amusements served to make the time pass agreeably. We enjoyed the pleasant sensation of being separated from the world, living, as it were, upon an unknown island, and consequently obliged to be sociable with each other.

Have you ever stopped to consider how much originality and spontaneity emanate from these various individuals who, on the preceding evening, did not even know each other, and who are now, for several days, condemned to lead a life of extreme intimacy, jointly defying the anger of the ocean, the terrible onslaught of the waves, the violence of the tempest and the agonizing monotony of the calm and sleepy water? Such a life becomes a sort of tragic existence, with its storms and its grandeurs, its monotony and its diversity; and that is why, perhaps, we embark upon that short voyage with mingled feelings of pleasure and fear.

But, during the past few years, a new sensation had been added to the life of the transatlantic traveler. The little floating island is now attached to the world from which it was once quite free. A bond united them, even in the very heart of the watery wastes of the Atlantic. That bond is the wireless telegraph, by means of which we receive news in the most mysterious manner. We know full well that the message is not transported by the medium of a hollow wire. No, the mystery is even more inexplicable, more romantic, and we must have recourse to the wings of the air in order to explain this new miracle. During the first day of the voyage, we felt that we were being followed, escorted, preceded even, by that distant voice, which, from time to time, whispered to one of us a few words from the receding world. Two friends spoke to me. Ten, twenty others sent gay or somber words of parting to other passengers.

On the second day, at a distance of five hundred miles from the French coast, in the midst of a violent storm, we received the following message by means of the wireless telegraph:

"Arsène Lupin is on your vessel, first cabin, blonde hair, wound right fore-arm, traveling alone under name of R........"

At that moment, a terrible flash of lightning rent the stormy skies. The electric waves were interrupted. The remainder of the dispatch never reached us. Of the name under which Arsène Lupin was concealing himself, we knew only the initial.

If the news had been of some other character, I have no doubt that the secret would have been carefully guarded by the telegraphic operator as well as by the officers of the vessel. But it was one of those events calculated to escape from the most rigorous discretion. The same day, no one knew how, the incident became a matter of current gossip and every passenger was aware that the famous Arsène Lupin was hiding in our midst.

Arsène Lupin in our midst! the irresponsible burglar whose exploits had been narrated in all the newspapers during the past few months! the mysterious individual with whom Ganimard, our shrewdest detective, had been engaged in an implacable conflict amidst interesting and picturesque surroundings. Arsène Lupin, the eccentric gentleman who operates only in the châteaux and salons, and who, one night, entered the residence of Baron Schormann, but emerged empty-handed, leaving, however, his card on which he had scribbled these words: "Arsène Lupin, gentleman-burglar, will return when the furniture is genuine." Arsène Lupin, the man of a thousand disguises: in turn a chauffeur, detective, bookmaker, Russian physician, Spanish bull-fighter, commercial traveler, robust youth, or decrepit old man.

Then consider this startling situation: Arsène Lupin was wandering about within the limited bounds of a transatlantic steamer; in that very small corner of the world, in that dining saloon, in that smoking room, in that music room! Arsène Lupin was, perhaps, this gentleman.... or that one.... my neighbor at the table.... the sharer of my stateroom....

"And this condition of affairs will last for five days!" exclaimed Miss Nelly Underdown, next morning. "It is unbearable! I hope he will be arrested."

Then, addressing me, she added:

"And you, Monsieur d'Andrézy, you are on intimate terms with the captain; surely you know something?"

I should have been delighted had I possessed any information that would interest Miss Nelly. She was one of those magnificent creatures who inevitably attract attention in every assembly. Wealth and beauty form an irresistible combination, and Nelly possessed both.

Educated in Paris under the care of a French mother, she was now going to visit her father, the millionaire Underdown of Chicago. She was accompanied by one of her friends, Lady Jerland.

At first, I had decided to open a flirtation with her; but, in the rapidly growing intimacy of the voyage, I was soon impressed by her charming manner and my feelings became too deep and reverential for a mere flirtation. Moreover, she accepted my attentions with a certain degree of favor. She condescended to laugh at my witticisms and display an interest in my stories. Yet I felt that I had a rival in the person of a young man with quiet and refined tastes; and it struck me, at times, that she preferred his taciturn humor to my Parisian frivolity. He formed one in the circle of admirers that surrounded Miss Nelly at the time she addressed to me the foregoing question. We were all comfortably seated in our deck-chairs. The storm of the preceding evening had cleared the sky. The weather was now delightful.

"I have no definite knowledge, mademoiselle," I replied, "but cannot we, ourselves, investigate the mystery quite as well as the detective Ganimard, the personal enemy of Arsène Lupin?"

"Oh! oh! you are progressing very fast, monsieur."

"Not at all, mademoiselle. In the first place, let me ask, do you find the problem a complicated one?"

"Very complicated."

"Have you forgotten the key we hold for the solution to the problem?"

"What key?"

"In the first place, Lupin calls himself Monsieur R———."

"Rather vague information," she replied.

"Secondly, he is traveling alone."

"Does that help you?" she asked.

"Thirdly, he is blonde."

"Well?"

"Then we have only to peruse the passenger-list, and proceed by process of elimination."

I had that list in my pocket. I took it out and glanced through it. Then I remarked:

"I find that there are only thirteen men on the passenger-list whose names begin with the letter R."

"Only thirteen?"

"Yes, in the first cabin. And of those thirteen, I find that nine of them are accompanied by women, children or servants. That leaves only four who are traveling alone. First, the Marquis de Raverdan———"

"Secretary to the American Ambassador," interrupted Miss Nelly. "I know him."

"Major Rawson," I continued.

"He is my uncle," someone said.

"Mon. Rivolta."

"Here!" exclaimed an Italian, whose face was concealed beneath a heavy black beard.

Miss Nelly burst into laughter, and exclaimed: "That gentleman can scarcely be called a blonde."

"Very well, then," I said, "we are forced to the conclusion that the guilty party is the last one on the list."

"What is his name?"

"Mon. Rozaine. Does anyone know him?"

No one answered. But Miss Nelly turned to the taciturn young man, whose attentions to her had annoyed me, and said:

"Well, Monsieur Rozaine, why do you not answer?"

All eyes were now turned upon him. He was a blonde. I must confess that I myself felt a shock of surprise, and the profound silence that followed her question indicated that the others present also viewed the situation with a feeling of sudden alarm. However, the idea was an absurd one, because the gentleman in question presented an air of the most perfect innocence.

"Why do I not answer?" he said. "Because, considering my name, my position as a solitary traveler and the color of my hair, I have already reached the same conclusion, and now think that I should be arrested."

He presented a strange appearance as he uttered these words. His thin lips were drawn closer than usual and his face was ghastly pale, whilst his eyes were streaked with blood. Of course, he was joking, yet his appearance and attitude impressed us strangely.

"But you have not the wound?" said Miss Nelly, naively.

"That is true," he replied, "I lack the wound."

Then he pulled up his sleeve, removing his cuff, and showed us his arm. But that action did not deceive me. He had shown us his left arm, and I was on the point of calling his attention to the fact, when another incident diverted our attention. Lady Jerland, Miss Nelly's friend, came running towards us in a state of great excitement, exclaiming:

"My jewels, my pearls! Someone has stolen them all!"

No, they were not all gone, as we soon found out. The thief had taken only part of them; a very curious thing. Of the diamond sunbursts, jeweled pendants, bracelets and necklaces, the thief had taken, not the largest but the finest and most valuable stones. The mountings were lying upon the table. I saw them there, despoiled of their jewels, like flowers from which the beautiful colored petals had been ruthlessly plucked. And this theft must have been committed at the time Lady Jerland was taking her tea; in broad daylight, in a stateroom opening on a much frequented corridor; moreover, the thief had been obliged to force open the door of the stateroom, search for the jewel-case, which was hidden at the bottom of a hat-box, open it, select his booty and remove it from the mountings.

Of course, all the passengers instantly reached the same conclusion; it was the work of Arsène Lupin.

That day, at the dinner table, the seats to the right and left of Rozaine remained vacant; and, during the evening, it was rumored that the captain had placed him under arrest, which information produced a feeling of safety and relief. We breathed once more. That evening, we resumed our games and dances. Miss Nelly, especially, displayed a spirit of thoughtless gayety which convinced me that if Rozaine's attentions had been agreeable to her in the beginning, she had already forgotten them. Her charm and good-humor completed my conquest. At midnight, under a bright moon, I declared my devotion with an ardor that did not seem to displease her.

But, next day, to our general amazement, Rozaine was at liberty. We learned that the evidence against him was not sufficient. He had produced documents that were perfectly regular, which showed that he was the son of a wealthy merchant of Bordeaux. Besides, his arms did not bear the slightest trace of a wound.

"Documents! Certificates of birth!" exclaimed the enemies of Rozaine, "of course, Arsène Lupin will furnish you as many as you desire. And as to the wound, he never had it, or he has removed it."

Then it was proven that, at the time of the theft, Rozaine was promenading on the deck. To which fact, his enemies replied that a man like Arsène Lupin could commit a crime without being actually present. And then, apart from all other circumstances, there remained one point which even the most skeptical could not answer: Who except Rozaine, was traveling alone, was a blonde, and bore a name beginning with R? To whom did the telegram point, if it were not Rozaine?

And when Rozaine, a few minutes before breakfast, came boldly toward our group, Miss Nelly and Lady Jerland arose and walked away.

An hour later, a manuscript circular was passed from hand to hand amongst the sailors, the stewards, and the passengers of all classes. It announced that Mon. Louis Rozaine offered a reward of ten thousand francs for the discovery of Arsène Lupin or other person in possession of the stolen jewels.

"And if no one assists me, I will unmask the scoundrel myself," declared Rozaine.

Rozaine against Arsène Lupin, or rather, according to current opinion, Arsène Lupin himself against Arsène Lupin; the contest promised to be interesting.

Nothing developed during the next two days. We saw Rozaine wandering about, day and night, searching, questioning, investigating. The captain, also, displayed commendable activity. He caused the vessel to be searched from stem to stern; ransacked every stateroom under the plausible theory that the jewels might be concealed anywhere, except in the thief's own room.

"I suppose they will find out something soon," remarked Miss Nelly to me. "He may be a wizard, but he cannot make diamonds and pearls become invisible."

"Certainly not," I replied, "but he should examine the lining of our hats and vests and everything we carry with us."

Then, exhibiting my Kodak, a 9x12 with which I had been photographing her in various poses, I added: "In an apparatus no larger than that, a person could hide all of Lady Jerland's jewels. He could pretend to take pictures and no one would suspect the game."

"But I have heard it said that every thief leaves some clue behind him."

"That may be generally true," I replied, "but there is one exception: Arsène Lupin."

"Why?"

"Because he concentrates his thoughts not only on the theft, but on all the circumstances connected with it that could serve as a clue to his identity."

"A few days ago, you were more confident."

"Yes, but since then I have seen him at work."

"And what do you think about it now?" she asked.

"Well, in my opinion, we are wasting our time."

And, as a matter of fact, the investigation had produced no result. But, in the meantime, the captain's watch had been stolen. He was furious. He quickened his efforts and watched Rozaine more closely than before. But, on the following day, the watch was found in the second officer's collar box.

This incident caused considerable astonishment, and displayed the humorous side of Arsène Lupin, burglar though he was, but dilettante as well. He combined business with pleasure. He reminded us of the author who almost died in a fit of laughter provoked by his own play. Certainly, he was an artist in his particular line of work, and whenever I saw Rozaine, gloomy and reserved, and thought of the double role that he was playing, I accorded him a certain measure of admiration.

On the following evening, the officer on deck duty heard groans emanating from the darkest corner of the ship. He approached and found a man lying there, his head enveloped in a thick gray scarf and his hands tied together with a heavy cord. It was

Rozaine. He had been assaulted, thrown down and robbed. A card, pinned to his coat, bore these words: "Arsène Lupin accepts with pleasure the ten thousand francs offered by Mon. Rozaine." As a matter of fact, the stolen pocket-book contained twenty thousand francs.

Of course, some accused the unfortunate man of having simulated this attack on himself. But, apart from the fact that he could not have bound himself in that manner, it was established that the writing on the card was entirely different from that of Rozaine, but, on the contrary, resembled the handwriting of Arsène Lupin as it was reproduced in an old newspaper found on board.

Thus it appeared that Rozaine was not Arsène Lupin; but was Rozaine, the son of a Bordeaux merchant. And the presence of Arsène Lupin was once more affirmed, and that in a most alarming manner.

Such was the state of terror amongst the passengers that none would remain alone in a stateroom or wander singly in unfrequented parts of the vessel. We clung together as a matter of safety. And yet the most intimate acquaintances were estranged by a mutual feeling of distrust. Arsène Lupin was, now, anybody and everybody. Our excited imaginations attributed to him miraculous and unlimited power. We supposed him capable of assuming the most unexpected disguises; of being, by turns, the highly respectable Major Rawson or the noble Marquis de Raverdan, or even—for we no longer stopped with the accusing letter of R—or even such or such a person well known to all of us, and having wife, children and servants.

The first wireless dispatches from America brought no news; at least, the captain did not communicate any to us. The silence was not reassuring.

Our last day on the steamer seemed interminable. We lived in constant fear of some disaster. This time, it would not be a simple theft or a comparatively harmless assault; it would be a crime, a murder. No one imagined that Arsène Lupin would confine himself to those two trifling offenses. Absolute master of the ship, the authorities powerless, he could do whatever he pleased; our property and lives were at his mercy.

Yet those were delightful hours for me, since they secured to me the confidence of Miss Nelly. Deeply moved by those startling events and being of a highly nervous nature, she spontaneously sought at my side a protection and security that I was pleased to give her. Inwardly, I blessed Arsène Lupin. Had he not been the means of bringing me and Miss Nelly closer to each other? Thanks to him, I could now indulge in delicious dreams of love and happiness—dreams that, I felt, were not unwelcome to Miss Nelly. Her smiling eyes authorized me to make them; the softness of her voice bade me hope.

As we approached the American shore, the active search for the thief was apparently abandoned, and we were anxiously awaiting the supreme moment in which the mysterious enigma would be explained. Who was Arsène Lupin? Under what name, under what disguise was the famous Arsène Lupin concealing himself? And, at last, that supreme moment arrived. If I live one hundred years, I shall not forget the slightest details of it.

"How pale you are, Miss Nelly," I said to my companion, as she leaned upon my arm, almost fainting.

"And you!" she replied, "ah! you are so changed."

"Just think! this is a most exciting moment, and I am delighted to spend it with you, Miss Nelly. I hope that your memory will sometimes revert—"

But she was not listening. She was nervous and excited. The gangway was placed in position, but, before we could use it, the uniformed customs officers came on board. Miss Nelly murmured:

"I shouldn't be surprised to hear that Arsène Lupin escaped from the vessel during the voyage."

"Perhaps he preferred death to dishonor, and plunged into the Atlantic rather than be arrested."

"Oh, do not laugh," she said.

Suddenly I started, and, in answer to her question, I said:

"Do you see that little old man standing at the bottom of the gangway?"

"With an umbrella and an olive-green coat?"

"It is Ganimard."

"Ganimard?"

"Yes, the celebrated detective who has sworn to capture Arsène Lupin. Ah! I can understand now why we did not receive any news from this side of the Atlantic. Ganimard was here! and he always keeps his business secret."

"Then you think he will arrest Arsène Lupin?"

"Who can tell? The unexpected always happens when Arsène Lupin is concerned in the affair."

"Oh!" she exclaimed, with that morbid curiosity peculiar to women, "I should like to see him arrested."

"You will have to be patient. No doubt, Arsène Lupin has already seen his enemy and will not be in a hurry to leave the steamer."

The passengers were now leaving the steamer. Leaning on his umbrella, with an air of careless indifference, Ganimard appeared to be paying no attention to the crowd that was hurrying down the gangway. The Marquis de Raverdan, Major Rawson, the Italian Rivolta, and many others had already left the vessel before Rozaine appeared. Poor Rozaine!

"Perhaps it is he, after all," said Miss Nelly to me. "What do you think?"

"I think it would be very interesting to have Ganimard and Rozaine in the same picture. You take the camera. I am loaded down."

I gave her the camera, but too late for her to use it. Rozaine was already passing the detective. An American officer, standing behind Ganimard, leaned forward and whispered in his ear. The French detective shrugged his shoulders and Rozaine passed on. Then, my God, who was Arsène Lupin?

"Yes," said Miss Nelly, aloud, "who can it be?"

Not more than twenty people now remained on board. She scrutinized them one by one, fearful that Arsène Lupin was not amongst them.

"We cannot wait much longer," I said to her.

She started toward the gangway. I followed. But we had not taken ten steps when Ganimard barred our passage.

"Well, what is it?" I exclaimed.

"One moment, monsieur. What's your hurry?"

"I am escorting mademoiselle."

"One moment," he repeated, in a tone of authority. Then, gazing into my eyes, he said:

"Arsène Lupin, is it not?"

I laughed, and replied: "No, simply Bernard d'Andrézy."

"Bernard d'Andrézy died in Macedonia three years ago."

"If Bernard d'Andrézy were dead, I should not be here. But you are mistaken. Here are my papers."

"They are his; and I can tell you exactly how they came into your possession."

"You are a fool!" I exclaimed. "Arsène Lupin sailed under the name of R——"

"Yes, another of your tricks; a false scent that deceived them at Havre. You play a good game, my boy, but this time luck is against you."

I hesitated a moment. Then he hit me a sharp blow on the right arm, which caused me to utter a cry of pain. He had struck the wound, yet unhealed, referred to in the telegram.

I was obliged to surrender. There was no alternative. I turned to Miss Nelly, who had heard everything. Our eyes met; then she glanced at the Kodak I had placed in her hands, and made a gesture that conveyed to me the impression that she understood everything. Yes, there, between the narrow folds of black leather, in the hollow centre of the small object that I had taken the precaution to place in her hands before Ganimard arrested me, it was there I had deposited Rozaine's twenty thousand francs and Lady Jerland's pearls and diamonds.

Oh! I pledge my oath that, at that solemn moment, when I was in the grasp of Ganimard and his two assistants, I was perfectly indifferent to everything, to my arrest, the hostility of the people, everything except this one question: what will Miss Nelly do with the things I had confided to her?

In the absence of that material and conclusive proof, I had nothing to fear; but would Miss Nelly decide to furnish that proof? Would she betray me? Would she act the part of an enemy who cannot forgive, or that of a woman whose scorn is softened by feelings of indulgence and involuntary sympathy?

She passed in front of me. I said nothing, but bowed very low. Mingled with the other passengers, she advanced to the gangway with my Kodak in her hand. It occurred to me that she would not dare to expose me publicly, but she might do so when she reached a more private place. However, when she had passed only a few feet down the gangway, with a movement of simulated awkwardness, she let the camera fall into the water between the vessel and the pier. Then she walked down the gangway, and was quickly lost to sight in the crowd. She had passed out of my life forever.

For a moment, I stood motionless. Then, to Ganimard's great astonishment, I muttered: "What a pity that I am not an honest man!"

Such was the story of his arrest as narrated to me by Arsène Lupin himself. The various incidents, which I shall record in writing at a later day, have established between us certain ties.... shall I say of friendship? Yes, I venture to believe that Arsène Lupin honors me with his friendship, and that it is through friendship that he occasionally calls on me, and brings, into the silence of my library, his youthful exuberance of spirits, the contagion of his enthusiasm, and the mirth of a man for whom destiny has naught but favors and smiles.

His portrait? How can I describe him? I have seen him twenty times and each time he was a different person; even he himself said to me on one occasion: "I no longer know who I am. I cannot recognize myself in the mirror." Certainly, he was a great actor, and possessed a marvelous faculty for disguising himself. Without the slightest effort, he could adopt the voice, gestures and mannerisms of another person.

"Why," said he, "why should I retain a definite form and feature? Why not avoid the danger of a personality that is ever the same? My actions will serve to identify me."

Then he added, with a touch of pride:

"So much the better if no one can ever say with absolute certainty: There is Arsène Lupin! The essential point is that the public may be able to refer to my work and say, without fear of mistake: Arsène Lupin did that!"

II. ARSÈNE LUPIN IN PRISON

There is no tourist worthy of the name who does not know the banks of the Seine, and has not noticed, in passing, the little feudal castle of the Malaquis, built upon a rock in the centre of the river. An arched bridge connects it with the shore. All around it, the calm waters of the great river play peacefully amongst the reeds, and the wagtails flutter over the moist crests of the stones.

The history of the Malaquis castle is stormy like its name, harsh like its outlines. It has passed through a long series of combats, sieges, assaults, rapines and massacres. A recital of the crimes that have been committed there would cause the stoutest heart to tremble. There are many mysterious legends connected with the castle, and they tell us of a famous subterranean tunnel that formerly led to the abbey of Jumieges and to the manor of Agnes Sorel, mistress of Charles VII.

In that ancient habitation of heroes and brigands, the Baron Nathan Cahorn now lived; or Baron Satan as he was formerly called on the Bourse, where he had acquired a fortune with incredible rapidity. The lords of Malaquis, absolutely ruined, had been obliged to sell the ancient castle at a great sacrifice. It contained an admirable collection of furniture, pictures, wood carvings, and faience. The Baron lived there alone, attended by three old servants. No one ever enters the place. No one had ever beheld the three Rubens that he possessed, his two Watteau, his Jean Goujon pulpit, and the many other treasures that he had acquired by a vast expenditure of money at public sales.

Baron Satan lived in constant fear, not for himself, but for the treasures that he had accumulated with such an earnest devotion and with so much perspicacity that the shrewdest merchant could not say that the Baron had ever erred in his taste or judgment. He loved them—his bibelots. He loved them intensely, like a miser; jealously, like a lover. Every day, at sunset, the iron gates at either end of the bridge and at the entrance to the court of honor are closed and barred. At the least touch on these gates, electric bells will ring throughout the castle.

One Thursday in September, a letter-carrier presented himself at the gate at the head of the bridge, and, as usual, it was the Baron himself who partially opened the heavy portal. He scrutinized the man as minutely as if he were a stranger, although the honest face and twinkling eyes of the postman had been familiar to the Baron for many years. The man laughed, as he said:

"It is only I, Monsieur le Baron. It is not another man wearing my cap and blouse."

"One can never tell," muttered the Baron.

The man handed him a number of newspapers, and then said:

"And now, Monsieur le Baron, here is something new."

"Something new?"

"Yes, a letter. A registered letter."

Living as a recluse, without friends or business relations, the baron never received any letters, and the one now presented to him immediately aroused within him a feeling of suspicion and distrust. It was like an evil omen. Who was this mysterious correspondent that dared to disturb the tranquility of his retreat?

"You must sign for it, Monsieur le Baron."

He signed; then took the letter, waited until the postman had disappeared beyond the bend in the road, and, after walking nervously to and fro for a few minutes, he leaned against the parapet of the bridge and opened the envelope. It contained a sheet of paper, bearing this heading: Prison de la Santé, Paris. He looked at the signature: Arsène Lupin. Then he read:

"Monsieur le Baron:

"There is, in the gallery in your castle, a picture of Philippe de Champaigne, of exquisite finish, which pleases me beyond measure. Your Rubens are also to my taste, as well as your smallest Watteau. In the salon to the right, I have noticed the Louis XIII cadence-table, the tapestries of Beauvais, the Empire gueridon signed 'Jacob,' and the Renaissance chest. In the salon to the left, all the cabinet full of jewels and miniatures.

"For the present, I will content myself with those articles that can be conveniently removed. I will therefore ask you to pack them carefully and ship them to me, charges prepaid, to the station at Batignolles, within eight days, otherwise I shall be obliged to remove them myself during the night of 27 September; but, under those circumstances, I shall not content myself with the articles above mentioned.

"Accept my apologies for any inconvenience I may cause you, and believe me to be your humble servant,

"Arsène Lupin."

"P. S.—Please do not send the largest Watteau. Although you paid thirty thousand francs for it, it is only a copy, the original having been burned, under the Directoire by Barras, during a night of debauchery. Consult the memoirs of Garat.

"I do not care for the Louis XV chatelaine, as I doubt its authenticity."

That letter completely upset the baron. Had it borne any other signature, he would have been greatly alarmed—but signed by Arsène Lupin!

As an habitual reader of the newspapers, he was versed in the history of recent crimes, and was therefore well acquainted with the exploits of the mysterious burglar. Of course, he knew that Lupin had been arrested in America by his enemy Ganimard and was at present incarcerated in the Prison de la Santé. But he knew also that any miracle might be expected from Arsène Lupin. Moreover, that exact knowledge of the castle, the location of the pictures and furniture, gave the affair an alarming aspect. How could he have acquired that information concerning things that no one had ever seen?

The baron raised his eyes and contemplated the stern outlines of the castle, its steep rocky pedestal, the depth of the surrounding water, and shrugged his shoulders. Certainly, there was no danger. No one in the world could force an entrance to the sanctuary that contained his priceless treasures.

No one, perhaps, but Arsène Lupin! For him, gates, walls and drawbridges did not exist. What use were the most formidable obstacles or the most careful precautions, if Arsène Lupin had decided to effect an entrance?

That evening, he wrote to the Procurer of the Republique at Rouen. He enclosed the threatening letter and solicited aid and protection.

The reply came at once to the effect that Arsène Lupin was in custody in the Prison de la Santé, under close surveillance, with no opportunity to write such a letter, which was, no doubt, the work of some imposter. But, as an act of precaution, the Procurer had submitted the letter to an expert in handwriting, who declared that, in spite of certain resemblances, the writing was not that of the prisoner.

But the words "in spite of certain resemblances" caught the attention of the baron; in them, he read the possibility of a doubt which appeared to him quite sufficient to warrant the intervention of the law. His fears increased. He read Lupin's letter over and over again. "I shall be obliged to remove them myself." And then there was the fixed date: the night of 27 September.

To confide in his servants was a proceeding repugnant to his nature; but now, for the first time in many years, he experienced the necessity of seeking counsel with someone. Abandoned by the legal official of his own district, and feeling unable to defend himself with his own resources, he was on the point of going to Paris to engage the services of a detective.

Two days passed; on the third day, he was filled with hope and joy as he read the following item in the 'Réveil de Caudebec', a newspaper published in a neighboring town:

"We have the pleasure of entertaining in our city, at the present time, the veteran detective Mon. Ganimard who acquired a world-wide reputation by his clever capture of Arsène Lupin. He has come here for rest and recreation, and, being an enthusiastic fisherman, he threatens to capture all the fish in our river."

Ganimard! Ah, here is the assistance desired by Baron Cahorn! Who could baffle the schemes of Arsène Lupin better than Ganimard, the patient and astute detective? He was the man for the place.

The baron did not hesitate. The town of Caudebec was only six kilometers from the castle, a short distance to a man whose step was accelerated by the hope of safety.

After several fruitless attempts to ascertain the detective's address, the baron visited the office of the 'Réveil,' situated on the quai. There he found the writer of the article who, approaching the window, exclaimed:

"Ganimard? Why, you are sure to see him somewhere on the quai with his fishing-pole. I met him there and chanced to read his name engraved on his rod. Ah, there he is now, under the trees."

"That little man, wearing a straw hat?"

"Exactly. He is a gruff fellow, with little to say."

Five minutes later, the baron approached the celebrated Ganimard, introduced himself, and sought to commence a conversation, but that was a failure. Then he broached the real object of his interview, and briefly stated his case. The other listened, motionless, with his attention riveted on his fishing-rod. When the baron had finished his story, the fisherman turned, with an air of profound pity, and said:

"Monsieur, it is not customary for thieves to warn people they are about to rob. Arsène Lupin, especially, would not commit such a folly."

"But—"

"Monsieur, if I had the least doubt, believe me, the pleasure of again capturing Arsène

Lupin would place me at your disposal. But, unfortunately, that young man is already under lock and key."

"He may have escaped."

"No one ever escaped from the Santé."

"But, he——"

"He, no more than any other."

"Yet——"

"Well, if he escapes, so much the better. I will catch him again. Meanwhile, you go home and sleep soundly. That will do for the present. You frighten the fish."

The conversation was ended. The baron returned to the castle, reassured to some extent by Ganimard's indifference. He examined the bolts, watched the servants, and, during the next forty-eight hours, he became almost persuaded that his fears were groundless. Certainly, as Ganimard had said, thieves do not warn people they are about to rob.

The fateful day was close at hand. It was now the twenty-sixth of September and nothing had happened. But at three o'clock the bell rang. A boy brought this telegram:

"No goods at Batignolles station. Prepare everything for tomorrow night. Arsène."

This telegram threw the baron into such a state of excitement that he even considered the advisability of yielding to Lupin's demands.

However, he hastened to Caudebec. Ganimard was fishing at the same place, seated on a campstool. Without a word, he handed him the telegram.

"Well, what of it?" said the detective.

"What of it? But it is tomorrow."

"What is tomorrow?"

"The robbery! The pillage of my collections!"

Ganimard laid down his fishing-rod, turned to the baron, and exclaimed, in a tone of impatience:

"Ah! Do you think I am going to bother myself about such a silly story as that!"

"How much do you ask to pass tomorrow night in the castle?"

"Not a sou. Now, leave me alone."

"Name your own price. I am rich and can pay it."

This offer disconcerted Ganimard, who replied, calmly:

"I am here on a vacation. I have no right to undertake such work."

"No one will know. I promise to keep it secret."

"Oh! nothing will happen."

"Come! three thousand francs. Will that be enough?"

The detective, after a moment's reflection, said:

"Very well. But I must warn you that you are throwing your money out of the window."

"I do not care."

"In that case... but, after all, what do we know about this devil Lupin! He may have quite a numerous band of robbers with him. Are you sure of your servants?"

"My faith——"

"Better not count on them. I will telegraph for two of my men to help me. And now, go! It is better for us not to be seen together. Tomorrow evening about nine o'clock."

. . .

The following day—the date fixed by Arsène Lupin—Baron Cahorn arranged all his panoply of war, furbished his weapons, and, like a sentinel, paced to and fro in front of the castle. He saw nothing, heard nothing. At half-past eight o'clock in the evening, he dismissed his servants. They occupied rooms in a wing of the building, in a retired spot, well removed from the main portion of the castle. Shortly thereafter, the baron heard the sound of approaching footsteps. It was Ganimard and his two assistants—great, powerful fellows with immense hands, and necks like bulls. After asking a few questions relating to the location of the various entrances and rooms, Ganimard carefully closed and barricaded all the doors and windows through which one could gain access to the threatened rooms. He inspected the walls, raised the tapestries, and finally installed his assistants in the central gallery which was located between the two salons.

"No nonsense! We are not here to sleep. At the slightest sound, open the windows of the court and call me. Pay attention also to the water-side. Ten metres of perpendicular rock is no obstacle to those devils."

Ganimard locked his assistants in the gallery, carried away the keys, and said to the baron:

"And now, to our post."

He had chosen for himself a small room located in the thick outer wall, between the two principal doors, and which, in former years, had been the watchman's quarters. A peep-hole opened upon the bridge; another on the court. In one corner, there was an opening to a tunnel.

"I believe you told me, Monsieur le Baron, that this tunnel is the only subterranean entrance to the castle and that it has been closed up for time immemorial?"

"Yes."

"Then, unless there is some other entrance, known only to Arsène Lupin, we are quite safe."

He placed three chairs together, stretched himself upon them, lighted his pipe and sighed:

"Really, Monsieur le Baron, I feel ashamed to accept your money for such a sinecure as this. I will tell the story to my friend Lupin. He will enjoy it immensely."

The baron did not laugh. He was anxiously listening, but heard nothing save the beating of his own heart. From time to time, he leaned over the tunnel and cast a fearful eye into its depths. He heard the clock strike eleven, twelve, one.

Suddenly, he seized Ganimard's arm. The latter leaped up, awakened from his sleep.

"Do you hear?" asked the baron, in a whisper.

"Yes."

"What is it?"

"I was snoring, I suppose."

"No, no, listen."

"Ah! yes, it is the horn of an automobile."

"Well?"

"Well! it is very improbable that Lupin would use an automobile like a battering-ram to demolish your castle. Come, Monsieur le Baron, return to your post. I am going to sleep. Good-night."

That was the only alarm. Ganimard resumed his interrupted slumbers, and the baron heard nothing except the regular snoring of his companion. At break of day, they left the room. The castle was enveloped in a profound calm; it was a peaceful dawn on the bosom of a tranquil river. They mounted the stairs, Cahorn radiant with joy, Ganimard calm as usual. They heard no sound; they saw nothing to arouse suspicion.

"What did I tell you, Monsieur le Baron? Really, I should not have accepted your offer. I am ashamed."

He unlocked the door and entered the gallery. Upon two chairs, with drooping heads and pendent arms, the detective's two assistants were asleep.

"Tonnerre de nom d'un chien!" exclaimed Ganimard. At the same moment, the baron cried out:

"The pictures! The credence!"

He stammered, choked, with arms outstretched toward the empty places, toward the denuded walls where naught remained but the useless nails and cords. The Watteau, disappeared! The Rubens, carried away! The tapestries taken down! The cabinets, despoiled of their jewels!

"And my Louis XVI candelabra! And the Regent chandelier!...And my twelfth-century Virgin!"

He ran from one spot to another in wildest despair. He recalled the purchase price of each article, added up the figures, counted his losses, pell-mell, in confused words and unfinished phrases. He stamped with rage; he groaned with grief. He acted like a ruined man whose only hope is suicide.

If anything could have consoled him, it would have been the stupefaction displayed by Ganimard. The famous detective did not move. He appeared to be petrified; he examined the room in a listless manner. The windows?.... closed. The locks on the doors?.... intact. Not a break in the ceiling; not a hole in the floor. Everything was in perfect order. The theft had been carried out methodically, according to a logical and inexorable plan.

"Arsène Lupin....Arsène Lupin," he muttered.

Suddenly, as if moved by anger, he rushed upon his two assistants and shook them violently. They did not awaken.

"The devil!" he cried. "Can it be possible?"

He leaned over them and, in turn, examined them closely. They were asleep; but their response was unnatural.

"They have been drugged," he said to the baron.

"By whom?"

"By him, of course, or his men under his discretion. That work bears his stamp."

"In that case, I am lost—nothing can be done."

"Nothing," assented Ganimard.

"It is dreadful; it is monstrous."

"Lodge a complaint."

"What good will that do?"

"Oh; it is well to try it. The law has some resources."

"The law! Bah! it is useless. You represent the law, and, at this moment, when you should be looking for a clue and trying to discover something, you do not even stir."

"Discover something with Arsène Lupin! Why, my dear monsieur, Arsène Lupin never leaves any clue behind him. He leaves nothing to chance. Sometimes I think he put himself in my way and simply allowed me to arrest him in America."

"Then, I must renounce my pictures! He has taken the gems of my collection. I would give a fortune to recover them. If there is no other way, let him name his own price."

Ganimard regarded the baron attentively, as he said:

"Now, that is sensible. Will you stick to it?"

"Yes, yes. But why?"

"An idea that I have."

"What is it?"

"We will discuss it later—if the official examination does not succeed. But, not one word about me, if you wish my assistance."

He added, between his teeth:

"It is true I have nothing to boast of in this affair."

The assistants were gradually regaining consciousness with the bewildered air of people who come out of an hypnotic sleep. They opened their eyes and looked about them in astonishment. Ganimard questioned them; they remembered nothing.

"But you must have seen some one?"

"No."

"Can't you remember?"

"No, no."

"Did you drink anything?"

They considered a moment, and then one of them replied:

"Yes, I drank a little water."

"Out of that carafe?"

"Yes."

"So did I," declared the other.

Ganimard smelled and tasted it. It had no particular taste and no odor.

"Come," he said, "we are wasting our time here. One can't decide an Arsène Lupin problem in five minutes. But, morbleu! I swear I will catch him again."

The same day, a charge of burglary was duly performed by Baron Cahorn against Arsène Lupin, a prisoner in the Prison de la Santé.

The baron afterwards regretted making the charge against Lupin when he saw his castle delivered over to the gendarmes, the procureur, the judge d'instruction, the newspaper reporters and photographers, and a throng of idle curiosity-seekers.

The affair soon became a topic of general discussion, and the name of Arsène Lupin excited the public imagination to such an extent that the newspapers filled their columns with the most fantastic stories of his exploits which found ready credence amongst their readers.

But the letter of Arsène Lupin that was published in the 'Echo de France' (no once ever knew how the newspaper obtained it), that letter in which Baron Cahorn was impudently warned of the coming theft, caused considerable excitement. The most fabulous theories were advanced. Some recalled the existence of the famous subterranean tunnels, and that was the line of research pursued by the officers of the law, who searched the house from top to bottom, questioned every stone, studied the wainscoting and the chimneys, the window-frames and the girders in the ceilings. By the light of torches, they examined the immense cellars where the lords of Malaquis were wont to store their munitions and provisions. They sounded the rocky foundation to its very centre. But it was all in vain. They discovered no trace of a subterranean tunnel. No secret passage existed.

But the eager public declared that the pictures and furniture could not vanish like so many ghosts. They are substantial, material things and require doors and windows for their exits and their entrances, and so do the people that remove them. Who were those people? How did they gain access to the castle? And how did they leave it?

The police officers of Rouen, convinced of their own impotence, solicited the assistance of the Parisian detective force. Mon. Dudouis, chief of the Sûreté, sent the best sleuths of the iron brigade. He himself spent forty-eight hours at the castle, but met with no success. Then he sent for Ganimard, whose past services had proved so useful when all else failed.

Ganimard listened, in silence, to the instructions of his superior; then, shaking his head, he said:

"In my opinion, it is useless to ransack the castle. The solution of the problem lies elsewhere."

"Where, then?"

"With Arsène Lupin."

"With Arsène Lupin! To support that theory, we must admit his intervention."

"I do admit it. In fact, I consider it quite certain."

"Come, Ganimard, that is absurd. Arsène Lupin is in prison."

"I grant you that Arsène Lupin is in prison, closely guarded; but he must have fetters on his feet, manacles on his wrists, and gag in his mouth before I change my opinion."

"Why so obstinate, Ganimard?"

"Because Arsène Lupin is the only man in France of sufficient calibre to invent and carry out a scheme of that magnitude."

"Mere words, Ganimard."

"But true ones. Look! What are they doing? Searching for subterranean passages, stones swinging on pivots, and other nonsense of that kind. But Lupin doesn't employ such old-fashioned methods. He is a modern cracksman, right up to date."

"And how would you proceed?"

"I should ask your permission to spend an hour with him."

"In his cell?"

"Yes. During the return trip from America we became very friendly, and I venture to say that if he can give me any information without compromising himself he will not hesitate to save me from incurring useless trouble."

It was shortly after noon when Ganimard entered the cell of Arsène Lupin. The latter, who was lying on his bed, raised his head and uttered a cry of apparent joy.

"Ah! This is a real surprise. My dear Ganimard, here!"

"Ganimard himself."

"In my chosen retreat, I have felt a desire for many things, but my fondest wish was to receive you here."

"Very kind of you, I am sure."

"Not at all. You know I hold you in the highest regard."

"I am proud of it."

"I have always said: Ganimard is our best detective. He is almost,—you see how candid I am!—he is almost as clever as Sherlock Holmes. But I am sorry that I cannot offer you anything better than this hard stool. And no refreshments! Not even a glass of beer! Of course, you will excuse me, as I am here only temporarily."

Ganimard smiled, and accepted the proffered seat. Then the prisoner continued:

"Mon Dieu, how pleased I am to see the face of an honest man. I am so tired of those devils of spies who come here ten times a day to ransack my pockets and my cell to satisfy themselves that I am not preparing to escape. The government is very solicitous on my account."

"It is quite right."

"Why so? I should be quite contented if they would allow me to live in my own quiet way."

"On other people's money."

"Quite so. That would be so simple. But here, I am joking, and you are, no doubt, in a hurry. So let us come to business, Ganimard. To what do I owe the honor of this visit?

"The Cahorn affair," declared Ganimard, frankly.

"Ah! Wait, one moment. You see I have had so many affairs! First, let me fix in my mind the circumstances of this particular case....Ah! yes, now I have it. The Cahorn affair, Malaquis castle, Seine-Inférieure....Two Rubens, a Watteau, and a few trifling articles."

"Trifling!"

"Oh! ma foi, all that is of slight importance. But it suffices to know that the affair interests you. How can I serve you, Ganimard?"

"Must I explain to you what steps the authorities have taken in the matter?"

"Not at all. I have read the newspapers and I will frankly state that you have made very little progress."

"And that is the reason I have come to see you."

"I am entirely at your service."

"In the first place, the Cahorn affair was managed by you?"

"From A to Z."

"The letter of warning? the telegram?"

"All mine. I ought to have the receipts somewhere."

Arsène opened the drawer of a small table of plain white wood which, with the bed and stool, constituted all the furniture in his cell, and took therefrom two scraps of paper which he handed to Ganimard.

"Ah!" exclaimed the detective, in surprise, "I though you were closely guarded and searched, and I find that you read the newspapers and collect postal receipts."

"Bah! these people are so stupid! They open the lining of my vest, they examine the soles of my shoes, they sound the walls of my cell, but they never imagine that Arsène Lupin would be foolish enough to choose such a simple hiding place."

Ganimard laughed, as he said:

"What a droll fellow you are! Really, you bewilder me. But, come now, tell me about the Cahorn affair."

"Oh! oh! not quite so fast! You would rob me of all my secrets; expose all my little tricks. That is a very serious matter."

"Was I wrong to count on your complaisance?"

"No, Ganimard, and since you insist——"

Arsène Lupin paced his cell two or three times, then, stopping before Ganimard, he asked:

"What do you think of my letter to the baron?"

"I think you were amusing yourself by playing to the gallery."

"Ah! playing to the gallery! Come, Ganimard, I thought you knew me better. Do I, Arsène Lupin, ever waste my time on such puerilities? Would I have written that letter if I could have robbed the baron without writing to him? I want you to understand that the letter was indispensable; it was the motor that set the whole machine in motion. Now, let us discuss together a scheme for the robbery of the Malaquis castle. Are you willing?"

"Yes, proceed."

"Well, let us suppose a castle carefully closed and barricaded like that of the Baron Cahorn. Am I to abandon my scheme and renounce the treasures that I covet, upon the pretext that the castle which holds them is inaccessible?"

"Evidently not."

"Should I make an assault upon the castle at the head of a band of adventurers as they did in ancient times?"

"That would be foolish."

"Can I gain admittance by stealth or cunning?"

"Impossible."

"Then there is only one way open to me. I must have the owner of the castle invite me to it."

"That is surely an original method."

"And how easy! Let us suppose that one day the owner receives a letter warning him that a notorious burglar known as Arsène Lupin is plotting to rob him. What will he do?"

"Send a letter to the Procureur."

"Who will laugh at him, *because the said Arsène Lupin is actually in prison.* Then, in his anxiety and fear, the simple man will ask the assistance of the first-comer, will he not?"

"Very likely."

"And if he happens to read in a country newspaper that a celebrated detective is spending his vacation in a neighboring town—"

"He will seek that detective."

"Of course. But, on the other hand, let us presume that, having foreseen that state of affairs, the said Arsène Lupin has requested one of his friends to visit Caudebec, make the acquaintance of the editor of the 'Réveil,' a newspaper to which the baron is a subscriber, and let said editor understand that such person is the celebrated detective—then, what will happen?"

"The editor will announce in the 'Réveil' the presence in Caudebec of said detective."

"Exactly; and one of two things will happen: either the fish—I mean Cahorn—will not bite, and nothing will happen; or, what is more likely, he will run and greedily swallow the bait. Thus, behold my Baron Cahorn imploring the assistance of one of my friends against me."

"Original, indeed!"

"Of course, the pseudo-detective at first refuses to give any assistance. On top of that comes the telegram from Arsène Lupin. The frightened baron rushes once more to my friend and offers him a definite sum of money for his services. My friend accepts and summons two members of our band, who, during the night, whilst Cahorn is under the watchful eye of his protector, removes certain articles by way of the window and lowers them with ropes into a nice little launch chartered for the occasion. Simple, isn't it?"

"Marvelous! Marvelous!" exclaimed Ganimard. "The boldness of the scheme and the ingenuity of all its details are beyond criticism. But who is the detective whose name and fame served as a magnet to attract the baron and draw him into your net?"

"There is only one name could do it—only one."

"And that is?"

"Arsène Lupin's personal enemy—the most illustrious Ganimard."

"I?"

"Yourself, Ganimard. And, really, it is very funny. If you go there, and the baron decides to talk, you will find that it will be your duty to arrest yourself, just as you arrested me in America. Hein! the revenge is really amusing: I cause Ganimard to arrest Ganimard."

Arsène Lupin laughed heartily. The detective, greatly vexed, bit his lips; to him the joke was quite devoid of humor. The arrival of a prison guard gave Ganimard an opportunity to recover himself. The man brought Arsène Lupin's luncheon, furnished by a neighboring restaurant. After depositing the tray upon the table, the guard retired. Lupin broke his bread, ate a few morsels, and continued:

"But, rest easy, my dear Ganimard, you will not go to Malaquis. I can tell you something that will astonish you: the Cahorn affair is on the point of being settled."

"Excuse me; I have just seen the Chief of the Sureté."

"What of that? Does Mon. Dudouis know my business better than I do myself? You will learn that Ganimard—excuse me—that the pseudo-Ganimard still remains on very good terms with the baron. The latter has authorized him to negotiate a very delicate transaction with me, and, at the present moment, in consideration of a certain sum, it is probable that the baron has recovered possession of his pictures and other treasures. And on their return, he will withdraw his complaint. Thus, there is no longer any theft, and the law must abandon the case."

Ganimard regarded the prisoner with a bewildered air.

"And how do you know all that?"

"I have just received the telegram I was expecting."

"You have just received a telegram?"

"This very moment, my dear friend. Out of politeness, I did not wish to read it in your presence. But if you will permit me—"

"You are joking, Lupin."

"My dear friend, if you will be so kind as to break that egg, you will learn for yourself that I am not joking."

Mechanically, Ganimard obeyed, and cracked the egg-shell with the blade of a knife. He uttered a cry of surprise. The shell contained nothing but a small piece of blue paper. At the request of Arsène he unfolded it. It was a telegram, or rather a portion of a telegram from which the post-marks had been removed. It read as follows:

"Contract closed. Hundred thousand balls delivered. All well."

"One hundred thousand balls?" said Ganimard.

"Yes, one hundred thousand francs. Very little, but then, you know, these are hard times....And I have some heavy bills to meet. If you only knew my budget.... living in the city comes very high."

Ganimard arose. His ill humor had disappeared. He reflected for a moment, glancing over the whole affair in an effort to discover a weak point; then, in a tone and manner that betrayed his admiration of the prisoner, he said:

"Fortunately, we do not have a dozen such as you to deal with; if we did, we would have to close up shop."

Arsène Lupin assumed a modest air, as he replied:

"Bah! a person must have some diversion to occupy his leisure hours, especially when he is in prison."

"What!" exclaimed Ganimard, "your trial, your defense, the examination—isn't that sufficient to occupy your mind?"

"No, because I have decided not to be present at my trial."

"Oh! oh!"

Arsène Lupin repeated, positively:

"I shall not be present at my trial."

"Really!"

"Ah! my dear monsieur, do you suppose I am going to rot upon the wet straw? You insult me. Arsène Lupin remains in prison just as long as it pleases him, and not one minute more."

"Perhaps it would have been more prudent if you had avoided getting there," said the detective, ironically.

"Ah! monsieur jests? Monsieur must remember that he had the honor to effect my arrest. Know then, my worthy friend, that no one, not even you, could have placed a hand upon me if a much more important event had not occupied my attention at that critical moment."

"You astonish me."

"A woman was looking at me, Ganimard, and I loved her. Do you fully understand what that means: to be under the eyes of a woman that one loves? I cared for nothing in the world but that. And that is why I am here."

"Permit me to say: you have been here a long time."

"In the first place, I wished to forget. Do not laugh; it was a delightful adventure and it is still a tender memory. Besides, I have been suffering from neurasthenia. Life is so feverish these days that it is necessary to take the 'rest cure' occasionally, and I find this spot a sovereign remedy for my tired nerves."

"Arsène Lupin, you are not a bad fellow, after all."

"Thank you," said Lupin. "Ganimard, this is Friday. On Wednesday next, at four o'clock in the afternoon, I will smoke my cigar at your house in the rue Pergolese."

"Arsène Lupin, I will expect you."

They shook hands like two old friends who valued each other at their true worth; then the detective stepped to the door.

"Ganimard!"

"What is it?" asked Ganimard, as he turned back.

"You have forgotten your watch."

"My watch?"

"Yes, it strayed into my pocket."

He returned the watch, excusing himself.

"Pardon me.... a bad habit. Because they have taken mine is no reason why I should take yours. Besides, I have a chronometer here that satisfies me fairly well."

He took from the drawer a large gold watch and heavy chain.

"From whose pocket did that come?" asked Ganimard.

Arsène Lupin gave a hasty glance at the initials engraved on the watch.

"J.B.....Who the devil can that be?....Ah! yes, I remember. Jules Bouvier, the judge who conducted my examination. A charming fellow!...."

III. THE ESCAPE OF ARSÈNE LUPIN

Arsène Lupin had just finished his repast and taken from his pocket an excellent cigar, with a gold band, which he was examining with unusual care, when the door of his cell was opened. He had barely time to throw the cigar into the drawer and move away from the table. The guard entered. It was the hour for exercise.

"I was waiting for you, my dear boy," exclaimed Lupin, in his accustomed good humor.

They went out together. As soon as they had disappeared at a turn in the corridor, two men entered the cell and commenced a minute examination of it. One was Inspector Dieuzy; the other was Inspector Folenfant. They wished to verify their suspicion that Arsène Lupin was in communication with his accomplices outside of the prison. On the preceding evening, the 'Grand Journal' had published these lines addressed to its court reporter:

"Monsieur:

"In a recent article you referred to me in most unjustifiable terms. Some days before the opening of my trial I will call you to account. Arsène Lupin."

The handwriting was certainly that of Arsène Lupin. Consequently, he sent letters; and, no doubt, received letters. It was certain that he was preparing for that escape thus arrogantly announced by him.

The situation had become intolerable. Acting in conjunction with the examining judge, the chief of the Sûreté, Mon. Dudouis, had visited the prison and instructed the gaoler in regard to the precautions necessary to insure Lupin's safety. At the same time, he sent the two men to examine the prisoner's cell. They raised every stone, ransacked the bed, did everything customary in such a case, but they discovered nothing, and were about to abandon their investigation when the guard entered hastily and said:

"The drawer.... look in the table-drawer. When I entered just now he was closing it."

They opened the drawer, and Dieuzy exclaimed:

"Ah! we have him this time."

Folenfant stopped him.

"Wait a moment. The chief will want to make an inventory."

"This is a very choice cigar."

"Leave it there, and notify the chief."

Two minutes later Mon. Dudouis examined the contents of the drawer. First he discovered a bundle of newspaper clippings relating to Arsène Lupin taken from the 'Argus de la Presse,' then a tobacco-box, a pipe, some paper called "onion-peel," and two books. He read the titles of the books. One was an English edition of Carlyle's "Hero-worship"; the other was a charming elzevir, in modern binding, the "Manual of Epictetus," a German translation published at Leyden in 1634. On examining the books, he found that all the pages were underlined and annotated. Were they prepared as a code for correspondence, or did they simply express the studious character of the reader? Then he examined the tobacco-box and the pipe. Finally, he took up the famous cigar with its gold band.

"Fichtre!" he exclaimed. "Our friend smokes a good cigar. It's a Henry Clay."

With the mechanical action of an habitual smoker, he placed the cigar close to his ear and squeezed it to make it crack. Immediately he uttered a cry of surprise. The cigar had yielded under the pressure of his fingers. He examined it more closely, and quickly discovered something white between the leaves of tobacco. Delicately, with the aid of a pin, he withdrew a roll of very thin paper, scarcely larger than a toothpick. It was a letter. He unrolled it, and found these words, written in a feminine handwriting:

"The basket has taken the place of the others. Eight out of ten are ready. On pressing the outer foot the plate goes downward. From twelve to sixteen every day, H-P will wait. But where? Reply at once. Rest easy; your friend is watching over you."

Mon. Dudouis reflected a moment, then said:

"It is quite clear.... the basket.... the eight compartments.... From twelve to sixteen means from twelve to four o'clock."

"But this H-P, that will wait?"

"H-P must mean automobile. H-P, horsepower, is the way they indicate strength of the motor. A twenty-four H-P is an automobile of twenty-four horsepower."

Then he rose, and asked:

"Had the prisoner finished his breakfast?"

"Yes."

"And as he has not yet read the message, which is proved by the condition of the cigar, it is probable that he had just received it."

"How?"

"In his food. Concealed in his bread or in a potato, perhaps."

"Impossible. His food was allowed to be brought in simply to trap him, but we have never found anything in it."

"We will look for Lupin's reply this evening. Detain him outside for a few minutes. I shall take this to the examining judge, and, if he agrees with me, we will have the letter photographed at once, and in an hour you can replace the letter in the drawer in a cigar similar to this. The prisoner must have no cause for suspicion."

It was not without a certain curiosity that Mon. Dudouis returned to the prison in the evening, accompanied by Inspector Dieuzy. Three empty plates were sitting on the stove in the corner.

"He has eaten?"

"Yes," replied the guard.

"Dieuzy, please cut that macaroni into very small pieces, and open that bread-roll....Nothing?"

"No, chief."

Mon. Dudouis examined the plates, the fork, the spoon, and the knife—an ordinary knife with a rounded blade. He turned the handle to the left; then to the right. It yielded and unscrewed. The knife was hollow, and served as a hiding-place for a sheet of paper.

"Peuh!" he said, "that is not very clever for a man like Arsène. But we mustn't lose any time. You, Dieuzy, go and search the restaurant."

Then he read the note:

"I trust to you, H-P will follow at a distance every day. I will go ahead. Au revoir, dear friend."

"At last," cried Mon. Dudouis, rubbing his hands gleefully, "I think we have the affair in our own hands. A little strategy on our part, and the escape will be a success in so far as the arrest of his confederates are concerned."

"But if Arsène Lupin slips through your fingers?" suggested the guard.

"We will have a sufficient number of men to prevent that. If, however, he displays too much cleverness, ma foi, so much the worse for him! As to his band of robbers, since the chief refuses to speak, the others must."

And, as a matter of fact, Arsène Lupin had very little to say. For several months, Mon. Jules Bouvier, the examining judge, had exerted himself in vain. The investigation had been reduced to a few uninteresting arguments between the judge and the advocate, Maître Danval, one of the leaders of the bar. From time to time, through courtesy, Arsène Lupin would speak. One day he said:

"Yes, monsieur, le judge, I quite agree with you: the robbery of the Crédit Lyonnais, the theft in the rue de Babylone, the issue of the counterfeit bank-notes, the burglaries at the various châteaux, Armesnil, Gouret, Imblevain, Groseillers, Malaquis, all my work, monsieur, I did it all."

"Then will you explain to me—"

"It is useless. I confess everything in a lump, everything and even ten times more than you know nothing about."

Wearied by his fruitless task, the judge had suspended his examinations, but he resumed them after the two intercepted messages were brought to his attention; and regularly, at mid-day, Arsène Lupin was taken from the prison to the Dépôt in the prison-van with a certain number of other prisoners. They returned about three or four o'clock.

Now, one afternoon, this return trip was made under unusual conditions. The other prisoners not having been examined, it was decided to take back Arsène Lupin first, thus he found himself alone in the vehicle.

These prison-vans, vulgarly called "panniers à salade"—or salad-baskets—are divided lengthwise by a central corridor from which open ten compartments, five on either side. Each compartment is so arranged that the occupant must assume and retain a sitting posture, and, consequently, the five prisoners are seated one upon the other, and yet separated one from the other by partitions. A municipal guard, standing at one end, watches over the corridor.

Arsène was placed in the third cell on the right, and the heavy vehicle started. He carefully calculated when they left the quai de l'Horloge, and when they passed the Palais de Justice. Then, about the centre of the bridge Saint Michel, with his outer foot, that is to say, his right foot, he pressed upon the metal plate that closed his cell. Immediately something clicked, and the metal plate moved. He was able to ascertain that he was located between the two wheels.

He waited, keeping a sharp look-out. The vehicle was proceeding slowly along the boulevard Saint Michel. At the corner of Saint Germain it stopped. A truck horse had fallen. The traffic having been interrupted, a vast throng of fiacres and omnibuses had gathered there. Arsène Lupin looked out. Another prison-van had stopped close to the one he occupied. He moved the plate still farther, put his foot on one of the spokes of the wheel and leaped to the ground. A coachman saw him, roared with laughter, then tried to raise an outcry, but his voice was lost in the noise of the traffic that had commenced to move again. Moreover, Arsène Lupin was already far away.

He had run for a few steps; but, once upon the sidewalk, he turned and looked around; he seemed to scent the wind like a person who is uncertain which direction to take. Then, having decided, he put his hands in his pockets, and, with the careless air of an idle stroller, he proceeded up the boulevard. It was a warm, bright autumn day, and the cafés were full. He took a seat on the terrace of one of them. He ordered a bock and a package of cigarettes. He emptied his glass slowly, smoked one cigarette and lighted a second. Then he asked the waiter to send the proprietor to him. When the proprietor came, Arsène spoke to him in a voice loud enough to be heard by everyone:

"I regret to say, monsieur, I have forgotten my pocketbook. Perhaps, on the strength of my name, you will be pleased to give me credit for a few days. I am Arsène Lupin."

The proprietor looked at him, thinking he was joking. But Arsène repeated:

"Lupin, prisoner at the Santé, but now a fugitive. I venture to assume that the name inspires you with perfect confidence in me."

And he walked away, amidst shouts of laughter, whilst the proprietor stood amazed.

Lupin strolled along the rue Soufflot, and turned into the rue Saint Jacques. He pursued his way slowly, smoking his cigarettes and looking into the shop-windows. At the Boulevard de Port Royal he took his bearings, discovered where he was, and then walked in the direction of the rue de la Santé. The high forbidding walls of the prison were now before him. He pulled his hat forward to shade his face; then, approaching the sentinel, he asked:

"Is this the prison de la Santé?"

"Yes."

"I wish to regain my cell. The van left me on the way, and I would not abuse—"

"Now, young man, move along—quick!" growled the sentinel.

"Pardon me, but I must pass through that gate. And if you prevent Arsène Lupin from entering the prison it will cost you dear, my friend."

"Arsène Lupin! What are you talking about!"

"I am sorry I haven't a card with me," said Arsène, fumbling in his pockets.

The sentinel eyed him from head to foot, in astonishment. Then, without a word, he rang a bell. The iron gate was partly opened, and Arsène stepped inside. Almost immediately he encountered the keeper of the prison, gesticulating and feigning a violent anger. Arsène smiled and said:

"Come, monsieur, don't play that game with me. What! they take the precaution to carry me alone in the van, prepare a nice little obstruction, and imagine I am going to take to my heels and rejoin my friends. Well, and what about the twenty agents of the Sûreté who accompanied us on foot, in fiacres and on bicycles? No, the arrangement did not please me. I should not have got away alive. Tell me, monsieur, did they count on that?"

He shrugged his shoulders, and added:

"I beg of you, monsieur, not to worry about me. When I wish to escape I shall not require any assistance."

On the second day thereafter, the 'Echo de France,' which had apparently become the official reporter of the exploits of Arsène Lupin,—it was said that he was one of its principal shareholders—published a most complete account of this attempted escape. The exact wording of the messages exchanged between the prisoner and his mysterious friend, the means by which correspondence was constructed, the complicity of the police, the promenade on the Boulevard Saint Michel, the incident at the café Soufflot, everything was disclosed. It was known that the search of the restaurant and its waiters by Inspector Dieuzy had been fruitless. And the public also learned an extraordinary thing which demonstrated the infinite variety of resources that Lupin possessed: the prison-van, in which he was being carried, was prepared for the occasion and substituted by his accomplices for one of the six vans which did service at the prison.

The next escape of Arsène Lupin was not doubted by anyone. He announced it himself, in categorical terms, in a reply to Mon. Bouvier on the day following his attempted escape. The judge having made a jest about the affair, Arsène was annoyed, and, firmly eyeing the judge, he said, emphatically:

"Listen to me, monsieur! I give you my word of honor that this attempted flight was simply preliminary to my general plan of escape."

"I do not understand," said the judge.

"It is not necessary that you should understand."

And when the judge, in the course of that examination which was reported at length in the columns of the 'Echo de France,' when the judge sought to resume his investigation, Arsène Lupin exclaimed, with an assumed air of lassitude:

"Mon Dieu, Mon Dieu, what's the use! All these questions are of no importance!"

"What! No importance?" cried the judge.

"No; because I shall not be present at the trial."

"You will not be present?"

"No; I have fully decided on that, and nothing will change my mind."

Such assurance combined with the inexplicable indiscretions that Arsène committed every day served to annoy and mystify the officers of the law. There were secrets known only to Arsène Lupin; secrets that he alone could divulge. But for what purpose did he reveal them? And how?

Arsène Lupin was changed to another cell. The judge closed his preliminary investigation. No further proceedings were taken in his case for a period of two months, during which time Arsène was seen almost constantly lying on his bed with his face turned toward the wall. The changing of his cell seemed to discourage him. He refused to see his advocate. He exchanged only a few necessary words with his keepers.

During the fortnight preceding his trial, he resumed his vigorous life. He complained of want of air. Consequently, early every morning he was allowed to exercise in the courtyard, guarded by two men.

Public curiosity had not died out; every day it expected to be regaled with news of his escape; and, it is true, he had gained a considerable amount of public sympathy by reason of his verve, his gayety, his diversity, his inventive genius and the mystery of his life. Arsène Lupin must escape. It was his inevitable fate. The public expected it, and was surprised that the event had been delayed so long. Every morning the Préfect of Police asked his secretary:

"Well, has he escaped yet?"

"No, Monsieur le Préfect."

"To-morrow, probably."

And, on the day before the trial, a gentleman called at the office of the 'Grand Journal,' asked to see the court reporter, threw his card in the reporter's face, and walked rapidly away. These words were written on the card: "Arsène Lupin always keeps his promises."

It was under these conditions that the trial commenced. An enormous crowd gathered at the court. Everybody wished to see the famous Arsène Lupin. They had a gleeful anticipation that the prisoner would play some audacious pranks upon the judge. Advocates and magistrats, reporters and men of the world, actresses and society women were crowded together on the benches provided for the public.

It was a dark, sombre day, with a steady downpour of rain. Only a dim light pervaded the courtroom, and the spectators caught a very indistinct view of the prisoner when the guards brought him in. But his heavy, shambling walk, the manner in which he dropped into his seat, and his passive, stupid appearance were not at all prepossessing. Several times his advocate—one of Mon. Danval's assistants—spoke to him, but he simply shook his head and said nothing.

The clerk read the indictment, then the judge spoke:

"Prisoner at the bar, stand up. Your name, age, and occupation?"

Not receiving any reply, the judge repeated:

"Your name? I ask you your name?"

A thick, slow voice muttered:

"Baudru, Désiré."

A murmur of surprise pervaded the courtroom. But the judge proceeded:

"Baudru, Désiré? Ah! a new alias! Well, as you have already assumed a dozen different names and this one is, no doubt, as imaginary as the others, we will adhere to the name of Arsène Lupin, by which you are more generally known."

The judge referred to his notes, and continued:

"For, despite the most diligent search, your past history remains unknown. Your case is unique in the annals of crime. We know not whom you are, whence you came, your birth and breeding—all is a mystery to us. Three years ago you appeared in our midst as Arsène Lupin, presenting to us a strange combination of intelligence and perversion, immorality and generosity. Our knowledge of your life prior to that date is vague and problematical. It may be that the man called Rostat who, eight years ago, worked with Dickson, the prestidigitator, was none other than Arsène Lupin. It is probable that the Russian student who, six years ago, attended the laboratory of Doctor Altier at the Saint Louis Hospital, and who often astonished the doctor by the ingenuity of his hypotheses on subjects of bacteriology and the boldness of his experiments in diseases of the skin, was none other than Arsène Lupin. It is probable, also, that Arsène Lupin was the professor who introduced the Japanese art of jiu-jitsu to the Parisian public. We have some reason to believe that Arsène Lupin was the bicyclist who won the Grand Prix de l'Exposition, received his ten thousand francs, and was never heard of again. Arsène Lupin may have been, also, the person who saved so many lives through the little dormer-window at the Charity Bazaar; and, at the same time, picked their pockets."

The judge paused for a moment, then continued:

"Such is that epoch which seems to have been utilized by you in a thorough preparation for the warfare you have since waged against society; a methodical apprenticeship in which you developed your strength, energy and skill to the highest point possible. Do you acknowledge the accuracy of these facts?"

During this discourse the prisoner had stood balancing himself, first on one foot, then on the other, with shoulders stooped and arms inert. Under the strongest light one could observe his extreme thinness, his hollow cheeks, his projecting cheek-bones, his earthen-colored face dotted with small red spots and framed in a rough, straggling beard. Prison life had caused him to age and wither. He had lost the youthful face and elegant figure we had seen portrayed so often in the newspapers.

It appeared as if he had not heard the question propounded by the judge. Twice it was repeated to him. Then he raised his eyes, seemed to reflect, then, making a desperate effort, he murmured:

"Baudru, Désiré."

The judge smiled, as he said:

"I do not understand the theory of your defense, Arsène Lupin. If you are seeking to avoid responsibility for your crimes on the ground of imbecility, such a line of defense is open to you. But I shall proceed with the trial and pay no heed to your vagaries."

He then narrated at length the various thefts, swindles and forgeries charged against Lupin. Sometimes he questioned the prisoner, but the latter simply grunted or remained silent. The examination of witnesses commenced. Some of the evidence given was immaterial; other portions of it seemed more important, but through all of it there ran a vein of contradictions and inconsistencies. A wearisome obscurity enveloped the proceedings, until Detective Ganimard was called as a witness; then interest was revived.

From the beginning the actions of the veteran detective appeared strange and unaccountable. He was nervous and ill at ease. Several times he looked at the prisoner, with obvious doubt and anxiety. Then, with his hands resting on the rail in front of him, he recounted the events in which he had participated, including his pursuit of the prisoner across Europe and his arrival in America. He was listened to with great avidity, as his capture of Arsène Lupin was well known to everyone through the medium of the press. Toward the close of his testimony, after referring to his conversations with Arsène Lupin, he stopped, twice, embarrassed and undecided. It was apparent that he was possessed of some thought which he feared to utter. The judge said to him, sympathetically:

"If you are ill, you may retire for the present."

"No, no, but——"

He stopped, looked sharply at the prisoner, and said:

"I ask permission to scrutinize the prisoner at closer range. There is some mystery about him that I must solve."

He approached the accused man, examined him attentively for several minutes, then returned to the witness-stand, and, in an almost solemn voice, he said:

"I declare, on oath, that the prisoner now before me is not Arsène Lupin."

A profound silence followed the statement. The judge, nonplused for a moment, exclaimed:

"Ah! What do you mean? That is absurd!"

The detective continued:

"At first sight there is a certain resemblance, but if you carefully consider the nose, the mouth, the hair, the color of skin, you will see that it is not Arsène Lupin. And the eyes! Did he ever have those alcoholic eyes!"

"Come, come, witness! What do you mean? Do you pretend to say that we are trying the wrong man?"

"In my opinion, yes. Arsène Lupin has, in some manner, contrived to put this poor devil in his place, unless this man is a willing accomplice."

This dramatic dénouement caused much laughter and excitement amongst the spectators. The judge adjourned the trial, and sent for Mon. Bouvier, the gaoler, and guards employed in the prison.

When the trial was resumed, Mon. Bouvier and the gaoler examined the accused and declared that there was only a very slight resemblance between the prisoner and Arsène Lupin.

"Well, then!" exclaimed the judge, "who is this man? Where does he come from? What is he in prison for?"

Two of the prison-guards were called and both of them declared that the prisoner was Arsène Lupin. The judged breathed once more.

But one of the guards then said:

"Yes, yes, I think it is he."

"What!" cried the judge, impatiently, "you *think* it is he! What do you mean by that?"

"Well, I saw very little of the prisoner. He was placed in my charge in the evening and, for two months, he seldom stirred, but laid on his bed with his face to the wall."

"What about the time prior to those two months?"

"Before that he occupied a cell in another part of the prison. He was not in cell 24."

Here the head gaoler interrupted, and said:

"We changed him to another cell after his attempted escape."

"But you, monsieur, you have seen him during those two months?"

"I had no occasion to see him. He was always quiet and orderly."

"And this prisoner is not Arsène Lupin?"

"No."

"Then who is he?" demanded the judge.

"I do not know."

"Then we have before us a man who was substituted for Arsène Lupin, two months ago. How do you explain that?"

"I cannot."

In absolute despair, the judge turned to the accused and addressed him in a conciliatory tone:

"Prisoner, can you tell me how, and since when, you became an inmate of the Prison de la Santé?"

The engaging manner of the judge was calculated to disarm the mistrust and awaken the understanding of the accused man. He tried to reply. Finally, under clever and gentle questioning, he succeeded in framing a few phrases from which the following story was gleaned: Two months ago he had been taken to the Dépôt, examined and released. As he was leaving the building, a free man, he was seized by two guards and placed in the prison-van. Since then he had occupied cell 24. He was contented there, plenty to eat, and he slept well—so he did not complain.

All that seemed probable; and, amidst the mirth and excitement of the spectators, the judge adjourned the trial until the story could be investigated and verified.

. . .

The following facts were at once established by an examination of the prison records: Eight weeks before a man named Baudru Désiré had slept at the Dépôt. He was released the next day, and left the Dépôt at two o'clock in the afternoon. On the same day at two o'clock, having been examined for the last time, Arsène Lupin left the Dépôt in a prison-van.

Had the guards made a mistake? Had they been deceived by the resemblance and carelessly substituted this man for their prisoner?

Another question suggested itself: Had the substitution been arranged in advance? In that event Baudru must have been an accomplice and must have caused his own arrest for the express purpose of taking Lupin's place. But then, by what miracle had such a plan, based on a series of improbable chances, been carried to success?

Baudru Désiré was turned over to the anthropological service; they had never seen anything like him. However, they easily traced his past history. He was known at Courbevois, at Asnières and at Levallois. He lived on alms and slept in one of those rag-picker's huts near the barrier de Ternes. He had disappeared from there a year ago.

Had he been enticed away by Arsène Lupin? There was no evidence to that effect. And even if that was so, it did not explain the flight of the prisoner. That still remained a mystery. Amongst twenty theories which sought to explain it, not one was satisfactory. Of the escape itself, there was no doubt; an escape that was incomprehensible, sensational, in which the public, as well as the officers of the law, could detect a carefully prepared plan, a combination of circumstances marvelously dove-tailed, whereof the dénouement fully justified the confident prediction of Arsène Lupin: "I shall not be present at my trial."

After a month of patient investigation, the problem remained unsolved. The poor devil of a Baudru could not be kept in prison indefinitely, and to place him on trial would be ridiculous. There was no charge against him. Consequently, he was released; but the chief of the Sûreté resolved to keep him under surveillance. This idea originated with Ganimard. From his point of view there was neither complicity nor chance. Baudru was an instrument upon which Arsène Lupin had played with his extraordinary skill. Baudru, when set at liberty, would lead them to Arsène Lupin or, at least, to some of his accomplices. The two inspectors, Folenfant and Dieuzy, were assigned to assist Ganimard.

One foggy morning in January the prison gates opened and Baudru Désiré stepped forth—a free man. At first he appeared to be quite embarrassed, and walked like a person who has no precise idea whither he is going. He followed the rue de la Santé and the rue Saint Jacques. He stopped in front of an old-clothes shop, removed his jacket and his vest, sold his vest on which he realized a few sous; then, replacing his jacket, he proceeded on his way. He crossed the Seine. At the Châtelet an omnibus passed him. He wished to enter it, but there was no place. The controller advised him to secure a number, so he entered the waiting-room.

Ganimard called to his two assistants, and, without removing his eyes from the waiting room, he said to them:

"Stop a carriage.... no, two. That will be better. I will go with one of you, and we will follow him."

The men obeyed. Yet Baudru did not appear. Ganimard entered the waiting-room. It was empty.

"Idiot that I am!" he muttered, "I forgot there was another exit."

There was an interior corridor extending from the waiting-room to the rue Saint Martin. Ganimard rushed through it and arrived just in time to observe Baudru upon the top of the Batignolles-Jardin de Plates omnibus as it was turning the corner of the rue de Rivoli. He ran and caught the omnibus. But he had lost his two assistants. He must continue the pursuit alone. In his anger he was inclined to seize the man by the collar without ceremony. Was it not with premeditation and by means of an ingenious ruse that his pretended imbecile had separated him from his assistants?

He looked at Baudru. The latter was asleep on the bench, his head rolling from side to side, his mouth half-opened, and an incredible expression of stupidity on his blotched face. No, such an adversary was incapable of deceiving old Ganimard. It was a stroke of luck—nothing more.

At the Galleries-Lafayette, the man leaped from the omnibus and took the La Muette tramway, following the boulevard Haussmann and the avenue Victor Hugo. Baudru alighted at La Muette station; and, with a nonchalant air, strolled into the Bois de Boulogne.

He wandered through one path after another, and sometimes retraced his steps. What was he seeking? Had he any definite object? At the end of an hour, he appeared to be faint from fatigue, and, noticing a bench, he sat down. The spot, not far from Auteuil, on the edge of a pond hidden amongst the trees, was absolutely deserted. After the lapse of another half-hour, Ganimard became impatient and resolved to speak to the man. He approached and took a seat beside Baudru, lighted a cigarette, traced some figures in the sand with the end of his cane, and said:

"It's a pleasant day."

No response. But, suddenly the man burst into laughter, a happy, mirthful laugh, spontaneous and irresistible. Ganimard felt his hair stand on end in horror and surprise. It was that laugh, that infernal laugh he knew so well!

With a sudden movement, he seized the man by the collar and looked at him with a keen, penetrating gaze; and found that he no longer saw the man Baudru. To be sure, he saw Baudru; but, at the same time, he saw the other, the real man, Lupin. He discovered the intense life in the eyes, he filled up the shrunken features, he perceived the real flesh beneath the flabby skin, the real mouth through the grimaces that deformed it. Those were the eyes and mouth of the other, and especially his keen, alert, mocking expression, so clear and youthful!

"Arsène Lupin, Arsène Lupin," he stammered.

Then, in a sudden fit of rage, he seized Lupin by the throat and tried to hold him down. In spite of his fifty years, he still possessed unusual strength, whilst his adversary was apparently in a weak condition. But the struggle was a brief one. Arsène Lupin made only a slight movement, and, as suddenly as he had made the attack, Ganimard released his hold. His right arm fell inert, useless.

"If you had taken lessons in jiu-jitsu at the quai des Orfèvres," said Lupin, "you would know that that blow is called udi-shi-ghi in Japanese. A second more, and I would have broken your arm and that would have been just what you deserve. I am surprised that you, an old friend whom I respect and before whom I voluntarily expose my incognito, should abuse my confidence in that violent manner. It is unworthy—Ah! What's the matter?"

Ganimard did not reply. That escape for which he deemed himself responsible—was it not he, Ganimard, who, by his sensational evidence, had led the court into serious error? That escape appeared to him like a dark cloud on his professional career. A tear rolled down his cheek to his gray moustache.

"Oh! mon Dieu, Ganimard, don't take it to heart. If you had not spoken, I would have arranged for some one else to do it. I couldn't allow poor Baudru Désiré to be convicted."

"Then," murmured Ganimard, "it was you that was there? And now you are here?"

"It is I, always I, only I."

"Can it be possible?"

"Oh, it is not the work of a sorcerer. Simply, as the judge remarked at the trial, the apprenticeship of a dozen years that equips a man to cope successfully with all the obstacles in life."

"But your face? Your eyes?"

"You can understand that if I worked eighteen months with Doctor Altier at the Saint-Louis hospital, it was not out of love for the work. I considered that he, who would one day have the honor of calling himself Arsène Lupin, ought to be exempt from the ordinary laws governing appearance and identity. Appearance? That can be modified at will. For instance, a hypodermic injection of paraffine will puff up the skin at the desired spot. Pyrogallic acid will change your skin to that of an Indian. The juice of the greater celandine will adorn you with the most beautiful eruptions and tumors. Another chemical affects the growth of your beard and hair; another changes the tone of your voice. Add to that two months of dieting in cell 24; exercises repeated a thousand times to enable me to hold my features in a certain grimace, to carry my head at a certain inclination, and adapt my back and shoulders to a stooping posture. Then five drops of atropine in the eyes to make them haggard and wild, and the trick is done."

"I do not understand how you deceived the guards."

"The change was progressive. The evolution was so gradual that they failed to notice it."

"But Baudru Désiré?"

"Baudru exists. He is a poor, harmless fellow whom I met last year; and, really, he bears a certain resemblance to me. Considering my arrest as a possible event, I took charge of Baudru and studied the points wherein we differed in appearance with a view to correct them in my own person. My friends caused him to remain at the Dépôt overnight, and to leave there next day about the same hour as I did—a coincidence easily arranged. Of course, it was necessary to have a record of his detention at the Dépôt in order to establish the fact that such a person was a reality; otherwise, the police would have sought elsewhere to find out my identity. But, in offering to them this excellent Baudru, it was inevitable, you understand, inevitable that they would seize upon him, and, despite the insurmountable difficulties of a substitution, they would prefer to believe in a substitution than confess their ignorance."

"Yes, yes, of course," said Ganimard.

"And then," exclaimed Arsène Lupin, "I held in my hands a trump-card: an anxious public watching and waiting for my escape. And that is the fatal error into which you fell, you and the others, in the course of that fascinating game pending between me and the officers of the law wherein the stake was my liberty. And you supposed that I was playing to the gallery; that I was intoxicated with my success. I, Arsène Lupin, guilty of such weakness! Oh, no! And, no longer ago than the Cahorn affair, you said: "When Arsène Lupin cries from the housetops that he will escape, he has some object in view." But, sapristi, you must understand that in order to escape I must create, in advance, a public belief in that escape, a belief amounting to an article of faith, an absolute conviction, a reality as glittering as the sun. And I did create that belief that Arsène Lupin would escape, that Arsène Lupin would not be present at his trial. And when you gave your evidence and said: "That man is not Arsène Lupin," everybody was prepared to believe you. Had one person doubted it, had any one uttered this simple restriction: Suppose it is Arsène Lupin?—from that moment, I was lost. If anyone had scrutinized my face, not imbued with the idea that I was not Arsène Lupin, as you and the others did at my trial, but with the idea that I might be Arsène Lupin; then, despite all my precautions, I should have been recognized. But I had no fear. Logically, psychologically, no once could entertain the idea that I was Arsène Lupin."

He grasped Ganimard's hand.

"Come, Ganimard, confess that on the Wednesday after our conversation in the prison de la Santé, you expected me at your house at four o'clock, exactly as I said I would go."

"And your prison-van?" said Ganimard, evading the question.

"A bluff! Some of my friends secured that old unused van and wished to make the attempt. But I considered it impractical without the concurrence of a number of unusual circumstances. However, I found it useful to carry out that attempted escape and give it the widest publicity. An audaciously planned escape, though not completed, gave to the succeeding one the character of reality simply by anticipation."

"So that the cigar...."

"Hollowed by myself, as well as the knife."

"And the letters?"

"Written by me."

"And the mysterious correspondent?"

"Did not exist."

Ganimard reflected a moment, then said:

"When the anthropological service had Baudru's case under consideration, why did they not perceive that his measurements coincided with those of Arsène Lupin?"

"My measurements are not in existence."

"Indeed!"

"At least, they are false. I have given considerable attention to that question. In the first place, the Bertillon system records the visible marks of identification—and you have seen that they are not infallible—and, after that, the measurements of the head, the fingers, the ears, etc. Of course, such measurements are more or less infallible."

"Absolutely."

"No; but it costs money to get around them. Before we left America, one of the employees of the service there accepted so much money to insert false figures in my measurements. Consequently, Baudru's measurements should not agree with those of Arsène Lupin."

After a short silence, Ganimard asked:

"What are you going to do now?"

"Now," replied Lupin, "I am going to take a rest, enjoy the best of food and drink and gradually recover my former healthy condition. It is all very well to become Baudru or some other person, on occasion, and to change your personality as you do your shirt, but you soon grow weary of the change. I feel exactly as I imagine the man who lost his shadow must have felt, and I shall be glad to be Arsène Lupin once more."

He walked to and fro for a few minutes, then, stopping in front of Ganimard, he said:

"You have nothing more to say, I suppose?"

"Yes. I should like to know if you intend to reveal the true state of facts connected with your escape. The mistake that I made——"

"Oh! no one will ever know that it was Arsène Lupin who was discharged. It is to my own interest to surround myself with mystery, and therefore I shall permit my escape to retain its almost miraculous character. So, have no fear on that score, my dear friend. I shall say nothing. And now, good-bye. I am going out to dinner this evening, and have only sufficient time to dress."

"I though you wanted a rest."

"Ah! there are duties to society that one cannot avoid. To-morrow, I shall rest."

"Where do you dine to-night?"

"With the British Ambassador!"

IV. THE MYSTERIOUS TRAVELLER

The evening before, I had sent my automobile to Rouen by the highway. I was to travel to Rouen by rail, on my way to visit some friends that live on the banks of the Seine.

At Paris, a few minutes before the train started, seven gentlemen entered my compartment; five of them were smoking. No matter that the journey was a short one, the thought of traveling with such a company was not agreeable to me, especially as the car was built on the old model, without a corridor. I picked up my overcoat, my newspapers and my time-table, and sought refuge in a neighboring compartment.

It was occupied by a lady, who, at sight of me, made a gesture of annoyance that did not escape my notice, and she leaned toward a gentleman who was standing on the step and was, no doubt, her husband. The gentleman scrutinized me closely, and, apparently, my appearance did not displease him, for he smiled as he spoke to his wife with the air of one who reassures a frightened child. She smiled also, and gave me a friendly glance as if she now understood that I was one of those gallant men with whom a woman can remain shut up for two hours in a little box, six feet square, and have nothing to fear.

Her husband said to her:

"I have an important appointment, my dear, and cannot wait any longer. Adieu."

He kissed her affectionately and went away. His wife threw him a few kisses and waved her handkerchief. The whistle sounded, and the train started.

At that precise moment, and despite the protests of the guards, the door was opened, and a man rushed into our compartment. My companion, who was standing and arranging her luggage, uttered a cry of terror and fell upon the seat. I am not a coward— far from it—but I confess that such intrusions at the last minute are always disconcerting. They have a suspicious, unnatural aspect.

However, the appearance of the new arrival greatly modified the unfavorable impression produced by his precipitant action. He was correctly and elegantly dressed, wore a tasteful cravat, correct gloves, and his face was refined and intelligent. But, where the devil had I seen that face before? Because, beyond all possible doubt, I had seen it.

And yet the memory of it was so vague and indistinct that I felt it would be useless to try to recall it at that time.

Then, directing my attention to the lady, I was amazed at the pallor and anxiety I saw in her face. She was looking at her neighbor—they occupied seats on the same side of the compartment—with an expression of intense alarm, and I perceived that one of her trembling hands was slowly gliding toward a little traveling bag that was lying on the seat about twenty inches from her. She finished by seizing it and nervously drawing it to her. Our eyes met, and I read in hers so much anxiety and fear that I could not refrain from speaking to her:

"Are you ill, madame? Shall I open the window?"

Her only reply was a gesture indicating that she was afraid of our companion. I smiled, as her husband had done, shrugged my shoulders, and explained to her, in pantomime, that she had nothing to fear, that I was there, and, besides, the gentleman appeared to be a very harmless individual. At that moment, he turned toward us, scrutinized both of us from head to foot, then settled down in his corner and paid us no more attention.

After a short silence, the lady, as if she had mustered all her energy to perform a desperate act, said to me, in an almost inaudible voice:

"Do you know who is on our train?"

"Who?"

"He.... he....I assure you...."

"Who is he?"

"Arsène Lupin!"

She had not taken her eyes off our companion, and it was to him rather than to me that she uttered the syllables of that disquieting name. He drew his hat over his face. Was that to conceal his agitation or, simply, to arrange himself for sleep? Then I said to her:

"Yesterday, through contumacy, Arsène Lupin was sentenced to twenty years' imprisonment at hard labor. Therefore it is improbable that he would be so imprudent, to-day, as to show himself in public. Moreover, the newspapers have announced his appearance in Turkey since his escape from the Santé."

"But he is on this train at the present moment," the lady proclaimed, with the obvious intention of being heard by our companion; "my husband is one of the directors in the penitentiary service, and it was the stationmaster himself who told us that a search was being made for Arsène Lupin."

"They may have been mistaken—"

"No; he was seen in the waiting-room. He bought a first-class ticket for Rouen."

"He has disappeared. The guard at the waiting-room door did not see him pass, and it is supposed that he had got into the express that leaves ten minutes after us."

"In that case, they will be sure to catch him."

"Unless, at the last moment, he leaped from that train to come here, into our train.... which is quite probable.... which is almost certain."

"If so, he will be arrested just the same; for the employees and guards would no doubt observe his passage from one train to the other, and, when we arrive at Rouen, they will arrest him there."

"Him—never! He will find some means of escape."

"In that case, I wish him 'bon voyage.'"

34

"But, in the meantime, think what he may do!"

"What?"

"I don't know. He may do anything."

She was greatly agitated, and, truly, the situation justified, to some extent, her nervous excitement. I was impelled to say to her:

"Of course, there are many strange coincidences, but you need have no fear. Admitting that Arsène Lupin is on this train, he will not commit any indiscretion; he will be only too happy to escape the peril that already threatens him."

My words did not reassure her, but she remained silent for a time. I unfolded my newspapers and read reports of Arsène Lupin's trial, but, as they contained nothing that was new to me, I was not greatly interested. Moreover, I was tired and sleepy. I felt my eyelids close and my head drop.

"But, monsieur, you are not going to sleep!"

She seized my newspaper, and looked at me with indignation.

"Certainly not," I said.

"That would be very imprudent."

"Of course," I assented.

I struggled to keep awake. I looked through the window at the landscape and the fleeting clouds, but in a short time all that became confused and indistinct; the image of the nervous lady and the drowsy gentleman were effaced from my memory, and I was buried in the soothing depths of a profound sleep. The tranquility of my response was soon disturbed by disquieting dreams, wherein a creature that had played the part and bore the name of Arsène Lupin held an important place. He appeared to me with his back laden with articles of value; he leaped over walls, and plundered castles. But the outlines of that creature, who was no longer Arsène Lupin, assumed a more definite form. He came toward me, growing larger and larger, leaped into the compartment with incredible agility, and landed squarely on my chest. With a cry of fright and pain, I awoke. The man, the traveller, our companion, with his knee on my breast, held me by the throat.

My sight was very indistinct, for my eyes were suffused with blood. I could see the lady, in a corner of the compartment, convulsed with fright. I tried even not to resist. Besides, I did not have the strength. My temples throbbed; I was almost strangled. One minute more, and I would have breathed my last. The man must have realized it, for he relaxed his grip, but did not remove his hand. Then he took a cord, in which he had prepared a slip-knot, and tied my wrists together. In an instant, I was bound, gagged, and helpless.

Certainly, he accomplished the trick with an ease and skill that revealed the hand of a master; he was, no doubt, a professional thief. Not a word, not a nervous movement; only coolness and audacity. And I was there, lying on the bench, bound like a mummy, I— Arsène Lupin!

It was anything but a laughing matter, and yet, despite the gravity of the situation, I keenly appreciated the humor and irony that it involved. Arsène Lupin seized and bound like a novice! robbed as if I were an unsophisticated rustic—for, you must understand, the scoundrel had deprived me of my purse and wallet! Arsène Lupin, a victim, duped, vanquished....What an adventure!

The lady did not move. He did not even notice her. He contented himself with picking up her traveling-bag that had fallen to the floor and taking from it the jewels, purse, and gold and silver trinkets that it contained. The lady opened her eyes, trembled with fear, drew the rings from her fingers and handed them to the man as if she wished to spare him unnecessary trouble. He took the rings and looked at her. She swooned.

Then, quite unruffled, he resumed his seat, lighted a cigarette, and proceeded to examine the treasure that he had acquired. The examination appeared to give him perfect satisfaction.

But I was not so well satisfied. I do not speak of the twelve thousand francs of which I had been unduly deprived: that was only a temporary loss, because I was certain that I would recover possession of that money after a very brief delay, together with the important papers contained in my wallet: plans, specifications, addresses, lists of correspondents, and compromising letters. But, for the moment, a more immediate and more serious question troubled me: How would this affair end? What would be the outcome of this adventure?

As you can imagine, the disturbance created by my passage through the Saint-Lazare station has not escaped my notice. Going to visit friends who knew me under the name of Guillaume Berlat, and amongst whom my resemblance to Arsène Lupin was a subject of many innocent jests, I could not assume a disguise, and my presence had been remarked. So, beyond question, the commissary of police at Rouen, notified by telegraph, and assisted by numerous agents, would be awaiting the train, would question all suspicious passengers, and proceed to search the cars.

Of course, I had foreseen all that, but it had not disturbed me, as I was certain that the police of Rouen would not be any shrewder than the police of Paris and that I could escape recognition; would it not be sufficient for me to carelessly display my card as "député," thanks to which I had inspired complete confidence in the gate-keeper at Saint-Lazare?—But the situation was greatly changed. I was no longer free. It was impossible to attempt one of my usual tricks. In one of the compartments, the commissary of police would find Mon. Arsène Lupin, bound hand and foot, as docile as a lamb, packed up, all ready to be dumped into a prison-van. He would have simply to accept delivery of the parcel, the same as if it were so much merchandise or a basket of fruit and vegetables. Yet, to avoid that shameful dénouement, what could I do?—bound and gagged, as I was? And the train was rushing on toward Rouen, the next and only station.

Another problem was presented, in which I was less interested, but the solution of which aroused my professional curiosity. What were the intentions of my rascally companion? Of course, if I had been alone, he could, on our arrival at Rouen, leave the car slowly and fearlessly. But the lady? As soon as the door of the compartment should be opened, the lady, now so quiet and humble, would scream and call for help. That was the dilemma that perplexed me! Why had he not reduced her to a helpless condition similar to mine? That would have given him ample time to disappear before his double crime was discovered.

He was still smoking, with his eyes fixed upon the window that was now being streaked with drops of rain. Once he turned, picked up my time-table, and consulted it.

The lady had to feign a continued lack of consciousness in order to deceive the enemy. But fits of coughing, provoked by the smoke, exposed her true condition. As to me, I was very uncomfortable, and very tired. And I meditated; I plotted.

The train was rushing on, joyously, intoxicated with its own speed.

Saint Etienne!....At that moment, the man arose and took two steps toward us, which caused the lady to utter a cry of alarm and fall into a genuine swoon. What was the man about to do? He lowered the window on our side. A heavy rain was now falling, and, by a gesture, the man expressed his annoyance at his not having an umbrella or an overcoat. He glanced at the rack. The lady's umbrella was there. He took it. He also took my overcoat and put it on.

We were now crossing the Seine. He turned up the bottoms of his trousers, then leaned over and raised the exterior latch of the door. Was he going to throw himself upon the track? At that speed, it would have been instant death. We now entered a tunnel. The man opened the door half-way and stood on the upper step. What folly! The darkness, the smoke, the noise, all gave a fantastic appearance to his actions. But suddenly, the train diminished its speed. A moment later it increased its speed, then slowed up again. Probably, some repairs were being made in that part of the tunnel which obliged the trains to diminish their speed, and the man was aware of the fact. He immediately stepped down to the lower step, closed the door behind him, and leaped to the ground. He was gone.

The lady immediately recovered her wits, and her first act was to lament the loss of her jewels. I gave her an imploring look. She understood, and quickly removed the gag that stifled me. She wished to untie the cords that bound me, but I prevented her.

"No, no, the police must see everything exactly as it stands. I want them to see what the rascal did to us."

"Suppose I pull the alarm-bell?"

"Too late. You should have done that when he made the attack on me."

"But he would have killed me. Ah! monsieur, didn't I tell you that he was on this train. I recognized him from his portrait. And now he has gone off with my jewels."

"Don't worry. The police will catch him."

"Catch Arsène Lupin! Never."

"That depends on you, madame. Listen. When we arrive at Rouen, be at the door and call. Make a noise. The police and the railway employees will come. Tell what you have seen: the assault made on me and the flight of Arsène Lupin. Give a description of him— soft hat, umbrella—yours—gray overcoat...."

"Yours," said she.

"What! mine? Not at all. It was his. I didn't have any."

"It seems to me he didn't have one when he came in."

"Yes, yes.... unless the coat was one that some one had forgotten and left in the rack. At all events, he had it when he went away, and that is the essential point. A gray overcoat— remember!.....Ah! I forgot. You must tell your name, first thing you do. Your husband's official position will stimulate the zeal of the police."

We arrived at the station. I gave her some further instructions in a rather imperious tone:

"Tell them my name—Guillaume Berlat. If necessary, say that you know me. That will save time. We must expedite the preliminary investigation. The important thing is the pursuit of Arsène Lupin. Your jewels, remember! Let there be no mistake. Guillaume Berlat, a friend of your husband."

"I understand....Guillaume Berlat."

She was already calling and gesticulating. As soon as the train stopped, several men entered the compartment. The critical moment had come.

Panting for breath, the lady exclaimed:

"Arsène Lupin.... he attacked us.... he stole my jewels....I am Madame Renaud.... my husband is a director of the penitentiary service....Ah! here is my brother, Georges Ardelle, director of the Crédit Rouennais.... you must know...."

She embraced a young man who had just joined us, and whom the commissary saluted. Then she continued, weeping:

"Yes, Arsène Lupin.... while monsieur was sleeping, he seized him by the throat....Mon. Berlat, a friend of my husband."

The commissary asked:

"But where is Arsène Lupin?"

"He leaped from the train, when passing through the tunnel."

"Are you sure that it was he?"

"Am I sure! I recognized him perfectly. Besides, he was seen at the Saint-Lazare station. He wore a soft hat——"

"No, a hard felt, like that," said the commissary, pointing to my hat.

"He had a soft hat, I am sure," repeated Madame Renaud, "and a gray overcoat."

"Yes, that is right," replied the commissary, "the telegram says he wore a gray overcoat with a black velvet collar."

"Exactly, a black velvet collar," exclaimed Madame Renaud, triumphantly.

I breathed freely. Ah! the excellent friend I had in that little woman.

The police agents had now released me. I bit my lips until they ran blood. Stooping over, with my handkerchief over my mouth, an attitude quite natural in a person who has remained for a long time in an uncomfortable position, and whose mouth shows the bloody marks of the gag, I addressed the commissary, in a weak voice:

"Monsieur, it was Arsène Lupin. There is no doubt about that. If we make haste, he can be caught yet. I think I may be of some service to you."

The railway car, in which the crime occurred, was detached from the train to serve as a mute witness at the official investigation. The train continued on its way to Havre. We were then conducted to the station-master's office through a crowd of curious spectators.

Then, I had a sudden access of doubt and discretion. Under some pretext or other, I must gain my automobile, and escape. To remain there was dangerous. Something might happen; for instance, a telegram from Paris, and I would be lost.

Yes, but what about my thief? Abandoned to my own resources, in an unfamiliar country, I could not hope to catch him.

"Bah! I must make the attempt," I said to myself. "It may be a difficult game, but an amusing one, and the stake is well worth the trouble."

And when the commissary asked us to repeat the story of the robbery, I exclaimed:

"Monsieur, really, Arsène Lupin is getting the start of us. My automobile is waiting in the courtyard. If you will be so kind as to use it, we can try...."

The commissary smiled, and replied:

"The idea is a good one; so good, indeed, that it is already being carried out. Two of my men have set out on bicycles. They have been gone for some time."

"Where did they go?"

"To the entrance of the tunnel. There, they will gather evidence, secure witnesses, and follow on the track of Arsène Lupin."

I could not refrain from shrugging my shoulders, as I replied:

"Your men will not secure any evidence or any witnesses."

"Really!"

"Arsène Lupin will not allow anyone to see him emerge from the tunnel. He will take the first road——"

"To Rouen, where we will arrest him."

"He will not go to Rouen."

"Then he will remain in the vicinity, where his capture will be even more certain."

"He will not remain in the vicinity."

"Oh! oh! And where will he hide?"

I looked at my watch, and said:

"At the present moment, Arsène Lupin is prowling around the station at Darnétal. At ten fifty, that is, in twenty-two minutes from now, he will take the train that goes from Rouen to Amiens."

"Do you think so? How do you know it?"

"Oh! it is quite simple. While we were in the car, Arsène Lupin consulted my railway guide. Why did he do it? Was there, not far from the spot where he disappeared, another line of railway, a station upon that line, and a train stopping at that station? On consulting my railway guide, I found such to be the case."

"Really, monsieur," said the commissary, "that is a marvelous deduction. I congratulate you on your skill."

I was now convinced that I had made a mistake in displaying so much cleverness. The commissary regarded me with astonishment, and I thought a slight suspicion entered his official mind....Oh! scarcely that, for the photographs distributed broadcast by the police department were too imperfect; they presented an Arsène Lupin so different from the one he had before him, that he could not possibly recognize me by it. But, all the same, he was troubled, confused and ill-at-ease.

"Mon Dieu! nothing stimulates the comprehension so much as the loss of a pocketbook and the desire to recover it. And it seems to me that if you will give me two of your men, we may be able...."

"Oh! I beg of you, monsieur le commissaire," cried Madame Renaud, "listen to Mon. Berlat."

The intervention of my excellent friend was decisive. Pronounced by her, the wife of an influential official, the name of Berlat became really my own, and gave me an identity that no mere suspicion could affect. The commissary arose, and said:

"Believe me, Monsieur Berlat, I shall be delighted to see you succeed. I am as much interested as you are in the arrest of Arsène Lupin."

He accompanied me to the automobile, and introduced two of his men, Honoré Massol and Gaston Delivet, who were assigned to assist me. My chauffer cranked up the car and I took my place at the wheel. A few seconds later, we left the station. I was saved.

Ah! I must confess that in rolling over the boulevards that surrounded the old Norman city, in my swift thirty-five horse-power Moreau-Lepton, I experienced a deep feeling of pride, and the motor responded, sympathetically to my desires. At right and left, the trees flew past us with startling rapidity, and I, free, out of danger, had simply to arrange my little personal affairs with the two honest representatives of the Rouen police who were sitting behind me. Arsène Lupin was going in search of Arsène Lupin!

Modest guardians of social order—Gaston Delivet and Honoré Massol—how valuable was your assistance! What would I have done without you? Without you, many times, at the cross-roads, I might have taken the wrong route! Without you, Arsène Lupin would have made a mistake, and the other would have escaped!

But the end was not yet. Far from it. I had yet to capture the thief and recover the stolen papers. Under no circumstances must my two acolytes be permitted to see those papers, much less to seize them. That was a point that might give me some difficulty.

We arrived at Darnétal three minutes after the departure of the train. True, I had the consolation of learning that a man wearing a gray overcoat with a black velvet collar had taken the train at the station. He had bought a second-class ticket for Amiens. Certainly, my début as detective was a promising one.

Delivet said to me:

"The train is express, and the next stop is Montérolier-Buchy in nineteen minutes. If we do not reach there before Arsène Lupin, he can proceed to Amiens, or change for the train going to Clères, and, from that point, reach Dieppe or Paris."

"How far to Montérolier?"

"Twenty-three kilometres."

"Twenty-three kilometres in nineteen minutes....We will be there ahead of him."

We were off again! Never had my faithful Moreau-Repton responded to my impatience with such ardor and regularity. It participated in my anxiety. It indorsed my determination. It comprehended my animosity against that rascally Arsène Lupin. The knave! The traitor!

"Turn to the right," cried Delivet, "then to the left."

We fairly flew, scarcely touching the ground. The mile-stones looked like little timid beasts that vanished at our approach. Suddenly, at a turn of the road, we saw a vortex of smoke. It was the Northern Express. For a kilometre, it was a struggle, side by side, but an unequal struggle in which the issue was certain. We won the race by twenty lengths.

In three seconds we were on the platform standing before the second-class carriages. The doors were opened, and some passengers alighted, but not my thief. We made a search through the compartments. No sign of Arsène Lupin.

"Sapristi!" I cried, "he must have recognized me in the automobile as we were racing, side by side, and he leaped from the train."

"Ah! there he is now! crossing the track."

I started in pursuit of the man, followed by my two acolytes, or rather followed by one of them, for the other, Massol, proved himself to be a runner of exceptional speed and endurance. In a few moments, he had made an appreciable gain upon the fugitive. The man noticed it, leaped over a hedge, scampered across a meadow, and entered a thick grove. When we reached this grove, Massol was waiting for us. He went no farther, for fear of losing us.

"Quite right, my dear friend," I said. "After such a run, our victim must be out of wind. We will catch him now."

I examined the surroundings with the idea of proceeding alone in the arrest of the fugitive, in order to recover my papers, concerning which the authorities would doubtless ask many disagreeable questions. Then I returned to my companions, and said:

"It is all quite easy. You, Massol, take your place at the left; you, Delivet, at the right. From there, you can observe the entire posterior line of the bush, and he cannot escape without you seeing him, except by that ravine, and I shall watch it. If he does not come out voluntarily, I will enter and drive him out toward one or the other of you. You have simply to wait. Ah! I forgot: in case I need you, a pistol shot."

Massol and Delivet walked away to their respective posts. As soon as they had disappeared, I entered the grove with the greatest precaution so as to be neither seen nor heard. I encountered dense thickets, through which narrow paths had been cut, but the overhanging boughs compelled me to adopt a stooping posture. One of these paths led to a clearing in which I found footsteps upon the wet grass. I followed them; they led me to the foot of a mound which was surmounted by a deserted, dilapidated hovel.

"He must be there," I said to myself. "It is a well-chosen retreat."

I crept cautiously to the side of the building. A slight noise informed me that he was there; and, then, through an opening, I saw him. His back was turned toward me. In two bounds, I was upon him. He tried to fire a revolver that he held in his hand. But he had no time. I threw him to the ground, in such a manner that his arms were beneath him, twisted and helpless, whilst I held him down with my knee on his breast.

"Listen, my boy," I whispered in his ear. "I am Arsène Lupin. You are to deliver over to me, immediately and gracefully, my pocketbook and the lady's jewels, and, in return therefore, I will save you from the police and enroll you amongst my friends. One word: yes or no?"

"Yes," he murmured.

"Very good. Your escape, this morning, was well planned. I congratulate you."

I arose. He fumbled in his pocket, drew out a large knife and tried to strike me with it.

"Imbecile!" I exclaimed.

With one hand, I parried the attack; with the other, I gave him a sharp blow on the carotid artery. He fell—stunned!

In my pocketbook, I recovered my papers and bank-notes. Out of curiosity, I took his. Upon an envelope, addressed to him, I read his name: Pierre Onfrey. It startled me. Pierre Onfrey, the assassin of the rue Lafontaine at Auteuil! Pierre Onfrey, he who had cut the throats of Madame Delbois and her two daughters. I leaned over him. Yes, those were the features which, in the compartment, had evoked in me the memory of a face I could not then recall.

But time was passing. I placed in an envelope two bank-notes of one hundred francs each, with a card bearing these words: "Arsène Lupin to his worthy colleagues Honoré Massol and Gaston Delivet, as a slight token of his gratitude." I placed it in a prominent spot in the room, where they would be sure to find it. Beside it, I placed Madame Renaud's handbag. Why could I not return it to the lady who had befriended me? I must confess that I had taken from it everything that possessed any interest or value, leaving there only a shell comb, a stick of rouge Dorin for the lips, and an empty purse. But, you know, business is business. And then, really, her husband is engaged in such a dishonorable vocation!

The man was becoming conscious. What was I to do? I was unable to save him or condemn him. So I took his revolver and fired a shot in the air.

"My two acolytes will come and attend to his case," I said to myself, as I hastened away by the road through the ravine. Twenty minutes later, I was seated in my automobile.

At four o'clock, I telegraphed to my friends at Rouen that an unexpected event would prevent me from making my promised visit. Between ourselves, considering what my friends must now know, my visit is postponed indefinitely. A cruel disillusion for them!

At six o'clock I was in Paris. The evening newspapers informed me that Pierre Onfrey had been captured at last.

Next day,—let us not despise the advantages of judicious advertising,—the 'Echo de France' published this sensational item:

"Yesterday, near Buchy, after numerous exciting incidents, Arsène Lupin effected the arrest of Pierre Onfrey. The assassin of the rue Lafontaine had robbed Madame Renaud, wife of the director in the penitentiary service, in a railway carriage on the Paris-Havre line. Arsène Lupin restored to Madame Renaud the hand-bag that contained her jewels, and gave a generous recompense to the two detectives who had assisted him in making that dramatic arrest."

V. THE QUEEN'S NECKLACE

Two or three times each year, on occasions of unusual importance, such as the balls at the Austrian Embassy or the soirées of Lady Billingstone, the Countess de Dreux-Soubise wore upon her white shoulders "The Queen's Necklace."

It was, indeed, the famous necklace, the legendary necklace that Bohmer and Bassenge, court jewelers, had made for Madame Du Barry; the veritable necklace that the Cardinal de Rohan-Soubise intended to give to Marie-Antoinette, Queen of France; and the same that the adventuress Jeanne de Valois, Countess de la Motte, had pulled to pieces one evening in February, 1785, with the aid of her husband and their accomplice, Rétaux de Villette.

To tell the truth, the mounting alone was genuine. Rétaux de Villette had kept it, whilst the Count de la Motte and his wife scattered to the four winds of heaven the beautiful stones so carefully chosen by Bohmer. Later, he sold the mounting to Gaston de Dreux-Soubise, nephew and heir of the Cardinal, who re-purchased the few diamonds that remained in the possession of the English jeweler, Jeffreys; supplemented them with other stones of the same size but of much inferior quality, and thus restored the marvelous necklace to the form in which it had come from the hands of Bohmer and Bassenge.

For nearly a century, the house of Dreux-Soubise had prided itself upon the possession of this historic jewel. Although adverse circumstances had greatly reduced their fortune, they preferred to curtail their household expenses rather than part with this relic of royalty. More particularly, the present count clung to it as a man clings to the home of his ancestors. As a matter of prudence, he had rented a safety-deposit box at the Crédit Lyonnais in which to keep it. He went for it himself on the afternoon of the day on which his wife wished to wear it, and he, himself, carried it back next morning.

On this particular evening, at the reception given at the Palais de Castille, the Countess achieved a remarkable success; and King Christian, in whose honor the fête was given, commented on her grace and beauty. The thousand facets of the diamond sparkled and shone like flames of fire about her shapely neck and shoulders, and it is safe to say that none but she could have borne the weight of such an ornament with so much ease and grace.

This was a double triumph, and the Count de Dreux was highly elated when they returned to their chamber in the old house of the faubourg Saint-Germain. He was proud of his wife, and quite as proud, perhaps, of the necklace that had conferred added luster to his noble house for generations. His wife, also, regarded the necklace with an almost childish vanity, and it was not without regret that she removed it from her shoulders and handed it to her husband who admired it as passionately as if he had never seen it before. Then, having placed it in its case of red leather, stamped with the Cardinal's arms, he passed into an adjoining room which was simply an alcove or cabinet that had been cut off from their chamber, and which could be entered only by means of a door at the foot of their bed. As he had done on previous occasions, he hid it on a high shelf amongst hat-boxes and piles of linen. He closed the door, and retired.

Next morning, he arose about nine o'clock, intending to go to the Crédit Lyonnais before breakfast. He dressed, drank a cup of coffee, and went to the stables to give his orders. The condition of one of the horses worried him. He caused it to be exercised in his presence. Then he returned to his wife, who had not yet left the chamber. Her maid was dressing her hair. When her husband entered, she asked:

"Are you going out?"

"Yes, as far as the bank."

"Of course. That is wise."

He entered the cabinet; but, after a few seconds, and without any sign of astonishment, he asked:

"Did you take it, my dear?"

"What?....No, I have not taken anything."

"You must have moved it."

"Not at all. I have not even opened that door."

He appeared at the door, disconcerted, and stammered, in a scarcely intelligible voice:

"You haven't....It wasn't you?....Then...."

She hastened to his assistance, and, together, they made a thorough search, throwing the boxes to the floor and overturning the piles of linen. Then the count said, quite discouraged:

"It is useless to look any more. I put it here, on this shelf."

"You must be mistaken."

"No, no, it was on this shelf—nowhere else."

They lighted a candle, as the room was quite dark, and then carried out all the linen and other articles that the room contained. And, when the room was emptied, they confessed, in despair, that the famous necklace had disappeared. Without losing time in vain lamentations, the countess notified the commissary of police, Mon. Valorbe, who came at once, and, after hearing their story, inquired of the count:

"Are you sure that no one passed through your chamber during the night?"

"Absolutely sure, as I am a very light sleeper. Besides, the chamber door was bolted, and I remember unbolting it this morning when my wife rang for her maid."

"And there is no other entrance to the cabinet?"

"None."

"No windows?"

"Yes, but it is closed up."

"I will look at it."

Candles were lighted, and Mon. Valorbe observed at once that the lower half of the window was covered by a large press which was, however, so narrow that it did not touch the casement on either side.

"On what does this window open?"

"A small inner court."

"And you have a floor above this?"

"Two; but, on a level with the servant's floor, there is a close grating over the court. That is why this room is so dark."

When the press was moved, they found that the window was fastened, which would not have been the case if anyone had entered that way.

"Unless," said the count, "they went out through our chamber."

"In that case, you would have found the door unbolted."

The commissary considered the situation for a moment, then asked the countess:

"Did any of your servants know that you wore the necklace last evening?"

"Certainly; I didn't conceal the fact. But nobody knew that it was hidden in that cabinet."

"No one?"

"No one.... unless...."

"Be quite sure, madam, as it is a very important point."

She turned to her husband, and said:

"I was thinking of Henriette."

"Henriette? She didn't know where we kept it."

"Are you sure?"

"Who is this woman Henriette?" asked Mon. Valorbe.

"A school-mate, who was disowned by her family for marrying beneath her. After her husband's death, I furnished an apartment in this house for her and her son. She is clever with her needle and has done some work for me."

"What floor is she on?"

"Same as ours.... at the end of the corridor.... and I think.... the window of her kitchen...."

"Opens on this little court, does it not?"

"Yes, just opposite ours."

Mon. Valorbe then asked to see Henriette. They went to her apartment; she was sewing, whilst her son Raoul, about six years old, was sitting beside her, reading. The commissary was surprised to see the wretched apartment that had been provided for the woman. It consisted of one room without a fireplace, and a very small room that served as a kitchen. The commissary proceeded to question her. She appeared to be overwhelmed on learning of the theft. Last evening she had herself dressed the countess and placed the necklace upon her shoulders.

"Good God!" she exclaimed, "it can't be possible!"

"And you have no idea? Not the least suspicion? Is it possible that the thief may have passed through your room?"

She laughed heartily, never supposing that she could be an object of suspicion.

"But I have not left my room. I never go out. And, perhaps, you have not seen?"

She opened the kitchen window, and said:

"See, it is at least three metres to the ledge of the opposite window."

"Who told you that we supposed the theft might have been committed in that way?"

"But.... the necklace was in the cabinet, wasn't it?"

"How do you know that?"

"Why, I have always known that it was kept there at night. It had been mentioned in my presence."

Her face, though still young, bore unmistakable traces of sorrow and resignation. And it now assumed an expression of anxiety as if some danger threatened her. She drew her son toward her. The child took her hand, and kissed it affectionately.

When they were alone again, the count said to the commissary:

"I do not suppose you suspect Henriette. I can answer for her. She is honesty itself."

"I quite agree with you," replied Mon. Valorbe. "At most, I thought there might have been an unconscious complicity. But I confess that even that theory must be abandoned, as it does not help solve the problem now before us."

The commissary of police abandoned the investigation, which was now taken up and completed by the examining judge. He questioned the servants, examined the condition of the bolt, experimented with the opening and closing of the cabinet window, and explored the little court from top to bottom. All was in vain. The bolt was intact. The window could not be opened or closed from the outside.

The inquiries especially concerned Henriette, for, in spite of everything, they always turned in her direction. They made a thorough investigation of her past life, and ascertained that, during the last three years, she had left the house only four times, and her business, on those occasions, was satisfactorily explained. As a matter of fact, she acted as chambermaid and seamstress to the countess, who treated her with great strictness and even severity.

At the end of a week, the examining judge had secured no more definite information than the commissary of police. The judge said:

"Admitting that we know the guilty party, which we do not, we are confronted by the fact that we do not know how the theft was committed. We are brought face to face with two obstacles: a door and a window—both closed and fastened. It is thus a double mystery. How could anyone enter, and, moreover, how could anyone escape, leaving behind him a bolted door and a fastened window?"

At the end of four months, the secret opinion of the judge was that the count and countess, being hard pressed for money, which was their normal condition, had sold the Queen's Necklace. He closed the investigation.

The loss of the famous jewel was a severe blow to the Dreux-Soubise. Their credit being no longer propped up by the reserve fund that such a treasure constituted, they found themselves confronted by more exacting creditors and money-lenders. They were obliged to cut down to the quick, to sell or mortgage every article that possessed any commercial value. In brief, it would have been their ruin, if two large legacies from some distant relatives had not saved them.

Their pride also suffered a downfall, as if they had lost a quartering from their escutcheon. And, strange to relate, it was upon her former schoolmate, Henriette, that the countess vented her spleen. Toward her, the countess displayed the most spiteful feelings, and even openly accused her. First, Henriette was relegated to the servants' quarters, and, next day, discharged.

For some time, the count and countess passed an uneventful life. They traveled a great deal. Only one incident of record occurred during that period. Some months after the departure of Henriette, the countess was surprised when she received and read the following letter, signed by Henriette:

"Madame,"

"I do not know how to thank you; for it was you, was it not, who sent me that? It could not have been anyone else. No one but you knows where I live. If I am wrong, excuse me, and accept my sincere thanks for your past favors...."

What did the letter mean? The present or past favors of the countess consisted principally of injustice and neglect. Why, then, this letter of thanks?

When asked for an explanation, Henriette replied that she had received a letter, through the mails, enclosing two bank-notes of one thousand francs each. The envelope, which she enclosed with her reply, bore the Paris post-mark, and was addressed in a handwriting that was obviously disguised. Now, whence came those two thousand francs? Who had sent them? And why had they sent them?

Henriette received a similar letter and a like sum of money twelve months later. And a third time; and a fourth; and each year for a period of six years, with this difference, that in the fifth and sixth years the sum was doubled. There was another difference: the post-office authorities having seized one of the letters under the pretext that it was not registered, the last two letters were duly sent according to the postal regulations, the first dated from Saint-Germain, the other from Suresnes. The writer signed the first one, "Anquety"; and the other, "Péchard." The addresses that he gave were false.

At the end of six years, Henriette died, and the mystery remained unsolved.

All these events are known to the public. The case was one of those which excite public interest, and it was a strange coincidence that this necklace, which had caused such a great commotion in France at the close of the eighteenth century, should create a similar commotion a century later. But what I am about to relate is known only to the parties directly interested and a few others from whom the count exacted a promise of secrecy. As it is probable that someday or other that promise will be broken, I have no hesitation in rending the veil and thus disclosing the key to the mystery, the explanation of the letter published in the morning papers two days ago; an extraordinary letter which increased, if possible, the mists and shadows that envelope this inscrutable drama.

Five days ago, a number of guests were dining with the Count de Dreux-Soubise. There were several ladies present, including his two nieces and his cousin, and the following gentlemen: the president of Essaville, the deputy Bochas, the chevalier Floriani, whom the count had known in Sicily, and General Marquis de Rouzières, an old club friend.

After the repast, coffee was served by the ladies, who gave the gentlemen permission to smoke their cigarettes, provided they would not desert the salon. The conversation was general, and finally one of the guests chanced to speak of celebrated crimes. And that gave the Marquis de Rouzières, who delighted to tease the count, an opportunity to mention the affair of the Queen's Necklace, a subject that the count detested.

Each one expressed his own opinion of the affair; and, of course, their various theories were not only contradictory but impossible.

"And you, monsieur," said the countess to the chevalier Floriani, "what is your opinion?"

"Oh! I—I have no opinion, madame."

All the guests protested; for the chevalier had just related in an entertaining manner various adventures in which he had participated with his father, a magistrate at Palermo, and which established his judgment and taste in such manners.

"I confess," said he, "I have sometimes succeeded in unraveling mysteries that the cleverest detectives have renounced; yet I do not claim to be Sherlock Holmes. Moreover, I know very little about the affair of the Queen's Necklace."

Everybody now turned to the count, who was thus obliged, quite unwillingly, to narrate all the circumstances connected with the theft. The chevalier listened, reflected, asked a few questions, and said:

"It is very strange.... at first sight, the problem appears to be a very simple one."

The count shrugged his shoulders. The others drew closer to the chevalier, who continued, in a dogmatic tone:

"As a general rule, in order to find the author of a crime or a theft, it is necessary to determine how that crime or theft was committed, or, at least, how it could have been committed. In the present case, nothing is more simple, because we are face to face, not with several theories, but with one positive fact, that is to say: the thief could only enter by the chamber door or the window of the cabinet. Now, a person cannot open a bolted door from the outside. Therefore, he must have entered through the window."

"But it was closed and fastened, and we found it fastened afterward," declared the count.

"In order to do that," continued Floriani, without heeding the interruption, "he had simply to construct a bridge, a plank or a ladder, between the balcony of the kitchen and the ledge of the window, and as the jewel-case——"

"But I repeat that the window was fastened," exclaimed the count, impatiently.

This time, Floriani was obliged to reply. He did so with the greatest tranquility, as if the objection was the most insignificant affair in the world.

"I will admit that it was; but is there not a transom in the upper part of the window?"

"How do you know that?"

"In the first place, that was customary in houses of that date; and, in the second place, without such a transom, the theft cannot be explained."

"Yes, there is one, but it was closed, the same as the window. Consequently, we did not pay attention to it."

"That was a mistake; for, if you had examined it, you would have found that it had been opened."

"But how?"

"I presume that, like all others, it opens by means of a wire with a ring on the lower end."

"Yes, but I do not see——"

"Now, through a hole in the window, a person could, by the aid of some instrument, let us say a poker with a hook at the end, grip the ring, pull down, and open the transom."

The count laughed and said:

"Excellent! excellent! Your scheme is very cleverly constructed, but you overlook one thing, monsieur, there is no hole in the window."

"There was a hole."

"Nonsense, we would have seen it."

"In order to see it, you must look for it, and no one has looked. The hole is there; it must be there, at the side of the window, in the putty. In a vertical direction, of course."

The count arose. He was greatly excited. He paced up and down the room, two or three times, in a nervous manner; then, approaching Floriani, said:

"Nobody has been in that room since; nothing has been changed."

"Very well, monsieur, you can easily satisfy yourself that my explanation is correct."

"It does not agree with the facts established by the examining judge. You have seen nothing, and yet you contradict all that we have seen and all that we know."

Floriani paid no attention to the count's petulance. He simply smiled and said:

"Mon Dieu, monsieur, I submit my theory; that is all. If I am mistaken, you can easily prove it."

"I will do so at once....I confess that your assurance——"

The count muttered a few more words; then suddenly rushed to the door and passed out. Not a word was uttered in his absence; and this profound silence gave the situation an air of almost tragic importance. Finally, the count returned. He was pale and nervous. He said to his friends, in a trembling voice:

"I beg your pardon.... the revelations of the chevalier were so unexpected....I should never have thought...."

His wife questioned him, eagerly:

"Speak.... what is it?"

He stammered: "The hole is there, at the very spot, at the side of the window——"

He seized the chevalier's arm, and said to him in an imperious tone:

"Now, monsieur, proceed. I admit that you are right so far, but now.... that is not all.... go on.... tell us the rest of it."

Floriani disengaged his arm gently, and, after a moment, continued:

"Well, in my opinion, this is what happened. The thief, knowing that the countess was going to wear the necklace that evening, had prepared his gangway or bridge during your absence. He watched you through the window and saw you hide the necklace. Afterward, he cut the glass and pulled the ring."

"Ah! but the distance was so great that it would be impossible for him to reach the window-fastening through the transom."

"Well, then, if he could not open the window by reaching through the transom, he must have crawled through the transom."

"Impossible; it is too small. No man could crawl through it."

"Then it was not a man," declared Floriani.

"What!"

"If the transom is too small to admit a man, it must have been a child."

"A child!"

"Did you not say that your friend Henriette had a son?"

"Yes; a son named Raoul."

"Then, in all probability, it was Raoul who committed the theft."

"What proof have you of that?"

"What proof! Plenty of it....For instance——"

He stopped, and reflected for a moment, then continued:

"For instance, that gangway or bridge. It is improbable that the child could have brought it in from outside the house and carried it away again without being observed.

48

He must have used something close at hand. In the little room used by Henriette as a kitchen, were there not some shelves against the wall on which she placed her pans and dishes?"

"Two shelves, to the best of my memory."

"Are you sure that those shelves are really fastened to the wooden brackets that support them? For, if they are not, we could be justified in presuming that the child removed them, fastened them together, and thus formed his bridge. Perhaps, also, since there was a stove, we might find the bent poker that he used to open the transom."

Without saying a word, the count left the room; and, this time, those present did not feel the nervous anxiety they had experienced the first time. They were confident that Floriani was right, and no one was surprised when the count returned and declared:

"It was the child. Everything proves it."

"You have seen the shelves and the poker?"

"Yes. The shelves have been unnailed, and the poker is there yet."

But the countess exclaimed:

"You had better say it was his mother. Henriette is the guilty party. She must have compelled her son——"

"No," declared the chevalier, "the mother had nothing to do with it."

"Nonsense! they occupied the same room. The child could not have done it without the mother's knowledge."

"True, they lived in the same room, but all this happened in the adjoining room, during the night, while the mother was asleep."

"And the necklace?" said the count. "It would have been found amongst the child's things."

"Pardon me! He had been out. That morning, on which you found him reading, he had just come from school, and perhaps the commissary of police, instead of wasting his time on the innocent mother, would have been better employed in searching the child's desk amongst his school-books."

"But how do you explain those two thousand francs that Henriette received each year? Are they not evidence of her complicity?"

"If she had been an accomplice, would she have thanked you for that money? And then, was she not closely watched? But the child, being free, could easily go to a neighboring city, negotiate with some dealer and sell him one diamond or two diamonds, as he might wish, upon condition that the money should be sent from Paris, and that proceeding could be repeated from year to year."

An indescribable anxiety oppressed the Dreux-Soubise and their guests. There was something in the tone and attitude of Floriani—something more than the chevalier's assurance which, from the beginning, had so annoyed the count. There was a touch of irony, that seemed rather hostile than sympathetic. But the count affected to laugh, as he said:

"All that is very ingenious and interesting, and I congratulate you upon your vivid imagination."

"No, not at all," replied Floriani, with the utmost gravity, "I imagine nothing. I simply describe the events as they must have occurred."

"But what do you know about them?"

"What you yourself have told me. I picture to myself the life of the mother and child down there in the country; the illness of the mother, the schemes of and inventions of the child to sell the precious stones in order to save his mother's life, or, at least, soothe her dying moments. Her illness overcomes her. She dies. Years roll on. The child becomes a man; and then—and now I will give my imagination a free rein—let us suppose that the man feels a desire to return to the home of his childhood, that he does so, and that he meets there certain people who suspect and accuse his mother.... do you realize the sorrow and anguish of such an interview in the very house wherein the original drama was played?"

His words seemed to echo for a few seconds in the ensuing silence, and one could read upon the faces of the Count and Countess de Dreux a bewildered effort to comprehend his meaning and, at the same time, the fear and anguish of such a comprehension. The count spoke at last, and said:

"Who are you, monsieur?"

"I? The chevalier Floriani, whom you met at Palermo, and whom you have been gracious enough to invite to your house on several occasions."

"Then what does this story mean?"

"Oh! nothing at all! It is simply a pastime, so far as I am concerned. I endeavor to depict the pleasure that Henriette's son, if he still lives, would have in telling you that he was the guilty party, and that he did it because his mother was unhappy, as she was on the point of losing the place of a.... servant, by which she lived, and because the child suffered at sight of his mother's sorrow."

He spoke with suppressed emotion, rose partially and inclined toward the countess. There could be no doubt that the chevalier Floriani was Henriette's son. His attitude and words proclaimed it. Besides, was it not his obvious intention and desire to be recognized as such?

The count hesitated. What action would he take against the audacious guest? Ring? Provoke a scandal? Unmask the man who had once robbed him? But that was a long time ago! And who would believe that absurd story about the guilty child? No; better far to accept the situation, and pretend not to comprehend the true meaning of it. So the count, turning to Floriani, exclaimed:

"Your story is very curious, very entertaining; I enjoyed it much. But what do you think has become of this young man, this model son? I hope he has not abandoned the career in which he made such a brilliant début."

"Oh! certainly not."

"After such a début! To steal the Queen's Necklace at six years of age; the celebrated necklace that was coveted by Marie-Antoinette!"

"And to steal it," remarked Floriani, falling in with the count's mood, "without costing him the slightest trouble, without anyone thinking to examine the condition of the window, or to observe that the window-sill was too clean—that window-sill which he had wiped in order to efface the marks he had made in the thick dust. We must admit that it was sufficient to turn the head of a boy at that age. It was all so easy. He had simply to desire the thing, and reach out his hand to get it."

"And he reached out his hand."

"Both hands," replied the chevalier, laughing.

His companions received a shock. What mystery surrounded the life of the so-called Floriani? How wonderful must have been the life of that adventurer, a thief at six years of age, and who, to-day, in search of excitement or, at most, to gratify a feeling of resentment, had come to brave his victim in her own house, audaciously, foolishly, and yet with all the grace and delicacy of a courteous guest!

He arose and approached the countess to bid her adieu. She recoiled, unconsciously. He smiled.

"Oh! Madame, you are afraid of me! Did I pursue my role of parlor-magician a step too far?"

She controlled herself, and replied, with her accustomed ease:

"Not at all, monsieur. The legend of that dutiful son interested me very much, and I am pleased to know that my necklace had such a brilliant destiny. But do you not think that the son of that woman, that Henriette, was the victim of hereditary influence in the choice of his vocation?"

He shuddered, feeling the point, and replied:

"I am sure of it; and, moreover, his natural tendency to crime must have been very strong or he would have been discouraged."

"Why so?"

"Because, as you must know, the majority of the diamonds were false. The only genuine stones were the few purchased from the English jeweler, the others having been sold, one by one, to meet the cruel necessities of life."

"It was still the Queen's Necklace, monsieur," replied the countess, haughtily, "and that is something that he, Henriette's son, could not appreciate."

"He was able to appreciate, madame, that, whether true or false, the necklace was nothing more than an object of parade, an emblem of senseless pride."

The count made a threatening gesture, but his wife stopped him.

"Monsieur," she said, "if the man to whom you allude has the slightest sense of honor—"

She stopped, intimidated by Floriani's cool manner.

"If that man has the slightest sense of honor," he repeated.

She felt that she would not gain anything by speaking to him in that manner, and in spite of her anger and indignation, trembling as she was from humiliated pride, she said to him, almost politely:

"Monsieur, the legend says that Rétaux de Villette, when in possession of the Queen's Necklace, did not disfigure the mounting. He understood that the diamonds were simply the ornament, the accessory, and that the mounting was the essential work, the creation of the artist, and he respected it accordingly. Do you think that this man had the same feeling?"

"I have no doubt that the mounting still exists. The child respected it."

"Well, monsieur, if you should happen to meet him, will you tell him that he unjustly keeps possession of a relic that is the property and pride of a certain family, and that, although the stones have been removed, the Queen's necklace still belongs to the house of Dreux-Soubise. It belongs to us as much as our name or our honor."

The chevalier replied, simply:

"I shall tell him, madame."

He bowed to her, saluted the count and the other guests, and departed.

. . .

Four days later, the countess de Dreux found upon the table in her chamber a red leather case bearing the cardinal's arms. She opened it, and found the Queen's Necklace.

But as all things must, in the life of a man who strives for unity and logic, converge toward the same goal—and as a little advertising never does any harm—on the following day, the 'Echo de France' published these sensational lines:

"The Queen's Necklace, the famous historical jewelry stolen from the family of Dreux-Soubise, has been recovered by Arsène Lupin, who hastened to restore it to its rightful owner. We cannot too highly commend such a delicate and chivalrous act."

VI. THE SEVEN OF HEARTS

I am frequently asked this question: "How did you make the acquaintance of Arsène Lupin?"

My connection with Arsène Lupin was well known. The details that I gather concerning that mysterious man, the irrefutable facts that I present, the new evidence that I produce, the interpretation that I place on certain acts of which the public has seen only the exterior manifestations without being able to discover the secret reasons or the invisible mechanism, all establish, if not an intimacy, at least amicable relations and regular confidences.

But how did I make his acquaintance? Why was I selected to be his historiographer? Why I, and not some one else?

The answer is simple: chance alone presided over my choice; my merit was not considered. It was chance that put me in his way. It was by chance that I was participant in one of his strangest and most mysterious adventures; and by chance that I was an actor in a drama of which he was the marvelous stage director; an obscure and intricate drama, bristling with such thrilling events that I feel a certain embarrassment in undertaking to describe it.

The first act takes place during that memorable night of 22 June, of which so much has already been said. And, for my part, I attribute the anomalous conduct of which I was guilty on that occasion to the unusual frame of mind in which I found myself on my return home. I had dined with some friends at the Cascade restaurant, and, the entire evening, whilst we smoked and the orchestra played melancholy waltzes, we talked only of crimes and thefts, and dark and frightful intrigues. That is always a poor overture to a night's sleep.

The Saint-Martins went away in an automobile. Jean Daspry—that delightful, heedless Daspry who, six months later, was killed in such a tragic manner on the frontier of Morocco—Jean Daspry and I returned on foot through the dark, warm night. When we arrived in front of the little house in which I had lived for a year at Neuilly, on the boulevard Maillot, he said to me:

"Are you afraid?"

"What an idea!"

"But this house is so isolated.... no neighbors.... vacant lots....Really, I am not a coward, and yet—"

"Well, you are very cheering, I must say."

"Oh! I say that as I would say anything else. The Saint-Martins have impressed me with their stories of brigands and thieves."

We shook hands and said good-night. I took out my key and opened the door.

"Well, that is good," I murmured, "Antoine has forgotten to light a candle."

Then I recalled the fact that Antoine was away; I had given him a short leave of absence. Forthwith, I was disagreeably oppressed by the darkness and silence of the night. I ascended the stairs on tiptoe, and reached my room as quickly as possible; then, contrary to my usual habit, I turned the key and pushed the bolt.

The light of my candle restored my courage. Yet I was careful to take my revolver from its case—a large, powerful weapon—and place it beside my bed. That precaution completed my reassurance. I laid down and, as usual, took a book from my night-table to read myself to sleep. Then I received a great surprise. Instead of the paper-knife with which I had marked my place on the preceding, I found an envelope, closed with five seals of red wax. I seized it eagerly. It was addressed to me, and marked: "Urgent."

A letter! A letter addressed to me! Who could have put it in that place? Nervously, I tore open the envelope, and read:

"From the moment you open this letter, whatever happens, whatever you may hear, do not move, do not utter one cry. Otherwise you are doomed."

I am not a coward, and, quite as well as another, I can face real danger, or smile at the visionary perils of imagination. But, let me repeat, I was in an anomalous condition of mind, with my nerves set on edge by the events of the evening. Besides, was there not, in my present situation, something startling and mysterious, calculated to disturb the most courageous spirit?

My feverish fingers clutched the sheet of paper, and I read and re-read those threatening words: "Do not move, do not utter one cry. Otherwise, you are doomed."

"Nonsense!" I thought. "It is a joke; the work of some cheerful idiot."

I was about to laugh—a good loud laugh. Who prevented me? What haunting fear compressed my throat?

At least, I would blow out the candle. No, I could not do it. "Do not move, or you are doomed," were the words he had written.

These auto-suggestions are frequently more imperious than the most positive realities; but why should I struggle against them? I had simply to close my eyes. I did so.

At that moment, I heard a slight noise, followed by crackling sounds, proceeding from a large room used by me as a library. A small room or antechamber was situated between the library and my bedchamber.

The approach of an actual danger greatly excited me, and I felt a desire to get up, seize my revolver, and rush into the library. I did not rise; I saw one of the curtains of the left window move. There was no doubt about it: the curtain had moved. It was still moving. And I saw—oh! I saw quite distinctly—in the narrow space between the curtains and the window, a human form; a bulky mass that prevented the curtains from hanging straight. And it is equally certain that the man saw me through the large meshes of the curtain. Then, I understood the situation. His mission was to guard me while the others carried away their booty. Should I rise and seize my revolver? Impossible! He was there! At the least movement, at the least cry, I was doomed.

Then came a terrific noise that shook the house; this was followed by lighter sounds, two or three together, like those of a hammer that rebounded. At least, that was the impression formed in my confused brain. These were mingled with other sounds, thus creating a veritable uproar which proved that the intruders were not only bold, but felt themselves secure from interruption.

They were right. I did not move. Was it cowardice? No, rather weakness, a total inability to move any portion of my body, combined with discretion; for why should I struggle? Behind that man, there were ten others who would come to his assistance. Should I risk my life to save a few tapestries and bibelots?

Throughout the night, my torture endured. Insufferable torture, terrible anguish! The noises had stopped, but I was in constant fear of their renewal. And the man! The man who was guarding me, weapon in hand. My fearful eyes remained cast in his direction. And my heart beat! And a profuse perspiration oozed from every pore of my body!

Suddenly, I experienced an immense relief; a milk-wagon, whose sound was familiar to me, passed along the boulevard; and, at the same time, I had an impression that the light of a new day was trying to steal through the closed window-blinds.

At last, daylight penetrated the room; other vehicles passed along the boulevard; and all the phantoms of the night vanished. Then I put one arm out of the bed, slowly and cautiously. My eyes were fixed upon the curtain, locating the exact spot at which I must fire; I made an exact calculation of the movements I must make; then, quickly, I seized my revolver and fired.

I leaped from my bed with a cry of deliverance, and rushed to the window. The bullet had passed through the curtain and the window-glass, but it had not touched the man— for the very good reason that there was none there. Nobody! Thus, during the entire night, I had been hypnotized by a fold of the curtain. And, during that time, the malefactors....Furiously, with an enthusiasm that nothing could have stopped, I turned the key, opened the door, crossed the antechamber, opened another door, and rushed into the library. But amazement stopped me on the threshold, panting, astounded, more astonished than I had been by the absence of the man. All the things that I supposed had been stolen, furniture, books, pictures, old tapestries, everything was in its proper place.

It was incredible. I could not believe my eyes. Notwithstanding that uproar, those noises of removal....I made a tour, I inspected the walls, I made a mental inventory of all the familiar objects. Nothing was missing. And, what was more disconcerting, there was no clue to the intruders, not a sign, not a chair disturbed, not the trace of a footstep.

"Well! Well!" I said to myself, pressing my hands on my bewildered head, "surely I am not crazy! I heard something!"

Inch by inch, I made a careful examination of the room. It was in vain. Unless I could consider this as a discovery: Under a small Persian rug, I found a card—an ordinary playing card. It was the seven of hearts; it was like any other seven of hearts in French playing-cards, with this slight but curious exception: The extreme point of each of the seven red spots or hearts was pierced by a hole, round and regular as if made with the point of an awl.

Nothing more. A card and a letter found in a book. But was not that sufficient to affirm that I had not been the plaything of a dream?

Throughout the day, I continued my searches in the library. It was a large room, much too large for the requirements of such a house, and the decoration of which attested the bizarre taste of its founder. The floor was a mosaic of multicolored stones, formed into large symmetrical designs. The walls were covered with a similar mosaic, arranged in panels, Pompeiian allegories, Byzantine compositions, frescoes of the Middle Ages. A Bacchus bestriding a cask. An emperor wearing a gold crown, a flowing beard, and holding a sword in his right hand.

Quite high, after the style of an artist's studio, there was a large window—the only one in the room. That window being always open at night, it was probable that the men had entered through it, by the aid of a ladder. But, again, there was no evidence. The bottom of the ladder would have left some marks in the soft earth beneath the window; but there were none. Nor were there any traces of footsteps in any part of the yard.

I had no idea of informing the police, because the facts I had before me were so absurd and inconsistent. They would laugh at me. However, as I was then a reporter on the staff of the 'Gil Blas,' I wrote a lengthy account of my adventure and it was published in the paper on the second day thereafter. The article attracted some attention, but no one took it seriously. They regarded it as a work of fiction rather than a story of real life. The Saint-Martins rallied me. But Daspry, who took an interest in such matters, came to see me, made a study of the affair, but reached no conclusion.

A few mornings later, the door-bell rang, and Antoine came to inform me that a gentleman desired to see me. He would not give his name. I directed Antoine to show him up. He was a man of about forty years of age with a very dark complexion, lively features, and whose correct dress, slightly frayed, proclaimed a taste that contrasted strangely with his rather vulgar manners. Without any preamble, he said to me—in a rough voice that confirmed my suspicion as to his social position:

"Monsieur, whilst in a café, I picked up a copy of the 'Gil Blas,' and read your article. It interested me very much.

"Thank you."

"And here I am."

"Ah!"

"Yes, to talk to you. Are all the facts related by you quite correct?"

"Absolutely so."

"Well, in that case, I can, perhaps, give you some information."

"Very well; proceed."

"No, not yet. First, I must be sure that the facts are exactly as you have related them."

"I have given you my word. What further proof do you want?"

"I must remain alone in this room."

"I do not understand," I said, with surprise.

"It's an idea that occurred to me when reading your article. Certain details established an extraordinary coincidence with another case that came under my notice. If I am mistaken, I shall say nothing more. And the only means of ascertaining the truth is by my remaining in the room alone."

What was at the bottom of this proposition? Later, I recalled that the man was exceedingly nervous; but, at the same time, although somewhat astonished, I found nothing particularly abnormal about the man or the request he had made. Moreover, my curiosity was aroused; so I replied:

"Very well. How much time do you require?"

"Oh! three minutes—not longer. Three minutes from now, I will rejoin you."

I left the room, and went downstairs. I took out my watch. One minute passed. Two minutes. Why did I feel so depressed? Why did those moments seem so solemn and weird? Two minutes and a half....Two minutes and three quarters. Then I heard a pistol shot.

I bounded up the stairs and entered the room. A cry of horror escaped me. In the middle of the room, the man was lying on his left side, motionless. Blood was flowing from a wound in his forehead. Near his hand was a revolver, still smoking.

But, in addition to this frightful spectacle, my attention was attracted by another object. At two feet from the body, upon the floor, I saw a playing-card. It was the seven of hearts. I picked it up. The lower extremity of each of the seven spots was pierced with a small round hole.

A half-hour later, the commissary of police arrived, then the coroner and the chief of the Sûreté, Mon. Dudouis. I had been careful not to touch the corpse. The preliminary inquiry was very brief, and disclosed nothing. There were no papers in the pockets of the deceased; no name upon his clothes; no initial upon his linen; nothing to give any clue to his identity. The room was in the same perfect order as before. The furniture had not been disturbed. Yet this man had not come to my house solely for the purpose of killing himself, or because he considered my place the most convenient one for his suicide! There must have been a motive for his act of despair, and that motive was, no doubt, the result of some new fact ascertained by him during the three minutes he was alone.

What was that fact? What had he seen? What frightful secret had been revealed to him? There was no answer to these questions. But, at the last moment, an incident occurred that appeared to us of considerable importance. As two policemen were raising the body to place it on a stretcher, the left hand thus being disturbed, a crumpled card fell from it. The card bore these words: "Georges Andermatt, 37 Rue de Berry."

What did that mean? Georges Andermatt was a rich banker in Paris, the founder and president of the Metal Exchange which had given such an impulse to the metallic industries in France. He lived in princely style; was the possessor of numerous automobiles, coaches, and an expensive racing-stable. His social affairs were very select, and Madame Andermatt was noted for her grace and beauty.

"Can that be the man's name?" I asked. ———————

The chief of the Sûreté leaned over him.

"It is not he. Mon. Andermatt is a thin man, and slightly grey."

"But why this card?"

"Have you a telephone, monsieur?"

"Yes, in the vestibule. Come with me."

He looked in the directory, and then asked for number 415.21.

"Is Mon. Andermatt at home?....Please tell him that Mon. Dudouis wished him to come at once to 102 Boulevard Maillot. Very important."

Twenty minutes later, Mon. Andermatt arrived in his automobile. After the circumstances had been explained to him, he was taken in to see the corpse. He displayed considerable emotion, and spoke, in a low tone, and apparently unwillingly:

"Etienne Varin," he said.

"You know him?"

"No.... or, at least, yes.... by sight only. His brother...."

"Ah! he has a brother?"

"Yes, Alfred Varin. He came to see me once on some matter of business....I forget what it was."

"Where does he live?"

"The two brothers live together—rue de Provence, I think."

"Do you know any reason why he should commit suicide?"

"None."

"He held a card in his hand. It was your card with your address."

"I do not understand that. It must have been there by some chance that will be disclosed by the investigation."

A very strange chance, I thought; and I felt that the others entertained the same impression.

I discovered the same impression in the papers next day, and amongst all my friends with whom I discussed the affair. Amid the mysteries that enveloped it, after the double discovery of the seven of hearts pierced with seven holes, after the two inscrutable events that had happened in my house, that visiting card promised to throw some light on the affair. Through it, the truth may be revealed. But, contrary to our expectations, Mon. Andermatt furnished no explanation. He said:

"I have told you all I know. What more can I do? I am greatly surprised that my card should be found in such a place, and I sincerely hope the point will be cleared up."

It was not. The official investigation established that the Varin brothers were of Swiss origin, had led a shifting life under various names, frequenting gambling resorts, associating with a band of foreigners who had been dispersed by the police after a series of robberies in which their participation was established only by their flight. At number 24 rue de Provence, where the Varin brothers had lived six years before, no one knew what had become of them.

I confess that, for my part, the case seemed to me so complicated and so mysterious that I did not think the problem would ever be solved, so I concluded to waste no more time upon it. But Jean Daspry, whom I frequently met at that period, became more and more interested in it each day. It was he who pointed out to me that item from a foreign newspaper which was reproduced and commented upon by the entire press. It was as follows:

"The first trial of a new model of submarine boat, which is expected to revolutionize naval warfare, will be given in presence of the former Emperor at a place that will be kept secret until the last minute. An indiscretion has revealed its name; it is called 'The Seven-of-Hearts.'"

The Seven-of-Hearts! That presented a new problem. Could a connection be established between the name of the sub-marine and the incidents which we have related? But a connection of what nature? What had happened here could have no possible relation with the sub-marine.

"What do you know about it?" said Daspry to me. "The most diverse effects often proceed from the same cause."

Two days later, the following foreign news item was received and published:

"It is said that the plans of the new sub-marine 'Seven-of-Hearts' were prepared by French engineers, who, having sought, in vain, the support of their compatriots, subsequently entered into negotiations with the British Admiralty, without success."

I do not wish to give undue publicity to certain delicate matters which once provoked considerable excitement. Yet, since all danger of injury therefrom has now come to an end, I must speak of the article that appeared in the 'Echo de France,' which aroused so much comment at that time, and which threw considerable light upon the mystery of the Seven-of-Hearts. This is the article as it was published over the signature of Salvator:

"THE AFFAIR OF THE SEVEN-OF-HEARTS.

"A CORNER OF THE VEIL RAISED.

"We will be brief. Ten years ago, a young mining engineer, Louis Lacombe, wishing to devote his time and fortune to certain studies, resigned his position he then held, and rented number 102 boulevard Maillot, a small house that had been recently built and decorated for an Italian count. Through the agency of the Varin brothers of Lausanne, one of whom assisted in the preliminary experiments and the other acted as financial agent, the young engineer was introduced to Georges Andermatt, the founder of the Metal Exchange.

"After several interviews, he succeeded in interesting the banker in a sub-marine boat on which he was working, and it was agreed that as soon as the invention was perfected, Mon. Andermatt would use his influence with the Minister of Marine to obtain a series of trials under the direction of the government. For two years, Louis Lacombe was a frequent visitor at Andermatt's house, and he submitted to the banker the various improvements he made upon his original plans, until one day, being satisfied with the perfection of his work, he asked Mon. Andermatt to communicate with the Minister of Marine. That day, Louis Lacombe dined at Mon. Andermatt's house. He left there about half-past eleven at night. He has not been seen since.

"A perusal of the newspapers of that date will show that the young man's family caused every possible inquiry to be made, but without success; and it was the general opinion that Louis Lacombe—who was known as an original and visionary youth—had quietly left for parts unknown.

"Let us accept that theory—improbable, though it be,—and let us consider another question, which is a most important one for our country: What has become of the plans of the sub-marine? Did Louis Lacombe carry them away? Are they destroyed?

"After making a thorough investigation, we are able to assert, positively, that the plans are in existence, and are now in the possession of the two brothers Varin. How did they acquire such a possession? That is a question not yet determined; nor do we know why they have not tried to sell them at an earlier date. Did they fear that their title to them would be called in question? If so, they have lost that fear, and we can announce definitely, that the plans of Louis Lacombe are now the property of foreign power, and we are in a position to publish the correspondence that passed between the Varin brothers and the representative of that power. The 'Seven-of-Hearts' invented by Louis Lacombe has been actually constructed by our neighbor.

"Will the invention fulfill the optimistic expectations of those who were concerned in that treacherous act?"

And a post-script adds:

"Later.—Our special correspondent informs us that the preliminary trial of the 'Seven-of-Hearts' has not been satisfactory. It is quite likely that the plans sold and delivered by the Varin brothers did not include the final document carried by Louis Lacombe to Mon. Andermatt on the day of his disappearance, a document that was indispensable to a thorough understanding of the invention. It contained a summary of the final conclusions of the inventor, and estimates and figures not contained

in the other papers. Without this document, the plans are incomplete; on the other hand, without the plans, the document is worthless.

"Now is the time to act and recover what belongs to us. It may be a difficult matter, but we rely upon the assistance of Mon. Andermatt. It will be to his interest to explain his conduct which has hitherto been so strange and inscrutable. He will explain not only why he concealed these facts at the time of the suicide of Etienne Varin, but also why he has never revealed the disappearance of the paper —a fact well known to him. He will tell why, during the last six years, he paid spies to watch the movements of the Varin brothers. We expect from him, not only words, but acts. And at once. Otherwise—-"

The threat was plainly expressed. But of what did it consist? What whip was Salvator, the anonymous writer of the article, holding over the head of Mon. Andermatt?

An army of reporters attacked the banker, and ten interviewers announced the scornful manner in which they were treated. Thereupon, the 'Echo de France' announced its position in these words:

"Whether Mon. Andermatt is willing or not, he will be, henceforth, our collaborator in the work we have undertaken."

Daspry and I were dining together on the day on which that announcement appeared. That evening, with the newspapers spread over my table, we discussed the affair and examined it from every point of view with that exasperation that a person feels when walking in the dark and finding himself constantly falling over the same obstacles. Suddenly, without any warning whatsoever, the door opened and a lady entered. Her face was hidden behind a thick veil. I rose at once and approached her.

"Is it you, monsieur, who lives here?" she asked.

"Yes, madame, but I do not understand—"

"The gate was not locked," she explained.

"But the vestibule door?"

She did not reply, and it occurred to me that she had used the servants' entrance. How did she know the way? Then there was a silence that was quite embarrassing. She looked at Daspry, and I was obliged to introduce him. I asked her to be seated and explain the object of her visit. She raised her veil, and I saw that she was a brunette with regular features and, though not handsome, she was attractive—principally, on account of her sad, dark eyes.

"I am Madame Andermatt," she said.

"Madame Andermatt!" I repeated, with astonishment.

After a brief pause, she continued with a voice and manner that were quite easy and natural:

"I have come to see you about that affair—you know. I thought I might be able to obtain some information—"

"Mon Dieu, madame, I know nothing but what has already appeared in the papers. But if you will point out in what way I can help you...."

"I do not know....I do not know."

Not until then did I suspect that her calm demeanor was assumed, and that some poignant grief was concealed beneath that air of tranquility. For a moment, we were silent and embarrassed. Then Daspry stepped forward, and said:

"Will you permit me to ask you a few questions?"

"Yes, yes," she cried. "I will answer."

"You will answer.... whatever those questions may be?"

"Yes."

"Did you know Louis Lacombe?" he asked.

"Yes, through my husband."

"When did you see him for the last time?"

"The evening he dined with us."

"At that time, was there anything to lead you to believe that you would never see him again?"

"No. But he had spoken of a trip to Russia—in a vague way."

"Then you expected to see him again?"

"Yes. He was to dine with us, two days later."

"How do you explain his disappearance?"

"I cannot explain it."

"And Mon. Andermatt?"

"I do not know."

"Yet the article published in the 'Echo de France' indicates——"

"Yes, that the Varin brothers had something to do with his disappearance."

"Is that your opinion?"

"Yes."

"On what do you base your opinion?"

"When he left our house, Louis Lacombe carried a satchel containing all the papers relating to his invention. Two days later, my husband, in a conversation with one of the Varin brothers, learned that the papers were in their possession."

"And he did not denounce them?"

"No."

"Why not?"

"Because there was something else in the satchel—something besides the papers of Louis Lacombe."

"What was it?"

She hesitated; was on the point of speaking, but, finally, remained silent. Daspry continued:

"I presume that is why your husband has kept a close watch over their movements instead of informing the police. He hoped to recover the papers and, at the same time, that compromising article which has enabled the two brothers to hold over him threats of exposure and blackmail."

"Over him, and over me."

"Ah! over you, also?"

"Over me, in particular."

She uttered the last words in a hollow voice. Daspry observed it; he paced to and fro for a moment, then, turning to her, asked:

"Had you written to Louis Lacombe?"

"Of course. My husband had business with him—"

"Apart from those business letters, had you written to Louis Lacombe.... other letters? Excuse my insistence, but it is absolutely necessary that I should know the truth. Did you write other letters?"

"Yes," she replied, blushing.

"And those letters came into the possession of the Varin brothers?"

"Yes."

"Does Mon. Andermatt know it?"

"He has not seen them, but Alfred Varin has told him of their existence and threatened to publish them if my husband should take any steps against him. My husband was afraid.... of a scandal."

"But he has tried to recover the letters?"

"I think so; but I do not know. You see, after that last interview with Alfred Varin, and after some harsh words between me and my husband in which he called me to account— we live as strangers."

"In that case, as you have nothing to lose, what do you fear?"

"I may be indifferent to him now, but I am the woman that he has loved, the one he would still love—oh! I am quite sure of that," she murmured, in a fervent voice, "he would still love me if he had not got hold of those cursed letters——"

"What! Did he succeed?....But the two brothers still defied him?"

"Yes, and they boasted of having a secure hiding-place."

"Well?"

"I believe my husband discovered that hiding-place."

"Ah! where was it?"

"Here."

"Here!" I cried in alarm.

"Yes. I always had that suspicion. Louis Lacombe was very ingenious and amused himself in his leisure hours, by making safes and locks. No doubt, the Varin brothers were aware of that fact and utilized one of Lacombe's safes in which to conceal the letters.... and other things, perhaps."

"But they did not live here," I said.

"Before you came, four months ago, the house had been vacant for some time. And they may have thought that your presence here would not interfere with them when they wanted to get the papers. But they did not count on my husband, who came here on the night of 22 June, forced the safe, took what he was seeking, and left his card to inform the two brothers that he feared them no more, and that their positions were now reversed. Two days later, after reading the article in the 'Gil Blas,' Etienne Varin came here, remained alone in this room, found the safe empty, and.... killed himself."

After a moment, Daspry said:

"A very simple theory....Has Mon. Andermatt spoken to you since then?"

"No."

"Has his attitude toward you changed in any way? Does he appear more gloomy, more anxious?"

"No, I haven't noticed any change."

"And yet you think he has secured the letters. Now, in my opinion, he has not got those letters, and it was not he who came here on the night of 22 June."

"Who was it, then?"

"The mysterious individual who is managing this affair, who holds all the threads in his hands, and whose invisible but far-reaching power we have felt from the beginning. It was he and his friends who entered this house on 22 June; it was he who discovered the hiding-place of the papers; it was he who left Mon. Andermatt's card; it is he who now holds the correspondence and the evidence of the treachery of the Varin brothers."

"Who is he?" I asked, impatiently.

"The man who writes letters to the 'Echo de France'.... Salvator! Have we not convincing evidence of that fact? Does he not mention in his letters certain details that no one could know, except the man who had thus discovered the secrets of the two brothers?"

"Well, then," stammered Madame Andermatt, in great alarm, "he has my letters also, and it is he who now threatens my husband. Mon Dieu! What am I to do?"

"Write to him," declared Daspry. "Confide in him without reserve. Tell him all you know and all you may hereafter learn. Your interest and his interest are the same. He is not working against Mon. Andermatt, but against Alfred Varin. Help him."

"How?"

"Has your husband the document that completes the plans of Louis Lacombe?"

"Yes."

"Tell that to Salvator, and, if possible, procure the document for him. Write to him at once. You risk nothing."

The advice was bold, dangerous even at first sight, but Madame Andermatt had no choice. Besides, as Daspry had said, she ran no risk. If the unknown writer were an enemy, that step would not aggravate the situation. If he were a stranger seeking to accomplish a particular purpose, he would attach to those letters only a secondary importance. Whatever might happen, it was the only solution offered to her, and she, in her anxiety, was only too glad to act on it. She thanked us effusively, and promised to keep us informed.

In fact, two days later, she sent us the following letter that she had received from Salvator:

"Have not found the letters, but I will get them. Rest easy. I am watching everything. S."

I looked at the letter. It was in the same handwriting as the note I found in my book on the night of 22 June.

Daspry was right. Salvator was, indeed, the originator of that affair.

We were beginning to see a little light coming out of the darkness that surrounded us, and an unexpected light was thrown on certain points; but other points yet remained obscure —for instance, the finding of the two seven-of-hearts. Perhaps I was unnecessarily concerned about those two cards whose seven punctured spots had appeared to me under such startling circumstances! Yet I could not refrain from asking myself: What role will they play in the drama? What importance do they bear? What conclusion must be drawn from the fact that the submarine constructed from the plans of Louis Lacombe bore the name of 'Seven-of-Hearts'?

Daspry gave little thought to the other two cards; he devoted all his attention to another problem which he considered more urgent; he was seeking the famous hiding-place.

"And who knows," said he, "I may find the letters that Salvator did not find—by inadvertence, perhaps. It is improbable that the Varin brothers would have removed from a spot, which they deemed inaccessible, the weapon which was so valuable to them."

And he continued to search. In a short time, the large room held no more secrets for him, so he extended his investigations to the other rooms. He examined the interior and the exterior, the stones of the foundation, the bricks in the walls; he raised the slates of the roof.

One day, he came with a pickaxe and a spade, gave me the spade, kept the pickaxe, pointed to the adjacent vacant lots, and said: "Come."

I followed him, but I lacked his enthusiasm. He divided the vacant land into several sections which he examined in turn. At last, in a corner, at the angle formed by the walls of two neighboring proprietors, a small pile of earth and gravel, covered with briers and grass, attracted his attention. He attacked it. I was obliged to help him. For an hour, under a hot sun, we labored without success. I was discouraged, but Daspry urged me on. His ardor was as strong as ever.

At last, Daspry's pickaxe unearthed some bones—the remains of a skeleton to which some scraps of clothing still hung. Suddenly, I turned pale. I had discovered, sticking in the earth, a small piece of iron cut in the form of a rectangle, on which I thought I could see red spots. I stooped and picked it up. That little iron plate was the exact size of a playing-card, and the red spots, made with red lead, were arranged upon it in a manner similar to the seven-of-hearts, and each spot was pierced with a round hole similar to the perforations in the two playing cards.

"Listen, Daspry, I have had enough of this. You can stay if it interests you. But I am going."

Was that simply the expression of my excited nerves? Or was it the result of a laborious task executed under a burning sun? I know that I trembled as I walked away, and that I went to bed, where I remained forty-eight hours, restless and feverish, haunted by skeletons that danced around me and threw their bleeding hearts at my head.

Daspry was faithful to me. He came to my house every day, and remained three or four hours, which he spent in the large room, ferreting, thumping, tapping.

"The letters are here, in this room," he said, from time to time, "they are here. I will stake my life on it."

On the morning of the third day I arose—feeble yet, but cured. A substantial breakfast cheered me up. But a letter that I received that afternoon contributed, more than anything else, to my complete recovery, and aroused in me a lively curiosity. This was the letter:

"*Monsieur,*

"*The drama, the first act of which transpired on the night of 22 June, is now drawing to a close. Force of circumstances compel me to bring the two principal actors in that drama face to face, and I wish that meeting to take place in your house, if you will be so kind as to give me the use of it for this evening from nine o'clock to eleven. It will be advisable to give your servant leave of absence for the evening, and, perhaps, you will be so kind as to leave the field open to the two adversaries. You will remember that when I visited your house on the night of 22 June, I took excellent care of your property.*

I feel that I would do you an injustice if I should doubt, for one moment, your absolute discretion in this affair. Your devoted,
    "SALVATOR."

I was amused at the facetious tone of his letter and also at the whimsical nature of his request. There was a charming display of confidence and candor in his language, and nothing in the world could have induced me to deceive him or repay his confidence with ingratitude.

I gave my servant a theatre ticket, and he left the house at eight o'clock. A few minutes later, Daspry arrived. I showed him the letter.

"Well?" said he.

"Well, I have left the garden gate unlocked, so anyone can enter."

"And you—are you going away?"

"Not at all. I intend to stay right here."

"But he asks you to go——"

"But I am not going. I will be discreet, but I am resolved to see what takes place."

"Ma foi!" exclaimed Daspry, laughing, "you are right, and I shall stay with you. I shouldn't like to miss it."

We were interrupted by the sound of the door-bell.

"Here already?" said Daspry, "twenty minutes ahead of time! Incredible!"

I went to the door and ushered in the visitor. It was Madame Andermatt. She was faint and nervous, and in a stammering voice, she ejaculated:

"My husband.... is coming.... he has an appointment.... they intend to give him the letters...."

"How do you know?" I asked.

"By chance. A message came for my husband while we were at dinner. The servant gave it to me by mistake. My husband grabbed it quickly, but he was too late. I had read it."

"You read it?"

"Yes. It was something like this: 'At nine o'clock this evening, be at Boulevard Maillot with the papers connected with the affair. In exchange, the letters.' So, after dinner, I hastened here."

"Unknown to your husband?"

"Yes."

"What do you think about it?" asked Daspry, turning to me.

"I think as you do, that Mon. Andermatt is one of the invited guests."

"Yes, but for what purpose?"

"That is what we are going to find out."

I led them to a large room. The three of us could hide comfortably behind the velvet chimney-mantle, and observe all that should happen in the room. We seated ourselves there, with Madame Andermatt in the centre.

The clock struck nine. A few minutes later, the garden gate creaked upon its hinges. I confess that I was greatly agitated. I was about to learn the key to the mystery. The startling events of the last few weeks were about to be explained, and, under my eyes, the last battle was going to be fought. Daspry seized the hand of Madame Andermatt, and said to her:

"Not a word, not a movement! Whatever you may see or hear, keep quiet!"

Some one entered. It was Alfred Varin. I recognized him at once, owing to the close resemblance he bore to his brother Etienne. There was the same slouching gait; the same cadaverous face covered with a black beard.

He entered with the nervous air of a man who is accustomed to fear the presence of traps and ambushes; who scents and avoids them. He glanced about the room, and I had the impression that the chimney, masked with a velvet portière, did not please him. He took three steps in our direction, when something caused him to turn and walk toward the old mosaic king, with the flowing beard and flamboyant sword, which he examined minutely, mounting on a chair and following with his fingers the outlines of the shoulders and head and feeling certain parts of the face. Suddenly, he leaped from the chair and walked away from it. He had heard the sound of approaching footsteps. Mon. Andermatt appeared at the door.

"You! You!" exclaimed the banker. "Was it you who brought me here?"

"I? By no means," protested Varin, in a rough, jerky voice that reminded me of his brother, "on the contrary, it was your letter that brought me here."

"My letter?"

"A letter signed by you, in which you offered——"

"I never wrote to you," declared Mon. Andermatt.

"You did not write to me!"

Instinctively, Varin was put on his guard, not against the banker, but against the unknown enemy who had drawn him into this trap. A second time, he looked in our direction, then walked toward the door. But Mon. Andermatt barred his passage.

"Well, where are you going, Varin?"

"There is something about this affair I don't like. I am going home. Good evening."

"One moment!"

"No need of that, Mon. Andermatt. I have nothing to say to you."

"But I have something to say to you, and this is a good time to say it."

"Let me pass."

"No, you will not pass."

Varin recoiled before the resolute attitude of the banker, as he muttered:

"Well, then, be quick about it."

One thing astonished me; and I have no doubt my two companions experienced a similar feeling. Why was Salvator not there? Was he not a necessary party at this conference? Or was he satisfied to let these two adversaries fight it out between themselves? At all events, his absence was a great disappointment, although it did not detract from the dramatic strength of the situation.

After a moment, Mon. Andermatt approached Varin and, face to face, eye to eye, said:

"Now, after all these years and when you have nothing more to fear, you can answer me candidly: What have you done with Louis Lacombe?"

"What a question! As if I knew anything about him!"

"You do know! You and your brother were his constant companions, almost lived with him in this very house. You knew all about his plans and his work. And the last night I ever saw Louis Lacombe, when I parted with him at my door, I saw two men slinking away in the shadows of the trees. That, I am ready to swear to."

"Well, what has that to do with me?"

"The two men were you and your brother."

"Prove it."

"The best proof is that, two days later, you yourself showed me the papers and the plans that belonged to Lacombe and offered to sell them. How did these papers come into your possession?"

"I have already told you, Mon. Andermatt, that we found them on Louis Lacombe's table, the morning after his disappearance."

"That is a lie!"

"Prove it."

"The law will prove it."

"Why did you not appeal to the law?"

"Why? Ah! Why—," stammered the banker, with a slight display of emotion.

"You know very well, Mon. Andermatt, if you had the least certainty of our guilt, our little threat would not have stopped you."

"What threat? Those letters? Do you suppose I ever gave those letters a moment's thought?"

"If you did not care for the letters, why did you offer me thousands of francs for their return? And why did you have my brother and me tracked like wild beasts?"

"To recover the plans."

"Nonsense! You wanted the letters. You knew that as soon as you had the letters in your possession, you could denounce us. Oh! no, I couldn't part with them!"

He laughed heartily, but stopped suddenly, and said:

"But, enough of this! We are merely going over old ground. We make no headway. We had better let things stand as they are."

"We will not let them stand as they are," said the banker, "and since you have referred to the letters, let me tell you that you will not leave this house until you deliver up those letters."

"I shall go when I please."

"You will not."

"Be careful, Mon. Andermatt. I warn you—"

"I say, you shall not go."

"We will see about that," cried Varin, in such a rage that Madame Andermatt could not suppress a cry of fear. Varin must have heard it, for he now tried to force his way out. Mon. Andermatt pushed him back. Then I saw him put his hand into his coat pocket.

"For the last time, let me pass," he cried.

"The letters, first!"

Varin drew a revolver and, pointing it at Mon. Andermatt, said:

"Yes or no?"

The banker stooped quickly. There was the sound of a pistol-shot. The weapon fell from Varin's hand. I was amazed. The shot was fired close to me. It was Daspry who had fired it at Varin, causing him to drop the revolver. In a moment, Daspry was standing between the two men, facing Varin; he said to him, with a sneer:

"You were lucky, my friend, very lucky. I fired at your hand and struck only the revolver."

Both of them looked at him, surprised. Then he turned to the banker, and said:

"I beg your pardon, monsieur, for meddling in your business; but, really, you play a very poor game. Let me hold the cards."

Turning again to Varin, Daspry said:

"It's between us two, comrade, and play fair, if you please. Hearts are trumps, and I play the seven."

Then Daspry held up, before Varin's bewildered eyes, the little iron plate, marked with the seven red spots. It was a terrible shock to Varin. With livid features, staring eyes, and an air of intense agony, the man seemed to be hypnotized at the sight of it.

"Who are you?" he gasped.

"One who meddles in other people's business, down to the very bottom."

"What do you want?"

"What you brought here tonight."

"I brought nothing."

"Yes, you did, or you wouldn't have come. This morning, you received an invitation to come here at nine o'clock, and bring with you all the papers held by you. You are here. Where are the papers?"

There was in Daspry's voice and manner a tone of authority that I did not understand; his manner was usually quite mild and conciliatory. Absolutely conquered, Varin placed his hand on one of his pockets, and said:

"The papers are here."

"All of them?"

"Yes."

"All that you took from Louis Lacombe and afterwards sold to Major von Lieben?"

"Yes."

"Are these the copies or the originals?"

"I have the originals."

"How much do you want for them?"

"One hundred thousand francs."

"You are crazy," said Daspry. "Why, the major gave you only twenty thousand, and that was like money thrown into the sea, as the boat was a failure at the preliminary trials."

"They didn't understand the plans."

"The plans are not complete."

"Then, why do you ask me for them?"

"Because I want them. I offer you five thousand francs—not a sou more."

"Ten thousand. Not a sou less."

"Agreed," said Daspry, who now turned to Mon. Andermatt, and said:

"Monsieur will kindly sign a check for the amount."

"But....I haven't got—"

"Your check-book? Here it is."

Astounded, Mon. Andermatt examined the check-book that Daspry handed to him.

"It is mine," he gasped. "How does that happen?"

"No idle words, monsieur, if you please. You have merely to sign."

The banker took out his fountain pen, filled out the check and signed it. Varin held out his hand for it.

"Put down your hand," said Daspry, "there is something more." Then, to the banker, he said: "You asked for some letters, did you not?"

"Yes, a package of letters."

"Where are they, Varin?"

"I haven't got them."

"Where are they, Varin?"

"I don't know. My brother had charge of them."

"They are hidden in this room."

"In that case, you know where they are."

"How should I know?"

"Was it not you who found the hiding-place? You appear to be as well informed.... as Salvator."

"The letters are not in the hiding-place."

"They are."

"Open it."

Varin looked at him, defiantly. Were not Daspry and Salvator the same person? Everything pointed to that conclusion. If so, Varin risked nothing in disclosing a hiding-place already known.

"Open it," repeated Daspry.

"I have not got the seven of hearts."

"Yes, here it is," said Daspry, handing him the iron plate. Varin recoiled in terror, and cried:

"No, no, I will not."

"Never mind," replied Daspry, as he walked toward the bearded king, climbed on a chair and applied the seven of hearts to the lower part of the sword in such a manner that the edges of the iron plate coincided exactly with the two edges of the sword. Then, with the assistance of an awl which he introduced alternately into each of the seven holes, he pressed upon seven of the little mosaic stones. As he pressed upon the seventh one, a clicking sound was heard, and the entire bust of the King turned upon a pivot, disclosing a large opening lined with steel. It was really a fire-proof safe.

"You can see, Varin, the safe is empty."

"So I see. Then, my brother has taken out the letters."

Daspry stepped down from the chair, approached Varin, and said:

"Now, no more nonsense with me. There is another hiding-place. Where is it?"

"There is none."

"Is it money you want? How much?"

"Ten thousand."

"Monsieur Andermatt, are those letters worth ten thousand francs to you?"

"Yes," said the banker, firmly.

Varin closed the safe, took the seven of hearts and placed it again on the sword at the same spot. He thrust the awl into each of the seven holes. There was the same clicking sound, but this time, strange to relate, it was only a portion of the safe that revolved on the pivot, disclosing quite a small safe that was built within the door of the larger one. The packet of letters was here, tied with a tape, and sealed. Varin handed the packet to Daspry. The latter turned to the banker, and asked:

"Is the check ready, Monsieur Andermatt?"

"Yes."

"And you have also the last document that you received from Louis Lacombe—the one that completes the plans of the sub-marine?"

"Yes."

The exchange was made. Daspry pocketed the document and the checks, and offered the packet of letters to Mon. Andermatt.

"This is what you wanted, Monsieur."

The banker hesitated a moment, as if he were afraid to touch those cursed letters that he had sought so eagerly. Then, with a nervous movement, he took them. Close to me, I heard a moan. I grasped Madame Andermatt's hand. It was cold.

"I believe, monsieur," said Daspry to the banker, "that our business is ended. Oh! no thanks. It was only by a mere chance that I have been able to do you a good turn. Good-night."

Mon. Andermatt retired. He carried with him the letters written by his wife to Louis Lacombe.

"Marvelous!" exclaimed Daspry, delighted. "Everything is coming our way. Now, we have only to close our little affair, comrade. You have the papers?"

"Here they are—all of them."

Daspry examined them carefully, and then placed them in his pocket.

"Quite right. You have kept your word," he said.

"But——"

"But what?"

"The two checks? The money?" said Varin, eagerly.

"Well, you have a great deal of assurance, my man. How dare you ask such a thing?"

"I ask only what is due to me."

"Can you ask pay for returning papers that you stole? Well, I think not!"

Varin was beside himself. He trembled with rage; his eyes were bloodshot.

"The money.... the twenty thousand...." he stammered.

"Impossible! I need it myself."

"The money!"

"Come, be reasonable, and don't get excited. It won't do you any good."

Daspry seized his arm so forcibly, that Varin uttered a cry of pain. Daspry continued:

"Now, you can go. The air will do you good. Perhaps you want me to show you the way. Ah! yes, we will go together to the vacant lot near here, and I will show you a little mound of earth and stones and under it——"

"That is false! That is false!"

"Oh! no, it is true. That little iron plate with the seven spots on it came from there. Louis Lacombe always carried it, and you buried it with the body—and with some other things that will prove very interesting to a judge and jury."

Varin covered his face with his hands, and muttered:

"All right, I am beaten. Say no more. But I want to ask you one question. I should like to know——"

"What is it?"

"Was there a little casket in the large safe?"

"Yes."

"Was it there on the night of 22 June?"

69

"Yes."

"What did it contain?"

"Everything that the Varin brothers had put in it—a very pretty collection of diamonds and pearls picked up here and there by the said brothers."

"And did you take it?"

"Of course I did. Do you blame me?"

"I understand.... it was the disappearance of that casket that caused my brother to kill himself."

"Probably. The disappearance of your correspondence was not a sufficient motive. But the disappearance of the casket....Is that all you wish to ask me?"

"One thing more: your name?"

"You ask that with an idea of seeking revenge."

"Parbleu! The tables may be turned. Today, you are on top. To-morrow——"

"It will be you."

"I hope so. Your name?"

"Arsène Lupin."

"Arsène Lupin!"

The man staggered, as though stunned by a heavy blow. Those two words had deprived him of all hope.

Daspry laughed, and said:

"Ah! did you imagine that a Monsieur Durand or Dupont could manage an affair like this? No, it required the skill and cunning of Arsène Lupin. And now that you have my name, go and prepare your revenge. Arsène Lupin will wait for you."

Then he pushed the bewildered Varin through the door.

"Daspry! Daspry!" I cried, pushing aside the curtain. He ran to me.

"What? What's the matter?"

"Madame Andermatt is ill."

He hastened to her, caused her to inhale some salts, and, while caring for her, questioned me:

"Well, what did it?"

"The letters of Louis Lacombe that you gave to her husband."

He struck his forehead and said:

"Did she think that I could do such a thing!...But, of course she would. Imbecile that I am!"

Madame Andermatt was now revived. Daspry took from his pocket a small package exactly similar to the one that Mon. Andermatt had carried away.

"Here are your letters, Madame. These are the genuine letters."

"But.... the others?"

"The others are the same, rewritten by me and carefully worded. Your husband will not find anything objectionable in them, and will never suspect the substitution since they were taken from the safe in his presence."

"But the handwriting——"

"There is no handwriting that cannot be imitated."

She thanked him in the same words she might have used to a man in her own social circle, so I concluded that she had not witnessed the final scene between Varin and Arsène Lupin. But the surprising revelation caused me considerable embarrassment. Lupin! My club companion was none other than Arsène Lupin. I could not realize it. But he said, quite at his ease:

"You can say farewell to Jean Daspry."

"Ah!"

"Yes, Jean Daspry is going on a long journey. I shall send him to Morocco. There, he may find a death worthy of him. I may say that that is his expectation."

"But Arsène Lupin will remain?"

"Oh! Decidedly. Arsène Lupin is simply at the threshold of his career, and he expects——"

I was impelled by curiosity to interrupt him, and, leading him away from the hearing of Madame Andermatt, I asked:

"Did you discover the smaller safe yourself—the one that held the letters?"

"Yes, after a great deal of trouble. I found it yesterday afternoon while you were asleep. And yet, God knows it was simple enough! But the simplest things are the ones that usually escape our notice." Then, showing me the seven-of-hearts, he added: "Of course I had guessed that, in order to open the larger safe, this card must be placed on the sword of the mosaic king."

"How did you guess that?"

"Quite easily. Through private information, I knew that fact when I came here on the evening of 22 June——"

"After you left me——"

"Yes, after turning the subject of our conversation to stories of crime and robbery which were sure to reduce you to such a nervous condition that you would not leave your bed, but would allow me to complete my search uninterrupted."

"The scheme worked perfectly."

"Well, I knew when I came here that there was a casket concealed in a safe with a secret lock, and that the seven-of-hearts was the key to that lock. I had merely to place the card upon the spot that was obviously intended for it. An hour's examination showed me where the spot was."

"One hour!"

"Observe the fellow in mosaic."

"The old emperor?"

"That old emperor is an exact representation of the king of hearts on all playing cards."

"That's right. But how does the seven of hearts open the larger safe at one time and the smaller safe at another time? And why did you open only the larger safe in the first instance? I mean on the night of 22 June."

"Why? Because I always placed the seven of hearts in the same way. I never changed the position. But, yesterday, I observed that by reversing the card, by turning it upside down, the arrangement of the seven spots on the mosaic was changed."

"Parbleu!"

"Of course, parbleu! But a person has to think of those things."

"There is something else: you did not know the history of those letters until Madame Andermatt——"

"Spoke of them before me? No. Because I found in the safe, besides the casket, nothing but the correspondence of the two brothers which disclosed their treachery in regard to the plans."

"Then it was by chance that you were led, first, to investigate the history of the two brothers, and then to search for the plans and documents relating to the sub-marine?"

"Simply by chance."

"For what purpose did you make the search?"

"Mon Dieu!" exclaimed Daspry, laughing, "how deeply interested you are!"

"The subject fascinates me."

"Very well, presently, after I have escorted Madame Andermatt to a carriage, and dispatched a short story to the 'Echo de France,' I will return and tell you all about it."

He sat down and wrote one of those short, clear-cut articles which served to amuse and mystify the public. Who does not recall the sensation that followed that article produced throughout the entire world?

"Arsène Lupin has solved the problem recently submitted by Salvator. Having acquired possession of all the documents and original plans of the engineer Louis Lacombe, he has placed them in the hands of the Minister of Marine, and he has headed a subscription list for the purpose of presenting to the nation the first submarine constructed from those plans. His subscription is twenty thousand francs."

"Twenty thousand francs! The checks of Mon. Andermatt?" I exclaimed, when he had given me the paper to read.

"Exactly. It was quite right that Varin should redeem his treachery."

And that is how I made the acquaintance of Arsène Lupin. That is how I learned that Jean Daspry, a member of my club, was none other than Arsène Lupin, gentleman-thief. That is how I formed very agreeable ties of friendship with that famous man, and, thanks to the confidence with which he honored me, how I became his very humble and faithful historiographer.

VII. MADAME IMBERT'S SAFE

At three o'clock in the morning, there were still half a dozen carriages in front of one of those small houses which form only the side of the boulevard Berthier. The door of that house opened, and a number of guests, male and female, emerged. The majority of them entered their carriages and were quickly driven away, leaving behind only two men who walked down Courcelles, where they parted, as one of them lived in that street. The other decided to return on foot as far as the Porte-Maillot. It was a beautiful winter's night, clear and cold; a night on which a brisk walk is agreeable and refreshing.

But, at the end of a few minutes, he had the disagreeable impression that he was being followed. Turning around, he saw a man skulking amongst the trees. He was not a coward; yet he felt it advisable to increase his speed. Then his pursuer commenced to run; and he deemed it prudent to draw his revolver and face him. But he had no time. The man rushed at him and attacked him violently. Immediately, they were engaged in a desperate struggle, wherein he felt that his unknown assailant had the advantage. He called for help, struggled, and was thrown down on a pile of gravel, seized by the throat, and gagged with a handkerchief that his assailant forced into his mouth. His eyes closed, and the man who was smothering him with his weight arose to defend himself against an unexpected attack. A blow from a cane and a kick from a boot; the man uttered two cries of pain, and fled, limping and cursing. Without deigning to pursue the fugitive, the new arrival stooped over the prostrate man and inquired:

"Are you hurt, monsieur?"

He was not injured, but he was dazed and unable to stand. His rescuer procured a carriage, placed him in it, and accompanied him to his house on the avenue de la Grande-Armée. On his arrival there, quite recovered, he overwhelmed his saviour with thanks.

"I owe you my life, monsieur, and I shall not forget it. I do not wish to alarm my wife at this time of night, but, to-morrow, she will be pleased to thank you personally. Come and breakfast with us. My name is Ludovic Imbert. May I ask yours?"

"Certainly, monsieur."

And he handed Mon. Imbert a card bearing the name: "Arsène Lupin."

At that time, Arsène Lupin did not enjoy the celebrity which the Cahorn affair, his escape from the Prison de la Santé, and other brilliant exploits, afterwards gained for him. He had not even used the name of Arsène Lupin. The name was specially invented to designate the rescuer of Mon. Imbert; that is to say, it was in that affair that Arsène Lupin was baptized. Fully armed and ready for the fray, it is true, but lacking the resources and authority which command success, Arsène Lupin was then merely an apprentice in a profession wherein he soon became a master.

With what a thrill of joy he recalled the invitation he received that night! At last, he had reached his goal! At last, he had undertaken a task worthy of his strength and skill! The Imbert millions! What a magnificent feast for an appetite like his!

He prepared a special toilet for the occasion; a shabby frock-coat, baggy trousers, a frayed silk hat, well-worn collar and cuffs, all quite correct in form, but bearing the unmistakable stamp of poverty. His cravat was a black ribbon pinned with a false diamond. Thus accoutred, he descended the stairs of the house in which he lived at Montmartre. At the third floor, without stopping, he rapped on a closed door with the head of his cane. He walked to the exterior boulevards. A tram-car was passing. He boarded it, and some one who had been following him took a seat beside him. It was the lodger who occupied the room on the third floor. A moment later, this man said to Lupin:

"Well, governor?"

"Well, it is all fixed."

"How?"

"I am going there to breakfast."

"You breakfast—there!"

"Certainly. Why not? I rescued Mon. Ludovic Imbert from certain death at your hands. Mon. Imbert is not devoid of gratitude. He invited me to breakfast."

There was a brief silence. Then the other said:

"But you are not going to throw up the scheme?"

"My dear boy," said Lupin, "When I arranged that little case of assault and battery, when I took the trouble at three o'clock in the morning, to rap you with my cane and tap you with my boot at the risk of injuring my only friend, it was not my intention to forego the advantages to be gained from a rescue so well arranged and executed. Oh! no, not at all."

"But the strange rumors we hear about their fortune?"

"Never mind about that. For six months, I have worked on this affair, investigated it, studied it, questioned the servants, the money-lenders and men of straw; for six months, I have shadowed the husband and wife. Consequently, I know what I am talking about. Whether the fortune came to them from old Brawford, as they pretend, or from some other source, I do not care. I know that it is a reality; that it exists. And some day it will be mine."

"Bigre! One hundred millions!"

"Let us say ten, or even five—that is enough! They have a safe full of bonds, and there will be the devil to pay if I can't get my hands on them."

The tram-car stopped at the Place de l'Etoile. The man whispered to Lupin:

"What am I to do now?"

"Nothing, at present. You will hear from me. There is no hurry."

Five minutes later, Arsène Lupin was ascending the magnificent flight of stairs in the Imbert mansion, and Mon. Imbert introduced him to his wife. Madame Gervaise Imbert was a short plump woman, and very talkative. She gave Lupin a cordial welcome.

"I desired that we should be alone to entertain our saviour," she said.

From the outset, they treated "our saviour" as an old and valued friend. By the time dessert was served, their friendship was well cemented, and private confidences were being exchanged. Arsène related the story of his life, the life of his father as a magistrate, the sorrows of his childhood, and his present difficulties. Gervaise, in turn, spoke of her youth, her marriage, the kindness of the aged Brawford, the hundred millions that she had inherited, the obstacles that prevented her from obtaining the enjoyment of her inheritance, the moneys she had been obliged to borrow at an exorbitant rate of interest, her endless contentions with Brawford's nephews, and the litigation! the injunctions! in fact, everything!

"Just think of it, Monsieur Lupin, the bonds are there, in my husband's office, and if we detach a single coupon, we lose everything! They are there, in our safe, and we dare not touch them."

Monsieur Lupin shivered at the bare idea of his proximity to so much wealth. Yet he felt quite certain that Monsieur Lupin would never suffer from the same difficulty as his fair hostess who declared she dare not touch the money.

"Ah! they are there!" he repeated, to himself; "they are there!"

A friendship formed under such circumstances soon led to closer relations. When discreetly questioned, Arsène Lupin confessed his poverty and distress. Immediately, the unfortunate young man was appointed private secretary to the Imberts, husband and wife, at a salary of one hundred francs a month. He was to come to the house every day and receive orders for his work, and a room on the second floor was set apart as his office. This room was directly over Mon. Imbert's office.

Arsène soon realized that his position as secretary was essentially a sinecure. During the first two months, he had only four important letters to recopy, and was called only once to Mon. Imbert's office; consequently, he had only one opportunity to contemplate, officially, the Imbert safe. Moreover, he noticed that the secretary was not invited to the social functions of the employer. But he did not complain, as he preferred to remain, modestly, in the shade and maintain his peace and freedom.

However, he was not wasting any time. From the beginning, he made clandestine visits to Mon. Imbert's office, and paid his respects to the safe, which was hermetically closed. It was an immense block of iron and steel, cold and stern in appearance, which could not be forced open by the ordinary tools of the burglar's trade. But Arsène Lupin was not discouraged.

"Where force fails, cunning prevails," he said to himself. "The essential thing is to be on the spot when the opportunity occurs. In the meantime, I must watch and wait."

He made immediately some preliminary preparations. After careful soundings made upon the floor of his room, he introduced a lead pipe which penetrated the ceiling of Mon. Imbert's office at a point between the two screeds of the cornice. By means of this pipe, he hoped to see and hear what transpired in the room below.

Henceforth, he passed his days stretched at full length upon the floor. He frequently saw the Imberts holding a consultation in front of the safe, investigating books and papers. When they turned the combination lock, he tried to learn the figures and the number of turns they made to the right and left. He watched their movements; he sought to catch their words. There was also a key necessary to complete the opening of the safe. What did they do with it? Did they hide it?

One day, he saw them leave the room without locking the safe. He descended the stairs quickly, and boldly entered the room. But they had returned.

"Oh! excuse me," he said, "I made a mistake in the door."

"Come in, Monsieur Lupin, come in," cried Madame Imbert, "are you not at home here? We want your advice. What bonds should we sell? The foreign securities or the government annuities?"

"But the injunction?" said Lupin, with surprise.

"Oh! it doesn't cover all the bonds."

She opened the door of the safe and withdrew a package of bonds. But her husband protested.

"No, no, Gervaise, it would be foolish to sell the foreign bonds. They are going up, whilst the annuities are as high as they ever will be. What do you think, my dear friend?"

The dear friend had no opinion; yet he advised the sacrifice of the annuities. Then she withdrew another package and, from it, she took a paper at random. It proved to be a three-per-cent annuity worth two thousand francs. Ludovic placed the package of bonds in his pocket. That afternoon, accompanied by his secretary, he sold the annuities to a stock-broker and realized forty-six thousand francs.

Whatever Madame Imbert might have said about it, Arsène Lupin did not feel at home in the Imbert house. On the contrary, his position there was a peculiar one. He learned that the servants did not even know his name. They called him "monsieur." Ludovic always spoke of him in the same way: "You will tell monsieur. Has monsieur arrived?" Why that mysterious appellation?

Moreover, after their first outburst of enthusiasm, the Imberts seldom spoke to him, and, although treating him with the consideration due to a benefactor, they gave him little or no attention. They appeared to regard him as an eccentric character who did not like to be disturbed, and they respected his isolation as if it were a stringent rule on his part. On one occasion, while passing through the vestibule, he heard Madame Imbert say to the two gentlemen:

"He is such a barbarian!"

"Very well," he said to himself, "I am a barbarian."

And, without seeking to solve the question of their strange conduct, he proceeded with the execution of his own plans. He had decided that he could not depend on chance, nor on the negligence of Madame Imbert, who carried the key of the safe, and who, on locking the safe, invariably scattered the letters forming the combination of the lock. Consequently, he must act for himself.

Finally, an incident precipitated matters; it was the vehement campaign instituted against the Imberts by certain newspapers that accused the Imberts of swindling. Arsène Lupin was present at certain family conferences when this new vicissitude was discussed. He decided that if he waited much longer, he would lose everything. During the next five days, instead of leaving the house about six o'clock, according to his usual habit, he locked himself in his room. It was supposed that he had gone out. But he was lying on the floor surveying the office of Mon. Imbert. During those five evenings, the favorable opportunity that he awaited did not take place. He left the house about midnight by a side door to which he held the key.

But on the sixth day, he learned that the Imberts, actuated by the malevolent insinuations of their enemies, proposed to make an inventory of the contents of the safe.

"They will do it to-night," thought Lupin.

And truly, after dinner, Imbert and his wife retired to the office and commenced to examine the books of account and the securities contained in the safe. Thus, one hour after another passed away. He heard the servants go upstairs to their rooms. No one now remained on the first floor. Midnight! The Imberts were still at work.

"I must get to work," murmured Lupin.

He opened his window. It opened on a court. Outside, everything was dark and quiet. He took from his desk a knotted rope, fastened it to the balcony in front of his window, and quietly descended as far as the window below, which was that of the of Imbert's office. He stood upon the balcony for a moment, motionless, with attentive ear and watchful eye, but the heavy curtains effectually concealed the interior of the room. He cautiously pushed on the double window. If no one had examined it, it ought to yield to the slightest pressure, for, during the afternoon, he had so fixed the bolt that it would not enter the staple.

The window yielded to his touch. Then, with infinite care, he pushed it open sufficiently to admit his head. He parted the curtains a few inches, looked in, and saw Mon. Imbert and his wife sitting in front of the safe, deeply absorbed in their work and speaking softly to each other at rare intervals.

He calculated the distance between him and them, considered the exact movements he would require to make in order to overcome them, one after the other, before they could call for help, and he was about to rush upon them, when Madame Imbert said:

"Ah! the room is getting quite cold. I am going to bed. And you, my dear?"

"I shall stay and finish."

"Finish! Why, that will take you all night."

"Not at all. An hour, at the most."

She retired. Twenty minutes, thirty minutes passed. Arsène pushed the window a little farther open. The curtains shook. He pushed once more. Mon. Imbert turned, and, seeing the curtains blown by the wind, he rose to close the window.

There was not a cry, not the trace of struggle. With a few precise moments, and without causing him the least injury, Arsène stunned him, wrapped the curtain about his head, bound him hand and foot, and did it all in such a manner that Mon. Imbert had no opportunity to recognize his assailant.

Quickly, he approached the safe, seized two packages that he placed under his arm, left the office, and opened the servants' gate. A carriage was stationed in the street.

"Take that, first—and follow me," he said to the coachman. He returned to the office, and, in two trips, they emptied the safe. Then Arsène went to his own room, removed the rope, and all other traces of his clandestine work.

A few hours later, Arsène Lupin and his assistant examined the stolen goods. Lupin was not disappointed, as he had foreseen that the wealth of the Imberts had been greatly exaggerated. It did not consist of hundreds of millions, nor even tens of millions. Yet it amounted to a very respectable sum, and Lupin expressed his satisfaction.

"Of course," he said, "there will be a considerable loss when we come to sell the bonds, as we will have to dispose of them surreptitiously at reduced prices. In the meantime, they will rest quietly in my desk awaiting a propitious moment."

Arsène saw no reason why he should not go to the Imbert house the next day. But a perusal of the morning papers revealed this startling fact: Ludovic and Gervaise Imbert had disappeared.

When the officers of the law seized the safe and opened it, they found there what Arsène Lupin had left—nothing.

Such are the facts; and I learned the sequel to them, one day, when Arsène Lupin was in a confidential mood. He was pacing to and fro in my room, with a nervous step and a feverish eye that were unusual to him.

"After all," I said to him, "it was your most successful venture."

Without making a direct reply, he said:

"There are some impenetrable secrets connected with that affair; some obscure points that escape my comprehension. For instance: What caused their flight? Why did they not take advantage of the help I unconsciously gave them? It would have been so simple to say: 'The hundred millions were in the safe. They are no longer there, because they have been stolen.'"

"They lost their nerve."

"Yes, that is it—they lost their nerve...On the other hand, it is true—"

"What is true?"

"Oh! nothing."

What was the meaning of Lupin's reticence? It was quite obvious that he had not told me everything; there was something he was loath to tell. His conduct puzzled me. It must indeed be a very serious matter to cause such a man as Arsène Lupin even a momentary hesitation. I threw out a few questions at random.

"Have you seen them since?"

"No."

"And have you never experienced the slightest degree of pity for those unfortunate people?"

"I!" he exclaimed, with a start.

His sudden excitement astonished me. Had I touched him on a sore spot? I continued:

"Of course. If you had not left them alone, they might have been able to face the danger, or, at least, made their escape with full pockets."

"What do you mean?" he said, indignantly. "I suppose you have an idea that my soul should be filled with remorse?"

"Call it remorse or regrets—anything you like——"

"They are not worth it."

"Have you no regrets or remorse for having stolen their fortune?"

"What fortune?"

"The packages of bonds you took from their safe."

"Oh! I stole their bonds, did I? I deprived them of a portion of their wealth? Is that my crime? Ah! my dear boy, you do not know the truth. You never imagined that those bonds were not worth the paper they were written on. Those bonds were false—they were counterfeit—every one of them—do you understand? THEY WERE COUNTERFEIT!"

I looked at him, astounded.

"Counterfeit! The four or five millions?"

"Yes, counterfeit!" he exclaimed, in a fit of rage. "Only so many scraps of paper! I couldn't raise a sou on the whole of them! And you ask me if I have any remorse. *They* are the ones who should have remorse and pity. They played me for a simpleton; and I fell into their trap. I was their latest victim, their most stupid gull!"

He was affected by genuine anger—the result of malice and wounded pride. He continued:

"From start to finish, I got the worst of it. Do you know the part I played in that affair, or rather the part they made me play? That of André Brawford! Yes, my boy, that is the truth, and I never suspected it. It was not until afterwards, on reading the newspapers, that the light finally dawned in my stupid brain. Whilst I was posing as his "saviour," as the gentleman who had risked his life to rescue Mon. Imbert from the clutches of an assassin, they were passing me off as Brawford. Wasn't that splendid? That eccentric individual who had a room on the second floor, that barbarian that was exhibited only at a distance, was Brawford, and Brawford was I! Thanks to me, and to the confidence that I inspired under the name of Brawford, they were enabled to borrow money from the bankers and other money-lenders. Ha! what an experience for a novice! And I swear to you that I shall profit by the lesson!"

He stopped, seized my arm, and said to me, in a tone of exasperation:

"My dear fellow, at this very moment, Gervaise Imbert owes me fifteen hundred francs."

I could not refrain from laughter, his rage was so grotesque. He was making a mountain out of a molehill. In a moment, he laughed himself, and said:

"Yes, my boy, fifteen hundred francs. You must know that I had not received one sou of my promised salary, and, more than that, she had borrowed from me the sum of fifteen hundred francs. All my youthful savings! And do you know why? To devote the money to charity! I am giving you a straight story. She wanted it for some poor people she was assisting—unknown to her husband. And my hard-earned money was wormed out of me by that silly pretense! Isn't it amusing, hein? Arsène Lupin done out of fifteen hundred francs by the fair lady from whom he stole four millions in counterfeit bonds! And what a vast amount of time and patience and cunning I expended to achieve that result! It was the first time in my life that I was played for a fool, and I frankly confess that I was fooled that time to the queen's taste!"

VIII. THE BLACK PEARL

A violent ringing of the bell awakened the concierge of number nine, avenue Hoche. She pulled the doorstring, grumbling:

"I thought everybody was in. It must be three o'clock!"

"Perhaps it is someone for the doctor," muttered her husband.

At that moment, a voice inquired:

"Doctor Harel .... what floor?"

"Third floor, left. But the doctor won't go out at night."

"He must go to-night."

The visitor entered the vestibule, ascended to the first floor, the second, the third, and, without stopping at the doctor's door, he continued to the fifth floor. There, he tried two keys. One of them fitted the lock.

"Ah! good!" he murmured, "that simplifies the business wonderfully. But before I commence work I had better arrange for my retreat. Let me see.... have I had sufficient time to rouse the doctor and be dismissed by him? Not yet.... a few minutes more."

At the end of ten minutes, he descended the stairs, grumbling noisily about the doctor. The concierge opened the door for him and heard it click behind him. But the door did not lock, as the man had quickly inserted a piece of iron in the lock in such a manner that the bolt could not enter. Then, quietly, he entered the house again, unknown to the concierge. In case of alarm, his retreat was assured. Noiselessly, he ascended to the fifth floor once more. In the antechamber, by the light of his electric lantern, he placed his hat and overcoat on one of the chairs, took a seat on another, and covered his heavy shoes with felt slippers.

"Ouf! Here I am—and how simple it was! I wonder why more people do not adopt the profitable and pleasant occupation of burglar. With a little care and reflection, it becomes a most delightful profession. Not too quiet and monotonous, of course, as it would then become wearisome."

He unfolded a detailed plan of the apartment.

"Let me commence by locating myself. Here, I see the vestibule in which I am sitting. On the street front, the drawing-room, the boudoir and dining-room. Useless to waste any time there, as it appears that the countess has a deplorable taste.... not a bibelot of any value!...Now, let's get down to business!... Ah! here is a corridor; it must lead to the bed chambers. At a distance of three metres, I should come to the door of the wardrobe-closet which connects with the chamber of the countess." He folded his plan, extinguished his lantern, and proceeded down the corridor, counting his distance, thus:

"One metre.... two metres.... three metres....Here is the door....Mon Dieu, how easy it is! Only a small, simple bolt now separates me from the chamber, and I know that the bolt is located exactly one metre, forty-three centimeters, from the floor. So that, thanks to a small incision I am about to make, I can soon get rid of the bolt."

He drew from his pocket the necessary instruments. Then the following idea occurred to him:

"Suppose, by chance, the door is not bolted. I will try it first."

He turned the knob, and the door opened.

"My brave Lupin, surely fortune favors you....What's to be done now? You know the situation of the rooms; you know the place in which the countess hides the black pearl. Therefore, in order to secure the black pearl, you have simply to be more silent than silence, more invisible than darkness itself."

Arsène Lupin was employed fully a half-hour in opening the second door—a glass door that led to the countess' bedchamber. But he accomplished it with so much skill and precaution, that even had the countess been awake, she would not have heard the slightest sound. According to the plan of the rooms, that he holds, he has merely to pass around a reclining chair and, beyond that, a small table close to the bed. On the table, there was a box of letter-paper, and the black pearl was concealed in that box. He stooped and crept cautiously over the carpet, following the outlines of the reclining-chair. When he reached the extremity of it, he stopped in order to repress the throbbing of his heart. Although he was not moved by any sense of fear, he found it impossible to overcome the nervous anxiety that one usually feels in the midst of profound silence. That circumstance astonished him, because he had passed through many more solemn moments without the slightest trace of emotion. No danger threatened him. Then why did his heart throb like an alarm-bell? Was it that sleeping woman who affected him? Was it the proximity of another pulsating heart?

He listened, and thought he could discern the rhythmical breathing of a person asleep. It gave him confidence, like the presence of a friend. He sought and found the armchair; then, by slow, cautious movements, advanced toward the table, feeling ahead of him with outstretched arm. His right had touched one of the feet of the table. Ah! now, he had simply to rise, take the pearl, and escape. That was fortunate, as his heart was leaping in his breast like a wild beast, and made so much noise that he feared it would waken the countess. By a powerful effort of the will, he subdued the wild throbbing of his heart, and was about to rise from the floor when his left hand encountered, lying on the floor, an object which he recognized as a candlestick—an overturned candlestick. A moment later, his hand encountered another object: a clock—one of those small traveling clocks, covered with leather.———

Well! What had happened? He could not understand. That candlestick, that clock; why were those articles not in their accustomed places? Ah! what had happened in the dread silence of the night?

Suddenly a cry escaped him. He had touched—oh! some strange, unutterable thing! "No! no!" he thought, "it cannot be. It is some fantasy of my excited brain." For twenty seconds, thirty seconds, he remained motionless, terrified, his forehead bathed with perspiration, and his fingers still retained the sensation of that dreadful contact.

Making a desperate effort, he ventured to extend his arm again. Once more, his hand encountered that strange, unutterable thing. He felt it. He must feel it and find out what it is. He found that it was hair, human hair, and a human face; and that face was cold, almost icy.

However frightful the circumstances may be, a man like Arsène Lupin controls himself and commands the situation as soon as he learns what it is. So, Arsène Lupin quickly brought his lantern into use. A woman was lying before him, covered with blood. Her neck and shoulders were covered with gaping wounds. He leaned over her and made a closer examination. She was dead.

"Dead! Dead!" he repeated, with a bewildered air.

He stared at those fixed eyes, that grim mouth, that livid flesh, and that blood—all that blood which had flowed over the carpet and congealed there in thick, black spots. He arose and turned on the electric lights. Then he beheld all the marks of a desperate struggle. The bed was in a state of great disorder. On the floor, the candlestick, and the clock, with the hands pointing to twenty minutes after eleven; then, further away, an overturned chair; and, everywhere, there was blood, spots of blood and pools of blood.

"And the black pearl?" he murmured.

The box of letter-paper was in its place. He opened it, eagerly. The jewel-case was there, but it was empty.

"Fichtre!" he muttered. "You boasted of your good fortune much too soon, my friend Lupin. With the countess lying cold and dead, and the black pearl vanished, the situation is anything but pleasant. Get out of here as soon as you can, or you may get into serious trouble."

Yet, he did not move.

"Get out of here? Yes, of course. Any person would, except Arsène Lupin. He has something better to do. Now, to proceed in an orderly way. At all events, you have a clear conscience. Let us suppose that you are the commissary of police and that you are proceeding to make an inquiry concerning this affair——Yes, but in order to do that, I require a clearer brain. Mine is muddled like a ragout."

He tumbled into an armchair, with his clenched hands pressed against his burning forehead.

The murder of the avenue Hoche is one of those which have recently surprised and puzzled the Parisian public, and, certainly, I should never have mentioned the affair if the veil of mystery had not been removed by Arsène Lupin himself. No one knew the exact truth of the case.

Who did not know—from having met her in the Bois—the fair Léotine Zalti, the once-famous cantatrice, wife and widow of the Count d'Andillot; the Zalti, whose luxury dazzled all Paris some twenty years ago; the Zalti who acquired an European reputation for the magnificence of her diamonds and pearls? It was said that she wore upon her shoulders the capital of several banking houses and the gold mines of numerous Australian companies. Skilful jewelers worked for Zalti as they had formerly wrought for kings and queens. And who does not remember the catastrophe in which all that wealth was swallowed up? Of all that marvelous collection, nothing remained except the famous black pearl. The black pearl! That is to say a fortune, if she had wished to part with it.

But she preferred to keep it, to live in a commonplace apartment with her companion, her cook, and a man-servant, rather than sell that inestimable jewel. There was a reason for it; a reason she was not afraid to disclose: the black pearl was the gift of an emperor! Almost ruined, and reduced to the most mediocre existence, she remained faithful to the companion of her happy and brilliant youth. The black pearl never left her possession. She wore it during the day, and, at night, concealed it in a place known to her alone.

All these facts, being republished in the columns of the public press, served to stimulate curiosity; and, strange to say, but quite obvious to those who have the key to the mystery, the arrest of the presumed assassin only complicated the question and prolonged the excitement. Two days later, the newspapers published the following item:

"Information has reached us of the arrest of Victor Danègre, the servant of the Countess d'Andillot. The evidence against him is clear and convincing. On the silken sleeve of his liveried waistcoat, which chief detective Dudouis found in his garret between the mattresses of his bed, several spots of blood were discovered. In addition, a cloth-covered button was missing from that garment, and this button was found beneath the bed of the victim.

"It is supposed that, after dinner, in place of going to his own room, Danègre slipped into the wardrobe-closet, and, through the glass door, had seen the countess hide the precious black pearl. This is simply a theory, as yet unverified by any evidence. There is, also, another obscure point. At seven o'clock in the morning, Danègre went to the tobacco-shop on the Boulevard de Courcelles; the concierge and the shop-keeper both affirm this fact. On the other hand, the countess' companion and cook, who sleep at the end of the hall, both declare that, when they arose at eight o'clock, the door of the antechamber and the door of the kitchen were locked. These two persons have been in the service of the countess for twenty years, and are above suspicion. The question is: How did Danègre leave the apartment? Did he have another key? These are matters that the police will investigate."

As a matter of fact, the police investigation threw no light on the mystery. It was learned that Victor Danègre was a dangerous criminal, a drunkard and a debauchee. But, as they proceeded with the investigation, the mystery deepened and new complications arose. In the first place, a young woman, Mlle. De Sinclèves, the cousin and sole heiress of the countess, declared that the countess, a month before her death, had written a letter to her and in it described the manner in which the black pearl was concealed. The letter disappeared the day after she received it. Who had stolen it?

Again, the concierge related how she had opened the door for a person who had inquired for Doctor Harel. On being questioned, the doctor testified that no one had rung his bell. Then who was that person? An accomplice?

The theory of an accomplice was thereupon adopted by the press and public, and also by Ganimard, the famous detective.

"Lupin is at the bottom of this affair," he said to the judge.

"Bah!" exclaimed the judge, "you have Lupin on the brain. You see him everywhere."

"I see him everywhere, because he is everywhere."

"Say rather that you see him every time you encounter something you cannot explain. Besides, you overlook the fact that the crime was committed at twenty minutes past eleven in the evening, as is shown by the clock, while the nocturnal visit, mentioned by the concierge, occurred at three o'clock in the morning."

Officers of the law frequently form a hasty conviction as to the guilt of a suspected person, and then distort all subsequent discoveries to conform to their established theory. The deplorable antecedents of Victor Danègre, habitual criminal, drunkard and rake, influenced the judge, and despite the fact that nothing new was discovered in corroboration of the early clues, his official opinion remained firm and unshaken. He closed his investigation, and, a few weeks later, the trial commenced. It proved to be slow and tedious. The judge was listless, and the public prosecutor presented the case in a careless manner. Under those circumstances, Danègre's counsel had an easy task. He pointed out the defects and inconsistencies of the case for the prosecution, and argued that the evidence was quite insufficient to convict the accused. Who had made the key, the indispensable key without which Danègre, on leaving the apartment, could not have locked the door behind him? Who had ever seen such a key, and what had become of it? Who had seen the assassin's knife, and where is it now?

"In any event," argued the prisoner's counsel, "the prosecution must prove, beyond any reasonable doubt, that the prisoner committed the murder. The prosecution must show that the mysterious individual who entered the house at three o'clock in the morning is not the guilty party. To be sure, the clock indicated eleven o'clock. But what of that? I contend, that proves nothing. The assassin could turn the hands of the clock to any hour he pleased, and thus deceive us in regard to the exact hour of the crime."

Victor Danègre was acquitted.

He left the prison on Friday about dusk in the evening, weak and depressed by his six months' imprisonment. The inquisition, the solitude, the trial, the deliberations of the jury, combined to fill him with a nervous fear. At night, he had been afflicted with terrible nightmares and haunted by weird visions of the scaffold. He was a mental and physical wreck.

Under the assumed name of Anatole Dufour, he rented a small room on the heights of Montmartre, and lived by doing odd jobs wherever he could find them. He led a pitiful existence. Three times, he obtained regular employment, only to be recognized and then discharged. Sometimes, he had an idea that men were following him—detectives, no doubt, who were seeking to trap and denounce him. He could almost feel the strong hand of the law clutching him by the collar.

One evening, as he was eating his dinner at a neighboring restaurant, a man entered and took a seat at the same table. He was a person about forty years of age, and wore a frock-coat of doubtful cleanliness. He ordered soup, vegetables, and a bottle of wine. After he had finished his soup, he turned his eyes on Danègre, and gazed at him intently. Danègre winced. He was certain that this was one of the men who had been following him for several weeks. What did he want? Danègre tried to rise, but failed. His limbs refused to support him. The man poured himself a glass of wine, and then filled Danègre's glass. The man raised his glass, and said:

"To your health, Victor Danègre."

Victor started in alarm, and stammered:

"I!....I!.... no, no....I swear to you...."

"You will swear what? That you are not yourself? The servant of the countess?"

"What servant? My name is Dufour. Ask the proprietor."

"Yes, Anatole Dufour to the proprietor of this restaurant, but Victor Danègre to the officers of the law."

"That's not true! Some one has lied to you."

The new-comer took a card from his pocket and handed it to Victor, who read on it: "Grimaudan, ex-inspector of the detective force. Private business transacted." Victor shuddered as he said:

"You are connected with the police?"

"No, not now, but I have a liking for the business and I continue to work at it in a manner more—profitable. From time to time I strike upon a golden opportunity—such as your case presents."

"My case?"

"Yes, yours. I assure you it is a most promising affair, provided you are inclined to be reasonable."

"But if I am not reasonable?"

"Oh! my good fellow, you are not in a position to refuse me anything I may ask."

"What is it.... you want?" stammered Victor, fearfully.

"Well, I will inform you in a few words. I am sent by Mademoiselle de Sinclèves, the heiress of the Countess d'Andillot."

"What for?"

"To recover the black pearl."

"Black pearl?"

"That you stole."

"But I haven't got it."

"You have it."

"If I had, then I would be the assassin."

"You are the assassin."

Danègre showed a forced smile.

"Fortunately for me, monsieur, the Assizecourt was not of your opinion. The jury returned an unanimous verdict of acquittal. And when a man has a clear conscience and twelve good men in his favor—"

The ex-inspector seized him by the arm and said:

"No fine phrases, my boy. Now, listen to me and weigh my words carefully. You will find they are worthy of your consideration. Now, Danègre, three weeks before the murder, you abstracted the cook's key to the servants' door, and had a duplicate key made by a locksmith named Outard, 244 rue Oberkampf."

"It's a lie—it's a lie!" growled Victor. "No person has seen that key. There is no such key."

"Here it is."

After a silence, Grimaudan continued:

"You killed the countess with a knife purchased by you at the Bazar de la Republique on the same day as you ordered the duplicate key. It has a triangular blade with a groove running from end to end."

"That is all nonsense. You are simply guessing at something you don't know. No one ever saw the knife."

"Here it is."

Victor Danègre recoiled. The ex-inspector continued:

"There are some spots of rust upon it. Shall I tell you how they came there?"

"Well!.... you have a key and a knife. Who can prove that they belong to me?"

"The locksmith, and the clerk from whom you bought the knife. I have already refreshed their memories, and, when you confront them, they cannot fail to recognize you."

His speech was dry and hard, with a tone of firmness and precision. Danègre was trembling with fear, and yet he struggled desperately to maintain an air of indifference.

"Is that all the evidence you have?"

"Oh! no, not at all. I have plenty more. For instance, after the crime, you went out the same way you had entered. But, in the centre of the wardrobe-room, being seized by some sudden fear, you leaned against the wall for support."

"How do you know that? No one could know such a thing," argued the desperate man.

"The police know nothing about it, of course. They never think of lighting a candle and examining the walls. But if they had done so, they would have found on the white plaster a faint red spot, quite distinct, however, to trace in it the imprint of your thumb which you had pressed against the wall while it was wet with blood. Now, as you are well aware, under the Bertillon system, thumb-marks are one of the principal means of identification."

Victor Danègre was livid; great drops of perspiration rolled down his face and fell upon the table. He gazed, with a wild look, at the strange man who had narrated the story of his crime as faithfully as if he had been an invisible witness to it. Overcome and powerless, Victor bowed his head. He felt that it was useless to struggle against this marvelous man. So he said:

"How much will you give me, if I give you the pearl?"

"Nothing."

"Oh! you are joking! Or do you mean that I should give you an article worth thousands and hundreds of thousands and get nothing in return?"

"You will get your life. Is that nothing?"

The unfortunate man shuddered. Then Grimaudan added, in a milder tone:

"Come, Danègre, that pearl has no value in your hands. It is quite impossible for you to sell it; so what is the use of your keeping it?"

"There are pawnbrokers.... and, some day, I will be able to get something for it."

"But that day may be too late."

"Why?"

"Because by that time you may be in the hands of the police, and, with the evidence that I can furnish—the knife, the key, the thumb-mark—what will become of you?"

Victor rested his head on his hands and reflected. He felt that he was lost, irremediably lost, and, at the same time, a sense of weariness and depression overcame him. He murmured, faintly:

"When must I give it to you?"

"To-night—within an hour."

"If I refuse?"

"If you refuse, I shall post this letter to the Procureur of the Republic; in which letter Mademoiselle de Sinclèves denounces you as the assassin."

Danègre poured out two glasses of wine which he drank in rapid succession, then, rising, said:

"Pay the bill, and let us go. I have had enough of the cursed affair."

Night had fallen. The two men walked down the rue Lepic and followed the exterior boulevards in the direction of the Place de l'Etoile. They pursued their way in silence; Victor had a stooping carriage and a dejected face. When they reached the Parc Monceau, he said:

"We are near the house."

"Parbleu! You only left the house once, before your arrest, and that was to go to the tobacco-shop."

"Here it is," said Danègre, in a dull voice.

They passed along the garden wall of the countess' house, and crossed a street on a corner of which stood the tobacco-shop. A few steps further on, Danègre stopped; his limbs shook beneath him, and he sank to a bench.

"Well! what now?" demanded his companion.

"It is there."

"Where? Come, now, no nonsense!"

"There—in front of us."

"Where?"

"Between two paving-stones."

"Which?"

"Look for it."

"Which stones?"

Victor made no reply.

"Ah; I see!" exclaimed Grimaudan, "you want me to pay for the information."

"No.... but....I am afraid I will starve to death."

"So! that is why you hesitate. Well, I'll not be hard on you. How much do you want?"

"Enough to buy a steerage pass to America."

"All right."

"And a hundred francs to keep me until I get work there."

"You shall have two hundred. Now, speak."

"Count the paving-stones to the right from the sewer-hole. The pearl is between the twelfth and thirteenth."

"In the gutter?"

"Yes, close to the sidewalk."

Grimaudan glanced around to see if anyone were looking. Some tram-cars and pedestrians were passing. But, bah, they will not suspect anything. He opened his pocketknife and thrust it between the twelfth and thirteenth stones.

"And if it is not there?" he said to Victor.

"It must be there, unless someone saw me stoop down and hide it."

Could it be possible that the back pearl had been cast into the mud and filth of the gutter to be picked up by the first comer? The black pearl—a fortune!

"How far down?" he asked.

"About ten centimetres."

He dug up the wet earth. The point of his knife struck something. He enlarged the hole with his finger. Then he abstracted the black pearl from its filthy hiding-place.

"Good! Here are your two hundred francs. I will send you the ticket for America."

On the following day, this article was published in the 'Echo de France,' and was copied by the leading newspapers throughout the world:

"Yesterday, the famous black pearl came into the possession of Arsène Lupin, who recovered it from the murderer of the Countess d'Andillot. In a short time, fac-similes of that precious jewel will be exhibited in London, St. Petersburg, Calcutta, Buenos Ayres and New York.

"Arsène Lupin will be pleased to consider all propositions submitted to him through his agents."

"And that is how crime is always punished and virtue rewarded," said Arsène Lupin, after he had told me the foregoing history of the black pearl.

"And that is how you, under the assumed name of Grimaudan, ex-inspector of detectives, were chosen by fate to deprive the criminal of the benefit of his crime."

"Exactly. And I confess that the affair gives me infinite satisfaction and pride. The forty minutes that I passed in the apartment of the Countess d'Andillot, after learning of her death, were the most thrilling and absorbing moments of my life. In those forty minutes, involved as I was in a most dangerous plight, I calmly studied the scene of the murder and reached the conclusion that the crime must have been committed by one of the house servants. I also decided that, in order to get the pearl, that servant must be arrested, and so I left the wainscoat button; it was necessary, also, for me to hold some convincing evidence of his guilt, so I carried away the knife which I found upon the floor, and the key which I found in the lock. I closed and locked the door, and erased the finger-marks from the plaster in the wardrobe-closet. In my opinion, that was one of those flashes—"

"Of genius," I said, interrupting.

"Of genius, if you wish. But, I flatter myself, it would not have occurred to the average mortal. To frame, instantly, the two elements of the problem—an arrest and an acquittal; to make use of the formidable machinery of the law to crush and humble my victim, and reduce him to a condition in which, when free, he would be certain to fall into the trap I was laying for him!"

"Poor devil—"

"Poor devil, do you say? Victor Danègre, the assassin! He might have descended to the lowest depths of vice and crime, if he had retained the black pearl. Now, he lives! Think of that: Victor Danègre is alive!"

"And you have the black pearl."

He took it out of one of the secret pockets of his wallet, examined it, gazed at it tenderly, and caressed it with loving fingers, and sighed, as he said:

"What cold Russian prince, what vain and foolish rajah may some day possess this priceless treasure! Or, perhaps, some American millionaire is destined to become the owner of this morsel of exquisite beauty that once adorned the fair bosom of Leontine Zalti, the Countess d'Andillot."

IX. SHERLOCK HOLMES ARRIVES TOO LATE

"It is really remarkable, Velmont, what a close resemblance you bear to Arsène Lupin!"

"How do you know?"

"Oh! like everyone else, from photographs, no two of which are alike, but each of them leaves the impression of a face.... something like yours."

Horace Velmont displayed some vexation.

"Quite so, my dear Devanne. And, believe me, you are not the first one who has noticed it."

"It is so striking," persisted Devanne, "that if you had not been recommended to me by my cousin d'Estevan, and if you were not the celebrated artist whose beautiful marine views I so admire, I have no doubt I should have warned the police of your presence in Dieppe."

This sally was greeted with an outburst of laughter. The large dining-hall of the Château de Thibermesnil contained on this occasion, besides Velmont, the following guests: Father Gélis, the parish priest, and a dozen officers whose regiments were quartered in the vicinity and who had accepted the invitation of the banker Georges Devanne and his mother. One of the officers then remarked:

"I understand that an exact description of Arsène Lupin has been furnished to all the police along this coast since his daring exploit on the Paris-Havre express."

"I suppose so," said Devanne. "That was three months ago; and a week later, I made the acquaintance of our friend Velmont at the casino, and, since then, he has honored me with several visits—an agreeable preamble to a more serious visit that he will pay me one of these days—or, rather, one of these nights."

This speech evoked another round of laughter, and the guests then passed into the ancient "Hall of the Guards," a vast room with a high ceiling, which occupied the entire lower part of the Tour Guillaume—William's Tower—and wherein Georges Devanne had collected the incomparable treasures which the lords of Thibermesnil had accumulated through many centuries. It contained ancient chests, credences, andirons and chandeliers. The stone walls were overhung with magnificent tapestries. The deep embrasures of the four windows were furnished with benches, and the Gothic windows were composed of small panes of colored glass set in a leaden frame. Between the door and the window to the left stood an immense bookcase of Renaissance style, on the pediment of which, in letters of gold, was the word "Thibermesnil," and, below it, the proud family device: "Fais ce que veulx" (Do what thou wishest). When the guests had lighted their cigars, Devanne resumed the conversation.

"And remember, Velmont, you have no time to lose; in fact, to-night is the last chance you will have."

"How so?" asked the painter, who appeared to regard the affair as a joke. Devanne was about to reply, when his mother mentioned to him to keep silent, but the excitement of the occasion and a desire to interest his guests urged him to speak.

"Bah!" he murmured. "I can tell it now. It won't do any harm."

The guests drew closer, and he commenced to speak with the satisfied air of a man who has an important announcement to make.

"To-morrow afternoon at four o'clock, Sherlock Holmes, the famous English detective, for whom such a thing as mystery does not exist; Sherlock Holmes, the most remarkable solver of enigmas the world has ever known, that marvelous man who would seem to be the creation of a romantic novelist—Sherlock Holmes will be my guest!"

Immediately, Devanne was the target of numerous eager questions. "Is Sherlock Holmes really coming?" "Is it so serious as that?" "Is Arsène Lupin really in this neighborhood?"

"Arsène Lupin and his band are not far away. Besides the robbery of the Baron Cahorn, he is credited with the thefts at Montigny, Gruchet and Crasville. And now it is my turn."

"Has he sent you a warning, as he did to Baron Cahorn?"

"No," replied Devanne, "he can't work the same trick twice."

"What then?"

"I will show you."

He rose, and pointing to a small empty space between the two enormous folios on one of the shelves of the bookcase, he said:

"There used to be a book there—a book of the sixteenth century entitled 'Chronique de Thibermesnil,' which contained the history of the castle since its construction by Duke Rollo on the site of a former feudal fortress. There were three engraved plates in the book;

one of which was a general view of the whole estate; another, the plan of the buildings; and the third—I call your attention to it, particularly—the third was the sketch of a subterranean passage, an entrance to which is outside the first line of ramparts, while the other end of the passage is here, in this very room. Well, that book disappeared a month ago."

"The deuce!" said Velmont, "that looks bad. But it doesn't seem to be a sufficient reason for sending for Sherlock Holmes."

"Certainly, that was not sufficient in itself, but another incident happened that gives the disappearance of the book a special significance. There was another copy of this book in the National Library at Paris, and the two books differed in certain details relating to the subterranean passage; for instance, each of them contained drawings and annotations, not printed, but written in ink and more or less effaced. I knew those facts, and I knew that the exact location of the passage could be determined only by a comparison of the two books. Now, the day after my book disappeared, the book was called for in the National Library by a reader who carried it away, and no one knows how the theft was effected."

The guests uttered many exclamations of surprise.

"Certainly, the affair looks serious," said one.

"Well, the police investigated the matter, and, as usual, discovered no clue whatever."

"They never do, when Arsène Lupin is concerned in it."

"Exactly; and so I decided to ask the assistance of Sherlock Holmes, who replied that he was ready and anxious to enter the lists with Arsène Lupin."

"What glory for Arsène Lupin!" said Velmont. "But if our national thief, as they call him, has no evil designs on your castle, Sherlock Holmes will have his trip in vain."

"There are other things that will interest him, such as the discovery of the subterranean passage."

"But you told us that one end of the passage was outside the ramparts and the other was in this very room!"

"Yes, but in what part of the room? The line which represents the passage on the charts ends here, with a small circle marked with the letters 'T.G.,' which no doubt stand for 'Tour Guillaume.' But the tower is round, and who can tell the exact spot at which the passage touches the tower?"

Devanne lighted a second cigar and poured himself a glass of Benedictine. His guests pressed him with questions and he was pleased to observe the interest that his remarks had created. Then he continued:

"The secret is lost. No one knows it. The legend is to the effect that the former lords of the castle transmitted the secret from father to son on their deathbeds, until Geoffroy, the last of the race, was beheaded during the Revolution in his nineteenth year."

"That is over a century ago. Surely, someone has looked for it since that time?"

"Yes, but they failed to find it. After I purchased the castle, I made a diligent search for it, but without success. You must remember that this tower is surrounded by water and connected with the castle only by a bridge; consequently, the passage must be underneath the old moat. The plan that was in the book in the National Library showed a series of stairs with a total of forty-eight steps, which indicates a depth of more than ten meters. You see, the mystery lies within the walls of this room, and yet I dislike to tear them down."

"Is there nothing to show where it is?"

"Nothing."

"Mon. Devanne, we should turn our attention to the two quotations," suggested Father Gélis.

"Oh!" exclaimed Mon. Devanne, laughing, "our worthy father is fond of reading memoirs and delving into the musty archives of the castle. Everything relating to Thibermesnil interests him greatly. But the quotations that he mentions only serve to complicate the mystery. He has read somewhere that two kings of France have known the key to the puzzle."

"Two kings of France! Who were they?"

"Henry the Fourth and Louis the Sixteenth. And the legend runs like this: On the eve of the battle of Arques, Henry the Fourth spent the night in this castle. At eleven o'clock in the evening, Louise de Tancarville, the prettiest woman in Normandy, was brought into the castle through the subterranean passage by Duke Edgard, who, at the same time, informed the king of the secret passage. Afterward, the king confided the secret to his minister Sully, who, in turn, relates the story in his book, "Royales Economies d'Etat," without making any comment upon it, but linking with it this incomprehensible sentence: 'Turn one eye on the bee that shakes, the other eye will lead to God!'"

After a brief silence, Velmont laughed and said:

"Certainly, it doesn't throw a dazzling light upon the subject."

"No; but Father Gélis claims that Sully concealed the key to the mystery in this strange sentence in order to keep the secret from the secretaries to whom he dictated his memoirs."

"That is an ingenious theory," said Velmont.

"Yes, and it may be nothing more; I cannot see that it throws any light on the mysterious riddle."

"And was it also to receive the visit of a lady that Louis the Sixteenth caused the passage to be opened?"

"I don't know," said Mon. Devanne. "All I can say is that the king stopped here one night in 1784, and that the famous Iron Casket found in the Louvre contained a paper bearing these words in the king's own writing: 'Thibermesnil 3-4-11.'"

Horace Velmont laughed heartily, and exclaimed:

"At last! And now that we have the magic key, where is the man who can fit it to the invisible lock?"

"Laugh as much as you please, monsieur," said Father Gélis, "but I am confident the solution is contained in those two sentences, and some day we will find a man able to interpret them."

"Sherlock Holmes is the man," said Mon. Devanne, "unless Arsène Lupin gets ahead of him. What is your opinion, Velmont?"

Velmont arose, placed his hand on Devanne's shoulder, and declared:

"I think that the information furnished by your book and the book of the National Library was deficient in a very important detail which you have now supplied. I thank you for it."

"What is it?"

"The missing key. Now that I have it, I can go to work at once," said Velmont.

"Of course; without losing a minute," said Devanne, smiling.

"Not even a second!" replied Velmont. "To-night, before the arrival of Sherlock Holmes, I must plunder your castle."

"You have no time to lose. Oh! by the way, I can drive you over this evening."

"To Dieppe?"

"Yes. I am going to meet Monsieur and Madame d'Androl and a young lady of their acquaintance who are to arrive by the midnight train."

Then addressing the officers, Devanne added:

"Gentlemen, I shall expect to see all of you at breakfast to-morrow."

The invitation was accepted. The company dispersed, and a few moments later Devanne and Velmont were speeding toward Dieppe in an automobile. Devanne dropped the artist in front of the Casino, and proceeded to the railway station. At twelve o'clock his friends alighted from the train. A half hour later the automobile was at the entrance to the castle. At one o'clock, after a light supper, they retired. The lights were extinguished, and the castle was enveloped in the darkness and silence of the night.

The moon appeared through a rift in the clouds, and filled the drawing-room with its bright white light. But only for a moment. Then the moon again retired behind its ethereal draperies, and darkness and silence reigned supreme. No sound could be heard, save the monotonous ticking of the clock. It struck two, and then continued its endless repetitions of the seconds. Then, three o'clock.

Suddenly, something clicked, like the opening and closing of a signal-disc that warns the passing train. A thin stream of light flashed to every corner of the room, like an arrow that leaves behind it a trail of light. It shot forth from the central fluting of a column that supported the pediment of the bookcase. It rested for a moment on the panel opposite like a glittering circle of burnished silver, then flashed in all directions like a guilty eye that scrutinizes every shadow. It disappeared for a short time, but burst forth again as a whole section of the bookcase revolved on a pivot and disclosed a large opening like a vault.

A man entered, carrying an electric lantern. He was followed by a second man, who carried a coil of rope and various tools. The leader inspected the room, listened a moment, and said:

"Call the others."

Then eight men, stout fellows with resolute faces, entered the room, and immediately commenced to remove the furnishings. Arsène Lupin passed quickly from one piece of furniture to another, examined each, and, according to its size or artistic value, he directed his men to take it or leave it. If ordered to be taken, it was carried to the gaping mouth of the tunnel, and ruthlessly thrust into the bowels of the earth. Such was the fate of six armchairs, six small Louis XV chairs, a quantity of Aubusson tapestries, some candelabra, paintings by Fragonard and Nattier, a bust by Houdon, and some statuettes. Sometimes, Lupin would linger before a beautiful chest or a superb picture, and sigh:

"That is too heavy.... too large.... what a pity!"

In forty minutes the room was dismantled; and it had been accomplished in such an orderly manner and with as little noise as if the various articles had been packed and wadded for the occasion.

Lupin said to the last man who departed by way of the tunnel:

"You need not come back. You understand, that as soon as the auto-van is loaded, you are to proceed to the grange at Roquefort."

"But you, patron?"

"Leave me the motor-cycle."

When the man had disappeared, Arsène Lupin pushed the section of the bookcase back into its place, carefully effaced the traces of the men's footsteps, raised a portière, and entered a gallery, which was the only means of communication between the tower and the castle. In the center of this gallery there was a glass cabinet which had attracted Lupin's attentions. It contained a valuable collection of watches, snuff-boxes, rings, chatelaines and miniatures of rare and beautiful workmanship. He forced the lock with a small jimmy, and experienced a great pleasure in handling those gold and silver ornaments, those exquisite and delicate works of art.

He carried a large linen bag, specially prepared for the removal of such knick-knacks. He filled it. Then he filled the pockets of his coat, waistcoat and trousers. And he was just placing over his left arm a number of pearl reticules when he heard a slight sound. He listened. No, he was not deceived. The noise continued. Then he remembered that, at one end of the gallery, there was a stairway leading to an unoccupied apartment, but which was probably occupied that night by the young lady whom Mon. Devanne had brought from Dieppe with his other visitors.

Immediately he extinguished his lantern, and had scarcely gained the friendly shelter of a window-embrasure, when the door at the top of the stairway was opened and a feeble light illuminated the gallery. He could feel—for, concealed by a curtain, he could not see—that a woman was cautiously descending the upper steps of the stairs. He hoped she would come no closer. Yet, she continued to descend, and even advanced some distance into the room. Then she uttered a faint cry. No doubt she had discovered the broken and dismantled cabinet.

She advanced again. Now he could smell the perfume, and hear the throbbing of her heart as she drew closer to the window where he was concealed. She passed so close that her skirt brushed against the window-curtain, and Lupin felt that she suspected the presence of another, behind her, in the shadow, within reach of her hand. He thought: "She is afraid. She will go away." But she did not go. The candle, that she carried in her trembling hand, grew brighter. She turned, hesitated a moment, appeared to listen, then suddenly drew aside the curtain.

They stood face to face. Arsène was astounded. He murmured, involuntarily:

"You—you—mademoiselle."

It was Miss Nelly. Miss Nelly! his fellow passenger on the transatlantic steamer, who had been the subject of his dreams on that memorable voyage, who had been a witness to his arrest, and who, rather than betray him, had dropped into the water the Kodak in which he had concealed the bank-notes and diamonds. Miss Nelly! that charming creature, the memory of whose face had sometimes cheered, sometimes saddened the long hours of imprisonment.

It was such an unexpected encounter that brought them face to face in that castle at that hour of the night, that they could not move, nor utter a word; they were amazed, hypnotized, each at the sudden apparition of the other. Trembling with emotion, Miss Nelly staggered to a seat. He remained standing in front of her.

Gradually, he realized the situation and conceived the impression he must have produced at that moment with his arms laden with knick-knacks, and his pockets and a linen sack overflowing with plunder. He was overcome with confusion, and he actually blushed to find himself in the position of a thief caught in the act. To her, henceforth, he was a thief, a man who puts his hand in another's pocket, who steals into houses and robs people while they sleep.

A watch fell upon the floor; then another. These were followed by other articles which slipped from his grasp one by one. Then, actuated by a sudden decision, he dropped the other articles into an armchair, emptied his pockets and unpacked his sack. He felt very uncomfortable in Nelly's presence, and stepped toward her with the intention of speaking to her, but she shuddered, rose quickly and fled toward the salon. The portière closed behind her. He followed her. She was standing trembling and amazed at the sight of the devastated room. He said to her, at once:

"To-morrow, at three o'clock, everything will be returned. The furniture will be brought back."

She made no reply, so he repeated:

"I promise it. To-morrow, at three o'clock. Nothing in the world could induce me to break that promise....To-morrow, at three o'clock."

Then followed a long silence that he dared not break, whilst the agitation of the young girl caused him a feeling of genuine regret. Quietly, without a word, he turned away, thinking: "I hope she will go away. I can't endure her presence." But the young girl suddenly spoke, and stammered:

"Listen.... footsteps....I hear someone...."

He looked at her with astonishment. She seemed to be overwhelmed by the thought of approaching peril.

"I don't hear anything," he said.

"But you must go—you must escape!"

"Why should I go?"

"Because—you must. Oh! do not remain here another minute. Go!"

She ran, quickly, to the door leading to the gallery and listened. No, there was no one there. Perhaps the noise was outside. She waited a moment, then returned reassured.

But Arsène Lupin had disappeared.

As soon as Mon. Devanne was informed of the pillage of his castle, he said to himself: It was Velmont who did it, and Velmont is Arsène Lupin. That theory explained everything, and there was no other plausible explanation. And yet the idea seemed preposterous. It was ridiculous to suppose that Velmont was anyone else than Velmont, the famous artist, and club-fellow of his cousin d'Estevan. So, when the captain of the gendarmes arrived to investigate the affair, Devanne did not even think of mentioning his absurd theory.

Throughout the forenoon there was a lively commotion at the castle. The gendarmes, the local police, the chief of police from Dieppe, the villagers, all circulated to and fro in the halls, examining every nook and corner that was open to their inspection. The approach of the maneuvering troops, the rattling fire of the musketry, added to the picturesque character of the scene.

The preliminary search furnished no clue. Neither the doors nor windows showed any signs of having been disturbed. Consequently, the removal of the goods must have been effected by means of the secret passage. Yet, there were no indications of footsteps on the floor, nor any unusual marks upon the walls.

Their investigations revealed, however, one curious fact that denoted the whimsical character of Arsène Lupin: the famous Chronique of the sixteenth century had been restored to its accustomed place in the library and, beside it, there was a similar book, which was none other than the volume stolen from the National Library.

At eleven o'clock the military officers arrived. Devanne welcomed them with his usual gayety; for, no matter how much chagrin he might suffer from the loss of his artistic treasures, his great wealth enabled him to bear his loss philosophically. His guests, Monsieur and Madame d'Androl and Miss Nelly, were introduced; and it was then noticed that one of the expected guests had not arrived. It was Horace Velmont. Would he come? His absence had awakened the suspicions of Mon. Devanne. But at twelve o'clock he arrived. Devanne exclaimed:

"Ah! here you are!"

"Why, am I not punctual?" asked Velmont.

"Yes, and I am surprised that you are.... after such a busy night! I suppose you know the news?"

"What news?"

"You have robbed the castle."

"Nonsense!" exclaimed Velmont, smiling.

"Exactly as I predicted. But, first escort Miss Underdown to the dining-room. Mademoiselle, allow me—"

He stopped, as he remarked the extreme agitation of the young girl. Then, recalling the incident, he said:

"Ah! of course, you met Arsène Lupin on the steamer, before his arrest, and you are astonished at the resemblance. Is that it?"

She did not reply. Velmont stood before her, smiling. He bowed. She took his proffered arm. He escorted her to her place, and took his seat opposite her. During the breakfast, the conversation related exclusively to Arsène Lupin, the stolen goods, the secret passage, and Sherlock Holmes. It was only at the close of the repast, when the conversation had drifted to other subjects, that Velmont took any part in it. Then he was, by turns, amusing and grave, talkative and pensive. And all his remarks seemed to be directed to the young girl. But she, quite absorbed, did not appear to hear them.

Coffee was served on the terrace overlooking the court of honor and the flower garden in front of the principal façade. The regimental band played on the lawn, and scores of soldiers and peasants wandered through the park.

Miss Nelly had not forgotten, for one moment, Lupin's solemn promise: "To-morrow, at three o'clock, everything will be returned."

At three o'clock! And the hands of the great clock in the right wing of the castle now marked twenty minutes to three. In spite of herself, her eyes wandered to the clock every minute. She also watched Velmont, who was calmly swinging to and fro in a comfortable rocking chair.

Ten minutes to three!....Five minutes to three!....Nelly was impatient and anxious. Was it possible that Arsène Lupin would carry out his promise at the appointed hour, when the castle, the courtyard, and the park were filled with people, and at the very moment when the officers of the law were pursuing their investigations? And yet....Arsène Lupin had given her his solemn promise. "It will be exactly as he said," thought she, so deeply was she impressed with the authority, energy and assurance of that remarkable man. To her, it no longer assumed the form of a miracle, but, on the contrary, a natural incident that must occur in the ordinary course of events. She blushed, and turned her head.

Three o'clock! The great clock struck slowly: one.... two.... three....Horace Velmont took out his watch, glanced at the clock, then returned the watch to his pocket. A few seconds passed in silence; and then the crowd in the courtyard parted to give passage to two wagons, that had just entered the park-gate, each drawn by two horses. They were army-wagons, such as are used for the transportation of provisions, tents, and other necessary military stores. They stopped in front of the main entrance, and a commissary-sergeant leaped from one of the wagons and inquired for Mon. Devanne. A moment later, that gentleman emerged from the house, descended the steps, and, under the canvas covers of the wagons, beheld his furniture, pictures and ornaments carefully packaged and arranged.

When questioned, the sergeant produced an order that he had received from the officer of the day. By that order, the second company of the fourth battalion were commanded to proceed to the crossroads of Halleux in the forest of Arques, gather up the furniture and other articles deposited there, and deliver same to Monsieur Georges Devanne, owner of the Thibermesnil castle, at three o'clock. Signed: Col. Beauvel.

"At the crossroads," explained the sergeant, "we found everything ready, lying on the grass, guarded by some passers-by. It seemed very strange, but the order was imperative."

One of the officers examined the signature. He declared it a forgery; but a clever imitation. The wagons were unloaded, and the goods restored to their proper places in the castle.

During this commotion, Nelly had remained alone at the extreme end of the terrace, absorbed by confused and distracted thoughts. Suddenly, she observed Velmont approaching her. She would have avoided him, but the balustrade that surrounded the terrace cut off her retreat. She was cornered. She could not move. A gleam of sunshine, passing through the scant foliage of a bamboo, lighted up her beautiful golden hair. Some one spoke to her in a low voice:

"Have I not kept my promise?"

Arsène Lupin stood close to her. No one else was near. He repeated, in a calm, soft voice:

"Have I not kept my promise?"

He expected a word of thanks, or at least some slight movement that would betray her interest in the fulfillment of his promise. But she remained silent.

Her scornful attitude annoyed Arsène Lupin; and he realized the vast distance that separated him from Miss Nelly, now that she had learned the truth. He would gladly have justified himself in her eyes, or at least pleaded extenuating circumstances, but he perceived the absurdity and futility of such an attempt. Finally, dominated by a surging flood of memories, he murmured:

"Ah! how long ago that was! You remember the long hours on the deck of the 'Provence.' Then, you carried a rose in your hand, a white rose like the one you carry to-day. I asked you for it. You pretended you did not hear me. After you had gone away, I found the rose—forgotten, no doubt—and I kept it."

She made no reply. She seemed to be far away. He continued:

"In memory of those happy hours, forget what you have learned since. Separate the past from the present. Do not regard me as the man you saw last night, but look at me, if only for a moment, as you did in those far-off days when I was Bernard d'Andrezy, for a short time. Will you, please?"

She raised her eyes and looked at him as he had requested. Then, without saying a word, she pointed to a ring he was wearing on his forefinger. Only the ring was visible; but the setting, which was turned toward the palm of his hand, consisted of a magnificent ruby. Arsène Lupin blushed. The ring belonged to Georges Devanne. He smiled bitterly, and said:

"You are right. Nothing can be changed. Arsène Lupin is now and always will be Arsène Lupin. To you, he cannot be even so much as a memory. Pardon me....I should have known that any attention I may now offer you is simply an insult. Forgive me."

He stepped aside, hat in hand. Nelly passed before him. He was inclined to detain her and beseech her forgiveness. But his courage failed, and he contented himself by following her with his eyes, as he had done when she descended the gangway to the pier at New York. She mounted the steps leading to the door, and disappeared within the house. He saw her no more.

A cloud obscured the sun. Arsène Lupin stood watching the imprints of her tiny feet in the sand. Suddenly, he gave a start. Upon the box which contained the bamboo, beside which Nelly had been standing, he saw the rose, the white rose which he had desired but dared not ask for. Forgotten, no doubt—it, also! But how—designedly or through distraction? He seized it eagerly. Some of its petals fell to the ground. He picked them up, one by one, like precious relics.

"Come!" he said to himself, "I have nothing more to do here. I must think of my safety, before Sherlock Holmes arrives."

The park was deserted, but some gendarmes were stationed at the park-gate. He entered a grove of pine trees, leaped over the wall, and, as a short cut to the railroad station, followed a path across the fields. After walking about ten minutes, he arrived at a spot where the road grew narrower and ran between two steep banks. In this ravine, he met a man traveling in the opposite direction. It was a man about fifty years of age, tall, smooth-shaven, and wearing clothes of a foreign cut. He carried a heavy cane, and a small satchel was strapped across his shoulder. When they met, the stranger spoke, with a slight English accent:

"Excuse me, monsieur, is this the way to the castle?"

"Yes, monsieur, straight ahead, and turn to the left when you come to the wall. They are expecting you."

"Ah!"

"Yes, my friend Devanne told us last night that you were coming, and I am delighted to be the first to welcome you. Sherlock Holmes has no more ardent admirer than.... myself."

There was a touch of irony in his voice that he quickly regretted, for Sherlock Holmes scrutinized him from head to foot with such a keen, penetrating eye that Arsène Lupin experienced the sensation of being seized, imprisoned and registered by that look more thoroughly and precisely than he had ever been by a camera.

"My negative is taken now," he thought, "and it will be useless to use a disguise with that man. He would look right through it. But, I wonder, has he recognized me?"

They bowed to each other as if about to part. But, at that moment, they heard a sound of horses' feet, accompanied by a clinking of steel. It was the gendarmes. The two men were obliged to draw back against the embankment, amongst the brushes, to avoid the horses. The gendarmes passed by, but, as they followed each other at a considerable distance, they were several minutes in doing so. And Lupin was thinking:

"It all depends on that question: has he recognized me? If so, he will probably take advantage of the opportunity. It is a trying situation."

When the last horseman had passed, Sherlock Holmes stepped forth and brushed the dust from his clothes. Then, for a moment, he and Arsène Lupin gazed at each other; and, if a person could have seen them at that moment, it would have been an interesting sight, and memorable as the first meeting of two remarkable men, so strange, so powerfully equipped, both of superior quality, and destined by fate, through their peculiar attributes, to hurl themselves one at the other like two equal forces that nature opposes, one against the other, in the realms of space.

Then the Englishman said: "Thank you, monsieur."

"You are quite welcome, replied Arsène Lupin."

They parted. Lupin went toward the railway station, and Sherlock Holmes continued on his way to the castle.

The local officers had given up the investigation after several hours of fruitless efforts, and the people at the castle were awaiting the arrival of the English detective with a lively curiosity. At first sight, they were a little disappointed on account of his commonplace appearance, which differed so greatly from the pictures they had formed of him in their own minds. He did not in any way resemble the romantic hero, the mysterious and diabolical personage that the name of Sherlock Holmes had evoked in their imaginations. However, Mon. Devanne exclaimed with much gusto:

"Ah! monsieur, you are here! I am delighted to see you. It is a long-deferred pleasure. Really, I scarcely regret what has happened, since it affords me the opportunity to meet you. But, how did you come?"

"By the train."

"But I sent my automobile to meet you at the station."

"An official reception, eh? with music and fireworks! Oh! no, not for me. That is not the way I do business," grumbled the Englishman.

This speech disconcerted Devanne, who replied, with a forced smile:

"Fortunately, the business has been greatly simplified since I wrote to you."

"In what way?"

"The robbery took place last night."

"If you had not announced my intended visit, it is probable the robbery would not have been committed last night."

"When, then?"

"To-morrow, or some other day."

"And in that case?"

"Lupin would have been trapped," said the detective.

"And my furniture?"

"Would not have been carried away."

"Ah! but my goods are here. They were brought back at three o'clock."

"By Lupin."

"By two army-wagons."

Sherlock Holmes put on his cap and adjusted his satchel. Devanne exclaimed, anxiously:

"But, monsieur, what are you going to do?"

"I am going home."

"Why?"

"Your goods have been returned; Arsène Lupin is far away—there is nothing for me to do."

"Yes, there is. I need your assistance. What happened yesterday, may happen again to-morrow, as we do not know how he entered, or how he escaped, or why, a few hours later, he returned the goods."

"Ah! you don't know—"

The idea of a problem to be solved quickened the interest of Sherlock Holmes.

"Very well, let us make a search—at once—and alone, if possible."

Devanne understood, and conducted the Englishman to the salon. In a dry, crisp voice, in sentences that seemed to have been prepared in advance, Holmes asked a number of questions about the events of the preceding evening, and enquired also concerning the guests and the members of the household. Then he examined the two volumes of the "Chronique," compared the plans of the subterranean passage, requested a repetition of the sentences discovered by Father Gélis, and then asked:

"Was yesterday the first time you have spoken those two sentences to any one?"

"Yes."

"You had never communicated then to Horace Velmont?"

"No."

"Well, order the automobile. I must leave in an hour."

"In an hour?"

"Yes; within that time, Arsène Lupin solved the problem that you placed before him."

"I.... placed before him—"

"Yes, Arsène Lupin or Horace Velmont—same thing."

"I thought so. Ah! the scoundrel!"

"Now, let us see," said Holmes, "last night at ten o'clock, you furnished Lupin with the information that he lacked, and that he had been seeking for many weeks. During the night, he found time to solve the problem, collect his men, and rob the castle. I shall be quite as expeditious."

He walked from end to end of the room, in deep thought, then sat down, crossed his long legs and closed his eyes.

Devanne waited, quite embarrassed. Thought he: "Is the man asleep? Or is he only meditating?" However, he left the room to give some orders, and when he returned he found the detective on his knees scrutinizing the carpet at the foot of the stairs in the gallery.

"What is it?" he enquired.

"Look.... there.... spots from a candle."

"You are right—and quite fresh."

"And you will also find them at the top of the stairs, and around the cabinet that

Arsène Lupin broke into, and from which he took the bibelots that he afterward placed in this armchair."

"What do you conclude from that?"

"Nothing. These facts would doubtless explain the cause for the restitution, but that is a side issue that I cannot wait to investigate. The main question is the secret passage. First, tell me, is there a chapel some two or three hundred metres from the castle?"

"Yes, a ruined chapel, containing the tomb of Duke Rollo."

"Tell your chauffer to wait for us near that chapel."

"My chauffer hasn't returned. If he had, they would have informed me. Do you think the secret passage runs to the chapel? What reason have—"

"I would ask you, monsieur," interrupted the detective, "to furnish me with a ladder and a lantern."

"What! do you require a ladder and a lantern?"

"Certainly, or I shouldn't have asked for them."

Devanne, somewhat disconcerted by this crude logic, rang the bell. The two articles were given with the sternness and precision of military commands.

"Place the ladder against the bookcase, to the left of the word Thibermesnil."

Devanne placed the ladder as directed, and the Englishman continued:

"More to the left.... to the right....There!....Now, climb up.... All the letters are in relief, aren't they?"

"Yes."

"First, turn the letter I one way or the other."

"Which one? There are two of them."

"The first one."

Devanne took hold of the letter, and exclaimed:

"Ah! yes, it turns toward the right. Who told you that?"

Sherlock Holmes did not reply to the question, but continued his directions:

"Now, take the letter B. Move it back and forth as you would a bolt."

Devanne did so, and, to his great surprise, it produced a clicking sound.

"Quite right," said Holmes. "Now, we will go to the other end of the word Thibermesnil, try the letter I, and see if it will open like a wicket."

With a certain degree of solemnity, Devanne seized the letter. It opened, but Devanne fell from the ladder, for the entire section of the bookcase, lying between the first and last letters of the words, turned on a pivot and disclosed the subterranean passage.

Sherlock Holmes said, coolly:

"You are not hurt?"

"No, no," said Devanne, as he rose to his feet, "not hurt, only bewildered. I can't understand now.... those letters turn.... the secret passage opens...."

"Certainly. Doesn't that agree exactly with the formula given by Sully? Turn one eye on the bee that shakes, the other eye will lead to God."

"But Louis the sixteenth?" asked Devanne.

"Louis the sixteenth was a clever locksmith. I have read a book he wrote about combination locks. It was a good idea on the part of the owner of Thibermesnil to show His Majesty a clever bit of mechanism. As an aid to his memory, the king wrote: 3-4-11, that is to say, the third, fourth and eleventh letters of the word."

"Exactly. I understand that. It explains how Lupin got out of the room, but it does not explain how he entered. And it is certain he came from the outside."

Sherlock Holmes lighted his lantern, and stepped into the passage.

"Look! All the mechanism is exposed here, like the works of a clock, and the reverse side of the letters can be reached. Lupin worked the combination from this side—that is all."

"What proof is there of that?"

"Proof? Why, look at that puddle of oil. Lupin foresaw that the wheels would require oiling."

"Did he know about the other entrance?"

"As well as I know it," said Holmes. "Follow me."

"Into that dark passage?"

"Are you afraid?"

"No, but are you sure you can find the way out?"

"With my eyes closed."

At first, they descended twelve steps, then twelve more, and, farther on, two other flights of twelve steps each. Then they walked through a long passageway, the brick walls of which showed the marks of successive restorations, and, in spots, were dripping with water. The earth, also, was very damp.

"We are passing under the pond," said Devanne, somewhat nervously.

At last, they came to a stairway of twelve steps, followed by three others of twelve steps each, which they mounted with difficulty, and then found themselves in a small cavity cut in the rock. They could go no further.

"The deuce!" muttered Holmes, "nothing but bare walls. This is provoking."

"Let us go back," said Devanne. "I have seen enough to satisfy me."

But the Englishman raised his eye and uttered a sigh of relief. There, he saw the same mechanism and the same word as before. He had merely to work the three letters. He did so, and a block of granite swung out of place. On the other side, this granite block formed the tombstone of Duke Rollo, and the word "Thibermesnil" was engraved on it in relief. Now, they were in the little ruined chapel, and the detective said:

"The other eye leads to God; that means, to the chapel."

"It is marvelous!" exclaimed Devanne, amazed at the clairvoyance and vivacity of the Englishman. "Can it be possible that those few words were sufficient for you?"

"Bah!" declared Holmes, "they weren't even necessary. In the chart in the book of the National Library, the drawing terminates at the left, as you know, in a circle, and at the right, as you do not know, in a cross. Now, that cross must refer to the chapel in which we now stand."

Poor Devanne could not believe his ears. It was all so new, so novel to him. He exclaimed:

"It is incredible, miraculous, and yet of a childish simplicity! How is it that no one has ever solved the mystery?"

"Because no one has ever united the essential elements, that is to say, the two books and the two sentences. No one, but Arsène Lupin and myself."

"But, Father Gélis and I knew all about those things, and, likewise—"

Holmes smiled, and said:

"Monsieur Devanne, everybody cannot solve riddles."

"I have been trying for ten years to accomplish what you did in ten minutes."

"Bah! I am used to it."

They emerged from the chapel, and found an automobile.

"Ah! there's an auto waiting for us."

"Yes, it is mine," said Devanne.

"Yours? You said your chauffeur hadn't returned."

They approached the machine, and Mon. Devanne questioned the chauffer:

"Edouard, who gave you orders to come here?"

"Why, it was Monsieur Velmont."

"Mon. Velmont? Did you meet him?"

"Near the railway station, and he told me to come to the chapel."

"To come to the chapel! What for?"

"To wait for you, monsieur, and your friend."

Devanne and Holmes exchanged looks, and Mon. Devanne said:

"He knew the mystery would be a simple one for you. It is a delicate compliment."

A smile of satisfaction lighted up the detective's serious features for a moment. The compliment pleased him. He shook his head, as he said:

"A clever man! I knew that when I saw him."

"Have you seen him?"

"I met him a short time ago—on my way from the station."

"And you knew it was Horace Velmont—I mean, Arsène Lupin?"

"That is right. I wonder how it came—"

"No, but I supposed it was—from a certain ironical speech he made."

"And you allowed him to escape?"

"Of course I did. And yet I had everything on my side, such as five gendarmes who passed us."

"Sacrableu!" cried Devanne. "You should have taken advantage of the opportunity."

"Really, monsieur," said the Englishman, haughtily, "when I encounter an adversary like Arsène Lupin, I do not take advantage of chance opportunities, I create them."

But time pressed, and since Lupin had been so kind as to send the automobile, they resolved to profit by it. They seated themselves in the comfortable limousine; Edouard took his place at the wheel, and away they went toward the railway station. Suddenly, Devanne's eyes fell upon a small package in one of the pockets of the carriage.

"Ah! what is that? A package! Whose is it? Why, it is for you."

"For me?"

"Yes, it is addressed: Sherlock Holmes, from Arsène Lupin."

The Englishman took the package, opened it, and found that it contained a watch.

"Ah!" he exclaimed, with an angry gesture.

"A watch," said Devanne. "How did it come there?"

The detective did not reply.

"Oh! it is your watch! Arsène Lupin returns your watch! But, in order to return it, he must have taken it. Ah! I see! He took your watch! That is a good one! Sherlock Holmes' watch stolen by Arsène Lupin! Mon Dieu! that is funny! Really.... you must excuse me....I can't help it."

He roared with laughter, unable to control himself. After which, he said, in a tone of earnest conviction:

"A clever man, indeed!"

The Englishman never moved a muscle. On the way to Dieppe, he never spoke a word, but fixed his gaze on the flying landscape. His silence was terrible, unfathomable, more violent than the wildest rage. At the railway station, he spoke calmly, but in a voice that impressed one with the vast energy and will power of that famous man. He said:

"Yes, he is a clever man, but someday I shall have the pleasure of placing on his shoulder the hand I now offer to you, Monsieur Devanne. And I believe that Arsène Lupin and Sherlock Holmes will meet again some day. Yes, the world is too small—we will meet—we must meet—and then—"

—The further startling and thrilling adventures of Arsène Lupin can be found in the book entitled "Arsène Lupin versus Herlock Sholmes."—

ARSÈNE LUPIN VERSUS HERLOCK
SHOLMES

I. LOTTERY TICKET NO. 514

On the eighth day of last December, Mon. Gerbois, professor of mathematics at the College of Versailles, while rummaging in an old curiosity-shop, unearthed a small mahogany writing-desk which pleased him very much on account of the multiplicity of its drawers.

"Just the thing for Suzanne's birthday present," thought he. And as he always tried to furnish some simple pleasures for his daughter, consistent with his modest income, he enquired the price, and, after some keen bargaining, purchased it for sixty-five francs. As he was giving his address to the shopkeeper, a young man, dressed with elegance and taste, who had been exploring the stock of antiques, caught sight of the writing-desk, and immediately enquired its price.

"It is sold," replied the shopkeeper.

"Ah! to this gentleman, I presume?"

Monsieur Gerbois bowed, and left the store, quite proud to be the possessor of an article which had attracted the attention of a gentleman of quality. But he had not taken a dozen steps in the street, when he was overtaken by the young man who, hat in hand and in a tone of perfect courtesy, thus addressed him:

"I beg your pardon, monsieur; I am going to ask you a question that you may deem impertinent. It is this: Did you have any special object in view when you bought that writing-desk?"

"No, I came across it by chance and it struck my fancy."

"But you do not care for it particularly?"

"Oh! I shall keep it—that is all."

"Because it is an antique, perhaps?"

"No; because it is convenient," declared Mon. Gerbois.

"In that case, you would consent to exchange it for another desk that would be quite as convenient and in better condition?"

"Oh! this one is in good condition, and I see no object in making an exchange."

"But——"

Mon. Gerbois is a man of irritable disposition and hasty temper. So he replied, testily:

"I beg of you, monsieur, do not insist."

But the young man firmly held his ground.

"I don't know how much you paid for it, monsieur, but I offer you double."

"No."

"Three times the amount."

"Oh! that will do," exclaimed the professor, impatiently; "I don't wish to sell it."

The young man stared at him for a moment in a manner that Mon. Gerbois would not readily forget, then turned and walked rapidly away.

An hour later, the desk was delivered at the professor's house on the Viroflay road. He called his daughter, and said:

"Here is something for you, Suzanne, provided you like it."

Suzanne was a pretty girl, with a gay and affectionate nature. She threw her arms around her father's neck and kissed him rapturously. To her, the desk had all the semblance of a royal gift. That evening, assisted by Hortense, the servant, she placed the desk in her room; then she dusted it, cleaned the drawers and pigeon-holes, and carefully arranged within it her papers, writing material, correspondence, a collection of post-cards, and some souvenirs of her cousin Philippe that she kept in secret.

Next morning, at half past seven, Mon. Gerbois went to the college. At ten o'clock, in pursuance of her usual custom, Suzanne went to meet him, and it was a great pleasure for him to see her slender figure and childish smile waiting for him at the college gate. They returned home together.

"And your writing desk—how is it this morning?"

"Marvelous! Hortense and I have polished the brass mountings until they look like gold."

"So you are pleased with it?"

"Pleased with it! Why, I don't see how I managed to get on without it for such a long time."

As they were walking up the pathway to the house, Mon. Gerbois said:

"Shall we go and take a look at it before breakfast?"

"Oh! yes, that's a splendid idea!"

She ascended the stairs ahead of her father, but, on arriving at the door of her room, she uttered a cry of surprise and dismay.

"What's the matter?" stammered Mon. Gerbois.

"The writing-desk is gone!"

When the police were called in, they were astonished at the admirable simplicity of the means employed by the thief. During Suzanne's absence, the servant had gone to market, and while the house was thus left unguarded, a drayman, wearing a badge—some of the neighbors saw it—stopped his cart in front of the house and rang twice. Not knowing that

Hortense was absent, the neighbors were not suspicious; consequently, the man carried on his work in peace and tranquility.

Apart from the desk, not a thing in the house had been disturbed. Even Suzanne's purse, which she had left upon the writing-desk, was found upon an adjacent table with its contents untouched. It was obvious that the thief had come with a set purpose, which rendered the crime even more mysterious; because, why did he assume so great a risk for such a trifling object?

The only clue the professor could furnish was the strange incident of the preceding evening. He declared:

"The young man was greatly provoked at my refusal, and I had an idea that he threatened me as he went away."

But the clue was a vague one. The shopkeeper could not throw any light on the affair. He did not know either of the gentlemen. As to the desk itself, he had purchased it for forty francs at an executor's sale at Chevreuse, and believed he had resold it at its fair value. The police investigation disclosed nothing more.

But Mon. Gerbois entertained the idea that he had suffered an enormous loss. There must have been a fortune concealed in a secret drawer, and that was the reason the young man had resorted to crime.

"My poor father, what would we have done with that fortune?" asked Suzanne.

"My child! with such a fortune, you could make a most advantageous marriage."

Suzanne sighed bitterly. Her aspirations soared no higher than her cousin Philippe, who was indeed a most deplorable object. And life, in the little house at Versailles, was not so happy and contented as of yore.

Two months passed away. Then came a succession of startling events, a strange blending of good luck and dire misfortune!

On the first day of February, at half-past five, Mon. Gerbois entered the house, carrying an evening paper, took a seat, put on his spectacles, and commenced to read. As politics did not interest him, he turned to the inside of the paper. Immediately his attention was attracted by an article entitled:

"Third Drawing of the Press Association Lottery.

"No. 514, series 23, draws a million."

The newspaper slipped from his fingers. The walls swam before his eyes, and his heart ceased to beat. He held No. 514, series 23. He had purchased it from a friend, to oblige him, without any thought of success, and behold, it was the lucky number!

Quickly, he took out his memorandum-book. Yes, he was quite right. The No. 514, series 23, was written there, on the inside of the cover. But the ticket?

He rushed to his desk to find the envelope-box in which he had placed the precious ticket; but the box was not there, and it suddenly occurred to him that it had not been there for several weeks. He heard footsteps on the gravel walk leading from the street.

He called:

"Suzanne! Suzanne!"

She was returning from a walk. She entered hastily. He stammered, in a choking voice:

"Suzanne ... the box ... the box of envelopes?"

"What box?"

"The one I bought at the Louvre ... one Saturday ... it was at the end of that table."

"Don't you remember, father, we put all those things away together."

"When?"

"The evening ... you know ... the same evening...."

"But where?... Tell me, quick!... Where?"

"Where? Why, in the writing-desk."

"In the writing-desk that was stolen?"

"Yes."

"Oh, mon Dieu!... In the stolen desk!"

He uttered the last sentence in a low voice, in a sort of stupor. Then he seized her hand, and in a still lower voice, he said:

"It contained a million, my child."

"Ah! father, why didn't you tell me?" she murmured, naively.

"A million!" he repeated. "It contained the ticket that drew the grand prize in the Press Lottery."

The colossal proportions of the disaster overwhelmed them, and for a long time they maintained a silence that they feared to break. At last, Suzanne said:

"But, father, they will pay you just the same."

"How? On what proof?"

"Must you have proof?"

"Of course."

"And you haven't any?"

"It was in the box."

"In the box that has disappeared."

"Yes; and now the thief will get the money."

"Oh! that would be terrible, father. You must prevent it."

For a moment he was silent; then, in an outburst of energy, he leaped up, stamped on the floor, and exclaimed:

"No, no, he shall not have that million; he shall not have it! Why should he have it? Ah! clever as he is, he can do nothing. If he goes to claim the money, they will arrest him. Ah! now, we will see, my fine fellow!"

"What will you do, father?"

"Defend our just rights, whatever happens! And we will succeed. The million francs belong to me, and I intend to have them."

A few minutes later, he sent this telegram:

"Governor Crédit Foncier
   "rue Capucines, Paris.
   "Am holder of No. 514, series 23. Oppose by all legal means any other claimant.
   "GERBOIS."

Almost at the same moment, the Crédit Foncier received the following telegram:

"No. 514, series 23, is in my possession.
   "ARSÈNE LUPIN."

Every time I undertake to relate one of the many extraordinary adventures that mark the life of Arsène Lupin, I experience a feeling of embarrassment, as it seems to me that the most commonplace of those adventures is already well known to my readers. In fact, there is not a movement of our "national thief," as he has been so aptly described, that has not been given the widest publicity, not an exploit that has not been studied in all its phases, not an action that has not been discussed with that particularity usually reserved for the recital of heroic deeds.

For instance, who does not know the strange history of "The Blonde Lady," with those curious episodes which were proclaimed by the newspapers with heavy black headlines, as follows: "Lottery Ticket No. 514!" ... "The Crime on the Avenue Henri-Martin!" ... "The Blue Diamond!" ... The interest created by the intervention of the celebrated English detective, Herlock Sholmes! The excitement aroused by the various vicissitudes which marked the struggle between those famous artists! And what a commotion on the boulevards, the day on which the newsboys announced: "Arrest of Arsène Lupin!"

My excuse for repeating these stories at this time is the fact that I produce the key to the enigma. Those adventures have always been enveloped in a certain degree of obscurity, which I now remove. I reproduce old newspaper articles, I relate old-time interviews, I present ancient letters; but I have arranged and classified all that material and reduced it to the exact truth. My collaborators in this work have been Arsène Lupin himself, and also the ineffable Wilson, the friend and confidant of Herlock Sholmes.

Everyone will recall the tremendous burst of laughter which greeted the publication of those two telegrams. The name "Arsène Lupin" was in itself a stimulus to curiosity, a promise of amusement for the gallery. And, in this case, the gallery means the entire world.

An investigation was immediately commenced by the Crédit Foncier, which established these facts: That ticket No. 514, series 23, had been sold by the Versailles branch office of the Lottery to an artillery officer named Bessy, who was afterward killed by a fall from his horse. Sometime before his death, he informed some of his comrades that he had transferred his ticket to a friend.

"And I am that friend," affirmed Mon. Gerbois.

"Prove it," replied the governor of the Crédit Foncier.

"Of course I can prove it. Twenty people can tell you that I was an intimate friend of Monsieur Bessy, and that we frequently met at the Café de la Place-d'Armes. It was there, one day, I purchased the ticket from him for twenty francs—simply as an accommodation to him.

"Have you any witnesses to that transaction?"

"No."

"Well, how do you expect to prove it?"

"By a letter he wrote to me."

"What letter?"

"A letter that was pinned to the ticket."

"Produce it."

"It was stolen at the same time as the ticket."

"Well, you must find it."

It was soon learned that Arsène Lupin had the letter. A short paragraph appeared in the *Echo de France*—which has the honor to be his official organ, and of which, it is said, he is one of the principal shareholders—the paragraph announced that Arsène Lupin had placed in the hands of Monsieur Detinan, his advocate and legal adviser, the letter that Monsieur Bessy had written to him—to him personally.

This announcement provoked an outburst of laughter. Arsène Lupin had engaged a lawyer! Arsène Lupin, conforming to the rules and customs of modern society, had appointed a legal representative in the person of a well-known member of the Parisian bar!

Mon. Detinan had never enjoyed the pleasure of meeting Arsène Lupin—a fact he deeply regretted—but he had actually been retained by that mysterious gentleman and felt greatly honored by the choice. He was prepared to defend the interests of his client to the best of his ability. He was pleased, even proud, to exhibit the letter of Mon. Bessy, but, although it proved the transfer of the ticket, it did not mention the name of the purchaser. It was simply addressed to "My Dear Friend."

"My Dear Friend! that is I," added Arsène Lupin, in a note attached to Mon. Bessy's letter. "And the best proof of that fact is that I hold the letter."

The swarm of reporters immediately rushed to see Mon. Gerbois, who could only repeat:

"My Dear Friend! that is I.... Arsène Lupin stole the letter with the lottery ticket."

"Let him prove it!" retorted Lupin to the reporters.

"He must have done it, because he stole the writing-desk!" exclaimed Mon. Gerbois before the same reporters.

"Let him prove it!" replied Lupin.

Such was the entertaining comedy enacted by the two claimants of ticket No. 514; and the calm demeanor of Arsène Lupin contrasted strangely with the nervous perturbation of poor Mon. Gerbois. The newspapers were filled with the lamentations of that unhappy man. He announced his misfortune with pathetic candor.

"Understand, gentlemen, it was Suzanne's dowry that the rascal stole! Personally, I don't care a straw for it,... but for Suzanne! Just think of it, a whole million! Ten times one hundred thousand francs! Ah! I knew very well that the desk contained a treasure!"

It was in vain to tell him that his adversary, when stealing the desk, was unaware that the lottery ticket was in it, and that, in any event, he could not foresee that the ticket would draw the grand prize. He would reply;

"Nonsense! of course, he knew it ... else why would he take the trouble to steal a poor, miserable desk?"

"For some unknown reason; but certainly not for a small scrap of paper which was then worth only twenty francs."

"A million francs! He knew it;... he knows everything! Ah! you do not know him—the scoundrel!... He hasn't robbed you of a million francs!"

The controversy would have lasted for a much longer time, but, on the twelfth day, Mon. Gerbois received from Arsène Lupin a letter, marked "confidential," which read as follows:

"Monsieur, the gallery is being amused at our expense. Do you not think it is time for us to be serious? The situation is this: I possess a ticket to which I have no legal right, and you have the legal right to a ticket you do not possess. Neither of us can do anything. You will not relinquish your rights to me; I will not deliver the ticket to you. Now, what is to be done?

"I see only one way out of the difficulty: Let us divide the spoils. A half-million for you; a half-million for me. Is not that a fair division? In my opinion, it is an equitable solution, and an immediate one. I will give you three days' time to consider the proposition. On Thursday morning I shall expect to read in the personal column of the Echo de France a discreet message addressed to M. Ars. Lup, expressing in veiled terms your consent to my offer. By so doing you will recover immediate possession of the ticket; then you can collect the money and send me half a million in a manner that I will describe to you later.

"In case of your refusal, I shall resort to other measures to accomplish the same result. But, apart from the very serious annoyances that such obstinacy on your part will cause you, it will cost you twenty-five thousand francs for supplementary expenses.

"Believe me, monsieur, I remain your devoted servant, ARSÈNE LUPIN."

In a fit of exasperation Mon. Gerbois committed the grave mistake of showing that letter and allowing a copy of it to be taken. His indignation overcame his discretion.

"Nothing! He shall have nothing!" he exclaimed, before a crowd of reporters. "To divide my property with him? Never! Let him tear up the ticket if he wishes!"

"Yet five hundred thousand francs is better than nothing."

"That is not the question. It is a question of my just right, and that right I will establish before the courts."

"What! attack Arsène Lupin? That would be amusing."

"No; but the Crédit Foncier. They must pay me the million francs."

"Without producing the ticket, or, at least, without proving that you bought it?"

"That proof exists, since Arsène Lupin admits that he stole the writing-desk."

"But would the word of Arsène Lupin carry any weight with the court?"

"No matter; I will fight it out."

The gallery shouted with glee; and wagers were freely made upon the result with the odds in favor of Lupin. On the following Thursday the personal column in the *Echo de France* was eagerly perused by the expectant public, but it contained nothing addressed to M. Ars. Lup. Mon. Gerbois had not replied to Arsène Lupin's letter. That was the declaration of war.

That evening the newspapers announced the abduction of Mlle. Suzanne Gerbois.

The most entertaining feature in what might be called the Arsène Lupin dramas is the comic attitude displayed by the Parisian police. Arsène Lupin talks, plans, writes, commands, threatens and executes as if the police did not exist. They never figure in his calculations.

And yet the police do their utmost. But what can they do against such a foe—a foe that scorns and ignores them?

Suzanne had left the house at twenty minutes to ten; such was the testimony of the servant. On leaving the college, at five minutes past ten, her father did not find her at the place she was accustomed to wait for him. Consequently, whatever had happened must have occurred during the course of Suzanne's walk from the house to the college. Two neighbors had met her about three hundred yards from the house. A lady had seen, on the avenue, a young girl corresponding to Suzanne's description. No one else had seen her.

Inquiries were made in all directions; the employees of the railways and street-car lines were questioned, but none of them had seen anything of the missing girl. However, at

Ville-d'Avray, they found a shopkeeper who had furnished gasoline to an automobile that had come from Paris on the day of the abduction. It was occupied by a blonde woman—extremely blonde, said the witness. An hour later, the automobile again passed through Ville-d'Avray on its way from Versailles to Paris. The shopkeeper declared that the automobile now contained a second woman who was heavily veiled. No doubt, it was Suzanne Gerbois.

The abduction must have taken place in broad daylight, on a frequented street, in the very heart of the town. How? And at what spot? Not a cry was heard; not a suspicious action had been seen. The shopkeeper described the automobile as a royal-blue limousine of twenty-four horse-power made by the firm of Peugeon & Co. Inquiries were then made at the Grand-Garage, managed by Madame Bob-Walthour, who made a specialty of abductions by automobile. It was learned that she had rented a Peugeon limousine on that day to a blonde woman whom she had never seen before nor since.

"Who was the chauffeur?"

"A young man named Ernest, whom I had engaged only the day before. He came well recommended."

"Is he here now?"

"No. He brought back the machine, but I haven't seen him since," said Madame Bob-Walthour.

"Do you know where we can find him?"

"You might see the people who recommended him to me. Here are the names."

Upon inquiry, it was learned that none of these people knew the man called Ernest. The recommendations were forged.

Such was the fate of every clue followed by the police. It ended nowhere. The mystery remained unsolved.

Mon. Gerbois had not the strength or courage to wage such an unequal battle. The disappearance of his daughter crushed him; he capitulated to the enemy. A short announcement in the *Echo de France* proclaimed his unconditional surrender.

Two days later, Mon. Gerbois visited the office of the Crédit Foncier and handed lottery ticket number 514, series 23, to the governor, who exclaimed, with surprise:

"Ah! you have it! He has returned it to you!"

"It was mislaid. That was all," replied Mon. Gerbois.

"But you pretended that it had been stolen."

"At first, I thought it had ... but here it is."

"We will require some evidence to establish your right to the ticket."

"Will the letter of the purchaser, Monsieur Bessy, be sufficient!"

"Yes, that will do."

"Here it is," said Mon. Gerbois, producing the letter.

"Very well. Leave these papers with us. The rules of the lottery allow us fifteen days' time to investigate your claim. I will let you know when to call for your money. I presume you desire, as much as I do, that this affair should be closed without further publicity."

"Quite so."

Mon. Gerbois and the governor henceforth maintained a discreet silence. But the secret was revealed in some way, for it was soon commonly known that Arsène Lupin had returned the lottery ticket to Mon. Gerbois. The public received the news with astonishment and admiration. Certainly, he was a bold gamester who thus threw upon the table a trump card of such importance as the precious ticket. But, it was true, he still retained a trump card of equal importance. However, if the young girl should escape? If the hostage held by Arsène Lupin should be rescued?

The police thought they had discovered the weak spot of the enemy, and now redoubled their efforts. Arsène Lupin disarmed by his own act, crushed by the wheels of his own machination, deprived of every sou of the coveted million ... public interest now centered in the camp of his adversary.

But it was necessary to find Suzanne. And they did not find her, nor did she escape. Consequently, it must be admitted, Arsène Lupin had won the first hand. But the game was not yet decided. The most difficult point remained. Mlle. Gerbois is in his possession, and he will hold her until he receives five hundred thousand francs. But how and where will such an exchange be made? For that purpose, a meeting must be arranged, and then what will prevent Mon. Gerbois from warning the police and, in that way, effecting the rescue of his daughter and, at the same time, keeping his money? The professor was interviewed, but he was extremely reticent. His answer was:

"I have nothing to say."

"And Mlle. Gerbois?"

"The search is being continued."

"But Arsène Lupin has written to you?"

"No."

"Do you swear to that?"

"No."

"Then it is true. What are his instructions?"

"I have nothing to say."

Then the interviewers attacked Mon. Detinan, and found him equally discreet.

"Monsieur Lupin is my client, and I cannot discuss his affairs," he replied, with an affected air of gravity.

These mysteries served to irritate the gallery. Obviously, some secret negotiations were in progress. Arsène Lupin had arranged and tightened the meshes of his net, while the police maintained a close watch, day and night, over Mon. Gerbois. And the three and only possible dénouements—the arrest, the triumph, or the ridiculous and pitiful abortion—were freely discussed; but the curiosity of the public was only partially satisfied, and it was reserved for these pages to reveal the exact truth of the affair.

On Monday, March 12th, Mon. Gerbois received a notice from the Crédit Foncier. On Wednesday, he took the one o'clock train for Paris. At two o'clock, a thousand bank-notes of one thousand francs each were delivered to him. Whilst he was counting them, one by one, in a state of nervous agitation—that money, which represented Suzanne's ransom—a carriage containing two men stopped at the curb a short distance from the bank. One of the men had grey hair and an unusually shrewd expression which formed a striking contrast to his shabby make-up. It was Detective Ganimard, the relentless enemy of Arsène Lupin. Ganimard said to his companion, Folenfant:

"In five minutes, we will see our clever friend Lupin. Is everything ready?"

"Yes."

"How many men have we?"

"Eight—two of them on bicycles."

"Enough, but not too many. On no account, must Gerbois escape us; if he does, it is all up. He will meet Lupin at the appointed place, give half a million in exchange for the girl, and the game will be over."

"But why doesn't Gerbois work with us? That would be the better way, and he could keep all the money himself."

"Yes, but he is afraid that if he deceives the other, he will not get his daughter."

"What other?"

"Lupin."

Ganimard pronounced the word in a solemn tone, somewhat timidly, as if he were speaking of some supernatural creature whose claws he already felt.

"It is very strange," remarked Folenfant, judiciously, "that we are obliged to protect this gentleman contrary to his own wishes."

"Yes, but Lupin always turns the world upside down," said Ganimard, mournfully.

A moment later, Mon. Gerbois appeared, and started up the street. At the end of the rue des Capucines, he turned into the boulevards, walking slowly, and stopping frequently to gaze at the shop-windows.

"Much too calm, too self-possessed," said Ganimard. "A man with a million in his pocket would not have that air of tranquility."

"What is he doing?"

"Oh! nothing, evidently.... But I have a suspicion that it is Lupin—yes, Lupin!"

At that moment, Mon. Gerbois stopped at a news-stand, purchased a paper, unfolded it and commenced to read it as he walked slowly away. A moment later, he gave a sudden bound into an automobile that was standing at the curb. Apparently, the machine had been waiting for him, as it started away rapidly, turned at the Madeleine and disappeared.

"Nom de nom!" cried Ganimard, "that's one of his old tricks!"

Ganimard hastened after the automobile around the Madeleine. Then, he burst into laughter. At the entrance to the Boulevard Malesherbes, the automobile had stopped and Mon. Gerbois had alighted.

"Quick, Folenfant, the chauffeur! It may be the man Ernest."

Folenfant interviewed the chauffeur. His name was Gaston; he was an employee of the automobile cab company; ten minutes ago, a gentleman had engaged him and told him to wait near the news-stand for another gentleman.

"And the second man—what address did he give?" asked Folenfant.

"No address. 'Boulevard Malesherbes ... avenue de Messine ... double pourboire.' That is all."

But, during this time, Mon. Gerbois had leaped into the first passing carriage.

"To the Concorde station, Metropolitan," he said to the driver.

He left the underground at the Place du Palais-Royal, ran to another carriage and ordered it to go to the Place de la Bourse. Then a second journey by the underground to the Avenue de Villiers, followed by a third carriage drive to number 25 rue Clapeyron.

Number 25 rue Clapeyron is separated from the Boulevard des Batignolles by the house which occupies the angle formed by the two streets. He ascended to the first floor and rang. A gentleman opened the door.

"Does Monsieur Detinan live here?"

"Yes, that is my name. Are you Monsieur Gerbois?"

"Yes."

"I was expecting you. Step in."

As Mon. Gerbois entered the lawyer's office, the clock struck three. He said:

"I am prompt to the minute. Is he here?"

"Not yet."

Mon. Gerbois took a seat, wiped his forehead, looked at his watch as if he did not know the time, and inquired, anxiously:

"Will he come?"

"Well, monsieur," replied the lawyer, "that I do not know, but I am quite as anxious and impatient as you are to find out. If he comes, he will run a great risk, as this house has been closely watched for the last two weeks. They distrust me."

"They suspect me, too. I am not sure whether the detectives lost sight of me or not on my way here."

"But you were—"

"It wouldn't be my fault," cried the professor, quickly. "You cannot reproach me. I promised to obey his orders, and I followed them to the very letter. I drew the money at the time fixed by him, and I came here in the manner directed by him. I have faithfully performed my part of the agreement—let him do his!"

After a short silence, he asked, anxiously:

"He will bring my daughter, won't he?"

"I expect so."

"But ... you have seen him?"

"I? No, not yet. He made the appointment by letter, saying both of you would be here, and asking me to dismiss my servants before three o'clock and admit no one while you were here. If I would not consent to that arrangement, I was to notify him by a few words in *the Echo de France*. But I am only too happy to oblige Mon. Lupin, and so I consented."

"Ah! how will this end?" moaned Mon. Gerbois.

He took the bank-notes from his pocket, placed them on the table and divided them into two equal parts. Then the two men sat there in silence. From time to time, Mon. Gerbois would listen. Did someone ring?... His nervousness increased every minute, and Monsieur Detinan also displayed considerable anxiety. At last, the lawyer lost his patience. He rose abruptly, and said:

"He will not come.... We shouldn't expect it. It would be folly on his part. He would run too great a risk."

And Mon. Gerbois, despondent, his hands resting on the bank-notes, stammered:

"Oh! Mon Dieu! I hope he will come. I would give the whole of that money to see my daughter again."

The door opened.

"Half of it will be sufficient, Monsieur Gerbois."

These words were spoken by a well-dressed young man who now entered the room and was immediately recognized by Mon. Gerbois as the person who had wished to buy the desk from him at Versailles. He rushed toward him.

"Where is my daughter—my Suzanne?"

Arsène Lupin carefully closed the door, and, while slowly removing his gloves, said to the lawyer:

"My dear maître, I am indebted to you very much for your kindness in consenting to defend my interests. I shall not forget it."

Mon. Detinan murmured:

"But you did not ring. I did not hear the door—"

"Doors and bells are things that should work without being heard. I am here, and that is the important point."

"My daughter! Suzanne! Where is she!" repeated the professor.

"Mon Dieu, monsieur," said Lupin, "what's your hurry? Your daughter will be here in a moment."

Lupin walked to and fro for a minute, then, with the pompous air of an orator, he said:

"Monsieur Gerbois, I congratulate you on the clever way in which you made the journey to this place."

Then, perceiving the two piles of bank-notes, he exclaimed:

"Ah! I see! the million is here. We will not lose any time. Permit me."

"One moment," said the lawyer, placing himself before the table. "Mlle. Gerbois has not yet arrived."

"Well?"

"Is not her presence indispensable?"

"I understand! I understand! Arsène Lupin inspires only a limited confidence. He might pocket the half-million and not restore the hostage. Ah! monsieur, people do not understand me. Because I have been obliged, by force of circumstances, to commit certain actions a little ... out of the ordinary, my good faith is impugned ... I, who have always observed the utmost scrupulosity and delicacy in business affairs. Besides, my dear monsieur if you have any fear, open the window and call. There are at least a dozen detectives in the street."

"Do you think so?"

Arsène Lupin raised the curtain.

"I think that Monsieur Gerbois could not throw Ganimard off the scent.... What did I tell you? There he is now."

"Is it possible!" exclaimed the professor. "But I swear to you—"

"That you have not betrayed me?... I do not doubt you, but those fellows are clever—sometimes. Ah! I can see Folenfant, and Greaume, and Dieuzy—all good friends of mine!"

Mon. Detinan looked at Lupin in amazement. What assurance! He laughed as merrily as if engaged in some childish sport, as if no danger threatened him. This unconcern reassured the lawyer more than the presence of the detectives. He left the table on which the bank-notes were lying. Arsène Lupin picked up one pile of bills after the other, took from each of them twenty-five bank-notes which he offered to Mon. Detinan, saying:

"The reward of your services to Monsieur Gerbois and Arsène Lupin. You well deserve it."

"You owe me nothing," replied the lawyer.

"What! After all the trouble we have caused you!"

"And all the pleasure you have given me!"

"That means, my dear monsieur, that you do not wish to accept anything from Arsène Lupin. See what it is to have a bad reputation."

He then offered the fifty thousand francs to Mon. Gerbois, saying:

"Monsieur, in memory of our pleasant interview, permit me to return you this as a wedding-gift to Mlle. Gerbois."

Mon. Gerbois took the money, but said:

"My daughter will not marry."

"She will not marry if you refuse your consent; but she wishes to marry."

"What do you know about it?"

"I know that young girls often dream of such things unknown to their parents. Fortunately, there are sometimes good genii like Arsène Lupin who discover their little secrets in the drawers of their writing desks."

"Did you find anything else?" asked the lawyer. "I confess I am curious to know why you took so much trouble to get possession of that desk."

"On account of its historic interest, my friend. Although despite the opinion of Monsieur Gerbois, the desk contained no treasure except the lottery ticket—and that was unknown to me—I had been seeking it for a long time. That writing-desk of yew and mahogany was discovered in the little house in which Marie Walêwska once lived in Boulogne, and, on one of the drawers there is this inscription: *'Dedicated to Napoleon I, Emperor of the French, by his very faithful servant, Mancion.'* And above it, these words, engraved with the point of a knife: 'To you, Marie.' Afterwards, Napoleon had a similar desk made for the Empress Josephine; so that the secretary that was so much admired at the Malmaison was only an imperfect copy of the one that will henceforth form part of my collection."

"Ah! if I had known, when in the shop, I would gladly have given it up to you," said the professor.

Arsène Lupin smiled, as he replied:

"And you would have had the advantage of keeping for your own use lottery ticket number 514."

"And you would not have found it necessary to abduct my daughter."

"Abduct your daughter?"

"Yes."

"My dear monsieur, you are mistaken. Mlle. Gerbois was not abducted."

"No?"

"Certainly not. Abduction means force or violence. And I assure you that she served as hostage of her own free will."

"Of her own free will!" repeated Mon. Gerbois, in amazement.

"In fact, she almost asked to be taken. Why, do you suppose that an intelligent young girl like Mlle. Gerbois, and who, moreover, nourishes an unacknowledged passion, would hesitate to do what was necessary to secure her dowry. Ah! I swear to you it was not difficult to make her understand that it was the only way to overcome your obstinacy."

Mon. Detinan was greatly amused. He replied to Lupin:

"But I should think it was more difficult to get her to listen to you. How did you approach her?"

"Oh! I didn't approach her myself. I have not the honor of her acquaintance. A friend of mine, a lady, carried on the negotiations."

"The blonde woman in the automobile, no doubt."

"Precisely. All arrangements were made at the first interview near the college. Since then, Mlle. Gerbois and her new friend have been travelling in Belgium and Holland in a manner that should prove most pleasing and instructive to a young girl. She will tell you all about it herself—"

The bell of the vestibule door rang, three rings in quick succession, followed by two isolated rings.

"It is she," said Lupin. "Monsieur Detinan, if you will be so kind—"

The lawyer hastened to the door.

Two young women entered. One of them threw herself into the arms of Mon. Gerbois. The other approached Lupin. The latter was a tall woman of a good figure, very pale complexion, and with blond hair, parted over her forehead in undulating waves, that glistened and shone like the setting sun. She was dressed in black, with no display of jeweled ornaments; but, on the contrary, her appearance indicated good taste and refined elegance. Arsène Lupin spoke a few words to her; then, bowing to Mlle. Gerbois, he said:

"I owe you an apology, mademoiselle, for all your troubles, but I hope you have not been too unhappy—"

"Unhappy! Why, I should have been very happy, indeed, if it hadn't been for leaving my poor father."

"Then all is for the best. Kiss him again, and take advantage of the opportunity—it is an excellent one—to speak to him about your cousin."

"My cousin! What do you mean? I don't understand."

"Of course, you understand. Your cousin Philippe. The young man whose letters you kept so carefully."

Suzanne blushed; but, following Lupin's advice, she again threw herself into her father's arms. Lupin gazed upon them with a tender look.

"Ah! Such is my reward for a virtuous act! What a touching picture! A happy father and a happy daughter! And to know that their joy is your work, Lupin! Hereafter these people will bless you, and reverently transmit your name unto their descendants, even unto the fourth generation. What a glorious reward, Lupin, for one act of kindness!"

He walked to the window.

"Is dear old Ganimard still waiting?... He would like very much to be present at this charming domestic scene!... Ah! he is not there.... Nor any of the others.... I don't see anyone. The deuce! The situation is becoming serious. I dare say they are already under the porte-cochere ... talking to the concierge, perhaps ... or, even, ascending the stairs!"

Mon. Gerbois made a sudden movement. Now, that his daughter had been restored to him, he saw the situation in a different light. To him, the arrest of his adversary meant half-a-million francs. Instinctively, he made a step forward. As if by chance, Lupin stood in his way.

"Where are you going, Monsieur Gerbois? To defend me against them! That is very kind of you, but I assure you it is not necessary. They are more worried than I."

Then he continued to speak, with calm deliberation:

"But, really, what do they know? That you are here, and, perhaps, that Mlle. Gerbois is here, for they may have seen her arrive with an unknown lady. But they do not imagine that I am here. How is it possible that I could be in a house that they ran-sacked from cellar to garret this morning? They suppose that the unknown lady was sent by me to make the exchange, and they will be ready to arrest her when she goes out—"

At that moment, the bell rang. With a brusque movement, Lupin seized Mon. Gerbois, and said to him, in an imperious tone:

"Do not move! Remember your daughter, and be prudent—otherwise—As to you, Monsieur Detinan, I have your promise."

Mon. Gerbois was rooted to the spot. The lawyer did not stir. Without the least sign of haste, Lupin picked up his hat and brushed the dust from off it with his sleeve.

"My dear Monsieur Detinan, if I can ever be of service to you.... My best wishes, Mademoiselle Suzanne, and my kind regards to Monsieur Philippe."

He drew a heavy gold watch from his pocket.

"Monsieur Gerbois, it is now forty-two minutes past three. At forty-six minutes past three, I give you permission to leave this room. Not one minute sooner than forty-six minutes past three."

"But they will force an entrance," suggested Mon. Detinan.

"You forget the law, my dear monsieur! Ganimard would never venture to violate the privacy of a French citizen. But, pardon me, time flies, and you are all slightly nervous."

He placed his watch on the table, opened the door of the room and addressing the blonde lady he said:

"Are you ready my dear?"

He drew back to let her pass, bowed respectfully to Mlle. Gerbois, and went out, closing the door behind him. Then they heard him in the vestibule, speaking, in a loud voice: "Good-day, Ganimard, how goes it? Remember me to Madame Ganimard. One of these days, I shall invite her to breakfast. Au revoir, Ganimard."

The bell rang violently, followed by repeated rings, and voices on the landing.

"Forty-five minutes," muttered Mon. Gerbois.

After a few seconds, he left the room and stepped into the vestibule. Arsène Lupin and the blonde lady had gone.

"Papa!... you mustn't! Wait!" cried Suzanne.

"Wait! you are foolish!... No quarter for that rascal!... And the half-million?"

He opened the outer door. Ganimard rushed in.

"That woman—where is she? And Lupin?"

"He was here ... he is here."

Ganimard uttered a cry of triumph.

"We have him. The house is surrounded."

"But the servant's stairway?" suggested Mon. Detinan.

"It leads to the court," said Ganimard. "There is only one exit—the street-door. Ten men are guarding it."

"But he didn't come in by the street-door, and he will not go out that way."

"What way, then?" asked Ganimard. "Through the air?"

He drew aside a curtain and exposed a long corridor leading to the kitchen. Ganimard ran along it and tried the door of the servants' stairway. It was locked. From the window he called to one of his assistants:

"Seen anyone?"

"No."

"Then they are still in the house!" he exclaimed. "They are hiding in one of the rooms! They cannot have escaped. Ah! Lupin, you fooled me before, but, this time, I get my revenge."

. . .

At seven o'clock in the evening, Mon. Dudonis, chief of the detective service, astonished at not receiving any news, visited the rue Clapeyron. He questioned the detectives who were guarding the house, then ascended to Mon. Detinan's apartment. The lawyer led him into his room. There, Mon. Dudonis beheld a man, or rather two legs kicking in the air, while the body to which they belonged was hidden in the depths of the chimney.

"Ohé!... Ohé!" gasped a stifled voice. And a more distant voice, from on high, replied: "Ohé!... Ohé!"

Mon. Dudonis laughed, and exclaimed:

"Here! Ganimard, have you turned chimney-sweep?"

The detective crawled out of the chimney. With his blackened face, his sooty clothes, and his feverish eyes, he was quite unrecognizable.

"I am looking for *him*," he growled.

"Who?"

"Arsène Lupin ... and his friend."

"Well, do you suppose they are hiding in the chimney?"

Ganimard arose, laid his sooty hand on the sleeve of his superior officer's coat, and exclaimed, angrily:

"Where do you think they are, chief? They must be somewhere! They are flesh and blood like you and me, and can't fade away like smoke."

"No, but they have faded away just the same."

"But how? How? The house is surrounded by our men—even on the roof."

"What about the adjoining house?"

"There's no communication with it."

"And the apartments on the other floors?"

"I know all the tenants. They have not seen anyone."

"Are you sure you know all of them?"

"Yes. The concierge answers for them. Besides, as an extra precaution, I have placed a man in each apartment. They can't escape. If I don't get them to-night, I will get them to-morrow. I shall sleep here."

He slept there that night and the two following nights. Three days and nights passed away without the discovery of the irrepressible Lupin or his female companion; more than that, Ganimard did not unearth the slightest clue on which to base a theory to explain their escape. For that reason, he adhered to his first opinion.

"There is no trace of their escape; therefore, they are here."

It may be that, at the bottom of his heart, his conviction was less firmly established, but he would not confess it. No, a thousand times, no! A man and a woman could not vanish like the evil spirits in a fairy tale. And, without losing his courage, he continued his searches, as if he expected to find the fugitives concealed in some impenetrable retreat, or embodied in the stone walls of the house.

II. THE BLUE DIAMOND

On the evening of March 27, at number 134 avenue Henri-Martin, in the house that he had inherited from his brother six months before, the old general Baron d'Hautrec, ambassador at Berlin under the second Empire, was asleep in a comfortable armchair, while his secretary was reading to him, and the Sister Auguste was warming his bed and preparing the night-lamp. At eleven o'clock, the Sister, who was obliged to return to the convent of her order at that hour, said to the secretary:

"Mademoiselle Antoinette, my work is finished; I am going."

"Very well, Sister."

"Do not forget that the cook is away, and that you are alone in the house with the servant."

"Have no fear for the Baron. I sleep in the adjoining room and always leave the door open."

The Sister left the house. A few moments later, Charles, the servant, came to receive his orders. The Baron was now awake, and spoke for himself.

"The usual orders, Charles: see that the electric bell rings in your room, and, at the first alarm, run for the doctor. Now, Mademoiselle Antoinette, how far did we get in our reading?"

"Is Monsieur not going to bed now?"

"No, no, I will go later. Besides, I don't need anyone."

Twenty minutes later, he was sleeping again, and Antoinette crept away on tiptoe. At that moment, Charles was closing the shutters on the lower floor. In the kitchen, he bolted the door leading to the garden, and, in the vestibule, he not only locked the door but hooked the chain as well. Then he ascended to his room on the third floor, went to bed, and was soon asleep.

Probably an hour had passed, when he leaped from his bed in alarm. The bell was ringing. It rang for some time, seven or eight seconds perhaps, without intermission.

"Well?" muttered Charles, recovering his wits, "another of the Baron's whims."

He dressed himself quickly, descended the stairs, stopped in front of the door, and rapped, according to his custom. He received no reply. He opened the door and entered.

"Ah! no light," he murmured. "What is that for?"

Then, in a low voice, he called:

"Mademoiselle?"

No reply.

"Are you there, mademoiselle? What's the matter? Is Monsieur le Baron ill?"

No reply. Nothing but a profound silence that soon became depressing. He took two steps forward; his foot struck a chair, and, having touched it, he noticed that it was overturned. Then, with his hand, he discovered other objects on the floor—a small table and a screen. Anxiously, he approached the wall, felt for the electric button, and turned on the light.

In the centre of the room, between the table and dressing-case, lay the body of his master, the Baron d'Hautrec.

"What!... It can't be possible!" he stammered.

He could not move. He stood there, with bulging eyes, gazing stupidly at the terrible disorder, the overturned chairs, a large crystal candelabra shattered in a thousand pieces, the clock lying on the marble hearthstone, all evidence of a fearful and desperate struggle. The handle of a stiletto glittered, not far from the corpse; the blade was stained with blood. A handkerchief, marked with red spots, was lying on the edge of the bed.

Charles recoiled with horror: the body lying at his feet extended itself for a moment, then shrunk up again; two or three tremors, and that was the end.

He stooped over the body. There was a clean-cut wound on the neck from which the blood was flowing and then congealing in a black pool on the carpet. The face retained an expression of extreme terror.

"Someone has killed him!" he muttered, "someone has killed him!"

Then he shuddered at the thought that there might be another dreadful crime. Did not the baron's secretary sleep in the adjoining room! Had not the assassin killed her also! He opened the door; the room was empty. He concluded that Antoinette had been abducted, or else she had gone away before the crime. He returned to the baron's chamber, his glance falling on the secretary, he noticed that that article of furniture remained intact. Then, he saw upon a table, beside a bunch of keys and a pocketbook that the baron placed there every night, a handful of golden louis. Charles seized the pocketbook, opened it, and found some bank-notes. He counted them; there were thirteen notes of one hundred francs each.

Instinctively, mechanically, he put the bank-notes in his pocket, rushed down the stairs, drew the bolt, unhooked the chain, closed the door behind him, and fled to the street.

Charles was an honest man. He had scarcely left the gate, when, cooled by the night air and the rain, he came to a sudden halt. Now, he saw his action in its true light, and it filled him with horror. He hailed a passing cab, and said to the driver:

"Go to the police-office, and bring the commissary. Hurry! There has been a murder in that house."

The cab-driver whipped his horse. Charles wished to return to the house, but found the gate locked. He had closed it himself when he came out, and it could not be opened from the outside. On the other hand, it was useless to ring, as there was no one in the house.

It was almost an hour before the arrival of the police. When they came, Charles told his story and handed the bank-notes to the commissary. A locksmith was summoned, and, after considerable difficulty, he succeeded in forcing open the garden gate and the vestibule door. The commissary of police entered the room first, but, immediately, turned to Charles and said:

"You told me that the room was in the greatest disorder."

Charles stood at the door, amazed, bewildered; all the furniture had been restored to its accustomed place. The small table was standing between the two windows, the chairs were upright, and the clock was on the centre of the mantel. The debris of the candelabra had been removed.

"Where is.... Monsieur le Baron?" stammered Charles.

"That's so!" exclaimed the officer, "where is the victim?"

He approached the bed, and drew aside a large sheet, under which reposed the Baron d'Hautrec, formerly French Ambassador at Berlin. Over him, lay his military coat, adorned with the Cross of Honor. His features were calm. His eyes were closed.

"Someone has been here," said Charles.

"How did they get in?"

"I don't know, but someone has been here during my absence. There was a stiletto on the floor—there! And a handkerchief, stained with blood, on the bed. They are not here now. They have been carried away. And some one has put the room in order."

"Who would do that?"

"The assassin."

"But we found all the doors locked."

"He must have remained in the house."

"Then he must be here yet, as you were in front of the house all the time."

Charles reflected a moment, then said, slowly:

"Yes ... of course.... I didn't go away from the gate."

"Who was the last person you saw with the baron?"

"Mademoiselle Antoinette, his secretary."

"What has become of her?"

"I don't know. Her bed wasn't occupied, so she must have gone out. I am not surprised at that, as she is young and pretty."

"But how could she leave the house?"

"By the door," said Charles.

"But you had bolted and chained it."

"Yes, but she must have left before that."

"And the crime was committed after her departure?"

"Of course," said the servant.

The house was searched from cellar to garret, but the assassin had fled. How? And when? Was it he or an accomplice who had returned to the scene of the crime and removed everything that might furnish a clue to his identity? Such were the questions the police were called upon to solve.

The coroner came at seven o'clock; and, at eight o'clock, Mon. Dudouis, the head of the detective service, arrived on the scene. They were followed by the Procureur of the Republic and the investigating magistrate. In addition to these officials, the house was overrun with policemen, detectives, newspaper reporters, photographers, and relatives and acquaintances of the murdered man.

A thorough search was made; they studied out the position of the corpse according to the information furnished by Charles; they questioned Sister Auguste when she arrived; but they discovered nothing new. Sister Auguste was astonished to learn of the disappearance of Antoinette Bréhat. She had engaged the young girl twelve days before, on excellent recommendations, and refused to believe that she would neglect her duty by leaving the house during the night.

"But, you see, she hasn't returned yet," said the magistrate, "and we are still confronted with the question: What has become of her?"

"I think she was abducted by the assassin," said Charles.

The theory was plausible, and was borne out by certain facts. Mon. Dudouis agreed with it. He said:

"Abducted? ma foi! that is not improbable."

"Not only improbable," said a voice, "but absolutely opposed to the facts. There is not a particle of evidence to support such a theory."

The voice was harsh, the accent sharp, and no one was surprised to learn that the speaker was Ganimard. In no one else, would they tolerate such a domineering tone.

"Ah! it is you, Ganimard!" exclaimed Mon. Dudouis. "I had not seen you before."

"I have been here since two o'clock."

"So you are interested in some things outside of lottery ticket number 514, the affair of the rue Clapeyron, the blonde lady and Arsène Lupin?"

"Ha-ha!" laughed the veteran detective. "I would not say that Lupin is a stranger to the present case. But let us forget the affair of the lottery ticket for a few moments, and try to unravel this new mystery."

Ganimard is not one of those celebrated detectives whose methods will create a school, or whose name will be immortalized in the criminal annals of his country. He is devoid of those flashes of genius which characterize the work of Dupin, Lecoq and Sherlock Holmes. Yet, it must be admitted, he possesses superior qualities of observation, sagacity, perseverance and even intuition. His merit lies in his absolute independence. Nothing troubles or influences him, except, perhaps, a sort of fascination that Arsène Lupin holds over him. However that may be, there is no doubt that his position on that morning, in the house of the late Baron d'Hautrec, was one of undoubted superiority, and his collaboration in the case was appreciated and desired by the investigating magistrate.

"In the first place," said Ganimard, "I will ask Monsieur Charles to be very particular on one point: He says that, on the occasion of his first visit to the room, various articles of furniture were overturned and strewn about the place; now, I ask him whether, on his second visit to the room, he found all those articles restored to their accustomed places—I mean, of course, correctly placed."

"Yes, all in their proper places," replied Charles.

"It is obvious, then, that the person who replaced them must have been familiar with the location of those articles."

The logic of this remark was apparent to his hearers. Ganimard continued:

"One more question, Monsieur Charles. You were awakened by the ringing of your bell. Now, who, do you think, rang it?"

"Monsieur le baron, of course."

"When could he ring it?"

"After the struggle ... when he was dying."

"Impossible; because you found him lying, unconscious, at a point more than four metres from the bell-button."

"Then he must have rung during the struggle."

"Impossible," declared Ganimard, "since the ringing, as you have said, was continuous and uninterrupted, and lasted seven or eight seconds. Do you think his antagonist would have permitted him to ring the bell in that leisurely manner?"

"Well, then, it was before the attack."

"Also, quite impossible, since you have told us that the lapse of time between the ringing of the bell and your entrance to the room was not more than three minutes. Therefore, if the baron rang before the attack, we are forced to the conclusion that the struggle, the murder and the flight of the assassin, all occurred within the short space of three minutes. I repeat: that is impossible."

"And yet," said the magistrate, "someone rang. If it were not the baron, who was it?"

"The murderer."

"For what purpose?"

"I do not know. But the fact that he did ring proves that he knew that the bell communicated with the servant's room. Now, who would know that, except an inmate of the house?"

Ganimard was drawing the meshes of his net closer and tighter. In a few clear and logical sentences, he had unfolded and defined his theory of the crime, so that it seemed quite natural when the magistrate said:

"As I understand it, Ganimard, you suspect the girl Antoinette Bréhat?"

"I do not suspect her; I accuse her."

"You accuse her of being an accomplice?"

"I accuse her of having killed Baron d'Hautrec."

"Nonsense! What proof have you?"

"The handful of hair I found in the right hand of the victim."

He produced the hair; it was of a beautiful blond color, and glittered like threads of gold. Charles looked at it, and said:

"That is Mademoiselle Antoinette's hair. There can be no doubt of it. And, then, there is another thing. I believe that the knife, which I saw on my first visit to the room, belonged to her. She used it to cut the leaves of books."

A long, dreadful silence followed, as if the crime had acquired an additional horror by reason of having been committed by a woman. At last, the magistrate said:

"Let us assume, until we are better informed, that the baron was killed by Antoinette Bréhat. We have yet to learn where she concealed herself after the crime, how she managed to return after Charles left the house, and how she made her escape after the arrival of the police. Have you formed any opinion on those points Ganimard?"

"None."

"Well, then, where do we stand?"

Ganimard was embarrassed. Finally, with a visible effort, he said:

"All I can say is that I find in this case the same method of procedure as we found in the affair of the lottery ticket number 514; the same phenomena, which might be termed the faculty of disappearing. Antoinette Bréhat has appeared and disappeared in this house as mysteriously as Arsène Lupin entered the house of Monsieur Detinan and escaped therefrom in the company of the blonde lady.

"Does that signify anything?"

"It does to me. I can see a probable connection between those two strange incidents. Antoinette Bréhat was hired by Sister Auguste twelve days ago, that is to say, on the day after the blonde Lady so cleverly slipped through my fingers. In the second place, the hair of the blonde Lady was exactly of the same brilliant golden hue as the hair found in this case."

"So that, in your opinion, Antoinette Bréhat—"

"Is the blonde Lady—precisely."

"And that Lupin had a hand in both cases?"

"Yes, that is my opinion."

This statement was greeted with an outburst of laughter. It came from Mon. Dudouis.

"Lupin! always Lupin! Lupin is into everything; Lupin is everywhere!"

"Yes, Lupin is into everything of any consequence," replied Ganimard, vexed at the ridicule of his superior.

"Well, so far as I see," observed Mon. Dudouis, "you have not discovered any motive for this crime. The secretary was not broken into, nor the pocketbook carried away. Even, a pile of gold was left upon the table."

"Yes, that is so," exclaimed Ganimard, "but the famous diamond?"

"What diamond?"

"The blue diamond! The celebrated diamond which formed part of the royal crown of France, and which was given by the Duke d'Aumale to Leonide Lebrun, and, at the death of Leonide Lebrun, was purchased by the Baron d'Hautrec as a souvenir of the charming comedienne that he had loved so well. That is one of those things that an old Parisian, like I, does not forget."

"It is obvious that if the blue diamond is not found, the motive for the crime is disclosed," said the magistrate. "But where should we search for it?"

"On the baron's finger," replied Charles. "He always wore the blue diamond on his left hand."

"I saw that hand, and there was only a plain gold ring on it," said Ganimard, as he approached the corpse.

"Look in the palm of the hand," replied the servant.

Ganimard opened the stiffened hand. The bezel was turned inward, and, in the centre of that bezel, the blue diamond shone with all its glorious splendor.

"The deuce!" muttered Ganimard, absolutely amazed, "I don't understand it."

"You will now apologize to Lupin for having suspected him, eh?" said Mon. Dudouis, laughing.

Ganimard paused for a moment's reflection, and then replied, sententiously:

"It is only when I do not understand things that I suspect Arsène Lupin."

Such were the facts established by the police on the day after the commission of that mysterious crime. Facts that were vague and incoherent in themselves, and which were not explained by any subsequent discoveries. The movements of Antoinette Bréhat remained as inexplicable as those of the blonde Lady, and the police discovered no trace of that mysterious creature with the golden hair who had killed Baron d'Hautrec and had failed to take from his finger the famous diamond that had once shone in the royal crown of France.

The heirs of the Baron d'Hautrec could not fail to benefit by such notoriety. They established in the house an exhibition of the furniture and other objects which were to be sold at the auction rooms of Drouot & Co. Modern furniture of indifferent taste, various objects of no artistic value ... but, in the centre of the room, in a case of purple velvet, protected by a glass globe, and guarded by two officers, was the famous blue diamond ring.

A large magnificent diamond of incomparable purity, and of that indefinite blue which the clear water receives from an unclouded sky, of that blue which can be detected in the whiteness of linen. Some admired, some enthused ... and some looked with horror on the chamber of the victim, on the spot where the corpse had lain, on the floor divested of its blood-stained carpet, and especially the walls, the unsurmountable walls over which the criminal must have passed. Some assured themselves that the marble mantel did not move, others imagined gaping holes, mouths of tunnels, secret connections with the sewers, and the catacombs—

The sale of the blue diamond took place at the salesroom of Drouot & Co. The place was crowded to suffocation, and the bidding was carried to the verge of folly. The sale was attended by all those who usually appear at similar events in Paris; those who buy, and those who make a pretense of being able to buy; bankers, brokers, artists, women of all classes, two cabinet ministers, an Italian tenor, an exiled king who, in order to maintain his credit, bid, with much ostentation, and in a loud voice, as high as one hundred thousand francs. One hundred thousand francs! He could offer that sum without any danger of his bid being accepted. The Italian tenor risked one hundred and fifty thousand, and a member of the Comédie-Française bid one hundred and seventy-five thousand francs.

When the bidding reached two hundred thousand francs, the smaller competitors fell out of the race. At two hundred and fifty thousand, only two bidders remained in the field: Herschmann, the well-known capitalist, the king of gold mines; and the Countess de Crozon, the wealthy American, whose collection of diamonds and precious stones is famed throughout the world.

"Two hundred and sixty thousand ... two hundred and seventy thousand ... seventy-five ... eighty...." exclaimed the auctioneer, as he glanced at the two competitors in succession. "Two hundred and eighty thousand for madame.... Do I hear any more?"

"Three hundred thousand," said Herschmann.

There was a short silence. The countess was standing, smiling, but pale from excitement. She was leaning against the back of the chair in front of her. She knew, and so did everyone present, that the issue of the duel was certain; logically, inevitably, it must terminate to the advantage of the capitalist, who had untold millions with which to indulge his caprices. However, the countess made another bid:

"Three hundred and five thousand."

Another silence. All eyes were now directed to the capitalist in the expectation that he would raise the bidding. But Herschmann was not paying any attention to the sale; his eyes were fixed on a sheet of paper which he held in his right hand, while the other hand held a torn envelope.

"Three hundred and five thousand," repeated the auctioneer. "Once!... Twice!... For the last time.... Do I hear any more?... Once!... Twice!... Am I offered any more? Last chance!..."

Herschmann did not move.

"Third and last time!... Sold!" exclaimed the auctioneer, as his hammer fell.

"Four hundred thousand," cried Herschman, starting up, as if the sound of the hammer had roused him from his stupor.

Too late; the auctioneer's decision was irrevocable. Some of Herschmann's acquaintances pressed around him. What was the matter? Why did he not speak sooner? He laughed, and said:

"Ma foi! I simply forgot—in a moment of abstraction."

"That is strange."

"You see, I just received a letter."

"And that letter was sufficient—"

"To distract my attention? Yes, for a moment."

Ganimard was there. He had come to witness the sale of the ring. He stopped one of the attendants of the auction room, and said:

"Was it you who carried the letter to Monsieur Herschmann?"

"Yes."

"Who gave it to you?"

"A lady."

"Where is she?"

"Where is she?... She was sitting down there ... the lady who wore a thick veil."

"She has gone?"

"Yes, just this moment."

Ganimard hastened to the door, and saw the lady descending the stairs. He ran after her. A crush of people delayed him at the entrance. When he reached the sidewalk, she had disappeared. He returned to the auction room, accosted Herschmann, introduced himself, and enquired about the letter. Herschmann handed it to him. It was carelessly scribbled in pencil, in a handwriting unknown to the capitalist, and contained these few words:

"The blue diamond brings misfortune. Remember the Baron d'Hautrec."

The vicissitudes of the blue diamond were not yet at an end. Although it had become well-known through the murder of the Baron d'Hautrec and the incidents at the auction-rooms, it was six months later that it attained even greater celebrity. During the following summer, the Countess de Crozon was robbed of the famous jewel she had taken so much trouble to acquire.

Let me recall that strange affair, of which the exciting and dramatic incidents sent a thrill through all of us, and over which I am now permitted to throw some light.

On the evening of August 10, the guests of the Count and Countess de Crozon were assembled in the drawing-room of the magnificent château which overlooks the Bay de Somme. To entertain her friends, the countess seated herself at the piano to play for them, after first placing her jewels on a small table near the piano, and, amongst them, was the ring of the Baron d'Hautrec.

An hour later, the count and the majority of the guests retired, including his two cousins and Madame de Réal, an intimate friend of the countess. The latter remained in the drawing-room with Herr Bleichen, the Austrian consul, and his wife.

They conversed for a time, and then the countess extinguished the large lamp that stood on a table in the centre of the room. At the same moment, Herr Bleichen extinguished the two piano lamps. There was a momentary darkness; then the consul lighted a candle, and the three of them retired to their rooms. But, as soon as she reached her apartment, the countess remembered her jewels and sent her maid to get them. When the maid returned with the jewels, she placed them on the mantel without the countess looking at them. Next day, Madame de Crozon found that one of her rings was missing; it was the blue diamond ring.

She informed her husband, and, after talking it over, they reached the conclusion that the maid was above suspicion, and that the guilty party must be Herr Bleichen.

The count notified the commissary of police at Amiens, who commenced an investigation and, discreetly, exercised a strict surveillance over the Austrian consul to prevent his disposing of the ring.

The château was surrounded by detectives day and night. Two weeks passed without incident. Then Herr Bleichen announced his intended departure. That day, a formal complaint was entered against him. The police made an official examination of his luggage. In a small satchel, the key to which was always carried by the consul himself, they found a bottle of dentifrice, and in that bottle they found the ring.

Madame Bleichen fainted. Her husband was placed under arrest.

Everyone will remember the line of defense adopted by the accused man. He declared that the ring must have been placed there by the Count de Crozen as an act of revenge. He said:

"The count is brutal and makes his wife very unhappy. She consulted me, and I advised her to get a divorce. The count heard of it in some way, and, to be revenged on me, he took the ring and placed it in my satchel."

The count and countess persisted in pressing the charge. Between the explanation which they gave and that of the consul, both equally possible and equally probable, the public had to choose. No new fact was discovered to turn the scale in either direction. A month of gossip, conjectures and investigations failed to produce a single ray of light.

Wearied of the excitement and notoriety, and incapable of securing the evidence necessary to sustain their charge against the consul, the count and countess at last sent to Paris for a detective competent to unravel the tangled threads of this mysterious skein. This brought Ganimard into the case.

For four days, the veteran detective searched the house from top to bottom, examined every foot of the ground, had long conferences with the maid, the chauffeur, the gardeners, the employees in the neighboring post-offices, visited the rooms that had been occupied by the various guests. Then, one morning, he disappeared without taking leave of his host or hostess. But a week later, they received this telegram:

"Please come to the Japanese Tea-room, rue Boissy d'Anglas, to-morrow, Friday, evening at five o'clock. Ganimard."

At five o'clock, Friday evening, their automobile stopped in front of number nine rue Boissy-d'Anglas. The old detective was standing on the sidewalk, waiting for them. Without a word, he conducted them to the first floor of the Japanese Tea-room. In one of the rooms, they met two men, whom Ganimard introduced in these words:

"Monsieur Gerbois, professor in the College of Versailles, from whom, you will remember, Arsène Lupin stole half a million; Monsieur Léonce d'Hautrec, nephew and sole legatee of the Baron d'Hautrec."

A few minutes later, another man arrived. It was Mon. Dudouis, head of the detective service, and he appeared to be in a particularly bad temper. He bowed, and then said:

"What's the trouble now, Ganimard? I received your telephone message asking me to come here. Is it anything of consequence?"

"Yes, chief, it is a very important matter. Within an hour, the last two cases to which I was assigned will have their dénouement here. It seemed to me that your presence was indispensable."

"And also the presence of Dieuzy and Folenfant, whom I noticed standing near the door as I came in?"

"Yes, chief."

"For what? Are you going to make an arrest, and you wish to do it with a flourish? Come, Ganimard, I am anxious to hear about it."

Ganimard hesitated a moment, then spoke with the obvious intention of making an impression on his hearers:

"In the first place, I wish to state that Herr Bleichen had nothing to do with the theft of the ring."

"Oh! oh!" exclaimed Mon. Dudouis, "that is a bold statement and a very serious one."

"And is that all you have discovered?" asked the Count de Crozon.

"Not at all. On the second day after the theft, three of your guests went on an automobile trip as far as Crécy. Two of them visited the famous battlefield; and, while they were there, the third party paid a hasty visit to the post-office, and mailed a small box, tied and sealed according to the regulations, and declared its value to be one hundred francs."

"I see nothing strange in that," said the count.

"Perhaps you will see something strange in it when I tell you that this person, in place of giving her true name, sent the box under the name of Rousseau, and the person to whom it was addressed, a certain Monsieur Beloux of Paris, moved his place of residence immediately after receiving the box, in other words, the ring."

"I presume you refer to one of my cousins d'Andelle?"

"No," replied Ganimard.

"Madame de Réal, then?"

"Yes."

"You accuse my friend, Madam de Réal?" cried the countess, shocked and amazed.

"I wish to ask you one question, madame," said Ganimard. "Was Madam de Réal present when you purchased the ring?"

"Yes, but we did not go there together."

"Did she advise you to buy the ring?"

The countess considered for a moment, then said:

"Yes, I think she mentioned it first—"

"Thank you, madame. Your answer establishes the fact that it was Madame de Réal who was the first to mention the ring, and it was she who advised you to buy it."

"But, I consider my friend is quite incapable—"

"Pardon me, countess, when I remind you that Madame de Réal is only a casual acquaintance and not your intimate friend, as the newspapers have announced. It was only last winter that you met her for the first time. Now, I can prove that everything she has told you about herself, her past life, and her relatives, is absolutely false; that Madame Blanche de Réal had no actual existence before she met you, and she has now ceased to exist."

"Well?"

"Well?" replied Ganimard.

"Your story is a very strange one," said the countess, "but it has no application to our case. If Madame de Réal had taken the ring, how do you explain the fact that it was found in Herr Bleichen's tooth-powder? Anyone who would take the risk and trouble of stealing the blue diamond would certainly keep it. What do you say to that?"

"I—nothing—but Madame de Réal will answer it."

"Oh! she does exist, then?"

"She does—and does not. I will explain in a few words. Three days ago, while reading a newspaper, I glanced over the list of hotel arrivals at Trouville, and there I read: 'Hôtel Beaurivage—Madame de Réal, etc.'

"I went to Trouville immediately, and interviewed the proprietor of the hotel. From the description and other information I received from him, I concluded that she was the very Madame de Réal that I was seeking; but she had left the hotel, giving her address in Paris as number three rue de Colisée. The day before yesterday I went to that address, and learned that there was no person there called Madame de Réal, but there was a Madame Réal, living on the second floor, who acted as a diamond broker and was frequently away from home. She had returned from a journey on the preceding evening. Yesterday, I called on her and, under an assumed name, I offered to act as an intermedium in the sale of some diamonds to certain wealthy friends of mine. She is to meet me here to-day to carry out that arrangement."

"What! You expect her to come here?"

"Yes, at half-past five."

"Are you sure it is she?"

"Madame de Réal of the Château de Crozon? Certainly. I have convincing evidence of that fact. But ... listen!... I hear Folenfant's signal."

It was a whistle. Ganimard arose quickly.

"There is no time to lose. Monsieur and Madame de Crozon, will you be kind enough to go into the next room. You also, Monsieur d'Hautrec, and you, Monsieur Gerbois. The door will remain open, and when I give the signal, you will come out. Of course, Chief, you will remain here."

"We may be disturbed by other people," said Mon. Dudouis.

"No. This is a new establishment, and the proprietor is one of my friends. He will not let anyone disturb us—except the blonde Lady."

"The blonde Lady! What do you mean?"

"Yes, the blonde Lady herself, chief; the friend and accomplice of Arsène Lupin, the mysterious blonde Lady against whom I hold convincing evidence; but, in addition to that, I wish to confront her with all the people she has robbed."

He looked through the window.

"I see her. She is coming in the door now. She can't escape: Folenfant and Dieuzy are guarding the door.... The blonde Lady is captured at last, Chief!"

A moment later a woman appeared at the door; she was tall and slender, with a very pale complexion and bright golden hair. Ganimard trembled with excitement; he could not move, nor utter a word. She was there, in front of him, at his mercy! What a victory over Arsène Lupin! And what a revenge! And, at the same time, the victory was such an easy one that he asked himself if the blonde Lady would not yet slip through his fingers by one of those miracles that usually terminated the exploits of Arsène Lupin. She remained standing near the door, surprised at the silence, and looked about her without any display of suspicion or fear.

"She will get away! She will disappear!" thought Ganimard.

Then he managed to get between her and the door. She turned to go out.

"No, no!" he said. "Why are you going away?"

"Really, monsieur, I do not understand what this means. Allow me—"

"There is no reason why you should go, madame, and very good reasons why you should remain."

"But—"

"It is useless, madame. You cannot go."

Trembling, she sat on a chair, and stammered:

"What is it you want?"

Ganimard had won the battle and captured the blonde Lady. He said to her:

"Allow me to present the friend I mentioned, who desires to purchase some diamonds. Have you procured the stones you promised to bring?"

"No—no—I don't know. I don't remember."

"Come! Jog your memory! A person of your acquaintance intended to send you a tinted stone.... 'Something like the blue diamond,' I said, laughing; and you replied: 'Exactly, I expect to have just what you want.' Do you remember?"

She made no reply. A small satchel fell from her hand. She picked it up quickly, and held it securely. Her hands trembled slightly.

"Come!" said Ganimard, "I see you have no confidence in us, Madame de Réal. I shall set you a good example by showing you what I have."

He took from his pocketbook a paper which he unfolded, and disclosed a lock of hair.

"These are a few hairs torn from the head of Antoinette Bréhat by the Baron d'Hautrec, which I found clasped in his dead hand. I have shown them to Mlle. Gerbois, who declares they are of the exact color of the hair of the blonde Lady. Besides, they are exactly the color of your hair—the identical color."

Madame Réal looked at him in bewilderment, as if she did not understand his meaning. He continued:

"And here are two perfume bottles, without labels, it is true, and empty, but still sufficiently impregnated with their odor to enable Mlle. Gerbois to recognize in them the perfume used by that blonde Lady who was her traveling companion for two weeks. Now, one of these bottles was found in the room that Madame de Réal occupied at the Château de Crozon, and the other in the room that you occupied at the Hôtel Beaurivage."

"What do you say?... The blonde Lady ... the Château de Crozon...."

The detective did not reply. He took from his pocket and placed on the table, side by side, four small sheets of paper. Then he said:

"I have, on these four pieces of paper, various specimens of handwriting; the first is the writing of Antoinette Bréhat; the second was written by the woman who sent the note to Baron Herschmann at the auction sale of the blue diamond; the third is that of Madame de Réal, written while she was stopping at the Château de Crozon; and the fourth is your handwriting, madame ... it is your name and address, which you gave to the porter of the Hôtel Beaurivage at Trouville. Now, compare the four handwritings. They are identical."

"What absurdity is this? really, monsieur, I do not understand. What does it mean?"

"It means, madame," exclaimed Ganimard, "that the blonde Lady, the friend and accomplice of Arsène Lupin, is none other than you, Madame Réal."

Ganimard went to the adjoining room and returned with Mon. Gerbois, whom he placed in front of Madame Réal, as he said:

"Monsieur Gerbois, is this the person who abducted your daughter, the woman you saw at the house of Monsieur Detinan?"

"No."

Ganimard was so surprised that he could not speak for a moment; finally, he said: "No?... You must be mistaken...."

"I am not mistaken. Madame is blonde, it is true, and in that respect resembles the blonde Lady; but, in all other respects, she is totally different."

"I can't believe it. You must be mistaken."

Ganimard called in his other witnesses.

"Monsieur d'Hautrec," he said, "do you recognize Antoinette Bréhat?"

"No, this is not the person I saw at my uncle's house."

"This woman is not Madame de Réal," declared the Count de Crozon.

That was the finishing touch. Ganimard was crushed. He was buried beneath the ruins of the structure he had erected with so much care and assurance. His pride was humbled, his spirit was broken, by the force of this unexpected blow.

Mon. Dudouis arose, and said:

"We owe you an apology, madame, for this unfortunate mistake. But, since your arrival here, I have noticed your nervous agitation. Something troubles you; may I ask what it is?"

"Mon Dieu, monsieur, I was afraid. My satchel contains diamonds to the value of a hundred thousand francs, and the conduct of your friend was rather suspicious."

"But you were frequently absent from Paris. How do you explain that?"

"I make frequent journeys to other cities in the course of my business. That is all."

Mon. Dudouis had nothing more to ask. He turned to his subordinate, and said:

"Your investigation has been very superficial, Ganimard, and your conduct toward this lady is really deplorable. You will come to my office to-morrow and explain it."

The interview was at an end, and Mon. Dudouis was about to leave the room when a most annoying incident occurred. Madame Réal turned to Ganimard, and said:

"I understand that you are Monsieur Ganimard. Am I right?"

"Yes."

"Then, this letter must be for you. I received it this morning. It was addressed to 'Mon. Justin Ganimard, care of Madame Réal.' I thought it was a joke, because I did not know you under that name, but it appears that your unknown correspondent knew of our rendezvous."

Ganimard was inclined to put the letter in his pocket unread, but he dared not do so in the presence of his superior, so he opened the envelope and read the letter aloud, in an almost inaudible tone:

"Once upon a time, there were a blonde Lady, a Lupin, and a Ganimard. Now, the wicked Ganimard had evil designs on the pretty blonde Lady, and the good Lupin was her friend and protector. When the good Lupin wished the blonde Lady to become the friend of the Countess de Crozon, he caused her to assume the name of Madame de Réal, which is a close resemblance to the name of a certain diamond broker, a woman with a pale complexion and golden hair. And the good Lupin said to himself: If ever the wicked Ganimard gets upon the track of the blonde Lady, how useful it will be to me if he should be diverted to the track of the honest diamond broker. A wise precaution that has borne good fruit. A little note sent to the newspaper read by the wicked Ganimard, a perfume bottle intentionally forgotten by the genuine blonde Lady at the Hôtel Beaurivage, the name and address of Madame Réal written on the hotel register by the genuine blonde Lady, and the trick is played. What do you think of it, Ganimard! I wished to tell you the true story of this affair, knowing that you would be the first to laugh over it. Really, it is quite amusing, and I have enjoyed it very much.

"Accept my best wishes, dear friend, and give my kind regards to the worthy Mon. Dudouis.

"ARSÈNE LUPIN."

"He knows everything," muttered Ganimard, but he did not see the humor of the situation as Lupin had predicted. "He knows some things I have never mentioned to anyone. How could he find out that I was going to invite you here, chief? How could he know that I had found the first perfume bottle? How could he find out those things?"

He stamped his feet and tore his hair—a prey to the most tragic despair. Mon. Dudouis felt sorry for him, and said:

"Come, Ganimard, never mind; try to do better next time."

And Mon. Dudouis left the room, accompanied by Madame Réal.

During the next ten minutes, Ganimard read and re-read the letter of Arsène Lupin. Monsieur and Madame de Crozon, Monsieur d'Hautrec and Monsieur Gerbois were holding an animated discussion in a corner of the room. At last, the count approached the detective, and said:

"My dear monsieur, after your investigation, we are no nearer the truth than we were before."

"Pardon me, but my investigation has established these facts: that the blonde Lady is the mysterious heroine of these exploits, and that Arsène Lupin directed them."

"Those facts do not solve the mystery; in fact, they render it more obscure. The blonde Lady commits a murder in order to steal the blue diamond, and yet she does not steal it. Afterward she steals it and gets rid of it by secretly giving it to another person. How do you explain her strange conduct?"

"I cannot explain it."

"Of course; but, perhaps, someone else can."

"Who?"

The Count hesitated, so the Countess replied, frankly:

"There is only one man besides yourself who is competent to enter the arena with Arsène Lupin and overcome him. Have you any objection to our engaging the services of Herlock Sholmes in this case?"

Ganimard was vexed at the question, but stammered a reply:

"No ... but ... I do not understand what——"

"Let me explain. All this mystery annoys me. I wish to have it cleared up. Monsieur Gerbois and Monsieur d'Hautrec have the same desire, and we have agreed to send for the celebrated English detective."

"You are right, madame," replied the detective, with a loyalty that did him credit, "you are right. Old Ganimard is not able to overcome Arsène Lupin. But will Herlock Sholmes succeed? I hope so, as I have the greatest admiration for him. But ... it is improbable."

"Do you mean to say that he will not succeed?"

"That is my opinion. I can foresee the result of a duel between Herlock Sholmes and Arsène Lupin. The Englishman will be defeated."

"But, in any event, can we count on your assistance?"

"Quite so, madame. I shall be pleased to render Monsieur Sholmes all possible assistance."

"Do you know his address?"

"Yes; 219 Parker street."

That evening Monsieur and Madame de Crozon withdrew the charge they had made against Herr Bleichen, and a joint letter was addressed to Herlock Sholmes.

III. HERLOCK SHOLMES OPENS HOSTILITIES

"What does monsieur wish?"

"Anything," replied Arsène Lupin, like a man who never worries over the details of a meal; "anything you like, but no meat or alcohol."

The waiter walked away, disdainfully.

"What! still a vegetarian?" I exclaimed.

"More so than ever," replied Lupin.

"Through taste, faith, or habit?"

"Hygiene."

"And do you never fall from grace?"

"Oh! yes ... when I am dining out ... and wish to avoid being considered eccentric."

We were dining near the Northern Railway station, in a little restaurant to which Arsène Lupin had invited me. Frequently he would send me a telegram asking me to meet him in some obscure restaurant, where we could enjoy a quiet dinner, well served, and which was always made interesting to me by his recital of some startling adventure theretofore unknown to me.

On that particular evening he appeared to be in a more lively mood than usual. He laughed and joked with careless animation, and with that delicate sarcasm that was habitual with him—a light and spontaneous sarcasm that was quite free from any tinge of malice. It was a pleasure to find him in that jovial mood, and I could not resist the desire to tell him so.

"Ah! yes," he exclaimed, "there are days in which I find life as bright and gay as a spring morning; then life seems to be an infinite treasure which I can never exhaust. And yet God knows I lead a careless existence!"

"Too much so, perhaps."

"Ah! but I tell you, the treasure is infinite. I can spend it with a lavish hand. I can cast my youth and strength to the four winds of Heaven, and it is replaced by a still younger and greater force. Besides, my life is so pleasant!... If I wished to do so, I might become— what shall I say?... An orator, a manufacturer, a politician.... But, I assure you, I shall never have such a desire. Arsène Lupin, I am; Arsène Lupin, I shall remain. I have made a vain search in history to find a career comparable to mine; a life better filled or more intense.... Napoleon? Yes, perhaps.... But Napoleon, toward the close of his career, when all Europe was trying to crush him, asked himself on the eve of each battle if it would not be his last."

Was he serious? Or was he joking? He became more animated as he proceeded:

"That is everything, do you understand, the danger! The continuous feeling of danger! To breathe it as you breathe the air, to scent it in every breath of wind, to detect it in every unusual sound.... And, in the midst of the tempest, to remain calm ... and not to stumble!

133

Otherwise, you are lost. There is only one sensation equal to it: that of the chauffeur in an automobile race. But that race lasts only a few hours; my race continues until death!"

"What fantasy!" I exclaimed. "And you wish me to believe that you have no particular motive for your adoption of that exciting life?"

"Come," he said, with a smile, "you are a clever psychologist. Work it out for yourself."

He poured himself a glass of water, drank it, and said:

"Did you read 'Le Temps' to-day?"

"No."

"Herlock Sholmes crossed the Channel this afternoon, and arrived in Paris about six o'clock."

"The deuce! What is he coming for?"

"A little journey he has undertaken at the request of the Count and Countess of Crozon, Monsieur Gerbois, and the nephew of Baron d'Hautrec. They met him at the Northern Railway station, took him to meet Ganimard, and, at this moment, the six of them are holding a consultation."

Despite a strong temptation to do so, I had never ventured to question Arsène Lupin concerning any action of his private life, unless he had first mentioned the subject to me. Up to that moment his name had not been mentioned, at least officially, in connection with the blue diamond. Consequently, I consumed my curiosity in patience. He continued:

"There is also in 'Le Temps' an interview with my old friend Ganimard, according to whom a certain blonde lady, who should be my friend, must have murdered the Baron d'Hautrec and tried to rob Madame de Crozon of her famous ring. And—what do you think?—he accuses me of being the instigator of those crimes."

I could not suppress a slight shudder. Was this true? Must I believe that his career of theft, his mode of existence, the logical result of such a life, had drawn that man into more serious crimes, including murder? I looked at him. He was so calm, and his eyes had such a frank expression! I observed his hands: they had been formed from a model of exceeding delicacy, long and slender; inoffensive, truly; and the hands of an artist....

"Ganimard has pipe-dreams," I said.

"No, no!" protested Lupin. "Ganimard has some cleverness; and, at times, almost inspiration."

"Inspiration!"

"Yes. For instance, that interview is a master-stroke. In the first place, he announces the coming of his English rival in order to put me on my guard, and make his task more difficult. In the second place, he indicates the exact point to which he has conducted the affair in order that Sholmes will not get credit for the work already done by Ganimard. That is good warfare."

"Whatever it may be, you have two adversaries to deal with, and such adversaries!"

"Oh! one of them doesn't count."

"And the other?"

"Sholmes? Oh! I confess he is a worthy foe; and that explains my present good humor. In the first place, it is a question of self-esteem; I am pleased to know that they consider me a subject worthy the attention of the celebrated English detective. In the next place, just imagine the pleasure a man, such as I, must experience in the thought of a duel with

Herlock Sholmes. But I shall be obliged to strain every muscle; he is a clever fellow, and will contest every inch of the ground."

"Then you consider him a strong opponent?"

"I do. As a detective, I believe, he has never had an equal. But I have one advantage over him; he is making the attack and I am simply defending myself. My rôle is the easier one. Besides, I am familiar with his method of warfare, and he does not know mine. I am prepared to show him a few new tricks that will give him something to think about."

He tapped the table with his fingers as he uttered the following sentences, with an air of keen delight:

"Arsène Lupin against Herlock Sholmes.... France against England.... Trafalgar will be revenged at last.... Ah! the rascal ... he doesn't suspect that I am prepared ... and a Lupin warned—"

He stopped suddenly, seized with a fit of coughing, and hid his face in his napkin, as if something had stuck in his throat.

"A bit of bread?" I inquired. "Drink some water."

"No, it isn't that," he replied, in a stifled voice.

"Then, what is it?"

"The want of air."

"Do you wish a window opened?"

"No, I shall go out. Give me my hat and overcoat, quick! I must go."

"What's the matter?"

"The two gentlemen who came in just now.... Look at the taller one ... now, when we go out, keep to my left, so he will not see me."

"The one who is sitting behind you?"

"Yes. I will explain it to you, outside."

"Who is it?"

"Herlock Sholmes."

He made a desperate effort to control himself, as if he were ashamed of his emotion, replaced his napkin, drank a glass of water, and, quite recovered, said to me, smiling:

"It is strange, hein, that I should be affected so easily, but that unexpected sight—"

"What have you to fear, since no one can recognize you, on account of your many transformations? Every time I see you it seems to me your face is changed; it's not at all familiar. I don't know why."

"But *he* would recognize me," said Lupin. "He has seen me only once; but, at that time, he made a mental photograph of me—not of my external appearance but of my very soul —not what I appear to be but just what I am. Do you understand? And then ... and then.... I did not expect to meet him here.... Such a strange encounter!... in this little restaurant...."

"Well, shall we go out?"

"No, not now," said Lupin.

"What are you going to do?"

"The better way is to act frankly ... to have confidence in him—trust him...."

"You will not speak to him?"

"Why not! It will be to my advantage to do so, and find out what he knows, and, perhaps, what he thinks. At present I have the feeling that his gaze is on my neck and shoulders, and that he is trying to remember where he has seen them before."

He reflected a moment. I observed a malicious smile at the corner of his mouth; then, obedient, I think, to a whim of his impulsive nature, and not to the necessities of the situation, he arose, turned around, and, with a bow and a joyous air, he said:

"By what lucky chance? Ah! I am delighted to see you. Permit me to introduce a friend of mine."

For a moment the Englishman was disconcerted; then he made a movement as if he would seize Arsène Lupin. The latter shook his head, and said:

"That would not be fair; besides, the movement would be an awkward one and ... quite useless."

The Englishman looked about him, as if in search of assistance.

"No use," said Lupin. "Besides, are you quite sure you can place your hand on me? Come, now, show me that you are a real Englishman and, therefore, a good sport."

This advice seemed to commend itself to the detective, for he partially rose and said, very formally:

"Monsieur Wilson, my friend and assistant—Monsieur Arsène Lupin."

Wilson's amazement evoked a laugh. With bulging eyes and gaping mouth, he looked from one to the other, as if unable to comprehend the situation. Herlock Sholmes laughed and said:

"Wilson, you should conceal your astonishment at an incident which is one of the most natural in the world."

"Why do you not arrest him?" stammered Wilson.

"Have you not observed, Wilson, that the gentleman is between me and the door, and only a few steps from the door. By the time I could move my little finger he would be outside."

"Don't let that make any difference," said Lupin, who now walked around the table and seated himself so that the Englishman was between him and the door—thus placing himself at the mercy of the foreigner.

Wilson looked at Sholmes to find out if he had the right to admire this act of wanton courage. The Englishman's face was impenetrable; but, a moment later, he called:

"Waiter!"

When the waiter came he ordered soda, beer and whisky. The treaty of peace was signed—until further orders. In a few moments the four men were conversing in an apparently friendly manner.

Herlock Sholmes is a man such as you might meet every day in the business world. He is about fifty years of age, and looks as if he might have passed his life in an office, adding up columns of dull figures or writing out formal statements of business accounts. There was nothing to distinguish him from the average citizen of London, except the appearance of his eyes, his terribly keen and penetrating eyes.

But then he is Herlock Sholmes—which means that he is a wonderful combination of intuition, observation, clairvoyance and ingenuity. One could readily believe that nature had been pleased to take the two most extraordinary detectives that the imagination of man has hitherto conceived, the Dupin of Edgar Allen Poe and the Lecoq of Emile Gaboriau, and, out of that material, constructed a new detective, more extraordinary and supernatural than either of them. And when a person reads the history of his exploits, which have made him famous throughout the entire world, he asks himself whether

Herlock Sholmes is not a mythical personage, a fictitious hero born in the brain of a great novelist—Conan Doyle, for instance.

When Arsène Lupin questioned him in regard to the length of his sojourn in France he turned the conversation into its proper channel by saying:

"That depends on you, monsieur."

"Oh!" exclaimed Lupin, laughing, "if it depends on me you can return to England to-night."

"That is a little too soon, but I expect to return in the course of eight or nine days—ten at the outside."

"Are you in such a hurry?"

"I have many cases to attend to; such as the robbery of the Anglo-Chinese Bank, the abduction of Lady Eccleston.... But, don't you think, Monsieur Lupin, that I can finish my business in Paris within a week?"

"Certainly, if you confine your efforts to the case of the blue diamond. It is, moreover, the length of time that I require to make preparations for my safety in case the solution of that affair should give you certain dangerous advantages over me."

"And yet," said the Englishman, "I expect to close the business in eight or ten days."

"And arrest me on the eleventh, perhaps?"

"No, the tenth is my limit."

Lupin shook his head thoughtfully, as he said:

"That will be difficult—very difficult."

"Difficult, perhaps, but possible, therefore certain—"

"Absolutely certain," said Wilson, as if he had clearly worked out the long series of operations which would conduct his collaborator to the desired result.

"Of course," said Herlock Sholmes, "I do not hold all the trump cards, as these cases are already several months old, and I lack certain information and clues upon which I am accustomed to base my investigations."

"Such as spots of mud and cigarette ashes," said Wilson, with an air of importance.

"In addition to the remarkable conclusions formed by Monsieur Ganimard, I have obtained all the articles written on the subject, and have formed a few deductions of my own."

"Some ideas which were suggested to us by analysis or hypothesis," added Wilson, sententiously.

"I wish to enquire," said Arsène Lupin, in that deferential tone which he employed in speaking to Sholmes, "would I be indiscreet if I were to ask you what opinion you have formed about the case?"

Really, it was a most exciting situation to see those two men facing each other across the table, engaged in an earnest discussion as if they were obliged to solve some abstruse problem or come to an agreement upon some controverted fact. Wilson was in the seventh heaven of delight. Herlock Sholmes filled his pipe slowly, lighted it, and said:

"This affair is much simpler than it appeared to be at first sight."

"Much simpler," said Wilson, as a faithful echo.

"I say 'this affair,' for, in my opinion, there is only one," said Sholmes. "The death of the Baron d'Hautrec, the story of the ring, and, let us not forget, the mystery of lottery ticket number 514, are only different phases of what one might call the mystery of the blonde Lady. Now, according to my view, it is simply a question of discovering the bond that unites those three episodes in the same story—the fact which proves the unity of the three events. Ganimard, whose judgment is rather superficial, finds that unity in the faculty of disappearance; that is, in the power of coming and going unseen and unheard. That theory does not satisfy me."

"Well, what is your idea?" asked Lupin.

"In my opinion," said Sholmes, "the characteristic feature of the three episodes is your design and purpose of leading the affair into a certain channel previously chosen by you. It is, on your part, more than a plan; it is a necessity, an indispensable condition of success."

"Can you furnish any details of your theory?"

"Certainly. For example, from the beginning of your conflict with Monsieur Gerbois, is it not evident that the apartment of Monsieur Detinan is the place selected by you, the inevitable spot where all the parties must meet? In your opinion, it was the only safe place, and you arranged a rendezvous there, publicly, one might say, for the blonde Lady and Mademoiselle Gerbois."

"The professor's daughter," added Wilson. "Now, let us consider the case of the blue diamond. Did you try to appropriate it while the Baron d'Hautrec possessed it! No. But the baron takes his brother's house. Six months later we have the intervention of Antoinette Bréhat and the first attempt. The diamond escapes you, and the sale is widely advertised to take place at the Drouot auction-rooms. Will it be a free and open sale? Is the richest amateur sure to carry off the jewel! No. Just as the banker Herschmann is on the point of buying the ring, a lady sends him a letter of warning, and it is the Countess de Crozon, prepared and influenced by the same lady, who becomes the purchaser of the diamond. Will the ring disappear at once? No; you lack the opportunity. Therefore, you must wait. At last the Countess goes to her château. That is what you were waiting for. The ring disappears."

"To reappear again in the tooth-powder of Herr Bleichen," remarked Lupin.

"Oh! such nonsense!" exclaimed Sholmes, striking the table with his fist, "don't tell me such a fairy tale. I am too old a fox to be led away by a false scent."

"What do you mean?"

"What do I mean?" said Sholmes, then paused a moment as if he wished to arrange his effect. At last he said:

"The blue diamond that was found in the tooth-powder was false. You kept the genuine stone."

Arsène Lupin remained silent for a moment; then, with his eyes fixed on the Englishman, he replied, calmly:

"You are impertinent, monsieur."

"Impertinent, indeed!" repeated Wilson, beaming with admiration.

"Yes," said Lupin, "and, yet, to do you credit, you have thrown a strong light on a very mysterious subject. Not a magistrate, not a special reporter, who has been engaged on this case, has come so near the truth. It is a marvelous display of intuition and logic."

"Oh! a person has simply to use his brains," said Herlock Sholmes, nattered at the homage of the expert criminal.

"And so few have any brains to use," replied Lupin. "And, now, that the field of conjectures has been narrowed down, and the rubbish cleared away——"

"Well, now, I have simply to discover why the three episodes were enacted at 25 rue

Clapeyron, 134 avenue Henri-Martin, and within the walls of the Château de Crozon and my work will be finished. What remains will be child's play. Don't you think so?"

"Yes, I think you are right."

"In that case, Monsieur Lupin, am I wrong in saying that my business will be finished in ten days?"

"In ten days you will know the whole truth," said Lupin.

"And you will be arrested."

"No."

"No?"

"In order that I may be arrested there must occur such a series of improbable and unexpected misfortunes that I cannot admit the possibility of such an event."

"We have a saying in England that 'the unexpected always happens.'"

They looked at each other for a moment calmly and fearlessly, without any display of bravado or malice. They met as equals in a contest of wit and skill. And this meeting was the formal crossing of swords, preliminary to the duel.

"Ah!" exclaimed Lupin, "at last I shall have an adversary worthy of the name—one whose defeat will be the proudest achievement in my career."

"Are you not afraid!" asked Wilson.

"Almost, Monsieur Wilson," replied Lupin, rising from his chair, "and the proof is that I am about to make a hasty retreat. Then, we will say ten days, Monsieur Sholmes?"

"Yes, ten days. This is Sunday. A week from next Wednesday, at eight o'clock in the evening, it will be all over."

"And I shall be in prison?"

"No doubt of it."

"Ha! not a pleasant outlook for a man who gets so much enjoyment out of life as I do. No cares, a lively interest in the affairs of the world, a justifiable contempt for the police, and the consoling sympathy of numerous friends and admirers. And now, behold, all that is about to be changed! It is the reverse side of the medal. After sunshine comes the rain. It is no longer a laughing matter. Adieu!"

"Hurry up!" said Wilson, full of solicitude for a person in whom Herlock Sholmes had inspired so much respect, "do not lose a minute."

"Not a minute, Monsieur Wilson; but I wish to express my pleasure at having met you, and to tell you how much I envy the master in having such a valuable assistant as you seem to be."

Then, after they had courteously saluted each other, like adversaries in a duel who entertain no feeling of malice but are obliged to fight by force of circumstances, Lupin seized me by the arm and drew me outside.

"What do you think of it, dear boy? The strange events of this evening will form an interesting chapter in the memoirs you are now preparing for me."

He closed the door of the restaurant behind us, and, after taking a few steps, he stopped and said:

"Do you smoke?"

"No. Nor do you, it seems to me."

"You are right, I don't."

He lighted a cigarette with a wax-match, which he shook several times in an effort to extinguish it. But he threw away the cigarette immediately, ran across the street, and joined two men who emerged from the shadows as if called by a signal. He conversed with them for a few minutes on the opposite sidewalk, and then returned to me.

"I beg your pardon, but I fear that cursed Sholmes is going to give me trouble. But, I assure you, he is not yet through with Arsène Lupin. He will find out what kind of fuel I use to warm my blood. And now—au revoir! The genial Wilson is right; there is not a moment to lose."

He walked away rapidly.

Thus ended the events of that exciting evening, or, at least, that part of them in which I was a participant. Subsequently, during the course of the evening, other stirring incidents occurred which have come to my knowledge through the courtesy of other members of that unique dinner-party.

At the very moment in which Lupin left me, Herlock Sholmes rose from the table, and looked at his watch.

"Twenty minutes to nine. At nine o'clock I am to meet the Count and Countess at the railway station."

"Then, we must be off!" exclaimed Wilson, between two drinks of whisky.

They left the restaurant.

"Wilson, don't look behind. We may be followed, and, in that case, let us act as if we did not care. Wilson, I want your opinion: why was Lupin in that restaurant?"

"To get something to eat," replied Wilson, quickly.

"Wilson, I must congratulate you on the accuracy of your deduction. I couldn't have done better myself."

Wilson blushed with pleasure, and Sholmes continued:

"To get something to eat. Very well, and, after that, probably, to assure himself whether I am going to the Château de Crozon, as announced by Ganimard in his interview. I must go in order not to disappoint him. But, in order to gain time on him, I shall not go."

"Ah!" said Wilson, nonplused.

"You, my friend, will walk down this street, take a carriage, two, three carriages. Return later and get the valises that we left at the station, and make for the Elysée-Palace at a galop."

"And when I reach the Elysée-Palace?"

"Engage a room, go to sleep, and await my orders."

Quite proud of the important rôle assigned to him, Wilson set out to perform his task. Herlock Sholmes proceeded to the railway station, bought a ticket, and repaired to the Amiens' express in which the Count and Countess de Crozon were already installed. He bowed to them, lighted his pipe, and had a quiet smoke in the corridor. The train started. Ten minutes later he took a seat beside the Countess, and said to her:

"Have you the ring here, madame?"

"Yes."

"Will you kindly let me see it?"

He took it, and examined it closely.

"Just as I suspected: it is a manufactured diamond."

"A manufactured diamond?"

"Yes; a new process which consists in submitting diamond dust to a tremendous heat until it melts and is then molded into a single stone."

"But my diamond is genuine."

"Yes, *your* diamond is; but this is not yours."

"Where is mine?"

"It is held by Arsène Lupin."

"And this stone?"

"Was substituted for yours, and slipped into Herr Bleichen's tooth-powder, where it was afterwards found."

"Then you think this is false?"

"Absolutely false."

The Countess was overwhelmed with surprise and grief, while her husband scrutinized the diamond with an incredulous air. Finally she stammered:

"Is it possible? And why did they not merely steal it and be done with it? And how did they steal it?"

"That is exactly what I am going to find out."

"At the Château de Crozon?"

"No. I shall leave the train at Creil and return to Paris. It is there the game between me and Arsène Lupin must be played. In fact, the game has commenced already, and Lupin thinks I am on my way to the château."

"But—"

"What does it matter to you, madame? The essential thing is your diamond, is it not?"

"Yes."

"Well, don't worry. I have just undertaken a much more difficult task than that. You have my promise that I will restore the true diamond to you within ten days."

The train slackened its speed. He put the false diamond in his pocket and opened the door. The Count cried out:

"That is the wrong side of the train. You are getting out on the tracks."

"That is my intention. If Lupin has anyone on my track, he will lose sight of me now. Adieu."

An employee protested in vain. After the departure of the train, the Englishman sought the station-master's office. Forty minutes later he leaped into a train that landed him in Paris shortly before midnight. He ran across the platform, entered the lunch-room, made his exit at another door, and jumped into a cab.

"Driver—rue Clapeyron."

Having reached the conclusion that he was not followed, he stopped the carriage at the end of the street, and proceeded to make a careful examination of Monsieur Detinan's house and the two adjoining houses. He made measurements of certain distances and entered the figures in his notebook.

"Driver—avenue Henri-Martin."

At the corner of the avenue and the rue de la Pompe, he dismissed the carriage, walked down the street to number 134, and performed the same operations in front of the house of the late Baron d'Hautrec and the two adjoining houses, measuring the width of the respective façades and calculating the depth of the little gardens that stood in front of them.

The avenue was deserted, and was very dark under its four rows of trees, between which, at considerable intervals, a few gas-lamps struggled in vain to light the deep shadows. One of them threw a dim light over a portion of the house, and Sholmes perceived the "To-let" sign posted on the gate, the neglected walks which encircled the small lawn, and the large bare windows of the vacant house.

"I suppose," he said to himself, "the house has been unoccupied since the death of the baron.... Ah! if I could only get in and view the scene of the murder!"

No sooner did the idea occur to him than he sought to put it in execution. But how could he manage it? He could not climb over the gate; it was too high. So he took from his pocket an electric lantern and a skeleton key which he always carried. Then, to his great surprise, he discovered that the gate was not locked; in fact, it was open about three or four inches. He entered the garden, and was careful to leave the gate as he had found it— partly open. But he had not taken many steps from the gate when he stopped. He had seen a light pass one of the windows on the second floor.

He saw the light pass a second window and a third, but he saw nothing else, except a silhouette outlined on the walls of the rooms. The light descended to the first floor, and, for a long time, wandered from room to room.

"Who the deuce is walking, at one o'clock in the morning, through the house in which the Baron d'Hautrec was killed?" Herlock Sholmes asked himself, deeply interested.

There was only one way to find out, and that was to enter the house himself. He did not hesitate, but started for the door of the house. However, at the moment when he crossed the streak of gaslight that came from the street-lamp, the man must have seen him, for the light in the house was suddenly extinguished and Herlock Sholmes did not see it again. Softly, he tried the door. It was open, also. Hearing no sound, he advanced through the hallway, encountered the foot of the stairs, and ascended to the first floor. Here there was the same silence, the same darkness.

He entered, one of the rooms and approached a window through which came a feeble light from the outside. On looking through the window he saw the man, who had no doubt descended by another stairway and escaped by another door. The man was threading his way through the shrubbery which bordered the wall that separated the two gardens.

"The deuce!" exclaimed Sholmes, "he is going to escape."

He hastened down the stairs and leaped over the steps in his eagerness to cut off the man's retreat. But he did not see anyone, and, owing to the darkness, it was several seconds before he was able to distinguish a bulky form moving through the shrubbery. This gave the Englishman food for reflection. Why had the man not made his escape, which he could have done so easily? Had he remained in order to watch the movements of the intruder who had disturbed him in his mysterious work?

"At all events," concluded Sholmes, "it is not Lupin; he would be more adroit. It may be one of his men."

For several minutes Herlock Sholmes remained motionless, with his gaze fixed on the adversary who, in his turn was watching the detective. But as that adversary had become passive, and as the Englishman was not one to consume his time in idle waiting, he examined his revolver to see if it was in good working order, remove his knife from its sheath, and walked toward the enemy with that cool effrontery and scorn of danger for which he had become famous.

He heard a clicking sound; it was his adversary preparing his revolver. Herlock

Sholmes dashed boldly into the thicket, and grappled with his foe. There was a sharp, desperate struggle, in the course of which Sholmes suspected that the man was trying to draw a knife. But the Englishman, believing his antagonist to be an accomplice of Arsène Lupin and anxious to win the first trick in the game with that redoubtable foe, fought with unusual strength and determination. He hurled his adversary to the ground, held him there with the weight of his body, and, gripping him by the throat with one hand, he used his free hand to take out his electric lantern, press the button, and throw the light over the face of his prisoner.

"Wilson!" he exclaimed, in amazement.

"Herlock Sholmes!" stammered a weak, stifled voice.

For a long time they remained silent, astounded, foolish. The shriek of an automobile rent the air. A slight breeze stirred the leaves. Suddenly, Herlock Sholmes seized his friend by the shoulders and shook him violently, as he cried:

"What are you doing here? Tell me.... What?... Did I tell you to hide in the bushes and spy on me?"

"Spy on you!" muttered Wilson, "why, I didn't know it was you."

"But what are you doing here? You ought to be in bed."

"I was in bed."

"You ought to be asleep."

"I was asleep."

"Well, what brought you here?" asked Sholmes.

"Your letter."

"My letter? I don't understand."

"Yes, a messenger brought it to me at the hotel."

"From me? Are you crazy?"

"It is true—I swear it."

"Where is the letter?"

Wilson handed him a sheet of paper, which he read by the light of his lantern. It was as follows:

"Wilson, come at once to avenue Henri-Martin. The house is empty. Inspect the whole place and make an exact plan. Then return to hotel.—Herlock Sholmes."

"I was measuring the rooms," said Wilson, "when I saw a shadow in the garden. I had only one idea——"

"That was to seize the shadow.... The idea was excellent.... But remember this, Wilson, whenever you receive a letter from me, be sure it is my handwriting and not a forgery."

"Ah!" exclaimed Wilson, as the truth dawned on him, "then the letter wasn't from you?"

"No."

"Who sent it, then?"

"Arsène Lupin."

"Why? For what purpose?" asked Wilson.

"I don't know, and that's what worries me. I don't understand why he took the trouble to disturb you. Of course, if he had sent me on such a foolish errand I wouldn't be surprised; but what was his object in disturbing you?"

"I must hurry back to the hotel."

"So must I, Wilson."

They arrived at the gate. Wilson, who was ahead, took hold of it and pulled.

"Ah! you closed it?" he said.

"No, I left it partly open."

Sholmes tried the gate; then, alarmed, he examined the lock. An oath escaped him:

"Good God! it is locked! locked with a key!"

He shook the gate with all his strength; then, realizing the futility of his efforts, he dropped his arms, discouraged, and muttered, in a jerky manner:

"I can see it all now—it is Lupin. He fore-saw that I would leave the train at Creil, and he prepared this neat little trap for me in case I should commence my investigation this evening. Moreover, he was kind enough to send me a companion to share my captivity. All done to make me lose a day, and, perhaps, also, to teach me to mind my own business."

"Do you mean to say we are prisoners?"

"Exactly. Herlock Sholmes and Wilson are the prisoners of Arsène Lupin. It's a bad beginning; but he laughs best who laughs last."

Wilson seized Sholmes' arm, and exclaimed:

"Look!... Look up there!... A light...."

A light shone through one of the windows of the first floor. Both of them ran to the house, and each ascended by the stairs he had used on coming out a short time before, and they met again at the entrance to the lighted chamber. A small piece of a candle was burning in the center of the room. Beside it there was a basket containing a bottle, a roasted chicken, and a loaf of bread.

Sholmes was greatly amused, and laughed heartily.

"Wonderful! we are invited to supper. It is really an enchanted place, a genuine fairy-land. Come, Wilson, cheer up! this is not a funeral. It's all very funny."

"Are you quite sure it is so very funny?" asked Wilson, in a lugubrious tone.

"Am I sure?" exclaimed Sholmes, with a gaiety that was too boisterous to be natural, "why, to tell the truth, it's the funniest thing I ever saw. It's a jolly good comedy! What a master of sarcasm this Arsène Lupin is! He makes a fool of you with the utmost grace and delicacy. I wouldn't miss this feast for all the money in the Bank of England. Come, Wilson, you grieve me. You should display that nobility of character which rises superior to misfortune. I don't see that you have any cause for complaint, really, I don't."

After a time, by dint of good humor and sarcasm, he managed to restore Wilson to his normal mood, and make him swallow a morsel of chicken and a glass of wine. But when the candle went out and they prepared to spend the night there, with the bare floor for a mattress and the hard wall for a pillow, the harsh and ridiculous side of the situation was impressed upon them. That particular incident will not form a pleasant page in the memoirs of the famous detective.

Next morning Wilson awoke, stiff and cold. A slight noise attracted his attention: Herlock Sholmes was kneeling on the floor, critically examining some grains of sand and studying some chalk-marks, now almost effaced, which formed certain figures and numbers, which figures he entered in his notebook.

Accompanied by Wilson, who was deeply interested in the work, he examined each room, and found similar chalk-marks in two other apartments. He noticed, also, two circles on the oaken panels, an arrow on a wainscot, and four figures on four steps of the stairs. At the end of an hour Wilson said:

"The figures are correct, aren't they?"

"I don't know; but, at all events, they mean something," replied Sholmes, who had forgotten the discomforts of the night in the joy created by his new discoveries.

"It is quite obvious," said Wilson, "they represent the number of pieces in the floor."

"Ah!"

"Yes. And the two circles indicate that the panels are false, as you can readily ascertain, and the arrow points in the direction in which the panels move."

Herlock Sholmes looked at Wilson, in astonishment.

"Ah! my dear friend, how do you know all that? Your clairvoyance makes my poor ability in that direction look quite insignificant."

"Oh! it is very simple," said Wilson, inflated with pride; "I examined those marks last night, according to your instructions, or, rather, according to the instructions of Arsène Lupin, since he wrote the letter you sent to me."

At that moment Wilson faced a greater danger than he had during his struggle in the garden with Herlock Sholmes. The latter now felt a furious desire to strangle him. But, dominating his feelings, Sholmes made a grimace which was intended for a smile, and said:

"Quite so, Wilson, you have done well, and your work shows commendable progress. But, tell me, have you exercised your powers of observation and analysis on any other points? I might profit by your deductions."

"Oh! no, I went no farther."

"That's a pity. Your début was such a promising one. But, since that is all, we may as well go."

"Go! but how can we get out?"

"The way all honest people go out: through the gate."

"But it is locked."

"It will be opened."

"By whom?"

"Please call the two policemen who are strolling down the avenue."

"But——"

"But what?"

"It is very humiliating. What will be said when it becomes known that Herlock Sholmes and Wilson were the prisoners of Arsène Lupin?"

"Of course, I understand they will roar with laughter," replied Herlock Sholmes, in a dry voice and with frowning features, "but we can't set up housekeeping in this place."

"And you will not try to find another way out?"

"No."

"But the man who brought us the basket of provisions did not cross the garden, coming or going. There is some other way out. Let us look for it, and not bother with the police."

"Your argument is sound, but you forget that all the detectives in Paris have been trying to find it for the last six months, and that I searched the house from top to bottom while you were asleep. Ah! my dear Wilson, we have not been accustomed to pursue such game as Arsène Lupin. He leaves no trail behind him."

. . .

At eleven o'clock, Herlock Sholmes and Wilson were liberated, and conducted to the nearest police station, where the commissary, after subjecting them to a severe examination, released them with an affectation of good-will that was quite exasperating.

"I am very sorry, messieurs, that this unfortunate incident has occurred. You will have a very poor opinion of French hospitality. Mon Dieu! what a night you must have passed! Ah! that rascally Lupin is no respecter of persons."

They took a carriage to their hotel. At the office Wilson asked for the key of his room.

After some search the clerk replied, much astonished:

"But, monsieur, you have given up the room."

"I gave it up? When?"

"This morning, by the letter your friend brought here."

"What friend?"

"The gentleman who brought your letter.... Ah! your card is still attached to the letter. Here they are."

Wilson looked at them. Certainly, it was one of his cards, and the letter was in his handwriting.

"Good Lord!" he muttered, "this is another of his tricks," and he added, aloud: "Where is my luggage?"

"Your friend took it."

"Ah!... and you gave it to him?"

"Certainly; on the strength of your letter and card."

"Of course ... of course."

They left the hotel and walked, slowly and thoughtfully, through the Champs-Elysées. The avenue was bright and cheerful beneath a clear autumn sun; the air was mild and pleasant.

At Rond-Point, Herlock Sholmes lighted his pipe. Then Wilson spoke:

"I can't understand you, Sholmes. You are so calm and unruffled. They play with you as a cat plays with a mouse, and yet you do not say a word."

Sholmes stopped, as he replied:

"Wilson, I was thinking of your card."

"Well?"

"The point is this: here is a man who, in view of a possible struggle with us, procures specimens of our handwriting, and who holds, in his possession, one or more of your cards. Now, have you considered how much precaution and skill those facts represent?"

"Well?"

"Well, Wilson, to overcome an enemy so well prepared and so thoroughly equipped requires the infinite shrewdness of ... of a Herlock Sholmes. And yet, as you have seen, Wilson, I have lost the first round."

At six o'clock the *Echo de France* published the following article in its evening edition:

"This morning Mon. Thenard, commissary of police in the sixteenth district, released Herlock Sholmes and his friend Wilson, both of whom had been locked in the house of the late Baron d'Hautrec, where they spent a very pleasant night—thanks to the thoughtful care and attention of Arsène Lupin."

"In addition to their other troubles, these gentlemen have been robbed of their valises, and, in consequence thereof, they have entered a formal complaint against Arsène Lupin."

"Arsène Lupin, satisfied that he has given them a mild reproof, hopes these gentlemen will not force him to resort to more stringent measures."

"Bah!" exclaimed Herlock Sholmes, crushing the paper in his hands, "that is only child's play! And that is the only criticism I have to make of Arsène Lupin: he plays to the gallery. There is that much of the fakir in him."

"Ah! Sholmes, you are a wonderful man! You have such a command over your temper. Nothing ever disturbs you."

"No, nothing disturbs me," replied Sholmes, in a voice that trembled from rage; "besides, what's the use of losing my temper?... I am quite confident of the final result; I shall have the last word."

IV. LIGHT IN THE DARKNESS

However well-tempered a man's character may be—and Herlock Sholmes is one of those men over whom ill-fortune has little or no hold—there are circumstances wherein the most courageous combatant feels the necessity of marshaling his forces before risking the chances of a battle.

"I shall take a vacation to-day," said Sholmes.

"And what shall I do?" asked Wilson.

"You, Wilson—let me see! You can buy some underwear and linen to replenish our wardrobe, while I take a rest."

"Very well, Sholmes, I will watch while you sleep."

Wilson uttered these words with all the importance of a sentinel on guard at the outpost, and therefore exposed to the greatest danger. His chest was expanded; his muscles were tense. Assuming a shrewd look, he scrutinized, officially, the little room in which they had fixed their abode.

"Very well, Wilson, you can watch. I shall occupy myself in the preparation of a line of attack more appropriate to the methods of the enemy we are called upon to meet. Do you see, Wilson, we have been deceived in this fellow Lupin. My opinion is that we must commence at the very beginning of this affair."

"And even before that, if possible. But have we sufficient time?"

"Nine days, dear boy. That is five too many."

The Englishman spent the entire afternoon in smoking and sleeping. He did not enter upon his new plan of attack until the following day. Then he said:

"Wilson, I am ready. Let us attack the enemy."

"Lead on, Macduff!" exclaimed Wilson, full of martial ardor. "I wish to fight in the front rank. Oh! have no fear. I shall do credit to my King and country, for I am an Englishman."

In the first place, Sholmes had three long and important interviews: With Monsieur Detinan, whose rooms he examined with the greatest care and precision; with Suzanne Gerbois, whom he questioned in regard to the blonde Lady; and with Sister Auguste, who had retired to the convent of the Visitandines since the murder of Baron d'Hautrec.

At each of these interviews Wilson had remained outside; and each time he asked: "Satisfactory?"

"Quite so."

"I was sure we were on the right track."

They paid a visit to the two houses adjoining that of the late Baron d'Hautrec in the avenue Henri-Martin; then they visited the rue Clapeyron, and, while he was examining the front of number 25, Sholmes said:

"All these houses must be connected by secret passages, but I can't find them."

For the first time in his life, Wilson doubted the omnipotence of his famous associate. Why did he now talk so much and accomplish so little?

"Why?" exclaimed Sholmes, in answer to Wilson's secret thought, "because, with this fellow Lupin, a person has to work in the dark, and, instead of deducting the truth from established facts, a man must extract it from his own brain, and afterward learn if it is supported by the facts in the case."

"But what about the secret passages?"

"They must exist. But even though I should discover them, and thus learn how Arsène Lupin made his entrance to the lawyer's house and how the blonde Lady escaped from the house of Baron d'Hautrec after the murder, what good would it do? How would it help me? Would it furnish me with a weapon of attack?"

"Let us attack him just the same," exclaimed Wilson, who had scarcely uttered these words when he jumped back with a cry of alarm. Something had fallen at their feet; it was a bag filled with sand which might have caused them serious injury if it had struck them.

Sholmes looked up. Some men were working on a scaffolding attached to the balcony at the fifth floor of the house. He said:

"We were lucky; one step more, and that heavy bag would have fallen on our heads. I wonder if—"

Moved by a sudden impulse, he rushed into the house, up the five flights of stairs, rang the bell, pushed his way into the apartment to the great surprise and alarm of the servant who came to the door, and made his way to the balcony in front of the house. But there was no one there.

"Where are the workmen who were here a moment ago?" he asked the servant.

"They have just gone."

"Which way did they go?"

"By the servants' stairs."

Sholmes leaned out of the window. He saw two men leaving the house, carrying bicycles. They mounted them and quickly disappeared around the corner.

"How long have they been working on this scaffolding?"

"Those men?... only since this morning. It's their first day."

Sholmes returned to the street, and joined Wilson. Together they returned to the hotel, and thus the second day ended in a mournful silence.

On the following day their programme was almost similar. They sat together on a bench in the avenue Henri-Martin, much to Wilson's disgust, who did not find it amusing to spend long hours watching the house in which the tragedy had occurred.

"What do you expect, Sholmes? That Arsène Lupin will walk out of the house?"

"No."

"That the blonde Lady will make her appearance?"

"No."

"What then?"

"I am looking for something to occur; some slight incident that will furnish me with a clue to work on."

"And if it does not occur!"

"Then I must, myself, create the spark that will set fire to the powder."

A solitary incident—and that of a disagreeable nature—broke the monotony of the forenoon.

A gentleman was riding along the avenue when his horse suddenly turned aside in such a manner that it ran against the bench on which they were sitting, and struck Sholmes a slight blow on the shoulder.

"Ha!" exclaimed Sholmes, "a little more and I would have had a broken shoulder."

The gentleman struggled with his horse. The Englishman drew his revolver and pointed it; but Wilson seized his arm, and said:

"Don't be foolish! What are you going to do! Kill the man!"

"Leave me alone, Wilson! Let go!"

During the brief struggle between Sholmes and Wilson the stranger rode away.

"Now, you can shoot," said Wilson, triumphantly, when the horseman was at some distance.

"Wilson, you're an idiot! Don't you understand that the man is an accomplice of Arsène Lupin?"

Sholmes was trembling from rage. Wilson stammered pitifully:

"What!... that man ... an accomplice?"

"Yes, the same as the workmen who tried to drop the bag of sand on us yesterday."

"It can't be possible!"

"Possible or not, there was only one way to prove it."

"By killing the man?"

"No—by killing the horse. If you hadn't grabbed my arm, I should have captured one of Lupin's accomplices. Now, do you understand the folly of your act?"

Throughout the afternoon both men were morose. They did not speak a word to each other. At five o'clock they visited the rue Clapeyron, but were careful to keep at a safe distance from the houses. However, three young men who were passing through the street, arm in arm, singing, ran against Sholmes and Wilson and refused to let them pass. Sholmes, who was in an ill humor, contested the right of way with them. After a brief struggle, Sholmes resorted to his fists. He struck one of the men a hard blow on the chest, another a blow in the face, and thus subdued two of his adversaries. Thereupon the three of them took to their heels and disappeared.

"Ah!" exclaimed Sholmes, "that does me good. I needed a little exercise."

But Wilson was leaning against the wall. Sholmes said:

"What's the matter, old chap? You're quite pale."

Wilson pointed to his left arm, which hung inert, and stammered:

"I don't know what it is. My arm pains me."

"Very much?... Is it serious?"

"Yes, I am afraid so."

He tried to raise his arm, but it was helpless. Sholmes felt it, gently at first, then in a rougher way, "to see how badly it was hurt," he said. He concluded that Wilson was really hurt, so he led him to a neighboring pharmacy, where a closer examination revealed the fact that the arm was broken and that Wilson was a candidate for the hospital. In the meantime they bared his arm and applied some remedies to ease his suffering.

"Come, come, old chap, cheer up!" said Sholmes, who was holding Wilson's arm, "in five or six weeks you will be all right again. But I will pay them back ... the rascals! Especially Lupin, for this is his work ... no doubt of that. I swear to you if ever——"

He stopped suddenly, dropped the arm—which caused Wilson such an access of pain that he almost fainted—and, striking his forehead, Sholmes said:

"Wilson, I have an idea. You know, I have one occasionally."

He stood for a moment, silent, with staring eyes, and then muttered, in short, sharp phrases:

"Yes, that's it ... that will explain all ... right at my feet ... and I didn't see it ... ah, parbleu! I should have thought of it before.... Wilson, I shall have good news for you."

Abruptly leaving his old friend, Sholmes ran into the street and went directly to the house known as number 25. On one of the stones, to the right of the door, he read this inscription: "Destange, architect, 1875."

There was a similar inscription on the house numbered 23.

Of course, there was nothing unusual in that. But what might be read on the houses in the avenue Henri-Martin?

A carriage was passing. He engaged it and directed the driver to take him to No. 134 avenue Henri-Martin. He was roused to a high pitch of excitement. He stood up in the carriage and urged the horse to greater speed. He offered extra pourboires to the driver. Quicker! Quicker!

How great was his anxiety as they turned from the rue de la Pompe! Had he caught a glimpse of the truth at last?

On one of the stones of the late Baron's house he read the words: "Destange, architect, 1874." And a similar inscription appeared on the two adjoining houses.

The reaction was such that he settled down in the seat of the carriage, trembling from joy. At last, a tiny ray of light had penetrated the dark shadows which encompassed these mysterious crimes! In the vast sombre forest wherein a thousand pathways crossed and re-crossed, he had discovered the first clue to the track followed by the enemy!

He entered a branch post office and obtained telephonic connection with the château de Crozon. The Countess answered the telephone call.

"Hello!... Is that you, madame?"

"Monsieur Sholmes, isn't it? Everything going all right?"

"Quite well, but I wish to ask you one question.... Hello!"

"Yes, I hear you."

"Tell me, when was the château de Crozon built?"

"It was destroyed by fire and rebuilt about thirty years ago."

"Who built it, and in what year?"

"There is an inscription on the front of the house which reads: 'Lucien Destange, architect, 1877.'"

"Thank you, madame, that is all. Good-bye."

He went away, murmuring: "Destange ... Lucien Destange ... that name has a familiar sound."

He noticed a public reading-room, entered, consulted a dictionary of modern biography, and copied the following information: "Lucien Destange, born 1840, Grand-Prix de Rome, officer of the Legion of Honor, author of several valuable books on architecture, etc...."

Then he returned to the pharmacy and found that Wilson had been taken to the hospital. There Sholmes found him with his arm in splints, and shivering with fever.

"Victory! Victory!" cried Sholmes. "I hold one end of the thread."

"Of what thread?"

"The one that leads to victory. I shall now be walking on solid ground, where there will be footprints, clues...."

"Cigarette ashes?" asked Wilson, whose curiosity had overcome his pain.

"And many other things! Just think, Wilson, I have found the mysterious link which unites the different adventures in which the blonde Lady played a part. Why did Lupin select those three houses for the scenes of his exploits?"

"Yes, why?"

"Because those three houses were built by the same architect. That was an easy problem, eh? Of course ... but who would have thought of it?"

"No one but you."

"And who, except I, knows that the same architect, by the use of analogous plans, has rendered it possible for a person to execute three distinct acts which, though miraculous in appearance, are, in reality, quite simple and easy?"

"That was a stroke of good luck."

"And it was time, dear boy, as I was becoming very impatient. You know, this is our fourth day."

"Out of ten."

"Oh! after this——"

Sholmes was excited, delighted, and gayer than usual.

"And when I think that these rascals might have attacked me in the street and broken my arm just as they did yours! Isn't that so, Wilson?"

Wilson simply shivered at the horrible thought. Sholmes continued:

"We must profit by the lesson. I can see, Wilson, that we were wrong to try and fight Lupin in the open, and leave ourselves exposed to his attacks."

"I can see it, and feel it, too, in my broken arm," said Wilson.

"You have one consolation, Wilson; that is, that I escaped. Now, I must be doubly cautious. In an open fight he will defeat me; but if I can work in the dark, unseen by him, I have the advantage, no matter how strong his forces may be."

"Ganimard might be of some assistance."

"Never! On the day that I can truly say: Arsène Lupin is there; I show you the quarry, and how to catch it; I shall go and see Ganimard at one of the two addresses that he gave me—his residence in the rue Pergolese, or at the Suisse tavern in the Place du Châtelet. But, until that time, I shall work alone."

He approached the bed, placed his hand on Wilson's shoulder—on the sore one, of course—and said to him:

"Take care of yourself, old fellow. Henceforth your rôle will be to keep two or three of

Arsène Lupin's men busy watching here in vain for my return to enquire about your health. It is a secret mission for you, eh?"

"Yes, and I shall do my best to fulfil it conscientiously. Then you do not expect to come here anymore?"

"What for?" asked Sholmes.

"I don't know ... of course.... I am getting on as well as possible. But, Herlock, do me a last service: give me a drink."

"A drink?"

"Yes, I am dying of thirst; and with my fever——"

"To be sure—directly——"

He made a pretense of getting some water, perceived a package of tobacco, lighted his pipe, and then, as if he had not heard his friend's request, he went away, whilst Wilson uttered a mute prayer for the inaccessible water.

"Monsieur Destange!"

The servant eyed from head to foot the person to whom he had opened the door of the house—the magnificent house that stood at the corner of the Place Malesherbes and the rue Montchanin—and at the sight of the man with gray hairs, badly shaved, dressed in a shabby black coat, with a body as ill-formed and ungracious as his face, he replied with the disdain which he thought the occasion warranted:

"Monsieur Destange may or may not be at home. That depends. Has monsieur a card?"

Monsieur did not have a card, but he had a letter of introduction and, after the servant had taken the letter to Mon. Destange, he was conducted into the presence of that gentleman who was sitting in a large circular room or rotunda which occupied one of the wings of the house. It was a library, and contained a profusion of books and architectural drawings. When the stranger entered, the architect said to him:

"You are Monsieur Stickmann?"

"Yes, monsieur."

"My secretary tells me that he is ill, and has sent you to continue the general catalogue of the books which he commenced under my direction, and, more particularly, the catalogue of German books. Are you familiar with that kind of work?"

"Yes, monsieur, quite so," he replied, with a strong German accent.

Under those circumstances the bargain was soon concluded, and Mon. Destange commenced work with his new secretary.

Herlock Sholmes had gained access to the house.

In order to escape the vigilance of Arsène Lupin and gain admittance to the house occupied by Lucien Destange and his daughter Clotilde, the famous detective had been compelled to resort to a number of stratagems, and, under a variety of names, to ingratiate himself into the good graces and confidence of a number of persons—in short, to live, during forty-eight hours, a most complicated life. During that time he had acquired the following information: Mon. Destange, having retired from active business on account of his failing health, now lived amongst the many books he had accumulated on the subject of architecture. He derived infinite pleasure in viewing and handling those dusty old volumes.

His daughter Clotilde was considered eccentric. She passed her time in another part of the house, and never went out.

"Of course," Sholmes said to himself, as he wrote in a register the titles of the books which Mon. Destange dictated to him, "all that is vague and incomplete, but it is quite a long step in advance. I shall surely solve one of these absorbing problems: Is Mon. Destange associated with Arsène Lupin? Does he continue to see him? Are the papers relating to the construction of the three houses still in existence? Will those papers not furnish me with the location of other houses of similar construction which Arsène Lupin and his associates will plunder in the future?

"Monsieur Destange, an accomplice of Arsène Lupin! That venerable man, an officer of the Legion of Honor, working in league with a burglar—such an idea was absurd! Besides, if we concede that such a complicity exists, how could Mon. Destange, thirty years ago, have possibly foreseen the thefts of Arsène Lupin, who was then an infant?"

No matter! The Englishman was implacable. With his marvelous scent, and that instinct which never fails him, he felt that he was in the heart of some strange mystery. Ever since he first entered the house, he had been under the influence of that impression, and yet he could not define the grounds on which he based his suspicions.

Up to the morning of the second day he had not made any significant discovery. At two o'clock of that day he saw Clotilde Destange for the first time; she came to the library in search of a book. She was about thirty years of age, a brunette, slow and silent in her movements, with features imbued with that expression of indifference which is characteristic of people who live a secluded life. She exchanged a few words with her father, and then retired, without even looking at Sholmes.

The afternoon dragged along monotonously. At five o'clock Mon. Destange announced his intention to go out. Sholmes was alone on the circular gallery that was constructed about ten feet above the floor of the rotunda. It was almost dark. He was on the point of going out, when he heard a slight sound and, at the same time, experienced the feeling that there was someone in the room. Several minutes passed before he saw or heard anything more. Then he shuddered; a shadowy form emerged from the gloom, quite close to him, upon the balcony. It seemed incredible. How long had this mysterious visitor been there? Whence did he come?

The strange man descended the steps and went directly to a large oaken cupboard. Sholmes was a keen observer of the man's movements. He watched him searching amongst the papers with which the cupboard was filled. What was he looking for?

Then the door opened and Mlle. Destange entered, speaking to someone who was following her:

"So you have decided not to go out, father?... Then I will make a light ... one second ... do not move...."

The strange man closed the cupboard and hid in the embrasure of a large window, drawing the curtains together. Did Mlle. Destange not see him? Did she not hear him? Calmly she turned on the electric lights; she and her father sat down close to each other. She opened a book she had brought with her, and commenced to read. After the lapse of a few minutes she said:

"Your secretary has gone."

"Yes, I don't see him."

"Do you like him as well as you did at first?" she asked, as if she were not aware of the illness of the real secretary and his replacement by Stickmann.

"Oh! yes."

Monsieur Destange's head bobbed from one side to the other. He was asleep. The girl resumed her reading. A moment later one of the window curtains was pushed back, and the strange man emerged and glided along the wall toward the door, which obliged him to pass behind Mon. Destange but in front of Clotilde, and brought him into the light so that Herlock Sholmes obtained a good view of the man's face. It was Arsène Lupin.

The Englishman was delighted. His forecast was verified; he had penetrated to the very heart of the mystery, and found Arsène Lupin to be the moving spirit in it.

Clotilde had not yet displayed any knowledge of his presence, although it was quite improbable that any movement of the intruder had escaped her notice. Lupin had almost reached the door and, in fact, his hand was already seeking the door-knob, when his coat brushed against a small table and knocked something to the floor. Monsieur Destange awoke with a start. Arsène Lupin was already standing in front of him, hat in hand, smiling.

"Maxime Bermond," exclaimed Mon. Destange, joyfully. "My dear Maxime, what lucky chance brings you here?"

"The wish to see you and Mademoiselle Destange."

"When did you return from your journey?"

"Yesterday."

"You must stay to dinner."

"No, thank you, I am sorry, but I have an appointment to dine with some friends at a restaurant."

"Come, to-morrow, then, Clotilde, you must urge him to come to-morrow. Ah! my dear Maxime.... I thought of you many times during your absence."

"Really?"

"Yes, I went through all my old papers in that cupboard, and found our last statement of account."

"What account?"

"Relating to the avenue Henri-Martin."

"Ah! do you keep such papers? What for?"

Then the three of them left the room, and continued their conversation in a small parlor which adjoined the library.

"Is it Lupin?" Sholmes asked himself, in a sudden access of doubt. Certainly, from all appearances, it was he; and yet it was also someone else who resembled Arsène Lupin in certain respects, and who still maintained his own individuality, features, and color of hair. Sholmes could hear Lupin's voice in the adjoining room. He was relating some stories at which Mon. Destange laughed heartily, and which even brought a smile to the lips of the melancholy Clotilde. And each of those smiles appeared to be the reward which Arsène Lupin was seeking, and which he was delighted to have secured. His success caused him to redouble his efforts and, insensibly, at the sound of that clear and happy voice, Clotilde's face brightened and lost that cold and listless expression which usually pervaded it.

"They love each other," thought Sholmes, "but what the deuce can there be in common between Clotilde Destange and Maxime Bermond? Does she know that Maxime is none other than Arsène Lupin?"

Until seven o'clock Sholmes was an anxious listener, seeking to profit by the conversation. Then, with infinite precaution, he descended from the gallery, crept along the side of the room to the door in such a manner that the people in the adjoining room did not see him.

When he reached the street Sholmes satisfied himself that there was neither an automobile nor a cab waiting there; then he slowly limped along the boulevard Malesherbes. He turned into an adjacent street, donned the overcoat which he had carried on his arm, altered the shape of his hat, assumed an upright carriage, and, thus transformed, returned to a place whence he could watch the door of Mon. Destange's house.

In a few minutes Arsène Lupin came out, and proceeded to walk toward the center of Paris by way of the rues de Constantinople and London. Herlock Sholmes followed at a distance of a hundred paces.

Exciting moments for the Englishman! He sniffed the air, eagerly, like a hound following a fresh scent. It seemed to him a delightful thing thus to follow his adversary. It was no longer Herlock Sholmes who was being watched, but Arsène Lupin, the invisible Arsène Lupin. He held him, so to speak, within the grasp of his eye, by an imperceptible bond that nothing could break. And he was pleased to think that the quarry belonged to him.

But he soon observed a suspicious circumstance. In the intervening space between him and Arsène Lupin he noticed several people traveling in the same direction, particularly two husky fellows in slouch hats on the left side of the street, and two others on the right wearing caps and smoking cigarettes. Of course, their presence in that vicinity may have been the result of chance, but Sholmes was more astonished when he observed that the four men stopped when Lupin entered a tobacco shop; and still more surprised when the four men started again after Lupin emerged from the shop, each keeping to his own side of the street.

"Curse it!" muttered Sholmes; "he is being followed."

He was annoyed at the idea that others were on the trail of Arsène Lupin; that someone might deprive him, not of the glory—he cared little for that—but of the immense pleasure of capturing, single-handed, the most formidable enemy he had ever met. And he felt that he was not mistaken; the men presented to Sholmes' experienced eye the appearance and manner of those who, while regulating their gait to that of another, wish to present a careless and natural air.

"Is this some of Ganimard's work?" muttered Sholmes. "Is he playing me false?"

He felt inclined to speak to one of the men with a view of acting in concert with him; but as they were now approaching the boulevard the crowd was becoming denser, and he was afraid he might lose sight of Lupin. So he quickened his pace and turned into the boulevard just in time to see Lupin ascending the steps of the Hungarian restaurant at the corner of the rue du Helder. The door of the restaurant was open, so that Sholmes, while sitting on a bench on the other side of the boulevard, could see Lupin take a seat at a table, luxuriously appointed and decorated with flowers, at which three gentlemen and two ladies of elegant appearance were already seated and who extended to Lupin a hearty greeting.

Sholmes now looked about for the four men and perceived them amongst a crowd of people who were listening to a gipsy orchestra that was playing in a neighboring café. It was a curious thing that they were paying no attention to Arsène Lupin, but seemed to be friendly with the people around them. One of them took a cigarette from his pocket and approached a gentleman who wore a frock coat and silk hat. The gentleman offered the other his cigar for a light, and Sholmes had the impression that they talked to each other much longer than the occasion demanded. Finally the gentleman approached the Hungarian restaurant, entered and looked around. When he caught sight of Lupin he advanced and spoke to him for a moment, then took a seat at an adjoining table. Sholmes now recognized this gentleman as the horseman who had tried to run him down in the avenue Henri-Martin.

Then Sholmes understood that these men were not tracking Arsène Lupin; they were a part of his band. They were watching over his safety. They were his bodyguard, his satellites, his vigilant escort. Wherever danger threatened Lupin, these confederates were at hand to avert it, ready to defend him. The four men were accomplices. The gentleman in the frock coat was an accomplice. These facts furnished the Englishman with food for reflection. Would he ever succeed in capturing that inaccessible individual? What unlimited power was possessed by such an organization, directed by such a chief!

He tore a leaf from his notebook, wrote a few lines in pencil, which he placed in an envelope, and said to a boy about fifteen years of age who was sitting on the bench beside him:

"Here, my boy; take a carriage and deliver this letter to the cashier of the Suisse tavern, Place du Châtelet. Be quick!"

He gave him a five-franc piece. The boy disappeared.

A half hour passed away. The crowd had grown larger, and Sholmes perceived only at intervals the accomplices of Arsène Lupin. Then someone brushed against him and whispered in his ear:

"Well? what is it, Monsieur Sholmes?"

"Ah! it is you, Ganimard?"

"Yes; I received your note at the tavern. What's the matter?"

"He is there."

"What do you mean?"

"There ... in the restaurant. Lean to the right.... Do you see him now?"

"No."

"He is pouring a glass of champagne for the lady."

"That is not Lupin."

"Yes, it is."

"But I tell you.... Ah! yet, it may be. It looks a great deal like him," said Ganimard, naively. "And the others—accomplices?"

"No; the lady sitting beside him is Lady Cliveden; the other is the Duchess de Cleath. The gentleman sitting opposite Lupin is the Spanish Ambassador to London."

Ganimard took a step forward. Sholmes retained him.

"Be prudent. You are alone."

"So is he."

"No, he has a number of men on the boulevard mounting guard. And inside the restaurant that gentleman——"

"And I, when I take Arsène Lupin by the collar and announce his name, I shall have the entire room on my side and all the waiters."

"I should prefer to have a few policemen."

"But, Monsieur Sholmes, we have no choice. We must catch him when we can."

He was right; Sholmes knew it. It was better to take advantage of the opportunity and make the attempt. Sholmes simply gave this advice to Ganimard:

"Conceal your identity as long as possible."

Sholmes glided behind a newspaper kiosk, whence he could still watch Lupin, who was leaning toward Lady Cliveden, talking and smiling.

Ganimard crossed the street, hands in his pockets, as if he were going down the boulevard, but when he reached the opposite sidewalk he turned quickly and bounded up the steps of the restaurant. There was a shrill whistle. Ganimard ran against the head waiter, who had suddenly planted himself in the doorway and now pushed Ganimard back with a show of indignation, as if he were an intruder whose presence would bring disgrace upon the restaurant. Ganimard was surprised. At the same moment the gentleman in the frock coat came out. He took the part of the detective and entered into an exciting argument with the waiter; both of them hung on to Ganimard, one pushing him in, the other pushing him out in such a manner that, despite all his efforts and despite his furious protestations, the unfortunate detective soon found himself on the sidewalk.

The struggling men were surrounded by a crowd. Two policemen, attracted by the noise, tried to force their way through the crowd, but encountered a mysterious resistance and could make no headway through the opposing backs and pressing shoulders of the mob.

But suddenly, as if by magic, the crowd parted and the passage to the restaurant was clear. The head waiter, recognizing his mistake, was profuse in his apologies; the gentleman in the frock coat ceased his efforts on behalf of the detective, the crowd dispersed, the policemen passed on, and Ganimard hastened to the table at which the six guests were sitting. But now there were only five! He looked around.... The only exit was the door.

"The person who was sitting here!" he cried to the five astonished guests. "Where is he?"

"Monsieur Destro?"

"No; Arsène Lupin!"

A waiter approached and said:

"The gentleman went upstairs."

Ganimard rushed up in the hope of finding him. The upper floor of the restaurant contained private dining-rooms and had a private stairway leading to the boulevard.

"No use looking for him now," muttered Ganimard. "He is far away by this time."

He was not far away—two hundred yards at most—in the Madeleine-Bastille omnibus, which was rolling along very peacefully with its three horses across the Place de l'Opéra toward the Boulevard des Capucines. Two sturdy fellows were talking together on the platform. On the roof of the omnibus near the stairs an old fellow was sleeping; it was Herlock Sholmes.

With bobbing head, rocked by the movement of the vehicle, the Englishman said to himself:

"If Wilson could see me now, how proud he would be of his collaborator!... Bah! It was easy to foresee that the game was lost, as soon as the man whistled; nothing could be done but watch the exits and see that our man did not escape. Really, Lupin makes life exciting and interesting."

At the terminal point Herlock Sholmes, by leaning over, saw Arsène Lupin leaving the omnibus, and as he passed in front of the men who formed his bodyguard Sholmes heard him say: "A l'Etoile."

"A l'Etoile, exactly, a rendezvous. I shall be there," thought Sholmes. "I will follow the two men."

Lupin took an automobile; but the men walked the entire distance, followed by Sholmes. They stopped at a narrow house, No. 40 rue Chalgrin, and rang the bell. Sholmes took his position in the shadow of a doorway, whence he could watch the house in question. A man opened one of the windows of the ground floor and closed the shutters. But the shutters did not reach to the top of the window. The impost was clear.

At the end of ten minutes a gentleman rang at the same door and a few minutes later another man came. A short time afterward an automobile stopped in front of the house, bringing two passengers: Arsène Lupin and a lady concealed beneath a large cloak and a thick veil.

"The blonde Lady, no doubt," said Sholmes to himself, as the automobile drove away.

Herlock Sholmes now approached the house, climbed to the window-ledge and, by standing on tiptoe, he was able to see through the window above the shutters. What did he see?

Arsène Lupin, leaning against the mantel, was speaking with considerable animation. The others were grouped around him, listening to him attentively. Amongst them Sholmes easily recognized the gentleman in the frock coat and he thought one of the other men resembled the head-waiter of the restaurant. As to the blonde Lady, she was seated in an armchair with her back to the window.

"They are holding a consultation," thought Sholmes. "They are worried over the incident at the restaurant and are holding a council of war. Ah! what a master stroke it would be to capture all of them at one fell stroke!"

One of them, having moved toward the door, Sholmes leaped to the ground and concealed himself in the shadow. The gentleman in the frock coat and the head-waiter left the house. A moment later a light appeared at the windows of the first floor, but the shutters were closed immediately and the upper part of the house was dark as well as the lower.

"Lupin and the woman are on the ground floor; the two confederates live on the upper floor," said Sholmes.

Sholmes remained there the greater part of the night, fearing that if he went away Arsène Lupin might leave during his absence. At four o'clock, seeing two policemen at the end of the street, he approached them, explained the situation and left them to watch the house. He went to Ganimard's residence in the rue Pergolese and wakened him.

"I have him yet," said Sholmes.

"Arsène Lupin?"

"Yes."

"If you haven't got any better hold on him than you had a while ago, I might as well go back to bed. But we may as well go to the station-house."

They went to the police station in the rue Mesnil and from there to the residence of the commissary, Mon. Decointre. Then, accompanied by half a dozen policemen, they went to the rue Chalgrin.

"Anything new?" asked Sholmes, addressing the two policemen.

"Nothing."

It was just breaking day when, after taking necessary measures to prevent escape, the commissary rang the bell and commenced to question the concierge. The woman was greatly frightened at this early morning invasion, and she trembled as she replied that there were no tenants on the ground floor.

"What! not a tenant?" exclaimed Ganimard.

"No; but on the first floor there are two men named Leroux. They have furnished the apartment on the ground floor for some country relations."

"A gentleman and lady."

"Yes."

"Who came here last night."

"Perhaps ... but I don't know ... I was asleep. But I don't think so, for the key is here. They did not ask for it."

With that key the commissary opened the door of the ground-floor apartment. It comprised only two rooms and they were empty.

"Impossible!" exclaimed Sholmes. "I saw both of them in this room."

"I don't doubt your word," said the commissary; "but they are not here now."

"Let us go to the first floor. They must be there."

"The first floor is occupied by two men named Leroux."

"We will examine the Messieurs Leroux."

They all ascended the stairs and the commissary rang. At the second ring a man opened the door; he was in his shirt-sleeves. Sholmes recognized him as one of Lupin's bodyguard. The man assumed a furious air:

"What do you mean by making such a row at this hour of the morning ... waking people up...."

But he stopped suddenly, astounded.

"God forgive me!... really, gentlemen, I didn't notice who it was. Why, it is Monsieur Decointre!... and you, Monsieur Ganimard. What can I do for you!"

Ganimard burst into an uncontrollable fit of laughter, which caused him to bend double and turn black in the face.

"Ah! it is you, Leroux," he stammered. "Oh! this is too funny! Leroux, an accomplice of Arsène Lupin! Oh, I shall die! and your brother, Leroux, where is he?"

"Edmond!" called the man. "It is Ganimard, who has come to visit us."

Another man appeared and at sight of him Ganimard's mirth redoubled.

"Oh! oh! we had no idea of this! Ah! my friends, you are in a bad fix now. Who would have ever suspected it?"

Turning to Sholmes, Ganimard introduced the man:

"Victor Leroux, a detective from our office, one of the best men in the iron brigade ... Edmond Leroux, chief clerk in the anthropometric service."

V. AN ABDUCTION

Herlock Sholmes said nothing. To protest? To accuse the two men? That would be useless. In the absence of evidence which he did not possess and had no time to seek, no one would believe him. Moreover, he was stifled with rage, but would not display his feelings before the triumphant Ganimard. So he bowed respectfully to the brothers Leroux, guardians of society, and retired.

In the vestibule he turned toward a low door which looked like the entrance to a cellar, and picked up a small red stone; it was a garnet. When he reached the street he turned and read on the front of the house this inscription: "Lucien Destange, architect, 1877."

The adjoining house, No. 42, bore the same inscription.

"Always the double passage—numbers 40 and 42 have a secret means of communication. Why didn't I think of that? I should have remained with the two policemen."

He met the policemen near the corner and said to them:

"Two people came out of house No. 42 during my absence, didn't they?"

"Yes; a gentleman and lady."

Ganimard approached. Sholmes took his arm, and as they walked down the street he said:

"Monsieur Ganimard, you have had a good laugh and will no doubt forgive me for the trouble I have caused you."

"Oh! there's no harm done; but it was a good joke."

"I admit that; but the best jokes have only a short life, and this one can't last much longer."

"I hope not."

"This is now the seventh day, and I can remain only three days more. Then I must return to London."

"Oh!"

"I wish to ask you to be in readiness, as I may call on you at any hour on Tuesday or Wednesday night."

"For an expedition of the same kind as we had to-night?"

"Yes, monsieur, the very same."

"With what result?"

"The capture of Arsène Lupin," replied Sholmes.

"Do you think so?"

"I swear it, on my honor, monsieur."

Sholmes bade Ganimard good-bye and went to the nearest hotel for a few hours' sleep; after which, refreshed and with renewed confidence in himself, he returned to the rue Chalgrin, slipped two louis into the hand of the concierge, assured himself that the brothers Leroux had gone out, learned that the house belonged to a Monsieur Harmingeat, and, provided with a candle, descended to the cellar through the low door near which he had found the garnet. At the bottom of the stairs he found another exactly like it.

"I am not mistaken," he thought; "this is the means of communication. Let me see if my skeleton-key will open the cellar reserved for the tenant of the ground floor. Yes; it will. Now, I will examine those cases of wine... oh! oh! here are some places where the dust has been cleared away ... and some footprints on the ground...."

A slight noise caused him to listen attentively. Quickly he pushed the door shut, blew out his candle and hid behind a pile of empty wine cases. After a few seconds he noticed that a portion of the wall swung on a pivot, the light of a lantern was thrown into the cellar, an arm appeared, then a man entered.

He was bent over, as if he were searching for something. He felt in the dust with his fingers and several times he threw something into a cardboard box that he carried in his left hand. Afterward he obliterated the traces of his footsteps, as well as the footprints left by Lupin and the blonde lady, and he was about to leave the cellar by the same way as he had entered, when he uttered a harsh cry and fell to the ground. Sholmes had leaped upon him. It was the work of a moment, and in the simplest manner in the world the man found himself stretched on the ground, bound and handcuffed. The Englishman leaned over him and said:

"Have you anything to say?... To tell what you know?"

The man replied by such an ironical smile that Sholmes realized the futility of questioning him. So he contented himself by exploring the pockets of his captive, but he found only a bunch of keys, a handkerchief and the small cardboard box which contained a dozen garnets similar to those which Sholmes had found.

Then what was he to do with the man? Wait until his friends came to his help and deliver all of them to the police? What good would that do? What advantage would that give him over Lupin?

He hesitated; but an examination of the box decided the question. The box bore this name and address: "Leonard, jeweler, rue de la Paix."

He resolved to abandon the man to his fate. He locked the cellar and left the house. At a branch post office he sent a telegram to Monsieur Destange, saying that he could not come that day. Then he went to see the jeweler and, handing him the garnets, said:

"Madame sent me with these stones. She wishes to have them reset."

Sholmes had struck the right key. The jeweler replied:

"Certainly; the lady telephoned to me. She said she would be here to-day."

Sholmes established himself on the sidewalk to wait for the lady, but it was five o'clock when he saw a heavily-veiled lady approach and enter the store. Through the window he saw her place on the counter a piece of antique jewelry set with garnets.

She went away almost immediately, walking quickly and passed through streets that were unknown to the Englishman. As it was now almost dark, he walked close behind her and followed her into a five-story house of double flats and, therefore, occupied by numerous tenants. At the second floor she stopped and entered. Two minutes later the Englishman commenced to try the keys on the bunch he had taken from the man in the rue Chalgrin. The fourth key fitted the lock.

Notwithstanding the darkness of the rooms, he perceived that they were absolutely empty, as if unoccupied, and the various doors were standing open so that he could see all the apartments. At the end of a corridor he perceived a ray of light and, by approaching on tiptoe and looking through the glass door, he saw the veiled lady who had removed her hat and dress and was now wearing a velvet dressing-gown. The discarded garments were lying on the only chair in the room and a lighted lamp stood on the mantel.

Then he saw her approach the fireplace and press what appeared to be the button of an electric bell. Immediately the panel to the right of the fireplace moved and slowly glided behind the adjoining panel, thus disclosing an opening large enough for a person to pass through. The lady disappeared through this opening, taking the lamp with her.

The operation was a very simple one. Sholmes adopted it and followed the lady. He found himself in total darkness and immediately he felt his face brushed by some soft articles. He lighted a match and found that he was in a very small room completely filled with cloaks and dresses suspended on hangers. He picked his way through until he reached a door that was draped with a portiere. He peeped through and, behold, the blonde lady was there, under his eyes, and almost within reach of his hand.

She extinguished the lamp and turned on the electric lights. Then for the first time Herlock Sholmes obtained a good look at her face. He was amazed. The woman, whom he had overtaken after so much trouble and after so many tricks and maneuvers, was none other than Clotilde Destange.

Clotilde Destange, the assassin of the Baron d'Hautrec and the thief who stole the blue diamond! Clotilde Destange, the mysterious friend of Arsène Lupin! And the blonde lady!

"Yes, I am only a stupid ass," thought Herlock Sholmes at that moment. "Because Lupin's friend was a blonde and Clotilde is a brunette, I never dreamed that they were the same person. But how could the blonde lady remain a blonde after the murder of the baron and the theft of the diamond?"

Sholmes could see a portion of the room; it was a boudoir, furnished with the most delightful luxury and exquisite taste, and adorned with beautiful tapestries and costly ornaments. A mahogany couch, upholstered in silk, was located on the side of the room opposite the door at which Sholmes was standing. Clotilde was sitting on this couch, motionless, her face covered by her hands. Then he perceived that she was weeping. Great tears rolled down her pale cheeks and fell, drop by drop, on the velvet corsage. The tears came thick and fast, as if their source were inexhaustible.

A door silently opened behind her and Arsène Lupin entered. He looked at her for a long time without making his presence known; then he approached her, knelt at her feet, pressed her head to his breast, folded her in his arms, and his actions indicated an infinite measure of love and sympathy. For a time not a word was uttered, but her tears became less abundant.

"I was so anxious to make you happy," he murmured.

"I am happy."

"No; you are crying.... Your tears break my heart, Clotilde."

The caressing and sympathetic tone of his voice soothed her, and she listened to him with an eager desire for hope and happiness. Her features were softened by a smile, and yet how sad a smile! He continued to speak in a tone of tender entreaty:

"You should not be unhappy, Clotilde; you have no cause to be."

She displayed her delicate white hands and said, solemnly:

"Yes, Maxime; so long as I see those hands I shall be sad."

"Why?"

"They are stained with blood."

"Hush! Do not think of that!" exclaimed Lupin. "The dead is past and gone. Do not resurrect it."

And he kissed the long, delicate hand, while she regarded him with a brighter smile as if each kiss effaced a portion of that dreadful memory.

"You must love me, Maxime; you must—because no woman will ever love you as I do. For your sake, I have done many things, not at your order or request, but in obedience to your secret desires. I have done things at which my will and conscience revolted, but there was some unknown power that I could not resist. What I did I did involuntarily, mechanically, because it helped you, because you wished it ... and I am ready to do it again to-morrow ... and always."

"Ah, Clotilde," he said, bitterly, "why did I draw you into my adventurous life? I should have remained the Maxime Bermond that you loved five years ago, and not have let you know the ... other man that I am."

She replied in a low voice:

"I love the other man, also, and I have nothing to regret."

"Yes, you regret your past life—the free and happy life you once enjoyed."

"I have no regrets when you are here," she said, passionately. "All faults and crimes disappear when I see you. When you are away I may suffer, and weep, and be horrified at what I have done; but when you come it is all forgotten. Your love wipes it all away. And I am happy again.... But you must love me!"

"I do not love you on compulsion, Clotilde. I love you simply because ... I love you."

"Are you sure of it?"

"I am just as sure of my own love as I am of yours. Only my life is a very active and exciting one, and I cannot spend as much time with you as I would like—just now."

"What is it? Some new danger? Tell me!"

"Oh! nothing serious. Only...."

"Only what?" she asked.

"Well, he is on our track."

"Who? Herlock Sholmes?"

"Yes; it was he who dragged Ganimard into that affair at the Hungarian restaurant. It was he who instructed the two policemen to watch the house in the rue Chalgrin. I have proof of it. Ganimard searched the house this morning and Sholmes was with him. Besides——"

"Besides? What?"

"Well, there is another thing. One of our men is missing."

"Who?"

"Jeanniot."

"The concierge?"

"Yes."

"Why, I sent him to the rue Chalgrin this morning to pick up the garnets that fell out of my brooch."

"There is no doubt, then, that Sholmes caught him."

"No; the garnets were delivered to the jeweler in the rue de la Paix."

"Then, what has become of him!"

"Oh! Maxime, I am afraid."

"There is nothing to be afraid of, but I confess the situation is very serious. What does he know? Where does he hide himself? His isolation is his strong card. I cannot reach him."

"What are you going to do?"

"Act with extreme prudence, Clotilde. Some time ago I decided to change my residence to a safer place, and Sholmes' appearance on the scene has prompted me to do so at once. When a man like that is on your track, you must be prepared for the worst. Well, I am making my preparations. Day after to-morrow, Wednesday, I shall move. At noon it will be finished. At two o'clock I shall leave the place, after removing the last trace of our residence there, which will be no small matter. Until then——"

"Well?"

"Until then we must not see each other and no one must see you, Clotilde. Do not go out. I have no fear for myself, but I have for you."

"That Englishman cannot possibly reach me."

"I am not so sure of that. He is a dangerous man. Yesterday I came here to search the cupboard that contains all of Monsieur Destange's old papers and records. There is danger there. There is danger everywhere. I feel that he is watching us—that he is drawing his net around us closer and closer. It is one of those intuitions which never deceive me."

"In that case, Maxime, go, and think no more of my tears. I shall be brave, and wait patiently until the danger is past. Adieu, Maxime."

They held one another for some time in a last fond embrace. And it was she that gently pushed him outside. Sholmes could hear the sound of their voices in the distance.

Emboldened by the necessities of the situation and the urgent need of bringing his investigation to a speedy termination, Sholmes proceeded to make an examination of the house in which he now found himself. He passed through Clotilde's boudoir into a corridor, at the end of which there was a stairway leading to the lower floor; he was about to descend this stairway when he heard voices below, which caused him to change his route. He followed the corridor, which was a circular one, and discovered another stairway, which he descended and found himself amidst surroundings that bore a familiar appearance. He passed through a door that stood partly open and entered a large circular room. It was Monsieur Destange's library.

"Ah! splendid!" he exclaimed. "Now I understand everything. The boudoir of Mademoiselle Clotilde—the blonde Lady—communicates with a room in the adjoining house, and that house does not front on the Place Malesherbes, but upon an adjacent street, the rue Montchanin, if I remember the name correctly.... And I now understand how Clotilde Destange can meet her lover and at the same time create the impression that she never leaves the house; and I understand also how Arsène Lupin was enabled to make his mysterious entrance to the gallery last night. Ah! there must be another connection between the library and the adjoining room. One more house full of ways that are dark! And no doubt Lucien Destange was the architect, as usual!... I should take advantage of this opportunity to examine the contents of the cupboard and perhaps learn the location of other houses with secret passages constructed by Monsieur Destange."

Sholmes ascended to the gallery and concealed himself behind some draperies, where he remained until late in the evening. At last a servant came and turned off the electric lights. An hour later the Englishman, by the light of his lantern, made his way to the cupboard. As he had surmised, it contained the architect's old papers, plans, specifications and books of account. It also contained a series of registers, arranged according to date, and Sholmes, having selected those of the most recent dates, searched in the indexes for the name "Harmingeat." He found it in one of the registers with a reference to page 63. Turning to that page, he read:

"Harmingeat, 40 rue Chalgrin."

This was followed by a detailed account of the work done in and about the installation of a furnace in the house. And in the margin of the book someone had written these words: "See account M.B."

"Ah! I thought so!" said Sholmes; "the account M.B. is the one I want. I shall learn from it the actual residence of Monsieur Lupin."

It was morning before he found that important account. It comprised sixteen pages, one of which was a copy of the page on which was described the work done for Mon. Harmingeat of the rue Chalgrin. Another page described the work performed for Mon. Vatinel as owner of the house at No. 25 rue Clapeyron. Another page was reserved for the Baron d'Hautrec, 134 avenue Henri-Martin; another was devoted to the Château de Crozon, and the eleven other pages to various owners of houses in Paris.

Sholmes made a list of those eleven names and addresses; after which he returned the books to their proper places, opened a window, jumped out onto the deserted street and closed the shutters behind him.

When he reached his room at the hotel he lighted his pipe with all the solemnity with which he was wont to characterize that act, and amidst clouds of smoke he studied the deductions that might be drawn from the account of M.B., or rather, from the account of Maxime Bermond alias Arsène Lupin.

At eight o'clock he sent the following message to Ganimard:

"I expect to pass through the rue Pergolese this forenoon and will inform you of a person whose arrest is of the highest importance. In any event, be at home to-night and to-morrow until noon and have at least thirty men at your service."

Then he engaged an automobile at the stand on the boulevard, choosing one whose chauffeur looked good-natured but dull-witted, and instructed him to drive to the Place Malesherbes, where he stopped him about one hundred feet from Monsieur Destange's house.

"My boy, close your carriage," he said to the chauffeur; "turn up the collar of your coat, for the wind is cold, and wait patiently. At the end of an hour and a half, crank up your machine. When I return we will go to the rue Pergolese."

As he was ascending the steps leading to the door a doubt entered his mind. Was it not a mistake on his part to be spending his time on the affairs of the blonde Lady, while Arsène Lupin was preparing to move? Would he not be better engaged in trying to find the abode of his adversary amongst the eleven houses on his list?

"Ah!" he exclaimed, "when the blonde Lady becomes my prisoner, I shall be master of the situation."

And he rang the bell.

Monsieur Destange was already in the library. They had been working only a few minutes, when Clotilde entered, bade her father good morning, entered the adjoining parlor and sat down to write. From his place Sholmes could see her leaning over the table and from time to time absorbed in deep meditation. After a short time he picked up a book and said to Monsieur Destange:

"Here is a book that Mademoiselle Destange asked me to bring to her when I found it."

He went into the little parlor, stood before Clotilde in such a manner that her father could not see her, and said:

"I am Monsieur Stickmann, your father's new secretary."

"Ah!" said Clotilde, without moving, "my father has changed his secretary? I didn't know it."

"Yes, mademoiselle, and I desire to speak with you."

"Kindly take a seat, monsieur; I have finished."

She added a few words to her letter, signed it, enclosed it in the envelope, sealed it, pushed her writing material away, rang the telephone, got in communication with her dressmaker, asked the latter to hasten the completion of a traveling dress, as she required it at once, and then, turning to Sholmes, she said:

"I am at your service, monsieur. But do you wish to speak before my father? Would not that be better?"

"No, mademoiselle; and I beg of you, do not raise your voice. It is better that Monsieur Destange should not hear us."

"For whose sake is it better?"

"Yours, mademoiselle."

"I cannot agree to hold any conversation with you that my father may not hear."

"But you must agree to this. It is imperative."

Both of them arose, eye to eye. She said:

"Speak, monsieur."

Still standing, he commenced:

"You will be so good as to pardon me if I am mistaken on certain points of secondary importance. I will guarantee, however, the general accuracy of my statements."

"Can we not dispense with these preliminaries, monsieur? Or are they necessary?"

Sholmes felt the young woman was on her guard, so he replied:

"Very well; I will come to the point. Five years ago your father made the acquaintance of a certain young man called Maxime Bermond, who was introduced as a contractor or an architect, I am not sure which it was; but it was one or the other. Monsieur Destange took a liking to the young man, and as the state of his health compelled him to retire from active business, he entrusted to Monsieur Bermond the execution of certain orders he had received from some of his old customers and which seemed to come within the scope of Monsieur Bermond's ability."

Herlock Sholmes stopped. It seemed to him that the girl's pallor had increased. Yet there was not the slightest tremor in her voice when she said:

"I know nothing about the circumstances to which you refer, monsieur, and I do not see in what way they can interest me."

"In this way, mademoiselle: You know, as well as I, that Maxime Bermond is also known by the name of Arsène Lupin."

She laughed, and said:

"Nonsense! Arsène Lupin? Maxime Bermond is Arsène Lupin? Oh! no! It isn't possible!"

"I have the honor to inform you of that fact, and since you refuse to understand my meaning, I will add that Arsène Lupin has found in this house a friend—more than a friend—and accomplice, blindly and passionately devoted to him."

Without emotion, or at least with so little emotion that Sholmes was astonished at her self-control, she declared:

"I do not understand your object, monsieur, and I do not care to; but I command you to say no more and leave this house."

"I have no intention of forcing my presence on you," replied Sholmes, with equal sang-froid, "but I shall not leave this house alone."

"And who will accompany you, monsieur?"

"You will."

"I?"

"Yes, mademoiselle, we will leave this house together, and you will follow me without one word of protest."

The strange feature of the foregoing interview was the absolute coolness of the two adversaries. It bore no resemblance to an implacable duel between two powerful wills; but, judging solely from their attitude and the tone of their voices, an onlooker would have supposed their conversation to be nothing more serious than a courteous argument over some impersonal subject.

Clotilde resumed her seat without deigning to reply to the last remark of Herlock Sholmes, except by a shrug of her shoulders. Sholmes looked at his watch and said:

"It is half-past ten. We will leave here in five minutes."

"Perhaps."

"If not, I shall go to Monsieur Destange, and tell him——"

"What?"

"The truth. I will tell him of the vicious life of Maxime Bermond, and I will tell him of the double life of his accomplice."

"Of his accomplice?"

"Yes, of the woman known as the blonde Lady, of the woman who was blonde."

"What proofs will you give him?"

"I will take him to the rue Chalgrin, and show him the secret passage made by Arsène Lupin's workmen,—while doing the work of which he had the control—between the houses numbered 40 and 42; the passage which you and he used two nights ago."

"Well?"

"I will then take Monsieur Destange to the house of Monsieur Detinan; we will descend the servant's stairway which was used by you and Arsène Lupin when you escaped from Ganimard, and we will search together the means of communication with the adjoining house, which fronts on the Boulevard des Batignolles, and not upon the rue Clapeyron."

"Well?"

"I will take Monsieur Destange to the château de Crozon, and it will be easy for him, who knows the nature of the work performed by Arsène Lupin in the restoration of the Château, to discover the secret passages constructed there by his workmen. It will thus be established that those passages allowed the blonde Lady to make a nocturnal visit to the Countess' room and take the blue diamond from the mantel; and, two weeks later, by similar means, to enter the room of Herr Bleichen and conceal the blue diamond in his tooth-powder—a strange action, I confess; a woman's revenge, perhaps; but I don't know, and I don't care."

"Well?"

"After that," said Herlock Sholmes, in a more serious tone, "I will take Monsieur Destange to 134 avenue Henri-Martin, and we will learn how the Baron d'Hautrec——"

"No, no, keep quiet," stammered the girl, struck with a sudden terror, "I forbid you!... you dare to say that it was I ... you accuse me?..."

"I accuse you of having killed the Baron d'Hautrec."

"No, no, it is a lie."

"You killed the Baron d'Hautrec, mademoiselle. You entered his service under the name of Antoinette Bréhat, for the purpose of stealing the blue diamond and you killed him."

"Keep quiet, monsieur," she implored him. "Since you know so much, you must know that I did not murder the baron."

"I did not say that you murdered him, mademoiselle. Baron d'Hautrec was subject to fits of insanity that only Sister Auguste could control. She told me so herself. In her absence, he must have attacked you, and in the course of the struggle you struck him in order to save your own life. Frightened at your awful situation, you rang the bell, and fled without even taking the blue diamond from the finger of your victim. A few minutes later you returned with one of Arsène Lupin's accomplices, who was a servant in the adjoining house, you placed the baron on the bed, you put the room in order, but you were afraid to take the blue diamond. Now, I have told you what happened on that night. I repeat, you did not murder the baron, and yet it was your hand that struck the blow."

She had crossed them over her forehead—those long delicate white hands—and kept them thus for a long time. At last, loosening her fingers, she said, in a voice rent by anguish:

"And do you intend to tell all that to my father?"

"Yes; and I will tell him that I have secured as witnesses: Mademoiselle Gerbois, who will recognize the blonde Lady; Sister Auguste, who will recognize Antoinette Bréhat; and the Countess de Crozon, who will recognize Madame de Réal. That is what I shall tell him."

"You will not dare," she said, recovering her self-possession in the face of an immediate peril.

He arose, and made a step toward the library. Clotilde stopped him:

"One moment, monsieur."

She paused, reflected a moment, and then, perfect mistress of herself, said:

"You are Herlock Sholmes?"

"Yes."

"What do you want of me?"

"What do I want? I am fighting a duel with Arsène Lupin, and I must win. The contest is now drawing to a climax, and I have an idea that a hostage as precious as you will give me an important advantage over my adversary. Therefore, you will follow me, mademoiselle; I will entrust you to one of my friends. As soon as the duel is ended, you will be set at liberty."

"Is that all?"

"That is all. I do not belong to the police service of this country, and, consequently, I do not consider that I am under any obligation ... to cause your arrest."

She appeared to have come to a decision ... yet she required a momentary respite. She closed her eyes, the better to concentrate her thoughts. Sholmes looked at her in surprise; she was now so tranquil and, apparently, indifferent to the dangers which threatened her. Sholmes thought: Does she believe that she is in danger? Probably not—since Lupin protects her. She has confidence in him. She believes that Lupin is omnipotent, and infallible.

"Mademoiselle," he said, "I told you that we would leave here in five minutes. That time has almost expired."

"Will you permit me to go to my room, monsieur, to get some necessary articles?"

"Certainly, mademoiselle; and I will wait for you in the rue Montchanin. Jeanniot, the concierge, is a friend of mine."

"Ah! you know...." she said, visibly alarmed.

"I know many things."

"Very well. I will ring for the maid."

The maid brought her hat and jacket. Then Sholmes said:

"You must give Monsieur Destange some reason for our departure, and, if possible, let your excuse serve for an absence of several days."

"That shall not be necessary. I shall be back very soon."

"They exchanged defiant glances and an ironic smile.

"What faith you have in him!" said Sholmes.

"Absolute."

"He does everything well, doesn't he? He succeeds in everything he undertakes. And whatever he does receives your approval and cooperation."

"I love him," she said, with a touch of passion in her voice.

"And you think that he will save you?"

She shrugged her shoulders, and, approaching her father, she said:

"I am going to deprive you of Monsieur Stickmann. We are going to the National Library."

"You will return for luncheon?"

"Perhaps ... no, I think not ... but don't be uneasy."

Then she said to Sholmes, in a firm voice:

"I am at your service, monsieur."

"Absolutely?"

"Quite so."

"I warn you that if you attempt to escape, I shall call the police and have you arrested. Do not forget that the blonde Lady is on parole."

"I give you my word of honor that I shall not attempt to escape."

"I believe you. Now, let us go."

They left the house together, as he had predicted.

The automobile was standing where Sholmes had left it. As they approached it, Sholmes could hear the rumbling of the motor. He opened the door, asked Clotilde to enter, and took a seat beside her. The machine started at once, gained the exterior boulevards, the avenue Hoche and the avenue de la Grande-Armée. Sholmes was considering his plans. He thought:

"Ganimard is at home. I will leave the girl in his care. Shall I tell him who she is? No, he would take her to prison at once, and that would spoil everything. When I am alone, I can consult my list of addresses taken from the 'account M.B.,' and run them down. To-night, or to-morrow morning at the latest, I shall go to Ganimard, as I agreed, and deliver into his hands Arsène Lupin and all his band."

He rubbed his hand, gleefully, at the thought that his duel with Lupin was drawing to a close, and he could not see any serious obstacle in the way of his success. And, yielding to an irrepressible desire to give vent to his feelings—an unusual desire on his part—he exclaimed:

"Excuse me, mademoiselle, if I am unable to conceal my satisfaction and delight. The battle has been a difficult one, and my success is, therefore, more enjoyable."

"A legitimate success, monsieur, of which you have a just right to be proud."

"Thank you. But where are we going? The chauffeur must have misunderstood my directions."

At that moment they were leaving Paris by the gate de Neuilly. That was strange, as the rue Pergolese is not outside the fortifications. Sholmes lowered the glass, and said:

"Chauffeur, you have made a mistake.... Rue Pergolese!"

The man made no reply. Sholmes repeated, in a louder voice:

"I told you to go to the rue Pergolese."

Still the man did not reply.

"Ah! but you are deaf, my friend. Or is he doing it on purpose? We are very much out of our way.... Rue Pergolese!... Turn back at once!... Rue Pergolese!"

The chauffeur made no sign of having heard the order. The Englishman fretted with impatience. He looked at Clotilde; a mysterious smile played upon her lips.

"Why do you laugh?" he said. "It is an awkward mistake, but it won't help you."

"Of course not," she replied.

Then an idea occurred to him. He rose and made a careful scrutiny of the chauffeur. His shoulders were not so broad; his bearing was not so stiff and mechanical. A cold perspiration covered his forehead and his hands clenched with sudden fear, as his mind was seized with the conviction that the chauffeur was Arsène Lupin.

"Well, Monsieur Sholmes, what do you think of our little ride?"

"Delightful, monsieur, really delightful," replied Sholmes.

Never in his life had he experienced so much difficulty in uttering a few simple words without a tremor, or without betraying his feelings in his voice. But quickly, by a sort of reaction, a flood of hatred and rage burst its bounds, overcame his self-control, and, brusquely drawing his revolver, he pointed it at Mademoiselle Destange.

"Lupin, stop, this minute, this second, or I fire at mademoiselle."

"I advise you to aim at the cheek if you wish to hit the temple," replied Lupin, without turning his head.

"Maxime, don't go so fast," said Clotilde, "the pavement is slippery and I am very timid."

She was smiling; her eyes were fixed on the pavement, over which the carriage was traveling at enormous speed.

"Let him stop! Let him stop!" said Sholmes to her, wild with rage, "I warn you that I am desperate."

The barrel of the revolver brushed the waving locks of her hair. She replied, calmly:

"Maxime is so imprudent. He is going so fast, I am really afraid of some accident."

Sholmes returned the weapon to his pocket and seized the handle of the door, as if to alight, despite the absurdity of such an act. Clotilde said to him:

"Be careful, monsieur, there is an automobile behind us."

He leaned over. There was an automobile close behind; a large machine of formidable aspect with its sharp prow and blood-red body, and holding four men clad in fur coats.

"Ah! I am well guarded," thought Sholmes. "I may as well be patient."

He folded his arms across his chest with that proud air of submission so frequently assumed by heroes when fate has turned against them. And while they crossed the river Seine and rushed through Suresnes, Rueil and Chatou, motionless and resigned, controlling his actions and his passions, he tried to explain to his own satisfaction by what miracle Arsène Lupin had substituted himself for the chauffeur. It was quite improbable that the honest-looking fellow he had selected on the boulevard that morning was an accomplice placed there in advance. And yet Arsène Lupin had received a warning in some way, and it must have been after he, Sholmes, had approached Clotilde in the house, because no one could have suspected his project prior to that time. Since then, Sholmes had not allowed Clotilde out of his sight.

Then an idea struck him: the telephone communication desired by Clotilde and her conversation with the dressmaker. Now, it was all quite clear to him. Even before he had spoken to her, simply upon his request to speak to her as the new secretary of Monsieur Destange, she had scented the danger, surmised the name and purpose of the visitor, and, calmly, naturally, as if she were performing a commonplace action of her every-day life, she had called Arsène Lupin to her assistance by some preconcerted signal.

How Arsène Lupin had come and caused himself to be substituted for the chauffeur were matters of trifling importance. That which affected Sholmes, even to the point of appeasing his fury, was the recollection of that incident whereby an ordinary woman, a sweetheart it is true, mastering her nerves, controlling her features, and subjugating the expression of her eyes, had completely deceived the astute detective Herlock Sholmes. How difficult to overcome an adversary who is aided by such confederates, and who, by the mere force of his authority, inspires in a woman so much courage and strength!

They crossed the Seine and climbed the hill at Saint-Germain; but, some five hundred metres beyond that town, the automobile slackened its speed. The other automobile advanced, and the two stopped, side by side. There was no one else in the neighborhood.

"Monsieur Sholmes," said Lupin, "kindly exchange to the other machine. Ours is really a very slow one."

"Indeed!" said Sholmes, calmly, convinced that he had no choice.

"Also, permit me to loan you a fur coat, as we will travel quite fast and the air is cool. And accept a couple of sandwiches, as we cannot tell when we will dine."

The four men alighted from the other automobile. One of them approached, and, as he raised his goggles, Sholmes recognized in him the gentleman in the frock coat that he had seen at the Hungarian restaurant. Lupin said to him:

"You will return this machine to the chauffeur from whom I hired it. He is waiting in the first wine-shop to the right as you go up the rue Legendre. You will give him the balance of the thousand francs I promised him.... Ah! yes, kindly give your goggles to Monsieur Sholmes."

He talked to Mlle. Destange for a moment, then took his place at the wheel and started, with Sholmes at his side and one of his men behind him. Lupin had not exaggerated when he said "we will travel quite fast." From the beginning he set a breakneck pace. The horizon rushed to meet them, as if attracted by some mysterious force, and disappeared instantly as though swallowed up in an abyss, into which many other things, such as trees, houses, fields and forests, were hurled with the tumultuous fury and haste of a torrent as it approached the cataract.

Sholmes and Lupin did not exchange a word. Above their heads the leaves of the poplars made a great noise like the waves of the sea, rhythmically arranged by the regular spacing of the trees. And the towns swept by like spectres: Manteo, Vernon, Gaillon. From one hill to the other, from Bon-Secours to Canteleu, Rouen, its suburbs, its harbor, its miles of wharves, Rouen seemed like the straggling street of a country village. And this was Duclair, Caudebec, the country of Caux which they skimmed over in their terrific flight, and Lillebonne, and Quillebeuf. Then, suddenly, they found themselves on the banks of the Seine, at the extremity of a little wharf, beside which lay a staunch sea-going yacht that emitted great volumes of black smoke from its funnel.

The automobile stopped. In two hours they had traveled over forty leagues.

A man, wearing a blue uniform and a goldlaced cap, came forward and saluted. Lupin said to him:

"All ready, captain? Did you receive my telegram?"

"Yes, I got it."

"Is *The Swallow* ready?"

"Yes, monsieur."

"Come, Monsieur Sholmes."

The Englishman looked around, saw a group of people on the terrace in front of a café, hesitated a moment, then, realizing that before he could secure any assistance he would be seized, carried aboard and placed in the bottom of the hold, he crossed the gang-plank and followed Lupin into the captain's cabin. It was quite a large room, scrupulously clean, and presented a cheerful appearance with its varnished woodwork and polished brass. Lupin closed the door and addressed Sholmes abruptly, and almost rudely, as he said:

"Well, what do you know?"

"Everything."

"Everything? Come, be precise."

His voice contained no longer that polite, if ironical, tone, which he had affected when speaking to the Englishman. Now, his voice had the imperious tone of a master accustomed to command and accustomed to be obeyed—even by a Herlock Sholmes. They measured each other by their looks, enemies now—open and implacable foes. Lupin spoke again, but in a milder tone:

"I have grown weary of your pursuit, and do not intend to waste any more time in avoiding the traps you lay for me. I warn you that my treatment of you will depend on your reply. Now, what do you know?"

"Everything, monsieur."

Arsène Lupin controlled his temper and said, in a jerky manner:

"I will tell you what you know. You know that, under the name of Maxime Bermond, I have ... *improved* fifteen houses that were originally constructed by Monsieur Destange."

"Yes."

"Of those fifteen houses, you have seen four."

"Yes."

"And you have a list of the other eleven."

"Yes."

"You made that list at Monsieur Destange's house on that night, no doubt."

"Yes."

"And you have an idea that, amongst those eleven houses, there is one that I have kept for the use of myself and my friends, and you have intrusted to Ganimard the task of finding my retreat."

"No."

"What does that signify?"

"It signifies that I choose to act alone, and do not want his help."

"Then I have nothing to fear, since you are in my hands."

"You have nothing to fear as long as I remain in your hands."

"You mean that you will not remain?"

"Yes."

Arsène Lupin approached the Englishman and, placing his hand on the latter's shoulder, said:

"Listen, monsieur; I am not in a humor to argue with you, and, unfortunately for you, you are not in a position to choose. So let us finish our business."

"Very well."

"You are going to give me your word of honor that you will not try to escape from this boat until you arrive in English waters."

"I give you my word of honor that I shall escape if I have an opportunity," replied the indomitable Sholmes.

"But, sapristi! you know quite well that at a word from me you would soon be rendered helpless. All these men will obey me blindly. At a sign from me they would place you in irons——"

"Irons can be broken."

"And throw you overboard ten miles from shore."

"I can swim."

"I hadn't thought of that," said Lupin, with a laugh. "Excuse me, master ... and let us finish. You will agree that I must take the measures necessary to protect myself and my friends."

"Certainly; but they will be useless."

"And yet you do not wish me to take them."

"It is your duty."

"Very well, then."

Lupin opened the door and called the captain and two sailors. The latter seized the Englishman, bound him hand and foot, and tied him to the captain's bunk.

"That will do," said Lupin. "It was only on account of your obstinacy and the unusual gravity of the situation, that I ventured to offer you this indignity."

The sailors retired. Lupin said to the captain:

"Let one of the crew remain here to look after Monsieur Sholmes, and you can give him as much of your own company as possible. Treat him with all due respect and consideration. He is not a prisoner, but a guest. What time have you, captain?"

"Five minutes after two."

Lupin consulted his watch, then looked at the clock that was attached to the wall of the cabin.

"Five minutes past two is right. How long will it take you to reach Southampton?"

"Nine hours, easy going."

"Make it eleven. You must not land there until after the departure of the midnight boat, which reaches Havre at eight o'clock in the morning. Do you understand, captain? Let me repeat: As it would be very dangerous for all of us to permit Monsieur to return to France by that boat, you must not reach Southampton before one o'clock in the morning."

"I understand."

"Au revoir, master; next year, in this world or in the next."

"Until to-morrow," replied Sholmes.

A few minutes later Sholmes heard the automobile going away, and at the same time the steam puffed violently in the depths of *The Swallow*. The boat had started for England. About three o'clock the vessel left the mouth of the river and plunged into the open sea. At that moment Sholmes was lying on the captain's bunk, sound asleep.

Next morning—it being the tenth and last day of the duel between Sholmes and Lupin— the *Echo de France* published this interesting bit of news:

"Yesterday a judgment of ejectment was entered in the case of Arsène Lupin against Herlock Sholmes, the English detective. Although signed at noon, the judgment was executed the same day. At one o'clock this morning Sholmes was landed at Southampton."

VI. SECOND ARREST OF ARSÈNE LUPIN

Since eight o'clock a dozen moving-vans had encumbered the rue Crevaux between the avenue du Bois-de-Boulogne and the avenue Bugeaud. Mon. Felix Davey was leaving the apartment in which he lived on the fourth floor of No. 8; and Mon. Dubreuil, who had united into a single apartment the fifth floor of the same house and the fifth floor of the two adjoining houses, was moving on the same day—a mere coincidence, since the gentlemen were unknown to each other—the vast collection of furniture regarding which so many foreign agents visited him every day.

A circumstance which had been noticed by some of the neighbors, but was not spoken of until later, was this: None of the twelve vans bore the name and address of the owner, and none of the men accompanying them visited the neighboring wine shops. They worked so diligently that the furniture was all out by eleven o'clock. Nothing remained but those scraps of papers and rags that are always left behind in the corners of the empty rooms.

Mon. Felix Davey, an elegant young man, dressed in the latest fashion, carried in his hand a walking-stick, the weight of which indicated that its owner possessed extraordinary biceps—Mon. Felix Davey walked calmly away and took a seat on a bench in the avenue du Bois-de-Boulogne facing the rue Pergolese. Close to him a woman, dressed in a neat but inexpensive costume, was reading a newspaper, whilst a child was playing with a shovel in a heap of sand.

After a few minutes Felix Davey spoke to the woman, without turning his head:

"Ganimard!"

"Went out at nine o'clock this morning."

"Where?"

"To police headquarters."

"Alone?"

"Yes."

"No telegram during the night?"

"No."

"Do they suspect you in the house?"

"No; I do some little things for Madame Ganimard, and she tells me everything her husband does. I have been with her all morning."

"Very well. Until further orders come here every day at eleven o'clock."

He rose and walked away in the direction of the Dauphine gate, stopping at the Chinese pavilion, where he partook of a frugal repast consisting of two eggs, with some fruit and vegetables. Then he returned to the rue Crevaux and said to the concierge:

"I will just glance through the rooms and then give you the keys."

He finished his inspection of the room that he had used as a library; then he seized the end of a gas-pipe, which hung down the side of the chimney. The pipe was bent and a hole made in the elbow. To this hole he fitted a small instrument in the form of an ear-trumpet and blew into it. A slight whistling sound came by way of reply. Placing the trumpet to his mouth, he said:

"Anyone around, Dubreuil?"

"No."

"May I come up!"

"Yes."

He returned the pipe to its place, saying to himself:

"How progressive we are! Our century abounds with little inventions which render life really charming and picturesque. And so amusing!... especially when a person knows how to enjoy life as I do."

He turned one of the marble mouldings of the mantel, and the entire half of the mantel moved, and the mirror above it glided in invisible grooves, disclosing an opening and the lower steps of a stairs built in the very body of the chimney; all very clean and complete— the stairs were constructed of polished metal and the walls of white tiles. He ascended the steps, and at the fifth floor there was the same opening in the chimney. Mon. Dubreuil was waiting for him.

"Have you finished in your rooms?"

"Yes."

"Everything cleared out?"

"Yes."

"And the people?"

"Only the three men on guard."

"Very well; come on."

They ascended to the upper floor by the same means, one after the other, and there found three men, one of whom was looking through the window.

"Anything new?"

"Nothing, governor."

"All quiet in the street?"

"Yes."

"In ten minutes I will be ready to leave. You will go also. But in the meantime if you see the least suspicious movement in the street, warn me."

"I have my finger on the alarm-bell all the time."

"Dubreuil, did you tell the moving men not to touch the wire of that bell?"

"Certainly; it is working all right."

"That is all I want to know."

The two gentlemen then descended to the apartment of Felix Davey and the latter, after adjusting the marble mantel, exclaimed, joyfully:

"Dubreuil, I should like to see the man who is able to discover all the ingenious devices, warning bells, net-works of electric wires and acoustic tubes, invisible passages, moving floors and hidden stairways. A real fairy-land!"

"What fame for Arsène Lupin!"

"Fame I could well dispense with. It's a pity to be compelled to leave a place so well equipped, and commence all over again, Dubreuil ... and on a new model, of course, for it would never do to duplicate this. Curse Herlock Sholmes!"

"Has he returned to Paris?"

"How could he? There has been only one boat come from Southampton and it left there at midnight; only one train from Havre, leaving there at eight o'clock this morning and due in Paris at eleven fifteen. As he could not catch the midnight boat at Southampton—and the instructions to the captain on that point were explicit—he cannot reach France until this evening via Newhaven and Dieppe."

"Do you think he will come back?"

"Yes; he never gives up. He will return to Paris; but it will be too late. We will be far away."

"And Mademoiselle Destange?"

"I am to see her in an hour."

"At her house?"

"Oh! no; she will not return there for several days. But you, Dubreuil, you must hurry. The loading of our goods will take a long time and you should be there to look after them."

"Are you sure that we are not being watched?"

"By whom? I am not afraid of anyone but Sholmes."

Dubreuil retired. Felix Davey made a last tour of the apartment, picked up two or three torn letters, then, noticing a piece of chalk, he took it and, on the dark paper of the drawing-room, drew a large frame and wrote within it the following:

"*Arsène Lupin, gentleman-burglar, lived here for five years at the beginning of the twentieth century.*"

This little pleasantry seemed to please him very much. He looked at it for a moment, whistling a lively air, then said to himself:

"Now that I have placed myself in touch with the historians of future generations, I can go. You must hurry, Herlock Sholmes, as I shall leave my present abode in three minutes, and your defeat will be an accomplished fact.... Two minutes more! you are keeping me waiting, Monsieur Sholmes.... One minute more! Are you not coming? Well, then, I proclaim your downfall and my apotheosis. And now I make my escape. Farewell, kingdom of Arsène Lupin! I shall never see you again. Farewell to the fifty-five rooms of the six apartments over which I reigned! Farewell, my own royal bed chamber!"

His outburst of joy was interrupted by the sharp ringing of a bell, which stopped twice, started again and then ceased. It was the alarm bell.

What was wrong? What unforeseen danger? Ganimard? No; that wasn't possible!

He was on the point of returning to his library and making his escape. But, first, he went to the window. There was no one in the street. Was the enemy already in the house? He listened and thought he could discern certain confused sounds. He hesitated no longer. He ran to his library, and as he crossed the threshold he heard the noise of a key being inserted in the lock of the vestibule door.

"The deuce!" he murmured; "I have no time to lose. The house may be surrounded. The servants' stairway—impossible! Fortunately, there is the chimney."

He pushed the moulding; it did not move. He made a greater effort—still it refused to move. At the same time he had the impression that the door below opened and that he could hear footsteps.

"Good God!" he cried; "I am lost if this cursed mechanism—"

He pushed with all his strength. Nothing moved—nothing! By some incredible accident, by some evil stroke of fortune, the mechanism, which had worked only a few moments ago, would not work now.

He was furious. The block of marble remained immovable. He uttered frightful imprecations on the senseless stone. Was his escape to be prevented by that stupid obstacle? He struck the marble wildly, madly; he hammered it, he cursed it.

"Ah! what's the matter, Monsieur Lupin? You seem to be displeased about something."

Lupin turned around. Herlock Sholmes stood before him!

Herlock Sholmes!... Lupin gazed at him with squinting eyes as if his sight were defective and misleading. Herlock Sholmes in Paris! Herlock Sholmes, whom he had shipped to England only the day before as a dangerous person, now stood before him free and victorious!... Ah! such a thing was nothing less than a miracle; it was contrary to all natural laws; it was the culmination of all that is illogical and abnormal.... Herlock Sholmes here—before his face!

And when the Englishman spoke his words were tinged with that keen sarcasm and mocking politeness with which his adversary had so often lashed him. He said:

"Monsieur Lupin, in, the first place I have the honor to inform you that at this time and place I blot from my memory forever all thoughts of the miserable night that you forced me to endure in the house of Baron d'Hautrec, of the injury done to my friend Wilson, of my abduction in the automobile, and of the voyage I took yesterday under your orders, bound to a very uncomfortable couch. But the joy of this moment effaces all those bitter memories. I forgive everything. I forget everything—I wipe out the debt. I am paid—and royally paid."

Lupin made no reply. So the Englishman continued:

"Don't you think so yourself?"

He appeared to insist as if demanding an acquiescence, as a sort of receipt in regard to the part.

After a moment's reflection, during which the Englishman felt that he was scrutinized to the very depth of his soul, Lupin declared:

"I presume, monsieur, that your conduct is based upon serious motives?"

"Very serious."

"The fact that you have escaped from my captain and his crew is only a secondary incident of our struggle. But the fact that you are here before me alone—understand, alone —face to face with Arsène Lupin, leads me to think that your revenge is as complete as possible."

"As complete as possible."

"This house?"

"Surrounded."

"The two adjoining houses?"

"Surrounded."

"The apartment above this?"

"The *three* apartments on the fifth floor that were formerly occupied by Monsieur Dubreuil are surrounded."

"So that——"

"So that you are captured, Monsieur Lupin—absolutely captured."

The feelings that Sholmes had experienced during his trip in the automobile were now suffered by Lupin, the same concentrated fury, the same revolt, and also, let us admit, the same loyalty of submission to force of circumstances. Equally brave in victory or defeat.

"Our accounts are squared, monsieur," said Lupin, frankly.

The Englishman was pleased with that confession. After a short silence Lupin, now quite self-possessed, said smiling:

"And I am not sorry! It becomes monotonous to win all the time. Yesterday I had only to stretch out my hand to finish you forever. Today I belong to you. The game is yours." Lupin laughed heartily and then continued: "At last the gallery will be entertained! Lupin in prison! How will he get out? In prison!... What an adventure!... Ah! Sholmes, life is just one damn thing after another!"

He pressed his closed hands to his temples as if to suppress the tumultuous joy that surged within him, and his actions indicated that he was moved by an uncontrollable mirth. At last, when he had recovered his self-possession, he approached the detective and said:

"And now what are you waiting for?"

"What am I waiting for?"

"Yes; Ganimard is here with his men—why don't they come in?"

"I asked him not to."

"And he consented?"

"I accepted his services on condition that he would be guided by me. Besides, he thinks that Felix Davey is only an accomplice of Arsène Lupin."

"Then I will repeat my question in another form. Why did you come in alone?"

"Because I wished to speak to you alone."

"Ah! ah! you have something to say to me."

That idea seemed to please Lupin immensely. There are certain circumstances in which words are preferable to deeds.

"Monsieur Sholmes, I am sorry I cannot offer you an easy chair. How would you like that broken box? Or perhaps you would prefer the window ledge? I am sure a glass of beer would be welcome ... light or dark?... But sit down, please."

"Thank you; we can talk as well standing up."

"Very well—proceed."

"I will be brief. The object of my sojourn in France was not to accomplish your arrest. If I have been led to pursue you, it was because I saw no other way to achieve my real object."

"Which was?"

"To recover the blue diamond."

"The blue diamond!"

"Certainly; since the one found in Herr Bleichen's tooth-powder was only an imitation."

"Quite right; the genuine diamond was taken by the blonde Lady. I made an exact duplicate of it and then, as I had designs on other jewels belonging to the Countess and as the Consul Herr Bleichen was already under suspicion, the aforesaid blonde Lady, in order to avert suspicion, slipped the false stone into the aforesaid Consul's luggage."

"While you kept the genuine diamond?"

"Of course."

"That diamond—I want it."

"I am very sorry, but it is impossible."

"I have promised it to the Countess de Crozon. I must have it."

"How will you get it, since it is in my possession?"

"That is precisely the reason—because it is in your possession."

"Oh! I am to give it to you?"

"Yes."

"Voluntarily?"

"I will buy it."

"Ah!" exclaimed Lupin, in an access of mirth, "you are certainly an Englishman. You treat this as a matter of business."

"It is a matter of business."

"Well? what is your offer?"

"The liberty of Mademoiselle Destange."

"Her liberty?... I didn't know she was under arrest."

"I will give Monsieur Ganimard the necessary information. When deprived of your protection, she can readily be taken."

Lupin laughed again, and said:

"My dear monsieur, you are offering me something you do not possess. Mademoiselle Destange is in a place of safety, and has nothing to fear. You must make me another offer."

The Englishman hesitated, visibly embarrassed and vexed. Then, placing his hand on the shoulder of his adversary, he said:

"And if I should propose to you-"

"My liberty?"

"No ... but I can leave the room to consult with Ganimard."

"And leave me alone!"

"Yes."

"Ah! mon dieu, what good would that be? The cursed mechanism will not work," said

Lupin, at the same time savagely pushing the moulding of the mantel. He stifled a cry of surprise; this time fortune favored him—the block of marble moved. It was his salvation; his hope of escape. In that event, why submit to the conditions imposed by Sholmes? He paced up and down the room, as if he were considering his reply. Then, in his turn, he placed his hand on the shoulder of his adversary, and said:

"All things considered, Monsieur Sholmes, I prefer to do my own business in my own way."

"But—"

"No, I don't require anyone's assistance."

"When Ganimard gets his hand on you, it will be all over. You can't escape from them."

"Who knows?"

"Come, that is foolish. Every door and window is guarded."

"Except one."

"Which?"

"*The one I will choose.*"

"Mere words! Your arrest is as good as made."

"Oh! no—not at all."

"Well?"

"I shall keep the blue diamond."

Sholmes looked at his watch, and said:

"It is now ten minutes to three. At three o'clock I shall call Ganimard."

"Well, then, we have ten minutes to chat. And to satisfy my curiosity, Monsieur Sholmes, I should like to know how you procured my address and my name of Felix Davey?"

Although his adversary's easy manner caused Sholmes some anxiety, he was willing to give Lupin the desired information since it reflected credit on his professional astuteness; so he replied:

"Your address? I got it from the blonde Lady."

"Clotilde!"

"Herself. Do you remember, yesterday morning, when I wished to take her away in the automobile, she telephoned to her dressmaker."

"Well?"

"Well, I understood, later, that you were the dressmaker. And last night, on the boat, by exercising my memory—and my memory is something I have good reason to be proud of—I was able to recollect the last two figures of your telephone number—73. Then, as I possessed a list of the houses you had 'improved,' it was an easy matter, on my arrival in Paris at eleven o'clock this morning, to search in the telephone directory and find there the name and address of Felix Davey. Having obtained that information, I asked the aid of Monsieur Ganimard."

"Admirable! I congratulate you. But bow did you manage to catch the eight o'clock train at Havre! How did you escape from *The Swallow*?"

"I did not escape."

"But——"

"You ordered the captain not to reach Southampton before one o'clock. He landed me there at midnight. I was able to catch the twelve o'clock boat for Havre."

"Did the captain betray me? I can't believe it."

"No, he did not betray you."

"Well, what then?"

"It was his watch."

"His watch?"

"Yes, I put it ahead one hour."

"How?"

"In the usual way, by turning the hands. We were sitting side by side, talking, and I was telling him some funny stories.... Why! he never saw me do it."

"Bravo! a very clever trick. I shall not forget it. But the clock that was hanging on the wall of the cabin?"

"Ah! the clock was a more difficult matter, as my feet were tied, but the sailor, who guarded me during the captain's absence, was kind enough to turn the hands for me."

"He? Nonsense! He wouldn't do it."

"Oh! but he didn't know the importance of his act. I told him I must catch the first train for London, at any price, and ... he allowed himself to be persuaded——"

"By means of——"

"By means of a slight gift, which the excellent fellow, loyal and true to his master, intends to send to you."

"What was it!"

"A mere trifle."

"But what?"

"The blue diamond."

"The blue diamond!"

"Yes, the false stone that you substituted for the Countess' diamond. She gave it to me."

There was a sudden explosion of violent laughter. Lupin laughed until the tears started in his eyes.

"Mon dieu, but it is funny! My false diamond palmed off on my innocent sailor! And the captain's watch! And the hands of the clock!"

Sholmes felt that the duel between him and Lupin was keener than ever. His marvelous instinct warned him that, behind his adversary's display of mirth, there was a shrewd intellect debating the ways and means to escape. Gradually Lupin approached the Englishman, who recoiled, and, unconsciously, slipped his hand into his watch-pocket.

"It is three o'clock, Monsieur Lupin."

"Three o'clock, already! What a pity! We were enjoying our chat so much."

"I am waiting for your answer."

"My answer? Mon dieu! but you are particular!... And so this is the last move in our little game—and the stake is my liberty!"

"Or the blue diamond."

"Very well. It's your play. What are you going to do!"

"I play the king," said Sholmes, as he fired his revolver.

"And I the ace," replied Lupin, as he struck at Sholmes with his fist.

Sholmes had fired into the air, as a signal to Ganimard, whose assistance he required. But Lupin's fist had caught Sholmes in the stomach, and caused him to double up with pain. Lupin rushed to the fireplace and set the marble slab in motion.... Too late! The door opened.

"Surrender, Lupin, or I fire!"

Ganimard, doubtless stationed closer than Lupin had thought, Ganimard was there, with his revolver turned on Lupin. And behind Ganimard there were twenty men, strong and ruthless fellows, who would beat him like a dog at the least sign of resistance.

"Hands down! I surrender!" said Lupin, calmly; and he folded his arms across his breast.

Everyone was amazed. In the room, divested of its furniture and hangings, Arsène Lupin's words sounded like an echo.... "I surrender!" ... It seemed incredible. No one would have been astonished if he had suddenly vanished through a trap, or if a section of the wall had rolled away and allowed him to escape. But he surrendered!

Ganimard advanced, nervously, and with all the gravity that the importance of the occasion demanded, he placed his hand on the shoulder of his adversary, and had the infinite pleasure of saying:

"I arrest you, Arsène Lupin."

"Brrr!" said Lupin, "you make me shiver, my dear Ganimard. What a lugubrious face! One would imagine you were speaking over the grave of a friend. For Heaven's sake, don't assume such a funereal air."

"I arrest you."

"Don't let that worry you! In the name of the law, of which he is a well-deserving pillar, Ganimard, the celebrated Parisian detective, arrests the wicked Arsène Lupin. An historic event, of which you will appreciate the true importance.... And it is the second time that it has happened. Bravo, Ganimard, you are sure of advancement in your chosen profession!"

And he held out his wrists for the hand-cuffs. Ganimard adjusted them in a most solemn manner. The numerous policemen, despite their customary presumption and the bitterness of their feelings toward Lupin, conducted themselves with becoming modesty, astonished at being permitted to gaze upon that mysterious and intangible creature.

"My poor Lupin," sighed our hero, "what would your aristocratic friends say if they should see you in this humiliating position?"

He pulled his wrists apart with all his strength. The veins in his forehead expanded. The links of the chain cut into his flesh. The chain fell off—broken.

"Another, comrades, that one was useless."

They placed two on him this time.

"Quite right," he said. "You cannot be too careful."

Then, counting the detectives and policemen, he said:

"How many are you, my friends? Twenty-five? Thirty? That's too many. I can't do anything. Ah! if there had been only fifteen!"

There was something fascinating about Lupin; it was the fascination of the great actor who plays his rôle with spirit and understanding, combined with assurance and ease. Sholmes regarded him as one might regard a beautiful painting with a due appreciation of all its perfection in coloring and technique. And he really thought that it was an equal struggle between those thirty men on one side, armed as they were with all the strength and majesty of the law, and, on the other side, that solitary individual, unarmed and handcuffed. Yes, the two sides were well-matched.

"Well, master," said Lupin to the Englishman, "this is your work. Thanks to you, Lupin is going to rot on the damp straw of a dungeon. Confess that your conscience pricks you a little, and that your soul is filled with remorse."

In spite of himself, Sholmes shrugged his shoulders, as if to say: "It's your own fault."

"Never! never!" exclaimed Lupin. "Give you the blue diamond? Oh! no, it has cost me too much trouble. I intend to keep it. On my occasion of my first visit to you in London—which will probably be next month—I will tell you my reasons. But will you be in London next month? Or do you prefer Vienna? Or Saint Petersburg?"

Then Lupin received a surprise. A bell commenced to ring. It was not the alarm-bell, but the bell of the telephone which was located between the two windows of the room and had not yet been removed.

The telephone! Ah! Who could it be? Who was about to fall into this unfortunate trap? Arsène Lupin exhibited an access of rage against the unlucky instrument as if he would like to break it into a thousand pieces and thus stifle the mysterious voice that was calling for him. But it was Ganimard who took down the receiver, and said:

"Hello!... Hello!... number 648.73 ... yes, this is it."

Then Sholmes stepped up, and, with an air of authority, pushed Ganimard aside, took the receiver, and covered the transmitter with his handkerchief in order to obscure the tone of his voice. At that moment he glanced toward Lupin, and the look which they exchanged indicated that the same idea had occurred to each of them, and that they foresaw the ultimate result of that theory: it was the blonde Lady who was telephoning. She wished to telephone to Felix Davey, or rather to Maxime Bermond, and it was to Sholmes she was about to speak. The Englishman said:

"Hello ... Hello!"

Then, after a silence, he said:

"Yes, it is I, Maxime."

The drama had commenced and was progressing with tragic precision. Lupin, the irrepressible and nonchalant Lupin, did not attempt to conceal his anxiety, and he strained every nerve in a desire to hear or, at least, to divine the purport of the conversation. And Sholmes continued, in reply to the mysterious voice:

"Hello!... Hello!... Yes, everything has been moved, and I am just ready to leave here and meet you as we agreed.... Where?... Where you are now.... Don't believe that he is here yet!..."

Sholmes stopped, seeking for words. It was clear that he was trying to question the girl without betraying himself, and that he was ignorant of her whereabouts. Moreover, Ganimard's presence seemed to embarrass him.... Ah! if some miracle would only interrupt that cursed conversation! Lupin prayed for it with all his strength, with all the intensity of his incited nerves! After a momentary pause, Sholmes continued:

"Hello!... Hello!... Do you hear me?... I can't hear you very well.... Can scarcely make out what you say.... Are you listening? Well, I think you had better return home.... No danger now.... But he is in England! I have received a telegram from Southampton announcing his arrival."

The sarcasm of those words! Sholmes uttered them with an inexpressible comfort. And he added:

"Very well, don't lose any time. I will meet you there."

He hung up the receiver.

"Monsieur Ganimard, can you furnish me with three men?"

"For the blonde Lady, eh?"

"Yes."

"You know who she is, and where she is?"

"Yes."

"Good! That settles Monsieur Lupin.... Folenfant, take two men, and go with Monsieur Sholmes."

The Englishman departed, accompanied by the three men.

The game was ended. The blonde Lady was, also, about to fall into the hands of the Englishman. Thanks to his commendable persistence and to a combination of fortuitous circumstances, the battle had resulted in a victory for the detective, and in irreparable disaster for Lupin.

"Monsieur Sholmes!"

The Englishman stopped.

"Monsieur Lupin?"

Lupin was clearly shattered by this final blow. His forehead was marked by deep wrinkles. He was sullen and dejected. However, he pulled himself together, and, notwithstanding his defeat, he exclaimed, in a cheerful tone:

"You will concede that fate has been against me. A few minutes ago, it prevented my escape through that chimney, and delivered me into your hands. Now, by means of the telephone, it presents you with the blonde Lady. I submit to its decrees."

"What do you mean?"

"I mean that I am ready to re-open our negotiation."

Sholmes took Ganimard aside and asked, in a manner that did not permit a reply, the authority to exchange a few words with the prisoner. Then he approached Lupin, and said, in a sharp, nervous tone:

"What do you want?"

"Mademoiselle Destange's liberty."

"You know the price."

"Yes."

"And you accept?"

"Yes; I accept your terms."

"Ah!" said the Englishman, in surprise, "but ... you refused ... for yourself——"

"Yes, I can look out for myself, Monsieur Sholmes, but now the question concerns a young woman ... and a woman I love. In France, understand, we have very decided ideas about such things. And Lupin has the same feelings as other people."

He spoke with simplicity and candor. Sholmes replied by an almost imperceptible inclination of his head, and murmured:

"Very well, the blue diamond."

"Take my cane, there, at the end of the mantel. Press on the head of the cane with one hand, and, with the other, turn the iron ferrule at the bottom."

Holmes took the cane and followed the directions. As he did so, the head of the cane divided and disclosed a cavity which contained a small ball of wax which, in turn, enclosed a diamond. He examined it. It was the blue diamond.

"Monsieur Lupin, Mademoiselle Destange is free."

"Is her future safety assured? Has she nothing to fear from you?"

"Neither from me, nor anyone else."

"How can you manage it?"

"Quite easily. I have forgotten her name and address."

"Thank you. And au revoir—for I will see you again, sometime, Monsieur Sholmes?"

"I have no doubt of it."

Then followed an animated conversation between Sholmes and Ganimard, which was abruptly terminated by the Englishman, who said:

"I am very sorry, Monsieur Ganimard, that we cannot agree on that point, but I have no time to waste trying to convince you. I leave for England within an hour."

"But ... the blonde Lady?"

"I do not know such a person."

"And yet, a moment ago——"

"You must take the affair as it stands. I have delivered Arsène Lupin into your hands. Here is the blue diamond, which you will have the pleasure of returning to the Countess de Crozon. What more do you want?"

"The blonde Lady."

"Find her."

Sholmes pulled his cap down over his forehead and walked rapidly away, like a man who is accustomed to go as soon as his business is finished.

"Bon voyage, monsieur," cried Lupin, "and, believe me, I shall never forget the friendly way in which our little business affairs have been arranged. My regards to Monsieur Wilson."

Not receiving any reply, Lupin added, sneeringly:

"That is what is called 'taking British leave.' Ah! their insular dignity lacks the flower of courtesy by which we are distinguished. Consider for a moment, Ganimard, what a charming exit a Frenchman would have made under similar circumstances! With what exquisite courtesy he would have masked his triumph!... But, God bless me, Ganimard, what are you doing? Making a search? Come, what's the use? There is nothing left—not even a scrap of paper. I assure you my archives are in a safe place."

"I am not so sure of that," replied Ganimard. "I must search everything."

Lupin submitted to the operation. Held by two detectives and surrounded by the others, he patiently endured the proceedings for twenty minutes, then he said:

"Hurry up, Ganimard, and finish!"

"You are in a hurry."

"Of course I am. An important appointment."

"At the police station?"

"No; in the city."

"Ah! at what time?"

"Two o'clock."

"It is three o'clock now."

"Just so; I will be late. And punctuality is one of my virtues."

"Well, give me five minutes."

"Not a second more," said Lupin.

"I am doing my best to expedite——"

"Oh! don't talk so much.... Still searching that cupboard? It is empty."

"Here are some letters."

"Old invoices, I presume!"

"No; a packet tied with a ribbon."

"A red ribbon? Oh! Ganimard, for God's sake, don't untie it!"

"From a woman?"

"Yes."

"A woman of the world?"

"The best in the world."

"Her name?"

"Madame Ganimard."

"Very funny! very funny!" exclaimed the detective.

At that moment the men, who had been sent to search the other rooms, returned and announced their failure to find anything. Lupin laughed and said:

"Parbleu! Did you expect to find my visiting list, or evidence of my business relations with the Emperor of Germany? But I can tell you what you should investigate, Ganimard: All the little mysteries of this apartment. For instance, that gas-pipe is a speaking tube. That chimney contains a stairway. That wall is hollow. And the marvelous system of bells! Ah! Ganimard, just press that button!"

Ganimard obeyed.

"Did you hear anything?" asked Lupin.

"No."

"Neither did I. And yet you notified my aeronaut to prepare the dirigible balloon which will soon carry us into the clouds.

"Come!" said Ganimard, who had completed his search; "we've had enough nonsense —let's be off."

He started away, followed by his men. Lupin did not move. His guardians pushed him in vain.

"Well," said Ganimard, "do you refuse to go?"

"Not at all. But it depends."

"On what?"

"Where you want to take me."

"To the station-house, of course."

"Then I refuse to go. I have no business there."

"Are you crazy?"

"Did I not tell you that I had an important appointment?"

"Lupin!"

"Why, Ganimard, I have an appointment with the blonde Lady, and do you suppose I would be so discourteous as to cause her a moment's anxiety? That would be very ungentlemanly."

"Listen, Lupin," said the detective, who was becoming annoyed by this persiflage; "I have been very patient with you, but I will endure no more. Follow me."

"Impossible; I have an appointment and I shall keep it."

"For the last time—follow me!"

"Im-pos-sible!"

At a sign from Ganimard two men seized Lupin by the arms; but they released him at once, uttering cries of pain. Lupin had thrust two long needles into them. The other men now rushed at Lupin with cries of rage and hatred, eager to avenge their comrades and to avenge themselves for the many affronts he had heaped upon them; and now they struck and beat him to their heart's desire. A violent blow on the temple felled Lupin to the floor.

"If you hurt him you will answer to me," growled Ganimard, in a rage.

He leaned over Lupin to ascertain his condition. Then, learning that he was breathing freely, Ganimard ordered his men to carry the prisoner by the head and feet, while he himself supported the body.

"Go gently, now!... Don't jolt him. Ah! the brutes would have killed him.... Well, Lupin, how goes it?"

"None too well, Ganimard ... you let them knock me out."

"It was your own fault; you were so obstinate," replied Ganimard. "But I hope they didn't hurt you."

They had left the apartment and were now on the landing. Lupin groaned and stammered:

"Ganimard ... the elevator ... they are breaking my bones."

"A good idea, an excellent idea," replied Ganimard. "Besides, the stairway is too narrow."

He summoned the elevator. They placed Lupin on the seat with the greatest care. Ganimard took his place beside him and said to his men:

"Go down the stairs and wait for me below. Understand?"

Ganimard closed the door of the elevator. Suddenly the elevator shot upward like a balloon released from its cable. Lupin burst into a fit of sardonic laughter.

"Good God!" cried Ganimard, as he made a frantic search in the dark for the button of descent. Having found it, he cried:

"The fifth floor! Watch the door of the fifth floor."

His assistants clambered up the stairs, two and three steps at a time. But this strange circumstance happened: The elevator seemed to break through the ceiling of the last floor, disappeared from the sight of Ganimard's assistants, suddenly made its appearance on the upper floor—the servants' floor—and stopped. Three men were there waiting for it. They opened the door. Two of them seized Ganimard, who, astonished at the sudden attack, scarcely made any defence. The other man carried off Lupin.

"I warned you, Ganimard ... about the dirigible balloon. Another time, don't be so tender-hearted. And, moreover, remember that Arsène Lupin doesn't allow himself to be struck and knocked down without sufficient reason. Adieu."

The door of the elevator was already closed on Ganimard, and the machine began to descend; and it all happened so quickly that the old detective reached the ground floor as soon as his assistants. Without exchanging a word they crossed the court and ascended the servants' stairway, which was the only way to reach the servants' floor through which the escape had been made.

A long corridor with several turns and bordered with little numbered rooms led to a door that was not locked. On the other side of this door and, therefore, in another house there was another corridor with similar turns and similar rooms, and at the end of it a servants' stairway. Ganimard descended it, crossed a court and a vestibule and found himself in the rue Picot. Then he understood the situation: the two houses, built the entire depth of the lots, touched at the rear, while the fronts of the houses faced upon two streets that ran parallel to each other at a distance of more than sixty metres apart.

He found the concierge and, showing his card, enquired:

"Did four men pass here just now?"

"Yes; the two servants from the fourth and fifth floors, with two friends."

"Who lives on the fourth and fifth floors?"

"Two men named Fauvel and their cousins, whose name is Provost. They moved to-day, leaving the two servants, who went away just now."

"Ah!" thought Ganimard; "what a grand opportunity we have missed! The entire band lived in these houses."

And he sank down on a chair in despair.

Forty minutes later two gentlemen were driven up to the station of the Northern Railway and hurried to the Calais express, followed by a porter who carried their valises. One of them had his arm in a sling, and the pallor of his face denoted some illness. The other man was in a jovial mood.

"We must hurry, Wilson, or we will miss the train.... Ah! Wilson, I shall never forget these ten days."

"Neither will I."

"Ah! it was a great struggle!"

"Superb!"

"A few repulses, here and there—"

"Of no consequence."

"And, at last, victory all along the line. Lupin arrested! The blue diamond recovered!"

"My arm broken!"

"What does a broken arm count for in such a victory as that?"

"Especially when it is my arm."

"Ah! yes, don't you remember, Wilson, that it was at the very time you were in the pharmacy, suffering like a hero, that I discovered the clue to the whole mystery?"

"How lucky!"

The doors of the carriages were being closed.

"All aboard. Hurry up, gentlemen!"

The porter climbed into an empty compartment and placed their valises in the rack, whilst Sholmes assisted the unfortunate Wilson.

"What's the matter, Wilson? You're not done up, are you? Come, pull your nerves together."

"My nerves are all right."

"Well, what is it, then?"

"I have only one hand."

"What of it?" exclaimed Sholmes, cheerfully. "You are not the only one who has had a broken arm. Cheer up!"

Sholmes handed the porter a piece of fifty centimes.

"Thank you, Monsieur Sholmes," said the porter.

The Englishman looked at him; it was Arsène Lupin.

"You!... you!" he stammered, absolutely astounded.

And Wilson brandished his sound arm in the manner of a man who demonstrates a fact as he said:

"You! you! but you were arrested! Sholmes told me so. When he left you Ganimard and thirty men had you in charge."

Lupin folded his arms and said, with an air of indignation:

"Did you suppose I would let you go away without bidding you adieu? After the very friendly relations that have always existed between us! That would be discourteous and ungrateful on my part."

The train whistled. Lupin continued:

"I beg your pardon, but have you everything you need? Tobacco and matches ... yes ... and the evening papers? You will find in them an account of my arrest—your last exploit, Monsieur Sholmes. And now, au revoir. Am delighted to have made your acquaintance. And if ever I can be of any service to you, I shall be only too happy...." He leaped to the platform and closed the door.

"Adieu," he repeated, waving his handkerchief. "Adieu.... I shall write to you.... You will write also, eh? And your arm broken, Wilson.... I am truly sorry.... I shall expect to hear from both of you. A postal card, now and then, simply address: Lupin, Paris. That is sufficient.... Adieu.... See you soon."

VII. THE JEWISH LAMP

Herlock Sholmes and Wilson were sitting in front of the fireplace, in comfortable armchairs, with the feet extended toward the grateful warmth of a glowing coke fire.

Sholmes' pipe, a short brier with a silver band, had gone out. He knocked out the ashes, filled it, lighted it, pulled the skirts of his dressing-gown over his knees, and drew from his pipe great puffs of smoke, which ascended toward the ceiling in scores of shadow rings.

Wilson gazed at him, as a dog lying curled up on a rug before the fire might look at his master, with great round eyes which have no hope other than to obey the least gesture of his owner. Was the master going to break the silence? Would he reveal to Wilson the subject of his reverie and admit his satellite into the charmed realm of his thoughts? When Sholmes had maintained his silent attitude for some time. Wilson ventured to speak:

"Everything seems quiet now. Not the shadow of a case to occupy our leisure moments."

Sholmes did not reply, but the rings of smoke emitted by Sholmes were better formed, and Wilson observed that his companion drew considerable pleasure from that trifling fact—an indication that the great man was not absorbed in any serious meditation. Wilson, discouraged, arose and went to the window.

The lonely street extended between the gloomy façades of grimy houses, unusually gloomy this morning by reason of a heavy downfall of rain. A cab passed; then another. Wilson made an entry of their numbers in his memorandum-book. One never knows!

"Ah!" he exclaimed, "the postman."

The man entered, shown in by the servant.

"Two registered letters, sir ... if you will sign, please?"

Sholmes signed the receipts, accompanied the man to the door, and was opening one of the letters as he returned.

"It seems to please you," remarked Wilson, after a moment's silence.

"This letter contains a very interesting proposition. You are anxious for a case—here's one. Read——"

Wilson read:

"Monsieur,

"I desire the benefit of your services and experience. I have been the victim of a serious theft, and the investigation has as yet been unsuccessful. I am sending to you by this mail a number of newspapers which will inform you of the affair, and if you will undertake the case, I will place my house at your disposal and ask you to fill in the enclosed check, signed by me, for whatever sum you require for your expenses.

"Kindly reply by telegraph, and much oblige,

"Your humble servant,

"Baron Victor d'Imblevalle,

"18 rue Murillo, Paris."

"Ah!" exclaimed Sholmes, "that sounds good ... a little trip to Paris ... and why not, Wilson? Since my famous duel with Arsène Lupin, I have not had an excuse to go there. I should be pleased to visit the capital of the world under less strenuous conditions."

He tore the check into four pieces and, while Wilson, whose arm had not yet regained its former strength, uttered bitter words against Paris and the Parisians, Sholmes opened the second envelope. Immediately, he made a gesture of annoyance, and a wrinkle appeared on his forehead during the reading of the letter; then, crushing the paper into a ball, he threw it, angrily, on the floor.

"Well? What's the matter?" asked Wilson, anxiously.

He picked up the ball of paper, unfolded it, and read, with increasing amazement:

"My Dear Monsieur:

"You know full well the admiration I have for you and the interest I take in your renown. Well, believe me, when I warn you to have nothing whatever to do with the case on which you have just now been called to Paris. Your intervention will cause much harm; your efforts will produce a most lamentable result; and you will be obliged to make a public confession of your defeat.

"Having a sincere desire to spare you such humiliation, I implore you, in the name of the friendship that unites us, to remain peacefully reposing at your own fireside.

"My best wishes to Monsieur Wilson, and, for yourself, the sincere regards of your devoted ARSÈNE LUPIN."

"Arsène Lupin!" repeated Wilson, astounded.

Sholmes struck the table with his fist, and exclaimed:

"Ah! he is pestering me already, the fool! He laughs at me as if I were a schoolboy! The public confession of my defeat! Didn't I force him to disgorge the blue diamond?"

"I tell you—he's afraid," suggested Wilson.

"Nonsense! Arsène Lupin is not afraid, and this taunting letter proves it."

"But how did he know that the Baron d'Imblevalle had written to you?"

"What do I know about it? You do ask some stupid questions, my boy."

"I thought ... I supposed——"

"What? That I am a clairvoyant? Or a sorcerer?"

"No, but I have seen you do some marvelous things."

"No person can perform *marvelous* things. I no more than you. I reflect, I deduct, I conclude—that is all; but I do not divine. Only fools divine."

Wilson assumed the attitude of a whipped cur, and resolved not to make a fool of himself by trying to divine why Sholmes paced the room with quick, nervous strides. But when Sholmes rang for the servant and ordered his valise, Wilson thought that he was in possession of a material fact which gave him the right to reflect, deduct and conclude that his associate was about to take a journey. The same mental operation permitted him to assert, with almost mathematical exactness:

"Sholmes, you are going to Paris."

"Possibly."

"And Lupin's affront impels you to go, rather than the desire to assist the Baron d'Imblevalle."

"Possibly."

"Sholmes, I shall go with you."

"Ah; ah! my old friend," exclaimed Sholmes, interrupting his walking, "you are not afraid that your right arm will meet the same fate as your left?"

"What can happen to me? You will be there."

"That's the way to talk, Wilson. We will show that clever Frenchman that he made a mistake when he threw his glove in our faces. Be quick, Wilson, we must catch the first train."

"Without waiting for the papers the baron has sent you?"

"What good are they?"

"I will send a telegram."

"No; if you do that, Arsène Lupin will know of my arrival. I wish to avoid that. This time, Wilson, we must fight under cover."

That afternoon, the two friends embarked at Dover. The passage was a delightful one. In the train from Calais to Paris, Sholmes had three hours sound sleep, while Wilson guarded the door of the compartment.

Sholmes awoke in good spirits. He was delighted at the idea of another duel with Arsène Lupin, and he rubbed his hands with the satisfied air of a man who looks forward to a pleasant vacation.

"At last!" exclaimed Wilson, "we are getting to work again."

And he rubbed his hands with the same satisfied air.

At the station, Sholmes took the wraps and, followed by Wilson, who carried the valises, he gave up his tickets and started off briskly.

"Fine weather, Wilson.... Blue sky and sunshine! Paris is giving us a royal reception."

"Yes, but what a crowd!"

"So much the better, Wilson, we will pass unnoticed. No one will recognize us in such a crowd."

"Is this Monsieur Sholmes?"

He stopped, somewhat puzzled. Who the deuce could thus address him by his name? A woman stood beside him; a young girl whose simple dress outlined her slender form and whose pretty face had a sad and anxious expression. She repeated her enquiry:

"You are Monsieur Sholmes?"

As he still remained silent, as much from confusion as from a habit of prudence, the girl asked a third time:

"Have I the honor of addressing Monsieur Sholmes?"

"What do you want?" he replied, testily, considering the incident a suspicious one.

"You must listen to me, Monsieur Sholmes, as it is a serious matter. I know that you are going to the rue Murillo."

"What do you say?"

"I know ... I know ... rue Murillo ... number 18. Well, you must not go ... no, you must not. I assure you that you will regret it. Do not think that I have any interest in the matter. I do it because it is right ... because my conscience tells me to do it."

Sholmes tried to get away, but she persisted:

"Oh! I beg of you, don't neglect my advice.... Ah! if I only knew how to convince you! Look at me! Look into my eyes! They are sincere ... they speak the truth."

She gazed at Sholmes, fearlessly but innocently, with those beautiful eyes, serious and clear, in which her very soul seemed to be reflected.

Wilson nodded his head, as he said:

"Mademoiselle looks honest."

"Yes," she implored, "and you must have confidence——"

"I have confidence in you, mademoiselle," replied Wilson.

"Oh, how happy you make me! And so has your friend? I feel it ... I am sure of it! What happiness! Everything will be all right now!... What a good idea of mine!... Ah! yes, there is a train for Calais in twenty minutes. You will take it.... Quick, follow me ... you must come this way ... there is just time."

She tried to drag them along. Sholmes seized her arm, and in as gentle a voice as he could assume, said to her:

"Excuse me, mademoiselle, if I cannot yield to your wishes, but I never abandon a task that I have once undertaken."

"I beseech you ... I implore you.... Ah if you could only understand!"

Sholmes passed outside and walked away at a quick pace. Wilson said to the girl:

"Have no fear ... he will be in at the finish. He never failed yet."

And he ran to overtake Sholmes.

HERLOCK SHOLMES—ARSÈNE LUPIN.

These words, in great black letters, met their gaze as soon as they left the railway station. A number of sandwich-men were parading through the street, one behind the other, carrying heavy canes with iron ferrules with which they struck the pavement in harmony, and, on their backs, they carried large posters, on which one could read the following notice:

THE MATCH BETWEEN HERLOCK SHOLMES
   AND ARSÈNE LUPIN. ARRIVAL OF THE ENGLISH
   CHAMPION. THE GREAT DETECTIVE ATTACKS

THE MYSTERY OF THE RUE MURILLO. READ THE
DETAILS IN THE "ECHO DE FRANCE".

Wilson shook his head, and said:

"Look at that, Sholmes, and we thought we were traveling incognito! I shouldn't be surprised to find the republican guard waiting for us at the rue Murillo to give us an official reception with toasts and champagne."

"Wilson, when you get funny, you get beastly funny," growled Sholmes.

Then he approached one of the sandwich-men with the obvious intention of seizing him in his powerful grip and crushing him, together with his infernal sign-board. There was quite a crowd gathered about the men, reading the notices, and joking and laughing.

Repressing a furious access of rage, Sholmes said to the man:

"When did they hire you?"

"This morning."

"How long have you been parading?"

"About an hour."

"But the boards were ready before that?"

"Oh, yes, they were ready when we went to the agency this morning."

So then it appears that Arsène Lupin had foreseen that he, Sholmes, would accept the challenge. More than that, the letter written by Lupin showed that he was eager for the fray and that he was prepared to measure swords once more with his formidable rival. Why? What motive could Arsène Lupin have in renewing the struggle?

Sholmes hesitated for a moment. Lupin must be very confident of his success to show so much insolence in advance; and was not he, Sholmes, falling into a trap by rushing into the battle at the first call for help?

However, he called a carriage.

"Come, Wilson!... Driver, 18 rue Murillo!" he exclaimed, with an outburst of his accustomed energy. With distended veins and clenched fists, as if he were about to engage in a boxing bout, he jumped into the carriage.

The rue Murillo is bordered with magnificent private residences, the rear of which overlook the Parc Monceau. One of the most pretentious of these houses is number 18, owned and occupied by the Baron d'Imblevalle and furnished in a luxurious manner consistent with the owner's taste and wealth. There was a courtyard in front of the house, and, in the rear, a garden well filled with trees whose branches mingle with those of the park.

After ringing the bell, the two Englishmen were admitted, crossed the courtyard, and were received at the door by a footman who showed them into a small parlor facing the garden in the rear of the house. They sat down and, glancing about, made a rapid inspection of the many valuable objects with which the room was filled.

"Everything very choice," murmured Wilson, "and in the best of taste. It is a safe deduction to make that those who had the leisure to collect these articles must now be at least fifty years of age."

The door opened, and the Baron d'Imblevalle entered, followed by his wife. Contrary to the deduction made by Wilson, they were both quite young, of elegant appearance, and vivacious in speech and action. They were profuse in their expressions of gratitude.

"So kind of you to come! Sorry to have caused you so much trouble! The theft now seems of little consequence, since it has procured us this pleasure."

"How charming these French people are!" thought Wilson, evolving one of his commonplace deductions.

"But time is money," exclaimed the baron, "especially your time, Monsieur Sholmes. So I will come to the point. Now, what do you think of the affair? Do you think you can succeed in it?"

"Before I can answer that I must know what it is about."

"I thought you knew."

"No; so I must ask you for full particulars, even to the smallest detail. First, what is the nature of the case?"

"A theft."

"When did it take place?"

"Last Saturday," replied the baron, "or, at least, some time during Saturday night or Sunday morning."

"That was six days ago. Now, you can tell me all about it."

"In the first place, monsieur, I must tell you that my wife and I, conforming to the manner of life that our position demands, go out very little. The education of our children, a few receptions, and the care and decoration of our house—such constitutes our life; and nearly all our evenings are spent in this little room, which is my wife's boudoir, and in which we have gathered a few artistic objects. Last Saturday night, about eleven o'clock, I turned off the electric lights, and my wife and I retired, as usual, to our room."

"Where is your room?"

"It adjoins this. That is the door. Next morning, that is to say, Sunday morning, I arose quite early. As Suzanne, my wife, was still asleep, I passed into the boudoir as quietly as possible so as not to wake her. What was my astonishment when I found that window open—as we had left it closed the evening before!"

"A servant——"

"No one enters here in the morning until we ring. Besides, I always take the precaution to bolt the second door which communicates with the ante-chamber. Therefore, the window must have been opened from the outside. Besides, I have some evidence of that: the second pane of glass from the right—close to the fastening—had been cut."

"And what does that window overlook?"

"As you can see for yourself, it opens on a little balcony, surrounded by a stone railing. Here, we are on the first floor, and you can see the garden behind the house and the iron fence which separates it from the Parc Monceau. It is quite certain that the thief came through the park, climbed the fence by the aid of a ladder, and thus reached the terrace below the window."

"That is quite certain, you say!"

"Well, in the soft earth on either side of the fence, they found the two holes made by the bottom of the ladder, and two similar holes can be seen below the window. And the stone railing of the balcony shows two scratches which were doubtless made by the contact of the ladder."

"Is the Parc Monceau closed at night?"

"No; but if it were, there is a house in course of erection at number 14, and a person could enter that way."

Herlock Sholmes reflected for a few minutes, and then said:

"Let us come down to the theft. It must have been committed in this room?"

"Yes; there was here, between that twelfth century Virgin and that tabernacle of chased silver, a small Jewish lamp. It has disappeared."

"And is that all?"

"That is all."

"Ah!... And what is a Jewish lamp?"

"One of those copper lamps used by the ancient Jews, consisting of a standard which supported a bowl containing the oil, and from this bowl projected several burners intended for the wicks."

"Upon the whole, an object of small value."

"No great value, of course. But this one contained a secret hiding-place in which we were accustomed to place a magnificent jewel, a chimera in gold, set with rubies and emeralds, which was of great value."

"Why did you hide it there?"

"Oh! I can't give any reason, monsieur, unless it was an odd fancy to utilize a hiding-place of that kind."

"Did anyone know it?"

"No."

"No one—except the thief," said Sholmes. "Otherwise he would not have taken the trouble to steal the lamp."

"Of course. But how could he know it, as it was only by accident that the secret mechanism of the lamp was revealed to us."

"A similar accident has revealed it to some one else ... a servant ... or an acquaintance. But let us proceed: I suppose the police have been notified?"

"Yes. The examining magistrate has completed his investigation. The reporter-detectives attached to the leading newspapers have also made their investigations. But, as I wrote to you, it seems to me the mystery will never be solved."

Sholmes arose, went to the window, examined the casement, the balcony, the terrace, studied the scratches on the stone railing with his magnifying-glass, and then requested Mon. d'Imblevalle to show him the garden.

Outside, Sholmes sat down in a rattan chair and gazed at the roof of the house in a dreamy way. Then he walked over to the two little wooden boxes with which they had covered the holes made in the ground by the bottom of the ladder with a view of preserving them intact. He raised the boxes, kneeled on the ground, scrutinized the holes and made some measurements. After making a similar examination of the holes near the fence, he and the baron returned to the boudoir where Madame d'Imblevalle was waiting for them. After a short silence Sholmes said:

"At the very outset of your story, baron, I was surprised at the very simple methods employed by the thief. To raise a ladder, cut a window-pane, select a valuable article, and walk out again—no, that is not the way such things are done. All that is too plain, too simple."

"Well, what do you think?"

"That the Jewish lamp was stolen under the direction of Arsène Lupin."

"Arsène Lupin!" exclaimed the baron.

"Yes, but he did not do it himself, as no one came from the outside. Perhaps a servant descended from the upper floor by means of a waterspout that I noticed when I was in the garden."

"What makes you think so?"

"Arsène Lupin would not leave this room empty-handed."

"Empty-handed! But he had the lamp."

"But that would not have prevented his taking that snuff-box, set with diamonds, or that opal necklace. When he leaves anything, it is because he can't carry it away."

"But the marks of the ladder outside?"

"A false scent. Placed there simply to avert suspicion."

"And the scratches on the balustrade?"

"A farce! They were made with a piece of sandpaper. See, here are scraps of the paper that I picked up in the garden."

"And what about the marks made by the bottom of the ladder?"

"Counterfeit! Examine the two rectangular holes below the window, and the two holes near the fence. They are of a similar form, but I find that the two holes near the house are closer to each other than the two holes near the fence. What does that fact suggest? To me, it suggested that the four holes were made by a piece of wood prepared for the purpose."

"The better proof would be the piece of wood itself."

"Here it is," said Sholmes, "I found it in the garden, under the box of a laurel tree."

The baron bowed to Sholmes in recognition of his skill. Only forty minutes had elapsed since the Englishman had entered the house, and he had already exploded all the theories theretofore formed, and which had been based on what appeared to be obvious and undeniable facts. But what now appeared to be the real facts of the case rested upon a more solid foundation, to-wit, the astute reasoning of a Herlock Sholmes.

"The accusation which you make against one of our household is a very serious matter," said the baroness. "Our servants have been with us a long time and none of them would betray our trust."

"If none of them has betrayed you, how can you explain the fact that I received this letter on the same day and by the same mail as the letter you wrote to me?"

He handed to the baroness the letter that he had received from Arsène Lupin. She exclaimed, in amazement:

"Arsène Lupin! How could he know?"

"Did you tell anyone that you had written to me?"

"No one," replied the baron. "The idea occurred to us the other evening at the dinner-table."

"Before the servants?"

"No, only our two children. Oh, no ... Sophie and Henriette had left the table, hadn't they, Suzanne?"

Madame d'Imblevalle, after a moment's reflection, replied:

"Yes, they had gone to Mademoiselle."

"Mademoiselle?" queried Sholmes.

"The governess, Mademoiselle Alice Demun."

"Does she take her meals with you?"

"No. Her meals are served in her room."

Wilson had an idea. He said:

"The letter written to my friend Herlock Sholmes was posted?"

"Of course."

"Who posted it?"

"Dominique, who has been my valet for twenty years," replied the baron. "Any search in that direction would be a waste of time."

"One never wastes his time when engaged in a search," said Wilson, sententiously.

This preliminary investigation now ended, and Sholmes asked permission to retire.

At dinner, an hour later, he saw Sophie and Henriette, the two children of the family, one was six and the other eight years of age. There was very little conversation at the table. Sholmes responded to the friendly advances of his hosts in such a curt manner that they were soon reduced to silence. When the coffee was served, Sholmes swallowed the contents of his cup, and rose to take his leave.

At that moment, a servant entered with a telephone message addressed to Sholmes. He opened it, and read:

"You have my enthusiastic admiration. The results attained by you in so short a time are simply marvelous. I am dismayed.
    "ARSÈNE LUPIN."

Sholmes made a gesture of indignation and handed the message to the baron, saying:

"What do you think now, monsieur? Are the walls of your house furnished with eyes and ears?"

"I don't understand it," said the baron, in amazement.

"Nor do I; but I do understand that Lupin has knowledge of everything that occurs in this house. He knows every movement, every word. There is no doubt of it. But how does he get his information? That is the first mystery I have to solve, and when I know that I will know everything."

That night, Wilson retired with the clear conscience of a man who has performed his whole duty and thus acquired an undoubted right to sleep and repose. So he fell asleep very quickly, and was soon enjoying the most delightful dreams in which he pursued Lupin and captured him single-handed; and the sensation was so vivid and exciting that it woke him from his sleep. Someone was standing at his bedside. He seized his revolver, and cried:

"Don't move, Lupin, or I'll fire."

"The deuce! Wilson, what do you mean?"

"Oh! it is you, Sholmes. Do you want me?"

"I want to show you something. Get up."

Sholmes led him to the window, and said:

"Look!... on the other side of the fence...."

"In the park?"

"Yes. What do you see?"

"I don't see anything."

"Yes, you do see something."

"Ah! of course, a shadow ... two of them."

"Yes, close to the fence. See, they are moving. Come, quick!"

Quickly they descended the stairs, and reached a room which opened into the garden. Through the glass door they could see the two shadowy forms in the same place.

"It is very strange," said Sholmes, "but it seems to me I can hear a noise inside the house."

"Inside the house? Impossible! Everybody is asleep."

"Well, listen——"

At that moment a low whistle came from the other side of the fence, and they perceived a dim light which appeared to come from the house.

"The baron must have turned on the light in his room. It is just above us."

"That must have been the noise you heard," said Wilson. "Perhaps they are watching the fence also."

Then there was a second whistle, softer than before.

"I don't understand it; I don't understand," said Sholmes, irritably.

"No more do I," confessed Wilson.

Sholmes turned the key, drew the bolt, and quietly opened the door. A third whistle, louder than before, and modulated to another form. And the noise above their heads became more pronounced. Sholmes said:

"It seems to be on the balcony outside the boudoir window."

He put his head through the half-opened door, but immediately recoiled, with a stifled oath. Then Wilson looked. Quite close to them there was a ladder, the upper end of which was resting on the balcony.

"The deuce!" said Sholmes, "there is someone in the boudoir. That is what we heard. Quick, let us remove the ladder."

But at that instant a man slid down the ladder and ran toward the spot where his accomplices were waiting for him outside the fence. He carried the ladder with him. Sholmes and Wilson pursued the man and overtook him just as he was placing the ladder against the fence. From the other side of the fence two shots were fired.

"Wounded?" cried Sholmes.

"No," replied Wilson.

Wilson seized the man by the body and tried to hold him, but the man turned and plunged a knife into Wilson's breast. He uttered a groan, staggered and fell.

"Damnation!" muttered Sholmes, "if they have killed him I will kill them."

He laid Wilson on the grass and rushed toward the ladder. Too late—the man had climbed the fence and, accompanied by his confederates, had fled through the bushes.

"Wilson, Wilson, it is not serious, hein? Merely a scratch."

The house door opened, and Monsieur d'Imblevalle appeared, followed by the servants, carrying candles.

"What's the matter?" asked the baron. "Is Monsieur Wilson wounded?"

"Oh! it's nothing—a mere scratch," repeated Sholmes, trying to deceive himself.

The blood was flowing profusely, and Wilson's face was livid. Twenty minutes later the doctor ascertained that the point of the knife had penetrated to within an inch and a half of the heart.

"An inch and a half of the heart! Wilson always was lucky!" said Sholmes, in an envious tone.

"Lucky ... lucky...." muttered the doctor.

"Of course! Why, with his robust constitution he will soon be out again."

"Six weeks in bed and two months of convalescence."

"Not more?"

"No, unless complications set in."

"Oh! the devil! what does he want complications for?"

Fully reassured, Sholmes joined the baron in the boudoir. This time the mysterious visitor had not exercised the same restraint. Ruthlessly, he had laid his vicious hand upon the diamond snuff-box, upon the opal necklace, and, in a general way, upon everything that could find a place in the greedy pockets of an enterprising burglar.

The window was still open; one of the window-panes had been neatly cut; and, in the morning, a summary investigation showed that the ladder belonged to the house then in course of construction.

"Now, you can see," said Mon. d'Imblevalle, with a touch of irony, "it is an exact repetition of the affair of the Jewish lamp."

"Yes, if we accept the first theory adopted by the police."

"Haven't you adopted it yet? Doesn't this second theft shatter your theory in regard to the first?"

"It only confirms it, monsieur."

"That is incredible! You have positive evidence that last night's theft was committed by an outsider, and yet you adhere to your theory that the Jewish lamp was stolen by someone in the house."

"Yes, I am sure of it."

"How do you explain it?"

"I do not explain anything, monsieur; I have established two facts which do not appear to have any relation to each other, and yet I am seeking the missing link that connects them."

His conviction seemed to be so earnest and positive that the baron submitted to it, and said:

"Very well, we will notify the police——"

"Not at all!" exclaimed the Englishman, quickly, "not at all! I intend to ask for their assistance when I need it—but not before."

"But the attack on your friend?"

"That's of no consequence. He is only wounded. Secure the license of the doctor. I shall be responsible for the legal side of the affair."

The next two days proved uneventful. Yet Sholmes was investigating the case with a minute care, and with a sense of wounded pride resulting from that audacious theft, committed under his nose, in spite of his presence and beyond his power to prevent it. He made a thorough investigation of the house and garden, interviewed the servants, and paid lengthy visits to the kitchen and stables. And, although his efforts were fruitless, he did not despair.

"I will succeed," he thought, "and the solution must be sought within the walls of this house. This affair is quite different from that of the blonde Lady, where I had to work in the dark, on unknown ground. This time I am on the battlefield itself. The enemy is not the elusive and invisible Lupin, but the accomplice, in flesh and blood, who lives and moves within the confines of this house. Let me secure the slightest clue and the game is mine!"

That clue was furnished to him by accident.

On the afternoon of the third day, when he entered a room located above the boudoir, which served as a study for the children, he found Henriette, the younger of the two sisters. She was looking for her scissors.

"You know," she said to Sholmes, "I make papers like that you received the other evening."

"The other evening?"

"Yes, just as dinner was over, you received a paper with marks on it ... you know, a telegram.... Well, I make them, too."

She left the room. To anyone else these words would seem to be nothing more than the insignificant remark of a child, and Sholmes himself listened to them with a distracted air and continued his investigation. But, suddenly, he ran after the child, and overtook her at the head of the stairs. He said to her:

"So you paste stamps and marks on papers?"

Henriette, very proudly, replied:

"Yes, I cut them out and paste them on."

"Who taught you that little game?"

"Mademoiselle ... my governess ... I have seen her do it often. She takes words out of the newspapers and pastes them——"

"What does she make out of them?"

"Telegrams and letters that she sends away."

Herlock Sholmes returned to the study, greatly puzzled by the information and seeking to draw from it a logical deduction. There was a pile of newspapers on the mantel. He opened them and found that many words and, in some places, entire lines had been cut out. But, after reading a few of the word's which preceded or followed, he decided that the missing words had been cut out at random—probably by the child. It was possible that one of the newspapers had been cut by mademoiselle; but how could he assure himself that such was the case?

Mechanically, Sholmes turned over the school-books on the table; then others which were lying on the shelf of a bookcase. Suddenly he uttered a cry of joy. In a corner of the bookcase, under a pile of old exercise books, he found a child's alphabet-book, in which the letters were ornamented with pictures, and on one of the pages of that book he discovered a place where a word had been removed. He examined it. It was a list of the days of the week. Monday, Tuesday, Wednesday, etc. The word "Saturday" was missing. Now, the theft of the Jewish lamp had occurred on a Saturday night.

Sholmes experienced that slight fluttering of the heart which always announced to him, in the clearest manner, that he had discovered the road which leads to victory. That ray of truth, that feeling of certainty, never deceived him.

With nervous fingers he hastened to examine the balance of the book. Very soon he made another discovery. It was a page composed of capital letters, followed by a line of figures. Nine of those letters and three of those figures had been carefully cut out. Sholmes made a list of the missing letters and figures in his memorandum book, in alphabetical and numerical order, and obtained the following result:

CDEHNOPEZ—237.

"Well? at first sight, it is a rather formidable puzzle," he murmured, "but, by transposing the letters and using all of them, is it possible to form one, two or three complete words?"

Sholmes tried it, in vain.

Only one solution seemed possible; it constantly appeared before him, no matter which way he tried to juggle the letters, until, at length, he was satisfied it was the true solution, since it harmonized with the logic of the facts and the general circumstances of the case.

As that page of the book did not contain any duplicate letters it was probable, in fact quite certain, that the words he could form from those letters would be incomplete, and that the original words had been completed with letters taken from other pages. Under those conditions he obtained the following solution, errors and omissions excepted:

REPOND Z—CH—237.

The first word was quite clear: répondez [reply], a letter E is missing because it occurs twice in the word, and the book furnished only one letter of each kind.

As to the second incomplete word, no doubt it formed, with the aid of the number 237, an address to which the reply was to be sent. They appointed Saturday as the time, and requested a reply to be sent to the address CH. 237.

Or, perhaps, CH. 237 was an address for a letter to be sent to the "general delivery" of some postoffice, or, again, they might form a part of some incomplete word. Sholmes searched the book once more, but did not discover that any other letters had been removed. Therefore, until further orders, he decided to adhere to the foregoing interpretation.

Henriette returned and observed what he was doing.

"Amusing, isn't it?"

"Yes, very amusing," he replied. "But, have you any other papers?... Or, rather, words already cut out that I can paste?"

"Papers?... No.... And Mademoiselle wouldn't like it."

"Mademoiselle?"

"Yes, she has scolded me already."

"Why?"

"Because I have told you some things ... and she says that a person should never tell things about those they love."

"You are quite right."

Henriette was delighted to receive his approbation, in fact so highly pleased that she took from a little silk bag that was pinned to her dress some scraps of cloth, three buttons, two cubes of sugar and, lastly, a piece of paper which she handed to Sholmes.

"See, I give it to you just the same."

It was the number of a cab—8,279.

"Where did this number come from?"

"It fell out of her pocketbook."

"When?"

"Sunday, at mass, when she was taking out some sous for the collection."

"Exactly! And now I shall tell you how to keep from being scolded again. Do not tell Mademoiselle that you saw me."

Sholmes then went to Mon. d'Imblevalle and questioned him in regard to Mademoiselle. The baron replied, indignantly:

"Alice Demun! How can you imagine such a thing? It is utterly impossible!"

"How long has she been in your service?"

"Only a year, but there is no one in the house in whom I have greater confidence."

"Why have I not seen her yet?"

"She has been away for a few days."

"But she is here now."

"Yes; since her return she has been watching at the bedside of your friend. She has all the qualities of a nurse ... gentle ... thoughtful ... Monsieur Wilson seems much pleased...."

"Ah!" said Sholmes, who had completely neglected to inquire about his friend. After a moment's reflection he asked:

"Did she go out on Sunday morning?"

"The day after the theft?"

"Yes."

The baron called his wife and asked her. She replied:

"Mademoiselle went to the eleven o'clock mass with the children, as usual."

"But before that?"

"Before that? No.... Let me see!... I was so upset by the theft ... but I remember now that, on the evening before, she asked permission to go out on Sunday morning ... to see a cousin who was passing through Paris, I think. But, surely, you don't suspect her?"

"Of course not ... but I would like to see her."

He went to Wilson's room. A woman dressed in a gray cloth dress, as in the hospitals, was bending over the invalid, giving him a drink. When she turned her face Sholmes recognized her as the young girl who had accosted him at the railway station.

Alice Demun smiled sweetly; her great serious, innocent eyes showed no sign of embarrassment. The Englishman tried to speak, muttered a few syllables, and stopped. Then she resumed her work, acting quite naturally under Sholmes' astonished gaze, moved the bottles, unrolled and rolled cotton bandages, and again regarded Sholmes with her charming smile of pure innocence.

He turned on his heels, descended the stairs, noticed Mon. d'Imblevalle's automobile in the courtyard, jumped into it, and went to Levallois, to the office of the cab company whose address was printed on the paper he had received from Henriette. The man who had driven carriage number 8,279 on Sunday morning not being there, Sholmes dismissed the automobile and waited for the man's return. He told Sholmes that he had picked up a woman in the vicinity of the Parc Monceau, a young woman dressed in black, wearing a heavy veil, and, apparently, quite nervous.

"Did she have a package?"

"Yes, quite a long package."

"Where did you take her?"

"Avenue des Ternes, corner of the Place Saint-Ferdinand. She remained there about ten minutes, and then returned to the Parc Monceau."

"Could you recognize the house in the avenue des Ternes?"

"Parbleu! Shall I take you there?"

"Presently. First take me to 36 quai des Orfèvres."

At the police office he saw Detective Ganimard.

"Monsieur Ganimard, are you at liberty?"

"If it has anything to do with Lupin—no!"

"It has something to do with Lupin."

"Then I do not go."

"What! you surrender——"

"I bow to the inevitable. I am tired of the unequal struggle, in which we are sure to be defeated. Lupin is stronger than I am—stronger than the two of us; therefore, we must surrender."

"I will not surrender."

"He will make you, as he has all others."

"And you would be pleased to see it—eh, Ganimard?"

"At all events, it is true," said Ganimard, frankly. "And since you are determined to pursue the game, I will go with you."

Together they entered the carriage and were driven to the avenue des Ternes. Upon their order the carriage stopped on the other side of the street, at some distance from the house, in front of a little café, on the terrace of which the two men took seats amongst the shrubbery. It was commencing to grow dark.

"Waiter," said Sholmes, "some writing material."

He wrote a note, recalled the waiter and gave him the letter with instructions to deliver it to the concierge of the house which he pointed out.

In a few minutes the concierge stood before them. Sholmes asked him if, on the Sunday morning, he had seen a young woman dressed in black.

"In black? Yes, about nine o'clock. She went to the second floor."

"Have you seen her often?"

"No, but for some time—well, during the last few weeks, I have seen her almost every day."

"And since Sunday?"

"Only once ... until to-day."

"What! Did she come to-day?"

"She is here now."

"Here now?"

"Yes, she came about ten minutes ago. Her carriage is standing in the Place Saint-Ferdinand, as usual. I met her at the door."

"Who is the occupant of the second floor?"

"There are two: a modiste, Mademoiselle Langeais, and a gentleman who rented two furnished rooms a month ago under the name of Bresson."

"Why do you say 'under the name'?"

"Because I have an idea that it is an assumed name. My wife takes care of his rooms, and ... well, there are not two shirts there with the same initials."

"Is he there much of the time?"

"No; he is nearly always out. He has not been here for three days."

"Was he here on Saturday night?"

"Saturday night?... Let me think.... Yes, Saturday night, he came in and stayed all night."

"What sort of a man is he?"

"Well, I can scarcely answer that. He is so changeable. He is, by turns, big, little, fat, thin ... dark and light. I do not always recognize him."

Ganimard and Sholmes exchanged looks.

"That is he, all right," said Ganimard.

"Ah!" said the concierge, "there is the girl now."

Mademoiselle had just emerged from the house and was walking toward her carriage in the Place Saint-Ferdinand.

"And there is Monsieur Bresson."

"Monsieur Bresson? Which is he?"

"The man with the parcel under his arm."

"But he is not looking after the girl. She is going to her carriage alone."

"Yes, I have never seen them together."

The two detectives had arisen. By the light of the street-lamps they recognized the form of Arsène Lupin, who had started off in a direction opposite to that taken by the girl.

"Which will you follow?" asked Ganimard.

"I will follow him, of course. He's the biggest game."

"Then I will follow the girl," proposed Ganimard.

"No, no," said Sholmes, quickly, who did not wish to disclose the girl's identity to Ganimard, "I know where to find her. Come with me."

They followed Lupin at a safe distance, taking care to conceal themselves as well as possible amongst the moving throng and behind the newspaper kiosks. They found the pursuit an easy one, as he walked steadily forward without turning to the right or left, but with a slight limp in the right leg, so slight as to require the keen eye of a professional observer to detect it. Ganimard observed it, and said:

"He is pretending to be lame. Ah! if we could only collect two or three policemen and pounce on our man! We run a chance to lose him."

But they did not meet any policemen before they reached the Porte des Ternes, and, having passed the fortifications, there was no prospect of receiving any assistance.

"We had better separate," said Sholmes, "as there are so few people on the street."

They were now on the Boulevard Victor-Hugo. They walked one on each side of the street, and kept well in the shadow of the trees. They continued thus for twenty minutes, when Lupin turned to the left and followed the Seine. Very soon they saw him descend to the edge of the river. He remained there only a few seconds, but they could not observe his movements. Then Lupin retraced his steps. His pursuers concealed themselves in the shadow of a gateway. Lupin passed in front of them. His parcel had disappeared. And as he walked away another man emerged from the shelter of a house and glided amongst the trees.

"He seems to be following him also," said Sholmes, in a low voice.

The pursuit continued, but was now embarrassed by the presence of the third man. Lupin returned the same way, passed through the Porte des Ternes, and re-entered the house in the avenue des Ternes.

The concierge was closing the house for the night when Ganimard presented himself.

"Did you see him?"

"Yes," replied the concierge, "I was putting out the gas on the landing when he closed and bolted his door."

"Is there any person with him?"

"No; he has no servant. He never eats here."

"Is there a servants' stairway?"

"No."

Ganimard said to Sholmes:

"I had better stand at the door of his room while you go for the commissary of police in the rue Demours."

"And if he should escape during that time?" said Sholmes.

"While I am here! He can't escape."

"One to one, with Lupin, is not an even chance for you."

"Well, I can't force the door. I have no right to do that, especially at night."

Sholmes shrugged his shoulders and said:

"When you arrest Lupin no one will question the methods by which you made the arrest. However, let us go up and ring, and see what happens then."

They ascended to the second floor. There was a double door at the left of the landing. Ganimard rang the bell. No reply. He rang again. Still no reply.

"Let us go in," said Sholmes.

"All right, come on," replied Ganimard.

Yet, they stood still, irresolute. Like people who hesitate when they ought to accomplish a decisive action they feared to move, and it seemed to them impossible that Arsène Lupin was there, so close to them, on the other side of that fragile door that could be broken down by one blow of the fist. But they knew Lupin too well to suppose that he would allow himself to be trapped in that stupid manner. No, no—a thousand times, no— Lupin was no longer there. Through the adjoining houses, over the roofs, by some conveniently prepared exit, he must have already made his escape, and, once more, it would only be Lupin's shadow that they would seize.

They shuddered as a slight noise, coming from the other side of the door, reached their ears. Then they had the impression, amounting almost to a certainty, that he was there, separated from them by that frail wooden door, and that he was listening to them, that he could hear them.

What was to be done? The situation was a serious one. In spite of their vast experience as detectives, they were so nervous and excited that they thought they could hear the beating of their own hearts. Ganimard questioned Sholmes by a look. Then he struck the door a violent blow with his fist. Immediately they heard the sound of footsteps, concerning which there was no attempt at concealment.

Ganimard shook the door. Then he and Sholmes, uniting their efforts, rushed at the door, and burst it open with their shoulders. Then they stood still, in surprise. A shot had been fired in the adjoining room. Another shot, and the sound of a falling body.

When they entered they saw the man lying on the floor with his face toward the marble mantel. His revolver had fallen from his hand. Ganimard stooped and turned the man's head. The face was covered with blood, which was flowing from two wounds, one in the cheek, the other in the temple.

"You can't recognize him for blood."

"No matter!" said Sholmes. "It is not Lupin."

"How do you know? You haven't even looked at him."

"Do you think that Arsène Lupin is the kind of a man that would kill himself?" asked Sholmes, with a sneer.

"But we thought we recognized him outside."

"We thought so, because the wish was father to the thought. That man has us bewitched."

"Then it must be one of his accomplices."

"The accomplices of Arsène Lupin do not kill themselves."

"Well, then, who is it?"

They searched the corpse. In one pocket Herlock Sholmes found an empty pocketbook; in another Ganimard found several louis. There were no marks of identification on any part of his clothing. In a trunk and two valises they found nothing but wearing apparel. On the mantel there was a pile of newspapers. Ganimard opened them. All of them contained articles referring to the theft of the Jewish lamp.

An hour later, when Ganimard and Sholmes left the house, they had acquired no further knowledge of the strange individual who had been driven to suicide by their untimely visit.

Who was he? Why had he killed himself? What was his connection with the affair of the Jewish lamp? Who had followed him on his return from the river? The situation involved many complex questions—many mysteries——

Herlock Sholmes went to bed in a very bad humor. Early next morning he received the following telephonic message:

"Arsène Lupin has the honor to inform you of his tragic death in the person of Monsieur Bresson, and requests the honor of your presence at the funeral service and burial, which will be held at the public expense on Thursday, 25 June."

VIII. THE SHIPWRECK

"That's what I don't like, Wilson," said Herlock Sholmes, after he had read Arsène Lupin's message; "that is what exasperates me in this affair—to feel that the cunning, mocking eye of that fellow follows me everywhere. He sees everything; he knows everything; he reads my inmost thoughts; he even foresees my slightest movement. Ah! he is possessed of a marvelous intuition, far surpassing that of the most instinctive woman, yes, surpassing even that of Herlock Sholmes himself. Nothing escapes him. I resemble an actor whose every step and movement are directed by a stage-manager; who says this and does that in obedience to a superior will. That is my position. Do you understand, Wilson?"

Certainly Wilson would have understood if his faculties had not been deadened by the profound slumber of a man whose temperature varies between one hundred and one hundred and three degrees. But whether he heard or not was a matter of no consequence to Herlock Sholmes, who continued:

"I have to concentrate all my energy and bring all my resources into action in order to make the slightest progress. And, fortunately for me, those petty annoyances are like so many pricks from a needle and serve only to stimulate me. As soon as the heat of the wound is appeased and the shock to my vanity has subsided I say to myself: 'Amuse yourself, my dear fellow, but remember that he who laughs last laughs best. Sooner or later you will betray yourself.' For you know, Wilson, it was Lupin himself, who, by his first dispatch and the observation that it suggested to little Henriette, disclosed to me the secret of his correspondence with Alice Hemun. Have you forgotten that circumstance, dear boy?"

But Wilson was asleep; and Sholmes, pacing to and fro, resumed his speech:

"And, now, things are not in a bad shape; a little obscure, perhaps, but the light is creeping in. In the first place, I must learn all about Monsieur Bresson. Ganimard and I will visit the bank of the river, at the spot where Bresson threw away the package, and the particular rôle of that gentleman will be known to me. After that the game will be played between me and Alice Demun. Rather a light-weight opponent, hein, Wilson? And do you not think that I will soon know the phrase represented by the letters clipped from the alphabet-book, and what the isolated letters—the 'C' and the 'H'—mean? That is all I want to know, Wilson."

Mademoiselle entered at that moment, and, observing Sholmes gesticulating, she said, in her sweetest manner:

"Monsieur Sholmes, I must scold you if you waken my patient. It isn't nice of you to disturb him. The doctor has ordered absolute rest."

He looked at her in silence, astonished, as on their first meeting, at her wonderful self-possession.

"Why do you look at me so, Monsieur Sholmes?... You seem to be trying to read my thoughts.... No?... Then what is it?"

She questioned him with the most innocent expression on her pretty face and in her frank blue eyes. A smile played upon her lips; and she displayed so much unaffected candor that the Englishman almost lost his temper. He approached her and said, in a low voice:

"Bresson killed himself last night."

She affected not to understand him; so he repeated:

"Bresson killed himself yesterday...."

She did not show the slightest emotion; she acted as if the matter did not concern or interest her in any way.

"You have been informed," said Sholmes, displaying his annoyance. "Otherwise, the news would have caused you to start, at least. Ah! you are stronger than I expected. But what's the use of your trying to conceal anything from me?"

He picked up the alphabet-book, which he had placed on a convenient table, and, opening it at the mutilated page, said:

"Will you tell me the order in which the missing letters should be arranged in order to express the exact wording of the message you sent to Bresson four days before the theft of the Jewish lamp?"

"The order?... Bresson?... the theft of the Jewish lamp?"

She repeated the words slowly, as if trying to grasp their meaning. He continued:

"Yes. Here are the letters employed ... on this bit of paper.... What did you say to Bresson?"

"The letters employed ... what did I say...."

Suddenly she burst into laughter:

"Ah! that is it! I understand! I am an accomplice in the crime! There is a Monsieur Bresson who stole the Jewish lamp and who has now committed suicide. And I am the friend of that gentleman. Oh! how absurd you are!"

"Whom did you go to see last night on the second floor of a house in the avenue des Ternes?"

"Who? My modiste, Mademoiselle Langeais. Do you suppose that my modiste and my friend Monsieur Bresson are the same person?"

Despite all he knew, Sholmes was now in doubt. A person can feign terror, joy, anxiety, in fact all emotions; but a person cannot feign absolute indifference or light, careless laughter. Yet he continued to question her:

"Why did you accost me the other evening at the Northern Railway station? And why did you entreat me to leave Paris immediately without investigating this theft?"

"Ah! you are too inquisitive, Monsieur Sholmes," she replied, still laughing in the most natural manner. "To punish you I will tell you nothing, and, besides, you must watch the patient while I go to the pharmacy on an urgent message. Au revoir."

She left the room.

"I am beaten ... by a girl," muttered Sholmes. "Not only did I get nothing out of her but I exposed my hand and put her on her guard."

And he recalled the affair of the blue diamond and his first interview with Clotilde Destange. Had not the blonde Lady met his question with the same unruffled serenity, and was he not once more face to face with one of those creatures who, under the protection and influence of Arsène Lupin, maintain the utmost coolness in the face of a terrible danger?

"Sholmes ... Sholmes...."

It was Wilson who called him. Sholmes approached the bed, and, leaning over, said:

"What's the matter, Wilson? Does your wound pain you?"

Wilson's lips moved, but he could not speak. At last, with a great effort, he stammered:

"No ... Sholmes ... it is not she ... that is impossible——"

"Come, Wilson, what do you know about it? I tell you that it is she! It is only when I meet one of Lupin's creatures, prepared and instructed by him, that I lose my head and make a fool of myself.... I bet you that within an hour Lupin will know all about our interview. Within an hour? What am I saying?... Why, he may know already. The visit to the pharmacy ... urgent message. All nonsense!... She has gone to telephone to Lupin."

Sholmes left the house hurriedly, went down the avenue de Messine, and was just in time to see Mademoiselle enter a pharmacy. Ten minutes later she emerged from the shop carrying some small packages and a bottle wrapped in white paper. But she had not proceeded far, when she was accosted by a man who, with hat in hand and an obsequious air, appeared to be asking for charity. She stopped, gave him something, and proceeded on her way.

"She spoke to him," said the Englishman to himself.

If not a certainty, it was at least an intuition, and quite sufficient to cause him to change his tactics. Leaving the girl to pursue her own course, he followed the suspected mendicant, who walked slowly to the avenue des Ternes and lingered for a long time around the house in which Bresson had lived, sometimes raising his eyes to the windows of the second floor and watching the people who entered the house.

At the end of an hour he climbed to the top of a tramcar going in the direction of Neuilly. Sholmes followed and took a seat behind the man, and beside a gentleman who was concealed behind the pages of a newspaper. At the fortifications the gentleman lowered the paper, and Sholmes recognized Ganimard, who thereupon whispered, as he pointed to the man in front:

"It is the man who followed Bresson last night. He has been watching the house for an hour."

"Anything new in regard to Bresson?" asked Sholmes.

"Yes, a letter came to his address this morning."

"This morning? Then it was posted yesterday before the sender could know of Bresson's death."

"Exactly. It is now in the possession of the examining magistrate. But I read it. It says: *He will not accept any compromise. He wants everything—the first thing as well as those of the second affair. Otherwise he will proceed.*"

"There is no signature," added Ganimard. "It seems to me those few lines won't help us much."

"I don't agree with you, Monsieur Ganimard. To me those few lines are very interesting."

"Why so? I can't see it."

"For reasons that are personal to me," replied Sholmes, with the indifference that he frequently displayed toward his colleague.

The tramcar stopped at the rue de Château, which was the terminus. The man descended and walked away quietly. Sholmes followed at so short a distance that Ganimard protested, saying:

"If he should turn around he will suspect us."

"He will not turn around."

"How do you know?"

"He is an accomplice of Arsène Lupin, and the fact that he walks in that manner, with his hands in his pockets, proves, in the first place, that he knows he is being followed and, in the second place, that he is not afraid."

"But I think we are keeping too close to him."

"Not too close to prevent his slipping through our fingers. He is too sure of himself."

"Ah! Look there! In front of that café there are two of the bicycle police. If I summon them to our assistance, how can the man slip through our fingers?"

"Well, our friend doesn't seem to be worried about it. In fact, he is asking for their assistance himself."

"Mon Dieu!" exclaimed Ganimard, "he has a nerve."

The man approached the two policemen just as they were mounting their bicycles. After a few words with them he leaped on a third bicycle, which was leaning against the wall of the café, and rode away at a fast pace, accompanied by the two policemen.

"Hein! one, two, three and away!" growled Sholmes. "And through, whose agency, Monsieur Ganimard? Two of your colleagues.... Ah! but Arsène Lupin has a wonderful organization! Bicycle policemen in his service!... I told you our man was too calm, too sure of himself."

"Well, then," said Ganimard, quite vexed, "what are we to do now? It is easy enough to laugh! Anyone can do that."

"Come, come, don't lose your temper! We will get our revenge. But, in the meantime, we need reinforcements."

"Folenfant is waiting for me at the end of the avenue de Neuilly."

"Well, go and get him and join me later. I will follow our fugitive."

Sholmes followed the bicycle tracks, which were plainly visible in the dust of the road as two of the machines were furnished with striated tires. Very soon he ascertained that the tracks were leading him to the edge of the Seine, and that the three men had turned in the direction taken by Bresson on the preceding evening. Thus he arrived at the gateway where he and Ganimard had concealed themselves, and, a little farther on, he discovered a mingling of the bicycle tracks which showed that the men had halted at that spot. Directly opposite there was a little point of land which projected into the river and, at the extremity thereof, an old boat was moored.

It was there that Bresson had thrown away the package, or, rather, had dropped it. Sholmes descended the bank and saw that the declivity was not steep and the water quite shallow, so it would be quite easy to recover the package, provided the three men had not forestalled him.

"No, that can't be," he thought, "they have not had time. A quarter of an hour at the most. And yet, why did they come this way?"

A fisherman was seated on the old boat. Sholmes asked him:

"Did you see three men on bicycles a few minutes ago?"

The fisherman made a negative gesture. But Sholmes insisted:

"Three men who stopped on the road just on top of the bank?"

The fisherman rested his pole under his arm, took a memorandum book from his pocket, wrote on one of the pages, tore it out, and handed it to Sholmes. The Englishman gave a start of surprise. In the middle of the paper which he held in his hand he saw the series of letters cut from the alphabet-book:

CDEHNOPRZEO—237.

The man resumed his fishing, sheltered from the sun by a large straw hat, with his coat and vest lying beside him. He was intently watching the cork attached to his line as it floated on the surface of the water.

There was a moment of silence—solemn and terrible.

"Is it he?" conjectured Sholmes, with an anxiety that was almost pitiful. Then the truth burst upon him:

"It is he! It is he! No one else could remain there so calmly, without the slightest display of anxiety, without the least fear of what might happen. And who else would know the story of those mysterious letters? Alice had warned him by means of her messenger."

Suddenly the Englishman felt that his hand—that his own hand had involuntarily seized the handle of his revolver, and that his eyes were fixed on the man's back, a little below the neck. One movement, and the drama would be finished; the life of the strange adventurer would come to a miserable end.

The fisherman did not stir.

Sholmes nervously toyed with his revolver, and experienced a wild desire to fire it and end everything; but the horror of such an act was repugnant to his nature. Death would be certain and would end all.

"Ah!" he thought, "let him get up and defend himself. If he doesn't, so much the worse for him. One second more ... and I fire...."

But a sound of footsteps behind him caused him to turn his head. It was Ganimard coming with some assistants.

Then, quickly changing his plans, Sholmes leaped into the boat, which was broken from its moorings by his sudden action; he pounced upon the man and seized him around the body. They rolled to the bottom of the boat together.

"Well, now!" exclaimed Lupin, struggling to free himself, "what does this mean? When one of us has conquered the other, what good will it do? You will not know what to do with me, nor I with you. We will remain here like two idiots."

The two oars slipped into the water. The boat drifted into the stream.

"Good Lord, what a fuss you make! A man of your age ought to know better! You act like a child."

Lupin succeeded in freeing himself from the grasp of the detective, who, thoroughly exasperated and ready to kill, put his hand in his pocket. He uttered an oath: Lupin had taken his revolver. Then he knelt down and tried to capture one of the lost oars in order to regain the shore, while Lupin was trying to capture the other oar in order to drive the boat down the river.

"It's gone! I can't reach it," said Lupin. "But it's of no consequence. If you get your oar I can prevent your using it. And you could do the same to me. But, you see, that is the way in this world, we act without any purpose or reason, as our efforts are in vain since Fate decides everything. Now, don't you see, Fate is on the side of his friend Lupin. The game is mine! The current favors me!"

The boat was slowly drifting down the river.

"Look out!" cried Lupin, quickly.

Someone on the bank was pointing a revolver. Lupin stooped, a shot was fired; it struck the water beyond the boat. Lupin burst into laughter.

"God bless me! It's my friend Ganimard! But it was very wrong of you to do that, Ganimard. You have no right to shoot except in self-defense. Does poor Lupin worry you so much that you forget yourself?... Now, be good, and don't shoot again!... If you do you will hit our English friend."

He stood behind Sholmes, facing Ganimard, and said:

"Now, Ganimard, I am ready! Aim for his heart!... Higher!... A little to the left.... Ah! you missed that time ... deuced bad shot.... Try again.... Your hand shakes, Ganimard.... Now, once more ... one, two, three, fire!... Missed!... Parbleu! the authorities furnish you with toy-pistols."

Lupin drew a long revolver and fired without taking aim. Ganimard put his hand to his hat: the bullet had passed through it.

"What do you think of that, Ganimard! Ah! that's a real revolver! A genuine English bulldog. It belongs to my friend, Herlock Sholmes."

And, with a laugh, he threw the revolver to the shore, where it landed at Ganimard's feet.

Sholmes could not withhold a smile of admiration. What a torrent of youthful spirits! And how he seemed to enjoy himself! It appeared as if the sensation of peril caused him a physical pleasure; and this extraordinary man had no other purpose in life than to seek for dangers simply for the amusement it afforded him in avoiding them.

Many people had now gathered on the banks of the river, and Ganimard and his men followed the boat as it slowly floated down the stream. Lupin's capture was a mathematical certainty.

"Confess, old fellow," said Lupin, turning to the Englishman, "that you would not exchange your present position for all the gold in the Transvaal! You are now in the first row of the orchestra chairs! But, in the first place, we must have the prologue ... after which we can leap, at one bound, to the fifth act of the drama, which will represent the capture or escape of Arsène Lupin. Therefore, I am going to ask you a plain question, to which I request a plain answer—a simple yes or no. Will you renounce this affair? At present I can repair the damage you have done; later it will be beyond my power. Is it a bargain?"

"No."

Lupin's face showed his disappointment and annoyance. He continued:

"I insist. More for your sake than my own, I insist, because I am certain you will be the first to regret your intervention. For the last time, yes or no?"

"No."

Lupin stooped down, removed one of the boards in the bottom of the boat, and, for some minutes, was engaged in a work the nature of which Sholmes could not discern. Then he arose, seated himself beside the Englishman, and said:

"I believe, monsieur, that we came to the river to-day for the same purpose: to recover the object which Bresson threw away. For my part I had invited a few friends to join me here, and I was on the point of making an examination of the bed of the river when my friends announced your approach. I confess that the news did not surprise me, as I have been notified every hour concerning the progress of your investigation. That was an easy matter. Whenever anything occurred in the rue Murillo that might interest me, simply a ring on the telephone and I was informed."

He stopped. The board that he had displaced in the bottom of the boat was rising and water was working into the boat all around it.

"The deuce! I didn't know how to fix it. I was afraid this old boat would leak. You are not afraid, monsieur?"

Sholmes shrugged his shoulders. Lupin continued:

"You will understand then, in those circumstances, and knowing in advance that you would be more eager to seek a battle than I would be to avoid it, I assure you I was not entirely displeased to enter into a contest of which the issue is quite certain, since I hold all the trump cards in my hand. And I desired that our meeting should be given the widest publicity in order that your defeat may be universally known, so that another Countess de Crozon or another Baron d'Imblevalle may not be tempted to solicit your aid against me. Besides, my dear monsieur—"

He stopped again and, using his half-closed hands as a lorgnette, he scanned the banks of the river.

"Mon Dieu! they have chartered a superb boat, a real war-vessel, and see how they are rowing. In five minutes they will be along-side, and I am lost. Monsieur Sholmes, a word of advice; you seize me, bind me and deliver me to the officers of the law. Does that programme please you?... Unless, in the meantime, we are shipwrecked, in which event we can do nothing but prepare our wills. What do you think?"

They exchanged looks. Sholmes now understood Lupin's scheme: he had scuttled the boat. And the water was rising. It had reached the soles of their boots. Then it covered their feet; but they did not move. It was half-way to their knees. The Englishman took out his tobacco, rolled a cigarette, and lighted it. Lupin continued to talk:

"But do not regard that offer as a confession of my weakness. I surrender to you in a battle in which I can achieve a victory in order to avoid a struggle upon a field not of my own choosing. In so doing I recognize the fact that Sholmes is the only enemy I fear, and announce my anxiety that Sholmes will not be diverted from my track. I take this opportunity to tell you these things since fate has accorded me the honor of a conversation with you. I have only one regret; it is that our conversation should have occurred while we are taking a foot-bath ... a situation that is lacking in dignity, I must confess.... What did I say? A foot-bath? It is worse than that."

The water had reached the board on which they were sitting, and the boat was gradually sinking.

Sholmes, smoking his cigarette, appeared to be calmly admiring the scenery. For nothing in the world, while face to face with that man who, while threatened by dangers, surrounded by a crowd, followed by a posse of police, maintained his equanimity and good humor, for nothing in the world would he, Sholmes, display the slightest sign of nervousness.

Each of them looked as if he might say: Should a person be disturbed by such trifles? Are not people drowned in a river every day? Is it such an unusual event as to deserve special attention? One chatted, whilst the other dreamed; both concealing their wounded pride beneath a mask of indifference.

One minute more and the boat will sink. Lupin continued his chatter:

"The important thing to know is whether we will sink before or after the arrival of the champions of the law. That is the main question. As to our shipwreck, that is a fore-gone conclusion. Now, monsieur, the hour has come in which we must make our wills. I give, devise and bequeath all my property to Herlock Sholmes, a citizen of England, for his own use and benefit. But, mon Dieu, how quickly the champions of the law are approaching! Ah! the brave fellows! It is a pleasure to watch them. Observe the precision of the oars! Ah! is it you, Brigadier Folenfant? Bravo! The idea of a war-vessel is an excellent one. I commend you to your superiors, Brigadier Folenfant.... Do you wish a medal? You shall have it. And your comrade Dieuzy, where is he?... Ah! yes, I think I see him on the left bank of the river at the head of a hundred natives. So that, if I escape shipwreck, I shall be captured on the left by Dieuzy and his natives, or, on the right, by Ganimard and the populace of Neuilly. An embarrassing dilemma!"

The boat entered an eddy; it swung around and Sholmes caught hold of the oarlocks. Lupin said to him:

"Monsieur, you should remove your coat. You will find it easier to swim without a coat. No? You refuse? Then I shall put on my own."

He donned his coat, buttoned it closely, the same as Sholmes, and said:

"What a discourteous man you are! And what a pity that you should be so stubborn in this affair, in which, of course, you display your strength, but, oh! so vainly! really, you mar your genius——"

"Monsieur Lupin," interrupted Sholmes, emerging from his silence, "you talk too much, and you frequently err through excess of confidence and through your frivolity."

"That is a severe reproach."

"Thus, without knowing it, you furnished me, only a moment ago, with the information I required."

"What! you required some information and you didn't tell me?"

"I had no occasion to ask you for it—you volunteered it. Within three hours I can deliver the key of the mystery to Monsieur d'Imblevalle. That is the only reply——"

He did not finish the sentence. The boat suddenly sank, taking both of the men down with it. It emerged immediately, with its keel in the air. Shouts were heard on either bank, succeeded by an anxious moment of silence. Then the shouts were renewed: one of the shipwrecked party had come to the surface.

It was Herlock Sholmes. He was an excellent swimmer, and struck out, with powerful strokes, for Folenfant's boat.

"Courage, Monsieur Sholmes," shouted Folenfant; "we are here. Keep it up ... we will get you ... a little more, Monsieur Sholmes ... catch the rope."

The Englishman seized the rope they had thrown to him. But, while they were hauling him into the boat, he heard a voice behind him, saying:

"The key of the mystery, monsieur, yes, you shall have it. I am astonished that you haven't got it already. What then? What good will it do you? By that time you will have lost the battle...."

Now comfortably installed astride the keel of the boat, Lupin continued his speech with solemn gestures, as if he hoped to convince his adversary.

"You must understand, my dear Sholmes, there is nothing to be done, absolutely nothing. You find yourself in the deplorable position of a gentleman——"

"Surrender, Lupin!" shouted Folenfant.

"You are an ill-bred fellow, Folenfant, to interrupt me in the middle of a sentence. I was saying——"

"Surrender, Lupin!"

"Oh! parbleu! Brigadier Folenfant, a man surrenders only when he is in danger. Surely, you do not pretend to say that I am in any danger."

"For the last time, Lupin, I call on you to surrender."

"Brigadier Folenfant, you have no intention of killing me; you may wish to wound me since you are afraid I may escape. But if by chance the wound prove mortal! Just think of your remorse! It would embitter your old age."

The shot was fired.

Lupin staggered, clutched at the keel of the boat for a moment, then let go and disappeared.

It was exactly three o'clock when the foregoing events transpired. Precisely at six o'clock, as he had foretold, Herlock Sholmes, dressed in trousers that were too short and a coat that was too small, which he had borrowed from an innkeeper at Neuilly, wearing a cap and a flannel shirt, entered the boudoir in the Rue Murillo, after having sent word to Monsieur and Madame d'Imblevalle that he desired an interview.

They found him walking up and down the room. And he looked so ludicrous in his strange costume that they could scarcely suppress their mirth. With pensive air and stooped shoulders, he walked like an automaton from the window to the door and from the door to the window, taking each time the same number of steps, and turning each time in the same manner.

He stopped, picked up a small ornament, examined it mechanically, and resumed his walk. At last, planting himself before them, he asked:

"Is Mademoiselle here?"

"Yes, she is in the garden with the children."'

"I wish Mademoiselle to be present at this interview."

"Is it necessary——"

"Have a little patience, monsieur. From the facts I am going to present to you, you will see the necessity for her presence here."

"Very well. Suzanne, will you call her?"

Madame d'Imblevalle arose, went out, and returned almost immediately, accompanied by Alice Demun. Mademoiselle, who was a trifle paler than usual, remained standing, leaning against a table, and without even asking why she had been called. Sholmes did not look at her, but, suddenly turning toward Monsieur d'Imblevalle, he said, in a tone which did not admit of a reply:

"After several days' investigation, monsieur, I must repeat what I told you when I first came here: the Jewish lamp was stolen by some one living in the house."

"The name of the guilty party?"

"I know it."

"Your proof?"

"I have sufficient to establish that fact."

"But we require more than that. We desire the restoration of the stolen goods."

"The Jewish lamp? It is in my possession."

"The opal necklace? The snuff-box?"

"The opal necklace, the snuff-box, and all the goods stolen on the second occasion are in my possession."

Sholmes delighted in these dramatic dialogues, and it pleased him to announce his victories in that curt manner. The baron and his wife were amazed, and looked at Sholmes with a silent curiosity, which was the highest praise.

He related to them, very minutely, what he had done during those three days. He told of his discovery of the alphabet book, wrote upon a sheet of paper the sentence formed by the missing letters, then related the journey of Bresson to the bank of the river and the suicide of the adventurer, and, finally, his struggle with Lupin, the shipwreck, and the disappearance of Lupin. When he had finished, the baron said, in a low voice:

"Now, you have told us everything except the name of the guilty party. Whom do you accuse?"

"I accuse the person who cut the letters from the alphabet book, and communicated with Arsène Lupin by means of those letters."

"How do you know that such correspondence was carried on with Arsène Lupin?"

"My information comes from Lupin himself."

He produced a piece of paper that was wet and crumpled. It was the page which Lupin had torn from his memorandum-book, and upon which he had written the phrase.

"And you will notice," said Sholmes, with satisfaction, "that he was not obliged to give me that sheet of paper, and, in that way, disclose his identity. Simple childishness on his part, and yet it gave me exactly the information I desired."

"What was it?" asked the baron. "I don't understand."

Sholmes took a pencil and made a fresh copy of the letters and figures.

"CDEHNOPRZEO—237."

"Well?" said the baron; "it is the formula you showed me yourself."

"No. If you had turned and returned that formula in every way, as I have done, you would have seen at first glance that this formula is not like the first one."

"In what respect do they differ?"

"This one has two more letters—an E and an O."

"Really; I hadn't noticed that."

"Join those two letters to the C and the H which remained after forming the word 'respondez,' and you will agree with me that the only possible word is ECHO."

"What does that mean?"

"It refers to the *Echo de France*, Lupin's newspaper, his official organ, the one in which he publishes his communications. Reply in the *Echo de France*, in the personal advertisements, under number 237. That is the key to the mystery, and Arsène Lupin was kind enough to furnish it to me. I went to the newspaper office."

"What did you find there?"

"I found the entire story of the relations between Arsène Lupin and his accomplice."

Sholmes produced seven newspapers which he opened at the fourth page and pointed to the following lines:

1. Ars. Lup. Lady implores protection. 540.
    2. 540. Awaiting particulars. A.L.
    3. A.L. Under domin. enemy. Lost.
    4. 540. Write address. Will make investigation.
    5. A.L. Murillo.
    6. 540. Park three o'clock. Violets.
    7. 237. Understand. Sat. Will be Sun. morn. park.

"And you call that the whole story!" exclaimed the baron.

"Yes, and if you will listen to me for a few minutes, I think I can convince you. In the first place, a lady who signs herself 540 implores the protection of Arsène Lupin, who replies by asking for particulars. The lady replies that she is under the domination of an enemy—who is Bresson, no doubt—and that she is lost if some one does not come to her assistance. Lupin is suspicious and does not yet venture to appoint an interview with the unknown woman, demands the address and proposes to make an investigation. The lady hesitates for four days—look at the dates—finally, under stress of circumstances and influenced by Bresson's threats, she gives the name of the street—Murillo. Next day, Arsène Lupin announces that he will be in the Park Monceau at three o'clock, and asks his unknown correspondent to wear a bouquet of violets as a means of identification. Then there is a lapse of eight days in the correspondence. Arsène Lupin and the lady do not require to correspond through the newspaper now, as they see each other or write directly. The scheme is arranged in this way: in order to satisfy Bresson's demands, the lady is to carry off the Jewish lamp. The date is not yet fixed. The lady who, as a matter of prudence, corresponds by means of letters cut out of a book, decides on Saturday and adds: *Reply Echo 237*. Lupin replies that it is understood and that he will be in the park on Sunday morning. Sunday morning, the theft takes place."

"Really, that is an excellent chain of circumstantial evidence and every link is complete," said the baron.

"The theft has taken place," continued Sholmes. "The lady goes out on Sunday morning, tells Lupin what she has done, and carries the Jewish lamp to Bresson. Everything occurs then exactly as Lupin had foreseen. The officers of the law, deceived by an open window, four holes in the ground and two scratches on the balcony railing, immediately advance the theory that the theft was committed by a burglar. The lady is safe."

"Yes, I confess the theory was a logical one," said the baron. "But the second theft—"

"The second theft was provoked by the first. The newspapers having related how the Jewish lamp had disappeared, some one conceived the idea of repeating the crime and carrying away what had been left. This time, it was not a simulated theft, but a real one, a genuine burglary, with ladders and other paraphernalia—"

"Lupin, of course—"

"No. Lupin does not act so stupidly. He doesn't fire at people for trifling reasons."

"Then, who was it?"

"Bresson, no doubt, and unknown to the lady whom he had menaced. It was Bresson who entered here; it was Bresson that I pursued; it was Bresson who wounded poor Wilson."

"Are you sure of it?"

"Absolutely. One of Bresson's accomplices wrote to him yesterday, before his suicide, a letter which proves that negotiations were pending between this accomplice and Lupin for the restitution of all the articles stolen from your house. Lupin demanded everything, *'the first thing* (that is, the Jewish lamp) *as well as those of the second affair.'* Moreover, he was watching Bresson. When the latter returned from the river last night, one of Lupin's men followed him as well as we."

"What was Bresson doing at the river?"

"Having been warned of the progress of my investigations——"

"Warned! by whom?"

"By the same lady, who justly feared that the discovery of the Jewish lamp would lead to the discovery of her own adventure. Thereupon, Bresson, having been warned, made into a package all the things that could compromise him and threw them into a place where he thought he could get them again when the danger was past. It was after his return, tracked by Ganimard and myself, having, no doubt, other sins on his conscience, that he lost his head and killed himself."

"But what did the package contain?"

"The Jewish lamp and your other ornaments."

"Then, they are not in your possession?"

"Immediately after Lupin's disappearance, I profited by the bath he had forced upon me, went to the spot selected by Bresson, where I found the stolen articles wrapped in some soiled linen. They are there, on the table."

Without a word, the baron cut the cord, tore open the wet linen, picked out the lamp, turned a screw in the foot, then divided the bowl of the lamp which opened in two equal parts and there he found the golden chimera, set with rubies and emeralds.

It was intact.

There was in that scene, so natural in appearance and which consisted of a simple exposition of facts, something which rendered it frightfully tragic—it was the formal, direct, irrefutable accusation that Sholmes launched in each of his words against Mademoiselle. And it was also the impressive silence of Alice Demun.

During that long, cruel accumulation of accusing circumstances heaped one upon another, not a muscle of her face had moved, not a trace of revolt or fear had marred the serenity of her limpid eyes. What were her thoughts. And, especially, what was she going to say at the solemn moment when it would become necessary for her to speak and defend herself in order to break the chain of evidence that Herlock Sholmes had so cleverly woven around her?

That moment had come, but the girl was silent.

"Speak! Speak!" cried Mon. d'Imblevalle.

She did not speak. So he insisted:

"One word will clear you. One word of denial, and I will believe you."

That word, she would not utter.

The baron paced to and fro in his excitement; then, addressing Sholmes, he said:

"No, monsieur, I cannot believe it, I do not believe it. There are impossible crimes! and this is opposed to all I know and to all that I have seen during the past year. No, I cannot believe it."

He placed his hand on the Englishman's shoulder, and said:

"But you yourself, monsieur, are you absolutely certain that you are right?"

Sholmes hesitated, like a man on whom a sudden demand is made and cannot frame an immediate reply. Then he smiled, and said:

"Only the person whom I accuse, by reason of her situation in your house, could know that the Jewish lamp contained that magnificent jewel."

"I cannot believe it," repeated the baron.

"Ask her."

It was, really, the very thing he would not have done, blinded by the confidence the girl had inspired in him. But he could no longer refrain from doing it. He approached her and, looking into her eyes, said:

"Was it you, mademoiselle? Was it you who took the jewel? Was it you who corresponded with Arsène Lupin and committed the theft?"

"It was I, monsieur," she replied.

She did not drop her head. Her face displayed no sign of shame or fear.

"Is it possible?" murmured Mon. d'Imblevalle. "I would never have believed it.... You are the last person in the world that I would have suspected. How did you do it?"

"I did it exactly as Monsieur Sholmes has told it. On Saturday night I came to the boudoir, took the lamp, and, in the morning I carried it ... to that man."

"No," said the baron; "what you pretend to have done is impossible."

"Impossible—why?"

"Because, in the morning I found the door of the boudoir bolted."

She blushed, and looked at Sholmes as if seeking his counsel. Sholmes was astonished at her embarrassment. Had she nothing to say? Did the confessions, which had corroborated the report that he, Sholmes, had made concerning the theft of the Jewish lamp, merely serve to mask a lie? Was she misleading them by a false confession?

The baron continued:

"That door was locked. I found the door exactly as I had left it the night before. If you entered by that door, as you pretend, some one must have opened it from the interior—

that is to say, from the boudoir or from our chamber. Now, there was no one inside these two rooms ... there was no one except my wife and myself."

Sholmes bowed his head and covered his face with his hands in order to conceal his emotion. A sudden light had entered his mind, that startled him and made him exceedingly uncomfortable. Everything was revealed to him, like the sudden lifting of a fog from the morning landscape. He was annoyed as well as ashamed, because his deductions were fallacious and his entire theory was wrong.

Alice Demun was innocent!

Alice Demun was innocent. That proposition explained the embarrassment he had experienced from the beginning in directing the terrible accusation against that young girl. Now, he saw the truth; he knew it. After a few seconds, he raised his head, and looked at Madame d'Imblevalle as naturally as he could. She was pale—with that unusual pallor which invades us in the relentless moments of our lives. Her hands, which she endeavored to conceal, were trembling as if stricken with palsy.

"One minute more," thought Sholmes, "and she will betray herself."

He placed himself between her and her husband in the desire to avert the awful danger which, *through his fault*, now threatened that man and woman. But, at sight of the baron, he was shocked to the very centre of his soul. The same dreadful idea had entered the mind of Monsieur d'Imblevalle. The same thought was at work in the brain of the husband. He understood, also! He saw the truth!

In desperation, Alice Demun hurled herself against the implacable truth, saying:

"You are right, monsieur. I made a mistake. I did not enter by this door. I came through the garden and the vestibule ... by aid of a ladder—"

It was a supreme effort of true devotion. But a useless effort! The words rang false. The voice did not carry conviction, and the poor girl no longer displayed those clear, fearless eyes and that natural air of innocence which had served her so well. Now, she bowed her head—vanquished.

The silence became painful. Madame d'Imblevalle was waiting for her husband's next move, overwhelmed with anxiety and fear. The baron appeared to be struggling against the dreadful suspicion, as if he would not submit to the overthrow of his happiness. Finally, he said to his wife:

"Speak! Explain!"

"I have nothing to tell you," she replied, in a very low voice, and with features drawn by anguish.

"So, then ... Mademoiselle...."

"Mademoiselle saved me ... through devotion ... through affection ... and accused herself...."

"Saved you from what? From whom?"

"From that man."

"Bresson?"

"Yes; it was I whom he held in fear by threats.... I met him at one of my friends'.... and I was foolish enough to listen to him. Oh! there was nothing that you cannot pardon. But I wrote him two letters ... letters which you will see.... I had to buy them back ... you know how.... Oh! have pity on me?... I have suffered so much!"

"You! You! Suzanne!"

He raised his clenched fists, ready to strike her, ready to kill her. But he dropped his arms, and murmured:

"You, Suzanne.... You!... Is it possible?"

By short detached sentences, she related the heartrending story, her dreadful awakening to the infamy of the man, her remorse, her fear, and she also told of Alice's devotion; how the young girl divined the sorrow of her mistress, wormed a confession out of her, wrote to Lupin, and devised the scheme of the theft in order to save her from Bresson.

"You, Suzanne, you," repeated Monsieur d'Imblevalle, bowed with grief and shame.... "How could you?"

❁

On the same evening, the steamer "City of London," which plies between Calais and Dover, was gliding slowly over the smooth sea. The night was dark; the wind was fainter than a zephyr. The majority of the passengers had retired to their cabins; but a few, more intrepid, were promenading on the deck or sleeping in large rocking-chairs, wrapped in their travelling-rugs. One could see, here and there, the light of a cigar, and one could hear, mingled with the soft murmur of the breeze, the faint sound of voices which were carefully subdued to harmonize with the deep silence of the night.

One of the passengers, who had been pacing to and fro upon the deck, stopped before a woman who was lying on a bench, scrutinized her, and, when she moved a little, he said:

"I thought you were asleep, Mademoiselle Alice."

"No, Monsieur Sholmes, I am not sleepy. I was thinking."

"Of what? If I may be so bold as to inquire?"

"I was thinking of Madame d'Imblevalle. She must be very unhappy. Her life is ruined."

"Oh! no, no," he replied quickly. "Her mistake was not a serious one. Monsieur d'Imblevalle will forgive and forget it. Why, even before we left, his manner toward her had softened."

"Perhaps ... but he will remember it for a long time ... and she will suffer a great deal."

"You love her?"

"Very much. It was my love for her that gave me strength to smile when I was trembling from fear, that gave me courage to look in your face when I desired to hide from your sight."

"And you are sorry to leave her?"

"Yes, very sorry. I have no relatives, no friends—but her."

"You will have friends," said the Englishman, who was affected by her sorrow. "I have promised that. I have relatives ... and some influence. I assure you that you will have no cause to regret coming to England."

"That may be, monsieur, but Madame d'Imblevalle will not be there."

Herlock Sholmes resumed his promenade upon the deck. After a few minutes, he took a seat near his travelling companion, filled his pipe, and struck four matches in a vain effort to light it. Then, as he had no more matches, he arose and said to a gentleman who was sitting near him:

"May I trouble you for a match?"

The gentleman opened a box of matches and struck one. The flame lighted up his face. Sholmes recognized him—it was Arsène Lupin.

If the Englishman had not given an almost imperceptible movement of surprise, Lupin would have supposed that his presence on board had been known to Sholmes, so well did he control his feelings and so natural was the easy manner in which he extended his hand to his adversary.

"How's the good health, Monsieur Lupin?"

"Bravo!" exclaimed Lupin, who could not repress a cry of admiration at the Englishman's sang-froid.

"Bravo? and why?"

"Why? Because I appear before you like a ghost, only a few hours after you saw me drowned in the Seine; and through pride—a quality that is essentially English—you evince not the slightest surprise. You greet me as a matter of course. Ah! I repeat: Bravo! Admirable!"

"There is nothing remarkable about it. From the manner in which you fell from the boat, I knew very well that you fell voluntarily, and that the bullet had not touched you."

"And you went away without knowing what had become of me?"

"What had become of you? Why, I knew that. There were at least five hundred people on the two banks of the river within a space of half-a-mile. If you escaped death, your capture was certain."

"And yet I am here."

"Monsieur Lupin, there are two men in the world at whom I am never astonished: in the first place, myself—and then, Arsène Lupin."

The treaty of peace was concluded.

If Sholmes had not been successful in his contests with Arsène Lupin; if Lupin remained the only enemy whose capture he must never hope to accomplish; if, in the course of their struggles, he had not always displayed a superiority, the Englishman had, none the less, by means of his extraordinary intuition and tenacity, succeeded in recovering the Jewish lamp as well as the blue diamond.

This time, perhaps, the finish had not been so brilliant, especially from the stand-point of the public spectators, since Sholmes was obliged to maintain a discreet silence in regard to the circumstances in which the Jewish lamp had been recovered, and to announce that he did not know the name of the thief. But as man to man, Arsène Lupin against Herlock Sholmes, detective against burglar, there was neither victor nor vanquished. Each of them had won corresponding victories.

Therefore they could now converse as courteous adversaries who had lain down their arms and held each other in high regard.

At Sholmes' request, Arsène Lupin related the strange story of his escape.

"If I may dignify it by calling it an escape," he said. "It was so simple! My friends were watching for me, as I had asked them to meet me there to recover the Jewish lamp. So, after remaining a good half-hour under the overturned boat, I took advantage of an occasion when Folenfant and his men were searching for my dead body along the bank of the river, to climb on top of the boat. Then my friends simply picked me up as they passed by in their motor-boat, and we sailed away under the staring eyes of an astonished multitude, including Ganimard and Folenfant."

"Very good," exclaimed Sholmes, "very neatly played. And now you have some business in England?"

"Yes, some accounts to square up.... But I forgot ... what about Monsieur d'Imblevalle?"

"He knows everything."

"All! my dear Sholmes, what did I tell you? The wrong is now irreparable. Would it not have been better to have allowed me to carry out the affair in my own way? In a day or two more, I should have recovered the stolen goods from Bresson, restored them to Monsieur d'Imblevalle, and those two honest citizens would have lived together in peace and happiness ever after. Instead of that—"

"Instead of that," said Sholmes, sneeringly, "I have mixed the cards and sown the seeds of discord in the bosom of a family that was under your protection."

"Mon Dieu! of course, I was protecting them. Must a person steal, cheat and wrong all the time?"

"Then you do good, also?"

"When I have the time. Besides, I find it amusing. Now, for instance, in our last adventure, I found it extremely diverting that I should be the good genius seeking to help and save unfortunate mortals, while you were the evil genius who dispensed only despair and tears."

"Tears! Tears!" protested Sholmes.

"Certainly! The d'Imblevalle household is demolished, and Alice Demun weeps."

"She could not remain any longer. Ganimard would have discovered her some day, and, through her, reached Madame d'Imblevalle."

"Quite right, monsieur; but whose fault is it?"

Two men passed by. Sholmes said to Lupin, in a friendly tone:

"Do you know those gentlemen?"

"I thought I recognized one of them as the captain of the steamer."

"And the other?"

"I don't know."

"It is Austin Gilett, who occupies in London a position similar to that of Monsieur Dudouis in Paris."

"Ah! how fortunate! Will you be so kind as to introduce me? Monsieur Dudouis is one of my best friends, and I shall be delighted to say as much of Monsieur Austin Gilett."

The two gentlemen passed again.

"And if I should take you at your word, Monsieur Lupin?" said Sholmes, rising, and seizing Lupin's wrist with a hand of iron.

"Why do you grasp me so tightly, monsieur? I am quite willing to follow you."

In fact, he allowed himself to be dragged along without the least resistance. The two gentlemen were disappearing from sight. Sholmes quickened his pace. His finger-nails even sank into Lupin's flesh.

"Come! Come!" he exclaimed, with a sort of feverish haste, in harmony with his action. "Come! quicker than that."

But he stopped suddenly. Alice Demun was following them.

"What are you doing, Mademoiselle? You need not come. You must not come!"

It was Lupin who replied:

"You will notice, monsieur, that she is not coming of her own free will. I am holding her wrist in the same tight grasp that you have on mine."

"Why!"

"Because I wish to present her also. Her part in the affair of the Jewish lamp is much more important than mine. Accomplice of Arsène Lupin, accomplice of Bresson, she has a right to tell her adventure with the Baroness d'Imblevalle—which will deeply interest Monsieur Gilett as an officer of the law. And by introducing her also, you will have carried your gracious intervention to the very limit, my dear Sholmes."

The Englishman released his hold on his prisoner's wrist. Lupin liberated Mademoiselle.

They stood looking at each other for a few seconds, silently and motionless. Then Sholmes returned to the bench and sat down, followed by Lupin and the girl. After a long silence, Lupin said: "You see, monsieur, whatever we may do, we will never be on the same side. You are on one side of the fence; I am on the other. We can exchange greetings, shake hands, converse a moment, but the fence is always there. You will remain Herlock Sholmes, detective, and I, Arsène Lupin, gentleman-burglar. And Herlock Sholmes will ever obey, more or less spontaneously, with more or less propriety, his instinct as a detective, which is to pursue the burglar and run him down, if possible. And Arsène Lupin, in obedience to his burglarious instinct, will always be occupied in avoiding the reach of the detective, and making sport of the detective, if he can do it. And, this time, he can do it. Ha-ha-ha!"

He burst into a loud laugh, cunning, cruel and odious.

Then, suddenly becoming serious, he addressed Alice Demun:

"You may be sure, mademoiselle, even when reduced to the last extremity, I shall not betray you. Arsène Lupin never betrays anyone—especially those whom he loves and admires. And, may I be permitted to say, I love and admire the brave, dear woman you have proved yourself to be."

He took from his pocket a visiting card, tore it in two, gave one-half of it to the girl, as he said, in a voice shaken with emotion:

"If Monsieur Sholmes' plans for you do not succeed, mademoiselle, go to Lady Strongborough—you can easily find her address—and give her that half of the card, and, at the same time, say to her: *Faithful friend*. Lady Strongborough will show you the true devotion of a sister."

"Thank you," said the girl; "I shall see her to-morrow."

"And now, Monsieur Sholmes," exclaimed Lupin, with the satisfied air of a gentleman who has fulfilled his duty, "I will say good-night. We will not land for an hour yet, so I will get that much rest."

He lay down on the bench, with his hands beneath his head.

In a short time the high cliffs of the English coast loomed up in the increasing light of a new-born day. The passengers emerged from the cabins and crowded the deck, eagerly gazing on the approaching shore. Austin Gilette passed by, accompanied by two men whom Sholmes recognized as sleuths from Scotland Yard.

Lupin was asleep, on his bench.

※

The further startling, wonderful and thrilling adventures of "Arsène Lupin" can be found in the book entitled "The Extraordinary Adventures of Arsène Lupin, Gentleman-Burglar."

THE CONFESSIONS OF ARSÈNE LUPIN

I. TWO HUNDRED THOUSAND FRANCS REWARD!...

"Lupin," I said, "tell me something about yourself."

"Why, what would you have me tell you? Everybody knows my life!" replied Lupin, who lay drowsing on the sofa in my study.

"Nobody knows it!" I protested. "People know from your letters in the newspapers that you were mixed up in this case, that you started that case. But the part which you played in it all, the plain facts of the story, the upshot of the mystery: these are things of which they know nothing."

"Pooh! A heap of uninteresting twaddle!"

"What! Your present of fifty thousand francs to Nicolas Dugrival's wife! Do you call that uninteresting? And what about the way in which you solved the puzzle of the three pictures?"

Lupin laughed:

"Yes, that was a queer puzzle, certainly. I can suggest a title for you if you like: what do you say to *The Sign of the Shadow*?"

"And your successes in society and with the fair sex?" I continued. "The dashing Arsène's love-affairs!... And the clue to your good actions? Those chapters in your life to which you have so often alluded under the names of *The Wedding-ring*, *Shadowed by Death*, and so on!... Why delay these confidences and confessions, my dear Lupin?... Come, do what I ask you!..."

It was at the time when Lupin, though already famous, had not yet fought his biggest battles; the time that preceded the great adventures of *The Hollow Needle* and *813*. He had not yet dreamt of annexing the accumulated treasures of the French Royal House[1] nor of changing the map of Europe under the Kaiser's nose[2]: he contented himself with milder surprises and humbler profits, making his daily effort, doing evil from day to day and doing a little good as well, naturally and for the love of the thing, like a whimsical and compassionate Don Quixote.

He was silent; and I insisted:

"Lupin, I wish you would!"

To my astonishment, he replied:

"Take a sheet of paper, old fellow, and a pencil."

I obeyed with alacrity, delighted at the thought that he at last meant to dictate to me some of those pages which he knows how to clothe with such vigour and fancy, pages which I, unfortunately, am obliged to spoil with tedious explanations and boring developments.

"Are you ready?" he asked.

"Quite."

"Write down, 20, 1, 11, 5, 14, 15."

"What?"

"Write it down, I tell you."

He was now sitting up, with his eyes turned to the open window and his fingers rolling a Turkish cigarette. He continued:

"Write down, 21, 14, 14, 5...."

He stopped. Then he went on:

"3, 5, 19, 19 ..."

And, after a pause:

"5, 18, 25 ..."

Was he mad? I looked at him hard and, presently, I saw that his eyes were no longer listless, as they had been a little before, but keen and attentive and that they seemed to be watching, somewhere, in space, a sight that apparently captivated them.

Meanwhile, he dictated, with intervals between each number:

"18, 9, 19, 11, 19 ..."

There was hardly anything to be seen through the window but a patch of blue sky on the right and the front of the building opposite, an old private house, whose shutters were closed as usual. There was nothing particular about all this, no detail that struck me as new among those which I had had before my eyes for years....

"1, 2...."

And suddenly I understood ... or rather I thought I understood, for how could I admit that Lupin, a man so essentially level-headed under his mask of frivolity, could waste his time upon such childish nonsense? What he was counting was the intermittent flashes of a ray of sunlight playing on the dingy front of the opposite house, at the height of the second floor!

"15, 22 ..." said Lupin.

The flash disappeared for a few seconds and then struck the house again, successively, at regular intervals, and disappeared once more.

I had instinctively counted the flashes and I said, aloud:

"5...."

"Caught the idea? I congratulate you!" he replied, sarcastically.

He went to the window and leant out, as though to discover the exact direction followed by the ray of light. Then he came and lay on the sofa again, saying:

"It's your turn now. Count away!"

The fellow seemed so positive that I did as he told me. Besides, I could not help confessing that there was something rather curious about the ordered frequency of those gleams on the front of the house opposite, those appearances and disappearances, turn and turn about, like so many flash signals.

They obviously came from a house on our side of the street, for the sun was entering my windows slantwise. It was as though some one were alternately opening and shutting a casement, or, more likely, amusing himself by making sunlight flashes with a pocket-mirror.

"It's a child having a game!" I cried, after a moment or two, feeling a little irritated by the trivial occupation that had been thrust upon me.

"Never mind, go on!"

And I counted away.... And I put down rows of figures.... And the sun continued to play in front of me, with mathematical precision.

"Well?" said Lupin, after a longer pause than usual.

"Why, it seems finished.... There has been nothing for some minutes...."

We waited and, as no more light flashed through space, I said, jestingly:

"My idea is that we have been wasting our time. A few figures on paper: a poor result!"

Lupin, without stirring from his sofa, rejoined:

"Oblige me, old chap, by putting in the place of each of those numbers the corresponding letter of the alphabet. Count A as 1, B as 2 and so on. Do you follow me?"

"But it's idiotic!"

"Absolutely idiotic, but we do such a lot of idiotic things in this life.... One more or less, you know!..."

I sat down to this silly work and wrote out the first letters:

"Take no...."

I broke off in surprise:

"Words!" I exclaimed. "Two English words meaning...."

"Go on, old chap."

And I went on and the next letters formed two more words, which I separated as they appeared. And, to my great amazement, a complete English sentence lay before my eyes.

"Done?" asked Lupin, after a time.

"Done!... By the way, there are mistakes in the spelling...."

"Never mind those and read it out, please.... Read slowly."

Thereupon I read out the following unfinished communication, which I will set down as it appeared on the paper in front of me:

"Take no unnecessary risks. Above all, avoid attacks, approach ennemy with great prudance and...."

I began to laugh:

"And there you are! *Fiat lux!* We're simply dazed with light! But, after all, Lupin, confess that this advice, dribbled out by a kitchen-maid, doesn't help you much!"

Lupin rose, without breaking his contemptuous silence, and took the sheet of paper.

I remembered soon after that, at this moment, I happened to look at the clock. It was eighteen minutes past five.

Lupin was standing with the paper in his hand; and I was able at my ease to watch, on his youthful features, that extraordinary mobility of expression which baffles all observers and constitutes his great strength and his chief safeguard. By what signs can one hope to identify a face which changes at pleasure, even without the help of make-up, and whose every transient expression seems to be the final, definite expression?... By what signs? There was one which I knew well, an invariable sign: Two little crossed wrinkles that marked his forehead whenever he made a powerful effort of concentration. And I saw it at that moment, saw the tiny tell-tale cross, plainly and deeply scored.

He put down the sheet of paper and muttered:

"Child's play!"

The clock struck half-past five.

"What!" I cried. "Have you succeeded?... In twelve minutes?..."

He took a few steps up and down the room, lit a cigarette and said:

"You might ring up Baron Repstein, if you don't mind, and tell him I shall be with him at ten o'clock this evening."

"Baron Repstein?" I asked. "The husband of the famous baroness?"

"Yes."

"Are you serious?"

"Quite serious."

Feeling absolutely at a loss, but incapable of resisting him, I opened the telephone-directory and unhooked the receiver. But, at that moment, Lupin stopped me with a peremptory gesture and said, with his eyes on the paper, which he had taken up again:

"No, don't say anything.... It's no use letting him know.... There's something more urgent ... a queer thing that puzzles me.... Why on earth wasn't the last sentence finished? Why is the sentence...."

He snatched up his hat and stick:

"Let's be off. If I'm not mistaken, this is a business that requires immediate solution; and I don't believe I *am* mistaken."

He put his arm through mine, as we went down the stairs, and said:

"I know what everybody knows. Baron Repstein, the company-promoter and racing-man, whose colt Etna won the Derby and the Grand Prix this year, has been victimized by his wife. The wife, who was well known for her fair hair, her dress and her extravagance, ran away a fortnight ago, taking with her a sum of three million francs, stolen from her husband, and quite a collection of diamonds, pearls and jewellery which the Princesse de Berny had placed in her hands and which she was supposed to buy. For two weeks the police have been pursuing the baroness across France and the continent: an easy job, as she scatters gold and jewels wherever she goes. They think they have her every moment. Two days ago, our champion detective, the egregious Ganimard, arrested a visitor at a big hotel in Belgium, a woman against whom the most positive evidence seemed to be heaped up. On enquiry, the lady turned out to be a notorious chorus-girl called Nelly Darbal. As for the baroness, she has vanished. The baron, on his side, has offered a reward of two hundred thousand francs to whosoever finds his wife. The money is in the hands of a solicitor. Moreover, he has sold his racing-stud, his house on the Boulevard Haussmann and his country-seat of Roquencourt in one lump, so that he may indemnify the Princesse de Berny for her loss."

"And the proceeds of the sale," I added, "are to be paid over at once. The papers say that the princess will have her money to-morrow. Only, frankly, I fail to see the connection between this story, which you have told very well, and the puzzling sentence...."

Lupin did not condescend to reply.

We had been walking down the street in which I live and had passed some four or five houses, when he stepped off the pavement and began to examine a block of flats, not of the latest construction, which looked as if it contained a large number of tenants:

"According to my calculations," he said, "this is where the signals came from, probably from that open window."

"On the third floor?"

"Yes."

He went to the portress and asked her:

"Does one of your tenants happen to be acquainted with Baron Repstein?"

"Why, of course!" replied the woman. "We have M. Lavernoux here, such a nice gentleman; he is the baron's secretary and agent. I look after his flat."

"And can we see him?"

"See him?... The poor gentleman is very ill."

"Ill?"

"He's been ill a fortnight ... ever since the trouble with the baroness.... He came home the next day with a temperature and took to his bed."

"But he gets up, surely?"

"Ah, that I can't say!"

"How do you mean, you can't say?"

"No, his doctor won't let any one into his room. He took my key from me."

"Who did?"

"The doctor. He comes and sees to his wants, two or three times a day. He left the house only twenty minutes ago ... an old gentleman with a grey beard and spectacles.... Walks quite bent.... But where are you going sir?"

"I'm going up, show me the way," said Lupin, with his foot on the stairs. "It's the third floor, isn't it, on the left?"

"But I mustn't!" moaned the portress, running after him. "Besides, I haven't the key ... the doctor...."

They climbed the three flights, one behind the other. On the landing, Lupin took a tool from his pocket and, disregarding the woman's protests, inserted it in the lock. The door yielded almost immediately. We went in.

At the back of a small dark room we saw a streak of light filtering through a door that had been left ajar. Lupin ran across the room and, on reaching the threshold, gave a cry:

"Too late! Oh, hang it all!"

The portress fell on her knees, as though fainting.

I entered the bedroom, in my turn, and saw a man lying half-dressed on the carpet, with his legs drawn up under him, his arms contorted and his face quite white, an emaciated, fleshless face, with the eyes still staring in terror and the mouth twisted into a hideous grin.

"He's dead," said Lupin, after a rapid examination.

"But why?" I exclaimed. "There's not a trace of blood!"

"Yes, yes, there is," replied Lupin, pointing to two or three drops that showed on the chest, through the open shirt. "Look, they must have taken him by the throat with one hand and pricked him to the heart with the other. I say, 'pricked,' because really the wound can't be seen. It suggests a hole made by a very long needle."

He looked on the floor, all round the corpse. There was nothing to attract his attention, except a little pocket-mirror, the little mirror with which M. Lavernoux had amused himself by making the sunbeams dance through space.

But, suddenly, as the portress was breaking into lamentations and calling for help, Lupin flung himself on her and shook her:

"Stop that!... Listen to me ... you can call out later.... Listen to me and answer me. It is most important. M. Lavernoux had a friend living in this street, had he not? On the same side, to the right? An intimate friend?"

"Yes."

"A friend whom he used to meet at the café in the evening and with whom he exchanged the illustrated papers?"

"Yes."

"Was the friend an Englishman?"

"Yes."

"What's his name?"

"Mr. Hargrove."

"Where does he live?"

"At No. 92 in this street."

"One word more: had that old doctor been attending him long?"

"No. I did not know him. He came on the evening when M. Lavernoux was taken ill."

Without another word, Lupin dragged me away once more, ran down the stairs and, once in the street, turned to the right, which took us past my flat again. Four doors further, he stopped at No. 92, a small, low-storied house, of which the ground-floor was occupied by the proprietor of a dram-shop, who stood smoking in his doorway, next to the entrance-passage. Lupin asked if Mr. Hargrove was at home.

"Mr. Hargrove went out about half-an-hour ago," said the publican. "He seemed very much excited and took a taxi-cab, a thing he doesn't often do."

"And you don't know...."

"Where he was going? Well, there's no secret about it He shouted it loud enough! 'Prefecture of Police' is what he said to the driver...."

Lupin was himself just hailing a taxi, when he changed his mind; and I heard him mutter:

"What's the good? He's got too much start of us...."

He asked if any one called after Mr. Hargrove had gone.

"Yes, an old gentleman with a grey beard and spectacles. He went up to Mr. Hargrove's, rang the bell, and went away again."

"I am much obliged," said Lupin, touching his hat.

He walked away slowly without speaking to me, wearing a thoughtful air. There was no doubt that the problem struck him as very difficult, and that he saw none too clearly in the darkness through which he seemed to be moving with such certainty.

He himself, for that matter, confessed to me:

"These are cases that require much more intuition than reflection. But this one, I may tell you, is well worth taking pains about."

We had now reached the boulevards. Lupin entered a public reading-room and spent a long time consulting the last fortnight's newspapers. Now and again, he mumbled:

"Yes ... yes ... of course ... it's only a guess, but it explains everything.... Well, a guess that answers every question is not far from being the truth...."

It was now dark. We dined at a little restaurant and I noticed that Lupin's face became gradually more animated. His gestures were more decided. He recovered his spirits, his liveliness. When we left, during the walk which he made me take along the Boulevard Haussmann, towards Baron Repstein's house, he was the real Lupin of the great occasions, the Lupin who had made up his mind to go in and win.

We slackened our pace just short of the Rue de Courcelles. Baron Repstein lived on the left-hand side, between this street and the Faubourg Saint-Honoré, in a three-storied private house of which we could see the front, decorated with columns and caryatides.

"Stop!" said Lupin, suddenly.

"What is it?"

"Another proof to confirm my supposition...."

"What proof? I see nothing."

"I do.... That's enough...."

He turned up the collar of his coat, lowered the brim of his soft hat and said:

"By Jove, it'll be a stiff fight! Go to bed, my friend. I'll tell you about my expedition to-morrow ... if it doesn't cost me my life."

"What are you talking about?"

"Oh, I know what I'm saying! I'm risking a lot. First of all, getting arrested, which isn't much. Next, getting killed, which is worse. But...." He gripped my shoulder. "But there's a third thing I'm risking, which is getting hold of two millions.... And, once I possess a capital of two millions, I'll show people what I can do! Good-night, old chap, and, if you never see me again...." He spouted Musset's lines:

> *"Plant a willow by my grave,*
> *The weeping willow that I love...."*

I walked away. Three minutes later—I am continuing the narrative as he told it to me next day—three minutes later, Lupin rang at the door of the Hôtel Repstein.

"Is monsieur le baron at home?"

"Yes," replied the butler, examining the intruder with an air of surprise, "but monsieur le baron does not see people as late as this."

"Does monsieur le baron know of the murder of M. Lavernoux, his land-agent?"

"Certainly."

"Well, please tell monsieur le baron that I have come about the murder and that there is not a moment to lose."

A voice called from above:

"Show the gentleman up, Antoine."

In obedience to this peremptory order, the butler led the way to the first floor. In an open doorway stood a gentleman whom Lupin recognized from his photograph in the papers as Baron Repstein, husband of the famous baroness and owner of Etna, the horse of the year.

He was an exceedingly tall, square-shouldered man. His clean-shaven face wore a pleasant, almost smiling expression, which was not affected by the sadness of his eyes. He was dressed in a well-cut morning-coat, with a tan waistcoat and a dark tie fastened with a pearl pin, the value of which struck Lupin as considerable.

He took Lupin into his study, a large, three-windowed room, lined with book-cases, sets of pigeonholes, an American desk and a safe. And he at once asked, with ill-concealed eagerness:

"Do you know anything?"

"Yes, monsieur le baron."

"About the murder of that poor Lavernoux?"

"Yes, monsieur le baron, and about madame le baronne also."

"Do you really mean it? Quick, I entreat you...."

He pushed forward a chair. Lupin sat down and began:

"Monsieur le baron, the circumstances are very serious. I will be brief."

"Yes, do, please."

"Well, monsieur le baron, in a few words, it amounts to this: five or six hours ago, Lavernoux, who, for the last fortnight, had been kept in a sort of enforced confinement by his doctor, Lavernoux—how shall I put it?—telegraphed certain revelations by means of signals which were partly taken down by me and which put me on the track of this case. He himself was surprised in the act of making this communication and was murdered."

"But by whom? By whom?"

"By his doctor."

"Who is this doctor?"

"I don't know. But one of M. Lavernoux's friends, an Englishman called Hargrove, the friend, in fact, with whom he was communicating, is bound to know and is also bound to know the exact and complete meaning of the communication, because, without waiting for the end, he jumped into a motor-cab and drove to the Prefecture of Police."

"Why? Why?... And what is the result of that step?"

"The result, monsieur le baron, is that your house is surrounded. There are twelve detectives under your windows. The moment the sun rises, they will enter in the name of the law and arrest the criminal."

"Then is Lavernoux's murderer concealed in my house? Who is he? One of the servants? But no, for you were speaking of a doctor!..."

"I would remark, monsieur le baron, that when this Mr. Hargrove went to the police to tell them of the revelations made by his friend Lavernoux, he was not aware that his friend Lavernoux was going to be murdered. The step taken by Mr Hargrove had to do with something else...."

"With what?"

"With the disappearance of madame la baronne, of which he knew the secret, thanks to the communication made by Lavernoux."

"What! They know at last! They have found the baroness! Where is she? And the jewels? And the money she robbed me of?"

Baron Repstein was talking in a great state of excitement. He rose and, almost shouting at Lupin, cried:

"Finish your story, sir! I can't endure this suspense!"

Lupin continued, in a slow and hesitating voice:

"The fact is ... you see ... it is rather difficult to explain ... for you and I are looking at the thing from a totally different point of view."

"I don't understand."

"And yet you ought to understand, monsieur le baron.... We begin by saying—I am quoting the newspapers—by saying, do we not, that Baroness Repstein knew all the secrets of your business and that she was able to open not only that safe over there, but also the one at the Crédit Lyonnais in which you kept your securities locked up?"

"Yes."

"Well, one evening, a fortnight ago, while you were at your club, Baroness Repstein, who, unknown to yourself, had converted all those securities into cash, left this house with a travelling-bag, containing your money and all the Princesse de Berny's jewels?"

"Yes."

"And, since then, she has not been seen?"

"No."

"Well, there is an excellent reason why she has not been seen."

"What reason?"

"This, that Baroness Repstein has been murdered...."

"Murdered!... The baroness!... But you're mad!"

"Murdered ... and probably that same evening."

"I tell you again, you are mad! How can the baroness have been murdered, when the police are following her tracks, so to speak, step by step?"

"They are following the tracks of another woman."

"What woman?"

"The murderer's accomplice."

"And who is the murderer?"

"The same man who, for the last fortnight, knowing that Lavernoux, through the situation which he occupied in this house, had discovered the truth, kept him imprisoned, forced him to silence, threatened him, terrorized him; the same man who, finding Lavernoux in the act of communicating with a friend, made away with him in cold blood by stabbing him to the heart."

"The doctor, therefore?"

"Yes."

"But who is this doctor? Who is this malevolent genius, this infernal being who appears and disappears, who slays in the dark and whom nobody suspects?"

"Can't you guess?"

"No."

"And do you want to know?"

"Do I want to know?... Why, speak, man, speak!... You know where he is hiding?"

"Yes."

"In this house?"

"Yes."

"And it is he whom the police are after?"

"Yes."

"And I know him?"

"Yes."

"Who is it?"

"You!"

"I!..."

Lupin had not been more than ten minutes with the baron; and the duel was commencing. The accusation was hurled, definitely, violently, implacably.

Lupin repeated:

"You yourself, got up in a false beard and a pair of spectacles, bent in two, like an old man. In short, you, Baron Repstein; and it is you for a very good reason, of which nobody has thought, which is that, if it was not you who contrived the whole plot, the case becomes inexplicable. Whereas, taking you as the criminal, you as murdering the baroness in order to get rid of her and run through those millions with another woman, you as murdering Lavernoux, your agent, in order to suppress an unimpeachable witness, oh, then the whole case is explained! Well, is it pretty clear? And are not you yourself convinced?"

The baron, who, throughout this conversation, had stood bending over his visitor, waiting for each of his words with feverish avidity, now drew himself up and looked at Lupin as though he undoubtedly had to do with a madman. When Lupin had finished speaking, the baron stepped back two or three paces, seemed on the point of uttering words which he ended by not saying, and then, without taking his eyes from his strange visitor, went to the fireplace and rang the bell.

Lupin did not make a movement. He waited smiling.

The butler entered. His master said:

"You can go to bed, Antoine. I will let this gentleman out."

"Shall I put out the lights, sir?"

"Leave a light in the hall."

Antoine left the room and the baron, after taking a revolver from his desk, at once came back to Lupin, put the weapon in his pocket and said, very calmly:

"You must excuse this little precaution, sir. I am obliged to take it in case you should be mad, though that does not seem likely. No, you are not mad. But you have come here with an object which I fail to grasp; and you have sprung upon me an accusation of so astounding a character that I am curious to know the reason. I have experienced so much disappointment and undergone so much suffering that an outrage of this kind leaves me indifferent. Continue, please."

His voice shook with emotion and his sad eyes seemed moist with tears.

Lupin shuddered. Had he made a mistake? Was the surmise which his intuition had suggested to him and which was based upon a frail groundwork of slight facts, was this surmise wrong?

His attention was caught by a detail: through the opening in the baron's waistcoat he saw the point of the pin fixed in the tie and was thus able to realize the unusual length of the pin. Moreover, the gold stem was triangular and formed a sort of miniature dagger, very thin and very delicate, yet formidable in an expert hand.

And Lupin had no doubt but that the pin attached to that magnificent pearl was the weapon which had pierced the heart of the unfortunate M. Lavernoux.

He muttered:

"You're jolly clever, monsieur le baron!"

The other, maintaining a rather scornful gravity, kept silence, as though he did not understand and as though waiting for the explanation to which he felt himself entitled. And, in spite of everything, this impassive attitude worried Arsène Lupin. Nevertheless, his conviction was so profound and, besides, he had staked so much on the adventure that he repeated:

"Yes, jolly clever, for it is evident that the baroness only obeyed your orders in realizing your securities and also in borrowing the princess's jewels on the pretence of buying them. And it is evident that the person who walked out of your house with a bag was not your wife, but an accomplice, that chorus-girl probably, and that it is your chorus-girl who is deliberately allowing herself to be chased across the continent by our worthy Ganimard. And I look upon the trick as marvelous. What does the woman risk, seeing that it is the baroness who is being looked for? And how could they look for any other woman than the baroness, seeing that you have promised a reward of two hundred thousand francs to the person who finds the baroness?... Oh, that two hundred thousand francs lodged with a solicitor: what a stroke of genius! It has dazzled the police! It has thrown dust in the eyes of the most clear-sighted! A gentleman who lodges two hundred thousand francs with a solicitor is a gentleman who speaks the truth.... So they go on hunting the baroness! And they leave you quietly to settle your affairs, to sell your stud and your two houses to the highest bidder and to prepare your flight! Heavens, what a joke!"

The baron did not wince. He walked up to Lupin and asked, without abandoning his imperturbable coolness:

"Who are you?"

Lupin burst out laughing.

"What can it matter who I am? Take it that I am an emissary of fate, looming out of the darkness for your destruction!"

He sprang from his chair, seized the baron by the shoulder and jerked out:

"Yes, for your destruction, my bold baron! Listen to me! Your wife's three millions, almost all the princess's jewels, the money you received to-day from the sale of your stud and your real estate: it's all there, in your pocket, or in that safe. Your flight is prepared. Look, I can see the leather of your portmanteau behind that hanging. The papers on your desk are in order. This very night, you would have done a guy. This very night, disguised beyond recognition, after taking all your precautions, you would have joined your chorus-girl, the creature for whose sake you have committed murder, that same Nelly Darbal, no doubt, whom Ganimard arrested in Belgium. But for one sudden, unforeseen obstacle: the police, the twelve detectives who, thanks to Lavernoux's revelations, have been posted under your windows. They've cooked your goose, old chap!... Well, I'll save you. A word through the telephone; and, by three or four o'clock in the morning, twenty of my friends will have removed the obstacle, polished off the twelve detectives, and you and I will slip away quietly. My conditions? Almost nothing; a trifle to you: we share the millions and the jewels. Is it a bargain?"

He was leaning over the baron, thundering at him with irresistible energy. The baron whispered:

"I'm beginning to understand. It's blackmail...."

"Blackmail or not, call it what you please, my boy, but you've got to go through with it and do as I say. And don't imagine that I shall give way at the last moment. Don't say to yourself, 'Here's a gentleman whom the fear of the police will cause to think twice. If I run a big risk in refusing, he also will be risking the handcuffs, the cells and the rest of it, seeing that we are both being hunted down like wild beasts.' That would be a mistake, monsieur le baron. I can always get out of it. It's a question of yourself, of yourself alone.... Your money or your life, my lord! Share and share alike ... if not, the scaffold! Is it a bargain?"

A quick movement. The baron released himself, grasped his revolver and fired.

But Lupin was prepared for the attack, the more so as the baron's face had lost its assurance and gradually, under the slow impulse of rage and fear, acquired an expression of almost bestial ferocity that heralded the rebellion so long kept under control.

He fired twice. Lupin first flung himself to one side and then dived at the baron's knees, seized him by both legs and brought him to the ground. The baron freed himself with an effort. The two enemies rolled over in each other's grip; and a stubborn, crafty, brutal, savage struggle followed.

Suddenly, Lupin felt a pain at his chest:

"You villain!" he yelled. "That's your Lavernoux trick; the tie-pin!"

Stiffening his muscles with a desperate effort, he overpowered the baron and clutched him by the throat victorious at last and omnipotent.

"You ass!" he cried. "If you hadn't shown your cards, I might have thrown up the game! You have such a look of the honest man about you! But what a biceps, my lord!... I thought for a moment.... But it's all over, now!... Come, my friend, hand us the pin and look cheerful.... No, that's what I call pulling a face.... I'm holding you too tight, perhaps? My lord's at his last gasp?... Come, be good!... That's it, just a wee bit of string round the wrists; do you allow me?... Why, you and I are agreeing like two brothers! It's touching!... At heart, you know, I'm rather fond of you.... And now, my bonnie lad, mind yourself! And a thousand apologies!..."

Half raising himself, with all his strength he caught the other a terrible blow in the pit of the stomach. The baron gave a gurgle and lay stunned and unconscious.

"That comes of having a deficient sense of logic, my friend," said Lupin. "I offered you half your money. Now I'll give you none at all ... provided I know where to find any of it. For that's the main thing. Where has the beggar hidden his dust? In the safe? By George, it'll be a tough job! Luckily, I have all the night before me...."

He began to feel in the baron's pockets, came upon a bunch of keys, first made sure that the portmanteau behind the curtain held no papers or jewels, and then went to the safe.

But, at that moment, he stopped short: he heard a noise somewhere. The servants? Impossible. Their attics were on the top floor. He listened. The noise came from below. And, suddenly, he understood: the detectives, who had heard the two shots, were banging at the front door, as was their duty, without waiting for daybreak. Then an electric bell rang, which Lupin recognized as that in the hall:

"By Jupiter!" he said. "Pretty work! Here are these jokers coming ... and just as we were about to gather the fruits of our laborious efforts! Tut, tut, Lupin, keep cool! What's expected of you? To open a safe, of which you don't know the secret, in thirty seconds.

235

That's a mere trifle to lose your head about! Come, all you have to do is to discover the secret! How many letters are there in the word? Four?"

He went on thinking, while talking and listening to the noise outside. He double-locked the door of the outer room and then came back to the safe:

"Four ciphers.... Four letters ... four letters.... Who can lend me a hand?... Who can give me just a tiny hint?... Who? Why, Lavernoux, of course! That good Lavernoux, seeing that he took the trouble to indulge in optical telegraphy at the risk of his life.... Lord, what a fool I am!... Why, of course, why, of course, that's it!... By Jove, this is too exciting!... Lupin, you must count ten and suppress that distracted beating of your heart. If not, it means bad work."

He counted ten and, now quite calm, knelt in front of the safe. He turned the four knobs with careful attention. Next, he examined the bunch of keys, selected one of them, then another, and attempted, in vain, to insert them in the lock:

"There's luck in odd numbers," he muttered, trying a third key. "Victory! This is the right one! Open Sesame, good old Sesame, open!"

The lock turned. The door moved on its hinges. Lupin pulled it to him, after taking out the bunch of keys:

"The millions are ours," he said. "Baron, I forgive you!"

And then he gave a single bound backward, hiccoughing with fright. His legs staggered beneath him. The keys jingled together in his fevered hand with a sinister sound. And, for twenty, for thirty seconds, despite the din that was being raised and the electric bells that kept ringing through the house, he stood there, wild-eyed, gazing at the most horrible, the most abominable sight: a woman's body, half-dressed, bent in two in the safe, crammed in, like an over-large parcel ... and fair hair hanging down ... and blood ... clots of blood ... and livid flesh, blue in places, decomposing, flaccid.

"The baroness!" he gasped. "The baroness!... Oh, the monster!..."

He roused himself from his torpor, suddenly, to spit in the murderer's face and pound him with his heels:

"Take that, you wretch!... Take that, you villain!... And, with it, the scaffold, the bran-basket!..."

Meanwhile, shouts came from the upper floors in reply to the detectives' ringing. Lupin heard footsteps scurrying down the stairs. It was time to think of beating a retreat.

In reality, this did not trouble him greatly. During his conversation with the baron, the enemy's extraordinary coolness had given him the feeling that there must be a private outlet. Besides, how could the baron have begun the fight, if he were not sure of escaping the police?

Lupin went into the next room. It looked out on the garden. At the moment when the detectives were entering the house, he flung his legs over the balcony and let himself down by a rain-pipe. He walked round the building. On the opposite side was a wall lined with shrubs. He slipped in between the shrubs and the wall and at once found a little door which he easily opened with one of the keys on the bunch. All that remained for him to do was to walk across a yard and pass through the empty rooms of a lodge; and in a few moments he found himself in the Rue du Faubourg Saint-Honoré. Of course—and this he had reckoned on—the police had not provided for this secret outlet.

. . .

"Well, what do you think of Baron Repstein?" cried Lupin, after giving me all the details of that tragic night. "What a dirty scoundrel! And how it teaches one to distrust appearances! I swear to you, the fellow looked a thoroughly honest man!"

"But what about the millions?" I asked. "The princess's jewels?"

"They were in the safe. I remember seeing the parcel."

"Well?"

"They are there still."

"Impossible!"

"They are, upon my word! I might tell you that I was afraid of the detectives, or else plead a sudden attack of delicacy. But the truth is simpler ... and more prosaic: the smell was too awful!..."

"What?"

"Yes, my dear fellow, the smell that came from that safe ... from that coffin.... No, I couldn't do it ... my head swam.... Another second and I should have been ill.... Isn't it silly?... Look, this is all I got from my expedition: the tie-pin.... The bed-rock value of the pearl is thirty thousand francs.... But all the same, I feel jolly well annoyed. What a sell!"

"One more question," I said. "The word that opened the safe!"

"Well?"

"How did you guess it?"

"Oh, quite easily! In fact, I am surprised that I didn't think of it sooner."

"Well, tell me."

"It was contained in the revelations telegraphed by that poor Lavernoux."

"What?"

"Just think, my dear chap, the mistakes in spelling...."

"The mistakes in spelling?"

"Why, of course! They were deliberate. Surely, you don't imagine that the agent, the private secretary of the baron—who was a company-promoter, mind you, and a racing-man—did not know English better than to spell 'necessery' with an 'e,' 'atack' with one 't,' 'ennemy' with two 'n's' and 'prudance' with an 'a'! The thing struck me at once. I put the four letters together and got 'Etna,' the name of the famous horse."

"And was that one word enough?"

"Of course! It was enough to start with, to put me on the scent of the Repstein case, of which all the papers were full, and, next, to make me guess that it was the key-word of the safe, because, on the one hand, Lavernoux knew the gruesome contents of the safe and, on the other, he was denouncing the baron. And it was in the same way that I was led to suppose that Lavernoux had a friend in the street, that they both frequented the same café, that they amused themselves by working out the problems and cryptograms in the illustrated papers and that they had contrived a way of exchanging telegrams from window to window."

"That makes it all quite simple!" I exclaimed.

"Very simple. And the incident once more shows that, in the discovery of crimes, there is something much more valuable than the examination of facts, than observations, deductions, inferences and all that stuff and nonsense. What I mean is, as I said before, intuition ... intuition and intelligence.... And Arsène Lupin, without boasting, is deficient in neither one nor the other!..."

II. THE WEDDING-RING

Yvonne d'Origny kissed her son and told him to be good:

"You know your grandmother d'Origny is not very fond of children. Now that she has sent for you to come and see her, you must show her what a sensible little boy you are." And, turning to the governess, "Don't forget, Fräulein, to bring him home immediately after dinner.... Is monsieur still in the house?"

"Yes, madame, monsieur le comte is in his study."

As soon as she was alone, Yvonne d'Origny walked to the window to catch a glimpse of her son as he left the house. He was out in the street in a moment, raised his head and blew her a kiss, as was his custom every day. Then the governess took his hand with, as Yvonne remarked to her surprise, a movement of unusual violence. Yvonne leant further out of the window and, when the boy reached the corner of the boulevard, she suddenly saw a man step out of a motor-car and go up to him. The man, in whom she recognized Bernard, her husband's confidential servant, took the child by the arm, made both him and the governess get into the car, and ordered the chauffeur to drive off.

The whole incident did not take ten seconds.

Yvonne, in her trepidation, ran to her bedroom, seized a wrap and went to the door. The door was locked; and there was no key in the lock.

She hurried back to the boudoir. The door of the boudoir also was locked.

Then, suddenly, the image of her husband appeared before her, that gloomy face which no smile ever lit up, those pitiless eyes in which, for years, she had felt so much hatred and malice.

"It's he ... it's he!" she said to herself. "He has taken the child.... Oh, it's horrible!"

She beat against the door with her fists, with her feet, then flew to the mantelpiece and pressed the bell fiercely.

The shrill sound rang through the house from top to bottom. The servants would be sure to come. Perhaps a crowd would gather in the street. And, impelled by a sort of despairing hope, she kept her finger on the button.

A key turned in the lock.... The door was flung wide open. The count appeared on the threshold of the boudoir. And the expression of his face was so terrible that Yvonne began to tremble.

He entered the room. Five or six steps separated him from her. With a supreme effort, she tried to stir, but all movement was impossible; and, when she attempted to speak, she could only flutter her lips and emit incoherent sounds. She felt herself lost. The thought of death unhinged her. Her knees gave way beneath her and she sank into a huddled heap, with a moan.

The count rushed at her and seized her by the throat:

"Hold your tongue ... don't call out!" he said, in a low voice. "That will be best for you!..."

Seeing that she was not attempting to defend herself, he loosened his hold of her and took from his pocket some strips of canvas ready rolled and of different lengths. In a few minutes, Yvonne was lying on a sofa, with her wrists and ankles bound and her arms fastened close to her body.

It was now dark in the boudoir. The count switched on the electric light and went to a little writing-desk where Yvonne was accustomed to keep her letters. Not succeeding in opening it, he picked the lock with a bent wire, emptied the drawers and collected all the contents into a bundle, which he carried off in a cardboard file:

"Waste of time, eh?" he grinned. "Nothing but bills and letters of no importance.... No proof against you.... Tah! I'll keep my son for all that; and I swear before Heaven that I will not let him go!"

As he was leaving the room, he was joined, near the door, by his man Bernard. The two stopped and talked, in a low voice; but Yvonne heard these words spoken by the servant:

"I have had an answer from the working jeweller. He says he holds himself at my disposal."

And the count replied:

"The thing is put off until twelve o'clock midday, to-morrow. My mother has just telephoned to say that she could not come before."

Then Yvonne heard the key turn in the lock and the sound of steps going down to the ground-floor, where her husband's study was.

She long lay inert, her brain reeling with vague, swift ideas that burnt her in passing, like flames. She remembered her husband's infamous behavior, his humiliating conduct to her, his threats, his plans for a divorce; and she gradually came to understand that she was the victim of a regular conspiracy, that the servants had been sent away until the following evening by their master's orders, that the governess had carried off her son by the count's instructions and with Bernard's assistance, that her son would not come back and that she would never see him again.

"My son!" she cried. "My son!..."

Exasperated by her grief, she stiffened herself, with every nerve, with every muscle tense, to make a violent effort. And she was astonished to find that her right hand, which the count had fastened too hurriedly, still retained a certain freedom.

Then a mad hope invaded her; and, slowly, patiently, she began the work of self-deliverance.

It was long in the doing. She needed a deal of time to widen the knot sufficiently and a deal of time afterward, when the hand was released, to undo those other bonds which tied her arms to her body and those which fastened her ankles.

Still, the thought of her son sustained her; and the last shackle fell as the clock struck eight. She was free!

She was no sooner on her feet than she flew to the window and flung back the latch, with the intention of calling the first passer-by. At that moment a policeman came walking along the pavement. She leant out. But the brisk evening air, striking her face, calmed her. She thought of the scandal, of the judicial investigation, of the cross-examination, of her son. O Heaven! What could she do to get him back? How could she escape? The count might appear at the least sound. And who knew but that, in a moment of fury ...?

She shivered from head to foot, seized with a sudden terror. The horror of death mingled, in her poor brain, with the thought of her son; and she stammered, with a choking throat:

"Help!... Help!..."

She stopped and said to herself, several times over, in a low voice, "Help!... Help!..." as though the word awakened an idea, a memory within her, and as though the hope of assistance no longer seemed to her impossible. For some minutes she remained absorbed in deep meditation, broken by fears and starts. Then, with an almost mechanical series of movements, she put out her arm to a little set of shelves hanging over the writing-desk, took down four books, one after the other, turned the pages with a distraught air, replaced them and ended by finding, between the pages of the fifth, a visiting-card on which her eyes spelt the name:

HORACE VELMONT,

followed by an address written in pencil:

CERCLE DE LA RUE ROYALE.

And her memory conjured up the strange thing which that man had said to her, a few years before, in that same house, on a day when she was at home to her friends:

"If ever a danger threatens you, if you need help, do not hesitate; post this card, which you see me put into this book; and, whatever the hour, whatever the obstacles, I will come."

With what a curious air he had spoken these words and how well he had conveyed the impression of certainty, of strength, of unlimited power, of indomitable daring!

Abruptly, unconsciously, acting under the impulse of an irresistible determination, the consequences of which she refused to anticipate, Yvonne, with the same automatic gestures, took a pneumatic-delivery envelope, slipped in the card, sealed it, directed it to "Horace Velmont, Cercle de la Rue Royale" and went to the open window. The policeman was walking up and down outside. She flung out the envelope, trusting to fate. Perhaps it would be picked up, treated as a lost letter and posted.

She had hardly completed this act when she realized its absurdity. It was mad to suppose that the message would reach the address and madder still to hope that the man to whom she was sending could come to her assistance, "whatever the hour, whatever the obstacles."

A reaction followed which was all the greater inasmuch as the effort had been swift and violent. Yvonne staggered, leant against a chair and, losing all energy, let herself fall.

The hours passed by, the dreary hours of winter evenings when nothing but the sound of carriages interrupts the silence of the street. The clock struck, pitilessly. In the half-sleep that numbed her limbs, Yvonne counted the strokes. She also heard certain noises, on different floors of the house, which told her that her husband had dined, that he was going up to his room, that he was going down again to his study. But all this seemed very shadowy to her; and her torpor was such that she did not even think of lying down on the sofa, in case he should come in....

The twelve strokes of midnight.... Then half-past twelve ... then one.... Yvonne thought of nothing, awaiting the events which were preparing and against which rebellion was useless. She pictured her son and herself as one pictures those beings who have suffered much and who suffer no more and who take each other in their loving arms. But a nightmare shattered this dream. For now those two beings were to be torn asunder; and she had the awful feeling, in her delirium, that she was crying and choking....

She leapt from her seat. The key had turned in the lock. The count was coming, attracted by her cries. Yvonne glanced round for a weapon with which to defend herself.

But the door was pushed back quickly and, astounded, as though the sight that presented itself before her eyes seemed to her the most inexplicable prodigy, she stammered:

"You!... You!..."

A man was walking up to her, in dress-clothes, with his opera-hat and cape under his arm, and this man, young, slender and elegant, she had recognized as Horace Velmont.

"You!" she repeated.

He said, with a bow:

"I beg your pardon, madame, but I did not receive your letter until very late."

"Is it possible? Is it possible that this is you ... that you were able to ...?"

He seemed greatly surprised:

"Did I not promise to come in answer to your call?"

"Yes ... but ..."

"Well, here I am," he said, with a smile.

He examined the strips of canvas from which Yvonne had succeeded in freeing herself and nodded his head, while continuing his inspection:

"So those are the means employed? The Comte d'Origny, I presume?... I also saw that he locked you in.... But then the pneumatic letter?... Ah, through the window!... How careless of you not to close it!"

He pushed both sides to. Yvonne took fright:

"Suppose they hear!"

"There is no one in the house. I have been over it."

"Still ..."

"Your husband went out ten minutes ago."

"Where is he?"

"With his mother, the Comtesse d'Origny."

"How do you know?"

"Oh, it's very simple! He was rung up by telephone and I awaited the result at the corner of this street and the boulevard. As I expected, the count came out hurriedly, followed by his man. I at once entered, with the aid of special keys."

He told this in the most natural way, just as one tells a meaningless anecdote in a drawing-room. But Yvonne, suddenly seized with fresh alarm, asked:

"Then it's not true?... His mother is not ill?... In that case, my husband will be coming back...."

"Certainly, the count will see that a trick has been played on him and in three quarters of an hour at the latest...."

"Let us go.... I don't want him to find me here.... I must go to my son...."

"One moment...."

"One moment!... But don't you know that they have taken him from me?... That they are hurting him, perhaps?..."

With set face and feverish gestures, she tried to push Velmont back. He, with great gentleness, compelled her to sit down and, leaning over her in a respectful attitude, said, in a serious voice:

"Listen, madame, and let us not waste time, when every minute is valuable. First of all, remember this: we met four times, six years ago.... And, on the fourth occasion, when I was speaking to you, in the drawing-room of this house, with too much—what shall I say? —with too much feeling, you gave me to understand that my visits were no longer welcome. Since that day I have not seen you. And, nevertheless, in spite of all, your faith in me was such that you kept the card which I put between the pages of that book and, six years later, you send for me and none other. That faith in me I ask you to continue. You must obey me blindly. Just as I surmounted every obstacle to come to you, so I will save you, whatever the position may be."

Horace Velmont's calmness, his masterful voice, with the friendly intonation, gradually quieted the countess. Though still very weak, she gained a fresh sense of ease and security in that man's presence.

"Have no fear," he went on. "The Comtesse d'Origny lives at the other end of the Bois de Vincennes. Allowing that your husband finds a motor-cab, it is impossible for him to be back before a quarter-past three. Well, it is twenty-five to three now. I swear to take you away at three o'clock exactly and to take you to your son. But I will not go before I know everything."

"What am I to do?" she asked.

"Answer me and very plainly. We have twenty minutes. It is enough. But it is not too much."

"Ask me what you want to know."

"Do you think that the count had any ... any murderous intentions?"

"No."

"Then it concerns your son?"

"Yes."

"He is taking him away, I suppose, because he wants to divorce you and marry another woman, a former friend of yours, whom you have turned out of your house. Is that it? Oh, I entreat you, answer me frankly! These are facts of public notoriety; and your hesitation, your scruples, must all cease, now that the matter concerns your son. So your husband wished to marry another woman?"

"Yes."

"The woman has no money. Your husband, on his side, has gambled away all his property and has no means beyond the allowance which he receives from his mother, the Comtesse d'Origny, and the income of a large fortune which your son inherited from two of your uncles. It is this fortune which your husband covets and which he would appropriate more easily if the child were placed in his hands. There is only one way: divorce. Am I right?"

"Yes."

"And what has prevented him until now is your refusal?"

"Yes, mine and that of my mother-in-law, whose religious feelings are opposed to divorce. The Comtesse d'Origny would only yield in case ..."

"In case ...?"

"In case they could prove me guilty of shameful conduct."

Velmont shrugged his shoulders:

"Therefore he is powerless to do anything against you or against your son. Both from the legal point of view and from that of his own interests, he stumbles against an obstacle which is the most insurmountable of all: the virtue of an honest woman. And yet, in spite of everything, he suddenly shows fight."

"What do you mean?"

"I mean that, if a man like the count, after so many hesitations and in the face of so many difficulties, risks so doubtful an adventure, it must be because he thinks he has command of weapons ..."

"What weapons?"

"I don't know. But they exist ... or else he would not have begun by taking away your son."

Yvonne gave way to her despair:

"Oh, this is horrible!... How do I know what he may have done, what he may have invented?"

"Try and think.... Recall your memories.... Tell me, in this desk which he has broken open, was there any sort of letter which he could possibly turn against you?"

"No ... only bills and addresses...."

"And, in the words he used to you, in his threats, is there nothing that allows you to guess?"

"Nothing."

"Still ... still," Velmont insisted, "there must be something." And he continued, "Has the count a particularly intimate friend ... in whom he confides?"

"No."

"Did anybody come to see him yesterday?"

"No, nobody."

"Was he alone when he bound you and locked you in?"

"At that moment, yes."

"But afterward?"

"His man, Bernard, joined him near the door and I heard them talking about a working jeweller...."

"Is that all?"

"And about something that was to happen the next day, that is, to-day, at twelve o'clock, because the Comtesse d'Origny could not come earlier."

Velmont reflected:

"Has that conversation any meaning that throws a light upon your husband's plans?"

"I don't see any."

"Where are your jewels?"

"My husband has sold them all."

"You have nothing at all left?"

"No."

"Not even a ring?"

"No," she said, showing her hands, "none except this."

"Which is your wedding-ring?"

"Which is my ... wedding—..."

She stopped, nonplussed. Velmont saw her flush as she stammered:

"Could it be possible?... But no ... no ... he doesn't know...."

Velmont at once pressed her with questions and Yvonne stood silent, motionless, anxious-faced. At last, she replied, in a low voice:

"This is not my wedding-ring. One day, long ago, it dropped from the mantelpiece in my bedroom, where I had put it a minute before and, hunt for it as I might, I could not find it again. So I ordered another, without saying anything about it ... and this is the one, on my hand...."

"Did the real ring bear the date of your wedding?"

"Yes ... the 23rd of October."

"And the second?"

"This one has no date."

He perceived a slight hesitation in her and a confusion which, in point of fact, she did not try to conceal.

"I implore you," he exclaimed, "don't hide anything from me.... You see how far we have gone in a few minutes, with a little logic and calmness.... Let us go on, I ask you as a favor."

"Are you sure," she said, "that it is necessary?"

"I am sure that the least detail is of importance and that we are nearly attaining our object. But we must hurry. This is a crucial moment."

"I have nothing to conceal," she said, proudly raising her head. "It was the most wretched and the most dangerous period of my life. While suffering humiliation at home, outside I was surrounded with attentions, with temptations, with pitfalls, like any woman who is seen to be neglected by her husband. Then I remembered: before my marriage, a man had been in love with me. I had guessed his unspoken love; and he has died since. I had the name of that man engraved inside the ring; and I wore it as a talisman. There was no love in me, because I was the wife of another. But, in my secret heart, there was a memory, a sad dream, something sweet and gentle that protected me...."

She had spoken slowly, without embarrassment, and Velmont did not doubt for a second that she was telling the absolute truth. He kept silent; and she, becoming anxious again, asked:

"Do you suppose ... that my husband ...?"

He took her hand and, while examining the plain gold ring, said:

"The puzzle lies here. Your husband, I don't know how, knows of the substitution of one ring for the other. His mother will be here at twelve o'clock. In the presence of witnesses, he will compel you to take off your ring; and, in this way, he will obtain the approval of his mother and, at the same time, will be able to obtain his divorce, because he will have the proof for which he was seeking."

"I am lost!" she moaned. "I am lost!"

"On the contrary, you are saved! Give me that ring ... and presently he will find another there, another which I will send you, to reach you before twelve, and which will bear the date of the 23rd of October. So...."

He suddenly broke off. While he was speaking, Yvonne's hand had turned ice-cold in his; and, raising his eyes, he saw that the young woman was pale, terribly pale:

"What's the matter? I beseech you ..."

She yielded to a fit of mad despair:

"This is the matter, that I am lost!... This is the matter, that I can't get the ring off! It has grown too small for me!... Do you understand?... It made no difference and I did not give it a thought.... But to-day ... this proof ... this accusation.... Oh, what torture!... Look ... it forms part of my finger ... it has grown into my flesh ... and I can't ... I can't...."

She pulled at the ring, vainly, with all her might, at the risk of injuring herself. But the flesh swelled up around the ring; and the ring did not budge.

"Oh!" she cried, seized with an idea that terrified her. "I remember ... the other night ... a nightmare I had.... It seemed to me that someone entered my room and caught hold of my hand.... And I could not wake up.... It was he! It was he! He had put me to sleep, I was sure of it ... and he was looking at the ring.... And presently he will pull it off before his mother's eyes.... Ah, I understand everything: that working jeweller!... He will cut it from my hand to-morrow.... You see, you see.... I am lost!..."

She hid her face in her hands and began to weep. But, amid the silence, the clock struck once ... and twice ... and yet once more. And Yvonne drew herself up with a jerk:

"There he is!" she cried. "He is coming!... It is three o'clock!... Let us go!..."

She grabbed at her cloak and ran to the door ... Velmont barred the way and, in a masterful tone:

"You shall not go!"

"My son.... I want to see him, to take him back...."

"You don't even know where he is!"

"I want to go."

"You shall not go!... It would be madness...."

He took her by the wrists. She tried to release herself; and Velmont had to employ a little force to overcome her resistance. In the end, he succeeded in getting her back to the sofa, then in laying her at full length and, at once, without heeding her lamentations, he took the canvas strips and fastened her wrists and ankles:

"Yes," he said, "It would be madness! Who would have set you free? Who would have opened that door for you? An accomplice? What an argument against you and what a pretty use your husband would make of it with his mother!... And, besides, what's the good? To run away means accepting divorce ... and what might that not lead to?... You must stay here...."

She sobbed:

"I'm frightened.... I'm frightened ... this ring burns me.... Break it.... Take it away.... Don't let him find it!"

"And if it is not found on your finger, who will have broken it? Again an accomplice.... No, you must face the music ... and face it boldly, for I answer for everything.... Believe me ... I answer for everything.... If I have to tackle the Comtesse d'Origny bodily and thus delay the interview.... If I had to come myself before noon ... it is the real wedding-ring that shall be taken from your finger—that I swear!—and your son shall be restored to you."

Swayed and subdued, Yvonne instinctively held out her hands to the bonds. When he stood up, she was bound as she had been before.

He looked round the room to make sure that no trace of his visit remained. Then he stooped over the countess again and whispered:

"Think of your son and, whatever happens, fear nothing.... I am watching over you."

She heard him open and shut the door of the boudoir and, a few minutes later, the hall-door.

At half-past three, a motor-cab drew up. The door downstairs was slammed again; and, almost immediately after, Yvonne saw her husband hurry in, with a furious look in his eyes. He ran up to her, felt to see if she was still fastened and, snatching her hand, examined the ring. Yvonne fainted....

. . .

She could not tell, when she woke, how long she had slept. But the broad light of day was filling the boudoir; and she perceived, at the first movement which she made, that her bonds were cut. Then she turned her head and saw her husband standing beside her, looking at her:

"My son ... my son ..." she moaned. "I want my son...."

He replied, in a voice of which she felt the jeering insolence:

"Our son is in a safe place. And, for the moment, it's a question not of him, but of you. We are face to face with each other, probably for the last time, and the explanation between us will be a very serious one. I must warn you that it will take place before my mother. Have you any objection?"

Yvonne tried to hide her agitation and answered:

"None at all."

"Can I send for her?"

"Yes. Leave me, in the meantime. I shall be ready when she comes."

"My mother is here."

"Your mother is here?" cried Yvonne, in dismay, remembering Horace Velmont's promise.

"What is there to astonish you in that?"

"And is it now ... is it at once that you want to ...?"

"Yes."

"Why?... Why not this evening?... Why not to-morrow?"

"To-day and now," declared the count. "A rather curious incident happened in the course of last night, an incident which I cannot account for and which decided me to hasten the explanation. Don't you want something to eat first?"

"No ... no...."

"Then I will go and fetch my mother."

He turned to Yvonne's bedroom. Yvonne glanced at the clock. It marked twenty-five minutes to eleven!

"Ah!" she said, with a shiver of fright.

Twenty-five minutes to eleven! Horace Velmont would not save her and nobody in the world and nothing in the world would save her, for there was no miracle that could place the wedding-ring upon her finger.

The count, returning with the Comtesse d'Origny, asked her to sit down. She was a tall, lank, angular woman, who had always displayed a hostile feeling to Yvonne. She did not even bid her daughter-in-law good-morning, showing that her mind was made up as regards the accusation:

"I don't think," she said, "that we need speak at length. In two words, my son maintains...."

"I don't maintain, mother," said the count, "I declare. I declare on my oath that, three months ago, during the holidays, the upholsterer, when laying the carpet in this room and the boudoir, found the wedding-ring which I gave my wife lying in a crack in the floor. Here is the ring. The date of the 23rd of October is engraved inside."

"Then," said the countess, "the ring which your wife carries...."

"That is another ring, which she ordered in exchange for the real one. Acting on my instructions, Bernard, my man, after long searching, ended by discovering in the outskirts of Paris, where he now lives, the little jeweller to whom she went. This man remembers perfectly and is willing to bear witness that his customer did not tell him to engrave a date, but a name. He has forgotten the name, but the man who used to work with him in his shop may be able to remember it. This working jeweller has been informed by letter that I required his services and he replied yesterday, placing himself at my disposal. Bernard went to fetch him at nine o'clock this morning. They are both waiting in my study."

He turned to his wife:

"Will you give me that ring of your own free will?"

"You know," she said, "from the other night, that it won't come off my finger."

"In that case, can I have the man up? He has the necessary implements with him."

"Yes," she said, in a voice faint as a whisper.

She was resigned. She conjured up the future as in a vision: the scandal, the decree of divorce pronounced against herself, the custody of the child awarded to the father; and she accepted this, thinking that she would carry off her son, that she would go with him to the ends of the earth and that the two of them would live alone together and happy....

Her mother-in-law said:

"You have been very thoughtless, Yvonne."

Yvonne was on the point of confessing to her and asking for her protection. But what was the good? How could the Comtesse d'Origny possibly believe her innocent? She made no reply.

Besides, the count at once returned, followed by his servant and by a man carrying a bag of tools under his arm.

And the count said to the man:

"You know what you have to do?"

"Yes," said the workman. "It's to cut a ring that's grown too small.... That's easily done.... A touch of the nippers...."

"And then you will see," said the count, "if the inscription inside the ring was the one you engraved."

Yvonne looked at the clock. It was ten minutes to eleven. She seemed to hear, somewhere in the house, a sound of voices raised in argument; and, in spite of herself, she felt a thrill of hope. Perhaps Velmont has succeeded.... But the sound was renewed; and she perceived that it was produced by some costermongers passing under her window and moving farther on.

It was all over. Horace Velmont had been unable to assist her. And she understood that, to recover her child, she must rely upon her own strength, for the promises of others are vain.

She made a movement of recoil. She had felt the workman's heavy hand on her hand; and that hateful touch revolted her.

The man apologized, awkwardly. The count said to his wife:

"You must make up your mind, you know."

Then she put out her slim and trembling hand to the workman, who took it, turned it over and rested it on the table, with the palm upward. Yvonne felt the cold steel. She longed to die, then and there; and, at once attracted by that idea of death, she thought of the poisons which she would buy and which would send her to sleep almost without her knowing it.

The operation did not take long. Inserted on the slant, the little steel pliers pushed back the flesh, made room for themselves and bit the ring. A strong effort ... and the ring broke. The two ends had only to be separated to remove the ring from the finger. The workman did so.

The count exclaimed, in triumph:

"At last! Now we shall see!... The proof is there! And we are all witnesses...."

He snatched up the ring and looked at the inscription. A cry of amazement escaped him. The ring bore the date of his marriage to Yvonne: "23rd of October"!...

We were sitting on the terrace at Monte Carlo. Lupin finished his story, lit a cigarette and calmly puffed the smoke into the blue air.

I said:

"Well?"

"Well what?"

"Why, the end of the story...."

"The end of the story? But what other end could there be?"

"Come ... you're joking ..."

"Not at all. Isn't that enough for you? The countess is saved. The count, not possessing the least proof against her, is compelled by his mother to forego the divorce and to give up the child. That is all. Since then, he has left his wife, who is living happily with her son, a fine lad of sixteen."

"Yes ... yes ... but the way in which the countess was saved?"

Lupin burst out laughing:

"My dear old chap"—Lupin sometimes condescends to address me in this affectionate manner—"my dear old chap, you may be rather smart at relating my exploits, but, by Jove, you do want to have the i's dotted for you! I assure you, the countess did not ask for explanations!"

"Very likely. But there's no pride about me," I added, laughing. "Dot those i's for me, will you?"

He took out a five-franc piece and closed his hand over it.

"What's in my hand?"

"A five-franc piece."

He opened his hand. The five-franc piece was gone.

"You see how easy it is! A working jeweller, with his nippers, cuts a ring with a date engraved upon it: 23rd of October. It's a simple little trick of sleight-of-hand, one of many which I have in my bag. By Jove, I didn't spend six months with Dickson, the conjurer,[3] for nothing!"

"But then ...?"

"Out with it!"

"The working jeweller?"

"Was Horace Velmont! Was good old Lupin! Leaving the countess at three o'clock in the morning, I employed the few remaining minutes before the husband's return to have a look round his study. On the table I found the letter from the working jeweller. The letter gave me the address. A bribe of a few louis enabled me to take the workman's place; and I arrived with a wedding-ring ready cut and engraved. Hocus-pocus! Pass!... The count couldn't make head or tail of it."

"Splendid!" I cried. And I added, a little chaffingly, in my turn, "But don't you think that you were humbugged a bit yourself, on this occasion?"

"Oh! And by whom, pray?"

"By the countess?"

"In what way?"

"Hang it all, that name engraved as a talisman!... The mysterious Adonis who loved her and suffered for her sake!... All that story seems very unlikely; and I wonder whether, Lupin though you be, you did not just drop upon a pretty love-story, absolutely genuine and ... none too innocent."

Lupin looked at me out of the corner of his eye:

"No," he said.

"How do you know?"

"If the countess made a misstatement in telling me that she knew that man before her marriage—and that he was dead—and if she really did love him in her secret heart, I, at least, have a positive proof that it was an ideal love and that he did not suspect it."

"And where is the proof?"

"It is inscribed inside the ring which I myself broke on the countess's finger ... and which I carry on me. Here it is. You can read the name she had engraved on it."

He handed me the ring. I read:

"Horace Velmont."

There was a moment of silence between Lupin and myself; and, noticing it, I also observed on his face a certain emotion, a tinge of melancholy.

I resumed:

"What made you tell me this story ... to which you have often alluded in my presence?"

"What made me ...?"

He drew my attention to a woman, still exceedingly handsome, who was passing on a young man's arm. She saw Lupin and bowed.

"It's she," he whispered. "She and her son."

"Then she recognized you?"

"She always recognizes me, whatever my disguise."

"But since the burglary at the Château de Thibermesnil,[4] the police have identified the two names of Arsène Lupin and Horace Velmont."

"Yes."

"Therefore she knows who you are."

"Yes."

"And she bows to you?" I exclaimed, in spite of myself.

He caught me by the arm and, fiercely:

"Do you think that I am Lupin to her? Do you think that I am a burglar in her eyes, a rogue, a cheat?... Why, I might be the lowest of miscreants, I might be a murderer even ... and still she would bow to me!"

"Why? Because she loved you once?"

"Rot! That would be an additional reason, on the contrary, why she should now despise me."

"What then?"

"I am the man who gave her back her son!"

III. THE SIGN OF THE SHADOW

"I received your telegram and here I am," said a gentleman with a grey moustache, who entered my study, dressed in a dark-brown frock-coat and a wide-brimmed hat, with a red ribbon in his buttonhole. "What's the matter?"

Had I not been expecting Arsène Lupin, I should certainly never have recognized him in the person of this old half-pay officer:

"What's the matter?" I echoed. "Oh, nothing much: a rather curious coincidence, that's all. And, as I know that you would just as soon clear up a mystery as plan one...."

"Well?"

"You seem in a great hurry!"

"I am ... unless the mystery in question is worth putting myself out for. So let us get to the point."

"Very well. Just begin by casting your eye on this little picture, which I picked up, a week or two ago, in a grimy old shop on the other side of the river. I bought it for the sake of its Empire frame, with the palm-leaf ornaments on the mouldings ... for the painting is execrable."

"Execrable, as you say," said Lupin, after he had examined it, "but the subject itself is rather nice. That corner of an old courtyard, with its rotunda of Greek columns, its sundial and its fish-pond and that ruined well with the Renascence roof and those stone steps and stone benches: all very picturesque."

"And genuine," I added. "The picture, good or bad, has never been taken out of its Empire frame. Besides, it is dated.... There, in the left-hand bottom corner: those red figures, 15. 4. 2, which obviously stand for 15 April, 1802."

"I dare say ... I dare say.... But you were speaking of a coincidence and, so far, I fail to see...."

I went to a corner of my study, took a telescope, fixed it on its stand and pointed it, through the open window, at the open window of a little room facing my flat, on the other side of the street. And I asked Lupin to look through it.

He stooped forward. The slanting rays of the morning sun lit up the room opposite, revealing a set of mahogany furniture, all very simple, a large bed and a child's bed hung with cretonne curtains.

"Ah!" cried Lupin, suddenly. "The same picture!"

"Exactly the same!" I said. "And the date: do you see the date, in red? 15. 4. 2."

"Yes, I see.... And who lives in that room?"

"A lady ... or, rather, a workwoman, for she has to work for her living ... needlework, hardly enough to keep herself and her child."

"What is her name?"

"Louise d'Ernemont.... From what I hear, she is the great-granddaughter of a farmer-general who was guillotined during the Terror."

"Yes, on the same day as André Chénier," said Lupin. "According to the memoirs of the time, this d'Ernemont was supposed to be a very rich man." He raised his head and said, "It's an interesting story.... Why did you wait before telling me?"

"Because this is the 15th of April."

"Well?"

"Well, I discovered yesterday—I heard them talking about it in the porter's box—that the 15th of April plays an important part in the life of Louise d'Ernemont."

"Nonsense!"

"Contrary to her usual habits, this woman who works every day of her life, who keeps her two rooms tidy, who cooks the lunch which her little girl eats when she comes home from the parish school ... this woman, on the 15th of April, goes out with the child at ten o'clock in the morning and does not return until nightfall. And this has happened for years and in all weathers. You must admit that there is something queer about this date which I find on an old picture, which is inscribed on another, similar picture and which controls the annual movements of the descendant of d'Ernemont the farmer-general."

"Yes, it's curious ... you're quite right," said Lupin, slowly. "And don't you know where she goes to?"

"Nobody knows. She does not confide in a soul. As a matter of fact, she talks very little."

"Are you sure of your information?"

"Absolutely. And the best proof of its accuracy is that here she comes."

A door had opened at the back of the room opposite, admitting a little girl of seven or eight, who came and looked out of the window. A lady appeared behind her, tall, good-looking still and wearing a sad and gentle air. Both of them were ready and dressed, in clothes which were simple in themselves, but which pointed to a love of neatness and a certain elegance on the part of the mother.

"You see," I whispered, "they are going out."

And presently the mother took the child by the hand and they left the room together.

Lupin caught up his hat:

"Are you coming?"

My curiosity was too great for me to raise the least objection. I went downstairs with Lupin.

As we stepped into the street, we saw my neighbor enter a baker's shop. She bought two rolls and placed them in a little basket which her daughter was carrying and which seemed already to contain some other provisions. Then they went in the direction of the outer boulevards and followed them as far as the Place de l'Étoile, where they turned down the Avenue Kléber to walk toward Passy.

Lupin strolled silently along, evidently obsessed by a train of thought which I was glad to have provoked. From time to time, he uttered a sentence which showed me the thread of his reflections; and I was able to see that the riddle remained as much a mystery to him as to myself.

Louise d'Ernemont, meanwhile, had branched off to the left, along the Rue Raynouard, a quiet old street in which Franklin and Balzac once lived, one of those streets which, lined with old-fashioned houses and walled gardens, give you the impression of being in a country-town. The Seine flows at the foot of the slope which the street crowns; and a number of lanes run down to the river.

My neighbor took one of these narrow, winding, deserted lanes. The first building, on the right, was a house the front of which faced the Rue Raynouard. Next came a moss-grown wall, of a height above the ordinary, supported by buttresses and bristling with broken glass. Half-way along the wall was a low, arched door. Louise d'Ernemont stopped in front of this door and opened it with a key which seemed to us enormous. Mother and child entered and closed the door.

"In any case," said Lupin, "she has nothing to conceal, for she has not looked round once...."

He had hardly finished his sentence when we heard the sound of footsteps behind us. It was two old beggars, a man and a woman, tattered, dirty, squalid, covered in rags. They passed us without paying the least attention to our presence. The man took from his wallet a key similar to my neighbor's and put it into the lock. The door closed behind them.

And, suddenly, at the top of the lane, came the noise of a motor-car stopping.... Lupin dragged me fifty yards lower down, to a corner in which we were able to hide. And we saw coming down the lane, carrying a little dog under her arm, a young and very much over-dressed woman, wearing a quantity of jewellery, a young woman whose eyes were too dark, her lips too red, her hair too fair. In front of the door, the same performance, with the same key.... The lady and the dog disappeared from view.

"This promises to be most amusing," said Lupin, chuckling. "What earthly connection can there be between those different people?"

There hove in sight successively two elderly ladies, lean and rather poverty-stricken in appearance, very much alike, evidently sisters; a footman in livery; an infantry corporal; a fat gentleman in a soiled and patched jacket-suit; and, lastly, a workman's family, father, mother, and four children, all six of them pale and sickly, looking like people who never eat their fill. And each of the newcomers carried a basket or string-bag filled with provisions.

"It's a picnic!" I cried.

"It grows more and more surprising," said Lupin, "and I sha'n't be satisfied till I know what is happening behind that wall."

To climb it was out of the question. We also saw that it finished, at the lower as well as at the upper end, at a house none of whose windows overlooked the enclosure which the wall contained.

During the next hour, no one else came along. We vainly cast about for a stratagem; and Lupin, whose fertile brain had exhausted every possible expedient, was about to go in search of a ladder, when, suddenly, the little door opened and one of the workman's children came out.

The boy ran up the lane to the Rue Raynouard. A few minutes later he returned, carrying two bottles of water, which he set down on the pavement to take the big key from his pocket.

By that time Lupin had left me and was strolling slowly along the wall. When the child, after entering the enclosure, pushed back the door Lupin sprang forward and stuck the point of his knife into the staple of the lock. The bolt failed to catch; and it became an easy matter to push the door ajar.

"That's done the trick!" said Lupin.

He cautiously put his hand through the doorway and then, to my great surprise, entered boldly. But, on following his example, I saw that, ten yards behind the wall, a clump of laurels formed a sort of curtain which allowed us to come up unobserved.

Lupin took his stand right in the middle of the clump. I joined him and, like him, pushed aside the branches of one of the shrubs. And the sight which presented itself to my eyes was so unexpected that I was unable to suppress an exclamation, while Lupin, on his side, muttered, between his teeth:

"By Jupiter! This is a funny job!"

We saw before us, within the confined space that lay between the two windowless houses, the identical scene represented in the old picture which I had bought at a second-hand dealer's!

The identical scene! At the back, against the opposite wall, the same Greek rotunda displayed its slender columns. In the middle, the same stone benches topped a circle of four steps that ran down to a fish-pond with moss-grown flags. On the left, the same well raised its wrought-iron roof; and, close at hand, the same sun-dial showed its slanting gnomon and its marble face.

The identical scene! And what added to the strangeness of the sight was the memory, obsessing Lupin and myself, of that date of the 15th of April, inscribed in a corner of the picture, and the thought that this very day was the 15th of April and that sixteen or seventeen people, so different in age, condition and manners, had chosen the 15th of April to come together in this forgotten corner of Paris!

All of them, at the moment when we caught sight of them, were sitting in separate groups on the benches and steps; and all were eating. Not very far from my neighbor and her daughter, the workman's family and the beggar couple were sharing their provisions; while the footman, the gentleman in the soiled suit, the infantry corporal and the two lean sisters were making a common stock of their sliced ham, their tins of sardines and their gruyère cheese.

The lady with the little dog alone, who had brought no food with her, sat apart from the others, who made a show of turning their backs upon her. But Louise d'Ernemont offered her a sandwich, whereupon her example was followed by the two sisters; and the corporal at once began to make himself as agreeable to the young person as he could.

It was now half-past one. The beggar-man took out his pipe, as did the fat gentleman; and, when they found that one had no tobacco and the other no matches, their needs soon brought them together. The men went and smoked by the rotunda and the women joined them. For that matter, all these people seemed to know one another quite well.

They were at some distance from where we were standing, so that we could not hear what they said. However, we gradually perceived that the conversation was becoming animated. The young person with the dog, in particular, who by this time appeared to be in great request, indulged in much voluble talk, accompanying her words with many gestures, which set the little dog barking furiously.

But, suddenly, there was an outcry, promptly followed by shouts of rage; and one and all, men and women alike, rushed in disorder toward the well. One of the workman's brats was at that moment coming out of it, fastened by his belt to the hook at the end of the rope; and the three other urchins were drawing him up by turning the handle. More active than the rest, the corporal flung himself upon him; and forthwith the footman and the fat gentleman seized hold of him also, while the beggars and the lean sisters came to blows with the workman and his family.

In a few seconds the little boy had not a stitch left on him beyond his shirt. The footman, who had taken possession of the rest of the clothes, ran away, pursued by the corporal, who snatched away the boy's breeches, which were next torn from the corporal by one of the lean sisters.

"They are mad!" I muttered, feeling absolutely at sea.

"Not at all, not at all," said Lupin.

"What! Do you mean to say that you can make head or tail of what is going on?"

He did not reply. The young lady with the little dog, tucking her pet under her arm, had started running after the child in the shirt, who uttered loud yells. The two of them raced round the laurel-clump in which we stood hidden; and the brat flung himself into his mother's arms.

At long last, Louise d'Ernemont, who had played a conciliatory part from the beginning, succeeded in allaying the tumult. Everybody sat down again; but there was a reaction in all those exasperated people and they remained motionless and silent, as though worn out with their exertions.

And time went by. Losing patience and beginning to feel the pangs of hunger, I went to the Rue Raynouard to fetch something to eat, which we divided while watching the actors in the incomprehensible comedy that was being performed before our eyes. They hardly stirred. Each minute that passed seemed to load them with increasing melancholy; and they sank into attitudes of discouragement, bent their backs more and more and sat absorbed in their meditations.

The afternoon wore on in this way, under a grey sky that shed a dreary light over the enclosure.

"Are they going to spend the night here?" I asked, in a bored voice.

But, at five o'clock or so, the fat gentleman in the soiled jacket-suit took out his watch. The others did the same and all, watch in hand, seemed to be anxiously awaiting an event of no little importance to themselves. The event did not take place, for, in fifteen or twenty minutes, the fat gentleman gave a gesture of despair, stood up and put on his hat.

Then lamentations broke forth. The two lean sisters and the workman's wife fell upon their knees and made the sign of the cross. The lady with the little dog and the beggar-woman kissed each other and sobbed; and we saw Louise d'Ernemont pressing her daughter sadly to her.

"Let's go," said Lupin.

"You think it's over?"

"Yes; and we have only just time to make ourselves scarce."

We went out unmolested. At the top of the lane, Lupin turned to the left and, leaving me outside, entered the first house in the Rue Raynouard, the one that backed on to the enclosure.

After talking for a few seconds to the porter, he joined me and we stopped a passing taxi-cab:

"No. 34 Rue de Turin," he said to the driver.

The ground-floor of No. 34 was occupied by a notary's office; and we were shown in, almost without waiting, to Maître Valandier, a smiling, pleasant-spoken man of a certain age.

Lupin introduced himself by the name of Captain Jeanniot, retired from the army. He said that he wanted to build a house to his own liking and that some one had suggested to him a plot of ground situated near the Rue Raynouard.

"But that plot is not for sale," said Maître Valandier.

"Oh, I was told...."

"You have been misinformed, I fear."

The lawyer rose, went to a cupboard and returned with a picture which he showed us. I was petrified. It was the same picture which I had bought, the same picture that hung in Louise d'Ernemont's room.

"This is a painting," he said, "of the plot of ground to which you refer. It is known as the Clos d'Ernemont."

"Precisely."

"Well, this close," continued the notary, "once formed part of a large garden belonging to d'Ernemont, the farmer-general, who was executed during the Terror. All that could be sold has been sold, piecemeal, by the heirs. But this last plot has remained and will remain in their joint possession ... unless...."

The notary began to laugh.

"Unless what?" asked Lupin.

"Well, it's quite a romance, a rather curious romance, in fact. I often amuse myself by looking through the voluminous documents of the case."

"Would it be indiscreet, if I asked ...?"

"Not at all, not at all," declared Maître Valandier, who seemed delighted, on the contrary, to have found a listener for his story. And, without waiting to be pressed, he began: "At the outbreak of the Revolution, Louis Agrippa d'Ernemont, on the pretence of joining his wife, who was staying at Geneva with their daughter Pauline, shut up his mansion in the Faubourg Saint-Germain, dismissed his servants and, with his son Charles, came and took up his abode in his pleasure-house at Passy, where he was known to nobody except an old and devoted serving-woman. He remained there in hiding for three years and he had every reason to hope that his retreat would not be discovered, when, one day, after luncheon, as he was having a nap, the old servant burst into his room. She had seen, at the end of the street, a patrol of armed men who seemed to be making for the house. Louis d'Ernemont got ready quickly and, at the moment when the men were knocking at the front door, disappeared through the door that led to the garden, shouting to his son, in a scared voice, to keep them talking, if only for five minutes. He may have intended to escape and found the outlets through the garden watched. In any case, he returned in six or seven minutes, replied very calmly to the questions put to him and raised no difficulty about accompanying the men. His son Charles, although only eighteen years of age, was arrested also."

"When did this happen?" asked Lupin.

"It happened on the 26th day of Germinal, Year II, that is to say, on the...."

Maître Valandier stopped, with his eyes fixed on a calendar that hung on the wall, and exclaimed:

"Why, it was on this very day! This is the 15th of April, the anniversary of the farmer-general's arrest."

"What an odd coincidence!" said Lupin. "And considering the period at which it took place, the arrest, no doubt, had serious consequences?"

"Oh, most serious!" said the notary, laughing. "Three months later, at the beginning of Thermidor, the farmer-general mounted the scaffold. His son Charles was forgotten in prison and their property was confiscated."

"The property was immense, I suppose?" said Lupin.

"Well, there you are! That's just where the thing becomes complicated. The property, which was, in fact, immense, could never be traced. It was discovered that the Faubourg

Saint-Germain mansion had been sold, before the Revolution, to an Englishman, together with all the country-seats and estates and all the jewels, securities and collections belonging to the farmer-general. The Convention instituted minute inquiries, as did the Directory afterward. But the inquiries led to no result."

"There remained, at any rate, the Passy house," said Lupin.

"The house at Passy was bought, for a mere song, by a delegate of the Commune, the very man who had arrested d'Ernemont, one Citizen Broquet. Citizen Broquet shut himself up in the house, barricaded the doors, fortified the walls and, when Charles d'Ernemont was at last set free and appeared outside, received him by firing a musket at him. Charles instituted one law-suit after another, lost them all and then proceeded to offer large sums of money. But Citizen Broquet proved intractable. He had bought the house and he stuck to the house; and he would have stuck to it until his death, if Charles had not obtained the support of Bonaparte. Citizen Broquet cleared out on the 12th of February, 1803; but Charles d'Ernemont's joy was so great and his brain, no doubt, had been so violently unhinged by all that he had gone through, that, on reaching the threshold of the house of which he had at last recovered the ownership, even before opening the door he began to dance and sing in the street. He had gone clean off his head."

"By Jove!" said Lupin. "And what became of him?"

"His mother and his sister Pauline, who had ended by marrying a cousin of the same name at Geneva, were both dead. The old servant-woman took care of him and they lived together in the Passy house. Years passed without any notable event; but, suddenly, in 1812, an unexpected incident happened. The old servant made a series of strange revelations on her death-bed, in the presence of two witnesses whom she sent for. She declared that the farmer-general had carried to his house at Passy a number of bags filled with gold and silver and that those bags had disappeared a few days before the arrest. According to earlier confidences made by Charles d'Ernemont, who had them from his father, the treasures were hidden in the garden, between the rotunda, the sun-dial and the well. In proof of her statement, she produced three pictures, or rather, for they were not yet framed, three canvases, which the farmer-general had painted during his captivity and which he had succeeded in conveying to her, with instructions to hand them to his wife, his son and his daughter. Tempted by the lure of wealth, Charles and the old servant had kept silence. Then came the law-suits, the recovery of the house, Charles's madness, the servant's own useless searches; and the treasures were still there."

"And they are there now," chuckled Lupin.

"And they will be there always," exclaimed Maître Valandier. "Unless ... unless Citizen Broquet, who no doubt smelt a rat, succeeded in ferreting them out. But this is an unlikely supposition, for Citizen Broquet died in extreme poverty."

"So then ...?"

"So then everybody began to hunt. The children of Pauline, the sister, hastened from Geneva. It was discovered that Charles had been secretly married and that he had sons. All these heirs set to work."

"But Charles himself?"

"Charles lived in the most absolute retirement. He did not leave his room."

"Never?"

"Well, that is the most extraordinary, the most astounding part of the story. Once a year, Charles d'Ernemont, impelled by a sort of subconscious will-power, came downstairs, took the exact road which his father had taken, walked across the garden and sat down either on the steps of the rotunda, which you see here, in the picture, or on the kerb of the well. At twenty-seven minutes past five, he rose and went indoors again; and until his death, which occurred in 1820, he never once failed to perform this incomprehensible pilgrimage. Well, the day on which this happened was invariably the 15th of April, the anniversary of the arrest."

Maître Valandier was no longer smiling and himself seemed impressed by the amazing story which he was telling us.

"And, since Charles's death?" asked Lupin, after a moment's reflection.

"Since that time," replied the lawyer, with a certain solemnity of manner, "for nearly a hundred years, the heirs of Charles and Pauline d'Ernemont have kept up the pilgrimage of the 15th of April. During the first few years they made the most thorough excavations. Every inch of the garden was searched, every clod of ground dug up. All this is now over. They take hardly any pains. All they do is, from time to time, for no particular reason, to turn over a stone or explore the well. For the most part, they are content to sit down on the steps of the rotunda, like the poor madman; and, like him, they wait. And that, you see, is the sad part of their destiny. In those hundred years, all these people who have succeeded one another, from father to son, have lost—what shall I say?—the energy of life. They have no courage left, no initiative. They wait. They wait for the 15th of April; and, when the 15th of April comes, they wait for a miracle to take place. Poverty has ended by overtaking every one of them. My predecessors and I have sold first the house, in order to build another which yields a better rent, followed by bits of the garden and further bits. But, as to that corner over there," pointing to the picture, "they would rather die than sell it. On this they are all agreed: Louise d'Ernemont, who is the direct heiress of Pauline, as well as the beggars, the workman, the footman, the circus-rider and so on, who represent the unfortunate Charles."

There was a fresh pause; and Lupin asked:

"What is your own opinion, Maître Valandier?"

"My private opinion is that there's nothing in it. What credit can we give to the statements of an old servant enfeebled by age? What importance can we attach to the crotchets of a madman? Besides, if the farmer-general had realized his fortune, don't you think that that fortune would have been found? One could manage to hide a paper, a document, in a confined space like that, but not treasures."

"Still, the pictures?..."

"Yes, of course. But, after all, are they a sufficient proof?"

Lupin bent over the copy which the solicitor had taken from the cupboard and, after examining it at length, said:

"You spoke of three pictures."

"Yes, the one which you see was handed to my predecessor by the heirs of Charles. Louise d'Ernemont possesses another. As for the third, no one knows what became of it."

Lupin looked at me and continued:

"And do they all bear the same date?"

"Yes, the date inscribed by Charles d'Ernemont when he had them framed, not long before his death.... The same date, that is to say the 15th of April, Year II, according to the revolutionary calendar, as the arrest took place in April, 1794."

"Oh, yes, of course," said Lupin. "The figure 2 means...."

He thought for a few moments and resumed:

"One more question, if I may. Did no one ever come forward to solve the problem?"

Maître Valandier threw up his arms:

"Goodness gracious me!" he cried. "Why, it was the plague of the office! One of my predecessors, Maître Turbon, was summoned to Passy no fewer than eighteen times, between 1820 and 1843, by the groups of heirs, whom fortune-tellers, clairvoyants, visionaries, impostors of all sorts had promised that they would discover the farmer-general's treasures. At last, we laid down a rule: any outsider applying to institute a search was to begin by depositing a certain sum."

"What sum?"

"A thousand francs."

"And did this have the effect of frightening them off?"

"No. Four years ago, an Hungarian hypnotist tried the experiment and made me waste a whole day. After that, we fixed the deposit at five thousand francs. In case of success, a third of the treasure goes to the finder. In case of failure, the deposit is forfeited to the heirs. Since then, I have been left in peace."

"Here are your five thousand francs."

The lawyer gave a start:

"Eh? What do you say?"

"I say," repeated Lupin, taking five bank-notes from his pocket and calmly spreading them on the table, "I say that here is the deposit of five thousand francs. Please give me a receipt and invite all the d'Ernemont heirs to meet me at Passy on the 15th of April next year."

The notary could not believe his senses. I myself, although Lupin had accustomed me to these surprises, was utterly taken back.

"Are you serious?" asked Maître Valandier.

"Perfectly serious."

"But, you know, I told you my opinion. All these improbable stories rest upon no evidence of any kind."

"I don't agree with you," said Lupin.

The notary gave him the look which we give to a person who is not quite right in his head. Then, accepting the situation, he took his pen and drew up a contract on stamped paper, acknowledging the payment of the deposit by Captain Jeanniot and promising him a third of such moneys as he should discover:

"If you change your mind," he added, "you might let me know a week before the time comes. I shall not inform the d'Ernemont family until the last moment, so as not to give those poor people too long a spell of hope."

"You can inform them this very day, Maître Valandier. It will make them spend a happier year."

We said good-bye. Outside, in the street, I cried:

"So you have hit upon something?"

"I?" replied Lupin. "Not a bit of it! And that's just what amuses me."

"But they have been searching for a hundred years!"

"It is not so much a matter of searching as of thinking. Now I have three hundred and sixty-five days to think in. It is a great deal more than I want; and I am afraid that I shall forget all about the business, interesting though it may be. Oblige me by reminding me, will you?"

I reminded him of it several times during the following months, though he never seemed to attach much importance to the matter. Then came a long period during which I had no opportunity of seeing him. It was the period, as I afterward learnt, of his visit to Armenia and of the terrible struggle on which he embarked against Abdul the Damned, a struggle which ended in the tyrant's downfall.

I used to write to him, however, at the address which he gave me and I was thus able to send him certain particulars which I had succeeded in gathering, here and there, about my neighbor Louise d'Ernemont, such as the love which she had conceived, a few years earlier, for a very rich young man, who still loved her, but who had been compelled by his family to throw her over; the young widow's despair, and the plucky life which she led with her little daughter.

Lupin replied to none of my letters. I did not know whether they reached him; and, meantime, the date was drawing near and I could not help wondering whether his numerous undertakings would not prevent him from keeping the appointment which he himself had fixed.

As a matter of fact, the morning of the 15th of April arrived and Lupin was not with me by the time I had finished lunch. It was a quarter-past twelve. I left my flat and took a cab to Passy.

I had no sooner entered the lane than I saw the workman's four brats standing outside the door in the wall. Maître Valandier, informed by them of my arrival, hastened in my direction:

"Well?" he cried. "Where's Captain Jeanniot?"

"Hasn't he come?"

"No; and I can assure you that everybody is very impatient to see him."

The different groups began to crowd round the lawyer; and I noticed that all those faces which I recognized had thrown off the gloomy and despondent expression which they wore a year ago.

"They are full of hope," said Maître Valandier, "and it is my fault. But what could I do? Your friend made such an impression upon me that I spoke to these good people with a confidence ... which I cannot say I feel. However, he seems a queer sort of fellow, this Captain Jeanniot of yours...."

He asked me many questions and I gave him a number of more or less fanciful details about the captain, to which the heirs listened, nodding their heads in appreciation of my remarks.

"Of course, the truth was bound to be discovered sooner or later," said the fat gentleman, in a tone of conviction.

The infantry corporal, dazzled by the captain's rank, did not entertain a doubt in his mind.

The lady with the little dog wanted to know if Captain Jeanniot was young.

But Louise d'Ernemont said:

"And suppose he does not come?"

"We shall still have the five thousand francs to divide," said the beggar-man.

For all that, Louise d'Ernemont's words had damped their enthusiasm. Their faces began to look sullen and I felt an atmosphere as of anguish weighing upon us.

At half-past one, the two lean sisters felt faint and sat down. Then the fat gentleman in the soiled suit suddenly rounded on the notary:

"It's you, Maître Valandier, who are to blame.... You ought to have brought the captain here by main force.... He's a humbug, that's quite clear."

He gave me a savage look, and the footman, in his turn, flung muttered curses at me.

I confess that their reproaches seemed to me well-founded and that Lupin's absence annoyed me greatly:

"He won't come now," I whispered to the lawyer.

And I was thinking of beating a retreat, when the eldest of the brats appeared at the door, yelling:

"There's some one coming!... A motor-cycle!..."

A motor was throbbing on the other side of the wall. A man on a motor-bicycle came tearing down the lane at the risk of breaking his neck. Suddenly, he put on his brakes, outside the door, and sprang from his machine.

Under the layer of dust which covered him from head to foot, we could see that his navy-blue reefer-suit, his carefully creased trousers, his black felt hat and patent-leather boots were not the clothes in which a man usually goes cycling.

"But that's not Captain Jeanniot!" shouted the notary, who failed to recognize him.

"Yes, it is," said Lupin, shaking hands with us. "I'm Captain Jeanniot right enough ... only I've shaved off my moustache.... Besides, Maître Valandier, here's your receipt."

He caught one of the workman's children by the arm and said:

"Run to the cab-rank and fetch a taxi to the corner of the Rue Raynouard. Look sharp! I have an urgent appointment to keep at two o'clock, or a quarter-past at the latest."

There was a murmur of protest. Captain Jeanniot took out his watch:

"Well! It's only twelve minutes to two! I have a good quarter of an hour before me. But, by Jingo, how tired I feel! And how hungry into the bargain!"

The corporal thrust his ammunition-bread into Lupin's hand; and he munched away at it as he sat down and said:

"You must forgive me. I was in the Marseilles express, which left the rails between Dijon and Laroche. There were twelve people killed and any number injured, whom I had to help. Then I found this motor-cycle in the luggage-van.... Maître Valandier, you must be good enough to restore it to the owner. You will find the label fastened to the handle-bar. Ah, you're back, my boy! Is the taxi there? At the corner of the Rue Raynouard? Capital!"

He looked at his watch again:

"Hullo! No time to lose!"

I stared at him with eager curiosity. But how great must the excitement of the d'Ernemont heirs have been! True, they had not the same faith in Captain Jeanniot that I had in Lupin. Nevertheless, their faces were pale and drawn. Captain Jeanniot turned slowly to the left and walked up to the sun-dial. The pedestal represented the figure of a man with a powerful torso, who bore on his shoulders a marble slab the surface of which had been so much worn by time that we could hardly distinguish the engraved lines that marked the hours. Above the slab, a Cupid, with outspread wings, held an arrow that served as a gnomon.

The captain stood leaning forward for a minute, with attentive eyes.

Then he said:

"Somebody lend me a knife, please."

A clock in the neighbourhood struck two. At that exact moment, the shadow of the arrow was thrown upon the sunlit dial along the line of a crack in the marble which divided the slab very nearly in half.

The captain took the knife handed to him. And with the point, very gently, he began to scratch the mixture of earth and moss that filled the narrow cleft.

Almost immediately, at a couple of inches from the edge, he stopped, as though his knife had encountered an obstacle, inserted his thumb and forefinger and withdrew a small object which he rubbed between the palms of his hands and gave to the lawyer:

"Here, Maître Valandier. Something to go on with."

It was an enormous diamond, the size of a hazelnut and beautifully cut.

The captain resumed his work. The next moment, a fresh stop. A second diamond, magnificent and brilliant as the first, appeared in sight.

And then came a third and a fourth.

In a minute's time, following the crack from one edge to the other and certainly without digging deeper than half an inch, the captain had taken out eighteen diamonds of the same size.

During this minute, there was not a cry, not a movement around the sun-dial. The heirs seemed paralyzed with a sort of stupor. Then the fat gentleman muttered:

"Geminy!"

And the corporal moaned:

"Oh, captain!... Oh, captain!..."

The two sisters fell in a dead faint. The lady with the little dog dropped on her knees and prayed, while the footman, staggering like a drunken man, held his head in his two hands, and Louise d'Ernemont wept.

When calm was restored and all became eager to thank Captain Jeanniot, they saw that he was gone.

Some years passed before I had an opportunity of talking to Lupin about this business. He was in a confidential vein and answered:

"The business of the eighteen diamonds? By Jove, when I think that three or four generations of my fellow-men had been hunting for the solution! And the eighteen diamonds were there all the time, under a little mud and dust!"

"But how did you guess?..."

"I did not guess. I reflected. I doubt if I need even have reflected. I was struck, from the beginning, by the fact that the whole circumstance was governed by one primary question: the question of time. When Charles d'Ernemont was still in possession of his wits, he wrote a date upon the three pictures. Later, in the gloom in which he was struggling, a faint glimmer of intelligence led him every year to the centre of the old garden; and the same faint glimmer led him away from it every year at the same moment, that is to say, at twenty-seven minutes past five. Something must have acted on the disordered machinery of his brain in this way. What was the superior force that controlled the poor madman's movements? Obviously, the instinctive notion of time represented by the sun-dial in the farmer-general's pictures. It was the annual revolution of the earth around the sun that brought Charles d'Ernemont back to the garden at a fixed date. And it was the earth's daily revolution upon its own axis that took him from it at a fixed hour, that is to say, at the hour, most likely, when the sun, concealed by objects different from those of to-day, ceased to light the Passy garden. Now of all this the sun-dial was the symbol. And that is why I at once knew where to look."

"But how did you settle the hour at which to begin looking?"

"Simply by the pictures. A man living at that time, such as Charles d'Ernemont, would have written either 26 Germinal, Year II, or else 15 April, 1794, but not 15 April, Year II. I was astounded that no one had thought of that."

"Then the figure 2 stood for two o'clock?"

"Evidently. And what must have happened was this: the farmer-general began by turning his fortune into solid gold and silver money. Then, by way of additional precaution, with this gold and silver he bought eighteen wonderful diamonds. When he was surprised by the arrival of the patrol, he fled into his garden. Which was the best place to hide the diamonds? Chance caused his eyes to light upon the sun-dial. It was two o'clock. The shadow of the arrow was then falling along the crack in the marble. He obeyed this sign of the shadow, rammed his eighteen diamonds into the dust and calmly went back and surrendered to the soldiers."

"But the shadow of the arrow coincides with the crack in the marble every day of the year and not only on the 15th of April."

"You forget, my dear chap, that we are dealing with a lunatic and that he remembered only this date of the 15th of April."

"Very well; but you, once you had solved the riddle, could easily have made your way into the enclosure and taken the diamonds."

"Quite true; and I should not have hesitated, if I had had to do with people of another description. But I really felt sorry for those poor wretches. And then you know the sort of idiot that Lupin is. The idea of appearing suddenly as a benevolent genius and amazing his kind would be enough to make him commit any sort of folly."

"Tah!" I cried. "The folly was not so great as all that. Six magnificent diamonds! How delighted the d'Ernemont heirs must have been to fulfil their part of the contract!"

Lupin looked at me and burst into uncontrollable laughter:

"So you haven't heard? Oh, what a joke! The delight of the d'Ernemont heirs!.... Why, my dear fellow, on the next day, that worthy Captain Jeanniot had so many mortal enemies! On the very next day, the two lean sisters and the fat gentleman organized an opposition. A contract? Not worth the paper it was written on, because, as could easily be proved, there was no such person as Captain Jeanniot. Where did that adventurer spring from? Just let him sue them and they'd soon show him what was what!"

"Louise d'Ernemont too?"

"No, Louise d'Ernemont protested against that piece of rascality. But what could she do against so many? Besides, now that she was rich, she got back her young man. I haven't heard of her since."

"So ...?"

"So, my dear fellow, I was caught in a trap, with not a leg to stand on, and I had to compromise and accept one modest diamond as my share, the smallest and the least handsome of the lot. That comes of doing one's best to help people!"

And Lupin grumbled between his teeth:

"Oh, gratitude!... All humbug!... Where should we honest men be if we had not our conscience and the satisfaction of duty performed to reward us?"

IV. THE INFERNAL TRAP

When the race was over, a crowd of people, streaming toward the exit from the grand stand, pushed against Nicolas Dugrival. He brought his hand smartly to the inside pocket of his jacket.

"What's the matter?" asked his wife.

"I still feel nervous ... with that money on me! I'm afraid of some nasty accident."

She muttered:

"And I can't understand you. How can you think of carrying such a sum about with you? Every farthing we possess! Lord knows, it cost us trouble enough to earn!"

"Pooh!" he said. "No one would guess that it is here, in my pocket-book."

"Yes, yes," she grumbled. "That young man-servant whom we discharged last week knew all about it, didn't he, Gabriel?"

"Yes, aunt," said a youth standing beside her.

Nicolas Dugrival, his wife and his nephew Gabriel were well-known figures at the race-meetings, where the regular frequenters saw them almost every day: Dugrival, a big, fat, red-faced man, who looked as if he knew how to enjoy life; his wife, also built on heavy lines, with a coarse, vulgar face, and always dressed in a plum-coloured silk much the worse for wear; the nephew, quite young, slender, with pale features, dark eyes and fair and rather curly hair.

As a rule, the couple remained seated throughout the afternoon. It was Gabriel who betted for his uncle, watching the horses in the paddock, picking up tips to right and left among the jockeys and stable-lads, running backward and forward between the stands and the *pari-mutuel*.

Luck had favoured them that day, for, three times, Dugrival's neighbours saw the young man come back and hand him money.

The fifth race was just finishing. Dugrival lit a cigar. At that moment, a gentleman in a tight-fitting brown suit, with a face ending in a peaked grey beard, came up to him and asked, in a confidential whisper:

"Does this happen to belong to you, sir?"

And he displayed a gold watch and chain.

Dugrival gave a start:

"Why, yes ... it's mine.... Look, here are my initials, N. G.: Nicolas Dugrival!"

And he at once, with a movement of terror, clapped his hand to his jacket-pocket. The note-case was still there.

"Ah," he said, greatly relieved, "that's a piece of luck!... But, all the same, how on earth was it done?... Do you know the scoundrel?"

"Yes, we've got him locked up. Pray come with me and we'll soon look into the matter."

"Whom have I the honour ...?"

"M. Delangle, detective-inspector. I have sent to let M. Marquenne, the magistrate, know."

Nicolas Dugrival went out with the inspector; and the two of them started for the commissary's office, some distance behind the grand stand. They were within fifty yards of it, when the inspector was accosted by a man who said to him, hurriedly:

"The fellow with the watch has blabbed; we are on the tracks of a whole gang. M. Marquenne wants you to wait for him at the *pari-mutuel* and to keep a look-out near the fourth booth."

There was a crowd outside the betting-booths and Inspector Delangle muttered:

"It's an absurd arrangement.... Whom am I to look out for?... That's just like M. Marquenne!..."

He pushed aside a group of people who were crowding too close upon him:

"By Jove, one has to use one's elbows here and keep a tight hold on one's purse. That's the way you got your watch pinched, M. Dugrival!"

"I can't understand...."

"Oh, if you knew how those gentry go to work! One never guesses what they're up to next. One of them treads on your foot, another gives you a poke in the eye with his stick and the third picks your pocket before you know where you are.... I've been had that way myself." He stopped and then continued, angrily. "But, bother it, what's the use of hanging about here! What a mob! It's unbearable!... Ah, there's M. Marquenne making signs to us!... One moment, please ... and be sure and wait for me here."

He shouldered his way through the crowd. Nicolas Dugrival followed him for a moment with his eyes. Once the inspector was out of sight, he stood a little to one side, to avoid being hustled.

A few minutes passed. The sixth race was about to start, when Dugrival saw his wife and nephew looking for him. He explained to them that Inspector Delangle was arranging matters with the magistrate.

"Have you your money still?" asked his wife.

"Why, of course I have!" he replied. "The inspector and I took good care, I assure you, not to let the crowd jostle us."

He felt his jacket, gave a stifled cry, thrust his hand into his pocket and began to stammer inarticulate syllables, while Mme. Dugrival gasped, in dismay:

"What is it? What's the matter?"

"Stolen!" he moaned. "The pocket-book ... the fifty notes!..."

"It's not true!" she screamed. "It's not true!"

"Yes, the inspector ... a common sharper ... he's the man...."

She uttered absolute yells:

"Thief! Thief! Stop thief!... My husband's been robbed!... Fifty thousand francs!... We are ruined!... Thief! Thief ..."

In a moment they were surrounded by policemen and taken to the commissary's office. Dugrival went like a lamb, absolutely bewildered. His wife continued to shriek at the top of her voice, piling up explanations, railing against the inspector:

"Have him looked for!... Have him found!... A brown suit.... A pointed beard.... Oh, the villain, to think what he's robbed us of!... Fifty thousand francs!... Why ... why, Dugrival, what are you doing?"

With one bound, she flung herself upon her husband. Too late! He had pressed the barrel of a revolver against his temple. A shot rang out. Dugrival fell. He was dead.

. . .

The reader cannot have forgotten the commotion made by the newspapers in connection with this case, nor how they jumped at the opportunity once more to accuse the police of carelessness and blundering. Was it conceivable that a pick-pocket could play the part of an inspector like that, in broad daylight and in a public place, and rob a respectable man with impunity?

Nicolas Dugrival's widow kept the controversy alive, thanks to her jeremiads and to the interviews which she granted on every hand. A reporter had secured a snapshot of her in front of her husband's body, holding up her hand and swearing to revenge his death. Her nephew Gabriel was standing beside her, with hatred pictured in his face. He, too, it appeared, in a few words uttered in a whisper, but in a tone of fierce determination, had taken an oath to pursue and catch the murderer.

The accounts described the humble apartment which they occupied at the Batignolles; and, as they had been robbed of all their means, a sporting-paper opened a subscription on their behalf.

As for the mysterious Delangle, he remained undiscovered. Two men were arrested, but had to be released forthwith. The police took up a number of clues, which were at once abandoned; more than one name was mentioned; and, lastly, they accused Arsène Lupin, an action which provoked the famous burglar's celebrated cable, dispatched from New York six days after the incident:

"Protest indignantly against calumny invented by baffled police. Send my condolences to unhappy victims. Instructing my bankers to remit them fifty thousand francs.
"LUPIN."

True enough, on the day after the publication of the cable, a stranger rang at Mme. Dugrival's door and handed her an envelope. The envelope contained fifty thousand-franc notes.

This theatrical stroke was not at all calculated to allay the universal comment. But an event soon occurred which provided any amount of additional excitement. Two days later, the people living in the same house as Mme. Dugrival and her nephew were awakened, at four o'clock in the morning, by horrible cries and shrill calls for help. They rushed to the flat. The porter succeeded in opening the door. By the light of a lantern carried by one of the neighbours, he found Gabriel stretched at full-length in his bedroom, with his wrists and ankles bound and a gag forced into his mouth, while, in the next room, Mme. Dugrival lay with her life's blood ebbing away through a great gash in her breast.

She whispered:

"The money.... I've been robbed.... All the notes gone...."

And she fainted away.

What had happened? Gabriel said—and, as soon as she was able to speak, Mme. Dugrival completed her nephew's story—that he was startled from his sleep by finding himself attacked by two men, one of whom gagged him, while the other fastened him down. He was unable to see the men in the dark, but he heard the noise of the struggle between them and his aunt. It was a terrible struggle, Mme. Dugrival declared. The ruffians, who obviously knew their way about, guided by some intuition, made straight for the little cupboard containing the money and, in spite of her resistance and outcries, laid hands upon the bundle of bank-notes. As they left, one of them, whom she had bitten in the arm, stabbed her with a knife, whereupon the men had both fled.

"Which way?" she was asked.

"Through the door of my bedroom and afterward, I suppose, through the hall-door."

"Impossible! The porter would have noticed them."

For the whole mystery lay in this: how had the ruffians entered the house and how did they manage to leave it? There was no outlet open to them. Was it one of the tenants? A careful inquiry proved the absurdity of such a supposition.

What then?

Chief-inspector Ganimard, who was placed in special charge of the case, confessed that he had never known anything more bewildering:

"It's very like Lupin," he said, "and yet it's not Lupin.... No, there's more in it than meets the eye, something very doubtful and suspicious.... Besides, if it were Lupin, why should he take back the fifty thousand francs which he sent? There's another question that puzzles me: what is the connection between the second robbery and the first, the one on the race-course? The whole thing is incomprehensible and I have a sort of feeling—which is very rare with me—that it is no use hunting. For my part, I give it up."

The examining-magistrate threw himself into the case with heart and soul. The reporters united their efforts with those of the police. A famous English sleuth-hound crossed the Channel. A wealthy American, whose head had been turned by detective-stories, offered a big reward to whosoever should supply the first information leading to the discovery of the truth. Six weeks later, no one was any the wiser. The public adopted Ganimard's view; and the examining-magistrate himself grew tired of struggling in a darkness which only became denser as time went on.

And life continued as usual with Dugrival's widow. Nursed by her nephew, she soon recovered from her wound. In the mornings, Gabriel settled her in an easy-chair at the dining-room window, did the rooms and then went out marketing. He cooked their lunch without even accepting the proffered assistance of the porter's wife.

Worried by the police investigations and especially by the requests for interviews, the aunt and nephew refused to see anybody. Not even the portress, whose chatter disturbed and wearied Mme. Dugrival, was admitted. She fell back upon Gabriel, whom she accosted each time that he passed her room:

"Take care, M. Gabriel, you're both of you being spied upon. There are men watching you. Why, only last night, my husband caught a fellow staring up at your windows."

"Nonsense!" said Gabriel. "It's all right. That's the police, protecting us."

One afternoon, at about four o'clock, there was a violent altercation between two costermongers at the bottom of the street. The porter's wife at once left her room to listen to the invectives which the adversaries were hurling at each other's heads. Her back was no sooner turned than a man, young, of medium height and dressed in a grey suit of irreproachable cut, slipped into the house and ran up the staircase.

When he came to the third floor, he rang the bell. Receiving no answer, he rang again. At the third summons, the door opened.

"Mme. Dugrival?" he asked, taking off his hat.

"Mme. Dugrival is still an invalid and unable to see any one," said Gabriel, who stood in the hall.

"It's most important that I should speak to her."

"I am her nephew and perhaps I could take her a message...."

"Very well," said the man. "Please tell Mme. Dugrival that an accident has supplied me with valuable information concerning the robbery from which she has suffered and that I should like to go over the flat and ascertain certain particulars for myself. I am accustomed to this sort of inquiry; and my call is sure to be of use to her."

Gabriel examined the visitor for a moment, reflected and said:

"In that case, I suppose my aunt will consent ... Pray come in."

He opened the door of the dining-room and stepped back to allow the other to pass. The stranger walked to the threshold, but, at the moment when he was crossing it, Gabriel raised his arm and, with a swift movement, struck him with a dagger over the right shoulder.

A burst of laughter rang through the room:

"Got him!" cried Mme. Dugrival, darting up from her chair. "Well done, Gabriel! But, I say, you haven't killed the scoundrel, have you?"

"I don't think so, aunt. It's a small blade and I didn't strike him too hard."

The man was staggering, with his hands stretched in front of him and his face deathly pale.

"You fool!" sneered the widow. "So you've fallen into the trap ... and a good job too! We've been looking out for you a long time. Come, my fine fellow, down with you! You don't care about it, do you? But you can't help yourself, you see. That's right: one knee on the ground, before the missus ... now the other knee.... How well we've been brought up!... Crash, there we go on the floor! Lord, if my poor Dugrival could only see him like that!... And now, Gabriel, to work!"

She went to her bedroom and opened one of the doors of a hanging wardrobe filled with dresses. Pulling these aside, she pushed open another door which formed the back of the wardrobe and led to a room in the next house:

"Help me carry him, Gabriel. And you'll nurse him as well as you can, won't you? For the present, he's worth his weight in gold to us, the artist!..."

The hours succeeded one another. Days passed.

One morning, the wounded man regained a moment's consciousness. He raised his eyelids and looked around him.

He was lying in a room larger than that in which he had been stabbed, a room sparsely furnished, with thick curtains hanging before the windows from top to bottom. There was light enough, however, to enable him to see young Gabriel Dugrival seated on a chair beside him and watching him.

"Ah, it's you, youngster!" he murmured. "I congratulate you, my lad. You have a sure and pretty touch with the dagger."

And he fell asleep again.

That day and the following days, he woke up several times and, each time, he saw the stripling's pale face, his thin lips and his dark eyes, with the hard look in them:

"You frighten me," he said. "If you have sworn to do for me, don't stand on ceremony. But cheer up, for goodness' sake. The thought of death has always struck me as the most humorous thing in the world. Whereas, with you, old chap, it simply becomes lugubrious. I prefer to go to sleep. Good-night!"

Still, Gabriel, in obedience to Mme. Dugrival's orders, continued to nurse him with the utmost care and attention. The patient was almost free from fever and was beginning to take beef-tea and milk. He gained a little strength and jested:

"When will the convalescent be allowed his first drive? Is the bath-chair there? Why, cheer up, stupid! You look like a weeping-willow contemplating a crime. Come, just one little smile for daddy!"

One day, on waking, he had a very unpleasant feeling of constraint. After a few efforts, he perceived that, during his sleep, his legs, chest and arms had been fastened to the bedstead with thin wire strands that cut into his flesh at the least movements.

"Ah," he said to his keeper, "this time it's the great performance! The chicken's going to be bled. Are you operating, Angel Gabriel? If so, see that your razor's nice and clean, old chap! The antiseptic treatment, *if* you please!"

But he was interrupted by the sound of a key grating in the lock. The door opposite opened and Mme. Dugrival appeared.

She approached slowly, took a chair and, producing a revolver from her pocket, cocked it and laid it on the table by the bedside.

"Brrrrr!" said the prisoner. "We might be at the Ambigu!... Fourth act: the Traitor's Doom. And the fair sex to do the deed.... The hand of the Graces.... What an honour!... Mme. Dugrival, I rely on you not to disfigure me."

"Hold your tongue, Lupin."

"Ah, so you know?... By Jove, how clever we are!"

"Hold your tongue, Lupin."

There was a solemn note in her voice that impressed the captive and compelled him to silence. He watched his two gaolers in turns. The bloated features and red complexion of Mme. Dugrival formed a striking contrast with her nephew's refined face; but they both wore the same air of implacable resolve.

The widow leant forward and said:

"Are you prepared to answer my questions?"

"Why not?"

"Then listen to me. How did you know that Dugrival carried all his money in his pocket?"

"Servants' gossip...."

"A young man-servant whom we had in our employ: was that it?"

"Yes."

"And did you steal Dugrival's watch in order to give it back to him and inspire him with confidence?"

"Yes."

She suppressed a movement of fury:

"You fool! You fool!... What! You rob my man, you drive him to kill himself and, instead of making tracks to the uttermost ends of the earth and hiding yourself, you go on playing Lupin in the heart of Paris!... Did you forget that I swore, on my dead husband's head, to find his murderer?"

"That's what staggers me," said Lupin. "How did you come to suspect me?"

"How? Why, you gave yourself away!"

"I did?..."

"Of course.... The fifty thousand francs...."

"Well, what about it? A present...."

"Yes, a present which you gave cabled instructions to have sent to me, so as to make believe that you were in America on the day of the races. A present, indeed! What humbug! The fact is, you didn't like to think of the poor fellow whom you had murdered. So you restored the money to the widow, publicly, of course, because you love playing to the gallery and ranting and posing, like the mountebank that you are. That was all very nicely thought out. Only, my fine fellow, you ought not to have sent me the selfsame notes that were stolen from Dugrival! Yes, you silly fool, the selfsame notes and no others! We knew the numbers, Dugrival and I did. And you were stupid enough to send the bundle to me. Now do you understand your folly?"

Lupin began to laugh:

"It was a pretty blunder, I confess. I'm not responsible; I gave different orders. But, all the same I can't blame any one except myself."

"Ah, so you admit it! You signed your theft and you signed your ruin at the same time. There was nothing left to be done but to find you. Find you? No, better than that. Sensible people don't find Lupin: they make him come to them! That was a masterly notion. It belongs to my young nephew, who loathes you as much as I do, if possible, and who knows you thoroughly, through reading all the books that have been written about you. He knows your prying nature, your need to be always plotting, your mania for hunting in the dark and unravelling what others have failed to unravel. He also knows that sort of sham kindness of yours, the driveling sentimentality that makes you shed crocodile tears over the people you victimize; And he planned the whole farce! He invented the story of the two burglars, the second theft of fifty thousand francs! Oh, I swear to you, before Heaven, that the stab which I gave myself with my own hands never hurt me! And I swear to you, before Heaven, that we spent a glorious time waiting for you, the boy and I, peeping out at your confederates who prowled under our windows, taking their bearings! And there was no mistake about it: you were bound to come! Seeing that you had restored the Widow Dugrival's fifty thousand francs, it was out of the question that you should allow the Widow Dugrival to be robbed of her fifty thousand francs! You were bound to come, attracted by the scent of the mystery. You were bound to come, for swagger, out of vanity! And you come!"

The widow gave a strident laugh:

"Well played, wasn't it? The Lupin of Lupins, the master of masters, inaccessible and invisible, caught in a trap by a woman and a boy!... Here he is in flesh and bone ... here he is with hands and feet tied, no more dangerous than a sparrow ... here is he ... here he is!..."

She shook with joy and began to pace the room, throwing sidelong glances at the bed, like a wild beast that does not for a moment take its eyes from its victim. And never had Lupin beheld greater hatred and savagery in any human being.

"Enough of this prattle," she said.

Suddenly restraining herself, she stalked back to him and, in a quite different tone, in a hollow voice, laying stress on every syllable:

"Thanks to the papers in your pocket, Lupin, I have made good use of the last twelve days. I know all your affairs, all your schemes, all your assumed names, all the organization of your band, all the lodgings which you possess in Paris and elsewhere. I have even visited one of them, the most secret, the one where you hide your papers, your ledgers and the whole story of your financial operations. The result of my investigations is very satisfactory. Here are four cheques, taken from four cheque-books and corresponding with four accounts which you keep at four different banks under four different names. I have filled in each of them for ten thousand francs. A larger figure would have been too risky. And, now, sign."

"By Jove!" said Lupin, sarcastically. "This is blackmail, my worthy Mme. Dugrival."

"That takes your breath away, what?"

"It takes my breath away, as you say."

"And you find an adversary who is a match for you?"

"The adversary is far beyond me. So the trap—let us call it infernal—the infernal trap into which I have fallen was laid not merely by a widow thirsting for revenge, but also by a first-rate business woman anxious to increase her capital?"

"Just so."

"My congratulations. And, while I think of it, used M. Dugrival perhaps to ...?"

"You have hit it, Lupin. After all, why conceal the fact? It will relieve your conscience. Yes, Lupin, Dugrival used to work on the same lines as yourself. Oh, not on the same scale!... We were modest people: a louis here, a louis there ... a purse or two which we trained Gabriel to pick up at the races.... And, in this way, we had made our little pile ... just enough to buy a small place in the country."

"I prefer it that way," said Lupin.

"That's all right! I'm only telling you, so that you may know that I am not a beginner and that you have nothing to hope for. A rescue? No. The room in which we now are communicates with my bedroom. It has a private outlet of which nobody knows. It was Dugrival's special apartment. He used to see his friends here. He kept his implements and tools here, his disguises ... his telephone even, as you perceive. So there's no hope, you see. Your accomplices have given up looking for you here. I have sent them off on another track. Your goose is cooked. Do you begin to realize the position?"

"Yes."

"Then sign the cheques."

"And, when I have signed them, shall I be free?"

"I must cash them first."

"And after that?"

"After that, on my soul, as I hope to be saved, you will be free."

"I don't trust you."

"Have you any choice?"

"That's true. Hand me the cheques."

She unfastened Lupin's right hand, gave him a pen and said:

"Don't forget that the four cheques require four different signatures and that the handwriting has to be altered in each case."

"Never fear."

He signed the cheques.

"Gabriel," said the widow, "it is ten o'clock. If I am not back by twelve, it will mean that this scoundrel has played me one of his tricks. At twelve o'clock, blow out his brains. I am leaving you the revolver with which your uncle shot himself. There are five bullets left out of the six. That will be ample."

She left the room, humming a tune as she went.

Lupin mumbled:

"I wouldn't give twopence for my life."

He shut his eyes for an instant and then, suddenly, said to Gabriel:

"How much?"

And, when the other did not appear to understand, he grew irritated:

"I mean what I say. How much? Answer me, can't you? We drive the same trade, you and I. I steal, thou stealest, we steal. So we ought to come to terms: that's what we are here for. Well? Is it a bargain? Shall we clear out together. I will give you a post in my gang, an easy, well-paid post. How much do you want for yourself? Ten thousand? Twenty thousand? Fix your own price; don't be shy. There's plenty to be had for the asking."

An angry shiver passed through his frame as he saw the impassive face of his keeper:

"Oh, the beggar won't even answer! Why, you can't have been so fond of old Dugrival as all that! Listen to me: if you consent to release me...."

But he interrupted himself. The young man's eyes wore the cruel expression which he knew so well. What was the use of trying to move him?

"Hang it all!" he snarled. "I'm not going to croak here, like a dog! Oh, if I could only...."

Stiffening all his muscles, he tried to burst his bonds, making a violent effort that drew a cry of pain from him; and he fell back upon his bed, exhausted.

"Well, well," he muttered, after a moment, "it's as the widow said: my goose is cooked. Nothing to be done. *De profundis*, Lupin."

A quarter of an hour passed, half an hour....

Gabriel, moving closer to Lupin, saw that his eyes were shut and that his breath came evenly, like that of a man sleeping. But Lupin said:

"Don't imagine that I'm asleep, youngster. No, people don't sleep at a moment like this. Only I am consoling myself. Needs must, eh?... And then I am thinking of what is to come after.... Exactly. I have a little theory of my own about that. You wouldn't think it, to look at me, but I believe in metempsychosis, in the transmigration of souls. It would take too long to explain, however.... I say, boy ... suppose we shook hands before we part? You won't? Then good-bye. Good health and a long life to you, Gabriel!..."

He closed his eyelids and did not stir again before Mme. Dugrival's return.

The widow entered with a lively step, at a few minutes before twelve. She seemed greatly excited:

"I have the money," she said to her nephew. "Run away. I'll join you in the motor down below."

"But...."

"I don't want your help to finish him off. I can do that alone. Still, if you feel like seeing the sort of a face a rogue can pull.... Pass me the weapon."

Gabriel handed her the revolver and the widow continued:

"Have you burnt our papers?"

"Yes."

"Then to work. And, as soon as he's done for, be off. The shots may bring the neighbours. They must find both the flats empty."

She went up to the bed:

"Are you ready, Lupin?"

"Ready's not the word: I'm burning with impatience."

"Have you any request to make of me?"

"None."

"Then...."

"One word, though."

"What is it?"

"If I meet Dugrival in the next world, what message am I to give him from you?"

She shrugged her shoulders and put the barrel of the revolver to Lupin's temple.

"That's it," he said, "and be sure your hand doesn't shake, my dear lady. It won't hurt you, I swear. Are you ready? At the word of command, eh? One ... two ... three...."

The widow pulled the trigger. A shot rang out.

"Is this death?" said Lupin. "That's funny! I should have thought it was something much more different from life!"

There was a second shot. Gabriel snatched the weapon from his aunt's hands and examined it:

"Ah," he exclaimed, "the bullets have been removed!... There are only the percussion-caps left!..."

His aunt and he stood motionless, for a moment, and confused:

"Impossible!" she blurted out. "Who could have done it?... An inspector?... The examining-magistrate?..."

She stopped and, in a low voice:

"Hark.... I hear a noise...."

They listened and the widow went into the hall. She returned, furious, exasperated by her failure and by the scare which she had received:

"There's nobody there.... It must have been the neighbours going out.... We have plenty of time.... Ah, Lupin, you were beginning to make merry!... The knife, Gabriel."

"It's in my room."

"Go and fetch it."

Gabriel hurried away. The widow stamped with rage:

"I've sworn to do it!... You've got to suffer, my fine fellow!... I swore to Dugrival that I would do it and I have repeated my oath every morning and evening since.... I have taken it on my knees, yes, on my knees, before Heaven that listens to me! It's my duty and my right to revenge my dead husband!... By the way, Lupin, you don't look quite as merry as you did!... Lord, one would almost think you were afraid!... He's afraid! He's afraid! I can see it in his eyes!... Come along, Gabriel, my boy!... Look at his eyes!... Look at his lips!... He's trembling!... Give me the knife, so that I may dig it into his heart while he's shivering.... Oh, you coward!... Quick, quick, Gabriel, the knife!..."

"I can't find it anywhere," said the young man, running back in dismay. "It has gone from my room! I can't make it out!"

"Never mind!" cried the Widow Dugrival, half demented. "All the better! I will do the business myself."

She seized Lupin by the throat, clutched him with her ten fingers, digging her nails into his flesh, and began to squeeze with all her might. Lupin uttered a hoarse rattle and gave himself up for lost.

Suddenly, there was a crash at the window. One of the panes was smashed to pieces.

"What's that? What is it?" stammered the widow, drawing herself erect, in alarm.

Gabriel, who had turned even paler than usual, murmured:

"I don't know.... I can't think...."

"Who can have done it?" said the widow.

She dared not move, waiting for what would come next. And one thing above all terrified her, the fact that there was no missile on the floor around them, although the pane of glass, as was clearly visible, had given way before the crash of a heavy and fairly large object, a stone, probably.

After a while, she looked under the bed, under the chest of drawers:

"Nothing," she said.

"No," said her nephew, who was also looking. And, resuming her seat, she said:

"I feel frightened ... my arms fail me ... you finish him off...."

Gabriel confessed:

"I'm frightened also."

"Still ... still," she stammered, "it's got to be done.... I swore it...."

Making one last effort, she returned to Lupin and gasped his neck with her stiff fingers. But Lupin, who was watching her pallid face, received a very clear sensation that she would not have the courage to kill him. To her he was becoming something sacred, invulnerable. A mysterious power was protecting him against every attack, a power which had already saved him three times by inexplicable means and which would find other means to protect him against the wiles of death.

She said to him, in a hoarse voice:

"How you must be laughing at me!"

"Not at all, upon my word. I should feel frightened myself, in your place."

"Nonsense, you scum of the earth! You imagine that you will be rescued ... that your friends are waiting outside? It's out of the question, my fine fellow."

"I know. It's not they defending me ... nobody's defending me...."

"Well, then?..."

"Well, all the same, there's something strange at the bottom of it, something fantastic and miraculous that makes your flesh creep, my fine lady."

"You villain!... You'll be laughing on the other side of your mouth before long."

"I doubt it."

"You wait and see."

She reflected once more and said to her nephew:

"What would you do?"

"Fasten his arm again and let's be off," he replied.

A hideous suggestion! It meant condemning Lupin to the most horrible of all deaths, death by starvation.

"No," said the widow. "He might still find a means of escape. I know something better than that."

She took down the receiver of the telephone, waited and asked:

"Number 82248, please."

And, after a second or two:

"Hullo!... Is that the Criminal Investigation Department?... Is Chief-inspector Ganimard there?... In twenty minutes, you say?... I'm sorry!... However!... When he comes, give him this message from Mme. Dugrival.... Yes, Mme. Nicolas Dugrival.... Ask him to come to my flat. Tell him to open the looking-glass door of my wardrobe; and, when he has done so, he will see that the wardrobe hides an outlet which makes my bedroom communicate with two other rooms. In one of these, he will find a man bound hand and foot. It is the thief, Dugrival's murderer.... You don't believe me?... Tell M. Ganimard; he'll believe me right enough.... Oh, I was almost forgetting to give you the man's name: Arsène Lupin!"

And, without another word, she replaced the receiver.

"There, Lupin, that's done. After all, I would just as soon have my revenge this way. How I shall hold my sides when I read the reports of the Lupin trial!... Are you coming, Gabriel?"

"Yes, aunt."

"Good-bye, Lupin. You and I sha'n't see each other again, I expect, for we are going abroad. But I promise to send you some sweets while you're in prison."

"Chocolates, mother! We'll eat them together!"

"Good-bye."

"*Au revoir.*"

The widow went out with her nephew, leaving Lupin fastened down to the bed.

He at once moved his free arm and tried to release himself; but he realized, at the first attempt, that he would never have the strength to break the wire strands that bound him. Exhausted with fever and pain, what could he do in the twenty minutes or so that were left to him before Ganimard's arrival?

Nor did he count upon his friends. True, he had been thrice saved from death; but this was evidently due to an astounding series of accidents and not to any interference on the part of his allies. Otherwise they would not have contented themselves with these extraordinary manifestations, but would have rescued him for good and all.

No, he must abandon all hope. Ganimard was coming. Ganimard would find him there. It was inevitable. There was no getting away from the fact.

And the prospect of what was coming irritated him singularly. He already heard his old enemy's gibes ringing in his ears. He foresaw the roars of laughter with which the incredible news would be greeted on the morrow. To be arrested in action, so to speak, on the battlefield, by an imposing detachment of adversaries, was one thing: but to be arrested, or rather picked up, scraped up, gathered up, in such condition, was really too silly. And Lupin, who had so often scoffed at others, felt all the ridicule that was falling to his share in this ending of the Dugrival business, all the bathos of allowing himself to be caught in the widow's infernal trap and finally of being "served up" to the police like a dish of game, roasted to a turn and nicely seasoned.

"Blow the widow!" he growled. "I had rather she had cut my throat and done with it."

He pricked up his ears. Some one was moving in the next room. Ganimard! No. Great as his eagerness would be, he could not be there yet. Besides, Ganimard would not have acted like that, would not have opened the door as gently as that other person was doing. What other person? Lupin remembered the three miraculous interventions to which he owed his life. Was it possible that there was really somebody who had protected him against the widow, and that that somebody was now attempting to rescue him? But, if so, who?

Unseen by Lupin, the stranger stooped behind the bed. Lupin heard the sound of the pliers attacking the wire strands and releasing him little by little. First his chest was freed, then his arms, then his legs.

And a voice said to him:

"You must get up and dress."

Feeling very weak, he half-raised himself in bed at the moment when the stranger rose from her stooping posture.

"Who are you?" he whispered. "Who are you?"

And a great surprise over came him.

By his side stood a woman, a woman dressed in black, with a lace shawl over her head, covering part of her face. And the woman, as far as he could judge, was young and of a graceful and slender stature.

"Who are you?" he repeated.

"You must come now," said the woman. "There's no time to lose."

"Can I?" asked Lupin, making a desperate effort. "I doubt if I have the strength."

"Drink this."

She poured some milk into a cup; and, as she handed it to him, her lace opened, leaving the face uncovered.

"You!" he stammered. "It's you!... It's you who ... it was you who were...."

He stared in amazement at this woman whose features presented so striking a resemblance to Gabriel's, whose delicate, regular face had the same pallor, whose mouth wore the same hard and forbidding expression. No sister could have borne so great a likeness to her brother. There was not a doubt possible: it was the identical person. And, without believing for a moment that Gabriel had concealed himself in a woman's clothes, Lupin, on the contrary, received the distinct impression that it was a woman standing beside him and that the stripling who had pursued him with his hatred and struck him with the dagger was in very deed a woman. In order to follow their trade with greater ease, the Dugrival pair had accustomed her to disguise herself as a boy.

"You ... you ...!" he repeated. "Who would have suspected ...?"

She emptied the contents of a phial into the cup:

"Drink this cordial," she said.

He hesitated, thinking of poison.

She added:

"It was I who saved you."

"Of course, of course," he said. "It was you who removed the bullets from the revolver?"

"Yes."

"And you who hid the knife?"

"Here it is, in my pocket."

"And you who smashed the window-pane while your aunt was throttling me?"

"Yes, it was I, with the paper-weight on the table: I threw it into the street."

"But why? Why?" he asked, in utter amazement.

"Drink the cordial."

"Didn't you want me to die? But then why did you stab me to begin with?"

"Drink the cordial."

He emptied the cup at a draught, without quite knowing the reason of his sudden confidence.

"Dress yourself ... quickly," she commanded, retiring to the window.

He obeyed and she came back to him, for he had dropped into a chair, exhausted.

"We must go now, we must, we have only just time.... Collect your strength."

She bent forward a little, so that he might lean on her shoulder, and turned toward the door and the staircase.

And Lupin walked as one walks in a dream, one of those queer dreams in which the most inconsequent things occur, a dream that was the happy sequel of the terrible nightmare in which he had lived for the past fortnight.

A thought struck him, however. He began to laugh:

"Poor Ganimard! Upon my word, the fellow has no luck, I would give twopence to see him coming to arrest me."

After descending the staircase with the aid of his companion, who supported him with incredible vigour, he found himself in the street, opposite a motor-car into which she helped him to mount.

"Right away," she said to the driver.

Lupin, dazed by the open air and the speed at which they were travelling, hardly took stock of the drive and of the incidents on the road. He recovered all his consciousness when he found himself at home in one of the flats which he occupied, looked after by his servant, to whom the girl gave a few rapid instructions.

"You can go," he said to the man.

But, when the girl turned to go as well, he held her back by a fold of her dress.

"No ... no ... you must first explain.... Why did you save me? Did you return unknown to your aunt? But why did you save me? Was it from pity?"

She did not answer. With her figure drawn up and her head flung back a little, she retained her hard and impenetrable air. Nevertheless, he thought he noticed that the lines of her mouth showed not so much cruelty as bitterness. Her eyes, her beautiful dark eyes, revealed melancholy. And Lupin, without as yet understanding, received a vague intuition of what was passing within her. He seized her hand. She pushed him away, with a start of revolt in which he felt hatred, almost repulsion. And, when he insisted, she cried:

"Let me be, will you?... Let me be!... Can't you see that I detest you?"

They looked at each other for a moment, Lupin disconcerted, she quivering and full of uneasiness, her pale face all flushed with unwonted colour.

He said to her, gently:

"If you detested me, you should have let me die.... It was simple enough.... Why didn't you?"

"Why?... Why?... How do I know?..."

Her face contracted. With a sudden movement, she hid it in her two hands; and he saw tears trickle between her fingers.

Greatly touched, he thought of addressing her in fond words, such as one would use to a little girl whom one wished to console, and of giving her good advice and saving her, in his turn, and snatching her from the bad life which she was leading, perhaps against her better nature.

But such words would have sounded ridiculous, coming from his lips, and he did not know what to say, now that he understood the whole story and was able to picture the young woman sitting beside his sick-bed, nursing the man whom she had wounded, admiring his pluck and gaiety, becoming attached to him, falling in love with him and thrice over, probably in spite of herself, under a sort of instinctive impulse, amid fits of spite and rage, saving him from death.

And all this was so strange, so unforeseen; Lupin was so much unmanned by his astonishment, that, this time, he did not try to retain her when she made for the door, backward, without taking her eyes from him.

She lowered her head, smiled for an instant and disappeared.

He rang the bell, quickly:

"Follow that woman," he said to his man. "Or no, stay where you are.... After all, it is better so...."

He sat brooding for a while, possessed by the girl's image. Then he revolved in his mind all that curious, stirring and tragic adventure, in which he had been so very near succumbing; and, taking a hand-glass from the table, he gazed for a long time and with a certain self-complacency at his features, which illness and pain had not succeeded in impairing to any great extent:

"Good looks count for something, after all!" he muttered.

V. THE RED SILK SCARF

On leaving his house one morning, at his usual early hour for going to the Law Courts, Chief-inspector Ganimard noticed the curious behavior of an individual who was walking along the Rue Pergolèse in front of him. Shabbily dressed and wearing a straw hat, though the day was the first of December, the man stooped at every thirty or forty yards to fasten his boot-lace, or pick up his stick, or for some other reason. And, each time, he took a little piece of orange-peel from his pocket and laid it stealthily on the kerb of the pavement. It was probably a mere display of eccentricity, a childish amusement to which no one else would have paid attention; but Ganimard was one of those shrewd observers who are indifferent to nothing that strikes their eyes and who are never satisfied until they know the secret cause of things. He therefore began to follow the man.

Now, at the moment when the fellow was turning to the right, into the Avenue de la Grande-Armée, the inspector caught him exchanging signals with a boy of twelve or thirteen, who was walking along the houses on the left-hand side. Twenty yards farther, the man stooped and turned up the bottom of his trousers legs. A bit of orange-peel marked the place. At the same moment, the boy stopped and, with a piece of chalk, drew a white cross, surrounded by a circle, on the wall of the house next to him.

The two continued on their way. A minute later, a fresh halt. The strange individual picked up a pin and dropped a piece of orange-peel; and the boy at once made a second cross on the wall and again drew a white circle round it.

"By Jove!" thought the chief-inspector, with a grunt of satisfaction. "This is rather promising.... What on earth can those two merchants be plotting?"

The two "merchants" went down the Avenue Friedland and the Rue du Faubourg-Saint-Honoré, but nothing occurred that was worthy of special mention. The double performance was repeated at almost regular intervals and, so to speak, mechanically. Nevertheless, it was obvious, on the one hand, that the man with the orange-peel did not do his part of the business until after he had picked out with a glance the house that was to be marked and, on the other hand, that the boy did not mark that particular house until after he had observed his companion's signal. It was certain, therefore, that there was an agreement between the two; and the proceedings presented no small interest in the chief-inspector's eyes.

At the Place Beauveau the man hesitated. Then, apparently making up his mind, he twice turned up and twice turned down the bottom of his trousers legs. Hereupon, the boy sat down on the kerb, opposite the sentry who was mounting guard outside the Ministry of the Interior, and marked the flagstone with two little crosses contained within two circles. The same ceremony was gone through a little further on, when they reached the Elysée. Only, on the pavement where the President's sentry was marching up and down, there were three signs instead of two.

"Hang it all!" muttered Ganimard, pale with excitement and thinking, in spite of himself, of his inveterate enemy, Lupin, whose name came to his mind whenever a mysterious circumstance presented itself. "Hang it all, what does it mean?"

He was nearly collaring and questioning the two "merchants." But he was too clever to commit so gross a blunder. The man with the orange-peel had now lit a cigarette; and the boy, also placing a cigarette-end between his lips, had gone up to him, apparently with the object of asking for a light.

They exchanged a few words. Quick as thought, the boy handed his companion an object which looked—at least, so the inspector believed—like a revolver. They both bent over this object; and the man, standing with his face to the wall, put his hand six times in his pocket and made a movement as though he were loading a weapon.

As soon as this was done, they walked briskly to the Rue de Surène; and the inspector, who followed them as closely as he was able to do without attracting their attention, saw them enter the gateway of an old house of which all the shutters were closed, with the exception of those on the third or top floor.

He hurried in after them. At the end of the carriage-entrance he saw a large courtyard, with a house-painter's sign at the back and a staircase on the left.

He went up the stairs and, as soon as he reached the first floor, ran still faster, because he heard, right up at the top, a din as of a free-fight.

When he came to the last landing he found the door open. He entered, listened for a second, caught the sound of a struggle, rushed to the room from which the sound appeared to proceed and remained standing on the threshold, very much out of breath and greatly surprised to see the man of the orange-peel and the boy banging the floor with chairs.

At that moment a third person walked out of an adjoining room. It was a young man of twenty-eight or thirty, wearing a pair of short whiskers in addition to his moustache, spectacles, and a smoking-jacket with an astrakhan collar and looking like a foreigner, a Russian.

"Good morning, Ganimard," he said. And turning to the two companions, "Thank you, my friends, and all my congratulations on the successful result. Here's the reward I promised you."

He gave them a hundred-franc note, pushed them outside and shut both doors.

"I am sorry, old chap," he said to Ganimard. "I wanted to talk to you ... wanted to talk to you badly."

He offered him his hand and, seeing that the inspector remained flabbergasted and that his face was still distorted with anger, he exclaimed:

"Why, you don't seem to understand!... And yet it's clear enough.... I wanted to see you particularly.... So what could I do?" And, pretending to reply to an objection, "No, no, old chap," he continued. "You're quite wrong. If I had written or telephoned, you would not have come ... or else you would have come with a regiment. Now I wanted to see you all alone; and I thought the best thing was to send those two decent fellows to meet you, with orders to scatter bits of orange-peel and draw crosses and circles, in short, to mark out your road to this place.... Why, you look quite bewildered! What is it? Perhaps you don't recognize me? Lupin.... Arsène Lupin.... Ransack your memory.... Doesn't the name remind you of anything?"

"You dirty scoundrel!" Ganimard snarled between his teeth.

Lupin seemed greatly distressed and, in an affectionate voice:

"Are you vexed? Yes, I can see it in your eyes.... The Dugrival business, I suppose? I ought to have waited for you to come and take me in charge?... There now, the thought never occurred to me! I promise you, next time...."

"You scum of the earth!" growled Ganimard.

"And I thinking I was giving you a treat! Upon my word, I did. I said to myself, 'That dear old Ganimard! We haven't met for an age. He'll simply rush at me when he sees me!'"

Ganimard, who had not yet stirred a limb, seemed to be waking from his stupor. He looked around him, looked at Lupin, visibly asked himself whether he would not do well to rush at him in reality and then, controlling himself, took hold of a chair and settled himself in it, as though he had suddenly made up his mind to listen to his enemy:

"Speak," he said. "And don't waste my time with any nonsense. I'm in a hurry."

"That's it," said Lupin, "let's talk. You can't imagine a quieter place than this. It's an old manor-house, which once stood in the open country, and it belongs to the Duc de Rochelaure. The duke, who has never lived in it, lets this floor to me and the outhouses to a painter and decorator. I always keep up a few establishments of this kind: it's a sound, practical plan. Here, in spite of my looking like a Russian nobleman, I am M. Daubreuil, an ex-cabinet-minister.... You understand, I had to select a rather overstocked profession, so as not to attract attention...."

"Do you think I care a hang about all this?" said Ganimard, interrupting him.

"Quite right, I'm wasting words and you're in a hurry. Forgive me. I sha'n't be long now.... Five minutes, that's all.... I'll start at once.... Have a cigar? No? Very well, no more will I."

He sat down also, drummed his fingers on the table, while thinking, and began in this fashion:

"On the 17th of October, 1599, on a warm and sunny autumn day ... Do you follow me?... But, now that I come to think of it, is it really necessary to go back to the reign of Henry IV, and tell you all about the building of the Pont-Neuf? No, I don't suppose you are very well up in French history; and I should only end by muddling you. Suffice it, then, for you to know that, last night, at one o'clock in the morning, a boatman passing under the last arch of the Pont-Neuf aforesaid, along the left bank of the river, heard something drop into the front part of his barge. The thing had been flung from the bridge and its evident destination was the bottom of the Seine. The bargee's dog rushed forward, barking, and, when the man reached the end of his craft, he saw the animal worrying a piece of newspaper that had served to wrap up a number of objects. He took from the dog such of the contents as had not fallen into the water, went to his cabin and examined them carefully. The result struck him as interesting; and, as the man is connected with one of my friends, he sent to let me know. This morning I was waked up and placed in possession of the facts and of the objects which the man had collected. Here they are."

He pointed to them, spread out on a table. There were, first of all, the torn pieces of a newspaper. Next came a large cut-glass inkstand, with a long piece of string fastened to the lid. There was a bit of broken glass and a sort of flexible cardboard, reduced to shreds. Lastly, there was a piece of bright scarlet silk, ending in a tassel of the same material and colour.

"You see our exhibits, friend of my youth," said Lupin. "No doubt, the problem would be more easily solved if we had the other objects which went overboard owing to the stupidity of the dog. But it seems to me, all the same, that we ought to be able to manage, with a little reflection and intelligence. And those are just your great qualities. How does the business strike you?"

Ganimard did not move a muscle. He was willing to stand Lupin's chaff, but his dignity commanded him not to speak a single word in answer nor even to give a nod or shake of the head that might have been taken to express approval or criticism.

"I see that we are entirely of one mind," continued Lupin, without appearing to remark the chief-inspector's silence. "And I can sum up the matter briefly, as told us by these exhibits. Yesterday evening, between nine and twelve o'clock, a showily dressed young woman was wounded with a knife and then caught round the throat and choked to death by a well-dressed gentleman, wearing a single eyeglass and interested in racing, with whom the aforesaid showily dressed young lady had been eating three meringues and a coffee éclair."

Lupin lit a cigarette and, taking Ganimard by the sleeve:

"Aha, that's up against you, chief-inspector! You thought that, in the domain of police deductions, such feats as those were prohibited to outsiders! Wrong, sir! Lupin juggles with inferences and deductions for all the world like a detective in a novel. My proofs are dazzling and absolutely simple."

And, pointing to the objects one by one, as he demonstrated his statement, he resumed:

"I said, after nine o'clock yesterday evening. This scrap of newspaper bears yesterday's date, with the words, 'Evening edition.' Also, you will see here, pasted to the paper, a bit of one of those yellow wrappers in which the subscribers' copies are sent out. These copies are always delivered by the nine o'clock post. Therefore, it was after nine o'clock. I said, a well-dressed man. Please observe that this tiny piece of glass has the round hole of a single eyeglass at one of the edges and that the single eyeglass is an essentially aristocratic article of wear. This well-dressed man walked into a pastry-cook's shop. Here is the very thin cardboard, shaped like a box, and still showing a little of the cream of the meringues and éclairs which were packed in it in the usual way. Having got his parcel, the gentleman with the eyeglass joined a young person whose eccentricity in the matter of dress is pretty clearly indicated by this bright-red silk scarf. Having joined her, for some reason as yet unknown he first stabbed her with a knife and then strangled her with the help of this same scarf. Take your magnifying glass, chief-inspector, and you will see, on the silk, stains of a darker red which are, here, the marks of a knife wiped on the scarf and, there, the marks of a hand, covered with blood, clutching the material. Having committed the murder, his next business is to leave no trace behind him. So he takes from his pocket, first, the newspaper to which he subscribes—a racing-paper, as you will see by glancing at the contents of this scrap; and you will have no difficulty in discovering the title—and, secondly, a cord, which, on inspection, turns out to be a length of whip-cord. These two details prove—do they not?—that our man is interested in racing and that he himself rides. Next, he picks up the fragments of his eyeglass, the cord of which has been broken in the struggle. He takes a pair of scissors—observe the hacking of the scissors—and cuts off the stained part of the scarf, leaving the other end, no doubt, in his victim's clenched hands. He makes a ball of the confectioner's cardboard box. He also puts in certain things that would have betrayed him, such as the knife, which must have slipped into the Seine. He wraps everything in the newspaper, ties it with the cord and fastens this cut-glass inkstand to it, as a make-weight. Then he makes himself scarce. A little later, the parcel falls into the waterman's barge. And there you are. Oof, it's hot work!... What do you say to the story?"

He looked at Ganimard to see what impression his speech had produced on the inspector. Ganimard did not depart from his attitude of silence.

Lupin began to laugh:

"As a matter of fact, you're annoyed and surprised. But you're suspicious as well: 'Why should that confounded Lupin hand the business over to me,' say you, 'instead of keeping it for himself, hunting down the murderer and rifling his pockets, if there was a robbery?' The question is quite logical, of course. But—there is a 'but'—I have no time, you see. I am full up with work at the present moment: a burglary in London, another at Lausanne, an exchange of children at Marseilles, to say nothing of having to save a young girl who is at this moment shadowed by death. That's always the way: it never rains but it pours. So I said to myself, 'Suppose I handed the business over to my dear old Ganimard? Now that it is half-solved for him, he is quite capable of succeeding. And what a service I shall be doing him! How magnificently he will be able to distinguish himself!' No sooner said than done. At eight o'clock in the morning, I sent the joker with the orange-peel to meet you. You swallowed the bait; and you were here by nine, all on edge and eager for the fray."

Lupin rose from his chair. He went over to the inspector and, with his eyes in Ganimard's, said:

"That's all. You now know the whole story. Presently, you will know the victim: some ballet-dancer, probably, some singer at a music-hall. On the other hand, the chances are that the criminal lives near the Pont-Neuf, most likely on the left bank. Lastly, here are all the exhibits. I make you a present of them. Set to work. I shall only keep this end of the scarf. If ever you want to piece the scarf together, bring me the other end, the one which the police will find round the victim's neck. Bring it me in four weeks from now to the day, that is to say, on the 29th of December, at ten o'clock in the morning. You can be sure of finding me here. And don't be afraid: this is all perfectly serious, friend of my youth; I swear it is. No humbug, honour bright. You can go straight ahead. Oh, by the way, when you arrest the fellow with the eyeglass, be a bit careful: he is left-handed! Good-bye, old dear, and good luck to you!"

Lupin spun round on his heel, went to the door, opened it and disappeared before Ganimard had even thought of taking a decision. The inspector rushed after him, but at once found that the handle of the door, by some trick of mechanism which he did not know, refused to turn. It took him ten minutes to unscrew the lock and ten minutes more to unscrew the lock of the hall-door. By the time that he had scrambled down the three flights of stairs, Ganimard had given up all hope of catching Arsène Lupin.

Besides, he was not thinking of it. Lupin inspired him with a queer, complex feeling, made up of fear, hatred, involuntary admiration and also the vague instinct that he, Ganimard, in spite of all his efforts, in spite of the persistency of his endeavours, would never get the better of this particular adversary. He pursued him from a sense of duty and pride, but with the continual dread of being taken in by that formidable hoaxer and scouted and fooled in the face of a public that was always only too willing to laugh at the chief-inspector's mishaps.

This business of the red scarf, in particular, struck him as most suspicious. It was interesting, certainly, in more ways than one, but so very improbable! And Lupin's explanation, apparently so logical, would never stand the test of a severe examination!

"No," said Ganimard, "this is all swank: a parcel of suppositions and guesswork based upon nothing at all. I'm not to be caught with chaff."

When he reached the headquarters of police, at 36 Quai des Orfèvres, he had quite made up his mind to treat the incident as though it had never happened.

He went up to the Criminal Investigation Department. Here, one of his fellow-inspectors said:

"Seen the chief?"

"No."

"He was asking for you just now."

"Oh, was he?"

"Yes, you had better go after him."

"Where?"

"To the Rue de Berne ... there was a murder there last night."

"Oh! Who's the victim?"

"I don't know exactly ... a music-hall singer, I believe."

Ganimard simply muttered:

"By Jove!"

Twenty minutes later he stepped out of the underground railway-station and made for the Rue de Berne.

The victim, who was known in the theatrical world by her stage-name of Jenny Saphir, occupied a small flat on the second floor of one of the houses. A policeman took the chief-inspector upstairs and showed him the way, through two sitting-rooms, to a bedroom, where he found the magistrates in charge of the inquiry, together with the divisional surgeon and M. Dudouis, the head of the detective-service.

Ganimard started at the first glance which he gave into the room. He saw, lying on a sofa, the corpse of a young woman whose hands clutched a strip of red silk! One of the shoulders, which appeared above the low-cut bodice, bore the marks of two wounds surrounded with clotted blood. The distorted and almost blackened features still bore an expression of frenzied terror.

The divisional surgeon, who had just finished his examination, said:

"My first conclusions are very clear. The victim was twice stabbed with a dagger and afterward strangled. The immediate cause of death was asphyxia."

"By Jove!" thought Ganimard again, remembering Lupin's words and the picture which he had drawn of the crime.

The examining-magistrate objected:

"But the neck shows no discoloration."

"She may have been strangled with a napkin or a handkerchief," said the doctor.

"Most probably," said the chief detective, "with this silk scarf, which the victim was wearing and a piece of which remains, as though she had clung to it with her two hands to protect herself."

"But why does only that piece remain?" asked the magistrate. "What has become of the other?"

"The other may have been stained with blood and carried off by the murderer. You can plainly distinguish the hurried slashing of the scissors."

"By Jove!" said Ganimard, between his teeth, for the third time. "That brute of a Lupin saw everything without seeing a thing!"

"And what about the motive of the murder?" asked the magistrate. "The locks have been forced, the cupboards turned upside down. Have you anything to tell me, M. Dudouis?"

The chief of the detective-service replied:

"I can at least suggest a supposition, derived from the statements made by the servant. The victim, who enjoyed a greater reputation on account of her looks than through her talent as a singer, went to Russia, two years ago, and brought back with her a magnificent sapphire, which she appears to have received from some person of importance at the court. Since then, she went by the name of Jenny Saphir and seems generally to have been very proud of that present, although, for prudence sake, she never wore it. I daresay that we shall not be far out if we presume the theft of the sapphire to have been the cause of the crime."

"But did the maid know where the stone was?"

"No, nobody did. And the disorder of the room would tend to prove that the murderer did not know either."

"We will question the maid," said the examining-magistrate.

M. Dudouis took the chief-inspector aside and said:

"You're looking very old-fashioned, Ganimard. What's the matter? Do you suspect anything?"

"Nothing at all, chief."

"That's a pity. We could do with a bit of showy work in the department. This is one of a number of crimes, all of the same class, of which we have failed to discover the perpetrator. This time we want the criminal ... and quickly!"

"A difficult job, chief."

"It's got to be done. Listen to me, Ganimard. According to what the maid says, Jenny Saphir led a very regular life. For a month past she was in the habit of frequently receiving visits, on her return from the music-hall, that is to say, at about half-past ten, from a man who would stay until midnight or so. 'He's a society man,' Jenny Saphir used to say, 'and he wants to marry me.' This society man took every precaution to avoid being seen, such as turning up his coat-collar and lowering the brim of his hat when he passed the porter's box. And Jenny Saphir always made a point of sending away her maid, even before he came. This is the man whom we have to find."

"Has he left no traces?"

"None at all. It is obvious that we have to deal with a very clever scoundrel, who prepared his crime beforehand and committed it with every possible chance of escaping unpunished. His arrest would be a great feather in our cap. I rely on you, Ganimard."

"Ah, you rely on me, chief?" replied the inspector. "Well, we shall see ... we shall see.... I don't say no.... Only...."

He seemed in a very nervous condition, and his agitation struck M. Dudouis.

"Only," continued Ganimard, "only I swear ... do you hear, chief? I swear...."

"What do you swear?"

"Nothing.... We shall see, chief ... we shall see...."

Ganimard did not finish his sentence until he was outside, alone. And he finished it aloud, stamping his foot, in a tone of the most violent anger:

"Only, I swear to Heaven that the arrest shall be effected by my own means, without my employing a single one of the clues with which that villain has supplied me. Ah, no! Ah, no!...."

Railing against Lupin, furious at being mixed up in this business and resolved, nevertheless, to get to the bottom of it, he wandered aimlessly about the streets. His brain was seething with irritation; and he tried to adjust his ideas a little and to discover, among the chaotic facts, some trifling detail, unperceived by all, unsuspected by Lupin himself, that might lead him to success.

He lunched hurriedly at a bar, resumed his stroll and suddenly stopped, petrified, astounded and confused. He was walking under the gateway of the very house in the Rue de Surène to which Lupin had enticed him a few hours earlier! A force stronger than his own will was drawing him there once more. The solution of the problem lay there. There and there alone were all the elements of the truth. Do and say what he would, Lupin's assertions were so precise, his calculations so accurate, that, worried to the innermost recesses of his being by so prodigious a display of perspicacity, he could not do other than take up the work at the point where his enemy had left it.

Abandoning all further resistance, he climbed the three flights of stairs. The door of the flat was open. No one had touched the exhibits. He put them in his pocket and walked away.

From that moment, he reasoned and acted, so to speak, mechanically, under the influence of the master whom he could not choose but obey.

Admitting that the unknown person whom he was seeking lived in the neighbourhood of the Pont-Neuf, it became necessary to discover, somewhere between that bridge and the Rue de Berne, the first-class confectioner's shop, open in the evenings, at which the cakes were bought. This did not take long to find. A pastry-cook near the Gare Saint-Lazare showed him some little cardboard boxes, identical in material and shape with the one in Ganimard's possession. Moreover, one of the shop-girls remembered having served, on the previous evening, a gentleman whose face was almost concealed in the collar of his fur coat, but whose eyeglass she had happened to notice.

"That's one clue checked," thought the inspector. "Our man wears an eyeglass."

He next collected the pieces of the racing-paper and showed them to a newsvendor, who easily recognized the *Turf Illustré*. Ganimard at once went to the offices of the *Turf* and asked to see the list of subscribers. Going through the list, he jotted down the names and addresses of all those who lived anywhere near the Pont-Neuf and principally— because Lupin had said so—those on the left bank of the river.

He then went back to the Criminal Investigation Department, took half a dozen men and packed them off with the necessary instructions.

At seven o'clock in the evening, the last of these men returned and brought good news with him. A certain M. Prévailles, a subscriber to the *Turf*, occupied an entresol flat on the Quai des Augustins. On the previous evening, he left his place, wearing a fur coat, took his letters and his paper, the *Turf Illustré*, from the porter's wife, walked away and returned home at midnight. This M. Prévailles wore a single eyeglass. He was a regular race-goer and himself owned several hacks which he either rode himself or jobbed out.

The inquiry had taken so short a time and the results obtained were so exactly in accordance with Lupin's predictions that Ganimard felt quite overcome on hearing the detective's report. Once more he was measuring the prodigious extent of the resources at Lupin's disposal. Never in the course of his life—and Ganimard was already well-advanced in years—had he come across such perspicacity, such a quick and far-seeing mind.

He went in search of M. Dudouis.

"Everything's ready, chief. Have you a warrant?"

"Eh?"

"I said, everything is ready for the arrest, chief."

"You know the name of Jenny Saphir's murderer?"

"Yes."

"But how? Explain yourself."

Ganimard had a sort of scruple of conscience, blushed a little and nevertheless replied:

"An accident, chief. The murderer threw everything that was likely to compromise him into the Seine. Part of the parcel was picked up and handed to me."

"By whom?"

"A boatman who refused to give his name, for fear of getting into trouble. But I had all the clues I wanted. It was not so difficult as I expected."

And the inspector described how he had gone to work.

"And you call that an accident!" cried M. Dudouis. "And you say that it was not difficult! Why, it's one of your finest performances! Finish it yourself, Ganimard, and be prudent."

Ganimard was eager to get the business done. He went to the Quai des Augustins with his men and distributed them around the house. He questioned the portress, who said that her tenant took his meals out of doors, but made a point of looking in after dinner.

A little before nine o'clock, in fact, leaning out of her window, she warned Ganimard, who at once gave a low whistle. A gentleman in a tall hat and a fur coat was coming along the pavement beside the Seine. He crossed the road and walked up to the house.

Ganimard stepped forward:

"M. Prévailles, I believe?"

"Yes, but who are you?"

"I have a commission to...."

He had not time to finish his sentence. At the sight of the men appearing out of the shadow, Prévailles quickly retreated to the wall and faced his adversaries, with his back to the door of a shop on the ground-floor, the shutters of which were closed.

"Stand back!" he cried. "I don't know you!"

His right hand brandished a heavy stick, while his left was slipped behind him and seemed to be trying to open the door.

Ganimard had an impression that the man might escape through this way and through some secret outlet:

"None of this nonsense," he said, moving closer to him. "You're caught.... You had better come quietly."

But, just as he was laying hold of Prévailles' stick, Ganimard remembered the warning which Lupin gave him: Prévailles was left-handed; and it was his revolver for which he was feeling behind his back.

The inspector ducked his head. He had noticed the man's sudden movement. Two reports rang out. No one was hit.

A second later, Prévailles received a blow under the chin from the butt-end of a revolver, which brought him down where he stood. He was entered at the Dépôt soon after nine o'clock.

Ganimard enjoyed a great reputation even at that time. But this capture, so quickly effected, by such very simple means, and at once made public by the police, won him a sudden celebrity. Prévailles was forthwith saddled with all the murders that had remained unpunished; and the newspapers vied with one another in extolling Ganimard's prowess.

The case was conducted briskly at the start. It was first of all ascertained that Prévailles, whose real name was Thomas Derocq, had already been in trouble. Moreover, the search instituted in his rooms, while not supplying any fresh proofs, at least led to the discovery of a ball of whip-cord similar to the cord used for doing up the parcel and also to the discovery of daggers which would have produced a wound similar to the wounds on the victim.

But, on the eighth day, everything was changed. Until then Prévailles had refused to reply to the questions put to him; but now, assisted by his counsel, he pleaded a circumstantial alibi and maintained that he was at the Folies-Bergère on the night of the murder.

As a matter of fact, the pockets of his dinner-jacket contained the counterfoil of a stall-ticket and a programme of the performance, both bearing the date of that evening.

"An alibi prepared in advance," objected the examining-magistrate.

"Prove it," said Prévailles.

The prisoner was confronted with the witnesses for the prosecution. The young lady from the confectioner's "thought she knew" the gentleman with the eyeglass. The hall-porter in the Rue de Berne "thought he knew" the gentleman who used to come to see Jenny Saphir. But nobody dared to make a more definite statement.

The examination, therefore, led to nothing of a precise character, provided no solid basis whereon to found a serious accusation.

The judge sent for Ganimard and told him of his difficulty.

"I can't possibly persist, at this rate. There is no evidence to support the charge."

"But surely you are convinced in your own mind, monsieur le juge d'instruction! Prévailles would never have resisted his arrest unless he was guilty."

"He says that he thought he was being assaulted. He also says that he never set eyes on Jenny Saphir; and, as a matter of fact, we can find no one to contradict his assertion.

Then again, admitting that the sapphire has been stolen, we have not been able to find it at his flat."

"Nor anywhere else," suggested Ganimard.

"Quite true, but that is no evidence against him. I'll tell you what we shall want, M. Ganimard, and that very soon: the other end of this red scarf."

"The other end?"

"Yes, for it is obvious that, if the murderer took it away with him, the reason was that the stuff is stained with the marks of the blood on his fingers."

Ganimard made no reply. For several days he had felt that the whole business was tending to this conclusion. There was no other proof possible. Given the silk scarf—and in no other circumstances—Prévailles' guilt was certain. Now Ganimard's position required that Prévailles' guilt should be established. He was responsible for the arrest, it had cast a glamour around him, he had been praised to the skies as the most formidable adversary of criminals; and he would look absolutely ridiculous if Prévailles were released.

Unfortunately, the one and only indispensable proof was in Lupin's pocket. How was he to get hold of it?

Ganimard cast about, exhausted himself with fresh investigations, went over the inquiry from start to finish, spent sleepless nights in turning over the mystery of the Rue de Berne, studied the records of Prévailles' life, sent ten men hunting after the invisible sapphire. Everything was useless.

On the 28th of December, the examining-magistrate stopped him in one of the passages of the Law Courts:

"Well, M. Ganimard, any news?"

"No, monsieur le juge d'instruction."

"Then I shall dismiss the case."

"Wait one day longer."

"What's the use? We want the other end of the scarf; have you got it?"

"I shall have it to-morrow."

"To-morrow!"

"Yes, but please lend me the piece in your possession."

"What if I do?"

"If you do, I promise to let you have the whole scarf complete."

"Very well, that's understood."

Ganimard followed the examining-magistrate to his room and came out with the piece of silk:

"Hang it all!" he growled. "Yes, I will go and fetch the proof and I shall have it too ... always presuming that Master Lupin has the courage to keep the appointment."

In point of fact, he did not doubt for a moment that Master Lupin would have this courage, and that was just what exasperated him. Why had Lupin insisted on this meeting? What was his object, in the circumstances?

Anxious, furious and full of hatred, he resolved to take every precaution necessary not only to prevent his falling into a trap himself, but to make his enemy fall into one, now that the opportunity offered. And, on the next day, which was the 29th of December, the date fixed by Lupin, after spending the night in studying the old manor-house in the Rue de Surène and convincing himself that there was no other outlet than the front door, he warned his men that he was going on a dangerous expedition and arrived with them on the field of battle.

He posted them in a café and gave them formal instructions: if he showed himself at one of the third-floor windows, or if he failed to return within an hour, the detectives were to enter the house and arrest any one who tried to leave it.

The chief-inspector made sure that his revolver was in working order and that he could take it from his pocket easily. Then he went upstairs.

He was surprised to find things as he had left them, the doors open and the locks broken. After ascertaining that the windows of the principal room looked out on the street, he visited the three other rooms that made up the flat. There was no one there.

"Master Lupin was afraid," he muttered, not without a certain satisfaction.

"Don't be silly," said a voice behind him.

Turning round, he saw an old workman, wearing a house-painter's long smock, standing in the doorway.

"You needn't bother your head," said the man. "It's I, Lupin. I have been working in the painter's shop since early morning. This is when we knock off for breakfast. So I came upstairs."

He looked at Ganimard with a quizzing smile and cried:

"'Pon my word, this is a gorgeous moment I owe you, old chap! I wouldn't sell it for ten years of your life; and yet you know how I love you! What do you think of it, artist? Wasn't it well thought out and well foreseen? Foreseen from alpha to omega? Did I understand the business? Did I penetrate the mystery of the scarf? I'm not saying that there were no holes in my argument, no links missing in the chain.... But what a masterpiece of intelligence! Ganimard, what a reconstruction of events! What an intuition of everything that had taken place and of everything that was going to take place, from the discovery of the crime to your arrival here in search of a proof! What really marvelous divination! Have you the scarf?"

"Yes, half of it. Have you the other?"

"Here it is. Let's compare."

They spread the two pieces of silk on the table. The cuts made by the scissors corresponded exactly. Moreover, the colours were identical.

"But I presume," said Lupin, "that this was not the only thing you came for. What you are interested in seeing is the marks of the blood. Come with me, Ganimard: it's rather dark in here."

They moved into the next room, which, though it overlooked the courtyard, was lighter; and Lupin held his piece of silk against the window-pane:

"Look," he said, making room for Ganimard.

The inspector gave a start of delight. The marks of the five fingers and the print of the palm were distinctly visible. The evidence was undeniable. The murderer had seized the stuff in his bloodstained hand, in the same hand that had stabbed Jenny Saphir, and tied the scarf round her neck.

"And it is the print of a left hand," observed Lupin. "Hence my warning, which had nothing miraculous about it, you see. For, though I admit, friend of my youth, that you may look upon me as a superior intelligence, I won't have you treat me as a wizard."

Ganimard had quickly pocketed the piece of silk. Lupin nodded his head in approval:

"Quite right, old boy, it's for you. I'm so glad you're glad! And, you see, there was no

trap about all this ... only the wish to oblige ... a service between friends, between pals....
And also, I confess, a little curiosity.... Yes, I wanted to examine this other piece of silk, the
one the police had.... Don't be afraid: I'll give it back to you.... Just a second...."

Lupin, with a careless movement, played with the tassel at the end of this half of the
scarf, while Ganimard listened to him in spite of himself:

"How ingenious these little bits of women's work are! Did you notice one detail in the
maid's evidence? Jenny Saphir was very handy with her needle and used to make all her
own hats and frocks. It is obvious that she made this scarf herself.... Besides, I noticed that
from the first. I am naturally curious, as I have already told you, and I made a thorough
examination of the piece of silk which you have just put in your pocket. Inside the tassel, I
found a little sacred medal, which the poor girl had stitched into it to bring her luck.
Touching, isn't it, Ganimard? A little medal of Our Lady of Good Succour."

The inspector felt greatly puzzled and did not take his eyes off the other. And Lupin
continued:

"Then I said to myself, 'How interesting it would be to explore the other half of the
scarf, the one which the police will find round the victim's neck!' For this other half, which
I hold in my hands at last, is finished off in the same way ... so I shall be able to see if it has
a hiding-place too and what's inside it.... But look, my friend, isn't it cleverly made? And
so simple! All you have to do is to take a skein of red cord and braid it round a wooden
cup, leaving a little recess, a little empty space in the middle, very small, of course, but
large enough to hold a medal of a saint ... or anything.... A precious stone, for instance....
Such as a sapphire...."

At that moment he finished pushing back the silk cord and, from the hollow of a cup
he took between his thumb and forefinger a wonderful blue stone, perfect in respect of
size and purity.

"Ha! What did I tell you, friend of my youth?"

He raised his head. The inspector had turned livid and was staring wild-eyed, as
though fascinated by the stone that sparkled before him. He at last realized the whole plot:

"You dirty scoundrel!" he muttered, repeating the insults which he had used at the
first interview. "You scum of the earth!"

The two men were standing one against the other.

"Give me back that," said the inspector.

Lupin held out the piece of silk.

"And the sapphire," said Ganimard, in a peremptory tone.

"Don't be silly."

"Give it back, or...."

"Or what, you idiot!" cried Lupin. "Look here, do you think I put you on to this soft
thing for nothing?"

"Give it back!"

"You haven't noticed what I've been about, that's plain! What! For four weeks I've
kept you on the move like a deer; and you want to ...! Come, Ganimard, old chap, pull
yourself together!... Don't you see that you've been playing the good dog for four weeks
on end?... Fetch it, Rover!... There's a nice blue pebble over there, which master can't get
at. Hunt it, Ganimard, fetch it ... bring it to master.... Ah, he's his master's own good little
dog!... Sit up! Beg!... Does'ms want a bit of sugar, then?..."

Ganimard, containing the anger that seethed within him, thought only of one thing, summoning his detectives. And, as the room in which he now was looked out on the courtyard, he tried gradually to work his way round to the communicating door. He would then run to the window and break one of the panes.

"All the same," continued Lupin, "what a pack of dunderheads you and the rest must be! You've had the silk all this time and not one of you ever thought of feeling it, not one of you ever asked himself the reason why the poor girl hung on to her scarf. Not one of you! You just acted at haphazard, without reflecting, without foreseeing anything...."

The inspector had attained his object. Taking advantage of a second when Lupin had turned away from him, he suddenly wheeled round and grasped the door-handle. But an oath escaped him: the handle did not budge.

Lupin burst into a fit of laughing:

"Not even that! You did not even foresee that! You lay a trap for me and you won't admit that I may perhaps smell the thing out beforehand.... And you allow yourself to be brought into this room without asking whether I am not bringing you here for a particular reason and without remembering that the locks are fitted with a special mechanism. Come now, speaking frankly, what do you think of it yourself?"

"What do I think of it?" roared Ganimard, beside himself with rage.

He had drawn his revolver and was pointing it straight at Lupin's face.

"Hands up!" he cried. "That's what I think of it!"

Lupin placed himself in front of him and shrugged his shoulders:

"Sold again!" he said.

"Hands up, I say, once more!"

"And sold again, say I. Your deadly weapon won't go off."

"What?"

"Old Catherine, your housekeeper, is in my service. She damped the charges this morning while you were having your breakfast coffee."

Ganimard made a furious gesture, pocketed the revolver and rushed at Lupin.

"Well?" said Lupin, stopping him short with a well-aimed kick on the shin.

Their clothes were almost touching. They exchanged defiant glances, the glances of two adversaries who mean to come to blows. Nevertheless, there was no fight. The recollection of the earlier struggles made any present struggle useless. And Ganimard, who remembered all his past failures, his vain attacks, Lupin's crushing reprisals, did not lift a limb. There was nothing to be done. He felt it. Lupin had forces at his command against which any individual force simply broke to pieces. So what was the good?

"I agree," said Lupin, in a friendly voice, as though answering Ganimard's unspoken thought, "you would do better to let things be as they are. Besides, friend of my youth, think of all that this incident has brought you: fame, the certainty of quick promotion and, thanks to that, the prospect of a happy and comfortable old age! Surely, you don't want the discovery of the sapphire and the head of poor Arsène Lupin in addition! It wouldn't be fair. To say nothing of the fact that poor Arsène Lupin saved your life.... Yes, sir! Who warned you, at this very spot, that Prévailles was left-handed?... And is this the way you thank me? It's not pretty of you, Ganimard. Upon my word, you make me blush for you!"

While chattering, Lupin had gone through the same performance as Ganimard and was now near the door. Ganimard saw that his foe was about to escape him. Forgetting all prudence, he tried to block his way and received a tremendous butt in the stomach, which sent him rolling to the opposite wall.

Lupin dexterously touched a spring, turned the handle, opened the door and slipped away, roaring with laughter as he went.

Twenty minutes later, when Ganimard at last succeeded in joining his men, one of them said to him:

"A house-painter left the house, as his mates were coming back from breakfast, and put a letter in my hand. 'Give that to your governor,' he said. 'Which governor?' I asked; but he was gone. I suppose it's meant for you."

"Let's have it."

Ganimard opened the letter. It was hurriedly scribbled in pencil and contained these words:

"This is to warn you, friend of my youth, against excessive credulity. When a fellow tells you that the cartridges in your revolver are damp, however great your confidence in that fellow may be, even though his name be Arsène Lupin, never allow yourself to be taken in. Fire first; and, if the fellow hops the twig, you will have acquired the proof (1) that the cartridges are not damp; and (2) that old Catherine is the most honest and respectable of housekeepers.

"One of these days, I hope to have the pleasure of making her acquaintance.

"Meanwhile, friend of my youth, believe me always affectionately and sincerely yours,

"ARSÈNE LUPIN."

VI. SHADOWED BY DEATH

After he had been round the walls of the property, Arsène Lupin returned to the spot from which he started. It was perfectly clear to him that there was no breach in the walls; and the only way of entering the extensive grounds of the Château de Maupertuis was through a little low door, firmly bolted on the inside, or through the principal gate, which was overlooked by the lodge.

"Very well," he said. "We must employ heroic methods."

Pushing his way into the copsewood where he had hidden his motor-bicycle, he unwound a length of twine from under the saddle and went to a place which he had noticed in the course of his exploration. At this place, which was situated far from the road, on the edge of a wood, a number of large trees, standing inside the park, overlapped the wall.

Lupin fastened a stone to the end of the string, threw it up and caught a thick branch, which he drew down to him and bestraddled. The branch, in recovering its position, raised him from the ground. He climbed over the wall, slipped down the tree, and sprang lightly on the grass.

It was winter; and, through the leafless boughs, across the undulating lawns, he could see the little Château de Maupertuis in the distance. Fearing lest he should be perceived, he concealed himself behind a clump of fir-trees. From there, with the aid of a field-glass, he studied the dark and melancholy front of the manor-house. All the windows were closed and, as it were, barricaded with solid shutters. The house might easily have been uninhabited.

"By Jove!" muttered Lupin. "It's not the liveliest of residences. I shall certainly not come here to end my days!"

But the clock struck three; one of the doors on the ground-floor opened; and the figure of a woman appeared, a very slender figure wrapped in a brown cloak.

The woman walked up and down for a few minutes and was at once surrounded by birds, to which she scattered crumbs of bread. Then she went down the stone steps that led to the middle lawn and skirted it, taking the path on the right.

With his field-glass, Lupin could distinctly see her coming in his direction. She was tall, fair-haired, graceful in appearance, and seemed to be quite a young girl. She walked with a sprightly step, looking at the pale December sun and amusing herself by breaking the little dead twigs on the shrubs along the road.

She had gone nearly two thirds of the distance that separated her from Lupin when there came a furious sound of barking and a huge dog, a colossal Danish boarhound, sprang from a neighbouring kennel and stood erect at the end of the chain by which it was fastened.

The girl moved a little to one side, without paying further attention to what was doubtless a daily incident. The dog grew angrier than ever, standing on its legs and dragging at its collar, at the risk of strangling itself.

Thirty or forty steps farther, yielding probably to an impulse of impatience, the girl turned round and made a gesture with her hand. The great Dane gave a start of rage, retreated to the back of its kennel and rushed out again, this time unfettered. The girl uttered a cry of mad terror. The dog was covering the space between them, trailing its broken chain behind it.

She began to run, to run with all her might, and screamed out desperately for help. But the dog came up with her in a few bounds.

She fell, at once exhausted, giving herself up for lost. The animal was already upon her, almost touching her.

At that exact moment a shot rang out. The dog turned a complete somersault, recovered its feet, tore the ground and then lay down, giving a number of hoarse, breathless howls, which ended in a dull moan and an indistinct gurgling. And that was all.

"Dead," said Lupin, who had hastened up at once, prepared, if necessary, to fire his revolver a second time.

The girl had risen and stood pale, still staggering. She looked in great surprise at this man whom she did not know and who had saved her life; and she whispered:

"Thank you.... I have had a great fright.... You were in the nick of time.... I thank you, monsieur."

Lupin took off his hat:

"Allow me to introduce myself, mademoiselle.... My name is Paul Daubreuil.... But before entering into any explanations, I must ask for one moment...."

He stooped over the dog's dead body and examined the chain at the part where the brute's effort had snapped it:

"That's it," he said, between his teeth. "It's just as I suspected. By Jupiter, things are moving rapidly!... I ought to have come earlier."

Returning to the girl's side, he said to her, speaking very quickly:

"Mademoiselle, we have not a minute to lose. My presence in these grounds is quite irregular. I do not wish to be surprised here; and this for reasons that concern yourself alone. Do you think that the report can have been heard at the house?"

The girl seemed already to have recovered from her emotion; and she replied, with a calmness that revealed all her pluck:

"I don't think so."

"Is your father in the house to-day?"

"My father is ill and has been in bed for months. Besides, his room looks out on the other front."

"And the servants?"

"Their quarters and the kitchen are also on the other side. No one ever comes to this part. I walk here myself, but nobody else does."

"It is probable, therefore, that I have not been seen either, especially as the trees hide us?"

"It is most probable."

"Then I can speak to you freely?"

"Certainly, but I don't understand...."

"You will, presently. Permit me to be brief. The point is this: four days ago, Mlle. Jeanne Darcieux...."

"That is my name," she said, smiling.

"Mlle. Jeanne Darcieux," continued Lupin, "wrote a letter to one of her friends, called Marceline, who lives at Versailles...."

"How do you know all that?" asked the girl, in astonishment. "I tore up the letter before I had finished it."

"And you flung the pieces on the edge of the road that runs from the house to Vendôme."

"That's true.... I had gone out walking...."

"The pieces were picked up and they came into my hands next day."

"Then ... you must have read them," said Jeanne Darcieux, betraying a certain annoyance by her manner.

"Yes, I committed that indiscretion; and I do not regret it, because I can save you."

"Save me? From what?"

"From death."

Lupin spoke this little sentence in a very distinct voice. The girl gave a shudder. Then she said:

"I am not threatened with death."

"Yes, you are, mademoiselle. At the end of October, you were reading on a bench on the terrace where you were accustomed to sit at the same hour every day, when a block of stone fell from the cornice above your head and you were within a few inches of being crushed."

"An accident...."

"One fine evening in November, you were walking in the kitchen-garden, by moonlight. A shot was fired, The bullet whizzed past your ear."

"At least, I thought so."

"Lastly, less than a week ago, the little wooden bridge that crosses the river in the park, two yards from the waterfall, gave way while you were on it. You were just able, by a miracle, to catch hold of the root of a tree."

Jeanne Darcieux tried to smile.

"Very well. But, as I wrote to Marceline, these are only a series of coincidences, of accidents...."

"No, mademoiselle, no. One accident of this sort is allowable.... So are two ... and even then!... But we have no right to suppose that the chapter of accidents, repeating the same act three times in such different and extraordinary circumstances, is a mere amusing coincidence. That is why I thought that I might presume to come to your assistance. And, as my intervention can be of no use unless it remains secret, I did not hesitate to make my way in here ... without walking through the gate. I came in the nick of time, as you said. Your enemy was attacking you once more."

"What!... Do you think?... No, it is impossible.... I refuse to believe...."

Lupin picked up the chain and, showing it to her:

"Look at the last link. There is no question but that it has been filed. Otherwise, so powerful a chain as this would never have yielded. Besides, you can see the mark of the file here."

Jeanne turned pale and her pretty features were distorted with terror:

"But who can bear me such a grudge?" she gasped. "It is terrible.... I have never done any one harm.... And yet you are certainly right.... Worse still...."

She finished her sentence in a lower voice:

"Worse still, I am wondering whether the same danger does not threaten my father."

"Has he been attacked also?"

"No, for he never stirs from his room. But his is such a mysterious illness!... He has no strength ... he cannot walk at all.... In addition to that, he is subject to fits of suffocation, as though his heart stopped beating.... Oh, what an awful thing!"

Lupin realized all the authority which he was able to assert at such a moment, and he said:

"Have no fear, mademoiselle. If you obey me blindly, I shall be sure to succeed."

"Yes ... yes ... I am quite willing ... but all this is so terrible...."

"Trust me, I beg of you. And please listen to me, I shall want a few particulars."

He rapped out a number of questions, which Jeanne Darcieux answered hurriedly:

"That animal was never let loose, was he?"

"Never."

"Who used to feed him?"

"The lodge-keeper. He brought him his food every evening."

"Consequently, he could go near him without being bitten?"

"Yes; and he only, for the dog was very savage."

"You don't suspect the man?"

"Oh, no!... Baptiste?... Never!"

"And you can't think of anybody?"

"No. Our servants are quite devoted to us. They are very fond of me."

"You have no friends staying in the house?"

"No."

"No brother?"

"No."

"Then your father is your only protector?"

"Yes; and I have told you the condition he is in."

"Have you told him of the different attempts?"

"Yes; and it was wrong of me to do so. Our doctor, old Dr. Guéroult, forbade me to cause him the least excitement."

"Your mother?..."

"I don't remember her. She died sixteen years ago ... just sixteen years ago."

"How old were you then?"

"I was not quite five years old."

"And were you living here?"

"We were living in Paris. My father only bought this place the year after."

Lupin was silent for a few moments. Then he concluded:

"Very well, mademoiselle, I am obliged to you. Those particulars are all I need for the present. Besides, it would not be wise for us to remain together longer."

"But," she said, "the lodge-keeper will find the dog soon.... Who will have killed him?"

"You, mademoiselle, to defend yourself against an attack."

"I never carry firearms."

"I am afraid you do," said Lupin, smiling, "because you killed the dog and there is no one but you who could have killed him. For that matter, let them think what they please. The great thing is that I shall not be suspected when I come to the house."

"To the house? Do you intend to?"

"Yes. I don't yet know how ... But I shall come.... This very evening.... So, once more, be easy in your mind. I will answer for everything."

Jeanne looked at him and, dominated by him, conquered by his air of assurance and good faith, she said, simply:

"I am quite easy."

"Then all will go well. Till this evening, mademoiselle."

"Till this evening."

She walked away; and Lupin, following her with his eyes until the moment when she disappeared round the corner of the house, murmured:

"What a pretty creature! It would be a pity if any harm were to come to her. Luckily, Arsène Lupin is keeping his weather-eye open."

Taking care not to be seen, with eyes and ears attentive to the least sight or sound, he inspected every nook and corner of the grounds, looked for the little low door which he had noticed outside and which was the door of the kitchen garden, drew the bolt, took the key and then skirted the walls and found himself once more near the tree which he had climbed. Two minutes later, he was mounting his motor-cycle.

The village of Maupertuis lay quite close to the estate. Lupin inquired and learnt that Dr. Guéroult lived next door to the church.

He rang, was shown into the consulting-room and introduced himself by his name of Paul Daubreuil, of the Rue de Surène, Paris, adding that he had official relations with the detective-service, a fact which he requested might be kept secret. He had become acquainted, by means of a torn letter, with the incidents that had endangered Mlle. Darcieux's life; and he had come to that young lady's assistance.

Dr. Guéroult, an old country practitioner, who idolized Jeanne, on hearing Lupin's explanations at once admitted that those incidents constituted undeniable proofs of a plot. He showed great concern, offered his visitor hospitality and kept him to dinner.

The two men talked at length. In the evening, they walked round to the manor-house together.

The doctor went to the sick man's room, which was on the first floor, and asked leave to bring up a young colleague, to whom he intended soon to make over his practice, when he retired.

Lupin, on entering, saw Jeanne Darcieux seated by her father's bedside. She suppressed a movement of surprise and, at a sign from the doctor, left the room.

The consultation thereupon took place in Lupin's presence. M. Darcieux's face was worn, with much suffering and his eyes were bright with fever. He complained particularly, that day, of his heart. After the auscultation, he questioned the doctor with obvious anxiety; and each reply seemed to give him relief. He also spoke of Jeanne and expressed his conviction that they were deceiving him and that his daughter had escaped yet more accidents. He continued perturbed, in spite of the doctor's denials. He wanted to have the police informed and inquiries set on foot.

But his excitement tired him and he gradually dropped off to sleep.

Lupin stopped the doctor in the passage:

"Come, doctor, give me your exact opinion. Do you think that M. Darcieux's illness can be attributed to an outside cause?"

"How do you mean?"

"Well, suppose that the same enemy should be interested in removing both father and daughter."

The doctor seemed struck by the suggestion.

"Upon my word, there is something in what you say.... The father's illness at times adopts such a very unusual character!... For instance, the paralysis of the legs, which is almost complete, ought to be accompanied by...."

The doctor reflected for a moment and then said in a low voice:

"You think it's poison, of course ... but what poison?... Besides, I see no toxic symptoms.... It would have to be.... But what are you doing? What's the matter?..."

The two men were talking outside a little sitting-room on the first floor, where Jeanne, seizing the opportunity while the doctor was with her father, had begun her evening meal. Lupin, who was watching her through the open door, saw her lift a cup to her lips and take a few sups.

Suddenly, he rushed at her and caught her by the arm:

"What are you drinking there?"

"Why," she said, taken aback, "only tea!"

"You pulled a face of disgust ... what made you do that?"

"I don't know ... I thought...."

"You thought what?"

"That ... that it tasted rather bitter.... But I expect that comes from the medicine I mixed with it."

"What medicine?"

"Some drops which I take at dinner ... the drops which you prescribed for me, you know, doctor."

"Yes," said Dr. Guéroult, "but that medicine has no taste of any kind.... You know it hasn't, Jeanne, for you have been taking it for a fortnight and this is the first time...."

"Quite right," said the girl, "and this does have a taste.... There—oh!—my mouth is still burning."

Dr. Guéroult now took a sip from the cup;

"Faugh!" he exclaimed, spitting it out again. "There's no mistake about it...."

Lupin, on his side, was examining the bottle containing the medicine; and he asked:

"Where is this bottle kept in the daytime?"

But Jeanne was unable to answer. She had put her hand to her heart and, wan-faced, with staring eyes, seemed to be suffering great pain:

"It hurts ... it hurts," she stammered.

The two men quickly carried her to her room and laid her on the bed:

"She ought to have an emetic," said Lupin.

"Open the cupboard," said the doctor. "You'll see a medicine-case.... Have you got it?... Take out one of those little tubes.... Yes, that one.... And now some hot water.... You'll find some on the tea-tray in the other room."

Jeanne's own maid came running up in answer to the bell. Lupin told her that Mlle. Darcieux had been taken unwell, for some unknown reason.

He next returned to the little dining-room, inspected the sideboard and the cupboards, went down to the kitchen and pretended that the doctor had sent him to ask about M. Darcieux's diet. Without appearing to do so, he catechized the cook, the butler, and Baptiste, the lodge-keeper, who had his meals at the manor-house with the servants. Then he went back to the doctor:

"Well?"

"She's asleep."

"Any danger?"

"No. Fortunately, she had only taken two or three sips. But this is the second time to-day that you have saved her life, as the analysis of this bottle will show."

"Quite superfluous to make an analysis, doctor. There is no doubt about the fact that there has been an attempt at poisoning."

"By whom?"

"I can't say. But the demon who is engineering all this business clearly knows the ways of the house. He comes and goes as he pleases, walks about in the park, files the dog's chain, mixes poison with the food and, in short, moves and acts precisely as though he were living the very life of her—or rather of those—whom he wants to put away."

"Ah! You really believe that M. Darcieux is threatened with the same danger?"

"I have not a doubt of it."

"Then it must be one of the servants? But that is most unlikely! Do you think ...?"

"I think nothing, doctor. I know nothing. All I can say is that the situation is most tragic and that we must be prepared for the worst. Death is here, doctor, shadowing the people in this house; and it will soon strike at those whom it is pursuing."

"What's to be done?"

"Watch, doctor. Let us pretend that we are alarmed about M. Darcieux's health and spend the night in here. The bedrooms of both the father and daughter are close by. If anything happens, we are sure to hear."

There was an easy-chair in the room. They arranged to sleep in it turn and turn about.

In reality, Lupin slept for only two or three hours. In the middle of the night he left the room, without disturbing his companion, carefully looked round the whole of the house and walked out through the principal gate.

He reached Paris on his motor-cycle at nine o'clock in the morning. Two of his friends, to whom he telephoned on the road, met him there. They all three spent the day in making searches which Lupin had planned out beforehand.

He set out again hurriedly at six o'clock; and never, perhaps, as he told me subsequently, did he risk his life with greater temerity than in his breakneck ride, at a mad rate of speed, on a foggy December evening, with the light of his lamp hardly able to pierce through the darkness.

He sprang from his bicycle outside the gate, which was still open, ran to the house and reached the first floor in a few bounds.

There was no one in the little dining-room.

Without hesitating, without knocking, he walked into Jeanne's bedroom:

"Ah, here you are!" he said, with a sigh of relief, seeing Jeanne and the doctor sitting side by side, talking.

"What? Any news?" asked the doctor, alarmed at seeing such a state of agitation in a man whose coolness he had had occasion to observe.

"No," said Lupin. "No news. And here?"

"None here, either. We have just left M. Darcieux. He has had an excellent day and he ate his dinner with a good appetite. As for Jeanne, you can see for yourself, she has all her pretty colour back again."

"Then she must go."

"Go? But it's out of the question!" protested the girl.

"You must go, you must!" cried Lupin, with real violence, stamping his foot on the floor.

He at once mastered himself, spoke a few words of apology and then, for three or four minutes, preserved a complete silence, which the doctor and Jeanne were careful not to disturb.

At last, he said to the young girl:

"You shall go to-morrow morning, mademoiselle. It will be only for one or two weeks. I will take you to your friend at Versailles, the one to whom you were writing. I entreat you to get everything ready to-night ... without concealment of any kind. Let the servants know that you are going.... On the other hand, the doctor will be good enough to tell M. Darcieux and give him to understand, with every possible precaution, that this journey is essential to your safety. Besides, he can join you as soon as his strength permits.... That's settled, is it not?"

"Yes," she said, absolutely dominated by Lupin's gentle and imperious voice.

"In that case," he said, "be as quick as you can ... and do not stir from your room...."

"But," said the girl, with a shudder, "am I to stay alone to-night?"

"Fear nothing. Should there be the least danger, the doctor and I will come back. Do not open your door unless you hear three very light taps."

Jeanne at once rang for her maid. The doctor went to M. Darcieux, while Lupin had some supper brought to him in the little dining-room.

"That's done," said the doctor, returning to him in twenty minutes' time. "M. Darcieux did not raise any great difficulty. As a matter of fact, he himself thinks it just as well that we should send Jeanne away."

They then went downstairs together and left the house.

On reaching the lodge, Lupin called the keeper.

"You can shut the gate, my man. If M. Darcieux should want us, send for us at once."

The clock of Maupertuis church struck ten. The sky was overcast with black clouds, through which the moon broke at moments.

The two men walked on for sixty or seventy yards.

They were nearing the village, when Lupin gripped his companion by the arm:

"Stop!"

"What on earth's the matter?" exclaimed the doctor.

"The matter is this," Lupin jerked out, "that, if my calculations turn out right, if I have not misjudged the business from start to finish, Mlle. Darcieux will be murdered before the night is out."

"Eh? What's that?" gasped the doctor, in dismay. "But then why did we go?"

"With the precise object that the miscreant, who is watching all our movements in the dark, may not postpone his crime and may perpetrate it, not at the hour chosen by himself, but at the hour which I have decided upon."

"Then we are returning to the manor-house?"

"Yes, of course we are, but separately."

"In that case, let us go at once."

"Listen to me, doctor," said Lupin, in a steady voice, "and let us waste no time in useless words. Above all, we must defeat any attempt to watch us. You will therefore go straight home and not come out again until you are quite certain that you have not been followed. You will then make for the walls of the property, keeping to the left, till you come to the little door of the kitchen-garden. Here is the key. When the church clock strikes eleven, open the door very gently and walk right up to the terrace at the back of the house. The fifth window is badly fastened. You have only to climb over the balcony. As soon as you are inside Mlle. Darcieux's room, bolt the door and don't budge. You quite understand, don't budge, either of you, whatever happens. I have noticed that Mlle. Darcieux leaves her dressing-room window ajar, isn't that so?"

"Yes, it's a habit which I taught her."

"That's the way they'll come."

"And you?"

"That's the way I shall come also."

"And do you know who the villain is?"

Lupin hesitated and then replied:

"No, I don't know.... And that is just how we shall find out. But, I implore you, keep cool. Not a word, not a movement, *whatever happens*!"

"I promise you."

"I want more than that, doctor. You must give me your word of honour."

"I give you my word of honour."

The doctor went away. Lupin at once climbed a neighbouring mound from which he could see the windows of the first and second floor. Several of them were lighted.

He waited for some little time. The lights went out one by one. Then, taking a direction opposite to that in which the doctor had gone, he branched off to the right and skirted the wall until he came to the clump of trees near which he had hidden his motor-cycle on the day before.

Eleven o'clock struck. He calculated the time which it would take the doctor to cross the kitchen-garden and make his way into the house.

"That's one point scored!" he muttered. "Everything's all right on that side. And now, Lupin to the rescue? The enemy won't be long before he plays his last trump ... and, by all the gods, I must be there!..."

He went through the same performance as on the first occasion, pulled down the branch and hoisted himself to the top of the wall, from which he was able to reach the bigger boughs of the tree.

Just then he pricked up his ears. He seemed to hear a rustling of dead leaves. And he actually perceived a dark form moving on the level thirty yards away:

"Hang it all!" he said to himself. "I'm done: the scoundrel has smelt a rat."

A moonbeam pierced through the clouds. Lupin distinctly saw the man take aim. He tried to jump to the ground and turned his head. But he felt something hit him in the chest, heard the sound of a report, uttered an angry oath and came crashing down from branch to branch, like a corpse.

Meanwhile, Doctor Guéroult, following Arsène Lupin's instructions, had climbed the ledge of the fifth window and groped his way to the first floor. On reaching Jeanne's room, he tapped lightly, three times, at the door and, immediately on entering, pushed the bolt:

"Lie down at once," he whispered to the girl, who had not taken off her things. "You must appear to have gone to bed. Brrrr, it's cold in here! Is the window open in your dressing-room?"

"Yes ... would you like me to ...?"

"No, leave it as it is. They are coming."

"They are coming!" spluttered Jeanne, in affright.

"Yes, beyond a doubt."

"But who? Do you suspect any one?"

"I don't know who.... I expect that there is some one hidden in the house ... or in the park."

"Oh, I feel so frightened!"

"Don't be frightened. The sportsman who's looking after you seems jolly clever and makes a point of playing a safe game. I expect he's on the look-out in the court."

The doctor put out the night-light, went to the window and raised the blind. A narrow cornice, running along the first story, prevented him from seeing more than a distant part of the courtyard; and he came back and sat down by the bed.

Some very painful minutes passed, minutes that appeared to them interminably long. The clock in the village struck; but, taken up as they were with all the little noises of the night, they hardly noticed the sound. They listened, listened, with all their nerves on edge:

"Did you hear?" whispered the doctor.

"Yes ... yes," said Jeanne, sitting up in bed.

"Lie down ... lie down," he said, presently. "There's some one coming."

There was a little tapping sound outside, against the cornice. Next came a series of indistinct noises, the nature of which they could not make out for certain. But they had a feeling that the window in the dressing-room was being opened wider, for they were buffeted by gusts of cold air.

Suddenly, it became quite clear: there was some one next door.

The doctor, whose hand was trembling a little, seized his revolver. Nevertheless, he did not move, remembering the formal orders which he had received and fearing to act against them.

The room was in absolute darkness; and they were unable to see where the adversary was. But they felt his presence.

They followed his invisible movements, the sound of his footsteps deadened by the carpet; and they did not doubt but that he had already crossed the threshold of the room.

And the adversary stopped. Of that they were certain. He was standing six steps away from the bed, motionless, undecided perhaps, seeking to pierce the darkness with his keen eyes.

Jeanne's hand, icy-cold and clammy, trembled in the doctor's grasp.

With his other hand, the doctor clutched his revolver, with his finger on the trigger. In spite of his pledged word, he did not hesitate. If the adversary touched the end of the bed, the shot would be fired at a venture.

The adversary took another step and then stopped again. And there was something awful about that silence, that impassive silence, that darkness in which those human beings were peering at one another, wildly.

Who was it looming in the murky darkness? Who was the man? What horrible enmity was it that turned his hand against the girl and what abominable aim was he pursuing?

Terrified though they were, Jeanne and the doctor thought only of that one thing: to see, to learn the truth, to gaze upon the adversary's face.

He took one more step and did not move again. It seemed to them that his figure stood out, darker, against the dark space and that his arm rose slowly, slowly....

A minute passed and then another minute....

And, suddenly, beyond the man, on the right a sharp click.... A bright light flashed, was flung upon the man, lit him full in the face, remorselessly.

Jeanne gave a cry of affright. She had seen—standing over her, with a dagger in his hand—she had seen ... her father!

Almost at the same time, though the light was already turned off, there came a report: the doctor had fired.

"Dash it all, don't shoot!" roared Lupin.

He threw his arms round the doctor, who choked out:

"Didn't you see?... Didn't you see?... Listen!... He's escaping!...."

"Let him escape: it's the best thing that could happen."

He pressed the spring of his electric lantern again, ran to the dressing-room, made certain that the man had disappeared and, returning quietly to the table, lit the lamp.

Jeanne lay on her bed, pallid, in a dead faint.

The doctor, huddled in his chair, emitted inarticulate sounds.

"Come," said Lupin, laughing, "pull yourself together. There is nothing to excite ourselves about: it's all over."

"Her father!... Her father!" moaned the old doctor.

"If you please, doctor, Mlle. Darcieux is ill. Look after her."

Without more words, Lupin went back to the dressing-room and stepped out on the window-ledge. A ladder stood against the ledge. He ran down it. Skirting the wall of the house, twenty steps farther, he tripped over the rungs of a rope-ladder, which he climbed and found himself in M. Darcieux's bedroom. The room was empty.

"Just so," he said. "My gentleman did not like the position and has cleared out. Here's wishing him a good journey.... And, of course, the door is bolted?... Exactly!... That is how our sick man, tricking his worthy medical attendant, used to get up at night in full security, fasten his rope-ladder to the balcony and prepare his little games. He's no fool, is friend Darcieux!"

He drew the bolts and returned to Jeanne's room. The doctor, who was just coming out of the doorway, drew him to the little dining-room:

"She's asleep, don't let us disturb her. She has had a bad shock and will take some time to recover."

Lupin poured himself out a glass of water and drank it down. Then he took a chair and, calmly:

"Pooh! She'll be all right by to-morrow."

"What do you say?"

"I say that she'll be all right by to-morrow."

"Why?"

"In the first place, because it did not strike me that Mlle. Darcieux felt any very great affection for her father."

"Never mind! Think of it: a father who tries to kill his daughter! A father who, for months on end, repeats his monstrous attempt four, five, six times over again!... Well, isn't that enough to blight a less sensitive soul than Jeanne's for good and all? What a hateful memory!"

"She will forget."

"One does not forget such a thing as that."

"She will forget, doctor, and for a very simple reason...."

"Explain yourself!"

"She is not M. Darcieux's daughter!"

"Eh?"

"I repeat, she is not that villain's daughter."

"What do you mean? M. Darcieux...."

"M. Darcieux is only her step-father. She had just been born when her father, her real father, died. Jeanne's mother then married a cousin of her husband's, a man bearing the same name, and she died within a year of her second wedding. She left Jeanne in M. Darcieux's charge. He first took her abroad and then bought this country-house; and, as nobody knew him in the neighbourhood, he represented the child as being his daughter. She herself did not know the truth about her birth."

The doctor sat confounded. He asked:

"Are you sure of your facts?"

"I spent my day in the town-halls of the Paris municipalities. I searched the registers, I interviewed two solicitors, I have seen all the documents. There is no doubt possible."

"But that does not explain the crime, or rather the series of crimes."

"Yes, it does," declared Lupin. "And, from the start, from the first hour when I meddled in this business, some words which Mlle. Darcieux used made me suspect that direction which my investigations must take. 'I was not quite five years old when my mother died,' she said. 'That was sixteen years ago.' Mlle. Darcieux, therefore, was nearly twenty-one, that is to say, she was on the verge of attaining her majority. I at once saw that this was an important detail. The day on which you reach your majority is the day on which your accounts are rendered. What was the financial position of Mlle. Darcieux, who was her mother's natural heiress? Of course, I did not think of the father for a second. To begin with, one can't imagine a thing like that; and then the farce which M. Darcieux was playing ... helpless, bedridden, ill...."

"Really ill," interrupted the doctor.

"All this diverted suspicion from him ... the more so as I believe that he himself was exposed to criminal attacks. But was there not in the family some person who would be interested in their removal? My journey to Paris revealed the truth to me: Mlle. Darcieux inherits a large fortune from her mother, of which her step-father draws the income. The solicitor was to have called a meeting of the family in Paris next month. The truth would have been out. It meant ruin to M. Darcieux."

"Then he had put no money by?"

"Yes, but he had lost a great deal as the result of unfortunate speculations."

"But, after all, Jeanne would not have taken the management of her fortune out of his hands!"

"There is one detail which you do not know, doctor, and which I learnt from reading the torn letter. Mlle. Darcieux is in love with the brother of Marceline, her Versailles friend; M. Darcieux was opposed to the marriage; and—you now see the reason—she was waiting until she came of age to be married."

"You're right," said the doctor, "you're right.... It meant his ruin."

"His absolute ruin. One chance of saving himself remained, the death of his step-daughter, of whom he is the next heir."

"Certainly, but on condition that no one suspected him."

"Of course; and that is why he contrived the series of accidents, so that the death might appear to be due to misadventure. And that is why I, on my side, wishing to bring things to a head, asked you to tell him of Mlle. Darcieux's impending departure. From that moment, it was no longer enough for the would-be sick man to wander about the grounds and the passages, in the dark, and execute some leisurely thought-out plan. No, he had to act, to act at once, without preparation, violently, dagger in hand. I had no doubt that he would decide to do it. And he did."

"Then he had no suspicions?"

"Of me, yes. He felt that I would return to-night, and he kept a watch at the place where I had already climbed the wall."

"Well?"

"Well," said Lupin, laughing, "I received a bullet full in the chest ... or rather my pocket-book received a bullet.... Here, you can see the hole.... So I tumbled from the tree, like a dead man. Thinking that he was rid of his only adversary, he went back to the house. I saw him prowl about for two hours. Then, making up his mind, he went to the coach-house, took a ladder and set it against the window. I had only to follow him."

The doctor reflected and said:

"You could have collared him earlier. Why did you let him come up? It was a sore trial for Jeanne ... and unnecessary."

"On the contrary, it was indispensable! Mlle. Darcieux would never have accepted the

303

truth. It was essential that she should see the murderer's very face. You must tell her all the circumstances when she wakes. She will soon be well again."

"But ... M. Darcieux?"

"You can explain his disappearance as you think best ... a sudden journey ... a fit of madness.... There will be a few inquiries.... And you may be sure that he will never be heard of again."

The doctor nodded his head:

"Yes ... that is so ... that is so ... you are right. You have managed all this business with extraordinary skill; and Jeanne owes you her life. She will thank you in person.... But now, can I be of use to you in any way? You told me that you were connected with the detective-service.... Will you allow me to write and praise your conduct, your courage?"

Lupin began to laugh:

"Certainly! A letter of that kind will do me a world of good. You might write to my immediate superior, Chief-inspector Ganimard. He will be glad to hear that his favourite officer, Paul Daubreuil, of the Rue de Surène, has once again distinguished himself by a brilliant action. As it happens, I have an appointment to meet him about a case of which you may have heard: the case of the red scarf.... How pleased my dear M. Ganimard will be!"

VII. A TRAGEDY IN THE FOREST OF MORGUES

The village was terror-stricken.

It was on a Sunday morning. The peasants of Saint-Nicolas and the neighbourhood were coming out of church and spreading across the square, when, suddenly, the women who were walking ahead and who had already turned into the high-road fell back with loud cries of dismay.

At the same moment, an enormous motor-car, looking like some appalling monster, came tearing into sight at a headlong rate of speed. Amid the shouts of the madly scattering people, it made straight for the church, swerved, just as it seemed about to dash itself to pieces against the steps, grazed the wall of the presbytery, regained the continuation of the national road, dashed along, turned the corner and disappeared, without, by some incomprehensible miracle, having so much as brushed against any of the persons crowding the square.

But they had seen! They had seen a man in the driver's seat, wrapped in a goat-skin coat, with a fur cap on his head and his face disguised in a pair of large goggles, and, with him, on the front of that seat, flung back, bent in two, a woman whose head, all covered with blood, hung down over the bonnet....

And they had heard! They had heard the woman's screams, screams of horror, screams of agony....

And it was all such a vision of hell and carnage that the people stood, for some seconds, motionless, stupefied.

"Blood!" roared somebody.

There was blood everywhere, on the cobblestones of the square, on the ground hardened by the first frosts of autumn; and, when a number of men and boys rushed off in pursuit of the motor, they had but to take those sinister marks for their guide.

The marks, on their part, followed the high-road, but in a very strange manner, going from one side to the other and leaving a zigzag track, in the wake of the tires, that made those who saw it shudder. How was it that the car had not bumped against that tree? How had it been righted, instead of smashing into that bank? What novice, what madman, what drunkard, what frightened criminal was driving that motor-car with such astounding bounds and swerves?

One of the peasants declared:

"They will never do the turn in the forest."

And another said:

"Of course they won't! She's bound to upset!"

The Forest of Morgues began at half a mile beyond Saint-Nicolas; and the road, which was straight up to that point, except for a slight bend where it left the village, started climbing, immediately after entering the forest, and made an abrupt turn among the rocks and trees. No motor-car was able to take this turn without first slackening speed. There were posts to give notice of the danger.

The breathless peasants reached the quincunx of beeches that formed the edge of the forest. And one of them at once cried:

"There you are!"

"What?"

"Upset!"

The car, a limousine, had turned turtle and lay smashed, twisted and shapeless. Beside it, the woman's dead body. But the most horrible, sordid, stupefying thing was the woman's head, crushed, flattened, invisible under a block of stone, a huge block of stone lodged there by some unknown and prodigious agency. As for the man in the goat-skin coat he was nowhere to be found.

He was not found on the scene of the accident. He was not found either in the neighbourhood. Moreover, some workmen coming down the Côte de Morgues declared that they had not seen anybody.

The man, therefore, had taken refuge in the woods.

The gendarmes, who were at once sent for, made a minute search, assisted by the peasants, but discovered nothing. In the same way, the examining-magistrates, after a close inquiry lasting for several days, found no clue capable of throwing the least light upon this inscrutable tragedy. On the contrary, the investigations only led to further mysteries and further improbabilities.

Thus it was ascertained that the block of stone came from where there had been a landslip, at least forty yards away. And the murderer, in a few minutes, had carried it all that distance and flung it on his victim's head.

On the other hand, the murderer, who was most certainly not hiding in the forest—for, if so, he must inevitably have been discovered, the forest being of limited extent—had the audacity, eight days after the crime, to come back to the turn on the hill and leave his goat-skin coat there. Why? With what object? There was nothing in the pockets of the coat, except a corkscrew and a napkin. What did it all mean?

Inquiries were made of the builder of the motor-car, who recognized the limousine as one which he had sold, three years ago, to a Russian. The said Russian, declared the manufacturer, had sold it again at once. To whom? No one knew. The car bore no number.

Then again, it was impossible to identify the dead woman's body. Her clothes and underclothing were not marked in any way. And the face was quite unknown.

Meanwhile, detectives were going along the national road in the direction opposite to that taken by the actors in this mysterious tragedy. But who was to prove that the car had followed that particular road on the previous night?

They examined every yard of the ground, they questioned everybody. At last, they succeeded in learning that, on the Saturday evening, a limousine had stopped outside a grocer's shop in a small town situated about two hundred miles from Saint-Nicolas, on a highway branching out of the national road. The driver had first filled his tank, bought some spare cans of petrol and lastly taken away a small stock of provisions: a ham, fruit, biscuits, wine and a half-bottle of Three Star brandy.

There was a lady on the driver's seat. She did not get down. The blinds of the limousine were drawn. One of these blinds was seen to move several times. The shopman was positive that there was somebody inside.

Presuming the shopman's evidence to be correct, then the problem became even more complicated, for, so far, no clue had revealed the presence of a third person.

Meanwhile, as the travellers had supplied themselves with provisions, it remained to be discovered what they had done with them and what had become of the remains.

The detectives retraced their steps. It was not until they came to the fork of the two roads, at a spot eleven or twelve miles from Saint-Nicolas, that they met a shepherd who, in answer to their questions, directed them to a neighbouring field, hidden from view behind the screen of bushes, where he had seen an empty bottle and other things.

The detectives were convinced at the first examination. The motor-car had stopped there; and the unknown travellers, probably after a night's rest in their car, had breakfasted and resumed their journey in the course of the morning.

One unmistakable proof was the half-bottle of Three Star brandy sold by the grocer. This bottle had its neck broken clean off with a stone. The stone employed for the purpose was picked up, as was the neck of the bottle, with its cork, covered with a tin-foil seal. The seal showed marks of attempts that had been made to uncork the bottle in the ordinary manner.

The detectives continued their search and followed a ditch that ran along the field at right angles to the road. It ended in a little spring, hidden under brambles, which seemed to emit an offensive smell. On lifting the brambles, they perceived a corpse, the corpse of a man whose head had been smashed in, so that it formed little more than a sort of pulp, swarming with vermin. The body was dressed in jacket and trousers of dark-brown leather. The pockets were empty: no papers, no pocket-book, no watch.

The grocer and his shopman were summoned and, two days later, formally identified, by his dress and figure, the traveller who had bought the petrol and provisions on the Saturday evening.

The whole case, therefore, had to be reopened on a fresh basis. The authorities were confronted with a tragedy no longer enacted by two persons, a man and a woman, of whom one had killed the other, but by three persons, including two victims, of whom one was the very man who was accused of killing his companion.

As to the murderer, there was no doubt: he was the person who travelled inside the motor-car and who took the precaution to remain concealed behind the curtains. He had first got rid of the driver and rifled his pockets and then, after wounding the woman, carried her off in a mad dash for death.

Given a fresh case, unexpected discoveries, unforeseen evidence, one might have hoped that the mystery would be cleared up, or, at least, that the inquiry would point a few steps along the road to the truth. But not at all. The corpse was simply placed beside the first corpse. New problems were added to the old. The accusation of murder was shifted from the one to the other. And there it ended. Outside those tangible, obvious facts there was nothing but darkness. The name of the woman, the name of the man, the name of the murderer were so many riddles. And then what had become of the murderer? If he had disappeared from one moment to the other, that in itself would have been a tolerably curious phenomenon. But the phenomenon was actually something very like a miracle, inasmuch as the murderer had not absolutely disappeared. He was there! He made a practice of returning to the scene of the catastrophe! In addition to the goat-skin coat, a fur cap was picked up one day; and, by way of an unparalleled prodigy, one morning, after a whole night spent on guard in the rock, beside the famous turning, the detectives found, on the grass of the turning itself, a pair of motor-goggles, broken, rusty, dirty, done for. How had the murderer managed to bring back those goggles unseen by the detectives? And, above all, why had he brought them back?

Men's brains reeled in the presence of such abnormalities. They were almost afraid to pursue the ambiguous adventure. They received the impression of a heavy, stifling, breathless atmosphere, which dimmed the eyes and baffled the most clear-sighted.

The magistrate in charge of the case fell ill. Four days later, his successor confessed that the matter was beyond him.

Two tramps were arrested and at once released. Another was pursued, but not caught; moreover, there was no evidence of any sort or kind against him. In short, it was nothing but one helpless muddle of mist and contradiction.

An accident, the merest accident led to the solution, or rather produced a series of circumstances that ended by leading to the solution. A reporter on the staff of an important Paris paper, who had been sent to make investigations on the spot, concluded his article with the following words:

"I repeat, therefore, that we must wait for fresh events, fresh facts; we must wait for some lucky accident. As things stand, we are simply wasting our time. The elements of truth are not even sufficient to suggest a plausible theory. We are in the midst of the most absolute, painful, impenetrable darkness. There is nothing to be done. All the Sherlock Holmeses in the world would not know what to make of the mystery, and Arsène Lupin himself, if he will allow me to say so, would have to pay forfeit here."

On the day after the appearance of that article, the newspaper in question printed this telegram:

"Have sometimes paid forfeit, but never over such a silly thing as this. The Saint-Nicolas tragedy is a mystery for babies.
"Arsène Lupin."

And the editor added:

"We insert this telegram as a matter of curiosity, for it is obviously the work of a wag. Arsène Lupin, past-master though he be in the art of practical joking, would be the last man to display such childish flippancy."

Two days elapsed; and then the paper published the famous letter, so precise and categorical in its conclusions, in which Arsène Lupin furnished the solution of the problem. I quote it in full:

"SIR:

"You have taken me on my weak side by defying me. You challenge me, and I accept the challenge. And I will begin by declaring once more that the Saint-Nicolas tragedy is a mystery for babies. I know nothing so simple, so natural; and the proof of the simplicity shall lie in the succinctness of my demonstration. It is contained in these few words: when a crime seems to go beyond the ordinary scope of things, when it seems unusual and stupid, then there are many chances that its explanation is to be found in superordinary, supernatural, superhuman motives.

"I say that there are many chances, for we must always allow for the part played by absurdity in the most logical and commonplace events. But, of course, it is impossible to see things as they are and not to take account of the absurd and the disproportionate.

"I was struck from the very beginning by that very evident character of unusualness. We have, first of all, the awkward, zigzag course of the motor-car, which would give one the impression that the car was driven by a novice. People have spoken of a drunkard or a madman, a justifiable supposition in itself. But neither madness nor drunkenness would account for the incredible strength required to transport, especially in so short a space of time, the stone with which the unfortunate woman's head was crushed. That proceeding called for a muscular power so great that I do not hesitate to look upon it as a second sign of the unusualness that marks the whole tragedy. And why move that enormous stone, to finish off the victim, when a mere pebble would have done the work? Why again was the murderer not killed, or at least reduced to a temporary state of helplessness, in the terrible somersault turned by the car? How did he disappear? And why, having disappeared, did he return to the scene of the accident? Why did he throw his fur coat there; then, on another day, his cap; then, on another day, his goggles?

"Unusual, useless, stupid acts.

"Why, besides, convey that wounded, dying woman on the driver's seat of the car, where everybody could see her? Why do that, instead of putting her inside, or flinging her into some corner, dead, just as the man was flung under the brambles in the ditch?

"Unusualness, stupidity.

"Everything in the whole story is absurd. Everything points to hesitation, incoherency, awkwardness, the silliness of a child or rather of a mad, blundering savage, of a brute.

"Look at the bottle of brandy. There was a corkscrew: it was found in the pocket of the great coat. Did the murderer use it? Yes, the marks of the corkscrew can be seen on the seal. But the operation was too complicated for him. He broke the neck with a stone. Always stones: observe that detail. They are the only weapon, the only implement which the creature employs. It is his customary weapon, his familiar implement. He kills the man with a stone, he kills the woman with a stone and he opens bottles with a stone!

"A brute, I repeat, a savage; disordered, unhinged, suddenly driven mad. By what? Why, of course, by that same brandy, which he swallowed at a draught while the driver and his companion were having breakfast in the field. He got out of the limousine, in which he was travelling, in his goat-skin coat and his fur cap, took the bottle, broke off the neck and drank. There is the whole story. Having drunk, he went raving mad and hit out at random, without reason. Then, seized with instinctive fear, dreading the inevitable punishment, he hid the body of the man. Then, like an idiot, he took up the wounded woman and ran away. He ran away in that motor-car which he did not know how to work, but which to him represented safety, escape from capture.

"But the money, you will ask, the stolen pocket-book? Why, who says that he was the thief? Who says that it was not some passing tramp, some labourer, guided by the stench of the corpse?

"Very well, you object, but the brute would have been found, as he is hiding somewhere near the turn, and as, after all, he must eat and drink.

"Well, well, I see that you have not yet understood. The simplest way, I suppose, to have done and to answer your objections is to make straight for the mark. Then let the gentlemen of the police and the gendarmerie themselves make straight for the mark. Let them take firearms. Let them explore the forest within a radius of two or three hundred yards from the turn, no more. But, instead of exploring with their heads down and their eyes fixed on the ground, let them look up into the air, yes, into the air, among the leaves and branches of the tallest oaks and the most unlikely beeches. And, believe me, they will see him. For he is there. He is there, bewildered, piteously at a loss, seeking for the man and woman whom he has killed, looking for them and waiting for them and not daring to go away and quite unable to understand.

"I myself am exceedingly sorry that I am kept in town by urgent private affairs and by some complicated matters of business which I have to set going, for I should much have liked to see the end of this rather curious adventure.

"Pray, therefore excuse me to my kind friends in the police and permit me to be, sir,

"Your obedient servant,

"ARSÈNE LUPIN."

The upshot will be remembered. The "gentlemen of the police and the gendarmerie" shrugged their shoulders and paid no attention to this lucubration. But four of the local country gentry took their rifles and went shooting, with their eyes fixed skyward, as though they meant to pot a few rooks. In half an hour they had caught sight of the murderer. Two shots, and he came tumbling from bough to bough. He was only wounded, and they took him alive.

That evening, a Paris paper, which did not yet know of the capture, printed the following paragraphs:

"Enquiries are being made after a M. and Mme. Bragoff, who landed at Marseilles six weeks ago and there hired a motor-car. They had been living in Australia for many years, during which time they had not visited Europe; and they wrote to the director of the Jardin d'Acclimatation, with whom they were in the habit of corresponding, that they were bringing with them a curious creature, of an entirely unknown species, of which it was difficult to say whether it was a man or a monkey.

"According to M. Bragoff, who is an eminent archæologist, the specimen in question is the anthropoid ape, or rather the ape-man, the existence of which had not hitherto been definitely proved. The structure is said to be exactly similar to that of *Pithecanthropus erectus*, discovered by Dr. Dubois in Java in 1891.

"This curious, intelligent and observant animal acted as its owner's servant on their property in Australia and used to clean their motor-car and even attempt to drive it.

"The question that is being asked is where are M. and Mme. Bragoff? Where is the strange primate that landed with them at Marseilles?"

The answer to this question was now made easy. Thanks to the hints supplied by Arsène Lupin, all the elements of the tragedy were known. Thanks to him, the culprit was in the hands of the law.

You can see him at the Jardin d'Acclimatation, where he is locked up under the name of "Three Stars." He is, in point of fact, a monkey; but he is also a man. He has the gentleness and the wisdom of the domestic animals and the sadness which they feel when their master dies. But he has many other qualities that bring him much closer to humanity: he is treacherous, cruel, idle, greedy and quarrelsome; and, above all, he is immoderately fond of brandy.

Apart from that, he is a monkey. Unless indeed ...!

A few days after Three Stars' arrest, I saw Arsène Lupin standing in front of his cage. Lupin was manifestly trying to solve this interesting problem for himself. I at once said, for I had set my heart upon having the matter out with him:

"You know, Lupin, that intervention of yours, your argument, your letter, in short, did not surprise me so much as you might think!"

"Oh, really?" he said, calmly. "And why?"

"Why? Because the incident has occurred before, seventy or eighty years ago. Edgar Allan Poe made it the subject of one of his finest tales. In those circumstances, the key to the riddle was easy enough to find."

Arsène Lupin took my arm, and walking away with me, said:

"When did you guess it, yourself?"

"On reading your letter," I confessed.

"And at what part of my letter?"

"At the end."

"At the end, eh? After I had dotted all the i's. So here is a crime which accident causes to be repeated, under quite different conditions, it is true, but still with the same sort of hero; and your eyes had to be opened, as well as other people's. It needed the assistance of my letter, the letter in which I amused myself—apart from the exigencies of the facts—by employing the argument and sometimes the identical words used by the American poet in a story which everybody has read. So you see that my letter was not absolutely useless and that one may safely venture to repeat to people things which they have learnt only to forget them."

Wherewith Lupin turned on his heel and burst out laughing in the face of an old monkey, who sat with the air of a philosopher, gravely meditating.

VIII. LUPIN'S MARRIAGE

"Monsieur Arsène Lupin has the honour to inform you of his approaching marriage with Mademoiselle Angélique de Sarzeau-Vendôme, Princesse de Bourbon-Condé, and to request the pleasure of your company at the wedding, which will take place at the church of Sainte-Clotilde...."

"The Duc de Sarzeau-Vendôme has the honour to inform you of the approaching marriage of his daughter Angélique, Princesse de Bourbon-Condé, with Monsieur Arsène Lupin, and to request...."

Jean Duc de Sarzeau-Vendôme could not finish reading the invitations which he held in his trembling hand. Pale with anger, his long, lean body shaking with tremors:

"There!" he gasped, handing the two communications to his daughter. "This is what our friends have received! This has been the talk of Paris since yesterday! What do you say to that dastardly insult, Angélique? What would your poor mother say to it, if she were alive?"

Angélique was tall and thin like her father, skinny and angular like him. She was thirty-three years of age, always dressed in black stuff, shy and retiring in manner, with a head too small in proportion to her height and narrowed on either side until the nose seemed to jut forth in protest against such parsimony. And yet it would be impossible to say that she was ugly, for her eyes were extremely beautiful, soft and grave, proud and a little sad: pathetic eyes which to see once was to remember.

She flushed with shame at hearing her father's words, which told her the scandal of which she was the victim. But, as she loved him, notwithstanding his harshness to her, his injustice and despotism, she said:

"Oh, I think it must be meant for a joke, father, to which we need pay no attention!"

"A joke? Why, every one is gossiping about it! A dozen papers have printed the confounded notice this morning, with satirical comments. They quote our pedigree, our ancestors, our illustrious dead. They pretend to take the thing seriously...."

"Still, no one could believe...."

"Of course not. But that doesn't prevent us from being the by-word of Paris."

"It will all be forgotten by to-morrow."

"To-morrow, my girl, people will remember that the name of Angélique de Sarzeau-Vendôme has been bandied about as it should not be. Oh, if I could find out the name of the scoundrel who has dared...."

At that moment, Hyacinthe, the duke's valet, came in and said that monsieur le duc was wanted on the telephone. Still fuming, he took down the receiver and growled:

"Well? Who is it? Yes, it's the Duc de Sarzeau-Vendôme speaking."

A voice replied:

"I want to apologize to you, monsieur le duc, and to Mlle. Angélique. It's my secretary's fault."

"Your secretary?"

"Yes, the invitations were only a rough draft which I meant to submit to you. Unfortunately my secretary thought...."

"But, tell me, monsieur, who are you?"

"What, monsieur le duc, don't you know my voice? The voice of your future son-in-law?"

"What!"

"Arsène Lupin."

The duke dropped into a chair. His face was livid.

"Arsène Lupin ... it's he ... Arsène Lupin...."

Angélique gave a smile:

"You see, father, it's only a joke, a hoax."

But the duke's rage broke out afresh and he began to walk up and down, moving his arms:

"I shall go to the police!... The fellow can't be allowed to make a fool of me in this way!... If there's any law left in the land, it must be stopped!"

Hyacinthe entered the room again. He brought two visiting-cards.

"Chotois? Lepetit? Don't know them."

"They are both journalists, monsieur le duc."

"What do they want?"

"They would like to speak to monsieur le duc with regard to ... the marriage...."

"Turn them out!" exclaimed the duke. "Kick them out! And tell the porter not to admit scum of that sort to my house in future."

"Please, father ..." Angélique ventured to say.

"As for you, shut up! If you had consented to marry one of your cousins when I wanted you to this wouldn't have happened."

The same evening, one of the two reporters printed, on the front page of his paper, a somewhat fanciful story of his expedition to the family mansion of the Sarzeau-Vendômes, in the Rue de Varennes, and expatiated pleasantly upon the old nobleman's wrathful protests.

The next morning, another newspaper published an interview with Arsène Lupin which was supposed to have taken place in a lobby at the Opera. Arsène Lupin retorted in a letter to the editor:

"I share my prospective father-in-law's indignation to the full. The sending out of the invitations was a gross breach of etiquette for which I am not responsible, but for which I wish to make a public apology. Why, sir, the date of the marriage is not yet fixed. My bride's father suggests early in May. She and I think that six weeks is really too long to wait!..."

That which gave a special piquancy to the affair and added immensely to the enjoyment of the friends of the family was the duke's well-known character: his pride and the uncompromising nature of his ideas and principles. Duc Jean was the last descendant of the Barons de Sarzeau, the most ancient family in Brittany; he was the lineal descendant of that Sarzeau who, upon marrying a Vendôme, refused to bear the new title which Louis XV forced upon him until after he had been imprisoned for ten years in the Bastille; and he had abandoned none of the prejudices of the old régime. In his youth, he followed the

Comte de Chambord into exile. In his old age, he refused a seat in the Chamber on the pretext that a Sarzeau could only sit with his peers.

The incident stung him to the quick. Nothing could pacify him. He cursed Lupin in good round terms, threatened him with every sort of punishment and rounded on his daughter:

"There, if you had only married!... After all you had plenty of chances. Your three cousins, Mussy, d'Emboise and Caorches, are noblemen of good descent, allied to the best families, fairly well-off; and they are still anxious to marry you. Why do you refuse them? Ah, because miss is a dreamer, a sentimentalist; and because her cousins are too fat, or too thin, or too coarse for her...."

She was, in fact, a dreamer. Left to her own devices from childhood, she had read all the books of chivalry, all the colourless romances of olden-time that littered the ancestral presses; and she looked upon life as a fairy-tale in which the beauteous maidens are always happy, while the others wait till death for the bridegroom who does not come. Why should she marry one of her cousins when they were only after her money, the millions which she had inherited from her mother? She might as well remain an old maid and go on dreaming....

She answered, gently:

"You will end by making yourself ill, father. Forget this silly business."

But how could he forget it? Every morning, some pin-prick renewed his wound. Three days running, Angélique received a wonderful sheaf of flowers, with Arsène Lupin's card peeping from it. The duke could not go to his club but a friend accosted him:

"That was a good one to-day!"

"What was?"

"Why, your son-in-law's latest! Haven't you seen it? Here, read it for yourself: 'M. Arsène Lupin is petitioning the Council of State for permission to add his wife's name to his own and to be known henceforth as Lupin de Sarzeau-Vendôme.'"

And, the next day, he read:

"As the young bride, by virtue of an unrepealed decree of Charles X, bears the title and arms of the Bourbon-Condés, of whom she is the heiress-of-line, the eldest son of the Lupins de Sarzeau-Vendôme will be styled Prince de Bourbon-Condé."

And, the day after, an advertisement.

"Exhibition of Mlle. de Sarzeau-Vendôme's trousseau at Messrs. ——'s Great Linen Warehouse. Each article marked with initials L. S. V."

Then an illustrated paper published a photographic scene: the duke, his daughter and his son-in-law sitting at a table playing three-handed auction-bridge.

And the date also was announced with a great flourish of trumpets: the 4th of May.

And particulars were given of the marriage-settlement. Lupin showed himself wonderfully disinterested. He was prepared to sign, the newspapers said, with his eyes closed, without knowing the figure of the dowry.

All these things drove the old duke crazy. His hatred of Lupin assumed morbid proportions. Much as it went against the grain, he called on the prefect of police, who advised him to be on his guard:

"We know the gentleman's ways; he is employing one of his favourite dodges. Forgive the expression, monsieur le duc, but he is 'nursing' you. Don't fall into the trap."

"What dodge? What trap?" asked the duke, anxiously.

"He is trying to make you lose your head and to lead you, by intimidation, to do something which you would refuse to do in cold blood."

"Still, M. Arsène Lupin can hardly hope that I will offer him my daughter's hand!"

"No, but he hopes that you will commit, to put it mildly, a blunder."

"What blunder?"

"Exactly that blunder which he wants you to commit."

"Then you think, monsieur le préfet ...?"

"I think the best thing you can do, monsieur le duc, is to go home, or, if all this excitement worries you, to run down to the country and stay there quietly, without upsetting yourself."

This conversation only increased the old duke's fears. Lupin appeared to him in the light of a terrible person, who employed diabolical methods and kept accomplices in every sphere of society. Prudence was the watchword.

And life, from that moment, became intolerable. The duke grew more crabbed and silent than ever and denied his door to all his old friends and even to Angélique's three suitors, her Cousins de Mussy, d'Emboise and de Caorches, who were none of them on speaking terms with the others, in consequence of their rivalry, and who were in the habit of calling, turn and turn about, every week.

For no earthly reason, he dismissed his butler and his coachman. But he dared not fill their places, for fear of engaging creatures of Arsène Lupin's; and his own man, Hyacinthe, in whom he had every confidence, having had him in his service for over forty years, had to take upon himself the laborious duties of the stables and the pantry.

"Come, father," said Angélique, trying to make him listen to common-sense. "I really can't see what you are afraid of. No one can force me into this ridiculous marriage."

"Well, of course, that's not what I'm afraid of."

"What then, father?"

"How can I tell? An abduction! A burglary! An act of violence! There is no doubt that the villain is scheming something; and there is also no doubt that we are surrounded by spies."

One afternoon, he received a newspaper in which the following paragraph was marked in red pencil:

"The signing of the marriage-contract is fixed for this evening, at the Sarzeau-Vendôme town-house. It will be quite a private ceremony and only a few privileged friends will be present to congratulate the happy pair. The witnesses to the contract on behalf of Mlle. de Sarzeau-Vendôme, the Prince de la Rochefoucauld-Limours and the Comte de Chartres, will be introduced by M. Arsène Lupin to the two gentlemen who have claimed the honour of acting as his groomsmen, namely, the prefect of police and the governor of the Santé Prison."

Ten minutes later, the duke sent his servant Hyacinthe to the post with three express messages. At four o'clock, in Angélique's presence, he saw the three cousins: Mussy, fat, heavy, pasty-faced; d'Emboise, slender, fresh-coloured and shy: Caorches, short, thin and unhealthy-looking: all three, old bachelors by this time, lacking distinction in dress or appearance.

The meeting was a short one. The duke had worked out his whole plan of campaign, a defensive campaign, of which he set forth the first stage in explicit terms:

"Angélique and I will leave Paris to-night for our place in Brittany. I rely on you, my three nephews, to help us get away. You, d'Emboise, will come and fetch us in your car, with the hood up. You, Mussy, will bring your big motor and kindly see to the luggage with Hyacinthe, my man. You, Caorches, will go to the Gare d'Orléans and book our berths in the sleeping-car for Vannes by the 10.40 train. Is that settled?"

The rest of the day passed without incident. The duke, to avoid any accidental indiscretion, waited until after dinner to tell Hyacinthe to pack a trunk and a portmanteau. Hyacinthe was to accompany them, as well as Angélique's maid.

At nine o'clock, all the other servants went to bed, by their master's order. At ten minutes to ten, the duke, who was completing his preparations, heard the sound of a motor-horn. The porter opened the gates of the courtyard. The duke, standing at the window, recognized d'Emboise's landaulette:

"Tell him I shall be down presently," he said to Hyacinthe, "and let mademoiselle know."

In a few minutes, as Hyacinthe did not return, he left his room. But he was attacked on the landing by two masked men, who gagged and bound him before he could utter a cry. And one of the men said to him, in a low voice:

"Take this as a first warning, monsieur le duc. If you persist in leaving Paris and refusing your consent, it will be a more serious matter."

And the same man said to his companion:

"Keep an eye on him. I will see to the young lady."

By that time, two other confederates had secured the lady's maid; and Angélique, herself gagged, lay fainting on a couch in her boudoir.

She came to almost immediately, under the stimulus of a bottle of salts held to her nostrils; and, when she opened her eyes, she saw bending over her a young man, in evening-clothes, with a smiling and friendly face, who said:

"I implore your forgiveness, mademoiselle. All these happenings are a trifle sudden and this behavior rather out of the way. But circumstances often compel us to deeds of which our conscience does not approve. Pray pardon me."

He took her hand very gently and slipped a broad gold ring on the girl's finger, saying:

"There, now we are engaged. Never forget the man who gave you this ring. He entreats you not to run away from him ... and to stay in Paris and await the proofs of his devotion. Have faith in him."

He said all this in so serious and respectful a voice, with so much authority and deference, that she had not the strength to resist. Their eyes met. He whispered:

"The exquisite purity of your eyes! It would be heavenly to live with those eyes upon one. Now close them...."

He withdrew. His accomplices followed suit. The car drove off, and the house in the Rue de Varennes remained still and silent until the moment when Angélique, regaining complete consciousness, called out for the servants.

They found the duke, Hyacinthe, the lady's maid and the porter and his wife all tightly bound. A few priceless ornaments had disappeared, as well as the duke's pocket-book and all his jewellery; tie pins, pearl studs, watch and so on.

The police were advised without delay. In the morning it appeared that, on the evening before, d'Emboise, when leaving his house in the motor-car, was stabbed by his own chauffeur and thrown, half-dead, into a deserted street. Mussy and Caorches had each received a telephone-message, purporting to come from the duke, countermanding their attendance.

Next week, without troubling further about the police investigation, without obeying the summons of the examining-magistrate, without even reading Arsène Lupin's letters to the papers on "the Varennes Flight," the duke, his daughter and his valet stealthily took a slow train for Vannes and arrived one evening, at the old feudal castle that towers over the headland of Sarzeau. The duke at once organized a defence with the aid of the Breton peasants, true mediæval vassals to a man. On the fourth day, Mussy arrived; on the fifth, Caorches; and, on the seventh, d'Emboise, whose wound was not as severe as had been feared.

The duke waited two days longer before communicating to those about him what, now that his escape had succeeded in spite of Lupin, he called the second part of his plan. He did so, in the presence of the three cousins, by a dictatorial order to Angélique, expressed in these peremptory terms:

"All this bother is upsetting me terribly. I have entered on a struggle with this man whose daring you have seen for yourself; and the struggle is killing me. I want to end it at all costs. There is only one way of doing so, Angélique, and that is for you to release me from all responsibility by accepting the hand of one of your cousins. Before a month is out, you must be the wife of Mussy, Caorches or d'Emboise. You have a free choice. Make your decision."

For four whole days Angélique wept and entreated her father, but in vain. She felt that he would be inflexible and that she must end by submitting to his wishes. She accepted:

"Whichever you please, father. I love none of them. So I may as well be unhappy with one as with the other."

Thereupon a fresh discussion ensued, as the duke wanted to compel her to make her own choice. She stood firm. Reluctantly and for financial considerations, he named d'Emboise.

The banns were published without delay.

From that moment, the watch in and around the castle was increased twofold, all the more inasmuch as Lupin's silence and the sudden cessation of the campaign which he had been conducting in the press could not but alarm the Duc de Sarzeau-Vendôme. It was obvious that the enemy was getting ready to strike and would endeavour to oppose the marriage by one of his characteristic moves.

Nevertheless, nothing happened: nothing two days before the ceremony, nothing on the day before, nothing on the morning itself. The marriage took place in the mayor's office, followed by the religious celebration in church; and the thing was done.

Then and not till then, the duke breathed freely. Notwithstanding his daughter's sadness, notwithstanding the embarrassed silence of his son-in-law, who found the situation a little trying, he rubbed his hands with an air of pleasure, as though he had achieved a brilliant victory:

"Tell them to lower the drawbridge," he said to Hyacinthe, "and to admit everybody. We have nothing more to fear from that scoundrel."

After the wedding-breakfast, he had wine served out to the peasants and clinked glasses with them. They danced and sang.

At three o'clock, he returned to the ground-floor rooms. It was the hour for his afternoon nap. He walked to the guard-room at the end of the suite. But he had no sooner placed his foot on the threshold than he stopped suddenly and exclaimed:

"What are you doing here, d'Emboise? Is this a joke?"

D'Emboise was standing before him, dressed as a Breton fisherman, in a dirty jacket and breeches, torn, patched and many sizes too large for him.

The duke seemed dumbfounded. He stared with eyes of amazement at that face which he knew and which, at the same time, roused memories of a very distant past within his brain. Then he strode abruptly to one of the windows overlooking the castle-terrace and called:

"Angélique!"

"What is it, father?" she asked, coming forward.

"Where's your husband?"

"Over there, father," said Angélique, pointing to d'Emboise, who was smoking a cigarette and reading, some way off.

The duke stumbled and fell into a chair, with a great shudder of fright:

"Oh, I shall go mad!"

But the man in the fisherman's garb knelt down before him and said:

"Look at me, uncle. You know me, don't you? I'm your nephew, the one who used to play here in the old days, the one whom you called Jacquot.... Just think a minute.... Here, look at this scar...."

"Yes, yes," stammered the duke, "I recognize you. It's Jacques. But the other one...."

He put his hands to his head:

"And yet, no, it can't be ... Explain yourself.... I don't understand.... I don't want to understand...."

There was a pause, during which the newcomer shut the window and closed the door leading to the next room. Then he came up to the old duke, touched him gently on the shoulder, to wake him from his torpor, and without further preface, as though to cut short any explanation that was not absolutely necessary, spoke as follows:

"Four years ago, that is to say, in the eleventh year of my voluntary exile, when I settled in the extreme south of Algeria, I made the acquaintance, in the course of a hunting-expedition arranged by a big Arab chief, of a man whose geniality, whose charm of manner, whose consummate prowess, whose indomitable pluck, whose combined humour and depth of mind fascinated me in the highest degree. The Comte d'Andrésy spent six weeks as my guest. After he left, we kept up a correspondence at regular intervals. I also often saw his name in the papers, in the society and sporting columns. He was to come back and I was preparing to receive him, three months ago, when, one evening as I was out riding, my two Arab attendants flung themselves upon me, bound me, blindfolded me and took me, travelling day and night, for a week, along deserted roads, to a bay on the coast, where five men awaited them. I was at once carried on board a small steam-yacht, which weighed anchor without delay. There was nothing to tell me who the men were nor what their object was in kidnapping me. They had locked me into a narrow cabin, secured by a massive door and lighted by a port-hole protected by two iron cross-bars. Every morning, a hand was inserted through a hatch between the next cabin and my own and placed on my bunk two or three pounds of bread, a good helping of food and a flagon of wine and removed the remains of yesterday's meals, which I put there for the purpose. From time to time, at night, the yacht stopped and I heard the sound of the boat rowing to some harbour and then returning, doubtless with provisions. Then we set out once more, without hurrying, as though on a cruise of people of our class, who travel for pleasure and are not pressed for time. Sometimes, standing on a chair, I would see the coastline, through my port-hole, too indistinctly, however, to locate it. And this lasted for weeks. One morning, in the ninth week, I perceived that the hatch had been left unfastened and I pushed it open. The cabin was empty at the time. With an effort, I was able to take a nail-file from a dressing-table. Two weeks after that, by dint of patient perseverance, I had succeeded in filing through the bars of my port-hole and I could have escaped that way, only, though I am a good swimmer, I soon grow tired. I had therefore to choose a moment when the yacht was not too far from the land. It was not until yesterday that, perched on my chair, I caught sight of the coast; and, in the evening, at sunset, I recognized, to my astonishment, the outlines of the Château de Sarzeau, with its pointed turrets and its square keep. I wondered if this was the goal of my mysterious voyage. All night long, we cruised in the offing. The same all day yesterday. At last, this morning, we put in at a distance which I considered favourable, all the more so as we were steaming through rocks under cover of which I could swim unobserved. But, just as I was about to make my escape, I noticed that the shutter of the hatch, which they thought they had closed, had once more opened of itself and was flapping against the partition. I again pushed it ajar from curiosity. Within arm's length was a little cupboard which I managed to open and in which my hand, groping at random, laid hold of a bundle of papers. This consisted of letters, letters containing instructions addressed to the pirates who held me prisoner. An hour later, when I wriggled through the port-hole and slipped into the sea, I knew all: the reasons for my abduction, the means employed, the object in view and the infamous scheme plotted during the last three months against the Duc de Sarzeau-Vendôme and his daughter. Unfortunately, it was too late. I was obliged, in order not to be seen from the yacht, to crouch in the cleft of a rock and did not reach land until mid-day. By the time that I had been to a fisherman's cabin, exchanged my clothes for his and come on here, it was three o'clock. On my arrival. I learnt that Angélique's marriage was celebrated this morning."

The old duke had not spoken a word. With his eyes riveted on the stranger's, he was listening in ever-increasing dismay. At times, the thought of the warnings given him by the prefect of police returned to his mind:

"They're nursing you, monsieur le duc, they are nursing you."

He said, in a hollow voice:

"Speak on ... finish your story.... All this is ghastly.... I don't understand it yet ... and I feel nervous...."

The stranger resumed:

"I am sorry to say, the story is easily pieced together and is summed up in a few sentences. It is like this: the Comte d'Andrésy remembered several things from his stay with me and from the confidences which I was foolish enough to make to him. First of all, I was your nephew and yet you had seen comparatively little of me, because I left Sarzeau when I was quite a child, and since then our intercourse was limited to the few weeks which I spent here, fifteen years ago, when I proposed for the hand of my Cousin Angélique; secondly, having broken with the past, I received no letters; lastly, there was a certain physical resemblance between d'Andrésy and myself which could be accentuated to such an extent as to become striking. His scheme was built up on those three points. He bribed my Arab servants to give him warning in case I left Algeria. Then he went back to Paris, bearing my name and made up to look exactly like me, came to see you, was invited to your house once a fortnight and lived under my name, which thus became one of the many aliases beneath which he conceals his real identity. Three months ago, when 'the apple was ripe,' as he says in his letters, he began the attack by a series of communications to the press; and, at the same time, fearing no doubt that some newspaper would tell me in Algeria the part that was being played under my name in Paris, he had me assaulted by my servants and kidnapped by his confederates. I need not explain any more in so far as you are concerned, uncle."

The Duc de Sarzeau-Vendôme was shaken with a fit of nervous trembling. The awful truth to which he refused to open his eyes appeared to him in its nakedness and assumed the hateful countenance of the enemy. He clutched his nephew's hands and said to him, fiercely, despairingly:

"It's Lupin, is it not?"

"Yes, uncle."

"And it's to him ... it's to him that I have given my daughter!"

"Yes, uncle, to him, who has stolen my name of Jacques d'Emboise from me and stolen your daughter from you. Angélique is the wedded wife of Arsène Lupin; and that in accordance with your orders. This letter in his handwriting bears witness to it. He has upset your whole life, thrown you off your balance, besieging your hours of waking and your nights of dreaming, rifling your town-house, until the moment when, seized with terror, you took refuge here, where, thinking that you would escape his artifices and his rapacity, you told your daughter to choose one of her three cousins, Mussy, d'Emboise or Caorches, as her husband.

"But why did she select that one rather than the others?"

"It was you who selected him, uncle."

"At random ... because he had the biggest income...."

"No, not at random, but on the insidious, persistent and very clever advice of your servant Hyacinthe."

The duke gave a start:

"What! Is Hyacinthe an accomplice?"

"No, not of Arsène Lupin, but of the man whom he believes to be d'Emboise and who promised to give him a hundred thousand francs within a week after the marriage."

"Oh, the villain!... He planned everything, foresaw everything...."

"Foresaw everything, uncle, down to shamming an attempt upon his life so as to avert suspicion, down to shamming a wound received in your service."

"But with what object? Why all these dastardly tricks?"

"Angélique has a fortune of eleven million francs. Your solicitor in Paris was to hand the securities next week to the counterfeit d'Emboise, who had only to realize them forthwith and disappear. But, this very morning, you yourself were to hand your son-in-law, as a personal wedding-present, five hundred thousand francs' worth of bearer-stock, which he has arranged to deliver to one of his accomplices at nine o'clock this evening, outside the castle, near the Great Oak, so that they may be negotiated to-morrow morning in Brussels."

The Duc de Sarzeau-Vendôme had risen from his seat and was stamping furiously up and down the room:

"At nine o'clock this evening?" he said. "We'll see about that.... We'll see about that.... I'll have the gendarmes here before then...."

"Arsène Lupin laughs at gendarmes."

"Let's telegraph to Paris."

"Yes, but how about the five hundred thousand francs?... And, still worse, uncle, the scandal?... Think of this: your daughter, Angélique de Sarzeau-Vendôme, married to that swindler, that thief.... No, no, it would never do...."

"What then?"

"What?..."

The nephew now rose and, stepping to a gun-rack, took down a rifle and laid it on the table, in front of the duke:

"Away in Algeria, uncle, on the verge of the desert, when we find ourselves face to face with a wild beast, we do not send for the gendarmes. We take our rifle and we shoot the wild beast. Otherwise, the beast would tear us to pieces with its claws."

"What do you mean?"

"I mean that, over there, I acquired the habit of dispensing with the gendarmes. It is a rather summary way of doing justice, but it is the best way, believe me, and to-day, in the present case, it is the only way. Once the beast is killed, you and I will bury it in some corner, unseen and unknown."

"And Angélique?"

"We will tell her later."

"What will become of her?"

"She will be my wife, the wife of the real d'Emboise. I desert her to-morrow and return to Algeria. The divorce will be granted in two months' time."

The duke listened, pale and staring, with set jaws. He whispered:

"Are you sure that his accomplices on the yacht will not inform him of your escape?"

"Not before to-morrow."

"So that ...?"

"So that inevitably, at nine o'clock this evening, Arsène Lupin, on his way to the Great Oak, will take the patrol-path that follows the old ramparts and skirts the ruins of the chapel. I shall be there, in the ruins."

"I shall be there too," said the Duc de Sarzeau-Vendôme, quietly, taking down a gun.

It was now five o'clock. The duke talked some time longer to his nephew, examined the weapons, loaded them with fresh cartridges. Then, when night came, he took d'Emboise through the dark passages to his bedroom and hid him in an adjoining closet.

Nothing further happened until dinner. The duke forced himself to keep calm during the meal. From time to time, he stole a glance at his son-in-law and was surprised at the likeness between him and the real d'Emboise. It was the same complexion, the same cast of features, the same cut of hair. Nevertheless, the look of the eye was different, keener in this case and brighter; and gradually the duke discovered minor details which had passed unperceived till then and which proved the fellow's imposture.

The party broke up after dinner. It was eight o'clock. The duke went to his room and released his nephew. Ten minutes later, under cover of the darkness, they slipped into the ruins, gun in hand.

Meanwhile, Angélique, accompanied by her husband, had gone to the suite of rooms which she occupied on the ground-floor of a tower that flanked the left wing. Her husband stopped at the entrance to the rooms and said:

"I am going for a short stroll, Angélique. May I come to you here, when I return?"

"Yes," she replied.

He left her and went up to the first floor, which had been assigned to him as his quarters. The moment he was alone, he locked the door, noiselessly opened a window that looked over the landscape and leant out. He saw a shadow at the foot of the tower, some hundred feet or more below him. He whistled and received a faint whistle in reply.

He then took from a cupboard a thick leather satchel, crammed with papers, wrapped it in a piece of black cloth and tied it up. Then he sat down at the table and wrote:

"Glad you got my message, for I think it unsafe to walk out of the castle with that large bundle of securities. Here they are. You will be in Paris, on your motor-cycle, in time to catch the morning train to Brussels, where you will hand over the bonds to Z.; and he will negotiate them at once.

"A. L.

"P. S.—As you pass by the Great Oak, tell our chaps that I'm coming. I have some instructions to give them. But everything is going well. No one here has the least suspicion."

He fastened the letter to the parcel and lowered both through the window with a length of string:

"Good," he said. "That's all right. It's a weight off my mind."

He waited a few minutes longer, stalking up and down the room and smiling at the portraits of two gallant gentlemen hanging on the wall:

"Horace de Sarzeau-Vendôme, marshal of France.... And you, the Great Condé ... I salute you, my ancestors both. Lupin de Sarzeau-Vendôme will show himself worthy of you."

At last, when the time came, he took his hat and went down. But, when he reached the ground-floor, Angélique burst from her rooms and exclaimed, with a distraught air:

"I say ... if you don't mind ... I think you had better...."

And then, without saying more, she went in again, leaving a vision of irresponsible terror in her husband's mind.

"She's out of sorts," he said to himself. "Marriage doesn't suit her."

He lit a cigarette and went out, without attaching importance to an incident that ought to have impressed him:

"Poor Angélique! This will all end in a divorce...."

The night outside was dark, with a cloudy sky.

The servants were closing the shutters of the castle. There was no light in the windows, it being the duke's habit to go to bed soon after dinner.

Lupin passed the gate-keeper's lodge and, as he put his foot on the drawbridge, said:

"Leave the gate open. I am going for a breath of air; I shall be back soon."

The patrol-path was on the right and ran along one of the old ramparts, which used to surround the castle with a second and much larger enclosure, until it ended at an almost demolished postern-gate. The park, which skirted a hillock and afterward followed the side of a deep valley, was bordered on the left by thick coppices.

"What a wonderful place for an ambush!" he said. "A regular cut-throat spot!"

He stopped, thinking that he heard a noise. But no, it was a rustling of the leaves. And yet a stone went rattling down the slopes, bounding against the rugged projections of the rock. But, strange to say, nothing seemed to disquiet him. The crisp sea-breeze came blowing over the plains of the headland; and he eagerly filled his lungs with it:

"What a thing it is to be alive!" he thought. "Still young, a member of the old nobility, a multi-millionaire: what could a man want more?"

At a short distance, he saw against the darkness the yet darker outline of the chapel, the ruins of which towered above the path. A few drops of rain began to fall; and he heard a clock strike nine. He quickened his pace. There was a short descent; then the path rose again. And suddenly, he stopped once more.

A hand had seized his.

He drew back, tried to release himself.

But some one stepped from the clump of trees against which he was brushing; and a voice said; "Ssh!... Not a word!..."

He recognized his wife, Angélique:

"What's the matter?" he asked.

She whispered, so low that he could hardly catch the words:

"They are lying in wait for you ... they are in there, in the ruins, with their guns...."

"Who?"

"Keep quiet.... Listen...."

They stood for a moment without stirring; then she said:

"They are not moving.... Perhaps they never heard me.... Let's go back...."

"But...."

"Come with me."

Her accent was so imperious that he obeyed without further question. But suddenly she took fright:

"Run!... They are coming!... I am sure of it!..."

True enough, they heard a sound of footsteps.

Then, swiftly, still holding him by the hand, she dragged him, with irresistible energy, along a shortcut, following its turns without hesitation in spite of the darkness and the brambles. And they very soon arrived at the drawbridge.

She put her arm in his. The gate-keeper touched his cap. They crossed the courtyard and entered the castle; and she led him to the corner tower in which both of them had their apartments:

"Come in here," she said.

"To your rooms?"

"Yes."

Two maids were sitting up for her. Their mistress ordered them to retire to their bedrooms, on the third floor.

Almost immediately after, there was a knock at the door of the outer room; and a voice called:

"Angélique!"

"Is that you, father?" she asked, suppressing her agitation.

"Yes. Is your husband here?"

"We have just come in."

"Tell him I want to speak to him. Ask him to come to my room. It's important."

"Very well, father, I'll send him to you."

She listened for a few seconds, then returned to the boudoir where her husband was and said:

"I am sure my father is still there."

He moved as though to go out:

"In that case, if he wants to speak to me...."

"My father is not alone," she said, quickly, blocking his way.

"Who is with him?"

"His nephew, Jacques d'Emboise."

There was a moment's silence. He looked at her with a certain astonishment, failing quite to understand his wife's attitude. But, without pausing to go into the matter:

"Ah, so that dear old d'Emboise is there?" he chuckled. "Then the fat's in the fire? Unless, indeed...."

"My father knows everything," she said. "I overheard a conversation between them just now. His nephew has read certain letters.... I hesitated at first about telling you.... Then I thought that my duty...."

He studied her afresh. But, at once conquered by the queerness of the situation, he burst out laughing:

"What? Don't my friends on board ship burn my letters? And they have let their prisoner escape? The idiots! Oh, when you don't see to everything yourself!... No matter, its distinctly humorous.... D'Emboise versus d'Emboise.... Oh, but suppose I were no longer recognized? Suppose d'Emboise himself were to confuse me with himself?"

He turned to a wash-hand-stand, took a towel, dipped it in the basin and soaped it and, in the twinkling of an eye, wiped the make-up from his face and altered the set of his hair:

"That's it," he said, showing himself to Angélique under the aspect in which she had seen him on the night of the burglary in Paris. "I feel more comfortable like this for a discussion with my father-in-law."

"Where are you going?" she cried, flinging herself in front of the door.

"Why, to join the gentlemen."

"You shall not pass!"

"Why not?"

"Suppose they kill you?"

"Kill me?"

"That's what they mean to do, to kill you ... to hide your body somewhere.... Who would know of it?"

"Very well," he said, "from their point of view, they are quite right. But, if I don't go to them, they will come here. That door won't stop them.... Nor you, I'm thinking. Therefore, it's better to have done with it."

"Follow me," commanded Angélique.

She took up the lamp that lit the room, went into her bedroom, pushed aside the wardrobe, which slid easily on hidden castors, pulled back an old tapestry-hanging, and said:

"Here is a door that has not been used for years. My father believes the key to be lost. I have it here. Unlock the door with it. A staircase in the wall will take you to the bottom of the tower. You need only draw the bolts of another door and you will be free."

He could hardly believe his ears. Suddenly, he grasped the meaning of Angélique's whole behavior. In front of that sad, plain, but wonderfully gentle face, he stood for a moment discountenanced, almost abashed. He no longer thought of laughing. A feeling of respect, mingled with remorse and kindness, overcame him.

"Why are you saving me?" he whispered.

"You are my husband."

He protested:

"No, no ... I have stolen that title. The law will never recognize my marriage."

"My father does not want a scandal," she said.

"Just so," he replied, sharply, "just so. I foresaw that; and that was why I had your cousin d'Emboise near at hand. Once I disappear, he becomes your husband. He is the man you have married in the eyes of men."

"You are the man I have married in the eyes of the Church."

"The Church! The Church! There are means of arranging matters with the Church.... Your marriage can be annulled."

"On what pretext that we can admit?"

He remained silent, thinking over all those points which he had not considered, all those points which were trivial and absurd for him, but which were serious for her, and he repeated several times:

"This is terrible ... this is terrible.... I should have anticipated...."

And, suddenly, seized with an idea, he clapped his hands and cried:

"There, I have it! I'm hand in glove with one of the chief figures at the Vatican. The Pope never refuses me anything. I shall obtain an audience and I have no doubt that the Holy Father, moved by my entreaties...."

His plan was so humorous and his delight so artless that Angélique could not help smiling; and she said:

"I am your wife in the eyes of God."

She gave him a look that showed neither scorn nor animosity, nor even anger; and he realized that she omitted to see in him the outlaw and the evil-doer and remembered only the man who was her husband and to whom the priest had bound her until the hour of death.

He took a step toward her and observed her more attentively. She did not lower her eyes at first. But she blushed. And never had he seen so pathetic a face, marked with such modesty and such dignity. He said to her, as on that first evening in Paris:

"Oh, your eyes ... the calm and sadness of your eyes ... the beauty of your eyes!"

She dropped her head and stammered:

"Go away ... go ..."

In the presence of her confusion, he received a quick intuition of the deeper feelings that stirred her, unknown to herself. To that spinster soul, of which he recognized the romantic power of imagination, the unsatisfied yearnings, the poring over old-world books, he suddenly represented, in that exceptional moment and in consequence of the unconventional circumstances of their meetings, somebody special, a Byronic hero, a chivalrous brigand of romance. One evening, in spite of all obstacles, he, the world-famed adventurer, already ennobled in song and story and exalted by his own audacity, had come to her and slipped the magic ring upon her finger: a mystic and passionate betrothal, as in the days of the *Corsair* and *Hernani*.... Greatly moved and touched, he was on the verge of giving way to an enthusiastic impulse and exclaiming:

"Let us go away together!... Let us fly!... You are my bride ... my wife.... Share my dangers, my sorrows and my joys.... It will be a strange and vigorous, a proud and magnificent life...."

But Angélique's eyes were raised to his again; and they were so pure and so noble that he blushed in his turn. This was not the woman to whom such words could be addressed.

He whispered:

"Forgive me.... I am a contemptible wretch.... I have wrecked your life...."

"No," she replied, softly. "On the contrary, you have shown me where my real life lies."

He was about to ask her to explain. But she had opened the door and was pointing the way to him. Nothing more could be spoken between them. He went out without a word, bowing very low as he passed.

A month later, Angélique de Sarzeau-Vendôme, Princesse de Bourbon-Condé, lawful wife of Arsène Lupin, took the veil and, under the name of Sister Marie-Auguste, buried herself within the walls of the Visitation Convent.

On the day of the ceremony, the mother superior of the convent received a heavy sealed envelope containing a letter with the following words:

"For Sister Marie-Auguste's poor."

Enclosed with the letter were five hundred bank-notes of a thousand francs each.

IX. THE INVISIBLE PRISONER

One day, at about four o'clock, as evening was drawing in, Farmer Goussot, with his four sons, returned from a day's shooting. They were stalwart men, all five of them, long of limb, broad-chested, with faces tanned by sun and wind. And all five displayed, planted on an enormous neck and shoulders, the same small head with the low forehead, thin lips, beaked nose and hard and repellent cast of countenance. They were feared and disliked by all around them. They were a money-grubbing, crafty family; and their word was not to be trusted.

On reaching the old barbican-wall that surrounds the Héberville property, the farmer opened a narrow, massive door, putting the big key back in his pocket after his sons had passed in. And he walked behind them, along the path that led through the orchards. Here and there stood great trees, stripped by the autumn winds, and clumps of pines, the last survivors of the ancient park now covered by old Goussot's farm.

One of the sons said:

"I hope mother has lit a log or two."

"There's smoke coming from the chimney," said the father.

The outhouses and the homestead showed at the end of a lawn; and, above them, the village church, whose steeple seemed to prick the clouds that trailed along the sky.

"All the guns unloaded?" asked old Goussot.

"Mine isn't," said the eldest. "I slipped in a bullet to blow a kestrel's head off...."

He was the one who was proudest of his skill. And he said to his brothers:

"Look at that bough, at the top of the cherry tree. See me snap it off."

On the bough sat a scarecrow, which had been there since spring and which protected the leafless branches with its idiot arms.

He raised his gun and fired.

The figure came tumbling down with large, comic gestures, and was caught on a big, lower branch, where it remained lying stiff on its stomach, with a great top hat on its head of rags and its hay-stuffed legs swaying from right to left above some water that flowed past the cherry tree through a wooden trough.

They all laughed. The father approved:

"A fine shot, my lad. Besides, the old boy was beginning to annoy me. I couldn't take my eyes from my plate at meals without catching sight of that oaf...."

They went a few steps farther. They were not more than thirty yards from the house, when the father stopped suddenly and said:

"Hullo! What's up?"

The sons also had stopped and stood listening. One of them said, under his breath:

"It comes from the house ... from the linen-room...."

And another spluttered:

"Sounds like moans.... And mother's alone!"

Suddenly, a frightful scream rang out. All five rushed forward. Another scream, followed by cries of despair.

"We're here! We're coming!" shouted the eldest, who was leading.

And, as it was a roundabout way to the door, he smashed in a window with his fist and sprang into the old people's bedroom. The room next to it was the linen-room, in which Mother Goussot spent most of her time.

"Damnation!" he said, seeing her lying on the floor, with blood all over her face. "Dad! Dad!"

"What? Where is she?" roared old Goussot, appearing on the scene. "Good lord, what's this?... What have they done to your mother?"

She pulled herself together and, with outstretched arm, stammered:

"Run after him!... This way!... This way!... I'm all right ... only a scratch or two.... But run, you! He's taken the money."

The father and sons gave a bound:

"He's taken the money!" bellowed old Goussot, rushing to the door to which his wife was pointing. "He's taken the money! Stop thief!"

But a sound of several voices rose at the end of the passage through which the other three sons were coming:

"I saw him! I saw him!"

"So did I! He ran up the stairs."

"No, there he is, he's coming down again!"

A mad steeplechase shook every floor in the house. Farmer Goussot, on reaching the end of the passage, caught sight of a man standing by the front door trying to open it. If he succeeded, it meant safety, escape through the market square and the back lanes of the village.

Interrupted as he was fumbling at the bolts, the man turning stupid, lost his head, charged at old Goussot and sent him spinning, dodged the eldest brother and, pursued by the four sons, doubled back down the long passage, ran into the old couple's bedroom, flung his legs through the broken window and disappeared.

The sons rushed after him across the lawns and orchards, now darkened by the falling night.

"The villain's done for," chuckled old Goussot. "There's no way out for him. The walls are too high. He's done for, the scoundrel!"

The two farm-hands returned, at that moment, from the village; and he told them what had happened and gave each of them a gun:

"If the swine shows his nose anywhere near the house," he said, "let fly at him. Give him no mercy!"

He told them where to stand, went to make sure that the farm-gates, which were only used for the carts, were locked, and, not till then, remembered that his wife might perhaps be in need of aid:

"Well, mother, how goes it?"

"Where is he? Have you got him?" she asked, in a breath.

"Yes, we're after him. The lads must have collared him by now."

The news quite restored her; and a nip of rum gave her the strength to drag herself to the bed, with old Goussot's assistance, and to tell her story. For that matter, there was not much to tell. She had just lit the fire in the living-hall; and she was knitting quietly at her bedroom window, waiting for the men to return, when she thought that she heard a slight grating sound in the linen-room next door:

"I must have left the cat in there," she thought to herself.

She went in, suspecting nothing, and was astonished to see the two doors of one of the linen-cupboards, the one in which they hid their money, wide open. She walked up to it, still without suspicion. There was a man there, hiding, with his back to the shelves.

"But how did he get in?" asked old Goussot.

"Through the passage, I suppose. We never keep the back door shut."

"And then did he go for you?"

"No, I went for him. He tried to get away."

"You should have let him."

"And what about the money?"

"Had he taken it by then?"

"Had he taken it! I saw the bundle of bank-notes in his hands, the sweep! I would have let him kill me sooner.... Oh, we had a sharp tussle, I give you my word!"

"Then he had no weapon?'

"No more than I did. We had our fingers, our nails and our teeth. Look here, where he bit me. And I yelled and screamed! Only, I'm an old woman you see.... I had to let go of him...."

"Do you know the man?"

"I'm pretty sure it was old Trainard."

"The tramp? Why, of course it's old Trainard!" cried the farmer. "I thought I knew him too.... Besides, he's been hanging round the house these last three days. The old vagabond must have smelt the money. Aha, Trainard, my man, we shall see some fun! A number-one hiding in the first place; and then the police.... I say, mother, you can get up now, can't you? Then go and fetch the neighbours.... Ask them to run for the gendarmes.... By the by, the attorney's youngster has a bicycle.... How that damned old Trainard scooted! He's got good legs for his age, he has. He can run like a hare!"

Goussot was holding his sides, reveling in the occurrence. He risked nothing by waiting. No power on earth could help the tramp escape or keep him from the sound thrashing which he had earned and from being conveyed, under safe escort, to the town gaol.

The farmer took a gun and went out to his two labourers:

"Anything fresh?"

"No, Farmer Goussot, not yet."

"We sha'n't have long to wait. Unless old Nick carries him over the walls...."

From time to time, they heard the four brothers hailing one another in the distance. The old bird was evidently making a fight for it, was more active than they would have thought. Still, with sturdy fellows like the Goussot brothers....

However, one of them returned, looking rather crestfallen, and made no secret of his opinion:

"It's no use keeping on at it for the present. It's pitch dark. The old chap must have crept into some hole. We'll hunt him out to-morrow."

"To-morrow! Why, lad, you're off your chump!" protested the farmer.

The eldest son now appeared, quite out of breath, and was of the same opinion as his brother. Why not wait till next day, seeing that the ruffian was as safe within the demesne as between the walls of a prison?

"Well, I'll go myself," cried old Goussot. "Light me a lantern, somebody!"

But, at that moment, three gendarmes arrived; and a number of village lads also came up to hear the latest.

The sergeant of gendarmes was a man of method. He first insisted on hearing the whole story, in full detail; then he stopped to think; then he questioned the four brothers, separately, and took his time for reflection after each deposition. When he had learnt from them that the tramp had fled toward the back of the estate, that he had been lost sight of repeatedly and that he had finally disappeared near a place known as the Crows' Knoll, he meditated once more and announced his conclusion:

"Better wait. Old Trainard might slip through our hands, amidst all the confusion of a pursuit in the dark, and then good-night, everybody!"

The farmer shrugged his shoulders and, cursing under his breath, yielded to the sergeant's arguments. That worthy organized a strict watch, distributed the brothers Goussot and the lads from the village under his men's eyes, made sure that the ladders were locked away and established his headquarters in the dining-room, where he and Farmer Goussot sat and nodded over a decanter of old brandy.

The night passed quietly. Every two hours, the sergeant went his rounds and inspected the posts. There were no alarms. Old Trainard did not budge from his hole.

The battle began at break of day.

It lasted four hours.

In those four hours, the thirteen acres of land within the walls were searched, explored, gone over in every direction by a score of men who beat the bushes with sticks, trampled over the tall grass, rummaged in the hollows of the trees and scattered the heaps of dry leaves. And old Trainard remained invisible.

"Well, this is a bit thick!" growled Goussot.

"Beats me altogether," retorted the sergeant.

And indeed there was no explaining the phenomenon. For, after all, apart from a few old clumps of laurels and spindle-trees, which were thoroughly beaten, all the trees were bare. There was no building, no shed, no stack, nothing, in short, that could serve as a hiding-place.

As for the wall, a careful inspection convinced even the sergeant that it was physically impossible to scale it.

In the afternoon, the investigations were begun all over again in the presence of the examining-magistrate and the public-prosecutor's deputy. The results were no more successful. Nay, worse, the officials looked upon the matter as so suspicious that they could not restrain their ill-humour and asked:

"Are you quite sure, Farmer Goussot, that you and your sons haven't been seeing double?"

"And what about my wife?" retorted the farmer, red with anger. "Did she see double when the scamp had her by the throat? Go and look at the marks, if you doubt me!"

"Very well. But then where is the scamp?"

"Here, between those four walls."

"Very well. Then ferret him out. We give it up. It's quite clear, that if a man were hidden within the precincts of this farm, we should have found him by now."

"I swear I'll lay hands on him, true as I stand here!" shouted Farmer Goussot. "It shall not be said that I've been robbed of six thousand francs. Yes, six thousand! There were three cows I sold; and then the wheat-crop; and then the apples. Six thousand-franc notes, which I was just going to take to the bank. Well, I swear to Heaven that the money's as good as in my pocket!"

"That's all right and I wish you luck," said the examining-magistrate, as he went away, followed by the deputy and the gendarmes.

The neighbours also walked off in a more or less facetious mood. And, by the end of the afternoon, none remained but the Goussots and the two farm-labourers.

Old Goussot at once explained his plan. By day, they were to search. At night, they were to keep an incessant watch. It would last as long as it had to. Hang it, old Trainard was a man like other men; and men have to eat and drink! Old Trainard must needs, therefore, come out of his earth to eat and drink.

"At most," said Goussot, "he can have a few crusts of bread in his pocket, or even pull up a root or two at night. But, as far as drink's concerned, no go. There's only the spring. And he'll be a clever dog if he gets near that."

He himself, that evening, took up his stand near the spring. Three hours later, his eldest son relieved him. The other brothers and the farm-hands slept in the house, each taking his turn of the watch and keeping all the lamps and candles lit, so that there might be no surprise.

So it went on for fourteen consecutive nights. And for fourteen days, while two of the men and Mother Goussot remained on guard, the five others explored the Héberville ground.

At the end of that fortnight, not a sign.

The farmer never ceased storming. He sent for a retired detective-inspector who lived in the neighbouring town. The inspector stayed with him for a whole week. He found neither old Trainard nor the least clue that could give them any hope of finding old Trainard.

"It's a bit thick!" repeated Farmer Goussot. "For he's there, the rascal! As far as being anywhere goes, he's there. So...."

Planting himself on the threshold, he railed at the enemy at the top of his voice:

"You blithering idiot, would you rather croak in your hole than fork out the money? Then croak, you pig!"

And Mother Goussot, in her turn, yelped, in her shrill voice:

"Is it prison you're afraid of? Hand over the notes and you can hook it!"

But old Trainard did not breathe a word; and the husband and wife tired their lungs in vain.

Shocking days passed. Farmer Goussot could no longer sleep, lay shivering with fever. The sons became morose and quarrelsome and never let their guns out of their hands, having no other idea but to shoot the tramp.

It was the one topic of conversation in the village; and the Goussot story, from being local at first, soon went the round of the press. Newspaper-reporters came from the assize-town, from Paris itself, and were rudely shown the door by Farmer Goussot.

"Each man his own house," he said. "You mind your business. I mind mine. It's nothing to do with any one."

"Still, Farmer Goussot...."

"Go to blazes!"

And he slammed the door in their face.

Old Trainard had now been hidden within the walls of Héberville for something like four weeks. The Goussots continued their search as doggedly and confidently as ever, but with daily decreasing hope, as though they were confronted with one of those mysterious obstacles which discourage human effort. And the idea that they would never see their money again began to take root in them.

One fine morning, at about ten o'clock, a motor-car, crossing the village square at full speed, broke down and came to a dead stop.

The driver, after a careful inspection, declared that the repairs would take some little time, whereupon the owner of the car resolved to wait at the inn and lunch. He was a gentleman on the right side of forty, with close-cropped side-whiskers and a pleasant expression of face; and he soon made himself at home with the people at the inn.

Of course, they told him the story of the Goussots. He had not heard it before, as he had been abroad; but it seemed to interest him greatly. He made them give him all the details, raised objections, discussed various theories with a number of people who were eating at the same table and ended by exclaiming:

"Nonsense! It can't be so intricate as all that. I have had some experience of this sort of thing. And, if I were on the premises...."

"That's easily arranged," said the inn-keeper. "I know Farmer Goussot.... He won't object...."

The request was soon made and granted. Old Goussot was in one of those frames of mind when we are less disposed to protest against outside interference. His wife, at any rate, was very firm:

"Let the gentleman come, if he wants to."

The gentleman paid his bill and instructed his driver to try the car on the high-road as soon as the repairs were finished:

"I shall want an hour," he said, "no more. Be ready in an hour's time."

Then he went to Farmer Goussot's.

He did not say much at the farm. Old Goussot, hoping against hope, was lavish with information, took his visitor along the walls down to the little door opening on the fields, produced the key and gave minute details of all the searches that had been made so far.

Oddly enough, the stranger, who hardly spoke, seemed not to listen either. He merely looked, with a rather vacant gaze. When they had been round the estate, old Goussot asked, anxiously:

"Well?"

"Well what?"

"Do you think you know?"

The visitor stood for a moment without answering. Then he said:

"No, nothing."

"Why, of course not!" cried the farmer, throwing up his arms. "How should you know! It's all hanky-panky. Shall I tell you what I think? Well, that old Trainard has been so jolly clever that he's lying dead in his hole ... and the bank-notes are rotting with him. Do you hear? You can take my word for it."

The gentleman said, very calmly:

"There's only one thing that interests me. The tramp, all said and done, was free at night and able to feed on what he could pick up. But how about drinking?"

"Out of the question!" shouted the farmer. "Quite out of the question! There's no water except this; and we have kept watch beside it every night."

"It's a spring. Where does it rise?"

"Here, where we stand."

"Is there enough pressure to bring it into the pool of itself?"

"Yes."

"And where does the water go when it runs out of the pool?"

"Into this pipe here, which goes under ground and carries it to the house, for use in the kitchen. So there's no way of drinking, seeing that we were there and that the spring is twenty yards from the house."

"Hasn't it rained during the last four weeks?"

"Not once: I've told you that already."

The stranger went to the spring and examined it. The trough was formed of a few boards of wood joined together just above the ground; and the water ran through it, slow and clear.

"The water's not more than a foot deep, is it?" he asked.

In order to measure it, he picked up from the grass a straw which he dipped into the pool. But, as he was stooping, he suddenly broke off and looked around him.

"Oh, how funny!" he said, bursting into a peal of laughter.

"Why, what's the matter?" spluttered old Goussot, rushing toward the pool, as though a man could have lain hidden between those narrow boards.

And Mother Goussot clasped her hands.

"What is it? Have you seen him? Where is he?"

"Neither in it nor under it," replied the stranger, who was still laughing.

He made for the house, eagerly followed by the farmer, the old woman and the four sons. The inn-keeper was there also, as were the people from the inn who had been watching the stranger's movements. And there was a dead silence, while they waited for the extraordinary disclosure.

"It's as I thought," he said, with an amused expression. "The old chap had to quench his thirst somewhere; and, as there was only the spring...."

"Oh, but look here," growled Farmer Goussot, "we should have seen him!"

"It was at night."

"We should have heard him ... and seen him too, as we were close by."

"So was he."

"And he drank the water from the pool?"

"Yes."

"How?"

"From a little way off."

"With what?"

"With this."

And the stranger showed the straw which he had picked up:

"There, here's the straw for the customer's long drink. You will see, there's more of it than usual: in fact, it is made of three straws stuck into one another. That was the first thing I noticed: those three straws fastened together. The proof is conclusive."

"But, hang it all, the proof of what?" cried Farmer Goussot, irritably.

The stranger took a shotgun from the rack.

"Is it loaded?" he asked.

"Yes," said the youngest of the brothers. "I use it to kill the sparrows with, for fun. It's small shot."

"Capital! A peppering where it won't hurt him will do the trick."

His face suddenly assumed a masterful look. He gripped the farmer by the arm and rapped out, in an imperious tone:

"Listen to me, Farmer Goussot. I'm not here to do policeman's work; and I won't have the poor beggar locked up at any price. Four weeks of starvation and fright is good enough for anybody. So you've got to swear to me, you and your sons, that you'll let him off without hurting him."

"He must hand over the money!"

"Well, of course. Do you swear?"

"I swear."

The gentleman walked back to the door-sill, at the entrance to the orchard. He took a quick aim, pointing his gun a little in the air, in the direction of the cherry tree which overhung the spring. He fired. A hoarse cry rang from the tree; and the scarecrow which had been straddling the main branch for a month past came tumbling to the ground, only to jump up at once and make off as fast as its legs could carry it.

There was a moment's amazement, followed by outcries. The sons darted in pursuit and were not long in coming up with the runaway, hampered as he was by his rags and weakened by privation. But the stranger was already protecting him against their wrath:

"Hands off there! This man belongs to me. I won't have him touched.... I hope I haven't stung you up too much, Trainard?"

Standing on his straw legs wrapped round with strips of tattered cloth, with his arms and his whole body clad in the same materials, his head swathed in linen, tightly packed like a sausage, the old chap still had the stiff appearance of a lay-figure. And the whole effect was so ludicrous and so unexpected that the onlookers screamed with laughter.

The stranger unbound his head; and they saw a veiled mask of tangled grey beard encroaching on every side upon a skeleton face lit up by two eyes burning with fever.

The laughter was louder than ever.

"The money! The six notes!" roared the farmer.

The stranger kept him at a distance:

"One moment ... we'll give you that back, sha'n't we, Trainard?"

And, taking his knife and cutting away the straw and cloth, he jested, cheerily:

"You poor old beggar, what a guy you look! But how on earth did you manage to pull off that trick? You must be confoundedly clever, or else you had the devil's own luck.... So, on the first night, you used the breathing-time they left you to rig yourself in these togs! Not a bad idea. Who could ever suspect a scarecrow?... They were so accustomed to seeing it stuck up in its tree! But, poor old daddy, how uncomfortable you must have felt, lying flat up there on your stomach, with your arms and legs dangling down! All day long, like that! The deuce of an attitude! And how you must have been put to it, when you ventured to move a limb, eh? And how you must have funked going to sleep!... And then you had to eat! And drink! And you heard the sentry and felt the barrel of his gun within a yard of your nose! Brrrr!... But the trickiest of all, you know, was your bit of straw!... Upon my word, when I think that, without a sound, without a movement so to speak, you had to fish out lengths of straw from your toggery, fix them end to end, let your apparatus down to the water and suck up the heavenly moisture drop by drop.... Upon my word, one could scream with admiration.... Well done, Trainard...." And he added, between his teeth, "Only you're in a very unappetizing state, my man. Haven't you washed yourself all this month, you old pig? After all, you had as much water as you wanted!... Here, you people, I hand him over to you. I'm going to wash my hands, that's what I'm going to do."

Farmer Goussot and his four sons grabbed at the prey which he was abandoning to them:

"Now then, come along, fork out the money."

Dazed as he was, the tramp still managed to simulate astonishment.

"Don't put on that idiot look," growled the farmer. "Come on. Out with the six notes...."

"What?... What do you want of me?" stammered old Trainard.

"The money ... on the nail...."

"What money?"

"The bank-notes."

"The bank-notes?"

"Oh, I'm getting sick of you! Here, lads...."

They laid the old fellow flat, tore off the rags that composed his clothes, felt and searched him all over.

There was nothing on him.

"You thief and you robber!" yelled old Goussot. "What have you done with it?"

The old beggar seemed more dazed than ever. Too cunning to confess, he kept on whining:

"What do you want of me?... Money? I haven't three sous to call my own...."

But his eyes, wide with wonder, remained fixed upon his clothes; and he himself seemed not to understand.

The Goussots' rage could no longer be restrained. They rained blows upon him, which did not improve matters. But the farmer was convinced that Trainard had hidden the money before turning himself into the scarecrow:

"Where have you put it, you scum? Out with it! In what part of the orchard have you hidden it?"

"The money?" repeated the tramp with a stupid look.

"Yes, the money! The money which you've buried somewhere.... Oh, if we don't find it, your goose is cooked!... We have witnesses, haven't we?... All of you, friends, eh? And then the gentleman...."

He turned, with the intention of addressing the stranger, in the direction of the spring, which was thirty or forty steps to the left. And he was quite surprised not to see him washing his hands there:

"Has he gone?" he asked.

Some one answered:

"No, he lit a cigarette and went for a stroll in the orchard."

"Oh, that's all right!" said the farmer. "He's the sort to find the notes for us, just as he found the man."

"Unless ..." said a voice.

"Unless what?" echoed the farmer. "What do you mean? Have you something in your head? Out with it, then! What is it?"

But he interrupted himself suddenly, seized with a doubt; and there was a moment's silence. The same idea dawned on all the country-folk. The stranger's arrival at Héberville, the breakdown of his motor, his manner of questioning the people at the inn and of gaining admission to the farm: were not all these part and parcel of a put-up job, the trick of a cracksman who had learnt the story from the papers and who had come to try his luck on the spot?...

"Jolly smart of him!" said the inn-keeper. "He must have taken the money from old Trainard's pocket, before our eyes, while he was searching him."

"Impossible!" spluttered Farmer Goussot. "He would have been seen going out that way ... by the house ... whereas he's strolling in the orchard."

Mother Goussot, all of a heap, suggested:

"The little door at the end, down there?..."

"The key never leaves me."

"But you showed it to him."

"Yes; and I took it back again.... Look, here it is."

He clapped his hand to his pocket and uttered a cry:

"Oh, dash it all, it's gone!... He's sneaked it!..."

He at once rushed away, followed and escorted by his sons and a number of the villagers.

When they were halfway down the orchard, they heard the throb of a motor-car, obviously the one belonging to the stranger, who had given orders to his chauffeur to wait for him at that lower entrance.

When the Goussots reached the door, they saw scrawled with a brick, on the worm-eaten panel, the two words:

"ARSÈNE LUPIN."

Stick to it as the angry Goussots might, they found it impossible to prove that old Trainard had stolen any money. Twenty persons had to bear witness that, when all was said, nothing was discovered on his person. He escaped with a few months' imprisonment for the assault.

He did not regret them. As soon as he was released, he was secretly informed that, every quarter, on a given date, at a given hour, under a given milestone on a given road, he would find three gold louis.

To a man like old Trainard that means wealth.

X. EDITH SWAN-NECK

"Arsène Lupin, what's your real opinion of Inspector Ganimard?"

"A very high one, my dear fellow."

"A very high one? Then why do you never miss a chance of turning him into ridicule?"

"It's a bad habit; and I'm sorry for it. But what can I say? It's the way of the world. Here's a decent detective-chap, here's a whole pack of decent men, who stand for law and order, who protect us against the apaches, who risk their lives for honest people like you and me; and we have nothing to give them in return but flouts and gibes. It's preposterous!"

"Bravo, Lupin! you're talking like a respectable ratepayer!"

"What else am I? I may have peculiar views about other people's property; but I assure you that it's very different when my own's at stake. By Jove, it doesn't do to lay hands on what belongs to me! Then I'm out for blood! Aha! It's *my* pocket, *my* money, *my* watch ... hands off! I have the soul of a conservative, my dear fellow, the instincts of a retired tradesman and a due respect for every sort of tradition and authority. And that is why Ganimard inspires me with no little gratitude and esteem."

"But not much admiration?"

"Plenty of admiration too. Over and above the dauntless courage which comes natural to all those gentry at the Criminal Investigation Department, Ganimard possesses very sterling qualities: decision, insight and judgment. I have watched him at work. He's somebody, when all's said. Do you know the Edith Swan-neck story, as it was called?"

"I know as much as everybody knows."

"That means that you don't know it at all. Well, that job was, I daresay, the one which I thought out most cleverly, with the utmost care and the utmost precaution, the one which I shrouded in the greatest darkness and mystery, the one which it took the biggest generalship to carry through. It was a regular game of chess, played according to strict scientific and mathematical rules. And yet Ganimard ended by unravelling the knot. Thanks to him, they know the truth to-day on the Quai des Orfèvres. And it is a truth quite out of the common, I assure you."

"May I hope to hear it?"

"Certainly ... one of these days ... when I have time.... But the Brunelli is dancing at the Opera to-night; and, if she were not to see me in my stall ...!"

I do not meet Lupin often. He confesses with difficulty, when it suits him. It was only gradually, by snatches, by odds and ends of confidences, that I was able to obtain the different incidents and to piece the story together in all its details.

The main features are well known and I will merely mention the facts.

Three years ago, when the train from Brest arrived at Rennes, the door of one of the luggage vans was found smashed in. This van had been booked by Colonel Sparmiento, a rich Brazilian, who was travelling with his wife in the same train. It contained a complete set of tapestry-hangings. The case in which one of these was packed had been broken open and the tapestry had disappeared.

Colonel Sparmiento started proceedings against the railway-company, claiming heavy damages, not only for the stolen tapestry, but also for the loss in value which the whole collection suffered in consequence of the theft.

The police instituted inquiries. The company offered a large reward. A fortnight later, a letter which had come undone in the post was opened by the authorities and revealed the fact that the theft had been carried out under the direction of Arsène Lupin and that a package was to leave next day for the United States. That same evening, the tapestry was discovered in a trunk deposited in the cloak-room at the Gare Saint-Lazare.

The scheme, therefore, had miscarried. Lupin felt the disappointment so much that he vented his ill-humour in a communication to Colonel Sparmiento, ending with the following words, which were clear enough for anybody:

"It was very considerate of me to take only one. Next time, I shall take the twelve. *Verbum sap.*
    "A. L."

Colonel Sparmiento had been living for some months in a house standing at the end of a small garden at the corner of the Rue de la Faisanderie and the Rue Dufresnoy. He was a rather thick-set, broad-shouldered man, with black hair and a swarthy skin, always well and quietly dressed. He was married to an extremely pretty but delicate Englishwoman, who was much upset by the business of the tapestries. From the first she implored her husband to sell them for what they would fetch. The Colonel had much too forcible and dogged a nature to yield to what he had every right to describe as a woman's fancies. He sold nothing, but he redoubled his precautions and adopted every measure that was likely to make an attempt at burglary impossible.

To begin with, so that he might confine his watch to the garden-front, he walled up all the windows on the ground-floor and the first floor overlooking the Rue Dufresnoy. Next, he enlisted the services of a firm which made a speciality of protecting private houses against robberies. Every window of the gallery in which the tapestries were hung was fitted with invisible burglar alarms, the position of which was known, to none but himself.

These, at the least touch, switched on all the electric lights and set a whole system of bells and gongs ringing.

In addition to this, the insurance companies to which he applied refused to grant policies to any considerable amount unless he consented to let three men, supplied by the companies and paid by himself, occupy the ground-floor of his house every night. They selected for the purpose three ex-detectives, tried and trustworthy men, all of whom hated Lupin like poison. As for the servants, the colonel had known them for years and was ready to vouch for them.

After taking these steps and organizing the defence of the house as though it were a fortress, the colonel gave a great house-warming, a sort of private view, to which he invited the members of both his clubs, as well as a certain number of ladies, journalists, art-patrons and critics.

They felt, as they passed through the garden-gate, much as if they were walking into a prison. The three private detectives, posted at the foot of the stairs, asked for each visitor's invitation card and eyed him up and down suspiciously, making him feel as though they were going to search his pockets or take his finger-prints.

The colonel, who received his guests on the first floor, made laughing apologies and seemed delighted at the opportunity of explaining the arrangements which he had invented to secure the safety of his hangings. His wife stood by him, looking charmingly young and pretty, fair-haired, pale and sinuous, with a sad and gentle expression, the expression of resignation often worn by those who are threatened by fate.

When all the guests had come, the garden-gates and the hall-doors were closed. Then everybody filed into the middle gallery, which was reached through two steel doors, while its windows, with their huge shutters, were protected by iron bars. This was where the twelve tapestries were kept.

They were matchless works of art and, taking their inspiration from the famous Bayeux Tapestry, attributed to Queen Matilda, they represented the story of the Norman Conquest. They had been ordered in the fourteenth century by the descendant of a man-at-arms in William the Conqueror's train; were executed by Jehan Gosset, a famous Arras weaver; and were discovered, five hundred years later, in an old Breton manor-house. On hearing of this, the colonel had struck a bargain for fifty thousand francs. They were worth ten times the money.

But the finest of the twelve hangings composing the set, the most uncommon because the subject had not been treated by Queen Matilda, was the one which Arsène Lupin had stolen and which had been so fortunately recovered. It portrayed Edith Swan-neck on the battlefield of Hastings, seeking among the dead for the body of her sweetheart Harold, last of the Saxon kings.

The guests were lost in enthusiasm over this tapestry, over the unsophisticated beauty of the design, over the faded colours, over the life-like grouping of the figures and the pitiful sadness of the scene. Poor Edith Swan-neck stood drooping like an overweighted lily. Her white gown revealed the lines of her languid figure. Her long, tapering hands were outstretched in a gesture of terror and entreaty. And nothing could be more mournful than her profile, over which flickered the most dejected and despairing of smiles.

"A harrowing smile," remarked one of the critics, to whom the others listened with deference. "A very charming smile, besides; and it reminds me, Colonel, of the smile of Mme. Sparmiento."

And seeing that the observation seemed to meet with approval, he enlarged upon his idea:

"There are other points of resemblance that struck me at once, such as the very graceful curve of the neck and the delicacy of the hands ... and also something about the figure, about the general attitude...."

"What you say is so true," said the colonel, "that I confess that it was this likeness that decided me to buy the hangings. And there was another reason, which was that, by a really curious chance, my wife's name happens to be Edith. I have called her Edith Swan-neck ever since." And the colonel added, with a laugh, "I hope that the coincidence will stop at this and that my dear Edith will never have to go in search of her true-love's body, like her prototype."

He laughed as he uttered these words, but his laugh met with no echo; and we find the same impression of awkward silence in all the accounts of the evening that appeared during the next few days. The people standing near him did not know what to say. One of them tried to jest:

"Your name isn't Harold, Colonel?"

"No, thank you," he declared, with continued merriment. "No, that's not my name; nor am I in the least like the Saxon king."

All have since agreed in stating that, at that moment, as the colonel finished speaking, the first alarm rang from the windows—the right or the middle window: opinions differ on this point—rang short and shrill on a single note. The peal of the alarm-bell was followed by an exclamation of terror uttered by Mme. Sparmiento, who caught hold of her husband's arm. He cried:

"What's the matter? What does this mean?"

The guests stood motionless, with their eyes staring at the windows. The colonel repeated:

"What does it mean? I don't understand. No one but myself knows where that bell is fixed...."

And, at that moment—here again the evidence is unanimous—at that moment came sudden, absolute darkness, followed immediately by the maddening din of all the bells and all the gongs, from top to bottom of the house, in every room and at every window.

For a few seconds, a stupid disorder, an insane terror, reigned. The women screamed. The men banged with their fists on the closed doors. They hustled and fought. People fell to the floor and were trampled under foot. It was like a panic-stricken crowd, scared by threatening flames or by a bursting shell. And, above the uproar, rose the colonel's voice, shouting:

"Silence!... Don't move!... It's all right!... The switch is over there, in the corner.... Wait a bit.... Here!"

He had pushed his way through his guests and reached a corner of the gallery; and, all at once, the electric light blazed up again, while the pandemonium of bells stopped.

Then, in the sudden light, a strange sight met the eyes. Two ladies had fainted. Mme. Sparmiento, hanging to her husband's arm, with her knees dragging on the floor, and livid in the face, appeared half dead. The men, pale, with their neckties awry, looked as if they had all been in the wars.

"The tapestries are there!" cried some one.

There was a great surprise, as though the disappearance of those hangings ought to have been the natural result and the only plausible explanation of the incident. But nothing had been moved. A few valuable pictures, hanging on the walls, were there still. And, though the same din had reverberated all over the house, though all the rooms had been thrown into darkness, the detectives had seen no one entering or trying to enter.

"Besides," said the colonel, "it's only the windows of the gallery that have alarms. Nobody but myself understands how they work; and I had not set them yet."

People laughed loudly at the way in which they had been frightened, but they laughed without conviction and in a more or less shamefaced fashion, for each of them was keenly alive to the absurdity of his conduct. And they had but one thought—to get out of that house where, say what you would, the atmosphere was one of agonizing anxiety.

Two journalists stayed behind, however; and the colonel joined them, after attending to Edith and handing her over to her maids. The three of them, together with the detectives, made a search that did not lead to the discovery of anything of the least interest. Then the colonel sent for some champagne; and the result was that it was not until a late hour—to be exact, a quarter to three in the morning—that the journalists took their leave, the colonel retired to his quarters, and the detectives withdrew to the room which had been set aside for them on the ground-floor.

They took the watch by turns, a watch consisting, in the first place, in keeping awake and, next, in looking round the garden and visiting the gallery at intervals.

These orders were scrupulously carried out, except between five and seven in the morning, when sleep gained the mastery and the men ceased to go their rounds. But it was broad daylight out of doors. Besides, if there had been the least sound of bells, would they not have woke up?

Nevertheless, when one of them, at twenty minutes past seven, opened the door of the gallery and flung back the shutters, he saw that the twelve tapestries were gone.

This man and the others were blamed afterward for not giving the alarm at once and for starting their own investigations before informing the colonel and telephoning to the local commissary. Yet this very excusable delay can hardly be said to have hampered the action of the police. In any case, the colonel was not told until half-past eight. He was dressed and ready to go out. The news did not seem to upset him beyond measure, or, at least, he managed to control his emotion. But the effort must have been too much for him, for he suddenly dropped into a chair and, for some moments, gave way to a regular fit of despair and anguish, most painful to behold in a man of his resolute appearance.

Recovering and mastering himself, he went to the gallery, stared at the bare walls and then sat down at a table and hastily scribbled a letter, which he put into an envelope and sealed.

"There," he said. "I'm in a hurry.... I have an important engagement.... Here is a letter for the commissary of police." And, seeing the detectives' eyes upon him, he added, "I am giving the commissary my views ... telling him of a suspicion that occurs to me.... He must follow it up.... I will do what I can...."

He left the house at a run, with excited gestures which the detectives were subsequently to remember.

A few minutes later, the commissary of police arrived. He was handed the letter, which contained the following words:

"I am at the end of my tether. The theft of those tapestries completes the crash which I have been trying to conceal for the past year. I bought them as a speculation and was hoping to get a million francs for them, thanks to the fuss that was made about them. As it was, an American offered me six hundred thousand. It meant my salvation. This means utter destruction.

"I hope that my dear wife will forgive the sorrow which I am bringing upon her. Her name will be on my lips at the last moment."

Mme. Sparmiento was informed. She remained aghast with horror, while inquiries were instituted and attempts made to trace the colonel's movements.

Late in the afternoon, a telephone-message came from Ville d'Avray. A gang of railway-men had found a man's body lying at the entrance to a tunnel after a train had passed. The body was hideously mutilated; the face had lost all resemblance to anything human. There were no papers in the pockets. But the description answered to that of the colonel.

Mme. Sparmiento arrived at Ville d'Avray, by motor-car, at seven o'clock in the evening. She was taken to a room at the railway-station. When the sheet that covered it was removed, Edith, Edith Swan-neck, recognized her husband's body.

In these circumstances, Lupin did not receive his usual good notices in the press:

"Let him look to himself," jeered one leader-writer, summing up the general opinion. "It would not take many exploits of this kind for him to forfeit the popularity which has not been grudged him hitherto. We have no use for Lupin, except when his rogueries are perpetrated at the expense of shady company-promoters, foreign adventurers, German barons, banks and financial companies. And, above all, no murders! A burglar we can put up with; but a murderer, no! If he is not directly guilty, he is at least responsible for this death. There is blood upon his hands; the arms on his escutcheon are stained gules...."

The public anger and disgust were increased by the pity which Edith's pale face aroused. The guests of the night before gave their version of what had happened, omitting none of the impressive details; and a legend formed straightway around the fair-haired Englishwoman, a legend that assumed a really tragic character, owing to the popular story of the swan-necked heroine.

And yet the public could not withhold its admiration of the extraordinary skill with which the theft had been effected. The police explained it, after a fashion. The detectives had noticed from the first and subsequently stated that one of the three windows of the gallery was wide open. There could be no doubt that Lupin and his confederates had entered through this window. It seemed a very plausible suggestion. Still, in that case, how were they able, first, to climb the garden railings, in coming and going, without being seen; secondly, to cross the garden and put up a ladder on the flower-border, without leaving the least trace behind; thirdly, to open the shutters and the window, without starting the bells and switching on the lights in the house?

The police accused the three detectives of complicity. The magistrate in charge of the case examined them at length, made minute inquiries into their private lives and stated formally that they were above all suspicion. As for the tapestries, there seemed to be no hope that they would be recovered.

It was at this moment that Chief-inspector Ganimard returned from India, where he had been hunting for Lupin on the strength of a number of most convincing proofs supplied by former confederates of Lupin himself. Feeling that he had once more been tricked by his everlasting adversary, fully believing that Lupin had dispatched him on this wild-goose chase so as to be rid of him during the business of the tapestries, he asked for a fortnight's leave of absence, called on Mme. Sparmiento and promised to avenge her husband.

Edith had reached the point at which not even the thought of vengeance relieves the sufferer's pain. She had dismissed the three detectives on the day of the funeral and engaged just one man and an old cook-housekeeper to take the place of the large staff of servants the sight of whom reminded her too cruelly of the past. Not caring what happened, she kept her room and left Ganimard free to act as he pleased.

He took up his quarters on the ground-floor and at once instituted a series of the most minute investigations. He started the inquiry afresh, questioned the people in the neighbourhood, studied the distribution of the rooms and set each of the burglar-alarms going thirty and forty times over.

At the end of the fortnight, he asked for an extension of leave. The chief of the detective-service, who was at that time M. Dudouis, came to see him and found him perched on the top of a ladder, in the gallery. That day, the chief-inspector admitted that all his searches had proved useless.

Two days later, however, M. Dudouis called again and discovered Ganimard in a very thoughtful frame of mind. A bundle of newspapers lay spread in front of him. At last, in reply to his superior's urgent questions, the chief-inspector muttered:

"I know nothing, chief, absolutely nothing; but there's a confounded notion worrying me.... Only it seems so absurd.... And then it doesn't explain things.... On the contrary, it confuses them rather...."

"Then ...?"

"Then I implore you, chief, to have a little patience ... to let me go my own way. But if I telephone to you, some day or other, suddenly, you must jump into a taxi, without losing a minute. It will mean that I have discovered the secret."

Forty-eight hours passed. Then, one morning, M. Dudouis received a telegram:

"Going to Lille.
    "GANIMARD."

"What the dickens can he want to go to Lille for?" wondered the chief-detective.

The day passed without news, followed by another day. But M. Dudouis had every confidence in Ganimard. He knew his man, knew that the old detective was not one of those people who excite themselves for nothing. When Ganimard "got a move on him," it meant that he had sound reasons for doing so.

As a matter of fact, on the evening of that second day, M. Dudouis was called to the telephone.

"Is that you, chief?"

"Is it Ganimard speaking?"

Cautious men both, they began by making sure of each other's identity. As soon as his mind was eased on this point, Ganimard continued, hurriedly:

"Ten men, chief, at once. And please come yourself."

"Where are you?"

"In the house, on the ground-floor. But I will wait for you just inside the garden-gate."

"I'll come at once. In a taxi, of course?"

"Yes, chief. Stop the taxi fifty yards from the house. I'll let you in when you whistle."

Things took place as Ganimard had arranged. Shortly after midnight, when all the lights were out on the upper floors, he slipped into the street and went to meet M. Dudouis. There was a hurried consultation. The officers distributed themselves as Ganimard ordered. Then the chief and the chief-inspector walked back together, noiselessly crossed the garden and closeted themselves with every precaution:

"Well, what's it all about?" asked M. Dudouis. "What does all this mean? Upon my word, we look like a pair of conspirators!"

But Ganimard was not laughing. His chief had never seen him in such a state of perturbation, nor heard him speak in a voice denoting such excitement:

"Any news, Ganimard?"

"Yes, chief, and ... this time ...! But I can hardly believe it myself.... And yet I'm not mistaken: I know the real truth.... It may be as unlikely as you please, but it is the truth, the whole truth and nothing but the truth."

He wiped away the drops of perspiration that trickled down his forehead and, after a further question from M. Dudouis, pulled himself together, swallowed a glass of water and began:

"Lupin has often got the better of me...."

"Look here, Ganimard," said M. Dudouis, interrupting him. "Why can't you come straight to the point? Tell me, in two words, what's happened."

"No, chief," retorted the chief-inspector, "it is essential that you should know the different stages which I have passed through. Excuse me, but I consider it indispensable." And he repeated: "I was saying, chief, that Lupin has often got the better of me and led me many a dance. But, in this contest in which I have always come out worst ... so far ... I have at least gained experience of his manner of play and learnt to know his tactics. Now, in the matter of the tapestries, it occurred to me almost from the start to set myself two problems. In the first place, Lupin, who never makes a move without knowing what he is after, was obviously aware that Colonel Sparmiento had come to the end of his money and that the loss of the tapestries might drive him to suicide. Nevertheless, Lupin, who hates the very thought of bloodshed, stole the tapestries."

"There was the inducement," said M. Dudouis, "of the five or six hundred thousand francs which they are worth."

"No, chief, I tell you once more, whatever the occasion might be, Lupin would not take life, nor be the cause of another person's death, for anything in this world, for millions and millions. That's the first point. In the second place, what was the object of all that disturbance, in the evening, during the house-warming party? Obviously, don't you think, to surround the business with an atmosphere of anxiety and terror, in the shortest possible time, and also to divert suspicion from the truth, which, otherwise, might easily have been suspected?... You seem not to understand, chief?"

"Upon my word, I do not!"

"As a matter of fact," said Ganimard, "as a matter of fact, it is not particularly plain. And I myself, when I put the problem before my mind in those same words, did not understand it very clearly.... And yet I felt that I was on the right track.... Yes, there was no doubt about it that Lupin wanted to divert suspicions ... to divert them to himself, Lupin, mark you ... so that the real person who was working the business might remain unknown...."

"A confederate," suggested M. Dudouis. "A confederate, moving among the visitors, who set the alarms going ... and who managed to hide in the house after the party had broken up."

"You're getting warm, chief, you're getting warm! It is certain that the tapestries, as they cannot have been stolen by any one making his way surreptitiously into the house, were stolen by somebody who remained in the house; and it is equally certain that, by taking the list of the people invited and inquiring into the antecedents of each of them, one might...."

"Well?"

"Well, chief, there's a 'but,' namely, that the three detectives had this list in their hands when the guests arrived and that they still had it when the guests left. Now sixty-three came in and sixty-three went away. So you see...."

"Then do you suppose a servant?..."

"No."

"The detectives?"

"No."

"But, still ... but, still," said the chief, impatiently, "if the robbery was committed from the inside...."

"That is beyond dispute," declared the inspector, whose excitement seemed to be nearing fever-point. "There is no question about it. All my investigations led to the same certainty. And my conviction gradually became so positive that I ended, one day, by drawing up this startling axiom: in theory and in fact, the robbery can only have been committed with the assistance of an accomplice staying in the house. Whereas there was no accomplice!"

"That's absurd," said Dudouis.

"Quite absurd," said Ganimard. "But, at the very moment when I uttered that absurd sentence, the truth flashed upon me."

"Eh?"

"Oh, a very dim, very incomplete, but still sufficient truth! With that clue to guide me, I was bound to find the way. Do you follow me, chief?"

M. Dudouis sat silent. The same phenomenon that had taken place in Ganimard was evidently taking place in him. He muttered:

"If it's not one of the guests, nor the servants, nor the private detectives, then there's no one left...."

"Yes, chief, there's one left...."

M. Dudouis started as though he had received a shock; and, in a voice that betrayed his excitement:

"But, look here, that's preposterous."

"Why?"

"Come, think for yourself!"

"Go on, chief: say what's in your mind."

"Nonsense! What do you mean?"

"Go on, chief."

"It's impossible! How can Sparmiento have been Lupin's accomplice?"

Ganimard gave a little chuckle.

"Exactly, Arsène Lupin's accomplice!... That explains everything. During the night, while the three detectives were downstairs watching, or sleeping rather, for Colonel Sparmiento had given them champagne to drink and perhaps doctored it beforehand, the said colonel took down the hangings and passed them out through the window of his bedroom. The room is on the second floor and looks out on another street, which was not watched, because the lower windows are walled up."

M. Dudouis reflected and then shrugged his shoulders:

"It's preposterous!" he repeated.

"Why?"

"Why? Because, if the colonel had been Arsène Lupin's accomplice, he would not have committed suicide after achieving his success."

"Who says that he committed suicide?"

"Why, he was found dead on the line!"

"I told you, there is no such thing as death with Lupin."

"Still, this was genuine enough. Besides, Mme. Sparmiento identified the body."

"I thought you would say that, chief. The argument worried me too. There was I, all of a sudden, with three people in front of me instead of one: first, Arsène Lupin, cracksman; secondly, Colonel Sparmiento, his accomplice; thirdly, a dead man. Spare us! It was too much of a good thing!"

Ganimard took a bundle of newspapers, untied it and handed one of them to Mr. Dudouis:

"You remember, chief, last time you were here, I was looking through the papers.... I wanted to see if something had not happened, at that period, that might bear upon the case and confirm my supposition. Please read this paragraph."

M. Dudouis took the paper and read aloud:

"Our Lille correspondent informs us that a curious incident has occurred in that town. A corpse has disappeared from the local morgue, the corpse of a man unknown who threw himself under the wheels of a steam tram-car on the day before. No one is able to suggest a reason for this disappearance."

M. Dudouis sat thinking and then asked:

"So ... you believe ...?"

"I have just come from Lille," replied Ganimard, "and my inquiries leave not a doubt in my mind. The corpse was removed on the same night on which Colonel Sparmiento gave his house-warming. It was taken straight to Ville d'Avray by motor-car; and the car remained near the railway-line until the evening."

"Near the tunnel, therefore," said M. Dudouis.

"Next to it, chief."

"So that the body which was found is merely that body, dressed in Colonel Sparmiento's clothes."

"Precisely, chief."

"Then Colonel Sparmiento is not dead?"

"No more dead than you or I, chief."

"But then why all these complications? Why the theft of one tapestry, followed by its recovery, followed by the theft of the twelve? Why that house-warming? Why that disturbance? Why everything? Your story won't hold water, Ganimard."

"Only because you, chief, like myself, have stopped halfway; because, strange as this story already sounds, we must go still farther, very much farther, in the direction of the improbable and the astounding. And why not, after all? Remember that we are dealing with Arsène Lupin. With him, is it not always just the improbable and the astounding that we must look for? Must we not always go straight for the maddest suppositions? And, when I say the maddest, I am using the wrong word. On the contrary, the whole thing is wonderfully logical and so simple that a child could understand it. Confederates only betray you. Why employ confederates, when it is so easy and so natural to act for yourself, by yourself, with your own hands and by the means within your own reach?"

"What are you saying?... What are you saying?... What are you saying?" cried M. Dudouis, in a sort of sing-song voice and a tone of bewilderment that increased with each separate exclamation.

Ganimard gave a fresh chuckle.

"Takes your breath away, chief, doesn't it? So it did mine, on the day when you came to see me here and when the notion was beginning to grow upon me. I was flabbergasted with astonishment. And yet I've had experience of my customer. I know what he's capable of.... But this, no, this was really a bit too stiff!"

"It's impossible! It's impossible!" said M. Dudouis, in a low voice.

"On the contrary, chief, it's quite possible and quite logical and quite normal. It's the threefold incarnation of one and the same individual. A schoolboy would solve the problem in a minute, by a simple process of elimination. Take away the dead man: there remains Sparmiento and Lupin. Take away Sparmiento...."

"There remains Lupin," muttered the chief-detective.

"Yes, chief, Lupin simply, Lupin in five letters and two syllables, Lupin taken out of his Brazilian skin, Lupin revived from the dead, Lupin translated, for the past six months, into Colonel Sparmiento, travelling in Brittany, hearing of the discovery of the twelve tapestries, buying them, planning the theft of the best of them, so as to draw attention to himself, Lupin, and divert it from himself, Sparmiento. Next, he brings about, in full view of the gaping public, a noisy contest between Lupin and Sparmiento or Sparmiento and Lupin, plots and gives the house-warming party, terrifies his guests and, when everything is ready, arranges for Lupin to steal Sparmiento's tapestries and for Sparmiento, Lupin's victim, to disappear from sight and die unsuspected, unsuspectable, regretted by his friends, pitied by the public and leaving behind him, to pocket the profits of the swindle...."

Ganimard stopped, looked the chief in the eyes and, in a voice that emphasized the importance of his words, concluded:

"Leaving behind him a disconsolate widow."

"Mme. Sparmiento! You really believe....?"

"Hang it all!" said the chief-inspector. "People don't work up a whole business of this sort, without seeing something ahead of them ... solid profits."

"But the profits, it seems to me, lie in the sale of the tapestries which Lupin will effect in America or elsewhere."

"First of all, yes. But Colonel Sparmiento could effect that sale just as well. And even better. So there's something more."

"Something more?"

"Come, chief, you're forgetting that Colonel Sparmiento has been the victim of an important robbery and that, though he may be dead, at least his widow remains. So it's his widow who will get the money."

"What money?"

"What money? Why, the money due to her! The insurance-money, of course!"

M. Dudouis was staggered. The whole business suddenly became clear to him, with its real meaning. He muttered:

"That's true!... That's true!... The colonel had insured his tapestries...."

"Rather! And for no trifle either."

"For how much?"

"Eight hundred thousand francs."

"Eight hundred thousand?"

"Just so. In five different companies."

"And has Mme. Sparmiento had the money?"

"She got a hundred and fifty thousand francs yesterday and two hundred thousand to-day, while I was away. The remaining payments are to be made in the course of this week."

"But this is terrible! You ought to have...."

"What, chief? To begin with, they took advantage of my absence to settle up accounts with the companies. I only heard about it on my return when I ran up against an insurance-manager whom I happen to know and took the opportunity of drawing him out."

The chief-detective was silent for some time, not knowing what to say. Then he mumbled:

"What a fellow, though!"

Ganimard nodded his head:

"Yes, chief, a blackguard, but, I can't help saying, a devil of a clever fellow. For his plan to succeed, he must have managed in such a way that, for four or five weeks, no one could express or even conceive the least suspicion of the part played by Colonel Sparmiento. All the indignation and all the inquiries had to be concentrated upon Lupin alone. In the last resort, people had to find themselves faced simply with a mournful, pitiful, penniless widow, poor Edith Swan-neck, a beautiful and legendary vision, a creature so pathetic that the gentlemen of the insurance-companies were almost glad to place something in her hands to relieve her poverty and her grief. That's what was wanted and that's what happened."

The two men were close together and did not take their eyes from each other's faces.

The chief asked:

"Who is that woman?"

"Sonia Kritchnoff."

"Sonia Kritchnoff?"

"Yes, the Russian girl whom I arrested last year at the time of the theft of the coronet, and whom Lupin helped to escape."[5]

"Are you sure?"

"Absolutely. I was put off the scent, like everybody else, by Lupin's machinations, and had paid no particular attention to her. But, when I knew the part which she was playing, I remembered. She is certainly Sonia, metamorphosed into an Englishwoman; Sonia, the most innocent-looking and the trickiest of actresses; Sonia, who would not hesitate to face death for love of Lupin."

"A good capture, Ganimard," said M. Dudouis, approvingly.

"I've something better still for you, chief!"

"Really? What?"

"Lupin's old foster-mother."

"Victoire?"[6]

"She has been here since Mme. Sparmiento began playing the widow; she's the cook."

"Oho!" said M. Dudouis. "My congratulations, Ganimard!"

"I've something for you, chief, that's even better than that!"

M. Dudouis gave a start. The inspector's hand clutched his and was shaking with excitement.

"What do you mean, Ganimard?"

"Do you think, chief, that I would have brought you here, at this late hour, if I had had nothing more attractive to offer you than Sonia and Victoire? Pah! They'd have kept!"

"You mean to say ...?" whispered M. Dudouis, at last, understanding the chief-inspector's agitation.

"You've guessed it, chief!"

"Is he here?"

"He's here."

"In hiding?"

"Not a bit of it. Simply in disguise. He's the man-servant."

This time, M. Dudouis did not utter a word nor make a gesture. Lupin's audacity confounded him.

Ganimard chuckled.

"It's no longer a threefold, but a fourfold incarnation. Edith Swan-neck might have blundered. The master's presence was necessary; and he had the cheek to return. For three weeks, he has been beside me during my inquiry, calmly following the progress made."

"Did you recognize him?"

"One doesn't recognize him. He has a knack of making-up his face and altering the proportions of his body so as to prevent any one from knowing him. Besides, I was miles from suspecting.... But, this evening, as I was watching Sonia in the shadow of the stairs, I heard Victoire speak to the man-servant and call him, 'Dearie.' A light flashed in upon me. 'Dearie!' That was what she always used to call him. And I knew where I was."

M. Dudouis seemed flustered, in his turn, by the presence of the enemy, so often pursued and always so intangible:

"We've got him, this time," he said, between his teeth. "We've got him; and he can't escape us."

"No, chief, he can't: neither he nor the two women."

"Where are they?"

"Sonia and Victoire are on the second floor; Lupin is on the third."

M. Dudouis suddenly became anxious:

"Why, it was through the windows of one of those floors that the tapestries were passed when they disappeared!"

"That's so, chief."

"In that case, Lupin can get away too. The windows look out on the Rue Dufresnoy."

"Of course they do, chief; but I have taken my precautions. The moment you arrived, I sent four of our men to keep watch under the windows in the Rue Dufresnoy. They have strict instructions to shoot, if any one appears at the windows and looks like coming down. Blank cartridges for the first shot, ball-cartridges for the next."

"Good, Ganimard! You have thought of everything. We'll wait here; and, immediately after sunrise...."

"Wait, chief? Stand on ceremony with that rascal? Bother about rules and regulations, legal hours and all that rot? And suppose he's not quite so polite to us and gives us the slip meanwhile? Suppose he plays us one of his Lupin tricks? No, no, we must have no nonsense! We've got him: let's collar him; and that without delay!"

And Ganimard, all a-quiver with indignant impatience, went out, walked across the garden and presently returned with half-a-dozen men:

"It's all right, chief. I've told them, in the Rue Dufresnoy, to get their revolvers out and aim at the windows. Come along."

These alarums and excursions had not been effected without a certain amount of noise, which was bound to be heard by the inhabitants of the house. M. Dudouis felt that his hand was forced. He made up his mind to act:

"Come on, then," he said.

The thing did not take long. The eight of them, Browning pistols in hand, went up the stairs without overmuch precaution, eager to surprise Lupin before he had time to organize his defences.

"Open the door!" roared Ganimard, rushing at the door of Mme. Sparmiento's bedroom.

A policeman smashed it in with his shoulder.

There was no one in the room; and no one in Victoire's bedroom either.

"They're all upstairs!" shouted Ganimard. "They've gone up to Lupin in his attic. Be careful now!"

All the eight ran up the third flight of stairs. To his great astonishment, Ganimard found the door of the attic open and the attic empty. And the other rooms were empty too.

"Blast them!" he cursed. "What's become of them?"

But the chief called him. M. Dudouis, who had gone down again to the second floor, noticed that one of the windows was not latched, but just pushed to:

"There," he said, to Ganimard, "that's the road they took, the road of the tapestries. I told you as much: the Rue Dufresnoy...."

"But our men would have fired on them," protested Ganimard, grinding his teeth with rage. "The street's guarded."

"They must have gone before the street was guarded."

"They were all three of them in their rooms when I rang you up, chief!"

"They must have gone while you were waiting for me in the garden."

"But why? Why? There was no reason why they should go to-day rather than to-morrow, or the next day, or next week, for that matter, when they had pocketed all the insurance-money!"

Yes, there was a reason; and Ganimard knew it when he saw, on the table, a letter addressed to himself and opened it and read it. The letter was worded in the style of the testimonials which we hand to people in our service who have given satisfaction:

"I, the undersigned, Arsène Lupin, gentleman-burglar, ex-colonel, ex-man-of-all-work, ex-corpse, hereby certify that the person of the name of Ganimard gave proof of the most remarkable qualities during his stay in this house. He was exemplary in his behavior, thoroughly devoted and attentive; and, unaided by the least clue, he foiled a part of my plans and saved the insurance-companies four hundred and fifty thousand francs. I congratulate him; and I am quite willing to overlook his blunder in not anticipating that the downstairs telephone communicates with the telephone in Sonia Kritchnoff's bedroom and that, when telephoning to Mr. Chief-detective, he was at the same time telephoning to me to clear out as fast as I could. It was a pardonable slip, which must not be allowed to dim the glamour of his services nor to detract from the merits of his victory.

"Having said this, I beg him to accept the homage of my admiration and of my sincere friendship.

"ARSÈNE LUPIN"

---

1. *The Hollow Needle*. By Maurice Leblanc. Translated by Alexander Teixeira de Mattos (Eveleigh Nash).
2. *813*. By Maurice Leblanc. Translated by Alexander Teixeira de Mattos (Mills & Boon).
3. *The Exploits of Arsène Lupin*. By Maurice Leblanc. Translated by Alexander Teixeira de Mattos (Cassell). IV. *The Escape of Arsène Lupin*.
4. *The Exploits of Arsène Lupin. IX. Holmlock Shears arrives too late.*
5. *Arsène Lupin*. The Novel of the Play. By Edgar Jepson and Maurice Leblanc (Mills & Boon).
6. *The Hollow Needle*. By Maurice Leblanc. Translated by Alexander Teixeira de Mattos (Nash). *813* By Maurice Leblanc. Translated by Alexander Teixeira de Mattos (Mills & Boon).

Made in United States
Troutdale, OR
10/26/2023

14018544R00217